# THE BLUEST EYE
# BELOVED
# JAZZ

## BY
# TONI MORRISON

*The Bluest Eye* (1970)

*Sula* (1974)

*Song of Solomon* (1977)

*Tar Baby* (1981)

*Beloved* (1987)

*Jazz* (1992)

*Playing in the Dark* (1992)

*Race-ing Justice, En-Gendering Power* (1992; editor)

*The Nobel Lecture in Literature* (1994)

*Birth of a Nation'hood* (1996; coeditor with
Claudia Brodsky Lacour)

*The Dancing Mind* (1996)

*Paradise* (1998)

# THE BLUEST EYE
# BELOVED
# JAZZ

## TONI MORRISON

Quality Paperback Book Club
New York

# THE BLUEST EYE

*To the two who gave me life*
*and the one who made me free*

Here is the house. It is green and white. It has a red door. It is very pretty. Here is the family. Mother, Father, Dick, and Jane live in the green-and-white house. They are very happy. See Jane. She has a red dress. She wants to play. Who will play with Jane? See the cat. It goes meow-meow. Come and play. Come play with Jane. The kitten will not play. See Mother. Mother is very nice. Mother, will you play with Jane? Mother laughs. Laugh, Mother, laugh. See Father. He is big and strong. Father, will you play with Jane? Father is smiling. Smile, Father, smile. See the dog. Bowwow goes the dog. Do you want to play with Jane? See the dog run. Run, dog, run. Look, look. Here comes a friend. The friend will play with Jane. They will play a good game. Play, Jane, play.

Here is the house it is green and white it has a red door it is very pretty here is the family mother father dick and jane live in the green-and-white house they are very happy see jane she has a red dress she wants to play who will play with jane see the cat it goes meow-meow come and play come play with jane the kitten will not play see mother mother is very nice mother will you play with jane mother laughs laugh mother laugh see father he is big and strong father will you play with jane father is smiling smile father smile see the dog bowwow goes the dog do you want to play do you want to play with jane see the dog run run dog run look look here comes a friend the friend will play with jane they will play a good game play jane play

Hereisthehouseitisgreenandwhiteithasareddooritisveryprettyhereisthefa
milymotherfatherdickandjaneliveinthegreenandwhitehousetheyareveryh
appyseejaneshehasareddressshewantstoplaywhowillplaywithjaneseetheca
titgoesmeowmeowcomeandplaycomeplaywithjanethekittenwillnotplays
eemothermotherisverynicemotherwillyouplaywithjanemotherlaughslau
ghmotherlaughseefatherheisbigandstrongfatherwillyouplaywithjanefath
erissmilingsmilefatherssmileseethedogbowwowgoesthedogdoyouwantto
playdoyouwanttoplaywithjaneseethedogrunrundogrunlooklookherecom
esafriendthefriendwillplaywithjanetheywillplayagoodgameplayjaneplay

*Quiet as it's kept, there were no marigolds in the fall of 1941. We thought, at the time, that it was because Pecola was having her father's baby that the marigolds did not grow. A little examination and much less melancholy would have proved to us that our seeds were not the only ones that did not sprout; nobody's did. Not even the gardens fronting the lake showed marigolds that year. But so deeply concerned were we with the health and safe delivery of Pecola's baby we could think of nothing but our own magic: if we planted the seeds, and said the right words over them, they would blossom, and everything would be all right.*

*It was a long time before my sister and I admitted to ourselves that no green was going to spring from our seeds. Once we knew, our guilt was relieved only by fights and mutual accusations about who was to blame. For years I thought my sister was right: it was my fault. I had planted them too far down in the earth. It never occurred to either of us that the earth itself might have been unyielding. We had dropped our seeds in our own little plot of black dirt just as Pecola's father had dropped his seeds in his own plot of black dirt. Our innocence and faith were no more productive than his lust or despair. What is clear now is that of all of that hope, fear, lust, love, and grief, nothing remains but Pecola and the unyielding earth. Cholly Breedlove is dead; our innocence too. The seeds shriveled and died; her baby too.*

*There is really nothing more to say—except why. But since why is difficult to handle, one must take refuge in how.*

Nuns go by as quiet as lust, and drunken men with sober eyes sing in the lobby of the Greek hotel. Rosemary Villanucci, our next-door friend who lives above her father's café, sits in a 1939 Buick eating bread and butter. She rolls down the window to tell my sister Frieda and me that we can't come in. We stare at her, wanting her bread, but more than that wanting to poke the arrogance out of her eyes and smash the pride of ownership that curls her chewing mouth. When she comes out of the car we will beat her up, make red marks on her white skin, and she will cry and ask us do we want her to pull her pants down. We will say no. We don't know what we should feel or do if she does, but whenever she asks us, we know she is offering us something precious and that our own pride must be asserted by refusing to accept.

School has started, and Frieda and I get new brown stockings and cod-liver oil. Grown-ups talk in tired, edgy voices about Zick's Coal Company and take us along in the evening to the railroad tracks where we fill burlap sacks with the tiny pieces of coal lying about. Later we walk home, glancing back to see the great carloads of slag being dumped, red hot and smoking, into the ravine that skirts the steel mill. The dying fire lights the sky with a dull orange glow. Frieda and I lag behind, staring at the patch of color surrounded by black. It is impossible not to feel a shiver when our feet leave the gravel path and sink into the dead grass in the field.

Our house is old, cold, and green. At night a kerosene lamp lights one large room. The others are braced in darkness, peopled by roaches and mice. Adults do not talk to us—they give us directions. They issue orders without providing information. When we trip and fall down they glance at us; if we cut or bruise ourselves, they ask us are we crazy. When we catch colds, they shake their heads in disgust at our lack of consideration. How, they ask us, do you expect anybody to get anything done if you all are sick? We cannot answer them. Our illness is treated with contempt, foul Black Draught, and castor oil that blunts our minds.

When, on a day after a trip to collect coal, I cough once, loudly, through bronchial tubes already packed tight with phlegm, my mother frowns. "Great Jesus. Get on in that bed. How many times do I have to tell you to wear something on your head? You must be the biggest fool in this town. Frieda? Get some rags and stuff that window."

Frieda restuffs the window. I trudge off to bed, full of guilt and self-pity. I lie down in my underwear, the metal in my black garters hurts my legs, but I do not take them off, for it is too cold to lie stockingless. It takes a long time for my body to heat its place in the bed. Once I have generated a silhouette of warmth, I dare not move, for there is a cold place one-half inch in any direction. No one speaks to me or asks how I feel. In an hour or two my mother comes. Her hands are large and rough, and when she rubs the Vicks salve on my chest, I am rigid with pain. She takes two fingers' full of it at a time, and massages my chest until I am faint. Just when I think I will tip over into a scream, she scoops out a little of the salve on her forefinger and puts it in my mouth, telling me to swallow. A hot flannel is wrapped about my neck and chest. I am covered up with heavy quilts and ordered to sweat, which I do—promptly.

Later I throw up, and my mother says, "What did you puke on the bed clothes for? Don't you have sense enough to hold your head out the bed? Now, look what you did. You think I got time for nothing but washing up your puke?"

The puke swaddles down the pillow onto the sheet—green-gray, with flecks of orange. It moves like the insides of an uncooked egg. Stubbornly clinging to its own mass, refusing to break up and be removed. How, I wonder, can it be so neat and nasty at the same time?

My mother's voice drones on. She is not talking to me. She is talking to the puke, but she is calling it my name: Claudia. She wipes it up as best she can and puts a scratchy towel over the large wet place. I lie down again. The rags have fallen from the window crack, and the air is cold. I dare not call her back and am reluctant to leave my warmth. My mother's anger humiliates me; her words chafe my cheeks, and I am crying. I do not know that she is not angry at me, but at my sickness. I believe she despises my weakness for letting the sickness "take holt." By and by I will not get sick; I will refuse to. But for now I am crying. I know I am making more snot, but I can't stop.

My sister comes in. Her eyes are full of sorrow. She sings to me: "When the deep purple falls over sleepy garden walls, someone thinks of me. . . ." I doze, thinking of plums, walls, and "someone."

But was it really like that? As painful as I remember? Only mildly. Or rather, it was a productive and fructifying pain. Love, thick and dark as Alaga syrup, eased up into that cracked window. I could smell it—taste it—sweet, musty, with an edge of wintergreen in its base—everywhere in that house. It stuck, along with my tongue, to the frosted windowpanes. It coated my chest, along with the salve, and when the flannel came undone in my sleep, the clear, sharp curves of air outlined its presence on my throat. And in the night, when my coughing was dry and tough, feet padded into the room, hands repinned the flannel, readjusted the quilt, and rested a moment on my forehead. So when I think of autumn, I think of somebody with hands who does not want me to die.

It was autumn too when Mr. Henry came. Our roomer. Our roomer. The words ballooned from the lips and hovered about our heads—silent, separate, and pleasantly mysterious. My mother was all ease and satisfaction in discussing his coming.

"You know him," she said to her friends. "Henry Washington. He's been living over there with Miss Della Jones on Thirteenth Street. But she's too addled now to keep up. So he's looking for another place."

"Oh, yes." Her friends do not hide their curiosity. "I been
wondering how long he was going to stay up there with her. They say
she's real bad off. Don't know who he is half the time, and nobody
else."

"Well, that old crazy nigger she married up with didn't help her
head none."

"Did you hear what he told folks when he left her?"

"Uh-uh. What?"

"Well, he run off with that trifling Peggy—from Elyria. You
know."

"One of Old Slack Bessie's girls?"

"That's the one. Well, somebody asked him why he left a nice good
church woman like Della for that heifer. You know Della always did
keep a good house. And he said the honest-to-God real reason was he
couldn't take no more of that violet water Della Jones used. Said he
wanted a woman to smell like a woman. Said Della was just too clean
for him."

"Old dog. Ain't that nasty!"

"You telling me. What kind of reasoning is that?"

"No kind. Some men just dogs."

"Is that what give her them strokes?"

"Must have helped. But you know, none of them girls wasn't too
bright. Remember that grinning Hattie? She wasn't never right.
And their Auntie Julia is still trotting up and down Sixteenth Street
talking to herself."

"Didn't she get put away?"

"Naw. County wouldn't take her. Said she wasn't harming
anybody."

"Well, she's harming me. You want something to scare the living
shit out of you, you get up at five-thirty in the morning like I do
and see that old hag floating by in that bonnet. Have mercy!"

They laugh.

Frieda and I are washing Mason jars. We do not hear their words, but with grown-ups we listen to and watch out for their voices.

"Well, I hope don't nobody let me roam around like that when I get senile. It's a shame."

"What they going to do about Della? Don't she have no people?"

"A sister's coming up from North Carolina to look after her. I expect she wants to get aholt of Della's house."

"Oh, come on. That's a evil thought, if ever I heard one."

"What you want to bet? Henry Washington said that sister ain't seen Della in fifteen years."

"I kind of thought Henry would marry her one of these days."

"That old woman?"

"Well, Henry ain't no chicken."

"No, but he ain't no buzzard, either."

"He ever been married to anybody?"

"No."

"How come? Somebody cut it off?"

"He's just picky."

"He ain't picky. You see anything around here you'd marry?"

"Well . . . no."

"He's just sensible. A steady worker with quiet ways. I hope it works out all right."

"It will. How much you charging?"

"Five dollars every two weeks."

"That'll be a big help to you."

"I'll say."

Their conversation is like a gently wicked dance: sound meets sound, curtsies, shimmies, and retires. Another sound enters but is upstaged by still another: the two circle each other and stop. Sometimes their words move in lofty spirals; other times they take strident leaps, and all of it is punctuated with warm-pulsed laughter—like the throb of a heart made of jelly. The edge, the curl, the thrust of their emotions is always clear to Frieda and me. We do not, cannot, know the meanings of all their words, for we are nine and ten years old. So we watch their faces, their hands, their feet, and listen for truth in timbre.

So when Mr. Henry arrived on a Saturday night, we smelled him. He smelled wonderful. Like trees and lemon vanishing cream, and Nu Nile Hair Oil and flecks of Sen-Sen.

He smiled a lot, showing small even teeth with a friendly gap in the middle. Frieda and I were not introduced to him—merely pointed out. Like, here is the bathroom; the clothes closet is here; and these are my kids, Frieda and Claudia; watch out for this window; it don't open all the way.

We looked sideways at him, saying nothing and expecting him to say nothing. Just to nod, as he had done at the clothes closet, acknowledging our existence. To our surprise, he spoke to us.

"Hello there. You must be Greta Garbo, and you must be Ginger Rogers."

We giggled. Even my father was startled into a smile.

"Want a penny?" He held out a shiny coin to us. Frieda lowered her head, too pleased to answer. I reached for it. He snapped his thumb and forefinger, and the penny disappeared. Our shock was laced with delight. We searched all over him, poking our fingers into his socks, looking up the inside back of his coat. If happiness is anticipation with certainty, we were happy. And while we waited for the coin to reappear, we knew we were amusing Mama and Daddy. Daddy was smiling, and Mama's eyes went soft as they followed our hands wandering over Mr. Henry's body.

We loved him. Even after what came later, there was no bitterness in our memory of him.

She slept in the bed with us. Frieda on the outside because she is brave—it never occurs to her that if in her sleep her hand hangs over the edge of the bed "something" will crawl out from under it and bite her fingers off. I sleep near the wall because that thought *has* occurred to me. Pecola, therefore, had to sleep in the middle.

Mama had told us two days earlier that a "case" was coming—a girl who had no place to go. The county had placed her in our house for a few days until they could decide what to do, or, more precisely, until the family was reunited. We were to be nice to her and not fight. Mama didn't know "what got into people," but that old Dog Breedlove had burned up his house, gone upside his wife's head, and everybody, as a result, was outdoors.

Outdoors, we knew, was the real terror of life. The threat of being outdoors surfaced frequently in those days. Every possibility of excess was curtailed with it. If somebody ate too much, he could end up outdoors. If somebody used too much coal, he could end up outdoors. People could gamble themselves outdoors, drink themselves outdoors. Sometimes mothers put their sons outdoors, and when that happened, regardless of what the son had done, all sympathy was with him. He was outdoors, and his own flesh had done it. To be put outdoors by a landlord was one thing—unfortunate, but an aspect of life over which you had no control, since you could not control your income. But to be slack enough to put oneself outdoors, or heartless enough to put one's own kin outdoors—that was criminal.

There is a difference between being put *out* and being put out*doors*. If you are put out, you go somewhere else; if you are outdoors, there is no place to go. The distinction was subtle but final. Outdoors was the end of something, an irrevocable, physical fact, defining and complementing our metaphysical condition. Being a minority in both caste and class, we moved about anyway on the hem of life, struggling to consolidate our weaknesses and hang on, or to creep singly up into the major folds of the garment. Our peripheral existence, however, was something we had learned to deal with—probably because it was abstract. But the concreteness of being outdoors was another matter—like the difference between the concept of death and being, in fact, dead. Dead doesn't change, and outdoors is here to stay.

Knowing that there was such a thing as outdoors bred in us a hunger for property, for ownership. The firm possession of a yard, a porch, a grape arbor. Propertied black people spent all their energies, all their love, on their nests. Like frenzied, desperate birds, they overdecorated everything; fussed and fidgeted over their hard-won homes; canned, jellied, and preserved all summer to fill the cupboards and shelves; they painted, picked, and poked at every corner of their houses. And these houses loomed like hothouse sunflowers among the rows of weeds that were the rented houses. Renting blacks cast furtive glances at these owned yards and porches, and made firmer commitments to buy themselves "some nice little old place." In the meantime, they saved, and scratched, and piled away what they could in the rented hovels, looking forward to the day of property.

Cholly Breedlove, then, a renting black, having put his family outdoors, had catapulted himself beyond the reaches of human consideration. He had joined the animals; was, indeed, an old dog, a snake, a ratty nigger. Mrs. Breedlove was staying with the woman she worked for; the boy, Sammy, was with some other family; and Pecola was to stay with us. Cholly was in jail.

She came with nothing. No little paper bag with the other dress, or a nightgown, or two pair of whitish cotton bloomers. She just appeared with a white woman and sat down.

We had fun in those few days Pecola was with us. Frieda and I stopped fighting each other and concentrated on our guest, trying hard to keep her from feeling outdoors.

When we discovered that she clearly did not want to dominate us, we liked her. She laughed when I clowned for her, and smiled and accepted gracefully the food gifts my sister gave her.

"Would you like some graham crackers?"

"I don't care."

Frieda brought her four graham crackers on a saucer and some milk in a blue-and-white Shirley Temple cup. She was a long time with the milk, and gazed fondly at the silhouette of Shirley Temple's dimpled

face. Frieda and she had a loving conversation about how cu-ute
Shirley Temple was. I couldn't join them in their adoration because I
hated Shirley. Not because she was cute, but because she danced with
Bojangles, who was *my* friend, *my* uncle, *my* daddy, and who ought to
have been soft-shoeing it and chuckling with me. Instead he was
enjoying, sharing, giving a lovely dance thing with one of those little
white girls whose socks never slid down under their heels. So I said, "I
like Jane Withers."

They gave me a puzzled look, decided I was incomprehensible, and
continued their reminiscing about old squint-eyed Shirley.

Younger than both Frieda and Pecola, I had not yet arrived at the
turning point in the development of my psyche which would allow me
to love her. What I felt at that time was unsullied hatred. But before
that I had felt a stranger, more frightening thing than hatred for all the
Shirley Temples of the world.

It had begun with Christmas and the gift of dolls. The big, the
special, the loving gift was always a big, blue-eyed Baby Doll. From
the clucking sounds of adults I knew that the doll represented what
they thought was my fondest wish. I was bemused with the thing
itself, and the way it looked. What was I supposed to do with it?
Pretend I was its mother? I had no interest in babies or the concept of
motherhood. I was interested only in humans my own age and size,
and could not generate any enthusiasm at the prospect of being a
mother. Motherhood was old age, and other remote possibilities. I
learned quickly, however, what I was expected to do with the doll:
rock it, fabricate storied situations around it, even sleep with it. Picture
books were full of little girls sleeping with their dolls. Raggedy Ann
dolls usually, but they were out of the question. I was physically
revolted by and secretly frightened of those round moronic eyes, the
pancake face, and orangeworms hair.

The other dolls, which were supposed to bring me great pleasure,
succeeded in doing quite the opposite. When I took it to bed, its hard
unyielding limbs resisted my flesh—the tapered fingertips on those

dimpled hands scratched. If, in sleep, I turned, the bone-cold head collided with my own. It was a most uncomfortable, patently aggressive sleeping companion. To hold it was no more rewarding. The starched gauze or lace on the cotton dress irritated any embrace. I had only one desire: to dismember it. To see of what it was made, to discover the dearness, to find the beauty, the desirability that had escaped me, but apparently only me. Adults, older girls, shops, magazines, newspapers, window signs—all the world had agreed that a blue-eyed, yellow-haired, pink-skinned doll was what every girl child treasured. "Here," they said, "this is beautiful, and if you are on this day 'worthy' you may have it." I fingered the face, wondering at the single-stroke eyebrows; picked at the pearly teeth stuck like two piano keys between red bowline lips. Traced the turned-up nose, poked the glassy blue eyeballs, twisted the yellow hair. I could not love it. But I could examine it to see what it was that all the world said was lovable. Break off the tiny fingers, bend the flat feet, loosen the hair, twist the head around, and the thing made one sound—a sound they said was the sweet and plaintive cry "Mama," but which sounded to me like the bleat of a dying lamb, or, more precisely, our icebox door opening on rusty hinges in July. Remove the cold and stupid eyeball, it would bleat still, "Ahhhhhh," take off the head, shake out the sawdust, crack the back against the brass bed rail, it would bleat still. The gauze back would split, and I could see the disk with six holes, the secret of the sound. A mere metal roundness.

Grown people frowned and fussed: "You-don't-know-how-to-take-care-of-nothing. I-never-had-a-baby-doll-in-my-whole-life-and-used-to-cry-my-eyes-out-for-them. Now-you-got-one-a-beautiful-one-and-you-tear-it-up-what's-the-matter-with-you?"

How strong was their outrage. Tears threatened to erase the aloofness of their authority. The emotion of years of unfulfilled longing preened in their voices. I did not know why I destroyed those dolls. But I did know that nobody ever asked me what I wanted for Christmas. Had any adult with the power to fulfill my desires taken me seriously and asked me what I wanted, they would have known that I did not want to have anything to own, or to possess any object. I wanted rather to feel something on Christmas day. The real question would have been, "Dear Claudia, what experience would you like on Christmas?" I could have spoken up, "I want to sit on the low stool in Big Mama's kitchen with my lap full of lilacs and listen to Big Papa play his violin for me alone." The lowness of the stool made for my body, the security and warmth of Big Mama's kitchen, the smell of the lilacs, the sound of the music, and, since it would be good to have all of my senses engaged, the taste of a peach, perhaps, afterward.

Instead I tasted and smelled the acridness of tin plates and cups designed for tea parties that bored me. Instead I looked with loathing on new dresses that required a hateful bath in a galvanized zinc tub before wearing. Slipping around on the zinc, no time to play or soak, for the water chilled too fast, no time to enjoy one's nakedness, only time to make curtains of soapy water careen down between the legs. Then the scratchy towels and the dreadful and humiliating absence of dirt. The irritable, unimaginative cleanliness. Gone the ink marks from legs and face, all my creations and accumulations of the day gone, and replaced by goose pimples.

I destroyed white baby dolls.

But the dismembering of dolls was not the true horror. The truly horrifying thing was the transference of the same impulses to little white girls. The indifference with which I could have axed them was shaken only by my desire to do so. To discover what eluded me: the secret of the magic they weaved on others. What made people look at them and say, "Awwwww," but not for me? The eye slide of black women as they approached them on the street, and the possessive gentleness of their touch as they handled them.

If I pinched them, their eyes—unlike the crazed glint of the baby doll's eyes—would fold in pain, and their cry would not be the sound of an icebox door, but a fascinating cry of pain. When I learned how repulsive this disinterested violence was, that it was repulsive because it was disinterested, my shame floundered about for refuge. The best hiding place was love. Thus the conversion from pristine sadism to fabricated hatred, to fraudulent love. It was a small step to Shirley Temple. I learned much later to worship her, just as I learned to delight in cleanliness, knowing, even as I learned, that the change was adjustment without improvement.

"Three quarts of milk. That's what was *in* that icebox yesterday. Three whole quarts. Now they ain't none. Not a drop. I don't mind folks coming in and getting what they want, but three quarts of milk! What the devil does *any*body need with *three* quarts of milk?"

The "folks" my mother was referring to was Pecola. The three of us, Pecola, Frieda, and I, listened to her downstairs in the kitchen fussing about the amount of milk Pecola had drunk. We knew she was fond of the Shirley Temple cup and took every opportunity to drink milk out of it just to handle and see sweet Shirley's face. My mother knew that Frieda and I hated milk and assumed Pecola drank it out of greediness. It was certainly not for us to "dispute" her. We didn't initiate talk with grown-ups; we answered their questions.

Ashamed of the insults that were being heaped on our friend, we just sat there: I picked toe jam, Frieda cleaned her fingernails with her teeth, and Pecola finger-traced some scars on her knee—her head cocked to one side. My mother's fussing soliloquies always irritated and depressed us. They were interminable, insulting, and although indirect (Mama never named anybody—just talked about folks and *some* people), extremely painful in their thrust. She would go on like that for hours, connecting one offense to another until all of the things that chagrined her were spewed out. Then, having told everybody and everything off, she would burst into song and sing the rest of the day. But it was such a long time before the singing part came. In the meantime, our stomachs jellying and our necks burning, we listened, avoided each other's eyes, and picked toe jam or whatever.

". . . I don't know what I'm supposed to be running here, a

charity ward, I guess. Time for me to get out of the *giving* line and get in the *getting* line. I guess I ain't sup*posed* to have nothing. I'm sup*posed* to end up in the poorhouse. Look like nothing I do is going to keep me out of there. Folks just spend all their time trying to figure out ways to send *me* to the poorhouse. I got about as much business with another mouth to feed as a cat has with side pockets. As if I don't have trouble enough trying to feed my own and keep out the poorhouse, now I got something else in here that's just going to *drink* me on in there. Well, naw, she ain't. Not long as I got strength in my body and a tongue in my head. There's a limit to everything. I ain't got nothing to just throw *away*. Don't *nobody* need *three* quarts of milk. Henry *Ford* don't need three quarts of milk. That's just downright *sinful*. I'm willing to do what I can for folks. Can't nobody say I ain't. But this has got to stop, and I'm just the one to stop it. Bible say watch as *well* as pray. Folks just dump they children off on you and go on 'bout they business. Ain't nobody even *peeped* in here to see whether that child has a loaf of bread. Look like they would just *peep* in to see whether I had a loaf of bread to give her. But naw. That thought don't cross they mind. That old trifling Cholly been out of jail *two* whole days and ain't been here *yet* to see if his own child was 'live or dead. She could be *dead* for all he know. And that *mama* neither. What kind of something is that?"

When Mama got around to Henry Ford and all those people who didn't care whether she had a loaf of bread, it was time to go. We wanted to miss the part about Roosevelt and the CCC camps.

Frieda got up and started down the stairs. Pecola and I followed, making a wide arc to avoid the kitchen doorway. We sat on the steps of the porch, where my mother's words could reach us only in spurts.

It was a lonesome Saturday. The house smelled of Fels Naphtha and the sharp odor of mustard greens cooking. Saturdays were lonesome, fussy, soapy days. Second in misery only to those tight, starchy, cough-drop Sundays, so full of "don'ts" and "set'cha self downs."

If my mother was in a singing mood, it wasn't so bad. She would sing about hard times, bad times, and somebody-done-gone-and-left-me times. But her voice was so sweet and her singing-eyes so melty I found myself longing for those hard times, yearning to be grown without "a thin di-i-ime to my name." I looked forward to the delicious time when "my man" would leave me, when I would "hate to see that evening sun go down . . ." 'cause then I would know "my man has left this town." Misery colored by the greens and blues in my mother's voice took all of the grief out of the words and left me with a conviction that pain was not only endurable, it was sweet.

But without song, those Saturdays sat on my head like a coal scuttle, and if Mama was fussing, as she was now, it was like somebody throwing stones at it.

". . . and here I am poor as a bowl of yak-me. What do they think I am? Some kind of Sandy Claus? Well, they can just take they stocking down 'cause it *ain't* Christmas. . . ."

We fidgeted.

"Let's do something," Frieda said.

"What do you want to do?" I asked.

"I don't know. Nothing." Frieda stared at the tops of the trees. Pecola looked at her feet.

"You want to go up to Mr. Henry's room and look at his girlie magazines?"

Frieda made an ugly face. She didn't like to look at dirty pictures. "Well," I continued, "we could look at his Bible. *That's* pretty." Frieda sucked her teeth and made a *phtt* sound with her lips. "O.K., then. We could go thread needles for the half-blind lady. She'll give us a penny."

Frieda snorted. "Her eyes look like snot. I don't feel like looking at them. What *you* want to do Pecola?"

"I don't care," she said. "Anything you want."

I had another idea. "We could go up the alley and see what's in the trash cans."

"Too cold," said Frieda. She was bored and irritable.

"I know. We could make some fudge."

"You kidding? With Mama in there fussing? When she starts fussing at the walls, you know she's gonna be at it all day. She wouldn't even let us."

"Well, let's go over to the Greek hotel and listen to them cuss."

"Oh, who wants to do *that?* Besides, they say the same old words all the time."

My supply of ideas exhausted, I began to concentrate on the white spots on my fingernails. The total signified the number of boyfriends I would have. Seven.

Mama's soliloquy slid into the silence ". . . Bible say feed the hungry. That's fine. That's all right. But I ain't feeding no elephants. . . . Anybody need three quarts of milk to *live* need to get out of here. They in the wrong place. What is this? Some kind of *dairy* farm?"

Suddenly Pecola bolted straight up, her eyes wide with terror. A whinnying sound came from her mouth.

"What's the matter with *you?*" Frieda stood up too.

Then we both looked where Pecola was staring. Blood was running down her legs. Some drops were on the steps. I leaped up. "Hey. You cut yourself? Look. It's all over your dress."

A brownish-red stain discolored the back of her dress. She kept whinnying, standing with her legs far apart.

Frieda said, "Oh. Lordy! I know. I know what that is!"

"What?" Pecola's fingers went to her mouth.

"That's ministratin'."

"What's that?"

"You know."

"Am I going to die?" she asked.

"Noooo. You won't die. It just means you can have a baby!"

"What?"

"How do *you* know?" I was sick and tired of Frieda knowing everything.

"Mildred told me, and Mama too."

"I don't believe it."

"You don't have to, dummy. Look. Wait here. Sit down, Pecola. Right here." Frieda was all authority and zest. "And you," she said to me, "you go get some water."

"Water?"

"Yes, stupid. Water. And be quiet, or Mama will hear you."

Pecola sat down again, a little less fear in her eyes. I went into the kitchen.

"What you want, girl?" Mama was rinsing curtains in the sink.

"Some water, ma'am."

"Right where I'm working, naturally. Well, get a glass. Not no clean one neither. Use that jar."

I got a Mason jar and filled it with water from the faucet. It seemed a long time filling.

"Don't nobody never want nothing till they see me at the sink. Then everybody got to drink water. . . ."

When the jar was full, I moved to leave the room.

"Where you going?"

"Outside."

"Drink that water right here!"

"I ain't gonna break nothing."

"You don't know what you gonna do."

"Yes, ma'am. I do. Lemme take it out. I won't spill none."

"You bed' not."

I got to the porch and stood there with the Mason jar of water. Pecola was crying.

"What you crying for? Does it hurt?"

She shook her head.

"Then stop slinging snot."

Frieda opened the back door. She had something tucked in her blouse. She looked at me in amazement and pointed to the jar. "What's that supposed to do?"

"You told me. You *said* get some water."

"Not a little old jar full. Lots of water. To scrub the steps with, dumbbell!"

"How was I supposed to know?"

"Yeah. How was you. Come on." She pulled Pecola up by the arm. "Let's go back here." They headed for the side of the house where the bushes were thick.

"Hey. What about me? I want to go."

"Shut uuuup," Frieda stage-whispered. "Mama will hear you. You wash the steps."

They disappeared around the corner of the house.

I was going to miss something. Again. Here was something important, and I had to stay behind and not see any of it. I poured the water on the steps, sloshed it with my shoe, and ran to join them.

Frieda was on her knees; a white rectangle of cotton was near her on the ground. She was pulling Pecola's pants off. "Come on. Step out of them." She managed to get the soiled pants down and flung them at me. "Here."

"What am I supposed to do with these?"

"Bury them, moron."

Frieda told Pecola to hold the cotton thing between her legs.

"How she gonna walk like that?" I asked.

Frieda didn't answer. Instead she took two safety pins from the hem of her skirt and began to pin the ends of the napkin to Pecola's dress.

I picked up the pants with two fingers and looked about for something to dig a hole with. A rustling noise in the bushes startled me, and turning toward it, I saw a pair of fascinated eyes in a dough-white face. Rosemary was watching us. I grabbed for her face and succeeded in scratching her nose. She screamed and jumped back.

"Mrs. MacTeer! Mrs. MacTeer!" Rosemary hollered. "Frieda and Claudia are out here playing nasty! Mrs. MacTeer!"

Mama opened the window and looked down at us.

"What?"

"They're playing nasty, Mrs. MacTeer. Look. And Claudia hit me 'cause I seen them!"

Mama slammed the window shut and came running out the back door.

"What you all doing? Oh. Uh-huh. Uh-huh. Playing nasty, huh?" She reached into the bushes and pulled off a switch. "I'd rather raise pigs than some nasty girls. Least I can slaughter *them!*"

We began to shriek. "No, Mama. No, ma'am. We wasn't! She's a liar! No, ma'am, Mama! No, ma'am, Mama!"

Mama grabbed Frieda by the shoulder, turned her around, and gave her three or four stinging cuts on her legs. "Gonna be nasty, huh? Naw you ain't!"

Frieda was destroyed. Whippings wounded and insulted her.

Mama looked at Pecola. "You too!" she said. "Child of mine or not!" She grabbed Pecola and spun her around. The safety pin snapped open on one end of the napkin, and Mama saw it fall from under her dress. The switch hovered in the air while Mama blinked. "What the devil is going on here?"

Frieda was sobbing. I, next in line, began to explain. "She was bleeding. We was just trying to stop the blood!"

Mama looked at Frieda for verification. Frieda nodded. "She's ministratin'. We was just helping."

Mama released Pecola and stood looking at her. Then she pulled both of them toward her, their heads against her stomach. Her eyes were sorry. "All right, all right. Now, stop crying. I didn't know. Come on, now. Get on in the house. Go on home, Rosemary. The show is over."

We trooped in, Frieda sobbing quietly, Pecola carrying a white tail, me carrying the little-girl-gone-to-woman pants.

Mama led us to the bathroom. She prodded Pecola inside, and taking the underwear from me, told us to stay out.

We could hear water running into the bathtub.

"You think she's going to drown her?"

"Oh, Claudia. You so dumb. She's just going to wash her clothes and all."

"Should we beat up Rosemary?"

"No. Leave her alone."

The water gushed, and over its gushing we could hear the music of my mother's laughter.

That night, in bed, the three of us lay still. We were full of awe and respect for Pecola. Lying next to a real person who was really ministratin' was somehow sacred. She was different from us now—grown-up-like. She, herself, felt the distance, but refused to lord it over us.

After a long while she spoke very softly. "Is it true that I can have a baby now?"

"Sure," said Frieda drowsily. "Sure you can."

"But . . . how?" Her voice was hollow with wonder.

"Oh," said Frieda, "somebody has to love you."

"Oh."

There was a long pause in which Pecola and I thought this over. It would involve, I supposed, "my man," who, before leaving me, would love me. But there weren't any babies in the songs my mother sang. Maybe that's why the women were sad: the men left before they could make a baby.

Then Pecola asked a question that had never entered my mind. "How do you do that? I mean, how do you get somebody to love you?" But Frieda was asleep. And I didn't know.

## HEREISTHEHOUSEITISGREENANDWHITEITHASAREDDO ORITISVERYPRETTYITISVERYPRETTYPRETTYPRETTYP

There is an abandoned store on the southeast corner of Broadway and Thirty-fifth Street in Lorain, Ohio. It does not recede into its background of leaden sky, nor harmonize with the gray frame houses and black telephone poles around it. Rather, it foists itself on the eye of the passerby in a manner that is both irritating and melancholy. Visitors who drive to this tiny town wonder why it has not been torn down, while pedestrians, who are residents of the neighborhood, simply look away when they pass it.

At one time, when the building housed a pizza parlor, people saw only slow-footed teen-aged boys huddled about the corner. These young boys met there to feel their groins, smoke cigarettes, and plan mild outrages. The smoke from their cigarettes they inhaled deeply, forcing it to fill their lungs, their hearts, their thighs, and keep at bay the shiveriness, the energy of their youth. They moved slowly, laughed slowly, but flicked the ashes from their cigarettes too quickly, too often, and exposed themselves, to those who were interested, as novices to the habit. But long before the sound of their lowing and the sight of their preening, the building was leased to a Hungarian baker, modestly famous for his brioche and poppy-seed rolls. Earlier than that, there was a real-estate office there, and even before that, some gypsies used it as a base of operations. The gypsy family gave the large plate-glass window as much distinction and character as it ever had. The girls of the family took turns sitting between yards of velvet draperies and Oriental rugs hanging at the windows. They looked out and occasionally smiled, or winked, or beckoned—only occasionally. Mostly they looked, their elaborate dresses, long-sleeved and long-skirted, hiding the nakedness that stood in their eyes.

So fluid has the population in that area been, that probably no one remembers longer, longer ago, before the time of the gypsies and the time of the teen-agers when the Breedloves lived there, nestled together in the storefront. Festering together in the debris of a realtor's whim. They slipped in and out of the box of peeling gray, making no stir in the neighborhood, no sound in the labor force, and no wave in the mayor's office. Each member of the family in his own cell of consciousness, each making his own patchwork quilt of reality—collecting fragments of experience here, pieces of information there. From the tiny impressions gleaned from one another, they created a sense of belonging and tried to make do with the way they found each other.

The plan of the living quarters was as unimaginative as a first-generation Greek landlord could contrive it to be. The large "store" area was partitioned into two rooms by beaverboard planks that did not reach to the ceiling. There was a living room, which the family called the front room, and the bedroom, where all the living was done. In the front room were two sofas, an upright piano, and a tiny artificial Christmas tree which had been there, decorated and dust-laden, for two years. The bedroom had three beds: a narrow iron bed for Sammy, fourteen years old, another for Pecola, eleven years old, and a double bed for Cholly and Mrs. Breedlove. In the center of the bedroom, for the even distribution of heat, stood a coal stove. Trunks, chairs, a small end table, and a cardboard "wardrobe" closet were placed around the walls. The kitchen was in the back of this apartment, a separate room. There were no bath facilities. Only a toilet bowl, inaccessible to the eye, if not the ear, of the tenants.

There is nothing more to say about the furnishings. They were anything but describable, having been conceived, manufactured, shipped, and sold in various states of thoughtlessness, greed, and indifference. The furniture had aged without ever having become familiar. People had owned it, but never known it. No one had lost a penny or a brooch under the cushions of either sofa and remembered the place and time of the loss or the finding. No one had clucked and said, "But I *had* it just a minute ago. I was sitting right there talking to . . ." or "Here it is. It must have slipped down while I was feeding the baby!" No one had given birth in one of the beds—or remembered with fondness the peeled paint places, because that's what the baby, when he learned to pull himself up, used to pick loose. No thrifty child had tucked a wad of gum under the table. No happy drunk—a friend of the family, with a fat neck, unmarried, you know, but God how he eats!—had sat at the piano and played "You Are My Sunshine." No young girl had stared at the tiny Christmas tree and remembered when she had decorated it, or wondered if that blue ball was going to hold, or if HE would ever come back to see it.

There were no memories among those pieces. Certainly no memories to be cherished. Occasionally an item provoked a physical reaction: an increase of acid irritation in the upper intestinal tract, a light flush of perspiration at the back of the neck as circumstances surrounding the piece of furniture were recalled. The sofa, for example. It had been purchased new, but the fabric had split straight across the back by the time it was delivered. The store would not take the responsibility. . . .

"Looka here, buddy. It was O.K. when I put it on the truck. The store can't do anything about it once it's on the truck. . . ." Listerine and Lucky Strike breath.

"But I don't want no tore couch if'n it's bought new." Pleading eyes and tightened testicles.

"Tough shit, buddy. *Your* tough shit. . . ."

You could hate a sofa, of course—that is, if you could hate a sofa. But it didn't matter. You still had to get together $4.80 a month. If you had to pay $4.80 a month for a sofa that started off split, no good, and humiliating—you couldn't take any joy in owning it. And the joylessness stank, pervading everything. The stink of it kept you from painting the beaverboard walls; from getting a matching piece of material for the chair; even from sewing up the split, which became a gash, which became a gaping chasm that exposed the cheap frame and cheaper upholstery. It withheld the refreshment in a sleep slept on it. It imposed a furtiveness on the loving done on it. Like a sore tooth that is not content to throb in isolation, but must diffuse its own pain to other parts of the body—making breathing difficult, vision limited, nerves unsettled, so a hated piece of furniture produces a fretful malaise that asserts itself throughout the house and limits the delight of things not related to it.

The only living thing in the Breedloves' house was the coal stove, which lived independently of everything and everyone, its fire being "out," "banked," or "up" at its own discretion, in spite of the fact that the family fed it and knew all the details of its regimen: sprinkle, do not dump, not too much. . . . The fire seemed to live, go down, or die according to its own schemata. In the morning, however, it always saw fit to die.

The Breedloves did not live in a storefront because they were having temporary difficulty adjusting to the cutbacks at the plant. They lived there because they were poor and black, and they stayed there because they believed they were ugly. Although their poverty was traditional and stultifying, it was not unique. But their ugliness was unique. No one could have convinced them that they were not relentlessly and aggressively ugly. Except for the father, Cholly, whose ugliness (the result of despair, dissipation, and violence directed toward petty things and weak people) was behavior, the rest of the family—Mrs. Breedlove, Sammy Breedlove, and Pecola Breedlove—wore their ugliness, put it on, so to speak, although it did not belong to them. The eyes, the small eyes set closely together under narrow foreheads. The low, irregular hairlines, which seemed even more irregular in contrast to the straight, heavy eyebrows which nearly met. Keen but crooked noses, with insolent nostrils. They had high cheekbones, and their ears turned forward. Shapely lips which called attention not to themselves but to the rest of the face. You looked at them and wondered why they were so ugly; you looked closely and could not find the source. Then you realized that it came from conviction, their conviction. It was as though some mysterious all-knowing master had given each one a cloak of ugliness to wear, and they had each accepted it without question. The master had said, "You are ugly people." They had looked about themselves and saw nothing to contradict the statement; saw, in fact, support for it leaning at them from every billboard, every movie, every glance. "Yes," they had said. "You are right." And they took the ugliness in their hands, threw it as a mantle over them, and went about the world with it. Dealing with it each according to his way. Mrs.

Breedlove handled hers as an actor does a prop: for the articulation of character, for support of a role she frequently imagined was hers—martyrdom. Sammy used his as a weapon to cause others pain. He adjusted his behavior to it, chose his companions on the basis of it: people who could be fascinated, even intimidated by it. And Pecola. She hid behind hers. Concealed, veiled, eclipsed—peeping out from behind the shroud very seldom, and then only to yearn for the return of her mask.

This family, on a Saturday morning in October, began, one by one, to stir out of their dreams of affluence and vengeance into the anonymous misery of their storefront.

Mrs. Breedlove slipped noiselessly out of bed, put a sweater on over her nightgown (which was an old day dress), and walked toward the kitchen. Her one good foot made hard, bony sounds; the twisted one whispered on the linoleum. In the kitchen she made noises with doors, faucets, and pans. The noises were hollow, but the threats they implied were not. Pecola opened her eyes and lay staring at the dead coal stove. Cholly mumbled, thrashed about in the bed for a minute, and then was quiet.

Even from where Pecola lay, she could smell Cholly's whiskey. The noises in the kitchen became louder and less hollow. There was direction and purpose in Mrs. Breedlove's movements that had nothing to do with the preparation of breakfast. This awareness, supported by ample evidence from the past, made Pecola tighten her stomach muscles and ration her breath.

Cholly had come home drunk. Unfortunately he had been too drunk to quarrel, so the whole business would have to erupt this morning. Because it had not taken place immediately, the oncoming fight would lack spontaneity; it would be calculated, uninspired, and deadly.

Mrs. Breedlove came swiftly into the room and stood at the foot of the bed where Cholly lay.

"I need some coal in this house."

Cholly did not move.

"Hear me?" Mrs. Breedlove jabbed Cholly's foot.

Cholly opened his eyes slowly. They were red and menacing. With no exception, Cholly had the meanest eyes in town.

"Awwwwww, woman!"

"I said I need some coal. It's as cold as a witch's tit in this house. Your whiskey ass wouldn't feel hellfire, but I'm cold. I got to do a lot of things, but I ain't got to freeze."

"Leave me lone."

"Not until you get me some coal. If working like a mule don't give me the right to be warm, what am I doing it for? You sure ain't bringing in nothing. If it was left up to you, we'd all be dead. . . ." Her voice was like an earache in the brain. ". . . If you think I'm going to wade out in the cold and get it myself, you'd better think again."

"I don't give a shit how you get it." A bubble of violence burst in his throat.

"You going to get your drunk self out of that bed and get me some coal or not?"

Silence.

"Cholly!"

Silence.

"Don't try me this morning, man. You say one more word, and I'll split you open!"

Silence.

"All right. All right. But if I sneeze once, just once, God help your butt!"

Sammy was awake now too, but pretending to be asleep. Pecola still held her stomach muscles taut and conserved her breath. They all knew that Mrs. Breedlove could have, would have, and had, gotten coal from the shed, or that Sammy or Pecola could be directed to get it. But the unquarreled evening hung like the first note of a dirge in sullenly expectant air. An escapade of drunkenness, no matter how routine, had its own ceremonial close. The tiny, undistinguished days that

Mrs. Breedlove lived were identified, grouped, and classed by these quarrels. They gave substance to the minutes and hours otherwise dim and unrecalled. They relieved the tiresomeness of poverty, gave grandeur to the dead rooms. In these violent breaks in routine that were themselves routine, she could display the style and imagination of what she believed to be her own true self. To deprive her of these fights was to deprive her of all the zest and reasonableness of life. Cholly, by his habitual drunkenness and orneriness, provided them both with the material they needed to make their lives tolerable. Mrs. Breedlove considered herself an upright and Christian woman, burdened with a no-count man, whom God wanted her to punish. (Cholly was beyond redemption, of course, and redemption was hardly the point—Mrs. Breedlove was not interested in Christ the Redeemer, but rather Christ the Judge.) Often she could be heard discoursing with Jesus about Cholly, pleading with Him to help her "strike the bastard down from his pea-knuckle of pride." And once when a drunken gesture catapulted Cholly into the red-hot stove, she screamed, "Get him, Jesus! Get him!" If Cholly had stopped drinking, she would never have forgiven Jesus. She needed Cholly's sins desperately. The lower he sank, the wilder and more irresponsible he became, the more splendid she and her task became. In the name of Jesus.

No less did Cholly need her. She was one of the few things abhorrent to him that he could touch and therefore hurt. He poured out on her the sum of all his inarticulate fury and aborted desires. Hating her, he could leave himself intact. When he was still very young, Cholly had been surprised in some bushes by two white men while he was newly but earnestly engaged in eliciting sexual pleasure from a little country girl. The men had shone a flashlight right on his behind. He had stopped, terrified. They chuckled. The beam of the flashlight did not move. "Go on," they said. "Go on and finish. And, nigger, make it good." The flashlight did not move. For some reason Cholly had not hated the white men; he hated, despised, the girl. Even a half-remembrance of this episode, along with myriad other humiliations, defeats, and emasculations, could stir him into flights of depravity that surprised himself—but only himself. Somehow he could not astound. He could only be astounded. So he gave that up, too.

Cholly and Mrs. Breedlove fought each other with a darkly brutal formalism that was paralleled only by their lovemaking. Tacitly they had agreed not to kill each other. He fought her the way a coward fights a man—with feet, the palms of his hands, and teeth. She, in turn, fought back in a purely feminine way—with frying pans and pokers, and occasionally a flat iron would sail toward his head. They did not talk, groan, or curse during these beatings. There was only the muted sound of falling things, and flesh on unsurprised flesh.

There was a difference in the reaction of the children to these battles. Sammy cursed for a while, or left the house, or threw himself into the fray. He was known, by the time he was fourteen, to have run away from home no less than twenty-seven times. Once he got to Buffalo and stayed three months. His returns, whether by force or circumstance, were sullen. Pecola, on the other hand, restricted by youth and sex, experimented with methods of endurance. Though the methods varied, the pain was as consistent as it was deep. She struggled between an overwhelming desire that one would kill the other, and a profound wish that she herself could die. Now she was whispering, "Don't, Mrs. Breedlove. Don't." Pecola, like Sammy and Cholly, always called her mother Mrs. Breedlove.

"Don't, Mrs. Breedlove. Don't."

But Mrs. Breedlove did.

By the grace, no doubt, of God, Mrs. Breedlove sneezed. Just once. She ran into the bedroom with a dishpan full of cold water and threw it in Cholly's face. He sat up, choking and spitting. Naked and ashen, he leaped from the bed, and with a flying tackle, grabbed his wife around the waist, and they hit the floor. Cholly picked her up and knocked her down with the back of his hand. She fell in a sitting position, her back supported by Sammy's bed frame. She had not let go of the dishpan, and began to hit at Cholly's thighs and groin with it. He put his foot in her chest, and she dropped the pan. Dropping to his knee, he struck her several times in the face, and she might have succumbed early had he not hit his hand against the metal bed frame when his wife ducked. Mrs. Breedlove took advantage of this momentary suspension of blows and slipped out of his reach. Sammy, who had watched in silence their struggling at his bedside, suddenly began to hit his father about the head with both fists, shouting "You naked fuck!" over and over and over. Mrs. Breedlove, having snatched up the round, flat stove lid, ran tippy-toe to Cholly as he was pulling himself up from his knees, and struck him two blows, knocking him right back into the senselessness out of which she had provoked him. Panting, she threw a quilt over him and let him lie.

Sammy screamed, "Kill him! Kill him!"

Mrs. Breedlove looked at Sammy with surprise. "Cut out that noise, boy." She put the stove lid back in place, and walked toward the kitchen. At the doorway she paused long enough to say to her son, "Get up from there anyhow. I need some coal."

Letting herself breathe easy now, Pecola covered her head with the quilt. The sick feeling, which she had tried to prevent by holding in her stomach, came quickly in spite of her precaution. There surged in her the desire to heave, but as always, she knew she would not.

"Please, God," she whispered into the palm of her hand. "Please make me disappear." She squeezed her eyes shut. Little parts of her body faded away. Now slowly, now with a rush. Slowly again. Her fingers went, one by one; then her arms disappeared all the way to the elbow. Her feet now. Yes, that was good. The legs all at once. It was hardest above the thighs. She had to be real still and pull. Her stomach would not go. But finally it, too, went away. Then her chest, her neck. The face was hard, too. Almost done, almost. Only her tight, tight eyes were left. They were always left.

Try as she might, she could never get her eyes to disappear. So what was the point? They were everything. Everything was there, in them. All of those pictures, all of those faces. She had long ago given up the idea of running away to see new pictures, new faces, as Sammy had so often done. He never took her, and he never thought about his going ahead of time, so it was never planned. It wouldn't have worked anyway. As long as she looked the way she did, as long as she was ugly, she would have to stay with these people. Somehow she belonged to them. Long hours she sat looking in the mirror, trying to discover the secret of the ugliness, the ugliness that made her ignored or despised at school, by teachers and classmates alike. She was the only member of her class who sat alone at a double desk. The first letter of her last name forced her to sit in the front of the room always. But what about Marie Appolonaire? Marie was in front of her, but she shared a desk with Luke Angelino. Her teachers had always treated her this way. They tried never to glance at her, and called on her only when everyone was required to respond. She also knew that when one of the girls at school wanted to be particularly insulting to a boy, or wanted to get an immediate response from him, she could say, "Bobby loves Pecola Breedlove! Bobby loves Pecola Breedlove!" and never fail to get peals of laughter from those in earshot, and mock anger from the accused.

It had occurred to Pecola some time ago that if her eyes, those eyes that held the pictures, and knew the sights—if those eyes of hers were different, that is to say, beautiful, she herself would be different. Her teeth were good, and at least her nose was not big and flat like some of those who were thought so cute. If she looked different, beautiful, maybe Cholly would be different, and Mrs. Breedlove too. Maybe they'd say, "Why, look at pretty-eyed Pecola. We mustn't do bad things in front of those pretty eyes."

*Pretty eyes. Pretty blue eyes. Big blue pretty eyes. Run, Jip, run. Jip runs, Alice runs. Alice has blue eyes. Jerry has blue eyes. Jerry runs. Alice runs. They run with their blue eyes. Four blue eyes. Four pretty blue eyes. Blue-sky eyes.*

*Blue-like Mrs. Forrest's blue blouse eyes. Morning-glory-blue-eyes. Alice-and-Jerry-blue-storybook-eyes.*

Each night, without fail, she prayed for blue eyes. Fervently, for a year she had prayed. Although somewhat discouraged, she was not without hope. To have something as wonderful as that happen would take a long, long time.

Thrown, in this way, into the binding conviction that only a miracle could relieve her, she would never know her beauty. She would see only what there was to see: the eyes of other people.

She walks down Garden Avenue to a small grocery store which sells penny candy. Three pennies are in her shoe—slipping back and forth between the sock and the inner sole. With each step she feels the painful press of the coins against her foot. A sweet, endurable, even cherished irritation, full of promise and delicate security. There is plenty of time to consider what to buy. Now, however, she moves down an avenue gently buffeted by the familiar and therefore loved images. The dandelions at the base of the telephone pole. Why, she wonders, do people call them weeds? She thought they were pretty. But grown-ups say, "Miss Dunion keeps her yard so nice. Not a dandelion anywhere." Hunkie women in black babushkas go into the fields with baskets to pull them up. But they do not want the yellow heads—only the jagged leaves. They make dandelion soup. Dandelion wine. Nobody loves the head of a dandelion. Maybe because they are so many, strong, and soon.

There was the sidewalk crack shaped like a Y, and the other one that lifted the concrete up from the dirt floor. Frequently her sloughing step had made her trip over that one. Skates would go well over this sidewalk—old it was, and smooth; it made the wheels glide evenly, with a mild whirr. The newly paved walks were bumpy and uncomfortable, and the sound of skate wheels on new walks was grating.

These and other inanimate things she saw and experienced. They were real to her. She knew them. They were the codes and touchstones of the world, capable of translation and possession. She owned the crack that made her stumble; she owned the clumps of dandelions whose white heads, last fall, she had blown away; whose yellow heads, this fall, she peered into. And owning them made her part of the world, and the world a part of her.

She climbs four wooden steps to the door of Yacobowski's Fresh Veg. Meat and Sundries Store. A bell tinkles as she opens it. Standing before the counter, she looks at the array of candies. All Mary Janes, she decides. Three for a penny. The resistant sweetness that breaks open at last to deliver peanut butter—the oil and salt which complement the sweet pull of caramel. A peal of anticipation unsettles her stomach.

She pulls off her shoe and takes out the three pennies. The gray head of Mr. Yacobowski looms up over the counter. He urges his eyes out of his thoughts to encounter her. Blue eyes. Blear-dropped. Slowly, like Indian summer moving imperceptibly toward fall, he looks toward her. Somewhere between retina and object, between vision and view, his eyes draw back, hesitate, and hover. At some fixed point in time and space he senses that he need not waste the effort of a glance. He does not see her, because for him there is nothing to see. How can a fifty-two-year-old white immigrant storekeeper with the taste of potatoes and beer in his mouth, his mind honed on the doe-eyed Virgin Mary, his sensibilities blunted by a permanent awareness of loss, *see* a little black girl? Nothing in his life even suggested that the feat was possible, not to say desirable or necessary.

"Yeah?"

She looks up at him and sees the vacuum where curiosity ought to lodge. And something more. The total absence of human recognition —the glazed separateness. She does not know what keeps his glance suspended. Perhaps because he is grown, or a man, and she a little girl. But she has seen interest, disgust, even anger in grown male eyes. Yet this vacuum is not new to her. It has an edge; somewhere in the bottom lid is the distaste. She has seen it lurking in the eyes of all white people. So. The distaste must be for her, her blackness. All things in her are flux and anticipation. But her blackness is static and dread. And it is the blackness that accounts for, that creates, the vacuum edged with distaste in white eyes.

She points her finger at the Mary Janes—a little black shaft of finger, its tip pressed on the display window. The quietly inoffensive assertion of a black child's attempt to communicate with a white adult.

"Them." The word is more sigh than sense.

"What? These? These?" Phlegm and impatience mingle in his voice.

She shakes her head, her fingertip fixed on the spot which, in her view, at any rate, identifies the Mary Janes. He cannot see her view— the angle of his vision, the slant of her finger, makes it incomprehensible to him. His lumpy red hand plops around in the glass casing like the agitated head of a chicken outraged by the loss of its body.

"Christ. Kantcha talk?"

His fingers brush the Mary Janes.

She nods.

"Well, why'nt you say so? One? How many?"

Pecola unfolds her fist, showing the three pennies. He scoots three Mary Janes toward her—three yellow rectangles in each packet. She holds the money toward him. He hesitates, not wanting to touch her hand. She does not know how to move the finger of her right hand from the display counter or how to get the coins out of her left hand. Finally he reaches over and takes the pennies from her hand. His nails graze her damp palm.

Outside, Pecola feels the inexplicable shame ebb.

Dandelions. A dart of affection leaps out from her to them. But they do not look at her and do not send love back. She thinks, "They *are* ugly. They *are* weeds." Preoccupied with that revelation, she trips on the sidewalk crack. Anger stirs and wakes in her; it opens its mouth, and like a hot-mouthed puppy, laps up the dredges of her shame.

Anger is better. There is a sense of being in anger. A reality and presence. An awareness of worth. It is a lovely surging. Her thoughts fall back to Mr. Yacobowski's eyes, his phlegmy voice. The anger will not hold; the puppy is too easily surfeited. Its thirst too quickly quenched, it sleeps. The shame wells up again, its muddy rivulets seeping into her eyes. What to do before the tears come. She remembers the Mary Janes.

Each pale yellow wrapper has a picture on it. A picture of little Mary Jane, for whom the candy is named. Smiling white face. Blond hair in gentle disarray, blue eyes looking at her out of a world of clean comfort. The eyes are petulant, mischievous. To Pecola they are simply pretty. She eats the candy, and its sweetness is good. To eat the candy is somehow to eat the eyes, eat Mary Jane. Love Mary Jane. Be Mary Jane.

Three pennies had bought her nine lovely orgasms with Mary Jane. Lovely Mary Jane, for whom a candy is named.

Three whores lived in the apartment above the Breedloves' storefront. China, Poland, and Miss Marie. Pecola loved them, visited them, and ran their errands. They, in turn, did not despise her.

On an October morning, the morning of the stove-lid triumph, Pecola climbed the stairs to their apartment.

Even before the door was opened to her tapping, she could hear Poland singing—her voice sweet and hard, like new strawberries:

> I got blues in my mealbarrel
> Blues up on the shelf
> I got blues in my mealbarrel
> Blues up on the shelf
> Blues in my bedroom
> Cause I'm sleepin' by myself

"Hi, dumplin'. Where your socks?" Marie seldom called Pecola the same thing twice, but invariably her epithets were fond ones chosen from menus and dishes that were forever uppermost in her mind.

"Hello, Miss Marie. Hello, Miss China. Hello, Miss Poland."

"You heard me. Where your socks? You as bare-legged as a yard dog."

"I couldn't find any."

"Couldn't find any? Must be somethin' in your house that loves socks."

China chuckled. Whenever something was missing, Marie attributed its disappearance to "something in the house that loved it." "There is somethin' in this house that loves brassieres," she would say with alarm.

Poland and China were getting ready for the evening. Poland, forever ironing, forever singing. China, sitting on a pale-green kitchen chair, forever and forever curling her hair. Marie never got ready.

The women were friendly, but slow to begin talk. Pecola always took the initiative with Marie, who, once inspired, was difficult to stop.

"How come you got so many boyfriends, Miss Marie?"

"*Boy*friends? *Boy*friends? Chittlin', I ain't seen a *boy* since nineteen and twenty-seven."

"You didn't see none then." China stuck the hot curlers into a tin of Nu Nile hair dressing. The oil hissed at the touch of the hot metal.

"How come, Miss Marie?" Pecola insisted.

"How come what? How come I ain't seen a boy since nineteen and twenty-seven? Because they ain't *been* no boys since then. That's when they stopped. Folks started gettin' born old."

"You mean that's when *you* got old," China said.

"I ain't never got old. Just fat."

"Same thing."

"You think 'cause you skinny, folks think you young? You'd make a haint buy a girdle."

"And you look like the north side of a southbound mule."

"All I know is, them bandy little legs of yours is every bit as old as mine."

"Don't worry 'bout my bandy legs. That's the first thing they push aside."

All three of the women laughed. Marie threw back her head. From deep inside, her laughter came like the sound of many rivers, freely, deeply, muddily, heading for the room of an open sea. China giggled spastically. Each gasp seemed to be yanked out of her by an unseen hand jerking an unseen string. Poland, who seldom spoke unless she was drunk, laughed without sound. When she was sober she hummed mostly or chanted blues songs, of which she knew many.

Pecola fingered the fringe of a scarf that lay on the back of a sofa. "I never seen nobody with as many boyfriends as you got, Miss Marie. How come they all love you?"

Marie opened a bottle of root beer. "What else they gone do? They know I'm rich and good-lookin'. They wants to put their toes in my curly hair, and get at my money."

"You rich, Miss Marie?"

"Puddin', I got money's mammy."

"Where you get it from? You don't do no work."

"Yeah," said China, "where you get it from?"

"Hoover give it me. I did him a favor once, for the F. B. and I."

"What'd you do?"

"I did him a favor. They wanted to catch this crook, you see. Name of Johnny. He was as low-down as they come. . . ."

"We *know* that." China arranged a curl.

". . . the F. B. and I. wanted him bad. He killed more people than TB. And if you *crossed* him? Whoa, Jesus! He'd run you as long as there was ground. Well, I was little and cute then. No more than ninety pounds, soaking wet."

"You ain't never been soaking wet," China said.

"Well, you ain't never been dry. Shut up. Let me tell you, sweetnin'. To tell it true, I was the only one could handle him. He'd go out and rob a bank or kill some people, and I'd say to him, soft-like, 'Johnny, you shouldn't do that.' And he'd say he just had to bring me pretty things. Lacy drawers and all. And every Saturday we'd get a case of beer and fry up some fish. We'd fry it in meal and egg batter, you know, and when it was all brown and crisp—not hard, though—we'd break open that cold beer. . . ." Marie's eyes went soft as the memory of just such a meal sometime, somewhere transfixed her. All her stories were subject to breaking down at descriptions of food. Pecola saw Marie's teeth settling down into the back of crisp sea bass; saw the fat fingers putting back into her mouth tiny flakes of white, hot meat that had escaped from her lips; she heard the "pop" of the beer-bottle cap; smelled the acridness of the first stream of vapor; felt the cold beeriness hit the tongue. She ended the daydream long before Marie.

"But what about the money?" she asked.

China hooted. "She's makin' like she's the Lady in Red that told on Dillinger. Dillinger wouldn't have come near you lessen he was going hunting in Africa and shoot you for a hippo."

"Well, this hippo had a ball back in Chicago. Whoa Jesus, ninety-nine!"

"How come you always say 'Whoa Jesus' and a number?" Pecola had long wanted to know.

"Because my mama taught me never to cuss."

"Did she teach you not to drop your drawers?" China asked.

"Didn't have none," said Marie. "Never saw a pair of drawers till I was fifteen, when I left Jackson and was doing day work in Cincinnati. My white lady gave me some old ones of hers. I thought they was some kind of stocking cap. I put it on my head when I dusted. When she saw me, she liked to fell out."

"You must have been one dumb somebody." China lit a cigarette and cooled her irons.

"How'd I know?" Marie paused. "And what's the use of putting on something you got to keep taking off all the time? Dewey never let me keep them on long enough to get used to them."

"Dewey who?" This was a somebody new to Pecola.

"Dewey who? Chicken! You never heard me tell of *Dewey?* " Marie was shocked by her negligence.

"No, ma'am."

"Oh, honey, you've missed half your life. Whoa Jesus, one-nine-five. You talkin' 'bout smooth! I met him when I was fourteen. We ran away and lived together like married for three years. You know all those klinker-tops you see runnin' up here? Fifty of 'em in a bowl wouldn't make a Dewey Prince ankle bone. Oh, Lord. How that man loved me!"

China arranged a fingerful of hair into a bang effect. "Then why he left you to sell tail?"

"Girl, when I found out I could sell it—that somebody would pay cold cash for it, you could have knocked me over with a feather."

Poland began to laugh. Soundlessly. "Me too. My auntie whipped me good that first time when I told her I didn't get no money. I said 'Money? For what? He didn't owe me nothin'.' She said, 'The hell he didn't!' "

They all dissolved in laughter.

Three merry gargoyles. Three merry harridans. Amused by a long-ago time of ignorance. They did not belong to those generations of prostitutes created in novels, with great and generous hearts, dedicated, because of the horror of circumstance, to ameliorating, the luckless, barren life of men, taking money incidentally and humbly for their "understanding." Nor were they from that sensitive breed of young girl, gone wrong at the hands of fate, forced to cultivate an outward brittleness in order to protect her springtime from further shock, but knowing full well she was cut out for better things, and could make the right man happy. Neither were they the sloppy, inadequate whores who, unable to make a living at it alone, turn to drug consumption and traffic or pimps to help complete their scheme of self-destruction, avoiding suicide only to punish the memory of some absent father or to sustain the misery of some silent mother. Except for Marie's fabled love for Dewey Prince, these women hated men, all men, without shame, apology, or discrimination. They abused their visitors with a scorn grown mechanical from use. Black men, white men, Puerto Ricans, Mexicans, Jews, Poles, whatever—all were inadequate and weak, all came under their jaundiced eyes and were the recipients of their disinterested wrath. They took delight in cheating them. On one occasion the town well knew, they lured a Jew up the stairs, pounced on him, all three, held him up by the heels, shook everything out of his pants pockets, and threw him out of the window.

Neither did they have respect for women, who, although not their colleagues, so to speak, nevertheless deceived their husbands—regularly or irregularly, it made no difference. "Sugar-coated whores," they called them, and did not yearn to be in their shoes. Their only respect was for what they would have described as "good Christian colored women." The woman whose reputation was spotless, and who tended to her family, who didn't drink or smoke or run around. These women had their undying, if covert, affection. They would sleep with their husbands, and take their money, but always with a vengeance.

Nor were they protective and solicitous of youthful innocence. They looked back on their own youth as a period of ignorance, and regretted that they had not made more of it. They were not young girls in whores' clothing, or whores regretting their loss of innocence. They were whores in whores' clothing, whores who had never been young and had no word for innocence. With Pecola they were as free as they were with each other. Marie concocted stories for her because she was a child, but the stories were breezy and rough. If Pecola had announced her intention to live the life they did, they would not have tried to dissuade her or voiced any alarm.

"You and Dewey Prince have any children, Miss Marie?"

"Yeah. Yeah. We had some." Marie fidgeted. She pulled a bobby pin from her hair and began to pick her teeth. That meant she didn't want to talk anymore.

Pecola went to the window and looked down at the empty street. A tuft of grass had forced its way up through a crack in the sidewalk,

only to meet a raw October wind. She thought of Dewey Prince and
how he loved Miss Marie. What did love feel like? she wondered.
How do grown-ups act when they love each other? Eat fish together?
Into her eyes came the picture of Cholly and Mrs. Breedlove in bed.
He making sounds as though he were in pain, as though something
had him by the throat and wouldn't let go. Terrible as his noises were,
they were not nearly as bad as the no noise at all from her mother. It
was as though she was not even there. Maybe that was love. Choking
sounds and silence.

Turning her eyes from the window, Pecola looked at the women.

China had changed her mind about the bangs and was arranging a
small but sturdy pompadour. She was adept in creating any number of
hair styles, but each one left her with a pinched and harassed look.
Then she applied makeup heavily. Now she gave herself surprised eyebrows and a cupid-bow mouth. Later she would make Oriental eyebrows and an evilly slashed mouth.

Poland, in her sweet strawberry voice, began another song:

> I know a boy who is sky-soft brown
> I know a boy who is sky-soft brown
> The dirt leaps for joy when his feet touch the ground.
> > His strut is a peacock
> > His eye is burning brass
> > His smile is sorghum syrup drippin' slow-sweet to the last
> I know a boy who is sky-soft brown

Marie sat shelling peanuts and popping them into her mouth. Pecola looked and looked at the women. Were they real? Marie belched,
softly, purringly, lovingly.

# Winter

❄

My daddy's face is a study. Winter moves into it and presides there. His eyes become a cliff of snow threatening to avalanche; his eyebrows bend like black limbs of leafless trees. His skin takes on the pale, cheerless yellow of winter sun; for a jaw he has the edges of a snowbound field dotted with stubble; his high forehead is the frozen sweep of the Erie, hiding currents of gelid thoughts that eddy in darkness. Wolf killer turned hawk fighter, he worked night and day to keep one from the door and the other from under the windowsills. A Vulcan guarding the flames, he gives us instructions about which doors to keep closed or opened for proper distribution of heat, lays kindling by, discusses qualities of coal, and teaches us how to rake, feed, and bank the fire. And he will not unrazor his lips until spring.

Winter tightened our heads with a band of cold and melted our eyes. We put pepper in the feet of our stockings, Vaseline on our faces, and stared through dark icebox mornings at four stewed prunes, slippery lumps of oatmeal, and cocoa with a roof of skin.

But mostly we waited for spring, when there could be gardens.

By the time this winter had stiffened itself into a hateful knot that nothing could loosen, something did loosen it, or rather someone. A someone who splintered the knot into silver threads that tangled us, netted us, made us long for the dull chafe of the previous boredom.

This disrupter of seasons was a new girl in school named Maureen Peal. A high-yellow dream child with long brown hair braided into two lynch ropes that hung down her back. She was rich, at least by our standards, as rich as the richest of the white girls, swaddled in comfort and care. The quality of her clothes threatened to derange Frieda and me. Patent-leather shoes with buckles, a cheaper version of which we got only at Easter and which had disintegrated by the end of May.

Fluffy sweaters the color of lemon drops tucked into skirts with pleats so orderly they astounded us. Brightly colored knee socks with white borders, a brown velvet coat trimmed in white rabbit fur, and a matching muff. There was a hint of spring in her sloe green eyes, something summery in her complexion, and a rich autumn ripeness in her walk.

She enchanted the entire school. When teachers called on her, they smiled encouragingly. Black boys didn't trip her in the halls; white boys didn't stone her, white girls didn't suck their teeth when she was assigned to be their work partners; black girls stepped aside when she wanted to use the sink in the girls' toilet, and their eyes genuflected under sliding lids. She never had to search for anybody to eat with in the cafeteria—they flocked to the table of her choice, where she opened fastidious lunches, shaming our jelly-stained bread with egg-salad sandwiches cut into four dainty squares, pink-frosted cupcakes, sticks of celery and carrots, proud, dark apples. She even bought and liked white milk.

Frieda and I were bemused, irritated, and fascinated by her. We looked hard for flaws to restore our equilibrium, but had to be content at first with uglying up her name, changing Maureen Peal to Meringue Pie. Later a minor epiphany was ours when we discovered that she had a dog tooth—a charming one to be sure—but a dog tooth nonetheless. And when we found out that she had been born with six fingers on each hand and that there was a little bump where each extra one had been removed, we smiled. They were small triumphs, but we took what we could get—snickering behind her back and calling her Six-finger-dog-tooth-meringue-pie. But we had to do it alone, for none of the other girls would cooperate with our hostility. They adored her.

When she was assigned a locker next to mine, I could indulge my jealousy four times a day. My sister and I both suspected that we were secretly prepared to be her friend, if she would let us, but I knew it would be a dangerous friendship, for when my eye traced the white border patterns of those Kelly-green knee socks, and felt the pull and slack of my brown stockings, I wanted to kick her. And when I thought of the unearned haughtiness in her eyes, I plotted accidental slammings of locker doors on her hand.

As locker friends, however, we got to know each other a little, and I was even able to hold a sensible conversation with her without visualizing her fall off a cliff, or giggling my way into what I thought was a clever insult.

One day, while I waited at the locker for Frieda, she joined me.

"Hi."

"Hi."

"Waiting for your sister?"

"Uh-huh."

"Which way do you go home?"

"Down Twenty-first Street to Broadway."

"Why don't you go down Twenty-second Street?"

" 'Cause I live on Twenty-first Street."

"Oh. I can walk that way, I guess. Partly, anyway."

"Free country."

Frieda came toward us, her brown stockings straining at the knees because she had tucked the toe under to hide a hole in the foot.

"Maureen's gonna walk part way with us."

Frieda and I exchanged glances, her eyes begging my restraint, mine promising nothing.

It was a false spring day, which, like Maureen, had pierced the shell of a deadening winter. There were puddles, mud, and an inviting warmth that deluded us. The kind of day on which we draped our coats over our heads, left our galoshes in school, and came down with croup the following day. We always responded to the slightest change in weather, the most minute shifts in time of day. Long before seeds were stirring, Frieda and I were scruffing and poking at the earth, swallowing air, drinking rain. . . .

As we emerged from the school with Maureen, we began to moult immediately. We put our head scarves in our coat pockets, and our coats on our heads. I was wondering how to maneuver Maureen's fur muff into a gutter when a commotion in the playground distracted us. A group of boys was circling and holding at bay a victim, Pecola Breedlove.

Bay Boy, Woodrow Cain, Buddy Wilson, Junie Bug—like a necklace of semiprecious stones they surrounded her. Heady with the smell of their own musk, thrilled by the easy power of a majority, they gaily harassed her.

"Black e mo. Black e mo. Yadaddsleepsnekked. Black e mo black e mo ya dadd sleeps nekked. Black e mo . . ."

They had extemporized a verse made up of two insults about matters over which the victim had no control; the color of her skin and speculations on the sleeping habits of an adult, wildly fitting in its incoherence. That they themselves were black, or that their own father had similarly relaxed habits was irrelevant. It was their contempt for their own blackness that gave the first insult its teeth. They seemed to have taken all of their smoothly cultivated ignorance, their exquisitely learned self-hatred, their elaborately designed hopelessness and sucked it all up into a fiery cone of scorn that had burned for ages in the hollows of their minds—cooled—and spilled over lips of outrage, consuming whatever was in its path. They danced a macabre ballet around the victim, whom, for their own sake, they were prepared to sacrifice to the flaming pit.

> Black e mo Black e mo Ya daddy sleeps nekked.
> Stch ta ta stch ta ta
> stach ta ta ta ta ta

Pecola edged around the circle crying. She had dropped her notebook, and covered her eyes with her hands.

We watched, afraid they might notice us and turn their energies our way. Then Frieda, with set lips and Mama's eyes, snatched her coat from her head and threw it on the ground. She ran toward them and brought her books down on Woodrow Cain's head. The circle broke. Woodrow Cain grabbed his head.

"Hey, girl!"

"You cut that out, you hear?" I had never heard Frieda's voice so loud and clear.

Maybe because Frieda was taller than he was, maybe because he saw her eyes, maybe because he had lost interest in the game, or maybe because he had a crush on Frieda, in any case Woodrow looked frightened just long enough to give her more courage.

"Leave her 'lone, or I'm gone tell everybody what you did!"

Woodrow did not answer; he just walled his eyes.

Bay Boy piped up, "Go on, gal. Ain't nobody bothering you."

"You shut up, Bullet Head." I had found my tongue.

"Who you calling Bullet Head?"

"I'm calling you Bullet Head, Bullet Head."

Frieda took Pecola's hand. "Come on."

"You want a fat lip?" Bay Boy drew back his fist at me.

"Yeah. Gimme one of yours."

"You gone get one."

Maureen appeared at my elbow, and the boys seemed reluctant to continue under her springtime eyes so wide with interest. They buckled in confusion, not willing to beat up three girls under her watchful gaze. So they listened to a budding male instinct that told them to pretend we were unworthy of their attention.

"Come on, man."

"Yeah. Come on. We ain't got time to fool with them."

Grumbling a few disinterested epithets, they moved away.

I picked up Pecola's notebook and Frieda's coat, and the four of us left the playground.

"Old Bullet Head, he's always picking on girls."

Frieda agreed with me. "Miss Forrester said he was incorrigival."

"Really?" I didn't know what that meant, but it had enough of a doom sound in it to be true of Bay Boy.

While Frieda and I clucked on about the near fight, Maureen, suddenly animated, put her velvet-sleeved arm through Pecola's and began to behave as though they were the closest of friends.

"I just moved here. My name is Maureen Peal. What's yours?"

"Pecola."

"Pecola? Wasn't that the name of the girl in *Imitation of Life?*"

"I don't know. What is that?"

"The picture show, you know. Where this mulatto girl hates her mother 'cause she is black and ugly but then cries at the funeral. It was real sad. Everybody cries in it. Claudette Colbert too."

"Oh." Pecola's voice was no more than a sigh.

"Anyway, her name was Pecola too. She was so pretty. When it comes back, I'm going to see it again. My mother has seen it four times."

Frieda and I walked behind them, surprised at Maureen's friendliness to Pecola, but pleased. Maybe she wasn't so bad, after all. Frieda had put her coat back on her head, and the two of us, so draped, trotted along enjoying the warm breeze and Frieda's heroics.

"You're in my gym class, aren't you?" Maureen asked Pecola.

"Yes."

"Miss Erkmeister's legs sure are bow. I bet she thinks they're cute. How come she gets to wear real shorts, and we have to wear those old bloomers? I want to die every time I put them on."

Pecola smiled but did not look at Maureen.

"Hey." Maureen stopped short. "There's an Isaley's. Want some ice cream? I have money."

She unzipped a hidden pocket in her muff and pulled out a multifolded dollar bill. I forgave her those knee socks.

"My uncle sued Isaley's." Maureen said to the three of us. "He sued the Isaley's in Akron. They said he was disorderly and that that was why they wouldn't serve him, but a friend of his, a policemen, came in and beared the witness, so the suit went through."

"What's a suit?"

"It's when you can beat them up if you want to and won't anybody do nothing. Our family does it all the time. We believe in suits."

At the entrance to Isaley's Maureen turned to Frieda and me, asking, "You all going to buy some ice cream?"

We looked at each other. "No," Frieda said.

Maureen disappeared into the store with Pecola.

Frieda looked placidly down the street; I opened my mouth, but quickly closed it. It was extremely important that the world not know that I fully expected Maureen to buy us some ice cream, that for the past 120 seconds I had been selecting the flavor, that I had begun to like Maureen, and that neither of us had a penny.

We supposed Maureen was being nice to Pecola because of the boys, and were embarrassed to be caught—even by each other—thinking that she would treat us, or that we deserved it as much as Pecola did.

The girls came out. Pecola with two dips of orange-pineapple, Maureen with black raspberry.

"You should have got some," she said. "They had all kinds. Don't eat down to the tip of the cone," she advised Pecola.

"Why?"

"Because there's a fly in there."

"How you know?"

"Oh, not really. A girl told me she found one in the bottom of hers once, and ever since then she throws that part away."

"Oh."

We passed the Dreamland Theater, and Betty Grable smiled down at us.

"Don't you just love her?" Maureen asked.

"Uh-huh," said Pecola.

I differed. "Hedy Lamarr is better."

Maureen agreed. "Ooooo yes. My mother told me that a girl named Audrey, she went to the beauty parlor where we lived before, and asked the lady to fix her hair like Hedy Lamarr's, and the lady said, 'Yeah, when you grow some hair like Hedy Lamarr's.' " She laughed long and sweet.

"Sounds crazy," said Frieda.

"She sure is. Do you know she doesn't even menstrate yet, and she's sixteen. Do you, yet?"

"Yes." Pecola glanced at us.

"So do I." Maureen made no attempt to disguise her pride. "Two months ago I started. My girl friend in Toledo, where we lived before, said when she started she was scared to death. Thought she had killed herself."

"Do you know what it's for?" Pecola asked the question as though hoping to provide the answer herself.

"For babies." Maureen raised two pencil-stroke eyebrows at the obviousness of the question. "Babies need blood when they are inside you, and if you are having a baby, then you don't menstrate. But when you're not having a baby, then you don't have to save the blood, so it comes out."

"How do babies get the blood?" asked Pecola.

"Through the like-line. You know. Where your belly button is. That is where the like-line grows from and pumps the blood to the baby."

"Well, if the belly buttons are to grow like-lines to give the baby blood, and only girls have babies, how come boys have belly buttons?"

Maureen hesitated. "I don't know," she admitted. "But boys have all sorts of things they don't need." Her tinkling laughter was somehow stronger than our nervous ones. She curled her tongue around the edge of the cone, scooping up a dollop of purple that made my eyes water. We were waiting for a stop light to change. Maureen kept scooping the ice cream from around the cone's edge with her tongue; she didn't bite the edge as I would have done. Her tongue circled the cone. Pecola had finished hers; Maureen evidently liked her things to last. While I was thinking about her ice cream, she must have been thinking about her last remark, for she said to Pecola, "Did you ever see a naked man?"

Pecola blinked, then looked away. "No. Where would I see a naked man?"

"I don't know. I just asked."

"I wouldn't even look at him, even if I did see him. That's dirty. Who wants to see a naked man?" Pecola was agitated. "Nobody's father would be naked in front of his own daughter. Not unless he was dirty too."

"I didn't say 'father.' I just said 'a naked man.' "

"Well . . ."

"How come you said 'father'?" Maureen wanted to know.

"Who else would she see, dog tooth?" I was glad to have a chance to show anger. Not only because of the ice cream, but because we had seen our own father naked and didn't care to be reminded of it and feel the shame brought on by the absence of shame. He had been walking down the hall from the bathroom into his bedroom and passed the open door of our room. We had lain there wide-eyed. He stopped and looked in, trying to see in the dark room whether we were really asleep—or was it his imagination that opened eyes were looking at him? Apparently he convinced himself that we were sleeping. He moved away, confident that his little girls would not lie open-eyed like that, staring, staring. When he had moved on, the dark took only him away, not his nakedness. That stayed in the room with us. Friendly-like.

"I'm not talking to you," said Maureen. "Besides, I don't care if she sees her father naked. She can look at him all day if she wants to. Who cares?"

"You do," said Frieda. "That's all you talk about."

"It is not."

"It is so. Boys, babies, and somebody's naked daddy. You must be boy-crazy."

"You better be quiet."

"Who's gonna make me?" Frieda put her hand on her hip and jutted her face toward Maureen.

"You all ready made. Mammy made."

"You stop talking about my mama."

"Well, you stop talking about my daddy."

"Who said anything about your old daddy?"

"You did."

"Well, you started it."

"I wasn't even talking to you. I was talking to Pecola."

"Yeah. About seeing her naked daddy."

"So what if she did see him?"

Pecola shouted, "I never saw my daddy naked. Never."

"You did too," Maureen snapped. "Bay Boy said so."

"I did not."

"You did."

"I did not."

"Did. Your own daddy, too!"

Pecola tucked her head in—a funny, sad, helpless movement. A kind of hunching of the shoulders, pulling in of the neck, as though she wanted to cover her ears.

"You stop talking about her daddy," I said.

"What do I care about her old black daddy?" asked Maureen.

"Black? Who you calling black?"

"You!"

"You think you so cute!" I swung at her and missed, hitting Pecola in the face. Furious at my clumsiness, I threw my notebook at her, but it caught her in the small of her velvet back, for she had turned and was flying across the street against traffic.

Safe on the other side, she screamed at us, "I *am* cute! And you ugly! Black and ugly black e mos. I *am* cute!"

She ran down the street, the green knee socks making her legs look like wild dandelion stems that had somehow lost their heads. The

weight of her remark stunned us, and it was a second or two before
Frieda and I collected ourselves enough to shout,
"Six-finger-dog-tooth-meringue-pie!" We chanted this most powerful
of our arsenal of insults as long as we could see the green stems and
rabbit fur.

Grown people frowned at the three girls on the curbside, two with
their coats draped over their heads, the collars framing the eyebrows
like nuns' habits, black garters showing where they bit the tops of
brown stockings that barely covered the knees, angry faces knotted like
dark cauliflowers.

Pecola stood a little apart from us, her eyes hinged in the direction
in which Maureen had fled. She seemed to fold into herself, like a
pleated wing. Her pain antagonized me. I wanted to open her up, crisp
her edges, ram a stick down that hunched and curving spine, force her
to stand erect and spit the misery out on the streets. But she held it in
where it could lap up into her eyes.

Frieda snatched her coat from her head. "Come on, Claudia. 'Bye,
Pecola."

We walked quickly at first, and then slower, pausing every now and
then to fasten garters, tie shoelaces, scratch, or examine old scars. We
were sinking under the wisdom, accuracy, and relevance of Maureen's
last words. If she was cute—and if anything could be believed, she
was—then we were not. And what did that mean? We were lesser.
Nicer, brighter, but still lesser. Dolls we could destroy, but we could
not destroy the honey voices of parents and aunts, the obedience in the
eyes of our peers, the slippery light in the eyes of our teachers when
they encountered the Maureen Peals of the world. What was the
secret? What did we lack? Why was it important? And so what?
Guileless and without vanity, we were still in love with ourselves then.
We felt comfortable in our skins, enjoyed the news that our senses
released to us, admired our dirt, cultivated our scars, and could not
comprehend this unworthiness. Jealousy we understood and thought
natural—a desire to have what somebody else had; but envy was a

strange, new feeling for us. And all the time we knew that Maureen Peal was not the Enemy and not worthy of such intense hatred. The *Thing* to fear was the *Thing* that made *her* beautiful, and not us.

The house was quiet when we opened the door. The acrid smell of simmering turnips filled our cheeks with sour saliva.

"Mama!"

There was no answer, but a sound of feet. Mr. Henry shuffled part of the way down the stairs. One thick, hairless leg leaned out of his bathrobe.

"Hello there, Greta Garbo; hello, Ginger Rogers."

We gave him the giggle he was accustomed to. "Hello, Mr. Henry. Where's Mama?"

"She went to your grandmaw's. Left word for you to cut off the turnips and eat some graham crackers till she got back. They in the kitchen."

We sat in silence at the kitchen table, crumbling the crackers into anthills. In a little while Mr. Henry came back down the stairs. Now he had his trousers on under his robe.

"Say. Wouldn't you all like some cream?"

"Oh, yes, sir."

"Here. Here's a quarter. Gone over to Isaley's and get yourself some cream. You been good girls, ain't you?"

His light-green words restored color to the day. "Yes, sir. Thank you, Mr. Henry. Will you tell Mama for us if she comes?"

"Sure. But she ain't due back for a spell."

Coatless, we left the house and had gotten all the way to the corner when Frieda said, "I don't want to go to Isaley's."

"What?"

"I don't want ice cream. I want potato chips."

"They got potato chips at Isaley's."

"I know, but why go all that long way? Miss Bertha got potato chips."

"But I want ice cream."

"No you don't, Claudia."

"I do too."

"Well, you go on to Isaley's. I'm going to Miss Bertha's."

"But you got the quarter, and I don't want to go all the way up there by myself."

"Then let's go to Miss Bertha's. You like her candy, don't you?"

"It's always stale, and she always runs out of stuff."

"Today is Friday. She orders fresh on Friday."

"And then that crazy old Soaphead Church lives there."

"So what? We're together. We'll run if he does anything at us."

"He scares me."

"Well, I don't want to go up by Isaley's. Suppose Meringue Pie is hanging around. You want to run into her, Claudia?"

"Come on, Frieda. I'll get candy."

Miss Bertha had a small candy, snuff, and tobacco store. One brick room sitting in her front yard. You had to peep in the door, and if she wasn't there, you knocked on the door of her house in back. This day she was sitting behind the counter reading a Bible in a tube of sunlight.

Frieda bought potato chips, and we got three Powerhouse bars for ten cents, and had a dime left. We hurried back home to sit under the lilac bushes on the side of the house. We always did our Candy Dance there so Rosemary could see us and get jealous. The Candy Dance was a humming, skipping, foot-tapping, eating, smacking combination that overtook us when we had sweets. Creeping between the bushes and the side of the house, we heard voices and laughter. We looked into the living-room window, expecting to see Mama. Instead we saw Mr. Henry and two women. In a playful manner, the way grandmothers do with babies, he was sucking the fingers of one of the women, whose laughter filled a tiny place over his head. The other woman was buttoning her coat. We knew immediately who they were, and our flesh crawled. One was China, and the other was called the Maginot Line. The back of my neck itched. These were the fancy women of the maroon nail polish that Mama and Big Mama hated. And in our house.

China was not too terrible, at least not in our imaginations. She was thin, aging, absentminded, and unaggressive. But the Maginot Line. That was the one my mother said she "wouldn't let eat out of one of her plates." That was the one church women never allowed their eyes to rest on. That was the one who had killed people, set them on fire, poisoned them, cooked them in lye. Although I thought the Maginot Line's face, hidden under all that fat, was really sweet, I had heard too many black and red words about her, seen too many mouths go triangle at the mention of her name, to dwell on any redeeming features she might have.

Showing brown teeth, China seemed to be genuinely enjoying Mr. Henry. The sight of him licking her fingers brought to mind the girlie magazines in his room. A cold wind blew somewhere in me, lifting little leaves of terror and obscure longing. I thought I saw a mild lonesomeness cross the face of the Maginot Line. But it may have been my own image that I saw in the slow flaring of her nostrils, in her eyes that reminded me of waterfalls in movies about Hawaii.

The Maginot Line yawned and said, "Come on, China. We can't hang in here all day. Them people be home soon." She moved toward the door.

Frieda and I dropped down to the ground, looking wildly into each other's eyes. When the women were some distance away, we went inside. Mr. Henry was in the kitchen opening a bottle of pop.

"Back already?"

"Yes, sir."

"Cream all gone?" His little teeth looked so kindly and helpless. Was that really our Mr. Henry with China's fingers?

"We got candy instead."

"You did huh? Ole sugar-tooth Greta Garbo."

He wiped the bottle sweat and turned it up to his lips—a gesture that made me uncomfortable.

"Who were those women, Mr. Henry?"

He choked on the pop and looked at Frieda. "What you say?"

"Those women," she repeated, "who just left. Who were they?"

"Oh." He laughed the grown-up getting-ready-to-lie laugh. A heh-heh we knew well.

"Those were some members of my Bible class. We read the scriptures together, and so they came today to read with me."

"Oh," said Frieda. I was looking at his house slippers to keep from seeing those kindly teeth frame a lie. He walked toward the stairs and then turned back to us.

"Bed' not mention it to your mother. She don't take to so much Bible study and don't like me having visitors, even if they good Christians."

"No, sir, Mr. Henry. We won't."

He rapidly mounted the stairs.

"Should we?" I asked. "Tell Mama?"

Frieda sighed. She had not even opened her Powerhouse bar or her potato chips, and now she traced the letters on the candy wrappers with her fingers. Suddenly she lifted her head and began to look all around the kitchen.

"No. I guess not. No plates are out."

"Plates? What you talking about now?"

"No plates are out. The Maginot Line didn't eat out of one of Mama's plates. Besides, Mama would just fuss all day if we told her."

We sat down and looked at the graham-cracker anthills we had made.

"We better cut off the turnips. They'll burn, and Mama will whip us," she said.

"I know."

"But if we let them burn, we won't have to eat them."

"Heyyy, what a lovely idea," I thought.

"Which you want? A whipping and no turnips, or turnips and no whippings?"

"I don't know. Maybe we could burn them just a little so Mama and Daddy can eat them, but we can say we can't."

"O.K."

I made a volcano out of my anthill.

"Frieda?"

"What?"

"What did Woodward do that you was gonna tell?"

"Wet the bed. Mrs. Cain told Mama he won't quit."

"Old nasty."

The sky was getting dark; I looked out of the window and saw snow falling. I poked my finger down into the mouth of my volcano, and it toppled, dispersing the golden grains into little swirls. The turnip pot crackled.

SEETHECATITGOESMEOWMEOWCOMEANDPLAYCOMEPL
AYWITHJANETHEKITTENWILLNOTPLAYPLAYPLAYPLA

They come from Mobile. Aiken. From Newport News. From Marietta.
From Meridian. And the sounds of these places in their mouths make
you think of love. When you ask them where they are from, they tilt
their heads and say "Mobile" and you think you've been kissed. They
say "Aiken" and you see a white butterfly glance off a fence with a torn
wing. They say "Nagadoches" and you want to say "Yes, I will." You
don't know what these towns are like, but you love what happens to
the air when they open their lips and let the names ease out.

Meridian. The sound of it opens the windows of a room like the
first four notes of a hymn. Few people can say the names of their home
towns with such sly affection. Perhaps because they don't have home
towns, just places where they were born. But these girls soak up the
juice of their home towns, and it never leaves them. They are thin
brown girls who have looked long at hollyhocks in the backyards of
Meridian, Mobile, Aiken, and Baton Rouge. And like hollyhocks they
are narrow, tall, and still. Their roots are deep, their stalks are firm, and
only the top blossom nods in the wind. They have the eyes of people
who can tell what time it is by the color of the sky. Such girls live in
quiet black neighborhoods where everybody is gainfully employed.
Where there are porch swings hanging from chains. Where the grass
is cut with a scythe, where rooster combs and sunflowers grow in the
yards, and pots of bleeding heart, ivy, and mother-in-law tongue line
the steps and windowsills. Such girls have bought watermelon and
snapbeans from the fruit man's wagon. They have put in the window
the cardboard sign that has a pound measure printed on each of three
edges—10 lbs., 25 lbs., 50 lbs.—and NO ICE on the fourth. These
particular brown girls from Mobile and Aiken are not like some of

their sisters. They are not fretful, nervous, or shrill; they do not have lovely black necks that stretch as though against an invisible collar; their eyes do not bite. These sugar-brown Mobile girls move through the streets without a stir. They are as sweet and plain as buttercake. Slim ankles; long, narrow feet. They wash themselves with orange-colored Lifebuoy soap, dust themselves with Cashmere Bouquet talc, clean their teeth with salt on a piece of rag, soften their skin with Jergens Lotion. They smell like wood, newspapers, and vanilla. They straighten their hair with Dixie Peach, and part it on the side. At night they curl it in paper from brown bags, tie a print scarf around their heads, and sleep with hands folded across their stomachs. They do not drink, smoke, or swear, and they still call sex "nookey." They sing second soprano in the choir, and although their voices are clear and steady, they are never picked to solo. They are in the second row, white blouses starched, blue skirts almost purple from ironing.

They go to land-grant colleges, normal schools, and learn how to do the white man's work with refinement: home economics to prepare his food; teacher education to instruct black children in obedience; music to soothe the weary master and entertain his blunted soul. Here they learn the rest of the lesson begun in those soft houses with porch swings and pots of bleeding heart: how to behave. The careful development of thrift, patience, high morals, and good manners. In short, how to get rid of the funkiness. The dreadful funkiness of passion, the funkiness of nature, the funkiness of the wide range of human emotions.

Wherever it erupts, this Funk, they wipe it away; where it crusts, they dissolve it; wherever it drips, flowers, or clings, they find it and fight it until it dies. They fight this battle all the way to the grave. The laugh that is a little too loud; the enunciation a little too round; the gesture a little too generous. They hold their behind in for fear of a sway too free; when they wear lipstick, they never cover the entire mouth for fear of lips too thick, and they worry, worry, worry about the edges of their hair.

They never seem to have boyfriends, but they always marry. Certain men watch them, without seeming to, and know that if such a girl is in his house, he will sleep on sheets boiled white, hung out to dry on juniper bushes, and pressed flat with a heavy iron. There will be pretty paper flowers decorating the picture of his mother, a large Bible in the front room. They feel secure. They know their work clothes will be mended, washed, and ironed on Monday, that their Sunday shirts will billow on hangers from the door jamb, stiffly starched and white. They look at her hands and know what she will do with biscuit dough; they smell the coffee and the fried ham; see the white, smoky grits with a dollop of butter on top. Her hips assure them that she will bear children easily and painlessly. And they are right.

What they do not know is that this plain brown girl will build her nest stick by stick, make it her own inviolable world, and stand guard over its every plant, weed, and doily, even against him. In silence will she return the lamp to where she put it in the first place; remove the dishes from the table as soon as the last bite is taken; wipe the doorknob after a greasy hand has touched it. A sidelong look will be enough to tell him to smoke on the back porch. Children will sense instantly that they cannot come into her yard to retrieve a ball. But the men do not know these things. Nor do they know that she will give him her body sparingly and partially. He must enter her surreptitiously, lifting the hem of her nightgown only to her navel. He must rest his weight on his elbows when they make love, ostensibly to avoid hurting her breasts but actually to keep her from having to touch or feel too much of him.

While he moves inside her, she will wonder why they didn't put the necessary but private parts of the body in some more convenient place —like the armpit, for example, or the palm of the hand. Someplace one could get to easily, and quickly, without undressing. She stiffens when she feels one of her paper curlers coming undone from the activity of love; imprints in her mind which one it is that is coming loose so she can quickly secure it once he is through. She hopes he will not sweat—

the damp may get into her hair; and that she will remain dry between her legs—she hates the glucking sound they make when she is moist. When she senses some spasm about to grip him, she will make rapid movements with her hips, press her fingernails into his back, suck in her breath, and pretend she is having an orgasm. She might wonder again, for the six hundredth time, what it would be like to have *that* feeling while her husband's penis is inside her. The closest thing to it was the time she was walking down the street and her napkin slipped free of her sanitary belt. It moved gently between her legs as she walked. Gently, ever so gently. And then a slight and distinctly delicious sensation collected in her crotch. As the delight grew, she had to stop in the street, hold her thighs together to contain it. That must be what it is like, she thinks, but it never happens while he is inside her. When he withdraws, she pulls her nightgown down, slips out of the bed and into the bathroom with relief.

Occasionally some living thing will engage her affections. A cat, perhaps, who will love her order, precision, and constancy; who will be as clean and quiet as she is. The cat will settle quietly on the windowsill and caress her with his eyes. She can hold him in her arms, letting his back paws struggle for footing on her breast and his forepaws cling to her shoulder. She can rub the smooth fur and feel the unresisting flesh underneath. At her gentlest touch he will preen, stretch, and open his mouth. And she will accept the strangely pleasant sensation that comes when he writhes beneath her hand and flattens his eyes with a surfeit of sensual delight. When she stands cooking at the table, he will circle about her shanks, and the trill of his fur spirals up her legs to her thighs, to make her fingers tremble a little in the pie dough.

Or, as she sits reading the "Uplifting Thoughts" in *The Liberty Magazine,* the cat will jump into her lap. She will fondle that soft hill of hair and let the warmth of the animal's body seep over and into the deeply private areas of her lap. Sometimes the magazine drops, and she opens her legs just a little, and the two of them will be still together, perhaps shifting a little together, sleeping a little together, until four o'clock, when the intruder comes home from work vaguely anxious about what's for dinner.

The cat will always know that he is first in her affections. Even after she bears a child. For she does bear a child—easily, and painlessly. But only one. A son. Named Junior.

One such girl from Mobile, or Meridian, or Aiken who did not sweat in her armpits nor between her thighs, who smelled of wood and vanilla, who had made soufflés in the Home Economics Department, moved with her husband, Louis, to Lorain, Ohio. Her name was Geraldine. There she built her nest, ironed shirts, potted bleeding hearts, played with her cat, and birthed Louis Junior.

Geraldine did not allow her baby, Junior, to cry. As long as his needs were physical, she could meet them—comfort and satiety. He was always brushed, bathed, oiled, and shod. Geraldine did not talk to him, coo to him, or indulge him in kissing bouts, but she saw that every other desire was fulfilled. It was not long before the child discovered the difference in his mother's behavior to himself and the cat. As he grew older, he learned how to direct his hatred of his mother to the cat, and spent some happy moments watching it suffer. The cat survived, because Geraldine was seldom away from home, and could effectively soothe the animal when Junior abused him.

Geraldine, Louis, Junior, and the cat lived next to the playground of Washington Irving School. Junior considered the playground his own, and the schoolchildren coveted his freedom to sleep late, go home for lunch, and dominate the playground after school. He hated to see the swings, slides, monkey bars, and seesaws empty and tried to get kids to stick around as long as possible. White kids; his mother did not like him to play with niggers. She had explained to him the difference between colored people and niggers. They were easily identifiable. Colored people were neat and quiet; niggers were dirty and loud. He belonged to the former group: he wore white shirts and blue trousers; his hair was cut as close to his scalp as possible to avoid any suggestion of

wool, the part was etched into his hair by the barber. In winter his
mother put Jergens Lotion on his face to keep the skin from becoming
ashen. Even though he was light-skinned, it was possible to ash. The
line between colored and nigger was not always clear; subtle and
telltale signs threatened to erode it, and the watch had to be constant.

Junior used to long to play with the black boys. More than anything
in the world he wanted to play King of the Mountain and have them
push him down the mound of dirt and roll over him. He wanted to
feel their hardness pressing on him, smell their wild blackness, and say
"Fuck you" with that lovely casualness. He wanted to sit with them on
curbstones and compare the sharpness of jackknives, the distance and
arcs of spitting. In the toilet he wanted to share with them the laurels
of being able to pee far and long. Bay Boy and P. L. had at one time
been his idols. Gradually he came to agree with his mother that neither Bay Boy nor P. L. was good enough for him. He played only with
Ralph Nisensky, who was two years younger, wore glasses, and didn't
want to *do* anything. More and more Junior enjoyed bullying girls. It
was easy making them scream and run. How he laughed when they fell
down and their bloomers showed. When they got up, their faces red
and crinkled, it made him feel good. The nigger girls he did not pick
on very much. They usually traveled in packs, and once when he threw
a stone at some of them, they chased, caught, and beat him witless. He
lied to his mother, saying Bay Boy did it. His mother was very upset.
His father just kept on reading the Lorain *Journal.*

When the mood struck him, he would call a child passing by to
come play on the swings or the seesaw. If the child wouldn't, or did
and left too soon, Junior threw gravel at him. He became a very good
shot.

Alternately bored and frightened at home, the playground was his
joy. On a day when he had been especially idle, he saw a very black
girl taking a shortcut through the playground. She kept her head down
as she walked. He had seen her many times before, standing alone, al-

ways alone, at recess. Nobody ever played with her. Probably, he thought, because she was ugly.

Now Junior called to her. "Hey! What are you doing walking through my yard?"

The girl stopped.

"Nobody can come through this yard 'less I say so."

"This ain't your yard. It's the school's."

"But I'm in charge of it."

The girl started to walk away.

"Wait." Junior walked toward her. "You can play in it if you want to. What's your name?"

"Pecola. I don't want to play."

"Come on. I'm not going to bother you."

"I got to go home."

"Say, you want to see something? I got something to show you."

"No. What is it?"

"Come on in my house. See, I live right there. Come on. I'll show you."

"Show me what?"

"Some kittens. We got some kittens. You can have one if you want."

"Real kittens?"

"Yeah. Come on."

He pulled gently at her dress. Pecola began to move toward his house. When he knew she had agreed, Junior ran ahead excitedly, stopping only to yell back at her to come on. He held the door open for her, smiling his encouragement. Pecola climbed the porch stairs and hesitated there, afraid to follow him. The house looked dark. Junior said, "There's nobody here. My ma's gone out, and my father's at work. Don't you want to see the kittens?"

Junior turned on the lights. Pecola stepped inside the door.

How beautiful, she thought. What a beautiful house. There was a big red-and-gold Bible on the dining-room table. Little lace doilies were everywhere—on arms and backs of chairs, in the center of a large dining table, on little tables. Potted plants were on all the windowsills. A color picture of Jesus Christ hung on a wall with the prettiest paper flowers fastened on the frame. She wanted to see everything slowly, slowly. But Junior kept saying, "Hey, you. Come on. Come on." He pulled her into another room, even more beautiful than the first. More doilies, a big lamp with green-and-gold base and white shade. There was even a rug on the floor, with enormous dark-red flowers. She was deep in admiration of the flowers when Junior said, "Here!" Pecola turned. "Here is your kitten!" he screeched. And he threw a big black cat right in her face. She sucked in her breath in fear and surprise and felt fur in her mouth. The cat clawed her face and chest in an effort to right itself, then leaped nimbly to the floor.

Junior was laughing and running around the room clutching his stomach delightedly. Pecola touched the scratched place on her face and felt tears coming. When she started toward the doorway, Junior leaped in front of her.

"You can't get out. You're my prisoner," he said. His eyes were merry but hard.

"You let me go."

"No!" He pushed her down, ran out the door that separated the rooms, and held it shut with his hands. Pecola's banging on the door increased his gasping, high-pitched laughter.

The tears came fast, and she held her face in her hands. When something soft and furry moved around her ankles, she jumped, and saw it was the cat. He wound himself in and about her legs. Momentarily distracted from her fear, she squatted down to touch him, her hands wet from the tears. The cat rubbed up against her knee. He was black all over, deep silky black, and his eyes, pointing down toward his nose, were bluish green. The light made them shine like blue ice. Pecola rubbed the cat's head; he whined, his tongue flicking with pleasure. The blue eyes in the black face held her.

Junior, curious at not hearing her sobs, opened the door, and saw her squatting down rubbing the cat's back. He saw the cat stretching its head and flattening its eyes. He had seen that expression many times as the animal responded to his mother's touch.

"Gimme my cat!" His voice broke. With a movement both awkward and sure he snatched the cat by one of its hind legs and began to swing it around his head in a circle.

"Stop that!" Pecola was screaming. The cat's free paws were stiffened, ready to grab anything to restore balance, its mouth wide, its eyes blue streaks of horror.

Still screaming, Pecola reached for Junior's hand. She heard her dress rip under her arm. Junior tried to push her away, but she grabbed the arm which was swinging the cat. They both fell, and in falling, Junior let go the cat, which, having been released in mid-motion, was thrown full force against the window. It slithered down and fell on the radiator behind the sofa. Except for a few shudders, it was still. There was only the slightest smell of singed fur.

Geraldine opened the door.

"What is this?" Her voice was mild, as though asking a perfectly reasonable question. "Who is this girl?"

"She killed our cat," said Junior. "Look." He pointed to the radiator, where the cat lay, its blue eyes closed, leaving only an empty, black, and helpless face.

Geraldine went to the radiator and picked up the cat. He was limp in her arms, but she rubbed her face in his fur. She looked at Pecola. Saw the dirty torn dress, the plaits sticking out on her head, hair matted where the plaits had come undone, the muddy shoes with the wad of gum peeping out from between the cheap soles, the soiled socks, one of which had been walked down into the heel of the shoe. She saw the safety pin holding the hem of the dress up. Up over the hump of the cat's back she looked at her. She had seen this little girl all of her life. Hanging out of windows over saloons in Mobile, crawling over the porches of shotgun houses on the edge of town, sitting in bus stations holding paper bags and crying to mothers who kept saying

"Shet up!" Hair uncombed, dresses falling apart, shoes untied and caked with dirt. They had stared at her with great uncomprehending eyes. Eyes that questioned nothing and asked everything. Unblinking and unabashed, they stared up at her. The end of the world lay in their eyes, and the beginning, and all the waste in between.

They were everywhere. They slept six in a bed, all their pee mixing together in the night as they wet their beds each in his own candy-and-potato-chip dream. In the long, hot days, they idled away, picking plaster from the walls and digging into the earth with sticks. They sat in little rows on street curbs, crowded into pews at church, taking space from the nice, neat, colored children; they clowned on the playgrounds, broke things in dime stores, ran in front of you on the street, made ice slides on the sloped sidewalks in winter. The girls grew up knowing nothing of girdles, and the boys announced their manhood by turning the bills of their caps backward. Grass wouldn't grow where they lived. Flowers died. Shades fell down. Tin cans and tires blossomed where they lived. They lived on cold black-eyed peas and orange pop. Like flies they hovered; like flies they settled. And this one had settled in her house. Up over the hump of the cat's back she looked.

"Get out," she said, her voice quiet. "You nasty little black bitch. Get out of my house."

The cat shuddered and flicked his tail.

Pecola backed out of the room, staring at the pretty milk-brown lady in the pretty gold-and-green house who was talking to her through the cat's fur. The pretty lady's words made the cat fur move; the breath of each word parted the fur. Pecola turned to find the front door and saw Jesus looking down at her with sad and unsurprised eyes, his long brown hair parted in the middle, the gay paper flowers twisted around his face.

Outside, the March wind blew into the rip in her dress. She held her head down against the cold. But she could not hold it low enough to avoid seeing the snowflakes falling and dying on the pavement.

# Spring

The first twigs are thin, green, and supple. They bend into a complete circle, but will not break. Their delicate, showy hopefulness shooting from forsythia and lilac bushes meant only a change in whipping style. They beat us differently in the spring. Instead of the dull pain of a winter strap, there were these new green switches that lost their sting long after the whipping was over. There was a nervous meanness in these long twigs that made us long for the steady stroke of a strap or the firm but honest slap of a hairbrush. Even now spring for me is shot through with the remembered ache of switchings, and forsythia holds no cheer.

Sunk in the grass of an empty lot on a spring Saturday, I split the stems of milkweed and thought about ants and peach pits and death and where the world went when I closed my eyes. I must have lain long in the grass, for the shadow that was in front of me when I left the house had disappeared when I went back. I entered the house, as the house was bursting with an uneasy quiet. Then I heard my mother singing something about trains and Arkansas. She came in the back door with some folded yellow curtains which she piled on the kitchen table. I sat down on the floor to listen to the song's story, and noticed how strangely she was behaving. She still had her hat on, and her shoes were dusty, as though she had been walking in deep dirt. She put on some water to boil and then swept the porch; then she hauled out the curtain stretcher, but instead of putting the damp curtains on it, she swept the porch again. All the time singing about trains and Arkansas.

When she finished, I went to look for Frieda. I found her upstairs lying on our bed, crying the tired, whimpering cry that follows the first wailings—mostly gasps and shudderings. I lay on the bed and looked at the tiny bunches of wild roses sprinkled over her dress. Many washings had faded their color and dimmed their outlines.

"What happened, Frieda?"

She lifted a swollen face from the crook of her arm. Shuddering still, she sat up, letting her thin legs dangle over the bedside. I knelt on the bed and picked up the hem of my dress to wipe her running nose. She never liked wiping noses on clothes, but this time she let me. It was the way Mama did with her apron.

"Did you get a whipping?"

She shook her head no.

"Then why you crying?"

"Because."

"Because what?"

"Mr. Henry."

"What'd he do?"

"Daddy beat him up."

"What for? The Maginot Line? Did he find out about the Maginot Line?"

"No."

"Well, what, then? Come on, Frieda. How come I can't know?"

"He . . . *picked* at me."

"Picked at you? You mean like Soaphead Church?"

"Sort of."

"He showed his privates at you?"

"Noooo. He touched me."

"Where?"

"Here and here." She pointed to the tiny breasts that, like two fallen acorns, scattered a few faded rose leaves on her dress.

"Really? How did it feel?"

"Oh, Claudia." She sounded put-out. I wasn't asking the right questions.

"It didn't feel like anything."

"But wasn't it supposed to? Feel good, I mean?" Frieda sucked her teeth. "What'd he do? Just walk up and pinch them?"

She sighed. "First he said how pretty I was. Then he grabbed my arm and touched me."

"Where was Mama and Daddy?"

"Over at the garden weeding."

"What'd you say when he did it?"

"Nothing. I just ran out the kitchen and went to the garden."

"Mama said we was never to cross the tracks by ourselves."

"Well, what would you do? Set there and let him pinch you?"

I looked at my chest. "I don't have nothing to pinch. I'm never going to have nothing."

"Oh, Claudia, you're jealous of everything. You *want* him to?"

"No, I just get tired of having everything last."

"You do not. What about scarlet fever? You had that first."

"Yes, but it didn't last. Anyway, what happened at the garden?"

"I told Mama, and she told Daddy, and we all come home, and he was gone, so we waited for him, and when Daddy saw him come up on the porch, he threw our old tricycle at his head and knocked him off the porch."

"Did he die?"

"Naw. He got up and started singing 'Nearer My God to Thee.' Then Mama hit him with a broom and told him to keep the Lord's name out of his mouth, but he wouldn't stop, and Daddy was cussing, and everybody was screaming."

"Oh, shoot, I always miss stuff."

"And Mr. Buford came running out with his gun, and Mama told him to go somewhere and sit down, and Daddy said no, give him the gun, and Mr. Buford did, and Mama screamed, and Mr. Henry shut up and started running, and Daddy shot at him and Mr. Henry jumped out of his shoes and kept on running in his socks. Then Rosemary came out and said that Daddy was going to jail, and I hit her."

"Real hard?"

"Real hard."

"Is that when Mama whipped you?"

"She didn't whip me, I told you."

"Then why you crying?"

"Miss Dunion came in after everybody was quiet, and Mama and Daddy was fussing about who let Mr. Henry in anyway, and she said that Mama should take me to the doctor, because I might be ruined, and Mama started screaming all over again."

"At you?"

"No. At Miss Dunion."

"But why were you crying?"

"I don't want to be *ruined!*"

"What's ruined?"

"You know. Like the Maginot Line. She's ruined. Mama said so." The tears came back.

An image of Frieda, big and fat, came to mind. Her thin legs swollen, her face surrounded by layers of rouged skin. I too begin to feel tears.

"But, Frieda, you could exercise and not eat."

She shrugged.

"Besides, what about China and Poland? They're ruined too, aren't they? And they ain't fat."

"That's because they drink whiskey. Mama says whiskey ate them up."

"You could drink whiskey."

"Where would I get whiskey?"

We thought about this. Nobody would sell it to us; we had no money, anyway. There was never any in our house. Who would have some?

"Pecola," I said. "Her father's always drunk. She can get us some."

"You think so?"

"Sure. Cholly's always drunk. Let's go ask her. We don't have to tell her what for."

"Now?"

"Sure, now."

"What'll we tell Mama?"

"Nothing. Let's just go out the back. One at a time. So she won't notice."

"O.K. You go first, Claudia."

We opened the fence gate at the bottom of the backyard and ran down the alley.

Pecola lived on the other side of Broadway. We had never been in her house, but we knew where it was. A two-story gray building that had been a store downstairs and had an apartment upstairs.

Nobody answered our knock on the front door, so we walked around to the side door. As we approached, we heard radio music and looked to see where it came from. Above us was the second-story porch, lined with slanting, rotting rails, and sitting on the porch was the Maginot Line herself. We stared up and automatically reached for the other's hand. A mountain of flesh, she lay rather than sat in a rocking chair. She had no shoes on, and each foot was poked between a railing: tiny baby toes at the tip of puffy feet; swollen ankles smoothed and tightened the skin; massive legs like tree stumps parted wide at the knees, over which spread two roads of soft flabby inner thigh that kissed each other deep in the shade of her dress and closed. A dark-brown root-beer bottle, like a burned limb, grew out of her dimpled hand. She looked at us down through the porch railings and emitted a low, long belch. Her eyes were as clean as rain, and again I remembered the waterfall. Neither of us could speak. Both of us imagined we were seeing what was to become of Frieda. The Maginot Line smiled at us.

"You all looking for somebody?"

I had to pull my tongue from the roof of my mouth to say, "Pecola—she live here?"

"Uh-huh, but she ain't here now. She gone to her mama's work place to git the wash."

"Yes, ma'am. She coming back?"

"Uh-huh. She got to hang up the clothes before the sun goes down."

"Oh."

"You can wait for her. Wanna come up here and wait?"

We exchanged glances. I looked back up at the broad cinnamon roads that met in the shadow of her dress.

Frieda said, "No, ma'am."

"Well," the Maginot Line seemed interested in our problem. "You can go to her mama's work place, but it's way over by the lake."

"Where by the lake?"

"That big white house with the wheelbarrow full of flowers."

It was a house that we knew, having admired the large white wheelbarrow tilted down on spoked wheels and planted with seasonal flowers.

"Ain't that too far for you all to go walking?"

Frieda scratched her knee.

"Why don't you wait for her? You can come up here. Want some pop?" Those rain-soaked eyes lit up, and her smile was full, not like the pinched and holding-back smile of other grown-ups.

I moved to go up the stairs, but Frieda said, "No, ma'am, we ain't allowed."

I was amazed at her courage, and frightened of her sassiness. The smile of the Maginot Line slipped. "Ain't 'llowed?"

"No'm."

"Ain't 'llowed to what?"

"Go in your house."

"Is that right?" The waterfalls were still. "How come?"

"My mama said so. My mama said you ruined."

The waterfalls began to run again. She put the root-beer bottle to her lips and drank it empty. With a graceful movement of the wrist, a gesture so quick and small we never really saw it, only remembered it afterward, she tossed the bottle over the rail at us. It split at our feet, and shards of brown glass dappled our legs before we could jump back. The Maginot Line put a fat hand on one of the folds of her stomach and laughed. At first just a deep humming with her mouth closed, then a larger, warmer sound. Laughter at once beautiful and frightening. She let her head tilt sideways, closed her eyes, and shook her massive trunk, letting the laughter fall like a wash of red leaves all around us. Scraps and curls of the laughter followed us as we ran. Our breath gave out at the same time our legs did. After we rested against a tree, our heads on crossed forearms, I said, "Let's go home."

Frieda was still angry—fighting, she believed, for her life. "No, we got to get it now."

"We can't go all the way to the lake."

"Yes we can. Come on."

"Mama gone get us."

"No she ain't. Besides, she can't do nothing but whip us."

That was true. She wouldn't kill us, or laugh a terrible laugh at us, or throw a bottle at us.

We walked down tree-lined streets of soft gray houses leaning like tired ladies. . . . The streets changed; houses looked more sturdy, their paint was newer, porch posts straighter, yards deeper. Then came brick houses set well back from the street, fronted by yards edged in shrubbery clipped into smooth cones and balls of velvet green.

The lakefront houses were the loveliest. Garden furniture, ornaments, windows like shiny eyeglasses, and no sign of life. The backyards of these houses fell away in green slopes down to a strip of sand, and then the blue Lake Erie, lapping all the way to Canada. The orange-patched sky of the steel-mill section never reached this part of town. This sky was always blue.

We reached Lake Shore Park, a city park laid out with rosebuds, fountains, bowling greens, picnic tables. It was empty now, but sweetly expectant of clean, white, well-behaved children and parents who would play there above the lake in summer before half-running, half-stumbling down the slope to the welcoming water. Black people were not allowed in the park, and so it filled our dreams.

Right before the entrance to the park was the large white house with the wheelbarrow full of flowers. Short crocus blades sheathed the purple-and-white hearts that so wished to be first they endured the chill and rain of early spring. The walkway was flagged in calculated disorder, hiding the cunning symmetry. Only fear of discovery and the knowledge that we did not belong kept us from loitering. We circled the proud house and went to the back.

There on the tiny railed stoop sat Pecola in a light red sweater and blue cotton dress. A little wagon was parked near her. She seemed glad to see us.

"Hi."

"Hi."

"What you all doing here?" She was smiling, and since it was a rare thing to see on her, I was surprised at the pleasure it gave me.

"We're looking for you."

"Who told you I was here?"

"The Maginot Line."

"Who is that?"

"That big fat lady. She lives over you."

"Oh, you mean Miss Marie. Her name is Miss Marie."

"Well, everybody calls her Miss Maginot Line. Ain't you scared?"

"Scared of what?"

"The Maginot Line."

Pecola looked genuinely puzzled. "What for?"

"Your mama let you go in her house? And eat out of her plates?"

"She don't know I go. Miss Marie is nice. They all nice."

"Oh, yeah," I said, "she tried to kill us."

"Who? Miss Marie? She don't bother nobody."

"Then how come your mama don't let you go in her house if she so nice?"

"I don't know. She say she's bad, but they ain't bad. They give me stuff all the time."

"What stuff?"

"Oh, lots of stuff, pretty dresses, and shoes. I got more shoes than I ever wear. And jewelry and candy and money. They take me to the movies, and once we went to the carnival. China gone take me to Cleveland to see the square, and Poland gone take me to Chicago to see the Loop. We going everywhere together."

"You lying. You don't have no pretty dresses."

"I do, too."

"Oh, come on, Pecola, what you telling us all that junk for?" Frieda asked.

"It ain't junk." Pecola stood up ready to defend her words, when the door opened.

Mrs. Breedlove stuck her head out the door and said, "What's going on out here? Pecola, who are these children?"

"That's Frieda and Claudia, Mrs. Breedlove."

"Whose girls are you?" She came all the way out on the stoop. She looked nicer than I had ever seen her, in her white uniform and her hair in a small pompadour.

"Mrs. MacTeer's girls, ma'am."

"Oh, yes. Live over on Twenty-first Street?"

"Yes, ma'am."

"What are you doing 'way over here?"

"Just walking. We came to see Pecola."

"Well, you better get on back. You can walk with Pecola. Come on in while I get the wash."

We stepped into the kitchen, a large spacious room. Mrs. Breedlove's skin glowed like taffeta in the reflection of white porcelain, white woodwork, polished cabinets, and brilliant copperware. Odors of meat, vegetables, and something freshly baked mixed with a scent of Fels Naphtha.

"I'm gone get the wash. You all stand stock still right there and

don't mess up nothing." She disappeared behind a white swinging
door, and we could hear the uneven flap of her footsteps as she
descended into the basement.

Another door opened, and in walked a little girl, smaller and
younger than all of us. She wore a pink sunback dress and pink fluffy
bedroom slippers with two bunny ears pointed up from the tips. Her
hair was corn yellow and bound in a thick ribbon. When she saw us,
fear danced across her face for a second. She looked anxiously around
the kitchen.

"Where's Polly?" she asked.

The familiar violence rose in me. Her calling Mrs. Breedlove Polly,
when even Pecola called her mother Mrs. Breedlove seemed reason
enough to scratch her.

"She's downstairs," I said.

"Polly!" she called.

"Look," Frieda whispered, "look at that." On the counter near the
stove in a silvery pan was a deep-dish berry cobbler. The purple juice
bursting here and there through crust. We moved closer.

"It's still hot," Frieda said.

Pecola stretched her hand to touch the pan, lightly, to see if it was
hot.

"Polly, come here," the little girl called again.

It may have been nervousness, awkwardness, but the pan tilted
under Pecola's fingers and fell to the floor, splattering blackish
blueberries everywhere. Most of the juice splashed on Pecola's legs,
and the burn must have been painful, for she cried out and began
hopping about just as Mrs. Breedlove entered with a tightly packed
laundry bag. In one gallop she was on Pecola, and with the back of her
hand knocked her to the floor. Pecola slid in the pie juice, one leg
folding under her. Mrs. Breedlove yanked her up by the arm, slapped
her again, and in a voice thin with anger, abused Pecola directly and
Frieda and me by implication.

"Crazy fool . . . my floor, mess . . . look what you . . ."

work . . . get on out . . . now that . . . crazy . . . my floor, my floor . . . my floor." Her words were hotter and darker than the smoking berries, and we backed away in dread.

The little girl in pink started to cry. Mrs. Breedlove turned to her. "Hush, baby, hush. Come here. Oh, Lord, look at your dress. Don't cry no more. Polly will change it." She went to the sink and turned tap water on a fresh towel. Over her shoulder she spit out words to us like rotten pieces of apple. "Pick up that wash and get on out of here, so I can get this mess cleaned up."

Pecola picked up the laundry bag, heavy with wet clothes, and we stepped hurriedly out the door. As Pecola put the laundry bag in the wagon, we could hear Mrs. Breedlove hushing and soothing the tears of the little pink-and-yellow girl.

"Who were they, Polly?"

"Don't worry none, baby."

"You gonna make another pie?"

" 'Course I will."

"Who were they, Polly?"

"Hush. Don't worry none," she whispered, and the honey in her words complemented the sundown spilling on the lake.

SEEMOTHERMOTHERISVERYNICEMOTHERWILLYOUPLA
YWITHJANEMOTHERLAUGHSLAUGHMOTHERLAUGHLA

The easiest thing to do would be to build a case out of her foot. That is what she herself did. But to find out the truth about how dreams die, one should never take the word of the dreamer. The end of her lovely beginning was probably the cavity in one of her front teeth. She preferred, however, to think always of her foot. Although she was the ninth of eleven children and lived on a ridge of red Alabama clay seven miles from the nearest road, the complete indifference with which a rusty nail was met when it punched clear through her foot during her second year of life saved Pauline Williams from total anonymity. The wound left her with a crooked, archless foot that flopped when she walked—not a limp that would have eventually twisted her spine, but a way of lifting the bad foot as though she were extracting it from little whirlpools that threatened to pull it under. Slight as it was, this deformity explained for her many things that would have been otherwise incomprehensible: why she alone of all the children had no nickname; why there were no funny jokes and anecdotes about funny things she had done; why no one ever remarked on her food preferences—no saving of the wing or neck for her—no cooking of the peas in a separate pot without rice because she did not like rice; why nobody teased her; why she never felt at home anywhere, or that she belonged anyplace. Her general feeling of separateness and unworthiness she blamed on her foot. Restricted, as a child, to this cocoon of her family's spinning, she cultivated quiet and private pleasures. She liked, most of all, to arrange things. To line things up in rows—jars on shelves at canning, peach pits on the step, sticks, stones, leaves—and the members of her family let these arrangements be. When by some accident somebody scattered her rows, they always stopped to retrieve them for her, and she was never angry, for it gave her a chance to rearrange them again. Whatever portable plurality she found, she organized into neat lines, according to their size, shape, or gradations of color. Just as she would never align a pine needle with the leaf of a cottonwood tree, she would never put the jars of tomatoes next to the green beans. During all of her four years of going to school, she was enchanted by numbers and depressed by words. She missed—without knowing what she missed— paints and crayons.

Near the beginning of World War I, the Williamses discovered, from returning neighbors and kin, the possibility of living better in another place. In shifts, lots, batches, mixed in with other families, they migrated, in six months and four journeys, to Kentucky, where there were mines and millwork.

*"When all us left from down home and was waiting down by the depot for the truck, it was nighttime. June bugs was shooting everywhere. They lighted up a tree leaf, and I seen a streak of green every now and again. That was the last time I seen real june bugs. These things up here ain't june bugs. They's something else. Folks here call them fireflies. Down home they was different. But I recollect that streak of green. I recollect it well."*

In Kentucky they lived in a real town, ten to fifteen houses on a single street, with water piped right into the kitchen. Ada and Fowler Williams found a five-room frame house for their family. The yard was bounded by a once-white fence against which Pauline's mother planted flowers and within which they kept a few chickens. Some of her brothers joined the Army, one sister died, and two got married, increasing the living space and giving the entire Kentucky venture a feel of luxury. The relocation was especially comfortable to Pauline, who was old enough to leave school. Mrs. Williams got a job cleaning and cooking for a white minister on the other side of town, and Pauline, now the oldest girl at home, took over the care of the house. She kept the fence in repair, pulling the pointed stakes erect, securing them with bits of

wire, collected eggs, swept, cooked, washed, and minded the two
younger children—a pair of twins called Chicken and Pie, who were
still in school. She was not only good at housekeeping, she enjoyed it.
After her parents left for work and the other children were at school or
in mines, the house was quiet. The stillness and isolation both calmed
and energized her. She could arrange and clean without interruption
until two o'clock, when Chicken and Pie came home.

When the war ended and the twins were ten years old, they too left
school to work. Pauline was fifteen, still keeping house, but with less
enthusiasm. Fantasies about men and love and touching were drawing
her mind and hands away from her work. Changes in weather began to
affect her, as did certain sights and sounds. These feelings translated
themselves to her in extreme melancholy. She thought of the death of
newborn things, lonely roads, and strangers who appear out of nowhere simply to hold one's hand, woods in which the sun was always
setting. In church especially did these dreams grow. The songs caressed
her, and while she tried to hold her mind on the wages of sin, her body
trembled for redemption, salvation, a mysterious rebirth that would
simply happen, with no effort on her part. In none of her fantasies was
she ever aggressive; she was usually idling by the river bank, or gathering berries in a field when a someone appeared, with gentle and penetrating eyes, who—with no exchange of words—understood; and before whose glance her foot straightened and her eyes dropped. The
someone had no face, no form, no voice, no odor. He was a simple
Presence, an all-embracing tenderness with strength and a promise of
rest. It did not matter that she had no idea of what to do or say to the
Presence—after the wordless knowing and the soundless touching, her
dreams disintegrated. But the Presence would know what to do. She
had only to lay her head on his chest and he would lead her away to
the sea, to the city, to the woods . . . forever.

There was a woman named Ivy who seemed to hold in her mouth
all of the sounds of Pauline's soul. Standing a little apart from the
choir, Ivy sang the dark sweetness that Pauline could not name; she

sang the death-defying death that Pauline yearned for; she sang of the Stranger who *knew* . . .

> Precious Lord take my hand
> Lead me on, let me stand
> I am tired, I am weak, I am worn.
> Through the storms, through the night
> Lead me on to the light
> Take my hand, precious Lord, lead me on.
>
> When my way grows drear
> Precious Lord linger near,
> When my life is almost gone
> Hear my cry hear my call
> Hold my hand lest I fall
> Take my hand, precious Lord, lead me on.

Thus it was that when the Stranger, the someone, did appear out of nowhere, Pauline was grateful but not surprised.

He came, strutting right out of a Kentucky sun on the hottest day of the year. He came big, he came strong, he came with yellow eyes, flaring nostrils, and he came with his own music.

Pauline was leaning idly on the fence, her arms resting on the cross-rail between the pickets. She had just put down some biscuit dough and was cleaning the flour from under her nails. Behind her at some distance she heard whistling. One of these rapid, high-note riffs that black boys make up as they go while sweeping, shoveling, or just walking along. A kind of city-street music where laughter belies anxiety, and joy is as short and straight as the blade of a pocketknife. She listened carefully to the music and let it pull her lips into a smile. The whistling got louder, and still she did not turn around, for she wanted it to last. While smiling to herself and holding fast to the break in somber thoughts, she felt something tickling her foot. She laughed aloud and turned to see. The whistler was bending down tickling her broken foot and kissing her leg. She could not stop her laughter—not until he looked up at her and she saw the Kentucky sun drenching the yellow, heavy-lidded eyes of Cholly Breedlove.

*"When I first seed Cholly, I want you to know it was like all the bits of color from that time down home when all us chil'ren went berry picking after a funeral and I put some in the pocket of my Sunday dress, and they mashed up and stained my hips. My whole dress was messed with purple, and it never did wash out. Not the dress nor me. I could feel that purple deep inside me. And that lemonade Mama used to make when Pap came in out the fields. It be cool and yellowish, with seeds floating near the bottom. And that streak of green them june bugs made on the trees the night we left from down home. All of them colors was in me. Just sitting there. So when Cholly come up and tickled my foot, it was like them berries, that lemonade, them streaks of green the june bugs made, all come together. Cholly was thin then, with real light eyes. He used to whistle, and when I heerd him, shivers come on my skin."*

Pauline and Cholly loved each other. He seemed to relish her company and even to enjoy her country ways and lack of knowledge about city things. He talked with her about her foot and asked, when they walked through the town or in the fields, if she were tired. Instead of ignoring her infirmity, pretending it was not there, he made it seem like something special and endearing. For the first time Pauline felt that her bad foot was an asset.

And he did touch her, firmly but gently, just as she had dreamed. But minus the gloom of setting suns and lonely river banks. She was secure and grateful; he was kind and lively. She had not known there was so much laughter in the world.

They agreed to marry and go 'way up north, where Cholly said steel mills were begging for workers. Young, loving, and full of energy, they came to Lorain, Ohio. Cholly found work in the steel mills right away, and Pauline started keeping house.

And then she lost her front tooth. But there must have been a speck, a brown speck easily mistaken for food but which did not leave, which sat on the enamel for months, and grew, until it cut into the surface and then to the brown putty underneath, finally eating away to the root, but avoiding the nerves, so its presence was not noticeable or uncomfortable. Then the weakened roots, having grown accustomed to the poison, responded one day to severe pressure, and the tooth fell free, leaving a ragged stump behind. But even before the little brown speck, there must have been the conditions, the setting that would allow it to exist in the first place.

In that young and growing Ohio town whose side streets, even, were paved with concrete, which sat on the edge of a calm blue lake, which boasted an affinity with Oberlin, the underground railroad station, just thirteen miles away, this melting pot on the lip of America facing the cold but receptive Canada—What could go wrong?

*"Me and Cholly was getting along good then. We come up north; supposed to be more jobs and all. We moved into two rooms up over a furniture store, and I set about housekeeping. Cholly was working at the steel plant, and everything was looking good. I don't know what all happened. Everything changed. It was hard to get to know folks up here, and I missed my people. I weren't used to so much white folks. The ones I seed before was something hateful, but they didn't come around too much. I mean, we didn't have too much truck with them. Just now and then in the fields, or at the commissary. But they want all over us. Up north they was everywhere—next door, downstairs, all over the streets—and colored folks few and far between. Northern colored folk was different too. Dicty-like. No better than whites for meanness. They could make you feel just as no-count, 'cept I didn't expect it from them. That was the lonesomest time of my life. I 'member looking out them front windows just waiting for Cholly to come home at three o'clock. I didn't even have a cat to talk to."*

In her loneliness, she turned to her husband for reassurance, entertainment, for things to fill the vacant places. Housework was not enough; there were only two rooms, and no yard to keep or move about in. The women in the town wore high-heeled shoes, and when Pauline tried to wear them, they aggravated her shuffle into a pronounced limp. Cholly was kindness still, but began to resist her total dependence on him. They were beginning to have less and less to say to each other. He had no problem finding other people and other things to occupy him—men were always climbing the stairs asking for him, and he was happy to accompany them, leaving her alone.

Pauline felt uncomfortable with the few black women she met. They were amused by her because she did not straighten her hair. When she tried to make up her face as they did, it came off rather badly. Their goading glances and private snickers at her way of talking (saying "chil'ren") and dressing developed in her a desire for new clothes. When Cholly began to quarrel about the money she wanted, she decided to go to work. Taking jobs as a day worker helped with the clothes, and even a few things for the apartment, but it did not help with Cholly. He was not pleased with her purchases and began to tell her so. Their marriage was shredded with quarrels. She was still no more than a girl, and still waiting for that plateau of happiness, that hand of a precious Lord who, when her way grew drear, would always linger near. Only now she had a clearer idea of what drear meant. Money became the focus of all their discussions, hers for clothes, his for drink. The sad thing was that Pauline did not really care for clothes and makeup. She merely wanted other women to cast favorable glances her way.

After several months of doing day work, she took a steady job in the home of a family of slender means and nervous, pretentious ways.

*"Cholly commenced to getting meaner and meaner and wanted to fight me all of the time. I give him as good as I got. Had to. Look like working for that woman and fighting Cholly was all I did. Tiresome. But I holt on to my jobs, even though working for that woman was more than a notion. It wasn't so much her meanness as just simpleminded. Her whole family was. Couldn't get along with one another worth nothing. You'd think with a pretty house*

*like that and all the money they could holt on to, they would enjoy one
another. She haul off and cry over the leastest thing. If one of her friends cut
her short on the telephone, she'd go to crying. She should of been glad she had
a telephone. I ain't got one yet. I recollect oncet how her baby brother who she
put through dentistry school didn't invite them to some big party he throwed.
They was a big to-do about that. Everybody stayed on the telephone for days.
Fussing and carrying on. She asked me, 'Pauline, what would you do if your
own brother had a party and didn't invite you?' I said ifn I really wanted to
go to that party, I reckoned I'd go anyhow. Never mind what he want. She
just sucked her teeth a little and made out like what I said was dumb. All the
while I was thinking how dumb she was. Whoever told her that her brother
was her friend? Folks can't like folks just 'cause they has the same mama. I
tried to like that woman myself. She was good about giving me stuff, but I
just couldn't like her. Soon as I worked up a good feeling on her account, she'd
do something ignorant and start in to telling me how to clean and do. If I left
her on her own, she'd drown in dirt. I didn't have to pick up after Chicken
and Pie the way I had to pick up after them. None of them knew so much as
how to wipe their behinds. I know, 'cause I did the washing. And couldn't pee
proper to save their lives. Her husband ain't hit the bowl yet. Nasty white
folks is about the nastiest things they is. But I would have stayed on 'cepting
for Cholly come over by where I was working and cut up so. He come there
drunk wanting some money. When that white woman see him, she turned red.
She tried to act strong-like, but she was scared bad. Anyway, she told Cholly
to get out or she would call the police. He cussed her and started pulling on
me. I would of gone upside his head, but I don't want no dealings with the
police. So I taken my things and left. I tried to get back, but she didn't want
me no more if I was going to stay with Cholly. She said she would let me stay
if I left him. I thought about that. But later on it didn't seem none too bright
for a black woman to leave a black man for a white woman. She didn't never
give me the eleven dollars she owed me, neither. That hurt bad. The gas man
had cut the gas off, and I couldn't cook none. I really begged that woman for
my money. I went to see her. She was mad as a wet hen. Kept on telling me I
owed her for uniforms and some old broken-down bed she give me. I didn't*

*know if I owed her or not, but I needed my money. She wouldn't let up none,
neither, even when I give her my word that Cholly wouldn't come back there
no more. Then I got so desperate I asked her if she would loan it to me. She
was quiet for a spell, and then she told me I shouldn't let a man take
advantage over me. That I should have more respect, and it was my husband's
duty to pay the bills, and if he couldn't, I should leave and get alimony. All
such simple stuff. What was he gone give me alimony on? I seen she didn't
understand that all I needed from her was my eleven dollars to pay the gas
man so I could cook. She couldn't get that one thing through her thick head.
'Are you going to leave him, Pauline?' she kept on saying. I thought she'd give
me my money if I said I would, so I said 'Yes, ma'am.' 'All right,' she said.
'You leave him, and then come back to work, and we'll let bygones be bygones.'
'Can I have my money today?' I said. 'No' she said. 'Only when you leave
him. I'm only thinking of you and your future. What good is he, Pauline,
what good is he to you?' How you going to answer a woman like that, who
don't know what good a man is, and say out of one side of her mouth she's
thinking of your future but won't give you your own money so you can buy
you something besides baloney to eat? So I said, 'No good, ma'am. He ain't no
good to me. But just the same, I think I'd best stay on.' She got up, and I left.
When I got outside, I felt pains in my crotch, I had held my legs together so
tight trying to make that woman understand. But I reckon now she couldn't
understand. She married a man with a slash in his face instead of a mouth.
So how could she understand?"*

One winter Pauline discovered she was pregnant. When she told
Cholly, he surprised her by being pleased. He began to drink less and
come home more often. They eased back into a relationship more like
the early days of their marriage, when he asked if she were tired or
wanted him to bring her something from the store. In this state of
ease, Pauline stopped doing day work and returned to her own housekeeping. But the loneliness in those two rooms had not gone away.
When the winter sun hit the peeling green paint of the kitchen chairs,
when the smoked hocks were boiling in the pot, when all she could

hear was the truck delivering furniture downstairs, she thought about back home, about how she had been all alone most of the time then too, but that this lonesomeness was different. Then she stopped staring at the green chairs, at the delivery truck; she went to the movies instead. There in the dark her memory was refreshed, and she succumbed to her earlier dreams. Along with the idea of romantic love, she was introduced to another—physical beauty. Probably the most destructive ideas in the history of human thought. Both originated in envy, thrived in insecurity, and ended in disillusion. In equating physical beauty with virtue, she stripped her mind, bound it, and collected self-contempt by the heap. She forgot lust and simple caring for. She regarded love as possessive mating, and romance as the goal of the spirit. It would be for her a well-spring from which she would draw the most destructive emotions, deceiving the lover and seeking to imprison the beloved, curtailing freedom in every way.

She was never able, after her education in the movies, to look at a face and not assign it some category in the scale of absolute beauty, and the scale was one she absorbed in full from the silver screen. There at last were the darkened woods, the lonely roads, the river banks, the gentle knowing eyes. There the flawed became whole, the blind sighted, and the lame and halt threw away their crutches. There death was dead, and people made every gesture in a cloud of music. There the black-and-white images came together, making a magnificent whole—all projected through the ray of light from above and behind.

It was really a simple pleasure, but she learned all there was to love and all there was to hate.

*"The onliest time I be happy seem like was when I was in the picture show. Every time I got, I went. I'd go early, before the show started. They'd cut off the lights, and everything be black. Then the screen would light up, and I'd move right on in them pictures. White men taking such good care of they women, and they all dressed up in big clean houses with the bathtubs right in the same room with the toilet. Them pictures gave me a lot of pleasure, but it*

*made coming home hard, and looking at Cholly hard. I don't know. I*
*'member one time I went to see Clark Gable and Jean Harlow. I fixed my hair*
*up like I'd seen hers on a magazine. A part on the side, with one little curl on*
*my forehead. It looked just like her. Well, almost just like. Anyway, I sat in*
*that show with my hair done up that way and had a good time. I thought I'd*
*see it through to the end again, and I got up to get me some candy. I was*
*sitting back in my seat, and I taken a big bite of that candy, and it pulled a*
*tooth right out of my mouth. I could of cried. I had good teeth, not a rotten*
*one in my head. I don't believe I ever did get over that. There I was, five*
*months pregnant, trying to look like Jean Harlow, and a front tooth gone.*
*Everything went then. Look like I just didn't care no more after that. I let my*
*hair go back, plaited it up, and settled down to just being ugly. I still went to*
*the pictures, though, but the meanness got worse. I wanted my tooth back.*
*Cholly poked fun at me, and we started fighting again. I tried to kill him. He*
*didn't hit me too hard, 'cause I were pregnant I guess, but the fights, once they*
*got started up again, kept up. He begin to make me madder than anything I*
*knowed, and I couldn't keep my hands off him. Well, I had that baby—a*
*boy—and after that got pregnant again with another one. But it weren't like*
*I thought it was gone be. I loved them and all, I guess, but maybe it was*
*having no money, or maybe it was Cholly, but they sure worried the life out of*
*me. Sometimes I'd catch myself hollering at them and beating them, and I'd*
*feel sorry for them, but I couldn't seem to stop. When I had the second one, a*
*girl, I 'member I said I'd love it no matter what it looked like. She looked like*
*a black ball of hair. I don't recollect trying to get pregnant that first time. But*
*that second time, I actually tried to get pregnant. Maybe 'cause I'd had one*
*already and wasn't scairt to do it. Anyway, I felt good, and wasn't thinking*
*on the carrying, just the baby itself. I used to talk to it whilst it be still in the*
*womb. Like good friends we was. You know. I be hanging wash and I*
*knowed lifting weren't good for it. I'd say to it holt on now I gone hang up*
*these few rags, don't get froggy; it be over soon. It wouldn't leap or nothing. Or*
*I be mixing something in a bowl for the other chile and I'd talk to it then too.*
*You know, just friendly talk. On up til the end I felted good about that baby.*
*I went to the hospital when my time come. So I could be easeful. I didn't want*

to have it at home like I done with the boy. They put me in a big room with a whole mess of women. The pains was coming, but not too bad. A little old doctor come to examine me. He had all sorts of stuff. He gloved his hand and put some kind of jelly on it and rammed it up between my legs. When he left off, some more doctors come. One old one and some young ones. The old one was learning the young ones about babies. Showing them how to do. When he got to me he said now these here women you don't have any trouble with. They deliver right away and with no pain. Just like horses. The young ones smiled a little. They looked at my stomach and between my legs. They never said nothing to me. Only one looked at me. Looked at my face, I mean. I looked right back at him. He dropped his eyes and turned red. He knowed, I reckon, that maybe I weren't no horse foaling. But them others. They didn't know. They went on. I seed them talking to them white women: 'How you feel? Gonna have twins?' Just shucking them, of course, but nice talk. Nice friendly talk. I got edgy, and when them pains got harder, I was glad. Glad to have something else to think about. I moaned something awful. The pains wasn't as bad as I let on, but I had to let them people know having a baby was more than a bowel movement. I hurt just like them white women. Just 'cause I wasn't hooping and hollering before didn't mean I wasn't feeling pain. What'd they think? That just 'cause I knowed how to have a baby with no fuss that my behind wasn't pulling and aching like theirs? Besides, that doctor don't know what he talking about. He must never seed no mare foal. Who say they don't have no pain? Just 'cause she don't cry? 'Cause she can't say it, they think it ain't there? If they looks in her eyes and see them eyeballs lolling back, see the sorrowful look, they'd know. Anyways, the baby come. Big old healthy thing. She looked different from what I thought. Reckon I talked to it so much before I conjured up a mind's eye view of it. So when I seed it, it was like looking at a picture of your mama when she was a girl. You knows who she is, but she don't look the same. They give her to me for a nursing, and she liked to pull my nipple off right away. She caught on fast. Not like Sammy, he was the hardest child to feed. But Pecola look like she knowed right off what to do. A right smart baby she was. I used to like to watch her. You know they makes them greedy sounds. Eyes all soft and wet. A cross between a puppy and

*a dying man. But I knowed she was ugly. Head full of pretty hair, but Lord
she was ugly."*

When Sammy and Pecola were still young Pauline had to go back
to work. She was older now, with no time for dreams and movies. It
was time to put all of the pieces together, make coherence where before there had been none. The children gave her this need; she herself
was no longer a child. So she became, and her process of becoming was
like most of ours: she developed a hatred for things that mystified or
obstructed her; acquired virtues that were easy to maintain; assigned
herself a role in the scheme of things; and harked back to simpler
times for gratification.

She took on the full responsibility and recognition of breadwinner
and returned to church. First, however, she moved out of the two
rooms into a spacious first floor of a building that had been built as a
store. She came into her own with the women who had despised her,
by being more moral than they; she avenged herself on Cholly by forcing him to indulge in the weaknesses she despised. She joined a church
where shouting was frowned upon, served on Stewardess Board No. 3,
and became a member of Ladies Circle No. 1. At prayer meeting she
moaned and sighed over Cholly's ways, and hoped God would help her
keep the children from the sins of the father. She stopped saying
"chil'ren" and said "childring" instead. She let another tooth fall, and
was outraged by painted ladies who thought only of clothes and men.
Holding Cholly as a model of sin and failure, she bore him like a
crown of thorns, and her children like a cross.

It was her good fortune to find a permanent job in the home of a
well-to-do family whose members were affectionate, appreciative, and
generous. She looked at their houses, smelled their linen, touched their
silk draperies, and loved all of it. The child's pink nightie, the stacks of
white pillow slips edged with embroidery, the sheets with top hems
picked out with blue cornflowers. She became what is known as an
ideal servant, for such a role filled practically all of her needs. When

she bathed the little Fisher girl, it was in a porcelain tub with silvery taps running infinite quantities of hot, clear water. She dried her in fluffy white towels and put her in cuddly night clothes. Then she brushed the yellow hair, enjoying the roll and slip of it between her fingers. No zinc tub, no buckets of stove-heated water, no flaky, stiff, grayish towels washed in a kitchen sink, dried in a dusty backyard, no tangled black puffs of rough wool to comb. Soon she stopped trying to keep her own house. The things she could afford to buy did not last, had no beauty or style, and were absorbed by the dingy storefront. More and more she neglected her house, her children, her man—they were like the afterthoughts one has just before sleep, the early-morning and late-evening edges of her day, the dark edges that made the daily life with the Fishers lighter, more delicate, more lovely. Here she could arrange things, clean things, line things up in neat rows. Here her foot flopped around on deep pile carpets, and there was no uneven sound. Here she found beauty, order, cleanliness, and praise. Mr. Fisher said, "I would rather sell her blueberry cobblers than real estate." She reigned over cupboards stacked high with food that would not be eaten for weeks, even months; she was queen of canned vegetables bought by the case, special fondants and ribbon candy curled up in tiny silver dishes. The creditors and service people who humiliated her when she went to them on her own behalf respected her, were even intimidated by her, when she spoke for the Fishers. She refused beef slightly dark or with edges not properly trimmed. The slightly reeking fish that she accepted for her own family she would all but throw in the fish man's face if he sent it to the Fisher house. Power, praise, and luxury were hers in this household. They even gave her what she had never had—a nickname—Polly. It was her pleasure to stand in her kitchen at the end of a day and survey her handiwork. Knowing there were soap bars by the dozen, bacon by the rasher, and reveling in her shiny pots and pans and polished floors. Hearing, "We'll never let her go. We could never find anybody like Polly. She will *not* leave the kitchen until everything is in order. Really, she is the ideal servant."

Pauline kept this order, this beauty, for herself, a private world, and never introduced it into her storefront, or to her children. Them she bent toward respectability, and in so doing taught them fear: fear of being clumsy, fear of being like their father, fear of not being loved by God, fear of madness like Cholly's mother's. Into her son she beat a loud desire to run away, and into her daughter she beat a fear of growing up, fear of other people, fear of life.

All the meaningfulness of her life was in her work. For her virtues were intact. She was an active church woman, did not drink, smoke, or carouse, defended herself mightily against Cholly, rose above him in every way, and felt she was fulfilling a mother's role conscientiously when she pointed out their father's faults to keep them from having them, or punished them when they showed any slovenliness, no matter how slight, when she worked twelve to sixteen hours a day to support them. And the world itself agreed with her.

It was only sometimes, sometimes, and then rarely, that she thought about the old days, or what her life had turned to. They were musings, idle thoughts, full sometimes of the old dreaminess, but not the kind of thing she cared to dwell on.

*"I started to leave him once, but something came up. Once, after he tried to set the house on fire, I was all set in my mind to go. I can't even 'member now what held me. He sure ain't give me much of a life. But it wasn't all bad. Sometimes things wasn't all bad. He used to come easing into bed sometimes, not too drunk. I make out like I'm asleep, 'cause it's late, and he taken three dollars out of my pocketbook that morning or something. I hear him breathing, but I don't look around. I can see in my mind's eye his black arms thrown back behind his head, the muscles like great big peach stones sanded down, with veins running like little swollen rivers down his arms. Without touching him I be feeling those ridges on the tips of my fingers. I sees the palms of his hands calloused to granite, and the long fingers curled up and still. I think about the thick, knotty hair on his chest, and the two big swells his breast muscles make. I want to rub my face hard in his chest and feel the hair*

*cut my skin. I know just where the hair growth slacks out—just above his navel—and how it picks up again and spreads out. Maybe he'll shift a little, and his leg will touch me, or I feel his flank just graze my behind. I don't move even yet. Then he lift his head, turn over, and put his hand on my waist. If I don't move, he'll move his hand over to pull and knead my stomach. Soft and slow-like. I still don't move, because I don't want him to stop. I want to pretend sleep and have him keep on rubbing my stomach. Then he will lean his head down and bite my tit. Then I don't want him to rub my stomach anymore. I want him to put his hand between my legs. I pretend to wake up, and turn to him, but not opening my legs. I want him to open them for me. He does, and I be soft and wet where his fingers are strong and hard. I be softer than I ever been before. All my strength in his hand. My brain curls up like wilted leaves. A funny, empty feeling is in my hands. I want to grab holt of something, so I hold his head. His mouth is under my chin. Then I don't want his hand between my legs no more, because I think I am softening away. I stretch my legs open, and he is on top of me. Too heavy to hold, and too light not to. He puts his thing in me. In me. In me. I wrap my feet around his back so he can't get away. His face is next to mine. The bed springs sounds like them crickets used to back home. He puts his fingers in mine, and we stretches our arms outwise like Jesus on the cross. I hold on tight. My fingers and my feet hold on tight, because everything else is going, going. I know he wants me to come first. But I can't. Not until he does. Not until I feel him loving me. Just me. Sinking into me. Not until I know that my flesh is all that be on his mind. That he couldn't stop if he had to. That he would die rather than take his thing out of me. Of me. Not until he has let go of all he has, and give it to me. To me. To me. When he does, I feel a power. I be strong, I be pretty, I be young. And then I wait. He shivers and tosses his head. Now I be strong enough, pretty enough, and young enough to let him make me come. I take my fingers out of his and put my hands on his behind. My legs drop back onto the bed. I don't make no noise, because the chil'ren might hear. I begin to feel those little bits of color floating up into me—deep in me. That streak of green from the june-bug light, the purple from the berries trickling along my thighs, Mama's lemonade yellow runs sweet in me. Then I feel like I'm laughing between my legs, and the laughing gets all mixed up with the colors, and I'm afraid I'll come, and afraid I won't. But I know I will. And I do. And it be rainbow all inside. And it lasts and lasts and lasts. I want to thank him, but don't know how, so I pat him like you do a baby. He asks me if I'm all right. I say yes. He gets off me and lies down to sleep. I want to say something, but I don't. I don't want to take my mind offen the rainbow. I should get up and go to the toilet, but I don't. Besides, Cholly is asleep with his leg throwed over me. I can't move and don't want to.*

*"But it ain't like that anymore. Most times he's thrashing away inside me before I'm woke, and through when I am. The rest of the time I can't even be next to his stinking drunk self. But I don't care 'bout it no more. My Maker will take care of me. I know He will. I know He will. Besides, it don't make no difference about this old earth. There is sure to be a glory. Only thing I miss sometimes is that rainbow. But like I say, I don't recollect it much anymore."*

## SEEFATHERHEISBIGANDSTRONGFATHERWILLYOUPLAY
## WITHJANEFATHERISSMILINGSMILEFATHERSMILESMILE

When Cholly was four days old, his mother wrapped him in two blankets and one newspaper and placed him on a junk heap by the railroad. His Great Aunt Jimmy, who had seen her niece carrying a bundle out of the back door, rescued him. She beat his mother with a razor strap and wouldn't let her near the baby after that. Aunt Jimmy raised Cholly herself, but took delight sometimes in telling him of how she had saved him. He gathered from her that his mother wasn't right in the head. But he never had a chance to find out, because she ran away shortly after the razor strap, and no one had heard of her since.

Cholly was grateful for having been saved. Except sometimes. Sometimes when he watched Aunt Jimmy eating collards with her fingers, sucking her four gold teeth, or smelled her when she wore the asafetida bag around her neck, or when she made him sleep with her for warmth in winter and he could see her old, wrinkled breasts sagging in her nightgown—then he wondered whether it would have been just as well to have died there. Down in the rim of a tire under a soft black Georgia sky.

He had four years of school before he got courage enough to ask his aunt who and where his father was.

"That Fuller boy, I believe it was," his aunt said. "He was hanging around then, but he taken off pretty quick before you was born. I think he gone to Macon. Him or his brother. Maybe both. I hear old man Fuller say something bout it once."

"What name he have?" asked Cholly.

"Fuller, Foolish."

"I mean what his given name?"

"Oh." She closed her eyes to think, and sighed. "Can't recollect nothing no more. Sam, was it? Yeh. Samuel. No. No, it wasn't. It was Samson. Samson Fuller."

"How come you all didn't name me Samson?" Cholly's voice was low.

"What for? He wasn't nowhere around when you was born. Your mama didn't name you nothing. The nine days wasn't up before she throwed you on the junk heap. When I got you I named you myself on the ninth day. You named after my dead brother. Charles Breedlove. A good man. Ain't no Samson never come to no good end."

Cholly didn't ask anything else.

Two years later he quit school to take a job at Tyson's Feed and Grain Store. He swept up, ran errands, weighed bags, and lifted them onto the drays. Sometimes they let him ride with the drayman. A nice old man called Blue Jack. Blue used to tell him old-timey stories about how it was when the Emancipation Proclamation came. How the black people hollered, cried, and sang. And ghost stories about how a white man cut off his wife's head and buried her in the swamp, and the headless body came out at night and went stumbling around the yard, knocking over stuff because it couldn't see, and crying all the time for a comb. They talked about the women Blue had had, and the fights he'd been in when he was younger, about how he talked his way out of getting lynched once, and how others hadn't.

Cholly loved Blue. Long after he was a man, he remembered the good times they had had. How on a July 4 at a church picnic a family was about to break open a watermelon. Several children were standing around watching. Blue was hovering about on the periphery of the circle—a faint smile of anticipation softening his face. The father of the family lifted the melon high over his head—his big arms looked taller than the trees to Cholly, and the melon blotted out the sun. Tall, head forward, eyes fastened on a rock, his arms higher than the pines, his hands holding a melon bigger than the sun, he paused an instant to get his bearing and secure his aim. Watching the figure etched against the bright blue sky, Cholly felt goose pimples popping along his arms and neck. He wondered if God looked like that. No. God was a nice old white man, with long white hair, flowing white beard, and little blue eyes that looked sad when people died and mean when they were bad It must be the devil who looks like that—holding the world in his hands, ready to dash it to the ground and spill the red guts so niggers could eat the sweet, warm insides. If the devil did look like that, Cholly preferred him. He never felt anything thinking about God, but just the idea of the devil excited him. And now the strong, black devil was blotting out the sun and getting ready to split open the world.

Far away somebody was playing a mouth organ; the music slithered over the cane fields and into the pine grove; it spiraled around the tree trunks and mixed itself with the pine scent, so Cholly couldn't tell the difference between the sound and the odor that hung about the heads of the people.

The man swung the melon down to the edge of a rock. A soft cry of disappointment accompanied the sound of smashed rind. The break was a bad one. The melon was jagged, and hunks of rind and red meat scattered on the grass.

Blue jumped. "Aw—awww," he moaned, "dere go da heart." His voice was both sad and pleased. Everybody looked to see the big red chunk from the very center of the melon, free of rind and sparse of seed which had rolled a little distance from Blue's feet. He stooped to pick it up. Blood red, its planes dull and blunted with sweetness, its edges rigid with juice. Too obvious, almost obscene, in the joy it promised.

"Go 'head, Blue," the father laughed. "You can have it."

Blue smiled and walked away. Little children scrambled for the pieces on the ground. Women picked out the seeds for the smallest ones and broke off little bits of the meat for themselves. Blue's eye caught Cholly's. He motioned to him. "Come on, boy. Les' you and me eat the heart."

Together the old man and the boy sat on the grass and shared the heart of the watermelon. The nasty-sweet guts of the earth.

It was in the spring, a very chilly spring, that Aunt Jimmy died of peach cobbler. She went to a camp meeting that took place after a rainstorm, and the damp wood of the benches was bad for her. For four or five days afterward, she felt poorly. Friends came to see about her. Some made camomile tea; others rubbed her with liniment. Miss Alice, her closest friend, read the Bible to her. Still she was declining. Advice was prolific, if contradictory.

"Don't eat no whites of eggs."

"Drink new milk."

"Chew on this root."

Aunt Jimmy ignored all but Miss Alice's Bible reading. She nodded in drowsy appreciation as the words from First Corinthians droned over her. Sweet amens fell from her lips as she was chastised for all her sins. But her body would not respond.

Finally it was decided to fetch M'Dear. M'Dear was a quiet woman who lived in a shack near the woods. She was a competent midwife and decisive diagnostician. Few could remember when M'Dear was not around. In any illness that could not be handled by ordinary means— known cures, intuition, or endurance—the word was always, "Fetch M'Dear."

When she arrived at Aunt Jimmy's house, Cholly was amazed at the sight of her. He had always pictured her as shriveled and hunched over, for he knew she was very, very old. But M'Dear loomed taller than the preacher who accompanied her. She must have been over six feet tall. Four big white knots of hair gave power and authority to her soft black face. Standing straight as a poker, she seemed to need her hickory stick not for support but for communication. She tapped it lightly on the floor as she looked down at Aunt Jimmy's wrinkled face. She stroked the knob with the thumb of her right hand while she ran her left one over Aunt Jimmy's body. The backs of her long fingers she placed on the patient's cheek, then placed her palm on the forehead. She ran her fingers through the sick woman's hair, lightly scratching the scalp, and then looking at what the fingernails revealed. She lifted

Aunt Jimmy's hand and looked closely at it—fingernails, back skin, the flesh of the palm she pressed with three fingertips. Later she put her ear on Aunt Jimmy's chest and stomach to listen. At M'Dear's request, the women pulled the slop jar from under the bed to show the stools. M'Dear tapped her stick while looking at them.

"Bury the slop jar and everything in it," she said to the women. To Aunt Jimmy she said, "You done caught cold in your womb. Drink pot liquor and nothing else."

"Will it pass?" asked Aunt Jimmy. "Is I'm gone be all right?"

"I reckon."

M'Dear turned and left the room. The preacher put her in his buggy to take her home.

That evening the women brought bowls of pot liquor from black-eyed peas, from mustards, from cabbage, from kale, from collards, from turnips, from beets, from green beans. Even the juice from a boiling hog jowl.

Two evenings later Aunt Jimmy had gained much strength. When Miss Alice and Mrs. Gaines stopped in to check on her, they remarked on her improvement. The three women sat talking about various miseries they had had, their cure or abatement, what had helped. Over and over again they returned to Aunt Jimmy's condition. Repeating its cause, what could have been done to prevent the misery from taking hold, and M'Dear's infallibility. Their voices blended into a threnody of nostalgia about pain. Rising and falling, complex in harmony, uncertain in pitch, but constant in the recitative of pain. They hugged the memories of illnesses to their bosoms. They licked their lips and clucked their tongues in fond remembrance of pains they had endured—childbirth, rheumatism, croup, sprains, backaches, piles. All of the bruises they had collected from moving about the earth—harvesting, cleaning, hoisting, pitching, stooping, kneeling, picking—always with young ones underfoot.

But they had been young once. The odor of their armpits and haunches had mingled into a lovely musk; their eyes had been furtive, their lips relaxed, and the delicate turn of their heads on those slim black necks had been like nothing other than a doe's. Their laughter had been more touch than sound.

Then they had grown. Edging into life from the back door. Becoming. Everybody in the world was in a position to give them orders. White women said, "Do this." White children said, "Give me that." White men said, "Come here." Black men said, "Lay down." The only people they need not take orders from were black children and each other. But they took all of that and re-created it in their own image. They ran the houses of white people, and knew it. When white men beat their men, they cleaned up the blood and went home to receive abuse from the victim. They beat their children with one hand and stole for them with the other. The hands that felled trees also cut umbilical cords; the hands that wrung the necks of chickens and butchered hogs also nudged African violets into bloom; the arms that loaded sheaves, bales, and sacks rocked babies into sleep. They patted biscuits into flaky ovals of innocence—and shrouded the dead. They plowed all day and came home to nestle like plums under the limbs of their men. The legs that straddled a mule's back were the same ones that straddled their men's hips. And the difference was all the difference there was.

Then they were old. Their bodies honed, their odor sour. Squatting in a cane field, stooping in a cotton field, kneeling by a river bank, they had carried a world on their heads. They had given over the lives of their own children and tendered their grandchildren. With relief they wrapped their heads in rags, and their breasts in flannel; eased their feet into felt. They were through with lust and lactation, beyond tears and terror. They alone could walk the roads of Mississippi, the lanes of Georgia, the fields of Alabama unmolested. They were old enough to be irritable when and where they chose, tired enough to look forward to death, disinterested enough to accept the idea of pain while ignoring the presence of pain. They were, in fact and at last, free. And the lives of these old black women were synthesized in their eyes—a purée of tragedy and humor, wickedness and serenity, truth and fantasy.

They chattered far into the night. Cholly listened and grew sleepy. The lullaby of grief enveloped him, rocked him, and at last numbed him. In his sleep the foul odor of an old woman's stools turned into the healthy smell of horse shit, and the voices of the three women were muted into the pleasant notes of a mouth organ. He was aware, in his sleep, of being curled up in a chair, his hands tucked between his thighs. In a dream his penis changed into a long hickory stick, and the hands caressing it were the hands of M'Dear.

On a wet Saturday night, before Aunt Jimmy felt strong enough to get out of the bed, Essie Foster brought her a peach cobbler. The old lady ate a piece, and the next morning when Cholly went to empty the slop jar, she was dead. Her mouth was a slackened O, and her hands, those long fingers with a man's hard nails, having done their laying by, could now be dainty on the sheet. One open eye looked at him as if to say, "Mind how you take holt of that jar, boy." Cholly stared back, unable to move, until a fly settled at the corner of her mouth. He fanned it away angrily, looked back at the eye, and did its bidding.

Aunt Jimmy's funeral was the first Cholly had ever attended. As a member of the family, one of the bereaved, he was the object of a great deal of attention. The ladies had cleaned the house, aired everything out, notified everybody, and stitched together what looked like a white wedding dress for Aunt Jimmy, a maiden lady, to wear when she met Jesus. They even produced a dark suit, white shirt, and tie for Cholly. The husband of one of them cut his hair. He was enclosed in fastidious tenderness. Nobody talked to him; that is, they treated him like the child he was, never engaging him in serious conversation; but they anticipated wishes he never had: meals appeared, hot water for the wooden tub, clothes laid out. At the wake he was allowed to fall asleep, and arms carried him to bed. Only on the third day after the death—the day of the funeral—did he have to share the spotlight. Aunt Jimmy's people came from nearby towns and farms. Her brother

O. V., his children and wife, and lots of cousins. But Cholly was still the major figure, because he was "Jimmy's boy, the last thing she loved," and "the one who found her." The solicitude of the women, the head pats of the men, pleased Cholly, and the creamy conversations fascinated him.

"What'd she die from?"

"Essie's pie."

"Don't say?"

"Uh-huh. She was doing fine, I saw her the very day before. Said she wanted me to bring her some black thread to patch some things for the boy. I should of known just from her wanting black thread that was a sign."

"Sure was."

"Just like Emma. 'Member? She kept asking for thread. Dropped dead that very evening."

"Yeah. Well, she was determined to have it. Kept on reminding me. I told her I had some to home, but naw, she wanted it new. So I sent Li'l June to get some that very morning when she was laying dead. I was just fixing to bring it over, 'long with a piece of sweet bread. You know how she craved my sweet bread."

"Sure did. Always bragged on it. She was a good friend to you."

"I believe it. Well, I had no more got my clothes on when Sally bust in the door hollering about how Cholly here had been over to Miss Alice saying she was dead. You could have knocked me over, I tell you."

"Guess Essie feels mighty bad."

"Oh, Lord, yes. But I told her the Lord giveth and the Lord taketh away. Wasn't her fault none. She makes good peach pies. But she bound to believe it was the pie did it, and I 'spect she right."·

"Well, she shouldn't worry herself none 'bout that. She was just doing what we all would of done."

"Yeah. 'Cause I was sure wrapping up that sweet bread, and that could of done it too."

"I doubts that. Sweet bread is pure. But a pie is the worse thing to give anybody ailing. I'm surprised Jimmy didn't know better."

"If she did, she wouldn't let on. She would have tried to please. You know how she was. So good."

"I'll say. Did she leave anything?"

"Not even a pocket handkerchief. The house belongs to some white folks in Clarksville."

"Oh, yeah? I thought she owned it."

"May have at one time. But not no more. I hear the insurance folks been down talking to her brother."

"How much do it come to?"

"Eighty-five dollars, I hear."

"That all?"

"Can she get in the ground on that?"

"Don't see how. When my daddy died last year this April it costed one hundred and fifty dollars. 'Course, we had to have everything just so. Now Jimmy's people may all have to chip in. That undertaker that lays out black folks ain't none too cheap."

"Seems a shame. She been paying on that insurance all her life."
"Don't I know?"

"Well, what about the boy? What he gone do?"

"Well, caint nobody find that mama, so Jimmy's brother gone take him back to his place. They say he got a nice place. Inside toilet and everything."

"That's nice. He seems like a good Christian man. And the boy need a man's hand."

"What time's the funeral?"

"Two clock. She ought to be in the ground by four."

"Where's the banquet? I heard Essie wanted it at her house."

"Naw, it's at Jimmy's. Her brother wanted it so."

"Well, it will be a big one. Everybody liked old Jimmy. Sure will miss her in the pew."

The funeral banquet was a peal of joy after the thunderous beauty of

the funeral. It was like a street tragedy with spontaneity tucked softly
into the corners of a highly formal structure. The deceased was the tragic hero, the survivors the innocent victims; there was the
omnipresence of the deity, strophe and antistrophe of the chorus of
mourners led by the preacher. There was grief over the waste of life,
the stunned wonder at the ways of God, and the restoration of order in
nature at the graveyard.

Thus the banquet was the exultation, the harmony, the acceptance
of physical frailty, joy in the termination of misery. Laughter, relief, a
steep hunger for food.

Cholly had not yet fully realized his aunt was dead. Everything was
so interesting. Even at the graveyard he felt nothing but curiosity, and
when his turn had come to view the body at the church, he had put his
hand out to touch the corpse to see if it were really ice cold like everybody said. But he drew his hand back quickly. Aunt Jimmy looked so
private, and it seemed wrong somehow to disturb that privacy. He had
trudged back to his pew dry-eyed amid tearful shrieks and shouts of
others, wondering if he should try to cry.

Back in his house, he was free to join in the gaiety and enjoy what
he really felt—a kind of carnival spirit. He ate greedily and felt good
enough to try to get to know his cousins. There was some question,
according to the adults, as to whether they were his real cousins or not,
since Jimmy's brother O. V. was only a half-brother, and Cholly's
mother had been the daughter of Jimmy's sister, but that sister was
from the second marriage of Jimmy's father, and O. V. was from the
first marriage.

One of these cousins interested Cholly in particular. He was about
fifteen or sixteen years old. Cholly went outside and found the boy
standing with some others near the tub where Aunt Jimmy used to
boil her clothes.

He ventured a tentative "Hey." They responded with another. The
fifteen-year-old named Jake offered Cholly a rolled-up cigarette. Cholly
took it, but when he held the cigarette at arm's length and stuck the

tip of it into the match flame, instead of putting it in his mouth and drawing on it, they laughed at him. Shamefaced, he threw the cigarette down. He felt it important to do something to reinstate himself with Jake. So when he asked Cholly if he knew any girls, Cholly said, "Sure."

All the girls Cholly knew were at the banquet, and he pointed to a cluster of them standing, hanging, draping on the back porch. Darlene too. Cholly hoped Jake wouldn't pick her.

"Let's get some and walk around," said Jake.

The two boys sauntered over to the porch. Cholly didn't know how to begin. Jake wrapped his legs around the rickety porch rail and just sat there staring off into space as though he had no interest in them at all. He was letting them look him over, and guardedly evaluating them in return.

The girls pretended they didn't see the boys and kept on chattering. Soon their talk got sharp; the gentle teasing they had been engaged in with each other changed to bitchiness, a serious kind of making fun. That was Jake's clue; the girls were reacting to him. They had gotten a whiff of his manhood and were shivering for a place in his attention.

Jake left the porch rail and walked right up to a girl named Suky, the one who had been most bitter in her making fun.

"Want to show me 'round?" He didn't even smile.

Cholly held his breath, waiting for Suky to shut Jake up. She was good at that, and well known for her sharp tongue. To his enormous surprise, she readily agreed, and even lowered her lashes. Taking courage, Cholly turned to Darlene and said, "Come on 'long. We just going down to the gully." He waited for her to screw up her face and say no, or what for, or some such thing. His feelings about her were mostly fear—fear that she would not like him, and fear that she would.

His second fear materialized. She smiled and jumped down the three leaning steps to join him. Her eyes were full of compassion, and Cholly remembered that he was the bereaved.

"If you want to," she said, "but not too far. Mama said we got to leave early, and its getting dark."

The four of them moved away. Some of the other boys had come to the porch and were about to begin that partly hostile, partly indifferent, partly desperate mating dance. Suky, Jake, Darlene, and Cholly walked through several backyards until they came to an open field. They ran across it and came to a dry riverbed lined with green. The object of the walk was a wild vineyard where the muscadine grew. Too new, too tight to have much sugar, they were eaten anyway. None of them wanted—not then—the grape's easy relinquishing of all its dark juice. The restraint, the holding off, the promise of sweetness that had yet to unfold, excited them more than full ripeness would have done. At last their teeth were on edge, and the boys diverted themselves by pelting the girls with the grapes. Their slim black boy wrists made G clefs in the air as they executed the tosses. The chase took Cholly and Darlene away from the lip of the gully, and when they paused for breath, Jake and Suky were nowhere in sight. Darlene's white cotton dress was stained with juice. Her big blue hair bow had come undone, and the sundown breeze was picking it up and fluttering it about her head. They were out of breath and sank down in the green-and-purple grass on the edge of the pine woods.

Cholly lay on his back panting. His mouth full of the taste of muscadine, listening to the pine needles rustling loudly in their anticipation of rain. The smell of promised rain, pine, and muscadine made him giddy. The sun had gone and pulled away its shreds of light. Turning his head to see where the moon was, Cholly caught sight of Darlene in moonlight behind him. She was huddled into a D—arms encircling drawn-up knees, on which she rested her head. Cholly could see her bloomers and the muscles of her young thighs.

"We bed' get on back," he said.

"Yeah." She stretched her legs flat on the ground and began to retie her hair ribbon. "Mama gone whup me."

"Naw she ain't."

"Uh-huh. She told me she would if I get dirty."

"You ain't dirty."

"I am too. Looka that." She dropped her hands from the ribbon and smoothed out a place on her dress where the grape stains were heaviest.

Cholly felt sorry for her; it was just as much his fault. Suddenly he realized that Aunt Jimmy was dead, for he missed the fear of being whipped. There was nobody to do it except Uncle O. V., and he was the bereaved too.

"Let me," he said. He rose to his knees facing her and tried to tie her ribbon. Darlene put her hands under his open shirt and rubbed the damp tight skin. When he looked at her in surprise, she stopped and laughed. He smiled and continued knotting the bow. She put her hands back under his shirt.

"Hold still," he said. "How I gone get this?"

She tickled his ribs with her fingertips. He giggled and grabbed his rib cage. They were on top of each other in a moment. She corkscrewing her hands into his clothes. He returning the play, digging into the neck of her dress, and then under her dress. When he got his hand in her bloomers, she suddenly stopped laughing and looked serious. Cholly, frightened, was about to take his hand away, but she held his wrist so he couldn't move it. He examined her then with his fingers, and she kissed his face and mouth. Cholly found her muscadine-lipped mouth distracting. Darlene released his head, shifted her body, and pulled down her pants. After some trouble with the buttons, Cholly dropped his pants down to his knees. Their bodies began to make sense to him, and it was not as difficult as he had thought it would be. She moaned a little, but the excitement collecting inside him made him close his eyes and regard her moans as no more than pine sighs over his head. Just as he felt an explosion threaten, Darlene froze and cried out. He thought he had hurt her, but when he looked at her face, she was staring wildly at something over his shoulder. He jerked around.

There stood two white men. One with a spirit lamp, the other with a flashlight. There was no mistake about their being white; he could smell it. Cholly jumped, trying to kneel, stand, and get his pants up all in one motion. The men had long guns.

"Hee hee hee heeeee." The snicker was a long asthmatic cough.

The other raced the flashlight all over Cholly and Darlene.

"Get on wid it, nigger," said the flashlight one.

"Sir?" said Cholly, trying to find a buttonhole.

"I said, get on wid it. An' make it good, nigger, make it good."

There was no place for Cholly's eyes to go. They slid about furtively searching for shelter, while his body remained paralyzed. The flashlight man lifted his gun down from his shoulder, and Cholly heard the clop of metal. He dropped back to his knees. Darlene had her head averted, her eyes staring out of the lamplight into the surrounding darkness and looking almost unconcerned, as though they had no part in the drama taking place around them. With a violence born of total helplessness, he pulled her dress up, lowered his trousers and underwear.

"Hee hee hee hee heeeeee."

Darlene put her hands over her face as Cholly began to simulate what had gone on before. He could do no more than make-believe. The flashlight made a moon on his behind.

"Hee hee hee hee heeee."

"Come on, coon. Faster. You ain't doing nothing for her."

"Hee hee hee hee heeee."

Cholly, moving faster, looked at Darlene. He hated her. He almost wished he could do it—hard, long, and painfully, he hated her so much. The flashlight wormed its way into his guts and turned the sweet taste of muscadine into rotten fetid bile. He stared at Darlene's hands covering her face in the moon and lamplight. They looked like baby claws.

"Hee hee hee hee heee."

Some dogs howled. "Thas them. Thas them. I know thas Old Honey."

"Yep," said the spirit lamp.

"Come on." The flashlight turned away, and one of them whistled to Honey.

"Wait," said the spirit lamp, "the coon ain't comed yet."

"Well, he have to come on his own time. Good luck, coon baby."

They crushed the pine needles underfoot. Cholly could hear them whistling for a long time, and then the dogs' answer no longer a howl, but warm excited yelps of recognition.

Cholly raised himself and in silence buttoned his trousers. Darlene did not move. Cholly wanted to strangle her, but instead he touched her leg with his foot. "We got to get, girl. Come on!"

She reached for her underwear with her eyes closed, and could not find them. The two of them patted about in the moonlight for the panties. When she found them, she put them on with the movements of an old woman. They walked away from the pine woods toward the road. He in front, she plopping along behind. It started to rain. "That's good," Cholly thought. "It will explain away our clothes."

When they got back to the house, some ten or twelve guests were still there. Jake was gone, Suky too. Some people had gone back for more helpings of food—potato pie, ribs. All were engrossed in early-night reminiscences about dreams, figures, premonitions. Their stuffed comfort was narcotic and had produced recollections and fabrications of hallucinations.

Cholly and Darlene's entrance produced only a mild stir.

"Ya'll soaked, ain't you?"

Darlene's mother was only vaguely fussy. She had eaten and drunk too much. Her shoes were under her chair, and the side snaps of her dress were opened. "Girl. Come on in here. Thought I told you . . ."

Some of the guests thought they would wait for the rain to slacken. Others, who had come in wagons, thought they'd best leave now. Cholly went into the little storeroom which had been made into a bed-

room for him. Three infants were sleeping on his cot. He took off his
rain- and pine-soaked clothes and put on his coveralls. He didn't know
where to go. Aunt Jimmy's room was out of the question, and Uncle
O. V. and his wife would be using it later anyway. He took a quilt
from a trunk, spread it on the floor, and lay down. Somebody was
brewing coffee, and he had a sharp craving for it, just before falling
asleep.

The next day was cleaning-out day, settling accounts, distributing
Aunt Jimmy's goods. Mouths were set in downward crescents, eyes
veiled, feet tentative.

Cholly floated about aimlessly, doing chores as he was told. All the
glamour and warmth the adults had given him on the previous day
were replaced by a sharpness that agreed with his mood. He could
think only of the flashlight, the muscadines, and Darlene's hands. And
when he was not thinking of them, the vacancy in his head was like
the space left by a newly pulled tooth still conscious of the rottenness
that had once filled it. Afraid of running into Darlene, he would not go
far from the house, but neither could he endure the atmosphere of his
dead Aunt's house. The picking through her things, the comments on
the "condition" of her goods. Sullen, irritable, he cultivated his hatred
of Darlene. Never did he once consider directing his hatred toward the
hunters. Such an emotion would have destroyed him. They were big,
white, armed men. He was small, black, helpless. His subconscious
knew what his conscious mind did not guess—that hating them would
have consumed him, burned him up like a piece of soft coal, leaving
only flakes of ash and a question mark of smoke. He was, in time, to
discover that hatred of white men—but not now. Not in impotence
but later, when the hatred could find sweet expression. For now, he
hated the one who had created the situation, the one who bore witness
to his failure, his impotence. The one whom he had not been able to
protect, to spare, to cover from the round moon glow of the flashlight.
The hee-hee-hee's. He recalled Darlene's dripping hair ribbon, flapping
against her face as they walked back in silence in the rain. The

loathing that galloped through him made him tremble. There was no one to talk to. Old Blue was too drunk too often these days to make sense. Besides, Cholly doubted if he could reveal his shame to Blue. He would have to lie a little to tell Blue, Blue the woman-killer. It seemed to him that lonely was much better than alone.

The day Cholly's uncle was ready to leave, when everything was packed, when the quarrels about who gets what had seethed down to a sticking gravy on everybody's tongue, Cholly sat on the back porch waiting. It had occurred to him that Darlene might be pregnant. It was a wildly irrational, completely uninformed idea, but the fear it produced was complete enough.

He had to get away. Never mind the fact that he was leaving that very day. A town or two away was not far enough, especially since he did not like or trust his uncle, and Darlene's mother could surely find him, and Uncle O. V. would turn him over to her. Cholly knew it was wrong to run out on a pregnant girl, and recalled, with sympathy, that his father had done just that. Now he understood. He knew then what he must do—find his father. His father would understand. Aunt Jimmy said he had gone to Macon.

With no more thought than a chick leaving its shell, he stepped off the porch. He had gotten a little way when he remembered the treasure; Aunt Jimmy had left something, and he had forgotten all about it. In a stove flue no longer used, she had hidden a little meal bag which she called her treasure. He slipped into the house and found the room empty. Digging into the flue, he encountered webs and soot, and then the soft bag. He sorted the money; fourteen one-dollar bills, two two-dollar bills, and lots of silver change . . . twenty-three dollars in all. Surely that would be enough to get to Macon. What a good, strong-sounding word, *Macon*.

Running away from home for a Georgia black boy was not a great problem. You just sneaked away and started walking. When night came you slept in a barn, if there were no dogs, a cane field, or an empty sawmill. You ate from the ground and bought root beer and licorice in little country stores. There was always an easy tale of woe to tell inquiring black adults, and whites didn't care, unless they were looking for sport.

When he was several days away, he could go to the back door of nice houses and tell the black cook or white mistress that he wanted a job weeding, plowing, picking, cleaning, and that he lived nearby. A week or more there, and he could take off. He lived this way through the turn of summer, and only the following October did he reach a town big enough to have a regular bus station. Dry-mouthed with excitement and apprehension, he went to the colored side of the counter to buy his ticket.

"How much to Macon, sir?"

"Eleven dollars. Five-fifty for children under twelve."

Cholly had twelve dollars and four cents.

"How old you be?"

"Just on twelve, sir, but my mama only give me ten dollars."

"You jest about the biggest twelve I ever seed."

"Please, sir, I got to get to Macon. My mama's sick."

"Thought you said you mama give you ten dollars."

"That's my play mama. My real mama is in Macon, sir."

"I reckon I knows a lying nigger when I sees one, but jest in case you ain't, jest in case one of them mammies is really dyin' and wants to see her little old smoke before she meets her maker, I gone do it."

Cholly heard nothing. The insults were part of the nuisances of life, like lice. He was happier than he had ever remembered being, except that time with Blue and the watermelon. The bus wasn't leaving for four hours, and the minutes of those hours struggled like gnats on fly paper—dying slow, exhausted with the fight to stay alive. Cholly was afraid to stir, even to relieve himself. The bus might leave while he was gone. Finally, rigid with constipation, he boarded the bus to Macon.

He found a window seat in the back all to himself, and all of Georgia slid before his eyes, until the sun shrugged out of sight. Even in the dark, he hungered to see, and only after the fiercest fight to keep his eyes open did he fall asleep. When he awoke it was very well into day, and a fat black lady was nudging him with a biscuit gashed with cold bacon. With the taste of bacon still in his teeth, they sidled into Macon.

At the end of the alley he could see men clustered like grapes. One large whooping voice spiraled over the heads of the bended forms. The kneeling forms, the leaning forms, all intent on one ground spot. As he came closer, he inhaled a rife and stimulating man smell. The men were gathered, just as the man in the pool hall had said, for and about dice and money. Each figure was decorated some way with the slight pieces of green. Some of them had separated their money, folded the bills around their fingers, clenched the fingers into fists, so the neat ends of the money stuck out in a blend of daintiness and violence. Others had stacked their bills, creased them down the middle, and held the wad as though they were about to deal cards. Still others had left their money in loosely crumpled balls. One man had money sticking out from under his cap. Another stroked his bills with a thumb and forefinger. There was more money in those black hands than Cholly had ever seen before. He shared their excitement, and the dry-mouthed apprehension on meeting his father gave way to the saliva flow of excitement. He glanced at the faces, looking for the one who might be his father. How would he know him? Would he look like a larger version of himself? At that moment Cholly could not remember what his own self looked like. He only knew he was fourteen years old, black, and already six feet tall. He searched the faces and saw only eyes, pleading eyes, cold eyes, eyes gone flat with malice, others laced with fear—all focused on the movement of a pair of dice that one man was throwing, snatching up, and throwing again. Chanting a kind of litany to which the others responded, rubbing the dice as though they were two hot coals, he whispered to them. Then with a whoop the cubes flew from his hand to a chorus of amazements and disappointments. Then the thrower scooped up money, and someone shouted, "Take it and crawl, you water dog, you, the best I know." There was some laughter, and a noticeable release of tension, during which some men exchanged money.

Cholly tapped an old white-haired man on the back.

"Can you tell me is Samson Fuller 'round here somewhere?"

"Fuller?" The name was familiar to the man's tongue. "I don't know, he here somewhere. They he is. In the brown jacket." The man pointed.

A man in a light-brown jacket stood at the far end of the group. He was gesturing in a quarrelsome, agitated manner with another man. Both of them had folded their faces in anger. Cholly edged around to where they stood, hardly believing he was at the end of his journey. There was his father, a man like any other man, but there indeed were his eyes, his mouth, his whole head. His shoulders lurked beneath that jacket, his voice, his hands—all real. They existed, really existed, somewhere. Right here. Cholly had always thought of his father as a giant of a man, so when he was very close it was with a shock that he discovered that he was taller than his father. In fact, he was staring at a balding spot on his father's head, which he suddenly wanted to stroke. While thus fascinated by the pitiable clean space hedged around by neglected tufts of wool, the man turned a hard, belligerent face to him.

"What you want, boy?"

"Uh. I mean . . . is you Samson Fuller?"

"Who sent you?"

"Huh?"

"You Melba's boy?"

"No, sir, I'm . . ." Cholly blinked. He could not remember his mother's name. Had he ever known it? What could he say? Whose boy was he? He couldn't say, "I'm your boy." That sounded disrespectful.

The man was impatient. "Something wrong with your head? Who told you to come after me?"

"Nobody." Cholly's hands were sweating. The man's eyes frightened him. "I just thought . . . I mean, I was just wandering around, and, uh, my name is Cholly. . . ."

But Fuller had turned back to the game that was about to begin anew. He bent down to toss a bill on the ground, and waited for a throw. When it was gone, he stood up and in a vexed and whiny voice shouted at Cholly, "Tell that bitch she get her money. Now, get the fuck outta my face!"

Cholly was a long time picking his foot up from the ground. He was trying to back up and walk away. Only with extreme effort could he get the first muscle to cooperate. When it did, he walked back up the alley, out of its shade, toward the blazing light of the street. As he emerged into the sun, he felt something in his legs give way. An orange crate with a picture of clasping hands pasted on its side was upended on the sidewalk. Cholly sat down on it. The sunshine dropped like honey on his head. A horse-drawn fruit wagon went by, its driver singing: "Fresh from the vine, sweet as sugar, red as wine."

Noises seemed to increase in volume. The clic-cloc of the women's heels, the laughter of idling men in doorways. There was a streetcar somewhere. Cholly sat. He knew if he was very still he would be all right. But then the trace of pain edged his eyes, and he had to use everything to send it away. If he was very still, he thought, and kept his eyes on one thing, the tears would not come. So he sat in the dripping honey sun, pulling every nerve and muscle into service to stop the fall of water from his eyes. While straining in this way, focusing every erg of energy on his eyes, his bowels suddenly opened up, and before he could realize what he knew, liquid stools were running down his legs. At the mouth of the alley where his father was, on an orange crate in the sun, on a street full of grown men and women, he had soiled himself like a baby.

In panic he wondered should he wait there, not moving until nighttime? No. His father would surely emerge and see him and laugh. Oh, Lord. He would laugh. Everybody would laugh. There was only one thing to do.

Cholly ran down the street, aware only of silence. People's mouths moved, their feet moved, a car jugged by—but with no sound. A door slammed in perfect soundlessness. His own feet made no sound. The air seemed to strangle him, hold him back. He was pushing through a world of invisible pine sap that threatened to smother him. Still he ran, seeing only silent moving things, until he came to the end of buildings, the beginning of open space, and saw the Ocmulgee River winding ahead. He scooted down a gravelly slope to a pier jutting out over the shallow water. Finding the deepest shadow under the pier, he crouched in it, behind one of the posts. He remained knotted there in fetal position, paralyzed, his fists covering his eyes, for a long time. No sound, no sight, only darkness and heat and the press of his knuckles on his eyelids. He even forgot his messed-up trousers.

Evening came. The dark, the warmth, the quiet, enclosed Cholly like the skin and flesh of an elderberry protecting its own seed.

Cholly stirred. The ache in his head was all he felt. Soon, like bright bits of glass, the events of that afternoon cut into him. At first he saw only money in black fingers, then he thought he was sitting on an uncomfortable chair, but when he looked, it turned out to be the head of a man, a head with a bald spot the size of an orange. When finally these bits merged into full memory, Cholly began to smell himself. He stood up and found himself weak, trembling, and dizzy. He leaned for a moment on the pier post, then took off his pants, underwear, socks, and shoes. He rubbed handfuls of dirt on his shoes; then he crawled to the river edge. He had to find the water's beginning with his hands, for he could not see it clearly. Slowly he swirled his clothes in the water and rubbed them until he thought they were clean. Back near his post, he took off his shirt and wrapped it around his waist, then spread his trousers and underwear on the ground. He squatted down and picked at the rotted wood of the pier. Suddenly he thought of his Aunt Jimmy, her asafetida bag, her four gold teeth, and the purple rag she wore around her head. With a longing that almost split him open, he thought of her handing him a bit of smoked hock out of her dish. He remembered just how she held it—clumsy-like, in three fingers, but with so much affection. No words, just picking up a bit of meat and holding it out to him. And then the tears rushed down his cheeks, to make a bouquet under his chin.

Three women are leaning out of two windows. They see the long clean neck of a new young boy and call to him. He goes to where they are. Inside, it is dark and warm. They give him lemonade in a Mason jar. As he drinks, their eyes float up to him through the bottom of the jar, through the slick sweet water. They give him back his manhood, which he takes aimlessly.

The pieces of Cholly's life could become coherent only in the head of a musician. Only those who talk their talk through the gold of curved metal, or in the touch of black-and-white rectangles and taut skins and strings echoing from wooden corridors, could give true form to his life. Only they would know how to connect the heart of a red watermelon to the asafetida bag to the muscadine to the flashlight on his behind to the fists of money to the lemonade in a Mason jar to a man called Blue and come up with what all of that meant in joy, in pain, in anger, in love, and give it its final and pervading ache of freedom. Only a musician would sense, know, without even knowing that he knew, that Cholly was free. Dangerously free. Free to feel whatever he felt—fear, guilt, shame, love, grief, pity. Free to be tender or violent, to whistle or weep. Free to sleep in doorways or between the white sheets of a singing woman. Free to take a job, free to leave it. He could go to jail and not feel imprisoned, for he had already seen the furtiveness in the eyes of his jailer, free to say, "No, suh," and smile, for he had already killed three white men. Free to take a woman's insults, for his body had already conquered hers. Free even to knock her in the head, for he had already cradled that head in his arms. Free to be gentle when she was sick, or mop her floor, for she knew what and where his maleness was. He was free to drink himself into a silly help-lessness, for he had already been a gandy dancer, done thirty days on a chain gang, and picked a woman's bullet out of the calf of his leg. He was free to live his fantasies, and free even to die, the how and the when of which held no interest for him. In those days, Cholly was truly free. Abandoned in a junk heap by his mother, rejected for a crap game by his father, there was nothing more to lose. He was alone with his own perceptions and appetites, and they alone interested him.

It was in this godlike state that he met Pauline Williams. And it was Pauline, or rather marrying her, that did for him what the flash-light did not do. The constantness, varietylessness, the sheer weight of sameness drove him to despair and froze his imagination. To be required to sleep with the same woman forever was a curious and unnatural idea to him; to be expected to dredge up enthusiasms for old acts, and routine ploys; he wondered at the arrogance of the female. When he had met Pauline in Kentucky, she was hanging over a fence scratching herself with a broken foot. The neatness, the charm, the joy he awakened in her made him want to nest with her. He had yet to discover what destroyed that desire. But he did not dwell on it. He thought rather of whatever had happened to the curiosity he used to feel. Nothing, nothing, interested him now. Not himself, not other people. Only in drink was there some break, some floodlight, and when that closed, there was oblivion.

But the aspect of married life that dumbfounded him and rendered him totally disfunctional was the appearance of children. Having no idea of how to raise children, and having never watched any parent raise himself, he could not even comprehend what such a relationship should be. Had he been interested in the accumulation of things, he could have thought of them as his material heirs; had he needed to prove himself to some nameless "others," he could have wanted them to excel in his own image and for his own sake. He had not been alone in the world since he was thirteen, knowing only a dying old woman who felt responsible for him, but whose age, sex, and interests were so remote from his own, he might have felt a stable connection between himself and the children. As it was, he reacted to them, and his reactions were based on what he felt at the moment.

So it was on a Saturday afternoon, in the thin light of spring, he staggered home reeling drunk and saw his daughter in the kitchen.

She was washing dishes. Her small back hunched over the sink. Cholly saw her dimly and could not tell what he saw or what he felt. Then he became aware that he was uncomfortable; next he felt the discomfort dissolve into pleasure. The sequence of his emotions was revulsion, guilt, pity, then love. His revulsion was a reaction to her young, helpless, hopeless presence. Her back hunched that way; her head to one side as though crouching from a permanent and unrelieved blow. Why did she have to look so whipped? She was a child—unburdened—why wasn't she happy? The clear statement of her misery was an accusation. He wanted to break her neck—but tenderly. Guilt and impotence rose in a bilious duet. What could he do for her—ever? What give her? What say to her? What could a burned-out black man say to the hunched back of his eleven-year-old daughter? If he looked into her face, he would see those haunted, loving eyes. The hauntedness would irritate him—the love would move him to fury. How dare she love him? Hadn't she any sense at all? What was he supposed to do about that? Return it? How? What could his calloused hands produce to make her smile? What of his knowledge of the world and of life could be useful to her? What could his heavy arms and befuddled brain accomplish that would earn him his own respect, that would in turn allow him to accept her love? His hatred of her slimed in his stomach and threatened to become vomit. But just before the puke moved from anticipation to sensation, she shifted her weight and stood on one foot scratching the back of her calf with her toe. It was a quiet and pitiful gesture. Her hands were going around and around a frying pan, scraping flecks of black into cold, greasy dishwater. The timid, tucked-in look of the scratching toe—that was what Pauline was doing the first time he saw her in Kentucky. Leaning over a fence staring at nothing in particular. The creamy toe of her bare foot scratching a velvet leg. It was such a small and simple gesture, but it filled him then with a wondering softness. Not the usual lust to part tight legs with his own, but a tenderness, a protectiveness. A desire to cover her foot with his hand and gently nibble away the itch from the calf with his teeth. He did it then, and startled Pauline into laughter. He did it now.

The tenderness welled up in him, and he sank to his knees, his eyes on the foot of his daughter. Crawling on all fours toward her, he raised his hand and caught the foot in an upward stroke. Pecola lost her balance and was about to careen to the floor. Cholly raised his other hand to her hips to save her from falling. He put his head down and nibbled at the back of her leg. His mouth trembled at the firm sweetness of the flesh. He closed his eyes, letting his fingers dig into her waist. The rigidness of her shocked body, the silence of her stunned throat, was better than Pauline's easy laughter had been. The confused mixture of his memories of Pauline and the doing of a wild and forbidden thing excited him, and a bolt of desire ran down his genitals, giving it length, and softening the lips of his anus. Surrounding all of this lust was a border of politeness. He wanted to fuck her—tenderly. But the tenderness would not hold. The tightness of her vagina was more than he could bear. His soul seemed to slip down to his guts and fly out into her, and the gigantic thrust he made into her then provoked the only sound she made—a hollow suck of air in the back of her throat. Like the rapid loss of air from a circus balloon.

Following the disintegration—the falling away—of sexual desire, he was conscious of her wet, soapy hands on his wrists, the fingers clenching, but whether her grip was from a hopeless but stubborn struggle to be free, or from some other emotion, he could not tell.

Removing himself from her was so painful to him he cut it short and snatched his genitals out of the dry harbor of her vagina. She appeared to have fainted. Cholly stood up and could see only her grayish panties, so sad and limp around her ankles. Again the hatred mixed with tenderness. The hatred would not let him pick her up; the tenderness forced him to cover her.

So when the child regained consciousness, she was lying on the kitchen floor under a heavy quilt, trying to connect the pain between her legs with the face of her mother looming over her.

SEETHEDOGBOWBOWGOESTHEDOGDOYOUWANTTOPL
AYDOYOUWANTTOPLAYWITHJANESEETHEDOGRUNR

Once there was an old man who loved things, for the slightest contact with people produced in him a faint but persistent nausea. He could not remember when this distaste began, nor could he remember ever being free of it. As a young boy he had been greatly disturbed by this revulsion which others did not seem to share, but having got a fine education, he learned, among other things, the word "misanthrope." Knowing his label provided him with both comfort and courage, he believed that to name an evil was to neutralize if not annihilate it. Then, too, he had read several books and made the acquaintance of several great misanthropes of the ages, whose spiritual company soothed him and provided him with yardsticks for measuring his whims, his yearnings, and his antipathies. Moreover, he found misanthropy an excellent means of developing character: when he subdued his revulsion and occasionally touched, helped, counseled, or befriended somebody, he was able to think of his behavior as generous and his intentions as noble. When he was enraged by some human effort or flaw, he was able to regard himself as discriminating, fastidious, and full of nice scruples.

As in the case of many misanthropes, his disdain for people led him into a profession designed to serve them. He was engaged in a line of work that was dependent solely on his ability to win the trust of others, and one in which the most intimate relationships were necessary. Having dallied with the priesthood in the Anglican Church, he abandoned it to become a caseworker. Time and misfortune, however, conspired against him, and he settled finally on a profession that brought him both freedom and satisfaction. He became a "Reader,

Adviser, and Interpreter of Dreams." It was a profession that suited him well. His hours were his own, the competition was slight, the clientele was already persuaded and therefore manageable, and he had numerous opportunities to witness human stupidity without sharing it or being compromised by it, and to nurture his fastidiousness by viewing physical decay. Although his income was small, he had no taste for luxury—his experience in the monastery had solidified his natural asceticism while it developed his preference for solitude. Celibacy was a haven, silence a shield.

All his life he had had a fondness for things—not the acquisition of wealth or beautiful objects, but a genuine love of worn objects: a coffee pot that had been his mother's, a welcome mat from the door of a rooming house he once lived in, a quilt from a Salvation Army store counter. It was as though his disdain of human contact had converted itself into a craving for things humans had touched. The residue of the human spirit smeared on inanimate objects was all he could withstand of humanity. To contemplate, for example, evidence of human foot-steps on the mat—absorb the smell of the quilt and wallow in the sweet certainty that many bodies had sweated, slept, dreamed, made love, been ill, and even died under it. Wherever he went, he took along his things, and was always searching for others. This thirst for worn things led him to casual but habitual examinations of trash barrels in alleys and wastebaskets in public places. . . .

All in all, his personality was an arabesque: intricate, symmetrical, balanced, and tightly constructed—except for one flaw. The careful de-sign was marred occasionally by rare but keen sexual cravings.

He could have been an active homosexual but lacked the courage. Bestiality did not occur to him, and sodomy was quite out of the ques-tion, for he did not experience sustained erections and could not endure the thought of somebody else's. And besides, the one thing that disgusted him more than entering and caressing a woman was caressing and being caressed by a man. In any case, his cravings, although intense, never relished physical contact. He abhorred flesh on flesh. Body odor, breath odor, overwhelmed him. The sight of dried matter in the corner of the eye, decayed or missing teeth, ear wax, blackheads, moles, blisters, skin crusts—all the natural excretions and protections the body was capable of—disquieted him. His attentions therefore gradually settled on those humans whose bodies were least offensive—children. And since he was too diffident to confront homosexuality, and since little boys were insulting, scary, and stubborn, he further limited his interests to little girls. They were usually manageable and frequently seductive. His sexuality was anything but lewd; his patronage of little girls smacked of innocence and was associated in his mind with cleanliness. He was what one might call a very clean old man.

A cinnamon-eyed West Indian with lightly browned skin.

Although his given name was printed on the sign in his kitchen window, and on the business cards he circulated, he was called by the townspeople Soaphead Church. No one knew where the "Church" part came from—perhaps somebody's recollection of his days as a guest preacher—those reverends who had been called but who had no flock or coop, and were constantly visiting other churches, sitting on the altar with the host preacher. But everybody knew what "Soaphead" meant—the tight, curly hair that took on and held a sheen and wave when pomaded with soap lather. A sort of primitive process.

He had been reared in a family proud of its academic accomplishments and its mixed blood—in fact, they believed the former was based on the latter. A Sir Whitcomb, some decaying British nobleman, who chose to disintegrate under a sun more easeful than England's, had introduced the white strain into the family in the early 1800's. Being a gentleman by order of the King, he had done the civilized thing for his mulatto bastard—provided it with three hundred pounds sterling, to the great satisfaction of the bastard's mother, who felt that fortune had smiled on her. The bastard too was grateful, and regarded as his life's goal the hoarding of this white strain. He bestowed his favors on a fifteen-year-old girl of similar parentage. She, like a good Victorian parody, learned from her husband all that was worth learning—to separate herself in body, mind, and spirit from all that suggested Africa; to cultivate the habits, tastes, preferences that her absent father-in-law and foolish mother-in-law would have approved.

They transferred this Anglophilia to their six children and sixteen grandchildren. Except for an occasional and unaccountable insurgent who chose a restive black, they married "up," lightening the family complexion and thinning out the family features.

With the confidence born of a conviction of superiority, they performed well at schools. They were industrious, orderly, and energetic, hoping to prove beyond a doubt De Gobineau's hypothesis that "all civilizations derive from the white race, that none can exist without its help, and that a society is great and brilliant only so far as it preserves the blood of the noble group that created it." Thus, they were seldom overlooked by schoolmasters who recommended promising students for study abroad. The men studied medicine, law, theology, and emerged repeatedly in the powerless government offices available to the native population. That they were corrupt in public and private practice, both lecherous and lascivious, was considered their noble right, and thoroughly enjoyed by most of the less gifted population.

As the years passed, due to the carelessness of some of the Whitcomb brothers, it became difficult to maintain their whiteness, and some distant and some not so distant relatives married each other. No obviously bad effects were noticed from these ill-advised unions, but one or two old maids or gardener boys marked a weakening of faculties and a disposition toward eccentricity in some of the children. Some flaw outside the usual alcoholism and lechery. They blamed the flaw on intermarriage with the family, however, not on the original genes of the decaying lord. In any case, there were flukes. No more than in any other family, to be sure, but more dangerous because more powerful. One of them was a religious fanatic who founded his own secret sect and fathered four sons, one of whom became a schoolmaster known for the precision of his justice and the control in his violence. This schoolmaster married a sweet, indolent half-Chinese girl for whom the fatigue of bearing a son was too much. She died soon after childbirth. Her son, named Elihue Micah Whitcomb, provided the schoolmaster with ample opportunity to work out his theories of education, discipline, and the good life. Little Elihue learned everything he needed to know well, particularly the fine art of self-deception. He read greedily but understood selectively, choosing the bits and pieces of other men's ideas that supported whatever predilection he had at the moment. Thus he chose to remember Hamlet's abuse of Ophelia, but not Christ's love of Mary Magdalene; Hamlet's frivolous politics, but not Christ's serious anarchy. He noticed Gibbon's acidity, but not his tolerance, Othello's love for the fair Desdemona, but not Iago's perverted love of Othello. The works he admired most were Dante's; those he despised most were Dostoyevsky's. For all his exposure to the best minds of the Western world, he allowed only the narrowest interpretation to touch him. He responded to his father's controlled violence by developing hard habits and a soft imagination. A hatred of, and fascination with, any hint of disorder or decay.

At seventeen, however, he met his Beatrice, who was three years his senior. A lovely, laughing big-legged girl who worked as a clerk in a Chinese department store. Velma. So strong was her affection and zest for life, she did not eliminate the frail, sickly Elihue from it. She found his fastidiousness and complete lack of humor touching, and longed to introduce him to the idea of delight. He resisted the introduction, but she married him anyway, only to discover that he was suffering from and enjoying an invincible melancholy. When she learned two months into the marriage how important his melancholy was to him, that he was very interested in altering her joy to a more academic gloom, that he equated lovemaking with communion and the Holy Grail, she simply left. She had not lived by the sea all those years, listened to the wharfman's songs all that time, to spend her life in the soundless cave of Elihue's mind.

He never got over her desertion. She was to have been the answer to his unstated, unacknowledged question—where was the life to counter the encroaching nonlife? Velma was to rescue him from the nonlife he had learned on the flat side of his father's belt. But he resisted her with such skill that she was finally driven out to escape the inevitable boredom produced by such a dainty life.

Young Elihue was saved from visible shattering by the steady hand of his father, who reminded him of the family's reputation and Velma's questionable one. He then pursued his studies with more vigor than before and decided at last to enter the ministry. When he was advised that he had no avocation, he left the island, came to America to study the then budding field of psychiatry. But the subject required too much truth, too many confrontations, and offered too little support to a failing ego. He drifted into sociology, then physical therapy. This diverse education continued for six years, when his father refused to support him any longer, until he "found" himself. Elihue, not knowing where to look, was thrown back on his own devices, and "found" himself quite unable to earn money. He began to sink into a rapidly fraying gentility, punctuated with a few of the white-collar occupations available to black people, regardless of their noble bloodlines, in America: desk clerk at a colored hotel in Chicago, insurance agent, traveling salesman for a cosmetics firm catering to blacks. He finally settled in Lorain, Ohio, in 1936, palming himself off as a minister, and inspiring awe with the way he spoke English. The women of the town early discovered his celibacy, and not being able to comprehend his rejection of them, decided that he was supernatural rather than unnatural.

Once he understood their decision, he quickly followed through, accepting the name (Soaphead Church) and the role they had given him. He rented a kind of back-room apartment from a deeply religious old lady named Bertha Reese. She was clean, quiet, and very close to total deafness. The lodgings were ideal in every way but one. Bertha Reese had an old dog, Bob, who, although as deaf and quiet as she, was not as clean. He slept most of his days away on the back porch, which was Elihue's entrance. The dog was too old to be of any use, and Bertha Reese had not the strength or presence of mind to care for him properly. She fed him, and watered him, left him alone. The dog was mangy; his exhausted eyes ran with a sea-green matter around which gnats and flies clustered. Soaphead was revolted by Bob and wished he would hurry up and die. He regarded this wish for the dog's death as humane, for he could not bear, he told himself, to see anything suffer. It did not occur to him that he was really concerned about his own suffering, since the dog had adjusted himself to frailty and old age. Soaphead finally determined to put an end to the animal's misery, and bought some poison with which to do it. Only the horror of having to go near him had prevented Soaphead from completing his mission. He waited for rage or blinding revulsion to spur him.

Living there among his worn things, rising early every morning from dreamless sleeps, he counseled those who sought his advice.

His business was dread. People came to him in dread, whispered in dread, wept and pleaded in dread. And dread was what he counseled.

Singly they found their way to his door, wrapped each in a shroud stitched with anger, yearning, pride, vengeance, loneliness, misery, defeat, and hunger. They asked for the simplest of things: love, health, and money. Make him love me. Tell me what this dream means. Help me get rid of this woman. Make my mother give me back my clothes. Stop my left hand from shaking. Keep my baby's ghost off the stove. Break so-and-so's fix. To all of these requests he addressed himself. His practice was to do what he was bid—not to suggest to a party that perhaps the request was unfair, mean, or hopeless.

With only occasional, and increasingly rare, encounters with the little girls he could persuade to be entertained by him, he lived rather peaceably among his things, admitting to no regrets. He was aware, of course, that something was awry in his life, and all lives, but put the problem where it belonged, at the foot of the Originator of Life. He believed that since decay, vice, filth, and disorder were pervasive, they must be in the Nature of Things. Evil existed because God had created it. He, God, had made a sloven and unforgivable error in judgment: designing an imperfect universe. Theologians justified the presence of corruption as a means by which men strove, were tested, and triumphed. A triumph of cosmic neatness. But this neatness, the neatness of Dante, was in the orderly sectioning and segregating of all levels of evil and decay. In the world it was not so. The most exquisite-looking ladies sat on toilets, and the most dreadful-looking had pure and holy yearnings. God had done a poor job, and Soaphead suspected that he himself could have done better. It was in fact a pity that the Maker had not sought his counsel.

Soaphead was reflecting once again on these thoughts one late hot afternoon when he heard a tap on his door. Opening it, he saw a little girl, quite unknown to him. She was about twelve or so, he thought, and seemed to him pitifully unattractive. When he asked her what she wanted, she did not answer, but held out to him one of his cards advertising his gifts and services: "If you are overcome with trouble and conditions that are not natural, I can remove them; Overcome Spells, Bad Luck, and Evil Influences. Remember, I am a true Spiritualist and Psychic Reader, born with power, and I will help you. Satisfaction in one visit. During many years of practice I have brought together many in marriage and reunited many who were separated. If you are unhappy, discouraged, or in distress, I can help you. Does bad luck seem to follow you? Has the one you love changed? I can tell you why. I will tell you who your enemies and friends are, and if the one you love is true or false. If you are sick, I can show you the way to health. I locate lost and stolen articles. Satisfaction guaranteed."

Soaphead Church told her to come in.

"What can I do for you, my child?"

She stood there, her hands folded across her stomach, a little protruding pot of tummy. "Maybe. Maybe you can do it for me."

"Do what for you?"

"I can't go to school no more. And I thought maybe you could help me."

"Help you how? Tell me. Don't be frightened."

"My eyes."

"What about your eyes?"

"I want them blue."

Soaphead pursed his lips, and let his tongue stroke a gold inlay. He thought it was at once the most fantastic and the most logical petition he had ever received. Here was an ugly little girl asking for beauty. A surge of love and understanding swept through him, but was quickly replaced by anger. Anger that he was powerless to help her. Of all the wishes people had brought him—money, love, revenge—this seemed to him the most poignant and the one most deserving of fulfillment. A little black girl who wanted to rise up out of the pit of her blackness and see the world with blue eyes. His outrage grew and felt like power. For the first time he honestly wished he could work miracles. Never before had he really wanted the true and holy power—only the power to make others believe he had it. It seemed so sad, so frivolous, that mere mortality, not judgment, kept him from it. Or did it?

With a trembling hand he made the sign of the cross over her. His flesh crawled; in that hot, dim little room of worn things, he was chilled.

"I can do nothing for you, my child. I am not a magician. I work only through the Lord. He sometimes uses me to help people. All I can do is offer myself to Him as the instrument through which he works. If He wants your wish granted, He will do it."

Soaphead walked to the window, his back to the girl. His mind raced, stumbled, and raced again. How to frame the next sentence? How to hang on to the feeling of power. His eye fell on old Bob sleeping on the porch.

"We must make, ah, some offering, that is, some contact with nature. Perhaps some simple creature might be the vehicle through which He will speak. Let us see."

He knelt down at the window, and moved his lips. After what seemed a suitable length of time, he rose and went to the icebox that stood near the other window. From it he removed a small packet wrapped in pinkish butcher paper. From a shelf he took a small brown bottle and sprinkled some of its contents on the substance inside the paper. He put the packet, partly opened, on the table.

"Take this food and give it to the creature sleeping on the porch. Make sure he eats it. And mark well how he behaves. If nothing happens, you will know that God has refused you. If the animal behaves strangely, your wish will be granted on the day following this one."

The girl picked up the packet; the odor of the dark, sticky meat made her want to vomit. She put a hand on her stomach.

"Courage. Courage, my child. These things are not granted to faint hearts."

She nodded and swallowed visibly, holding down the vomit. Soaphead opened the door, and she stepped over the threshold.

"Good-bye, God bless," he said and quickly shut the door. At the window he stood watching her, his eyebrows pulled together into waves of compassion, his tongue fondling the worn gold in his upper jaw. He saw the girl bending down to the sleeping dog, who, at her touch, opened one liquid eye, matted in the corners with what looked like green glue. She reached out and touched the dog's head, stroking him gently. She placed the meat on the floor of the porch, near his nose. The odor roused him; he lifted his head, and got up to smell it better. He ate it in three or four gulps. The girl stroked his head again, and the dog looked up at her with soft triangle eyes. Suddenly he coughed, the cough of a phlegmy old man—and got to his feet. The girl jumped. The dog gagged, his mouth chomping the air, and promptly fell down. He tried to raise himself, could not, tried again, and half-fell down the steps. Choking, stumbling, he moved like a broken toy around the yard. The girl's mouth was open, a little petal of tongue showing. She made a wild, pointless gesture with one hand and then covered her mouth with both hands. She was trying not to vomit. The dog fell again, a spasm jerking his body. Then he was quiet. The girl's hands covering her mouth, she backed away a few feet, then turned, ran out of the yard and down the walk.

Soaphead Church went to the table. He sat down, with folded hands balancing his forehead on the balls of his thumbs. Then he rose and went to a tiny night table with a drawer, from which he took paper and a fountain pen. A bottle of ink was on the same shelf that held the poison. With these things he sat again at the table. Slowly, carefully, relishing his penmanship, he wrote the following letter:

Att: TO HE WHO GREATLY ENNOBLED HUMAN NATURE
BY CREATING IT
Dear God:

The Purpose of this letter is to familiarize you with facts which either have escaped your notice, or which you have chosen to ignore.

Once upon a time I lived greenly and youngish on one of your islands. An island of the archipelago in the South Atlantic between North and South America, enclosing the Caribbean Sea and the Gulf of Mexico: divided into the Greater Antilles, the Lesser Antilles, and the Bahama Islands. Not the Windward or Leeward Island colonies, mark you, but within, of course, the Greater of the two Antilles (while the precision of my prose may be, at times, laborious, it is necessary that I identify myself to you clearly).

Now.

We in this colony took as our own the most dramatic, and the most obvious, of our white master's characteristics, which were, of course, their worst. In retaining the identity of our race, we held fast to those characteristics most gratifying to sustain and least troublesome to maintain. Consequently we were not royal but snobbish, not aristocratic but class-conscious; we believed authority was cruelty to our inferiors, and education was being at school. We mistook violence for passion, indolence for leisure, and thought recklessness was freedom. We raised our children and reared our crops; we let infants grow, and property develop. Our manhood was defined by acquisitions. Our womanhood by acquiescence. And the smell of your fruit and the labor of your days we abhorred.

This morning, before the little black girl came, I cried—for Velma. Oh, not aloud. There is no wind to carry, bear, or even refuse to bear, a sound so heavy with regret. But in my silent own lone way, I cried—for Velma. You need to know about Velma to understand what I did today.

She (Velma) left me the way people leave a hotel room. A hotel room is a place to be when you are doing something else. Of itself it is of no consequence to one's major scheme. A hotel room is convenient. But its convenience is limited to the time you need it while you are in that particular town on that particular business; you hope it is comfortable, but prefer, rather, that it be anonymous. It is not, after all, where you *live.*

When you no longer need it, you pay a little something for its use; say, "Thank you, sir," and when your business in that town is over, you go away from that room. Does anybody regret leaving a hotel room? Does anybody, who has a home, a real home somewhere, want to stay there? Does anybody look back with affection, or even disgust, at a hotel room when they leave it? You can only love or despise whatever *living* was done in that room. But the room itself? But you take a souvenir. Not, oh, not, to remember the room. To remember, rather, the time and the place of your business, your adventure. What can anyone feel for a hotel room? One doesn't any more feel for a hotel room than one expects a hotel room to feel for its occupant.

That, heavenly, heavenly Father, was how she left me; or rather, she never left me, because she was never ever there.

You remember, do you, how and of what we are made? Let me tell you now about the breasts of little girls. I apologize for the inappropriateness (is that it?), the imbalance of loving them at awkward times of day, and in awkward places, and the tastelessness of loving those which belonged to members of my family. Do I have to apologize for loving strangers?

But you too are amiss here, Lord. How, why, did you allow it to happen? How is it I could lift my eyes from the contemplation of Your Body and fall deeply into the contemplation of theirs? The buds. The buds on some of these saplings. They were mean, you know, mean and tender. Mean little buds resisting the touch, springing like rubber. But aggressive. Daring me to touch. Commanding me to touch. Not a bit shy, as you'd suppose. They stuck out at me, oh yes, at me. Slender-chested, finger-chested lassies. Have you ever seen them, Lord? I mean, really seen them? One could not see them and not love them. You who made them must have considered them lovely even as an idea— how much more lovely is the manifestation of that idea. I couldn't, as you must recall, keep my hands, my mouth, off them. Salt-sweet. Like not quite ripe strawberries covered with the light salt sweat of running days and hopping, skipping, jumping hours.

The love of them—the touch, taste, and feel of them—was not just an easy luxurious human vice; they were, for me, A Thing To Do Instead. Instead of papa, instead of the Cloth, instead of Velma, and I *chose* not to do without them. But I didn't go into the church. At least I didn't do that. As to what I did do? I told people I knew all about You. That I had received Your Powers. It was not a complete *lie;* but it was a *complete* lie. I should never have, I admit, I should never have taken their money in exchange for well-phrased, well-placed, well-faced lies. But, mark you, I hated it. Not for a moment did I love the lies or the money.

But consider: The woman who left the hotel room.

Consider: The greentime, the noontime of the archipelago.

Consider: Their hopeful eyes that were outdone only by their hoping breasts.

Consider: How I needed a comfortable evil to prevent my knowing what I could not bear to know.

Consider: How I hated and despised the money.

And now, consider: Not according to my just deserts, but according to *my* mercy, the little black girl that came a-looning at me today. Tell me, Lord, how could you leave a lass so long so lone that she could find her way to me? How could you? I weep for you, Lord. And it is because I weep for You that I had to do your work for You.

Do you know what she came for? Blue eyes. New, blue eyes, she said. Like she was buying shoes. "I'd like a pair of new blue eyes." She must have asked you for them for a very long time, and you hadn't replied. (A habit, I could have told her, a long-ago habit broken for Job —but no more.) She came to *me* for them. She had one of my cards. (Card enclosed.) By the way, I added the Micah—Micah Elihue Whitcomb. But I am called Soaphead Church. I cannot remember how or why I got the name. What makes one name more a person than another? Is the name the real thing, then? And the person only what his name says? Is that why to the simplest and friendliest of questions: "What is your name?" put to you by Moses, You would not say, and said instead "I am who I am." Like Popeye? I Yam What I Yam? Afraid you were, weren't you, to give out your name? Afraid they would know the name and then know you? Then they wouldn't fear you? It's quite all right. Don't be vexed. I mean no offense. I understand. I have been a bad man too, and an unhappy man too. But someday *I* will die. I was always so kind. Why do I have to die? The little girls. The little girls are the only things I'll miss. Do you know that when I touched their sturdy little tits and bit them—just a little—I felt I was being friendly? I didn't want to kiss their mouths or sleep in the bed with them or take a child bride for my own. Playful, I felt, and friendly. Not like the newspapers said. Not like the people whispered. And they didn't mind at all. Not at all. Remember how so many of them came back? No one would even try to understand that. If I'd been hurting them, would they have come back? Two of them, Doreen and Sugar Babe, they'd come together. I gave them mints, money, and they'd eat ice cream with their legs open while I played with them. It was like a party. And there wasn't nastiness, and there wasn't any filth, and there wasn't any odor, and there wasn't any groaning—just the light white laughter of little girls and me. And there wasn't any look— any long funny look—any long funny Velma look afterward. No look that makes you feel dirty afterward. That makes you want to die. With little girls it is all clean and good and friendly.

You have to understand that, Lord. You said, "Suffer little children to come unto me, and harm them not." Did you forget? Did you forget about the children? Yes. You forgot. You let them go wanting, sit on road shoulders, crying next to their dead mothers. I've seen them charred, lame, halt. You forgot, Lord. You forgot how and when to be God.

That's why I changed the little black girl's eyes for her, and I didn't touch her; not a finger did I lay on her. But I gave her those blue eyes she wanted. Not for pleasure, and not for money. I did what You did not, could not, would not do: I looked at that ugly little black girl, and I loved her. I played You. And it was a very good show!

I, I have caused a miracle. I gave her the eyes. I gave her the blue, blue, two blue eyes. Cobalt blue. A streak of it right out of your own blue heaven. No one else will see her blue eyes. But *she* will. And she will live happily ever after. I, I have found it meet and right so to do.

Now you are jealous. You are jealous of me.

You see? I, too, have created. Not aboriginally, like you, but creation is a heady wine, more for the taster than the brewer.

Having therefore imbibed, as it were, of the nectar, I am not afraid of You, of Death, not even of Life, and it's all right about Velma; and it's all right about Papa; and it's all right about the Greater and the Lesser Antilles. Quite all right. Quite.

With kindest regards, I remain,

Your,

Micah Elihue Whitcomb

Soaphead Church folded the sheets of paper into three equal parts and slipped them into an envelope. Although he had no seal, he longed for sealing wax. He removed a cigar box from under the bed and rummaged about in it. There were some of his most precious things: a sliver of jade that had dislodged from a cuff link at the Chicago hotel; a gold pendant shaped like a Y with a piece of coral attached to it that had belonged to the mother he never knew; four large hairpins that Velma had left on the rim of the bathroom sink; a powder blue grosgrain ribbon from the head of a little girl named Precious Jewel; a blackened faucet head from the sink in a jail cell in Cincinnati; two marbles he had found under a bench in Morningside Park on a very fine spring day; an old Lucky Hart catalog that smelled still of nut-brown and mocha face powder, and lemon vanishing cream. Distracted by his things, he forgot what he had been looking for. The effort to recall was too great; there was a buzzing in his head, and a wash of fatigue overcame him. He closed his box, eased himself out on the bed, and slipped into an ivory sleep from which he could not hear the tiny yelps of an old lady who had come out of her candy store and found the still carcass of an old dog named Bob.

I have only to break into the tightness of a strawberry, and I see summer—its dust and lowering skies. It remains for me a season of storms. The parched days and sticky nights are undistinguished in my mind, but the storms, the violent sudden storms, both frightened and quenched me. But my memory is uncertain; I recall a summer storm in the town where we lived and imagine a summer my mother knew in 1929. There was a tornado that year, she said, that blew away half of south Lorain. I mix up her summer with my own. Biting the strawberry, thinking of storms, I see her. A slim young girl in a pink crepe dress. One hand is on her hip; the other lolls about her thigh—waiting. The wind swoops her up, high above the houses, but she is still standing, hand on hip. Smiling. The anticipation and promise in her lolling hand are not altered by the holocaust. In the summer tornado of 1929, my mother's hand is unextinguished. She is strong, smiling, and relaxed while the world falls down about her. So much for memory. Public fact becomes private reality, and the seasons of a Midwestern town become the *Moirai* of our small lives.

The summer was already thick when Frieda and I received our seeds. We had waited since April for the magic package containing the packets and packets of seeds we were to sell for five cents each, which would entitle us to a new bicycle. We believed it, and spent a major part of every day trooping about the town selling them. Although Mama had restricted us to the homes of people she knew or the neighborhoods familiar to us, we knocked on all doors, and floated in and out of every house that opened to us: twelve-room houses that sheltered half as many families, smelling of grease and urine; tiny wooden four-room houses tucked into bushes near the railroad tracks; the up-over places—apartments up over fish markets, butcher shops, furniture stores, saloons, restaurants; tidy brick houses with flowered carpets and glass bowls with fluted edges.

During that summer of the seed selling we thought about the money, thought about the seeds, and listened with only half an ear to what people were saying. In the houses of people who knew us we were asked to come in and sit, given cold water or lemonade; and while we sat there being refreshed, the people continued their conversations or went about their chores. Little by little we began to piece a story together, a secret, terrible, awful story. And it was only after two or three such vaguely overheard conversations that we realized that the story was about Pecola. Properly placed, the fragments of talk ran like this:

"Did you hear about that girl?"

"What? Pregnant?"

"Yas. But guess who?"

"Who? I don't know all these little old boys."

"That's just it. Ain't no little old boy. They say it's Cholly."

"Cholly? Her daddy?"

"Uh-huh."

"Lord. Have mercy. That dirty nigger."

" 'Member that time he tried to burn them up? I knew he was crazy for sure then."

"What's she gone do? The mama?"

"Keep on like she been, I reckon. He taken off."

"County ain't gone let her keep that baby, is they?"

"Don't know."

"None of them Breedloves seem right anyhow. That boy is off somewhere every minute, and the girl was always foolish."

"Don't nobody know nothing about them anyway. Where they come from or nothing. Don't seem to have no people."

"What you reckon make him do a thing like that?"

"Beats me. Just nasty."

"Well, they ought to take her out of school."

"Ought to. She carry some of the blame."

"Oh, come on. She ain't but twelve or so."

"Yeah. But you never know. How come she didn't fight him?"

"Maybe she did."

"Yeah? You never know."

"Well, it probably won't live. They say the way her mama beat her she lucky to be alive herself."

"She be lucky if it don't live. Bound to be the ugliest thing walking."

"Can't help but be. Ought to be a law: two ugly people doubling up like that to make more ugly. Be better off in the ground."

"Well, I wouldn't worry none. It be a miracle if it live."

Our astonishment was short-lived, for it gave way to a curious kind of defensive shame; we were embarrassed for Pecola, hurt for her, and finally we just felt sorry for her. Our sorrow drove out all thoughts of the new bicycle. And I believe our sorrow was the more intense because nobody else seemed to share it. They were disgusted, amused, shocked, outraged, or even excited by the story. But we listened for the one who would say, "Poor little girl," or, "Poor baby," but there was only head-wagging where those words should have been. We looked for eyes creased with concern, but saw only veils.

I thought about the baby that everybody wanted dead, and saw it very clearly. It was in a dark, wet place, its head covered with great O's of wool, the black face holding, like nickels, two clean black eyes, the flared nose, kissing-thick lips, and the living, breathing silk of black skin. No synthetic yellow bangs suspended over marble-blue eyes, no pinched nose and bowline mouth. More strongly than my fondness for Pecola, I felt a need for someone to want the black baby to live—just to counteract the universal love of white baby dolls, Shirley Temples, and Maureen Peals. And Frieda must have felt the same thing. We did not think of the fact that Pecola was not married; lots of girls had babies who were not married. And we did not dwell on the fact that the baby's father was Pecola's father too; the process of having a baby

by any male was incomprehensible to us—at least she knew her father.
We thought only of this overwhelming hatred for the unborn baby.
We remembered Mrs. Breedlove knocking Pecola down and soothing
the pink tears of the frozen doll baby that sounded like the door of our
icebox. We remembered the knuckled eyes of schoolchildren under the
gaze of Meringue Pie and the eyes of these same children when they
looked at Pecola. Or maybe we didn't remember; we just knew. We
had defended ourselves since memory against everything and
everybody, considered all speech a code to be broken by us, and all
gestures subject to careful analysis; we had become headstrong,
devious, and arrogant. Nobody paid us any attention, so we paid very
good attention to ourselves. Our limitations were not known to
us—not then. Our only handicap was our size; people gave us orders
because they were bigger and stronger. So it was with confidence,
strengthened by pity and pride, that we decided to change the course of
events and alter a human life.

"What we gone do, Frieda?"

"What can we do? Miss Johnson said it would be a miracle if it
lived."

"So let's make it a miracle."

"Yeah, but how?"

"We could pray."

"That's not enough. Remember last time with the bird?"

"That was different; it was half-dead when we found it."

"I don't care, I still think we have to do something really strong this
time."

"Let's ask Him to let Pecola's baby live and promise to be good for
a whole month."

"O.K. But we better give up something so He'll know we really
mean it this time."

"Give up what? We ain't got nothing. Nothing but the seed
money, two dollars."

"We could give that. Or, you know what? We could give up the bicycle. Bury the money and . . . plant the seeds."

"All of the money?"

"Claudia, do you want to do it or not?"

"O.K. I just thought . . . O.K."

"We have to do it *right*, now. We'll bury the money over by her house so we can't go back and dig it up, and we'll plant the seeds out back of our house so we can watch over them. And when they come up, we'll know everything is all right. All right?"

"All right. Only let me sing this time. You say the magic words."

LOOKLOOKHERECOMESAFRIENDTHEFRIENDWILLPLAY
WITHJANETHEYWILLPLAYAGOODGAMEPLAYJANEPLA

*How many times a minute are you going to look inside that old thing?*
I didn't look in a long time.
*You did too–*
So what? I can look if I want to.
*I didn't say you couldn't. I just don't know why you have to look every minute. They aren't going anywhere.*
I know it. I just like to look.
*You scared they might go away?*
Of course not. How can they go away?
*The others went away.*
They didn't go away. They changed.
*Go away. Change. What's the difference?*
A lot. Mr. Soaphead said they would last forever.
*Forever and ever Amen?*
Yes, if you want to know.
*You don't have to be so smarty when you talk to me.*
I'm not being smarty. You started it.
*I'd just like to do something else besides watch you stare in that mirror.*
You're just jealous.
*I am not.*
You are. You wish you had them.
*Ha. What would I look like with blue eyes?*
Nothing much.
*If you're going to keep this up, I may as well go on off by myself.*
No. Don't go. What you want to do?
*We could go outside and play, I guess.*
But it's too hot.

*You can take your old mirror. Put it in your coat pocket, and you can look at yourself up and down the street.*

Boy! I never would have thought you'd be so jealous.

*Oh, come on!*

You are.

*Are what?*

Jealous.

*O.K. So I'm jealous.*

See. I told you.

*No. I told you.*

Are they really nice?

*Yes. Very nice.*

Just "very nice"?

*Really, truly, very nice.*

Really, truly, bluely nice?

*Oh, God. You are crazy.*

I am not!

*I didn't meant it that way.*

Well, what did you mean?

*Come on. It's too hot in here.*

Wait a minute. I can't find my shoes.

*Here they are.*

Oh. Thank you.

*Got your mirror?*

Yes dearie. . . .

*Well, let's go then. . . . Ow!*

What's the matter?

*The sun is too bright. It hurts my eyes.*

Not mine. I don't even blink. Look. I can look right at the sun.

*Don't do that.*

Why not? It doesn't hurt. I don't even have to blink.

*Well, blink anyway. You make me feel funny, staring at the sun like that.*

Feel funny how?

*I don't know.*

Yes, you do. Feel funny how?

*I told you, I don't know.*

Why don't you look at me when you say that? You're looking drop-eyed like Mrs. Breedlove.

*Mrs. Breedlove look drop-eyed at you?*

Yes. Now she does. Ever since I got my blue eyes, she look away from me all of the time. Do you suppose she's jealous too?

*Could be. They are pretty, you know.*

I know. He really did a good job. Everybody's jealous. Every time I look at somebody, they look off.

*Is that why nobody has told you how pretty they are?*

Sure it is. Can you imagine? Something like that happening to a person, and nobody but nobody saying anything about it? They all try to pretend they don't see them. Isn't that funny? . . . I said, isn't that funny?

*Yes.*

You are the only one who tells me how pretty they are.

*Yes.*

You are a real friend. I'm sorry about picking on you before. I mean, saying you were jealous and all.

*That's all right.*

No. Really. You are my very best friend. Why didn't I know you before?

*You didn't need me before.*

Didn't need you?

*I mean . . . you were so unhappy before. I guess you didn't notice me before.*

I guess you're right. And I was so lonely for friends. And you were right here. Right before my eyes.

*No, honey. Right after your eyes.*

What?

*What does Maureen think about your eyes?*

She doesn't say anything about them. Has she said anything to you about them?

*No. Nothing.*

Do you like Maureen?

*Oh. She's all right. For a half-white girl, that is.*

I know what you mean. But would you like to be her friend? I mean, would you like to go around with her or anything?

*No.*

Me neither. But she sure is popular.

*Who wants to be popular?*

Not me.

*Me neither.*

But you couldn't be popular anyway. You don't even go to school.

*You don't either.*

I know. But I used to.

*What did you stop for?*

They made me.

*Who made you?*

I don't know. After that first day at school when I had my blue eyes. Well, the next day they had Mrs. Breedlove come out. Now I don't go anymore. But I don't care.

*You don't?*

No, I don't. They're just prejudiced, that's all.

*Yes, they sure are prejudiced.*

Just because I got blue eyes, bluer than theirs, they're prejudiced.

*That's right.*

They are bluer, aren't they?

*Oh, yes. Much bluer.*

Bluer than Joanna's?

*Much bluer than Joanna's.*

And bluer than Michelena's?

*Much bluer than Michelena's.*

I thought so. Did Michelena say anything to you about my eyes?

*No. Nothing.*

Did you say anything to her?

*No.*

How come?

*How come what?*

How come you don't talk to anybody?

*I talk to you.*

Besides me.

*I don't like anybody besides you.*

Where do you live?

*I told you once.*

What is your mother's name?

*Why are you so busy meddling me?*

I just wondered. You don't talk to anybody. You don't go to school. And nobody talks to you.

*How do you know nobody talks to me?*

They don't. When you're in the house with me, even Mrs. Breedlove doesn't say anything to you. Ever. Sometimes I wonder if she even sees you.

*Why wouldn't she see me?*

I don't know. She almost walks right over you.

*Maybe she doesn't feel too good since Cholly's gone.*

Oh, yes. You must be right.

*She probably misses him.*

I don't know why she would. All he did was get drunk and beat her up.

*Well, you know how grown-ups are.*

Yes. No. How are they?

*Well, she probably loved him anyway.*

HIM?

*Sure. Why not? Anyway, if she didn't love him, she sure let him do it to her a lot.*

That's nothing.

*How do you know?*

I saw them all the time. She didn't like it.

*Then why'd she let him do it to her?*

Because he made her.

*How could somebody make you do something like that?*

Easy.

*Oh, yeah? How easy?*

They just make you, that's all.

*I guess you're right. And Cholly could make anybody do anything.*

He could not.

*He made you, didn't he?*

Shut up!

*I was only teasing.*

Shut up!

*O.K. O.K.*

He just tried, see? He didn't do anything. You hear me?

*I'm shutting up.*

You'd better. I don't like that kind of talk.

*I said I'm shutting up.*

You always talk so dirty. Who told you about that, anyway?

*I forget.*

Sammy?

*No. You did.*

I did not.

*You did. You said he tried to do it to you when you were sleeping on the couch.*

See there! You don't even know what you're talking about. It was when I was washing dishes.

*Oh, yes. Dishes.*

By myself. In the kitchen.

*Well, I'm glad you didn't let him.*

Yes.

*Did you?*

Did I what?

*Let him.*

Now who's crazy?

*I am, I guess.*

You sure are.

*Still . . .*

Well. Go ahead. Still what?

*I wonder what it would be like.*

Horrible.

*Really?*

Yes. Horrible.

*Then why didn't you tell Mrs. Breedlove?*

I did tell her!

*I don't mean about the first time. I mean about the second time, when you were sleeping on the couch.*

I wasn't sleeping! I was reading!

*You don't have to shout.*

You don't understand anything, do you? She didn't even believe me when I told her.

*So that's why you didn't tell her about the second time?*

She wouldn't have believed me then either.

*You're right. No use telling her when she wouldn't believe you.*

That's what I'm trying to get through your thick head.

*O.K. I understand now. Just about.*

What do you mean, just about?

*You sure are mean today.*

You keep on saying mean and sneaky things. I thought you were my friend.

*I am. I am.*

Then leave me alone about Cholly.

*OK.*

There's nothing more to say about him, anyway. He's gone, anyway.

*Yes. Good riddance.*

Yes. Good riddance.

*And Sammy's gone too.*

And Sammy's gone too.

*So there's no use talking about it. I mean them.*

No. No use at all.

*It's all over now.*

Yes.

*And you don't have to be afraid of Cholly coming at you anymore.*

No.

*That was horrible, wasn't it?*

Yes.

*The second time too?*

Yes.

*Really? The second time too?*

Leave me alone! You better leave me alone.

*Can't you take a joke? I was only funning.*

I don't like to talk about dirty things.

*Me neither. Let's talk about something else.*

What? What will we talk about?

*Why, your eyes.*

Oh, yes. My eyes. My blue eyes. Let me look again.

*See how pretty they are.*

Yes. They get prettier each time I look at them.

*They are the prettiest I've ever seen.*

Really?

*Oh, yes.*

Prettier than the sky?

*Oh, yes. Much prettier than the sky.*

Prettier than Alice-and-Jerry Storybook eyes?

*Oh, yes. Much prettier than Alice-and-Jerry Storybook eyes.*

And prettier than Joanna's?

*Oh, yes. And bluer too.*

Bluer than Michelena's?

*Yes.*

Are you sure?

*Of course I'm sure.*

You don't sound sure. . . .

*Well, I am sure. Unless. . . .*

Unless what?

*Oh, nothing. I was just thinking about a lady I saw yesterday. Her eyes sure were blue. But no. Not bluer than yours.*

Are you sure?

*Yes. I remember them now. Yours are bluer.*

I'm glad.

*Me too. I'd hate to think that there was anybody around with bluer eyes than yours. I'm sure there isn't. Not around here, anyway.*

But you don't know, do you? You haven't seen everybody, have you?

*No. I haven't.*

So there could be, couldn't there?

*Not hardly.*

But maybe. Maybe. You said "around here." Nobody "around here" probably has bluer eyes. What about someplace else? Even if my eyes are bluer than Joanna's and bluer than Michelena's and bluer than that lady's you saw, suppose there is somebody way off somewhere with bluer eyes than mine?

*Don't be silly.*

There could be. Couldn't there?

*Not hardly.*

But suppose. Suppose a long way off. In Cincinnati, say, there is somebody whose eyes are bluer than mine? Suppose there are *two* people with bluer eyes?

*So what? You asked for blue eyes. You got blue eyes.*

He should have made them bluer.

*Who?*

Mr. Soaphead.

*Did you say what color blue you wanted them?*
No. I forgot.
*Oh. Well.*
Look. Look over there. At that girl. Look at her eyes. Are they bluer than mine?
*No, I don't think so.*
Did you look real good?
*Yes.*
Here comes someone. Look at his. See if they're bluer.
*You're being silly. I'm not going to look at everybody's eyes.*
You have to.
*No I don't.*
Please. If there is somebody with bluer eyes than mine, then maybe there is somebody with the bluest eyes. The bluest eyes in the whole world.
*That's just too bad, isn't it?*
Please help me look.
*No.*
But suppose my eyes aren't blue enough?
*Blue enough for what?*
Blue enough for . . . I don't know. Blue enough for something. Blue enough . . . for you!
*I'm not going to play with you anymore.*
Oh. Don't leave me.
*Yes. I am.*
Why? Are you mad at me?
*Yes.*
Because my eyes aren't blue enough? Because I don't have the bluest eyes?
*No. Because you're acting silly.*
Don't go. Don't leave me. Will you come back if I get them?
*Get what?*
The bluest eyes. Will you come back then?

*Of course I will. I'm just going away for a little while.*
You promise?
*Sure. I'll be back. Right before your very eyes.*

So it was.

A little black girl yearns for the blue eyes of a little white girl, and the horror at the heart of her yearning is exceeded only by the evil of fulfillment.

We saw her sometimes, Frieda and I—after the baby came too soon and died. After the gossip and the slow wagging of heads. She was so sad to see. Grown people looked away; children, those who were not frightened by her, laughed outright.

The damage done was total. She spent her days, her tendril, sap-green days, walking up and down, up and down, her head jerking to the beat of a drummer so distant only she could hear. Elbows bent, hands on shoulders, she flailed her arms like a bird in an eternal, grotesquely futile effort to fly. Beating the air, a winged but grounded bird, intent on the blue void it could not reach—could not even see—but which filled the valleys of the mind.

We tried to see her without looking at her, and never, never went near. Not because she was absurd, or repulsive, or because we were frightened, but because we had failed her. Our flowers never grew. I was convinced that Frieda was right, that I had planted them too deeply. How could I have been so sloven? So we avoided Pecola Breedlove—forever.

And the years folded up like pocket handkerchiefs. Sammy left town long ago; Cholly died in the workhouse; Mrs. Breedlove still does housework. And Pecola is somewhere in that little brown house she and her mother moved to on the edge of town, where you can see her even now, once in a while. The birdlike gestures are worn away to a mere picking and plucking her way between the tire rims and the sunflowers, between Coke bottles and milkweed, among all the waste and beauty of the world—which is what she herself was. All of our waste which we dumped on her and which she absorbed. And all of our beauty, which was hers first and which she gave to us. All of us—all who knew her—felt so wholesome after we cleaned ourselves on her. We were so beautiful when we stood astride her ugliness. Her simplicity decorated us, her guilt sanctified us, her pain made us glow with health, her awkwardness made us think we had a sense of humor. Her inarticulateness made us believe we were eloquent. Her poverty kept us generous. Even her waking dreams we used—to silence our own nightmares. And she let us, and thereby deserved our contempt. We honed our egos on her, padded our characters with her frailty, and yawned in the fantasy of our strength.

And fantasy it was, for we were not strong, only aggressive; we were not free, merely licensed; we were not compassionate, we were polite; not good, but well behaved. We courted death in order to call ourselves brave, and hid like thieves from life. We substituted good grammar for intellect; we switched habits to simulate maturity; we rearranged lies and called it truth, seeing in the new pattern of an old idea the Revelation and the Word.

She, however, stepped over into madness, a madness which protected her from us simply because it bored us in the end.

Oh, some of us "loved" her. The Maginot Line. And Cholly loved her. I'm sure he did. He, at any rate, was the one who loved her enough to touch her, envelop her, give something of himself to her. But his touch was fatal, and the something he gave her filled the matrix of her agony with death. Love is never any better than the lover. Wicked people love wickedly, violent people love violently, weak people love weakly, stupid people love stupidly, but the love of a free man is never safe. There is no gift for the beloved. The lover alone possesses his gift of love. The loved one is shorn, neutralized, frozen in the glare of the lover's inward eye.

And now when I see her searching the garbage—for what? The thing we assassinated? I talk about how I did *not* plant the seeds too

deeply, how it was the fault of the earth, the land, of our town. I even
think now that the land of the entire country was hostile to marigolds
that year. This soil is bad for certain kinds of flowers. Certain seeds it
will not nurture, certain fruit it will not bear, and when the land kills
of its own volition, we acquiesce and say the victim had no right to
live. We are wrong, of course, but it doesn't matter. It's too late. At
least on the edge of my town, among the garbage and the sunflowers of
my town, it's much, much, much too late.

*Afterword*

We had just started elementary school. She said she wanted blue eyes. I looked around to picture her with them and was violently repelled by what I imagined she would look like if she had her wish. The sorrow in her voice seemed to call for sympathy, and I faked it for her, but, astonished by the desecration she proposed, I "got mad" at her instead.

Until that moment I had seen the pretty, the lovely, the nice, the ugly, and although I had certainly used the word "beautiful," I had never experienced its shock—the force of which was equaled by the knowledge that no one else recognized it, not even, or especially, the one who possessed it.

It must have been more than the face I was examining: the silence of the street in the early afternoon, the light, the atmosphere of confession. In any case it was the first time I knew beautiful. Had imagined it for myself. Beauty was not simply something to behold; it was something one could *do*.

*The Bluest Eye* was my effort to say something about that; to say something about why she had not, or possibly ever would have, the experience of what she possessed and also why she prayed for so radical an alteration. Implicit in her desire was racial self-loathing. And twenty years later I was still wondering about how one learns that. Who told her? Who made her feel that it was better to be a freak than what she was? Who had looked at her and found her so wanting, so small a weight on the beauty scale? The novel pecks away at the gaze that condemned her.

The reclamation of racial beauty in the sixties stirred these thoughts, made me think about the necessity for the claim. Why, although reviled by others, could this beauty not be taken for granted within the community? Why did it need wide public articulation to exist? These are not clever questions. But in 1962 when I began this story, and in 1965 when it began to be a book, the answers were not as obvious to me as they quickly became and are now. The assertion of racial beauty was not a reaction to the self-mocking, humorous critique of cultural/racial foibles common in all groups, but against the damaging internalization of assumptions of immutable inferiority originating in an outside gaze. I focused, therefore, on how something as grotesque as the demonization of an entire race could take root inside the most delicate member of society: a child; the most vulnerable member: a female. In trying to dramatize the devastation that even casual racial contempt can cause, I chose a unique situation, not a representative one. The extremity of Pecola's case stemmed largely from a crippled and crippling family—unlike the average black family and unlike the narrator's. But singular as Pecola's life was, I believed some aspects of her woundability were lodged in all young girls. In exploring the social and domestic aggression that could cause a child to literally fall apart, I mounted a series of rejections, some routine, some exceptional, some monstrous, all the while trying hard to avoid complicity in the demonization process Pecola was subjected to. That is, I did not want to dehumanize the characters who trashed Pecola and contributed to her collapse.

One problem was centering: the weight of the novel's inquiry on so delicate and vulnerable a character could smash her and lead readers into the comfort of pitying her rather than into an interrogation of themselves for the smashing. My solution—break the narrative into parts that had to be reassembled by the reader—seemed to me a good idea, the execution of which does not satisfy me now. Besides, it didn't work: many readers remain touched but not moved.

The other problem, of course, was language. Holding the despising glance while sabotaging it was difficult. The novel tried to hit the raw nerve of racial self-contempt, expose it, then soothe it not with narcotics but with language that replicated the agency I discovered in my first experience of beauty. Because that moment was so racially infused (my revulsion at what my school friend wanted: very blue eyes in a very black skin; the harm she was doing to *my* concept of the beautiful), the struggle was for writing that was indisputably black. I don't yet know quite what that is, but neither that nor the attempts to disqualify an effort to find out keeps me from trying to pursue it.

Some time ago I did the best job I could of describing strategies for grounding my work in race-specific yet race-free prose. Prose free of racial hierarchy and triumphalism. Parts of that description are as follows.

The opening phrase of the first sentence, "Quiet as it's kept," had several attractions for me. First, it was a familiar phrase, familiar to me as a child listening to adults; to black women conversing with one another, telling a story, an anecdote, gossip about some one or event within the circle, the family, the neighborhood. The words are conspiratorial. "Shh, don't tell anyone else," and "No one is allowed to know this." It is a secret between us and a secret that is being kept from us. The conspiracy is both held and withheld, exposed and sustained. In some sense it was precisely what the act of writing the book was: the public exposure of a private confidence. In order to comprehend fully the duality of that position, one needs to be reminded of the political climate in which the writing took place, 1965–69, a time of great social upheaval in the lives of black people. The publication (as opposed to the writing) involved the exposure; the writing was the disclosure of secrets, secrets "we" shared and those withheld from us by ourselves and by the world outside the community.

"Quiet as it's kept" is also a figure of speech that is written, in this instance, but clearly chosen for how speakerly it is, how it speaks and bespeaks a particular world and its ambience. Further, in addition to its "back fence" connotation, its suggestion of illicit gossip, of thrilling revelation, there is also, in the "whisper," the assumption (on the part of the reader) that the teller is on the inside, knows something others do not, and is going to be generous with this privileged information. The intimacy I was aiming for, the intimacy between the reader and the page, could start up immediately because the secret is being shared, at best, and eavesdropped upon, at the least. Sudden familiarity or instant intimacy seemed crucial to me. I did not want the reader to have time to wonder, "What do I have to do, to give up, in order to read this? What defense do I need, what distance maintain?'' Because I know (and the reader does not—he or she has to wait for the second sentence) that this is a terrible story about things one would rather not know anything about.

What, then, is the Big Secret about to be shared? The thing we (reader and I) are "in" on? A botanical aberration. Pollution, perhaps. A skip, perhaps, in the natural order of things: a September, an autumn, a fall without marigolds. Bright, common, strong and sturdy marigolds. When? In 1941, and since that is a momentous year (the beginning of World War II for the United States), the "fall" of 1941, just before the declaration of war, has a "closet" innuendo. In the temperate zone where there is a season known as "fall" during which one expects marigolds to be at their peak, in the months before the beginning of U.S. participation in World War II, something grim is about to be divulged. The next sentence will make it clear that the sayer, the one who knows, is a child speaking, mimicking the adult black women on the porch or in the backyard. The opening phrase is an effort to be grown-up about this shocking information. The point of view of a child alters the priority an adult would assign the information. "We thought . . . it was because Pecola was having her father's baby that the marigolds did not grow" foregrounds the flowers, backgrounds illicit, traumatic, incomprehensible sex coming to its dreaded fruition. This forgrounding of "trivial" information and backgrounding of shocking knowledge secures the point of view but gives the reader pause about whether the voice of children can be trusted at all or is more trustworthy than an adult's. The reader is thereby protected from a confrontation too soon with the painful details, while simultaneously provoked into a desire to know them. The novelty, I thought, would be in having this story of female violation revealed from the vantage point of the victims or could-be victims of rape—the persons no one inquired of (certainly not in 1965): the girls themselves. And since the victim does not have the vocabulary to understand the violence or its context, gullible, vulnerable girlfriends, looking back as the knowing adults they pretended to be in the beginning, would have to do that for her, and would have to fill those silences with their own reflective lives. Thus, the opening provides the stroke that announces something more than a secret shared, but a silence broken, a void filled, an unspeakable thing spoken at last. And it draws the connection between a minor destabilization in seasonal flora and the insignificant destruction of a black girl. Of course "minor" and "insignificant" represent the outside world's view—for the girls, both phenomena are earthshaking depositories of information they spend that whole year of childhood (and afterward) trying to fathom, and cannot. If they have any success, it will be in transferring the problem of fathoming to the presumably adult reader, to the inner circle of listeners. At the least they have distributed the weight of these problematical questions to a larger constituency, and justified the public exposure of a privacy. If the conspiracy that the opening words announce is entered into by the reader, then the book can be seen to open with its close: a speculation on the disruption of "nature" as being a social disruption with tragic individual consequences in which the reader, as part of the population of the text, is implicated.

However, a problem lies in the central chamber of the novel. The shattered world I built (to complement what is happening to Pecola), its pieces held together by seasons in childtime and commenting at every turn on the incompatible and barren white-family primer, does not in its present form handle effectively the silence at its center: the void that is Pecola's "unbeing." It should have had a shape—like the emptiness left by a boom or a cry. It required a sophistication unavailable to me, and some deft manipulation of the voices around her. She is not *seen* by herself until she hallucinates a self. And the fact of her hallucination becomes a kind of outside-the-book conversation.

Also, although I was pressing for a female expressiveness, it eluded me for the most part, and I had to content myself with female personae because I was not able to secure throughout the work the feminine subtext that is present in the opening sentence (the women gossiping, eager and aghast in "Quiet as it's kept"). The shambles this struggle became is most evident in the section on Pauline Breedlove, where I resorted to two voices, hers and the urging narrator's, both of which are extremely unsatisfactory to me. It is interesting to me now that where I thought I would have the most difficulty subverting the language to a feminine mode, I had the least: connecting Cholly's "rape" by the whitemen to his own of his daughter. This most masculine act of aggression becomes feminized in my language, "passive," and, I think, more accurately repellent when deprived of the male "glamour of shame" rape is (or once was) routinely given.

My choices of language (speakerly, aural, colloquial), my reliance for full comprehension on codes embedded in black culture, my effort to effect immediate co-conspiracy and intimacy (without any distancing, explanatory fabric), as well as my attempt to shape a silence while breaking it are attempts to transfigure the complexity and wealth of Black-American culture into a language worthy of the culture.

Thinking back now on the problems expressive language presented to me, I am amazed by their currency, their tenacity. Hearing "civilized" languages debase humans, watching cultural exorcisms debase literature, seeing oneself preserved in the amber of disqualifying metaphors—I can say that my narrative project is as difficult today as it was thirty years ago.

With very few exceptions, the initial publication of *The Bluest Eye* was like Pecola's life: dismissed, trivialized, misread. And it has taken twenty-five years to gain for her the respectful publication this edition is.

Princeton, New Jersey
November, 1993

# BELOVED

*Sixty Million*
*and more*

*I will call them my people,*
*which were not my people;*
*and her beloved,*
*which was not beloved.*

ROMANS 9:25

# One

124 WAS SPITEFUL. Full of a baby's venom. The women in the house knew it and so did the children. For years each put up with the spite in his own way, but by 1873 Sethe and her daughter Denver were its only victims. The grandmother, Baby Suggs, was dead, and the sons, Howard and Buglar, had run away by the time they were thirteen years old—as soon as merely looking in a mirror shattered it (that was the signal for Buglar); as soon as two tiny hand prints appeared in the cake (that was it for Howard). Neither boy waited to see more; another kettleful of chickpeas smoking in a heap on the floor; soda crackers crumbled and strewn in a line next to the door-sill. Nor did they wait for one of the relief periods: the weeks, months even, when nothing was disturbed. No. Each one fled at once—the moment the house committed what was for him the one insult not to be borne or witnessed a second time. Within two months, in the dead of winter, leaving their grandmother, Baby Suggs; Sethe, their mother; and their little sister, Denver, all by themselves in the gray and white house on Bluestone Road. It didn't have a number then, because Cincinnati didn't stretch that far. In fact, Ohio had been calling itself a state only seventy years when first one brother and then the next stuffed quilt packing into his hat, snatched up his shoes, and crept away from the lively spite the house felt for them.

Baby Suggs didn't even raise her head. From her sickbed she heard them go but that wasn't the reason she lay still. It was a wonder to her that her grandsons had taken so long to realize that every house wasn't like the one on Bluestone Road. Suspended between the nastiness of life and the meanness of the dead, she couldn't get interested in leaving life or living it, let alone the fright of two creeping-off boys. Her past had been like her present—intolerable—and since she knew death was anything but forgetfulness, she used the little energy left her for pondering color.

"Bring a little lavender in, if you got any. Pink, if you don't."

And Sethe would oblige her with anything from fabric to her own tongue. Winter in Ohio was especially rough if you had an appetite for color. Sky provided the only drama, and counting on a Cincinnati horizon for life's principal joy was reckless indeed. So Sethe and the girl Denver did what they could, and what the house permitted, for her. Together they waged a perfunctory battle against the outrageous behavior of that place; against turned-over slop jars, smacks on the behind, and gusts of sour air. For they understood the source of the outrage as well as they knew the source of light.

Baby Suggs died shortly after the brothers left, with no interest whatsoever in their leave-taking or hers, and right afterward Sethe and Denver decided to end the persecution by calling forth the ghost that tried them so. Perhaps a conversation, they thought, an exchange of views or something would help. So they held hands and said, "Come on. Come on. You may as well just come on."

The sideboard took a step forward but nothing else did.

"Grandma Baby must be stopping it," said Denver. She was ten and still mad at Baby Suggs for dying.

Sethe opened her eyes. "I doubt that," she said.

"Then why don't it come?"

"You forgetting how little it is," said her mother. "She wasn't even two years old when she died. Too little to understand. Too little to talk much even."

"Maybe she don't want to understand," said Denver.

"Maybe. But if she'd only come, I could make it clear to her." Sethe released her daughter's hand and together they pushed the sideboard back against the wall. Outside a driver whipped his horse into the gallop local people felt necessary when they passed 124.

"For a baby she throws a powerful spell," said Denver.

"No more powerful than the way I loved her," Sethe answered and there it was again. The welcoming cool of unchiseled headstones;

the one she selected to lean against on tiptoe, her knees wide open as any grave. Pink as a fingernail it was, and sprinkled with glittering chips. Ten minutes, he said. You got ten minutes I'll do it for free.

Ten minutes for seven letters. With another ten could she have gotten "Dearly" too? She had not thought to ask him and it bothered her still that it might have been possible—that for twenty minutes, a half hour, say, she could have had the whole thing, every word she heard the preacher say at the funeral (and all there was to say, surely) engraved on her baby's headstone: Dearly Beloved. But what she got, settled for, was the one word that mattered. She thought it would be enough, rutting among the headstones with the engraver, his young son looking on, the anger in his face so old; the appetite in it quite new. That should certainly be enough. Enough to answer one more preacher, one more abolitionist and a town full of disgust.

Counting on the stillness of her own soul, she had forgotten the other one: the soul of her baby girl. Who would have thought that a little old baby could harbor so much rage? Rutting among the stones under the eyes of the engraver's son was not enough. Not only did she have to live out her years in a house palsied by the baby's fury at having its throat cut, but those ten minutes she spent pressed up against dawn-colored stone studded with star chips, her knees wide open as the grave, were longer than life, more alive, more pulsating than the baby blood that soaked her fingers like oil.

"We could move," she suggested once to her mother-in-law.

"What'd be the point?" asked Baby Suggs. "Not a house in the country ain't packed to its rafters with some dead Negro's grief. We lucky this ghost is a baby. My husband's spirit was to come back in here? or yours? Don't talk to me. You lucky. You got three left. Three pulling at your skirts and just one raising hell from the other side. Be thankful, why don't you? I had eight. Every one of them gone away from me. Four taken, four chased, and all, I expect, worrying somebody's house into evil." Baby Suggs rubbed her eyebrows. "My first-born. All I can remember of her is how she loved the burned bottom of bread. Can you beat that? Eight children and that's all I remember."

"That's all you let yourself remember," Sethe had told her, but she was down to one herself—one alive, that is—the boys chased off by the dead one, and her memory of Buglar was fading fast. Howard at least had a head shape nobody could forget. As for the rest, she worked hard to remember as close to nothing as was safe. Unfortunately her brain was devious. She might be hurrying across a field, running practically, to get to the pump quickly and rinse the chamomile sap from her legs. Nothing else would be in her mind. The picture of the men coming to nurse her was as lifeless as the nerves in her back where the skin buckled like a washboard. Nor was there the faintest scent of ink or the cherry gum and oak bark from which it was made. Nothing. Just the breeze cooling her face as she rushed toward water. And then sopping the chamomile away with pump water and rags, her mind fixed on getting every last bit of sap off—on her carelessness in taking a shortcut across the field just to save a half mile, and not noticing how high the weeds had grown until the itching was all the way to her knees. Then something. The plash of water, the sight of her shoes and stockings awry on the path where she had flung them; or Here Boy lapping in the puddle near her feet, and suddenly there was Sweet Home rolling, rolling, rolling out before her eyes, and although there was not a leaf on that farm that did not make her want to scream, it rolled itself out before her in shameless beauty. It never looked as terrible as it was and it made her wonder if hell was a pretty place too. Fire and brimstone all right, but hidden in lacy groves. Boys hanging from the most beautiful sycamores in the world. It shamed her—remembering the wonderful soughing trees rather than the boys. Try as she might to make it otherwise, the sycamores beat out the children every time and she could not forgive her memory for that.

When the last of the chamomile was gone, she went around to the front of the house, collecting her shoes and stockings on the way. As if to punish her further for her terrible memory, sitting on the porch not forty feet away was Paul D, the last of the Sweet Home men. And although she could never mistake his face for another's, she said, "Is that you?"

"What's left." He stood up and smiled. "How you been, girl, besides barefoot?"

When she laughed it came out loose and young. "Messed up my legs back yonder. Chamomile."

He made a face as though tasting a teaspoon of something bitter. "I don't want to even hear 'bout it. Always did hate that stuff."

Sethe balled up her stockings and jammed them into her pocket. "Come on in."

"Porch is fine, Sethe. Cool out here." He sat back down and looked at the meadow on the other side of the road, knowing the eagerness he felt would be in his eyes.

"Eighteen years," she said softly.

"Eighteen," he repeated. "And I swear I been walking every one of em. Mind if I join you?" He nodded toward her feet and began unlacing his shoes.

"You want to soak them? Let me get you a basin of water." She moved closer to him to enter the house.

"No, uh uh. Can't baby feet. A whole lot more tramping they got to do yet."

"You can't leave right away, Paul D. You got to stay awhile."

"Well, long enough to see Baby Suggs, anyway. Where is she?"

"Dead."

"Aw no. When?"

"Eight years now. Almost nine."

"Was it hard? I hope she didn't die hard."

Sethe shook her head. "Soft as cream. Being alive was the hard part. Sorry you missed her though. Is that what you came by for?"

"That's some of what I came for. The rest is you. But if all the truth be known, I go anywhere these days. Anywhere they let me sit down."

"You looking good."

"Devil's confusion. He lets me look good long as I feel bad." He looked at her and the word "bad" took on another meaning.

Sethe smiled. This is the way they were—had been. All of the Sweet Home men, before and after Halle, treated her to a mild brotherly flirtation, so subtle you had to scratch for it.

Except for a heap more hair and some waiting in his eyes, he looked the way he had in Kentucky. Peachstone skin; straight-backed. For a man with an immobile face it was amazing how ready it was to smile, or blaze or be sorry with you. As though all you had to do was get his attention and right away he produced the feeling you were feeling. With less than a blink, his face seemed to change—underneath it lay the activity.

"I wouldn't have to ask about him, would I? You'd tell me if there was anything to tell, wouldn't you?" Sethe looked down at her feet and saw again the sycamores.

"I'd tell you. Sure I'd tell you. I don't know any more now than I did then." Except for the churn, he thought, and you don't need to know that. "You must think he's still alive."

"No. I think he's dead. It's not being sure that keeps him alive."

"What did Baby Suggs think?"

"Same, but to listen to her, all her children is dead. Claimed she felt each one go the very day and hour."

"When she say Halle went?"

"Eighteen fifty-five. The day my baby was born."

"You had that baby, did you? Never thought you'd make it." He chuckled. "Running off pregnant."

"Had to. Couldn't be no waiting." She lowered her head and thought, as he did, how unlikely it was that she had made it. And if it hadn't been for that girl looking for velvet, she never would have.

"All by yourself too." He was proud of her and annoyed by her. Proud she had done it; annoyed that she had not needed Halle or him in the doing.

"Almost by myself. Not all by myself. A whitegirl helped me."

"Then she helped herself too, God bless her."

"You could stay the night, Paul D."

"You don't sound too steady in the offer."

Sethe glanced beyond his shoulder toward the closed door. "Oh it's truly meant. I just hope you'll pardon my house. Come on in. Talk to Denver while I cook you something."

Paul D tied his shoes together, hung them over his shoulder and followed her through the door straight into a pool of red and undulating light that locked him where he stood.

"You got company?" he whispered, frowning.

"Off and on," said Sethe.

"Good God." He backed out the door onto the porch. "What kind of evil you got in here?"

"It's not evil, just sad. Come on. Just step through."

He looked at her then, closely. Closer than he had when she first rounded the house on wet and shining legs, holding her shoes and stockings up in one hand, her skirts in the other. Halle's girl—the one with iron eyes and backbone to match. He had never seen her hair in Kentucky. And though her face was eighteen years older than when last he saw her, it was softer now. Because of the hair. A face too still for comfort; irises the same color as her skin, which, in that still face, used to make him think of a mask with mercifully punched-out eyes. Halle's woman. Pregnant every year including the year she sat by the fire telling him she was going to run. Her three children she had already packed into a wagonload of others in a caravan of Negroes crossing the river. They were to be left with Halle's mother near Cincinnati. Even in that tiny shack, leaning so close to the fire you could smell the heat in her dress, her eyes did not pick up a flicker of light. They were like two wells into which he had trouble gazing. Even punched out they needed to be covered, lidded, marked with some sign to warn folks of what that emptiness held. So he looked instead at the fire while she told him, because her husband was not there for the telling. Mr. Garner was dead and his wife had a lump in her neck the size of a sweet potato and unable to speak to anyone. She leaned as close to the fire as her pregnant belly allowed and told him, Paul D, the last of the Sweet Home men.

There had been six of them who belonged to the farm, Sethe the only female. Mrs. Garner, crying like a baby, had sold his brother to pay off the debts that surfaced the minute she was widowed. Then schoolteacher arrived to put things in order. But what he did broke three more Sweet Home men and punched the glittering iron out of Sethe's eyes, leaving two open wells that did not reflect firelight.

Now the iron was back but the face, softened by hair, made him trust her enough to step inside her door smack into a pool of pulsing red light.

She was right. It was sad. Walking through it, a wave of grief soaked him so thoroughly he wanted to cry. It seemed a long way to the normal light surrounding the table, but he made it—dry-eyed and lucky.

"You said she died soft. Soft as cream," he reminded her.

"That's not Baby Suggs," she said.

"Who then?"

"My daughter. The one I sent ahead with the boys."

"She didn't live?"

"No. The one I was carrying when I run away is all I got left. Boys gone too. Both of em walked off just before Baby Suggs died."

Paul D looked at the spot where the grief had soaked him. The red was gone but a kind of weeping clung to the air where it had been.

Probably best, he thought. If a Negro got legs he ought to use them. Sit down too long, somebody will figure out a way to tie them up. Still . . . if her boys were gone . . .

"No man? You here by yourself?"

"Me and Denver," she said.

"That all right by you?"

"That's all right by me."

She saw his skepticism and went on. "I cook at a restaurant in town. And I sew a little on the sly."

Paul D smiled then, remembering the bedding dress. Sethe was thirteen when she came to Sweet Home and already iron-eyed. She was a timely present for Mrs. Garner who had lost Baby Suggs to her husband's high principles. The five Sweet Home men looked at the new girl and decided to let her be. They were young and so sick with the absence of women they had taken to calves. Yet they let the iron-eyed girl be, so she could choose in spite of the fact that each one would have beaten the others to mush to have her. It took her a year to choose—a long, tough year of thrashing on pallets eaten up with dreams of her. A year of yearning, when rape seemed the solitary gift of life. The restraint they had exercised possible only because they were Sweet Home men—the ones Mr. Garner bragged about while other farmers shook their heads in warning at the phrase.

"Y'all got boys," he told them. "Young boys, old boys, picky boys, stroppin boys. Now at Sweet Home, my niggers is men every one of em. Bought em thataway, raised em thataway. Men every one."

"Beg to differ, Garner. Ain't no nigger men."

"Not if you scared, they ain't." Garner's smile was wide. "But if you a man yourself, you'll want your niggers to be men too."

"I wouldn't have no nigger men round my wife."

It was the reaction Garner loved and waited for. "Neither would I," he said. "Neither would I," and there was always a pause before the neighbor, or stranger, or peddler, or brother-in-law or whoever it was got the meaning. Then a fierce argument, sometimes a fight, and Garner came home bruised and pleased, having demonstrated one more time what a real Kentuckian was: one tough enough and smart enough to make and call his own niggers men.

And so they were: Paul D Garner, Paul F Garner, Paul A Garner, Halle Suggs and Sixo, the wild man. All in their twenties, minus women, fucking cows, dreaming of rape, thrashing on pallets, rubbing their thighs and waiting for the new girl—the one who took Baby Suggs' place after Halle bought her with five years of Sundays. Maybe that was why she chose him. A twenty-year-old man so in love with his mother he gave up five years of Sabbaths just to see her sit down for a change was a serious recommendation.

She waited a year. And the Sweet Home men abused cows while they waited with her. She chose Halle and for their first bedding she sewed herself a dress on the sly.

"Won't you stay on awhile? Can't nobody catch up on eighteen years in a day."

Out of the dimness of the room in which they sat, a white staircase climbed toward the blue-and-white wallpaper of the second floor. Paul D could see just the beginning of the paper; discreet flecks of yellow sprinkled among a blizzard of snowdrops all backed by blue. The luminous white of the railing and steps kept him glancing toward it. Every sense he had told him the air above the stairwell was charmed and very thin. But the girl who walked down out of that air was round and brown with the face of an alert doll.

Paul D looked at the girl and then at Sethe who smiled saying, "Here she is my Denver. This is Paul D, honey, from Sweet Home."

"Good morning, Mr. D."

"Garner, baby. Paul D Garner."

"Yes sir."

"Glad to get a look at you. Last time I saw your mama, you were pushing out the front of her dress."

"Still is," Sethe smiled, "provided she can get in it."

Denver stood on the bottom step and was suddenly hot and shy. It had been a long time since anybody (good-willed whitewoman, preacher, speaker or newspaperman) sat at their table, their sympathetic voices called liar by the revulsion in their eyes. For twelve years, long before Grandma Baby died, there had been no visitors of any sort and certainly no friends. No coloredpeople. Certainly no hazelnut man with too long hair and no notebook, no charcoal, no oranges, no questions. Someone her mother wanted to talk to and would even consider talking to while barefoot. Looking, in fact acting, like a girl instead of the quiet, queenly woman Denver had known all her life. The one who never looked away, who when a man got stomped to death by a mare right in front of Sawyer's restaurant did not look away; and when a sow began eating her own litter did not look away then either. And when the baby's spirit picked up Here Boy and slammed him into the wall hard enough to break two of his legs and dislocate his eye, so hard he went into convulsions and chewed up his tongue, still her mother had not looked away. She had taken a hammer, knocked the dog unconscious, wiped away the blood and saliva, pushed his eye back in his head and set his leg bones. He recovered, mute and off-balance, more because of his untrustworthy eye than his bent legs, and winter, summer, drizzle or dry, nothing could persuade him to enter the house again.

Now here was this woman with the presence of mind to repair a dog gone savage with pain rocking her crossed ankles and looking away from her own daughter's body. As though the size of it was more than vision could bear. And neither she nor he had on shoes. Hot, shy, now Denver was lonely. All that leaving: first her brothers, then her grandmother—serious losses since there were no children willing to circle her in a game or hang by their knees from her porch railing. None of that had mattered as long as her mother did not look away as she was doing now, making Denver long, downright *long*, for a sign of spite from the baby ghost.

"She's a fine-looking young lady," said Paul D. "Fine-looking. Got her daddy's sweet face."

"You know my father?"

"Knew him. Knew him well."

"Did he, Ma'am?" Denver fought an urge to realign her affection.

"Of course he knew your daddy. I told you, he's from Sweet Home."

Denver sat down on the bottom step. There was nowhere else gracefully to go. They were a twosome, saying "Your daddy" and "Sweet Home" in a way that made it clear both belonged to them and not to her. That her own father's absence was not hers. Once the absence had belonged to Grandma Baby—a son, deeply mourned because he was the one who had bought her out of there. Then it was her mother's absent husband. Now it was this hazelnut stranger's absent friend. Only those who knew him ("knew him well") could claim his absence for themselves. Just as only those who lived in Sweet Home could remember it, whisper it and glance sideways at one another while they did. Again she wished for the baby ghost—its anger thrilling her now where it used to wear her out. Wear her out.

"We have a ghost in here," she said, and it worked. They were not a twosome anymore. Her mother left off swinging her feet and being girlish. Memory of Sweet Home dropped away from the eyes of the man she was being girlish for. He looked quickly up the lightning-white stairs behind her.

"So I hear," he said. "But sad, your mama said. Not evil."

"No sir," said Denver, "not evil. But not sad either."

"What then?"

"Rebuked. Lonely and rebuked."

"Is that right?" Paul D turned to Sethe.

"I don't know about lonely," said Denver's mother. "Mad, maybe, but I don't see how it could be lonely spending every minute with us like it does."

"Must be something you got it wants."

Sethe shrugged. "It's just a baby."

"My sister," said Denver. "She died in this house."

Paul D scratched the hair under his jaw. "Reminds me of that headless bride back behind Sweet Home. Remember that, Sethe? Used to roam them woods regular."

"How could I forget? Worrisome . . ."

"How come everybody run off from Sweet Home can't stop talking about it? Look like if it was so sweet you would have stayed."

"Girl, who you talking to?"

Paul D laughed. "True, true. She's right, Sethe. It wasn't sweet and it sure wasn't home." He shook his head.

"But it's where we were," said Sethe. "All together. Comes back whether we want it to or not." She shivered a little. A light ripple of skin on her arm, which she caressed back into sleep. "Denver," she said, "start up that stove. Can't have a friend stop by and don't feed him."

"Don't go to any trouble on my account," Paul D said.

"Bread ain't trouble. The rest I brought back from where I work. Least I can do, cooking from dawn to noon, is bring dinner home. You got any objections to pike?"

"If he don't object to me I don't object to him."

At it again, thought Denver. Her back to them, she jostled the kindlin and almost lost the fire. "Why don't you spend the night, Mr. Garner? You and Ma'am can talk about Sweet Home all night long."

Sethe took two swift steps to the stove, but before she could yank Denver's collar, the girl leaned forward and began to cry.

"What is the matter with you? I never knew you to behave this way."

"Leave her be," said Paul D. "I'm a stranger to her."

"That's just it. She got no cause to act up with a stranger. Oh baby, what is it? Did something happen?"

But Denver was shaking now and sobbing so she could not speak. The tears she had not shed for nine years wetting her far too womanly breasts.

"I can't no more. I can't no more."

"Can't what? What can't you?"

"I can't live here. I don't know where to go or what to do, but I can't live here. Nobody speaks to us. Nobody comes by. Boys don't like me. Girls don't either."

"Honey, honey."

"What's she talking 'bout nobody speaks to you?" asked Paul D.

"It's the house. People don't—"

"It's not! It's not the house. It's us! And it's you!"

"Denver!"

"Leave off, Sethe. It's hard for a young girl living in a haunted house. That can't be easy."

"It's easier than some other things."

"Think, Sethe. I'm a grown man with nothing new left to see or do and I'm telling you it ain't easy. Maybe you all ought to move. Who owns this house?"

Over Denver's shoulder Sethe shot Paul D a look of snow. "What you care?"

"They won't let you leave?"

"No."

"Sethe."

"No moving. No leaving. It's all right the way it is."

"You going to tell me it's all right with this child half out of her mind?"

Something in the house braced, and in the listening quiet that followed Sethe spoke.

"I got a tree on my back and a haint in my house, and nothing in between but the daughter I am holding in my arms. No more running—from nothing. I will never run from another thing on this earth. I took one journey and I paid for the ticket, but let me tell you something, Paul D Garner: it cost too much! Do you hear me? It cost too much. Now sit down and eat with us or leave us be."

Paul D fished in his vest for a little pouch of tobacco—concentrating on its contents and the knot of its string while Sethe led Denver into the keeping room that opened off the large room he was sitting in. He had no smoking papers, so he fiddled with the pouch and listened through the open door to Sethe quieting her daughter. When she came back she avoided his look and went straight to a small table next to the stove. Her back was to him and he could see all the hair he wanted without the distraction of her face.

"What tree on your back?"

"Huh." Sethe put a bowl on the table and reached under it for flour.

"What tree on your back? Is something growing on your back? I don't see nothing growing on your back."

"It's there all the same."

"Who told you that?"

"Whitegirl. That's what she called it. I've never seen it and never will. But that's what she said it looked like. A chokecherry tree. Trunk, branches, and even leaves. Tiny little chokecherry leaves. But that was eighteen years ago. Could have cherries too now for all I know."

Sethe took a little spit from the tip of her tongue with her forefinger. Quickly, lightly she touched the stove. Then she trailed her fingers through the flour, parting, separating small hills and ridges of it, looking for mites. Finding none, she poured soda and salt into the crease of her folded hand and tossed both into the flour. Then she reached into a can and scooped half a handful of lard. Deftly she squeezed the flour through it, then with her left hand sprinkling water, she formed the dough.

"I had milk," she said. "I was pregnant with Denver but I had milk for my baby girl. I hadn't stopped nursing her when I sent her on ahead with Howard and Buglar."

Now she rolled the dough out with a wooden pin. "Anybody could smell me long before he saw me. And when he saw me he'd see the drops of it on the front of my dress. Nothing I could do about that. All I knew was I had to get my milk to my baby girl. Nobody was going to nurse her like me. Nobody was going to get it to her fast enough, or take it away when she had enough and didn't know it. Nobody knew that she couldn't pass her air if you held her up on your shoulder, only if she was lying on my knees. Nobody knew that but me and nobody had her milk but me. I told that to the women in the wagon. Told them to put sugar water in cloth to suck from so when I got there in a few days she wouldn't have forgot me. The milk would be there and I would be there with it."

"Men don't know nothing much," said Paul D, tucking his pouch back into his vest pocket, "but they do know a suckling can't be away from its mother for long."

"Then they know what it's like to send your children off when your breasts are full."

"We was talking 'bout a tree, Sethe."

"After I left you, those boys came in there and took my milk. That's what they came in there for. Held me down and took it. I told Mrs. Garner on em. She had that lump and couldn't speak but her eyes rolled out tears. Them boys found out I told on em. School-teacher made one open up my back, and when it closed it made a tree. It grows there still."

"They used cowhide on you?"

"And they took my milk."

"They beat you and you was pregnant?"

"And they took my milk!"

The fat white circles of dough lined the pan in rows. Once more Sethe touched a wet forefinger to the stove. She opened the oven door and slid the pan of biscuits in. As she raised up from the heat she felt Paul D behind her and his hands under her breasts. She straightened up and knew, but could not feel, that his cheek was pressing into the branches of her chokecherry tree.

Not even trying, he had become the kind of man who could walk into a house and make the women cry. Because with him, in his presence, they could. There was something blessed in his manner. Women saw him and wanted to weep—to tell him that their chest hurt and their knees did too. Strong women and wise saw him and told him things they only told each other: that way past the Change of Life, desire in them had suddenly become enormous, greedy, more savage than when they were fifteen, and that it embarrassed them and made them sad; that secretly they longed to die—to be quit of it—that sleep was more precious to them than any waking day. Young girls sidled up to him to confess or describe how well-dressed the visitations were that had followed them straight from their dreams. Therefore, although he did not understand why this was so, he was not surprised when Denver dripped tears into the stovefire. Nor, fifteen minutes later, after telling him about her stolen milk, her mother wept as well. Behind her, bending down, his body an arc of kindness, he held her breasts in the palms of his hands. He rubbed his cheek on her back and learned that way her sorrow, the roots of it; its wide trunk and intricate branches. Raising his fingers to the hooks of her dress, he knew without seeing them or hearing any sigh that the tears were coming fast. And when the top of her dress was around her hips and he saw the sculpture her back had become, like the decorative work of an ironsmith too passionate for display, he could think but not say, "Aw, Lord, girl." And he would tolerate no peace until he had touched every ridge and leaf of it with his mouth, none of which Sethe could feel because her back skin had been dead for years. What she knew was that the responsibility for her breasts, at last, was in somebody else's hands.

Would there be a little space, she wondered, a little time, some way to hold off eventfulness, to push busyness into the corners of the room and just stand there a minute or two, naked from shoulder blade to waist, relieved of the weight of her breasts, smelling the stolen milk again and the pleasure of baking bread? Maybe this one time she could stop dead still in the middle of a cooking meal—not even leave the stove—and feel the hurt her back ought to. Trust things and remember things because the last of the Sweet Home men was there to catch her if she sank?

The stove didn't shudder as it adjusted to its heat. Denver wasn't stirring in the next room. The pulse of red light hadn't come back and Paul D had not trembled since 1856 and then for eighty-three days in a row. Locked up and chained down, his hands shook so bad he couldn't smoke or even scratch properly. Now he was trembling again but in the legs this time. It took him a while to realize that his legs were not shaking because of worry, but because the floorboards were and the grinding, shoving floor was only part of it. The house itself was pitching. Sethe slid to the floor and struggled to get back into her dress. While down on all fours, as though she were holding her house down on the ground, Denver burst from the keeping room, terror in her eyes, a vague smile on her lips.

"God damn it! Hush up!" Paul D was shouting, falling, reaching for anchor. "Leave the place alone! Get the hell out!" A table rushed toward him and he grabbed its leg. Somehow he managed to stand at an angle and, holding the table by two legs, he bashed it about, wrecking everything, screaming back at the screaming house. "You want to fight, come on! God damn it! She got enough without you. She got enough!"

The quaking slowed to an occasional lurch, but Paul D did not stop whipping the table around until everything was rock quiet. Sweating and breathing hard, he leaned against the wall in the space the sideboard left. Sethe was still crouched next to the stove, clutching her salvaged shoes to her chest. The three of them, Sethe, Denver, and Paul D, breathed to the same beat, like one tired person. Another breathing was just as tired.

It was gone. Denver wandered through the silence to the stove. She ashed over the fire and pulled the pan of biscuits from the oven. The jelly cupboard was on its back, its contents lying in a heap in the corner of the bottom shelf. She took out a jar, and, looking around for a plate, found half of one by the door. These things she carried out to the porch steps, where she sat down.

The two of them had gone up there. Stepping lightly, easy-footed, they had climbed the white stairs, leaving her down below. She pried the wire from the top of the jar and then the lid. Under it was cloth and under that a thin cake of wax. She removed it all and coaxed the jelly onto one half of the half a plate. She took a biscuit and pulled off its black top. Smoke curled from the soft white insides.

She missed her brothers. Buglar and Howard would be twenty-two and twenty-three now. Although they had been polite to her during the quiet time and gave her the whole top of the bed, she remembered how it was before: the pleasure they had sitting clustered on the white stairs—she between the knees of Howard or Buglar—while they made up die-witch! stories with proven ways of killing her dead. And Baby Suggs telling her things in the keeping room. She smelled like bark in the day and leaves at night, for Denver would not sleep in her old room after her brothers ran away.

Now her mother was upstairs with the man who had gotten rid of the only other company she had. Denver dipped a bit of bread into the jelly. Slowly, methodically, miserably she ate it.

NOT QUITE in a hurry, but losing no time, Sethe and Paul D climbed the white stairs. Overwhelmed as much by the downright luck of finding her house and her in it as by the certainty of giving her his sex, Paul D dropped twenty-five years from his recent memory. A stair step before him was Baby Suggs' replacement, the new girl they dreamed of at night and fucked cows for at dawn while waiting for her to choose. Merely kissing the wrought iron on her back had shook the house, had made it necessary for him to beat it to pieces. Now he would do more.

She led him to the top of the stairs, where light came straight from the sky because the second-story windows of that house had been placed in the pitched ceiling and not the walls. There were two rooms and she took him into one of them, hoping he wouldn't mind the fact that she was not prepared; that though she could remember desire, she had forgotten how it worked; the clutch and helplessness that resided in the hands; how blindness was altered so that what leapt to the eye were places to lie down, and all else—door knobs, straps, hooks, the sadness that crouched in corners, and the passing of time—was interference.

It was over before they could get their clothes off. Half-dressed and short of breath, they lay side by side resentful of one another and the skylight above them. His dreaming of her had been too long and too long ago. Her deprivation had been not having any dreams of her own at all. Now they were sorry and too shy to make talk.

Sethe lay on her back, her head turned from him. Out of the corner of his eye, Paul D saw the float of her breasts and disliked it, the spread-away, flat roundness of them that he could definitely live without, never mind that downstairs he had held them as though they were the most expensive part of himself. And the wrought-iron maze he had explored in the kitchen like a gold miner pawing through pay dirt was in fact a revolting clump of scars. Not a tree, as she said. Maybe shaped like one, but nothing like any tree he knew because trees were inviting; things you could trust and be near; talk to if you wanted to as he frequently did since way back when he took the midday meal in the fields of Sweet Home. Always in the same place if he could, and choosing the place had been hard because Sweet Home had more pretty trees than any farm around. His choice he called Brother, and sat under it, alone sometimes, sometimes with Halle or the other Pauls, but more often with Sixo, who was gentle then and still speaking English. Indigo with a flame-red tongue, Sixo experimented with night-cooked potatoes, trying to pin down exactly when to put smoking-hot rocks in a hole, potatoes on top, and cover the whole thing with twigs so that by the time they broke for the meal, hitched the animals, left the field and got to Brother, the po- tatoes would be at the peak of perfection. He might get up in the middle of the night, go all the way out there, start the earth-over by starlight; or he would make the stones less hot and put the next day's potatoes on them right after the meal. He never got it right, but they ate those undercooked, overcooked, dried-out or raw potatoes any- way, laughing, spitting and giving him advice.

Time never worked the way Sixo thought, so of course he never got it right. Once he plotted down to the minute a thirty-mile trip to see a woman. He left on a Saturday when the moon was in the place he wanted it to be, arrived at her cabin before church on Sunday and had just enough time to say good morning before he had to start back again so he'd make the field call on time Monday morning. He had walked for seventeen hours, sat down for one, turned around and walked seventeen more. Halle and the Pauls spent the whole day covering Sixo's fatigue from Mr. Garner. They ate no potatoes that day, sweet or white. Sprawled near Brother, his flame-red tongue hidden from them, his indigo face closed, Sixo slept through dinner like a corpse. Now *there* was a man, and *that* was a tree. Himself lying in the bed and the "tree" lying next to him didn't compare.

Paul D looked through the window above his feet and folded his hands behind his head. An elbow grazed Sethe's shoulder. The touch of cloth on her skin startled her. She had forgotten he had not taken off his shirt. Dog, she thought, and then remembered that she had not allowed him the time for taking it off. Nor herself time to take off her petticoat, and considering she had begun undressing before she saw him on the porch, that her shoes and stockings were already in her hand and she had never put them back on; that he had looked at her wet bare feet and asked to join her; that when she rose to cook he had undressed her further; considering how quickly they had started getting naked, you'd think by now they would be. But maybe a man was nothing but a man, which is what Baby Suggs always said. They encouraged you to put some of your weight in their hands and soon as you felt how light and lovely that was, they studied your scars and tribulations, after which they did what he had done: ran her children out and tore up the house.

She needed to get up from there, go downstairs and piece it all back together. This house he told her to leave as though a house was a little thing—a shirtwaist or a sewing basket you could walk off from or give away any old time. She who had never had one but this one; she who left a dirt floor to come to this one; she who had to bring a fistful of salsify into Mrs. Garner's kitchen every day just to be able to work in it, feel like some part of it was hers, because she wanted to love the work she did, to take the ugly out of it, and the only way she could feel at home on Sweet Home was if she picked some pretty growing thing and took it with her. The day she forgot was the day butter wouldn't come or the brine in the barrel blistered her arms.

At least it seemed so. A few yellow flowers on the table, some myrtle tied around the handle of the flatiron holding the door open for a breeze calmed her, and when Mrs. Garner and she sat down to sort bristle, or make ink, she felt fine. Fine. Not scared of the men beyond. The five who slept in quarters near her, but never came in the night. Just touched their raggedy hats when they saw her and stared. And if she brought food to them in the fields, bacon and bread wrapped in a piece of clean sheeting, they never took it from her hands. They stood back and waited for her to put it on the ground (at the foot of a tree) and leave. Either they did not want to take anything from her, or did not want her to see them eat. Twice or three times she lingered. Hidden behind honeysuckle she watched them. How different they were without her, how they laughed and played and urinated and sang. All but Sixo, who laughed once—at the very end. Halle, of course, was the nicest. Baby Suggs' eighth and last child, who rented himself out all over the county to buy her away from there. But he too, as it turned out, was nothing but a man.

"A man ain't nothing but a man," said Baby Suggs. "But a son? Well now, that's *somebody*."

It made sense for a lot of reasons because in all of Baby's life, as well as Sethe's own, men and women were moved around like checkers. Anybody Baby Suggs knew, let alone loved, who hadn't run off or been hanged, got rented out, loaned out, bought up, brought back, stored up, mortgaged, won, stolen or seized. So Baby's eight children had six fathers. What she called the nastiness of life was the shock she received upon learning that nobody stopped playing checkers just because the pieces included her children. Halle she was able to keep the longest. Twenty years. A lifetime. Given to her, no doubt, to make up for *hearing* that her two girls, neither of whom had their adult teeth, were sold and gone and she had not been able to wave goodbye. To make up for coupling with a straw boss for four months in exchange for keeping her third child, a boy, with her—only to have him traded for lumber in the spring of the next year and to find herself pregnant by the man who promised not to and did. That child she could not love and the rest she would not. "God take what He would," she said. And He did, and He did, and He did and then gave her Halle who gave her freedom when it didn't mean a thing.

Sethe had the amazing luck of six whole years of marriage to that "somebody" son who had fathered every one of her children. A blessing she was reckless enough to take for granted, lean on, as though Sweet Home really was one. As though a handful of myrtle stuck in the handle of a pressing iron propped against the door in a whitewoman's kitchen could make it hers. As though mint sprig in the mouth changed the breath as well as its odor. A bigger fool never lived.

Sethe started to turn over on her stomach but changed her mind. She did not want to call Paul D's attention back to her, so she settled for crossing her ankles.

But Paul D noticed the movement as well as the change in her breathing. He felt obliged to try again, slower this time, but the appetite was gone. Actually it was a good feeling—not wanting her. Twenty-five years and blip! The kind of thing Sixo would do—like the time he arranged a meeting with Patsy the Thirty-Mile Woman. It took three months and two thirty-four-mile round trips to do it. To persuade her to walk one-third of the way toward him, to a place he knew. A deserted stone structure that Redmen used way back when they thought the land was theirs. Sixo discovered it on one of his night creeps, and asked its permission to enter. Inside, having felt what it felt like, he asked the Redmen's Presence if he could bring his woman there. It said yes and Sixo painstakingly instructed her how to get there, exactly when to start out, how his welcoming or warning whistles would sound. Since neither could go anywhere on business of their own, and since the Thirty-Mile Woman was already fourteen and scheduled for somebody's arms, the danger was real. When he arrived, she had not. He whistled and got no answer. He went into the Redmen's deserted lodge. She was not there. He returned to the meeting spot. She was not there. He waited longer. She still did not come. He grew frightened for her and walked down the road in the direction she should be coming from. Three or four miles, and he stopped. It was hopeless to go on that way, so he stood in the wind and asked for help. Listening close for some sign, he heard a whimper. He turned toward it, waited and heard it again. Uncautious now, he hollered her name. She answered in a voice that sounded like life to him—not death. "Not move!" he shouted. "Breathe hard I can find you." He did. She believed she was already at the meeting place and was crying because she thought he had not kept his promise. Now it was too late for the rendezvous to happen at the Redmen's house, so they dropped where they were. Later he punctured her calf to simulate snakebite so she could use it in some way as an excuse for not being on time to shake worms from tobacco leaves. He gave her detailed directions about following the stream as a shortcut back, and saw her off. When he got to the road it was very light and he had his clothes in his hands. Suddenly from around a bend a wagon trundled toward him. Its driver, wide-eyed, raised a whip while the woman seated beside him covered her face. But Sixo had already melted into the woods before the lash could unfurl itself on his indigo behind.

He told the story to Paul F, Halle, Paul A and Paul D in the peculiar way that made them cry-laugh. Sixo went among trees at night. For dancing, he said, to keep his bloodlines open, he said. Privately, alone, he did it. None of the rest of them had seen him at it, but they could imagine it, and the picture they pictured made them eager to laugh at him—in daylight, that is, when it was safe.

But that was before he stopped speaking English because there was no future in it. Because of the Thirty-Mile Woman Sixo was the only one not paralyzed by yearning for Sethe. Nothing could be as good as the sex with her Paul D had been imagining off and on for twenty-five years. His foolishness made him smile and think fondly of himself as he turned over on his side, facing her. Sethe's eyes were closed, her hair a mess. Looked at this way, minus the polished eyes, her face was not so attractive. So it must have been her eyes that kept him both guarded and stirred up. Without them her face was manageable—a face he could handle. Maybe if she would keep them closed like that . . . But no, there was her mouth. Nice. Halle never knew what he had.

Although her eyes were closed, Sethe knew his gaze was on her face, and a paper picture of just how bad she must look raised itself up before her mind's eye. Still, there was no mockery coming from his gaze. Soft. It felt soft in a waiting kind of way. He was not judging her—or rather he was judging but not comparing her. Not since Halle had a man looked at her that way: not loving or passionate, but interested, as though he were examining an ear of corn for quality. Halle was more like a brother than a husband. His care suggested a family relationship rather than a man's laying claim. For years they saw each other in full daylight only on Sundays. The rest of the time they spoke or touched or ate in darkness. Predawn darkness and the afterlight of sunset. So looking at each other intently was a Sunday-morning pleasure and Halle examined her as though storing up what he saw in sunlight for the shadow he saw the rest of the week. And he had so little time. After his Sweet Home work and on Sunday afternoons was the debt work he owed for his mother. When he asked her to be his wife, Sethe happily agreed and then was stuck not knowing the next step. There should be a ceremony, shouldn't there? A preacher, some dancing, a party, a something. She and Mrs. Garner were the only women there, so she decided to ask her.

"Halle and me want to be married, Mrs. Garner."

"So I heard." She smiled. "He talked to Mr. Garner about it. Are you already expecting?"

"No, ma'am."

"Well, you will be. You know that, don't you?"

"Yes, ma'am."

"Halle's nice, Sethe. He'll be good to you."

"But I mean we want to get married."

"You just said so. And I said all right."

"Is there a wedding?"

Mrs. Garner put down her cooking spoon. Laughing a little, she touched Sethe on the head, saying, "You are one sweet child." And then no more.

Sethe made a dress on the sly and Halle hung his hitching rope from a nail on the wall of her cabin. And there on top of a mattress on top of the dirt floor of the cabin they coupled for the third time, the first two having been in the tiny cornfield Mr. Garner kept because it was a crop animals could use as well as humans. Both Halle and Sethe were under the impression that they were hidden. Scrunched down among the stalks they couldn't see anything, including the corn tops waving over their heads and visible to everyone else.

Sethe smiled at her and Halle's stupidity. Even the crows knew and came to look. Uncrossing her ankles, she managed not to laugh aloud.

The jump, thought Paul D, from a calf to a girl wasn't all that mighty. Not the leap Halle believed it would be. And taking her in the corn rather than her quarters, a yard away from the cabins of the others who had lost out, was a gesture of tenderness. Halle wanted privacy for her and got public display. Who could miss a ripple in a cornfield on a quiet cloudless day? He, Sixo and both of the Pauls sat under Brother pouring water from a gourd over their heads, and through eyes streaming with well water, they watched the confusion of tassels in the field below. It had been hard, hard, hard sitting there erect as dogs, watching corn stalks dance at noon. The water running over their heads made it worse.

Paul D sighed and turned over. Sethe took the opportunity afforded by his movement to shift as well. Looking at Paul D's back, she remembered that some of the corn stalks broke, folded down over Halle's back, and among the things her fingers clutched were husk and cornsilk hair.

How loose the silk. How jailed down the juice.

The jealous admiration of the watching men melted with the feast of new corn they allowed themselves that night. Plucked from the broken stalks that Mr. Garner could not doubt was the fault of the raccoon. Paul F wanted his roasted; Paul A wanted his boiled and now Paul D couldn't remember how finally they'd cooked those ears too young to eat. What he did remember was parting the hair to get to the tip, the edge of his fingernail just under, so as not to graze a single kernel.

The pulling down of the tight sheath, the ripping sound always convinced her it hurt.

As soon as one strip of husk was down, the rest obeyed and the ear yielded up to him its shy rows, exposed at last. How loose the silk. How quick the jailed-up flavor ran free.

No matter what all your teeth and wet fingers anticipated, there was no accounting for the way that simple joy could shake you.

How loose the silk. How fine and loose and free.

DENVER'S SECRETS were sweet. Accompanied every time by wild veronica until she discovered cologne. The first bottle was a gift, the next she stole from her mother and hid among boxwood until it froze and cracked. That was the year winter came in a hurry at suppertime and stayed eight months. One of the War years when Miss Bodwin, the whitewoman, brought Christmas cologne for her mother and herself, oranges for the boys and another good wool shawl for Baby Suggs. Talking of a war full of dead people, she looked happy—flush-faced, and although her voice was heavy as a man's, she smelled like a roomful of flowers—excitement that Denver could have all for herself in the boxwood. Back beyond 124 was a narrow field that stopped itself at a wood. On the yonder side of these woods, a stream. In these woods, between the field and the stream, hidden by post oaks, five boxwood bushes, planted in a ring, had started stretching toward each other four feet off the ground to form a round, empty room seven feet high, its walls fifty inches of murmuring leaves.

Bent low, Denver could crawl into this room, and once there she could stand all the way up in emerald light.

It began as a little girl's houseplay, but as her desires changed, so did the play. Quiet, primate and completely secret except for the noisome cologne signal that thrilled the rabbits before it confused them. First a playroom (where the silence was softer), then a refuge (from her brothers' fright), soon the place became the point. In that bower, closed off from the hurt of the hurt world, Denver's imagination produced its own hunger and its own food, which she badly needed because loneliness wore her out. *Wore her out.* Veiled and protected by the live green walls, she felt ripe and clear, and salvation was as easy as a wish.

Once when she was in the boxwood, an autumn long before Paul D moved into the house with her mother, she was made suddenly cold by a combination of wind and the perfume on her skin. She dressed herself, bent down to leave and stood up in snowfall: a thin and whipping snow very like the picture her mother had painted as she described the circumstances of Denver's birth in a canoe straddled by a whitegirl for whom she was named.

Shivering, Denver approached the house, regarding it, as she always did, as a person rather than a structure. A person that wept, sighed, trembled and fell into fits. Her steps and her gaze were the cautious ones of a child approaching a nervous, idle relative (someone dependent but proud). A breastplate of darkness hid all the windows except one. Its dim glow came from Baby Suggs' room. When Denver looked in, she saw her mother on her knees in prayer, which was not unusual. What was unusual (even for a girl who had lived all her life in a house peopled by the living activity of the dead) was that a white dress knelt down next to her mother and had its sleeve around her mother's waist. And it was the tender embrace of the dress sleeve that made Denver remember the details of her birth— that and the thin, whipping snow she was standing in, like the fruit of common flowers. The dress and her mother together looked like two friendly grown-up women—one (the dress) helping out the other. And the magic of her birth, its miracle in fact, testified to that friendliness as did her own name.

Easily she stepped into the told story that lay before her eyes on the path she followed away from the window. There was only one door to the house and to get to it from the back you had to walk all the way around to the front of 124, past the storeroom, past the cold house, the privy, the shed, on around to the porch. And to get to the part of the story she liked best, she had to start way back: hear the birds in the thick woods, the crunch of leaves underfoot; see her mother making her way up into the hills where no houses were likely to be. How Sethe was walking on two feet meant for standing still. How they were so swollen she could not see her arch or feel her ankles. Her leg shaft ended in a loaf of flesh scalloped by five toenails. But she could not, would not, stop, for when she did the little antelope rammed her with horns and pawed the ground of her womb with impatient hooves. While she was walking, it seemed to graze, quietly—so she walked, on two feet meant, in this sixth month of pregnancy, for standing still. Still, near a kettle; still, at the churn; still, at the tub and ironing board. Milk, sticky and sour on her dress, attracted every small flying thing from gnats to grasshoppers. By the time she reached the hill skirt she had long ago stopped waving them off. The clanging in her head, begun as a churchbell heard from a distance, was by then a tight cap of pealing bells around her ears. She sank and had to look down to see whether she was in a hole or kneeling. Nothing was alive but her nipples and the little antelope. Finally, she was horizontal—or must have been because blades of wild onion were scratching her temple and her cheek. Concerned as she was for the life of her children's mother, Sethe told Denver, she remembered thinking: "Well, at least I don't have to take another step." A dying thought if ever there was one, and she waited for the little antelope to protest, and why she thought of an antelope Sethe could not imagine since she had never seen one. She guessed it must have been an invention held on to from before Sweet Home, when she was very young. Of that place where she was born (Carolina maybe? or was it Louisiana?) she remembered only song and dance. Not even her own mother, who was pointed out to her by the eight-year-old child who watched over the young ones—pointed out as the one among many backs turned away from her, stooping in a watery field. Patiently Sethe waited for this particular back to gain the row's end and stand. What she saw was a cloth hat as opposed to a straw one, singularity enough in that world of cooing women each of whom was called Ma'am.

"Seth—thuh."

"Ma'am."

"Hold on to the baby."

"Yes, Ma'am."

"Seth—thuh."

"Ma'am."

"Get some kindlin in here."

"Yes, Ma'am."

Oh but when they sang. And oh but when they danced and sometimes they danced the antelope. The men as well as the ma'ams, one of whom was certainly her own. They shifted shapes and became something other. Some unchained, demanding other whose feet knew her pulse better than she did. Just like this one in her stomach.

"I believe this baby's ma'am is gonna die in wild onions on the bloody side of the Ohio River." That's what was on her mind and what she told Denver. Her exact words. And it didn't seem such a bad idea, all in all, in view of the step she would not have to take, but the thought of herself stretched out dead while the little antelope lived on—an hour? a day? a day and a night?—in her lifeless body grieved her so she made the groan that made the person walking on a path not ten yards away halt and stand right still. Sethe had not heard the walking, but suddenly she heard the standing still and then she smelled the hair. The voice, saying, "Who's in there?" was all she needed to know that she was about to be discovered by a white-boy. That he too had mossy teeth, an appetite. That on a ridge of pine near the Ohio River, trying to get to her three children, one of whom was starving for the food she carried; that after her husband had disappeared; that after her milk had been stolen, her back pulped, her children orphaned, she was not to have an easeful death. No.

She told Denver that a *something* came up out of the earth into her—like a freezing, but moving too, like jaws inside. "Look like I was just cold jaws grinding," she said. Suddenly she was eager for his eyes, to bite into them; to gnaw his cheek.

"I was hungry," she told Denver, "just as hungry as I could be for his eyes. I couldn't wait."

So she raised up on her elbow and dragged herself, one pull, two, three, four, toward the young white voice talking about "Who that back in there?"

" 'Come see,' I was thinking. 'Be the last thing you behold,' and sure enough here come the feet so I thought well that's where I'll have to start God do what He would, I'm gonna eat his feet off. I'm laughing now, but it's true. I wasn't just set to do it. I was hungry to do it. Like a snake. All jaws and hungry.

"It wasn't no whiteboy at all. Was a girl. The raggediest-looking trash you ever saw saying, 'Look there. A nigger. If that don't beat all.' "

And now the part Denver loved the best:

Her name was Amy and she needed beef and pot liquor like nobody in this world. Arms like cane stalks and enough hair for four or five heads. Slow-moving eyes. She didn't look at anything quick. Talked so much it wasn't clear how she could breathe at the same time. And those cane-stalk arms, as it turned out, were as strong as iron.

"You 'bout the scariest-looking something I ever seen. What you doing back up in here?"

Down in the grass, like the snake she believed she was, Sethe opened her mouth, and instead of fangs and a split tongue, out shot the truth.

"Running," Sethe told her. It was the first word she had spoken all day and it came out thick because of her tender tongue.

"Them the feet you running on? My Jesus my." She squatted down and stared at Sethe's feet. "You got anything on you, gal, pass for food?"

"No." Sethe tried to shift to a sitting position but couldn't.

"I like to die I'm so hungry." The girl moved her eyes slowly, examining the greenery around her. "Thought there'd be huckleberries. Look like it. That's why I come up in here. Didn't expect to find no nigger woman. If they was any, birds ate em. You like huckleberries?"

"I'm having a baby, miss."

Amy looked at her. "That mean you don't have no appetite? Well I got to eat me something."

Combing her hair with her fingers, she carefully surveyed the landscape once more. Satisfied nothing edible was around, she stood up to go and Sethe's heart stood up too at the thought of being left alone in the grass without a fang in her head.

"Where you on your way to, miss?"

She turned and looked at Sethe with freshly lit eyes. "Boston. Get me some velvet. It's a store there called Wilson. I seen the pictures of it and they have the prettiest velvet. They don't believe I'm a get it, but I am."

Sethe nodded and shifted her elbow. "Your ma'am know you on the lookout for velvet?"

The girl shook her hair out of her face. "My mama worked for these here people to pay for her passage. But then she had me and since she died right after, well, they said I had to work for em to pay it off. I did, but now I want me some velvet."

They did not look directly at each other, not straight into the eyes anyway. Yet they slipped effortlessly into yard chat about nothing in particular—except one lay on the ground.

"Boston," said Sethe. "Is that far?"

"Ooooh, yeah. A hundred miles. Maybe more."

"Must be velvet closer by."

"Not like in Boston. Boston got the best. Be so pretty on me. You ever touch it?"

"No, miss. I never touched no velvet." Sethe didn't know if it was the voice, or Boston or velvet, but while the whitegirl talked, the baby slept. Not one butt or kick, so she guessed her luck had turned.

"Ever see any?" she asked Sethe. "I bet you never even seen any."

"If I did I didn't know it. What's it like, velvet?"

Amy dragged her eyes over Sethe's face as though she would never give out so confidential a piece of information as that to a perfect stranger.

"What they call you?" she asked.

However far she was from Sweet Home, there was no point in giving out her real name to the first person she saw. "Lu," said Sethe. "They call me Lu."

"Well, Lu, velvet is like the world was just born. Clean and new and so smooth. The velvet I seen was brown, but in Boston they got all colors. Carmine. That means red but when you talk about velvet you got to say 'carmine.' " She raised her eyes to the sky and then, as though she had wasted enough time away from Boston, she moved off saying, "I gotta go."

Picking her way through the brush she hollered back to Sethe, "What you gonna do, just lay there and foal?"

"I can't get up from here," said Sethe.

"What?" She stopped and turned to hear.

"I said I can't get up."

Amy drew her arm across her nose and came slowly back to where Sethe lay. "It's a house back yonder," she said.

"A house?"

"Mmmmm. I passed it. Ain't no regular house with people in it though. A lean-to, kinda."

"How far?"

"Make a difference, does it? You stay the night here snake get you."

"Well he may as well come on. I can't stand up let alone walk and God help me, miss, I can't crawl."

"Sure you can, Lu. Come on," said Amy and, with a toss of hair enough for five heads, she moved toward the path.

So she crawled and Amy walked alongside her, and when Sethe needed to rest, Amy stopped too and talked some more about Boston and velvet and good things to eat. The sound of that voice, like a sixteen-year-old boy's, going on and on and on, kept the little antelope quiet and grazing. During the whole hateful crawl to the lean-to, it never bucked once.

Nothing of Sethe's was intact by the time they reached it except the cloth that covered her hair. Below her bloody knees, there was no feeling at all; her chest was two cushions of pins. It was the voice full of velvet and Boston and good things to eat that urged her along and made her think that maybe she wasn't, after all, just a crawling graveyard for a six-month baby's last hours.

The lean-to was full of leaves, which Amy pushed into a pile for Sethe to lie on. Then she gathered rocks, covered them with more leaves and made Sethe put her feet on them, saying: "I know a woman had her feet cut off they was so swole." And she made sawing gestures with the blade of her hand across Sethe's ankles. "Zzz Zzz Zzz Zzz."

"I used to be a good size. Nice arms and everything. Wouldn't think it, would you? That was before they put me in the root cellar. I was fishing off the Beaver once. Catfish in Beaver River sweet as chicken. Well I was just fishing there and a nigger floated right by me. I don't like drowned people, you? Your feet remind me of him. All swole like."

Then she did the magic: lifted Sethe's feet and legs and massaged them until she cried salt tears.

"It's gonna hurt, now," said Amy. "Anything dead coming back to life hurts."

A truth for all times, thought Denver. Maybe the white dress holding its arm around her mother's waist was in pain. If so, it could mean the baby ghost had plans. When she opened the door, Sethe was just leaving the keeping room.

"I saw a white dress holding on to you," Denver said.

"White? Maybe it was my bedding dress. Describe it to me."

"Had a high neck. Whole mess of buttons coming down the back."

"Buttons. Well, that lets out my bedding dress. I never had a button on nothing."

"Did Grandma Baby?"

Sethe shook her head. "She couldn't handle them. Even on her shoes. What else?"

"A bunch at the back. On the sit-down part."

"A bustle? It had a bustle?"

"I don't know what it's called."

"Sort of gathered-like? Below the waist in the back?"

"Um hm."

"A rich lady's dress. Silk?"

"Cotton, look like."

"Lisle probably. White cotton lisle. You say it was holding on to me. How?"

"Like you. It looked just like you. Kneeling next to you while you were praying. Had its arm around your waist."

"Well, I'll be."

"What were you praying for, Ma'am?"

"Not *for* anything. I don't pray anymore. I just talk."

"What were you talking about?"

"You won't understand, baby."

"Yes, I will."

"I was talking about time. It's so hard for me to believe in it. Some things go. Pass on. Some things just stay. I used to think it was my rememory. You know. Some things you forget. Other things you never do. But it's not. Places, places are still there. If a house burns down, it's gone, but the place—the picture of it—stays, and not just in my rememory, but out there, in the world. What I remember is a picture floating around out there outside my head. I mean, even if I don't think it, even if I die, the picture of what I did, or knew, or saw is still out there. Right in the place where it happened."

"Can other people see it?" asked Denver.

"Oh, yes. Oh, yes, yes, yes. Someday you be walking down the road and you hear something or see something going on. So clear. And you think it's you thinking it up. A thought picture. But no. It's when you bump into a rememory that belongs to somebody else. Where I was before I came here, that place is real. It's never going away. Even if the whole farm—every tree and grass blade of it dies. The picture is still there and what's more, if you go there—you who never was there—if you go there and stand in the place where it was, it will happen again; it will be there for you, waiting for you. So, Denver, you can't never go there. Never. Because even though it's all over—over and done with—it's going to always be there waiting for you. That's how come I had to get all my children out. No matter what."

Denver picked at her fingernails. "If it's still there, waiting, that must mean that nothing ever dies."

Sethe looked right in Denver's face. "Nothing ever does," she said.

"You never told me all what happened. Just that they whipped you and you run off, pregnant. With me."

"Nothing to tell except schoolteacher. He was a little man. Short. Always wore a collar, even in the fields. A schoolteacher, she said. That made her feel good that her husband's sister's husband had book learning and was willing to come farm Sweet Home after Mr. Garner passed. The men could have done it, even with Paul F sold. But it was like Halle said. She didn't want to be the only white person on the farm and a woman too. So she was satisfied when the school-teacher agreed to come. He brought two boys with him. Sons or nephews. I don't know. They called him Onka and had pretty manners, all of em. Talked soft and spit in handkerchiefs. Gentle in a lot of ways. You know, the kind who know Jesus by His first name, but out of politeness never use it even to His face. A pretty good farmer, Halle said. Not strong as Mr. Garner but smart enough. He liked the ink I made. It was her recipe, but he preferred how I mixed it and it was important to him because at night he sat down to write in his book. It was a book about us but we didn't know that right away. We just thought it was his manner to ask us questions. He commenced to carry round a notebook and write down what we said. I still think it was them questions that tore Sixo up. Tore him up for all time."

She stopped.

Denver knew that her mother was through with it—for now anyway. The single slow blink of her eyes; the bottom lip sliding up slowly to cover the top; and then a nostril sigh, like the snuff of a candle flame—signs that Sethe had reached the point beyond which she would not go.

"Well, I think the baby got plans," said Denver.

"What plans?"

"I don't know, but the dress holding on to you got to mean something."

"Maybe," said Sethe. "Maybe it does have plans."

Whatever they were or might have been, Paul D messed them up for good. With a table and a loud male voice he had rid 124 of its claim to local fame. Denver had taught herself to take pride in the condemnation Negroes heaped on them; the assumption that the haunting was done by an evil thing looking for more. None of them knew the downright pleasure of enchantment, of not suspecting but *knowing* the things behind things. Her brothers had known, but it scared them; Grandma Baby knew, but it saddened her. None could appreciate the safety of ghost company. Even Sethe didn't love it. She just took it for granted—like a sudden change in the weather.

But it was gone now. Whooshed away in the blast of a hazelnut man's shout, leaving Denver's world flat, mostly, with the exception of an emerald closet standing seven feet high in the woods. Her mother had secrets—things she wouldn't tell; things she halfway told. Well, Denver had them too. And hers were sweet—sweet as lily-of-the-valley cologne.

Sethe had given little thought to the white dress until Paul D came, and then she remembered Denver's interpretation: plans. The morning after the first night with Paul D, Sethe smiled just thinking about what the word could mean. It was a luxury she had not had in eighteen years and only that once. Before and since, all her effort was directed not on avoiding pain but on getting through it as quickly as possible. The one set of plans she had made—getting away from Sweet Home—went awry so completely she never dared life by making more.

Yet the morning she woke up next to Paul D, the word her daughter had used a few years ago did cross her mind and she thought about what Denver had seen kneeling next to her, and thought also of the temptation to trust and remember that gripped her as she stood before the cooking stove in his arms. Would it be all right? Would it be all right to go ahead and feel? Go ahead and *count on something?*

She couldn't think clearly, lying next to him listening to his breathing, so carefully, carefully, she had left the bed.

Kneeling in the keeping room where she usually went to talk-think it was clear why Baby Suggs was so starved for color. There wasn't any except for two orange squares in a quilt that made the absence shout. The walls of the room were slate-colored, the floor earth-brown, the wooden dresser the color of itself, curtains white, and the dominating feature, the quilt over an iron cot, was made up of scraps of blue serge, black, brown and gray wool—the full range of the dark and the muted that thrift and modesty allowed. In that sober field, two patches of orange looked wild—like life in the raw.

Sethe looked at her hands, her bottle-green sleeves, and thought how little color there was in the house and how strange that she had not missed it the way Baby did. Deliberate, she thought, it must be deliberate, because the last color she remembered was the pink chips in the headstone of her baby girl. After that she became as color conscious as a hen. Every dawn she worked at fruit pies, potato dishes and vegetables while the cook did the soup, meat and all the rest. And she could not remember remembering a molly apple or a yellow squash. Every dawn she saw the dawn, but never acknowledged or remarked its color. There was something wrong with that. It was as though one day she saw red baby blood, another day the pink gravestone chips, and that was the last of it.

124 was so full of strong feeling perhaps she was oblivious to the loss of anything at all. There was a time when she scanned the fields every morning and every evening for her boys. When she stood at the open window, unmindful of flies, her head cocked to her left shoulder, her eyes searching to the right for them. Cloud shadow on the road, an old woman, a wandering goat untethered and gnawing bramble—each one looked at first like Howard—no, Buglar. Little by little she stopped and their thirteen-year-old faces faded completely into their baby ones, which came to her only in sleep. When her dreams roamed outside 124, anywhere they wished, she saw them sometimes in beautiful trees, their little legs barely visible in the leaves. Sometimes they ran along the railroad track laughing, too loud, apparently, to hear her because they never did turn around. When she woke the house crowded in on her: there was the door where the soda crackers were lined up in a row; the white stairs her baby girl loved to climb; the corner where Baby Suggs mended shoes, a pile of which were still in the cold room; the exact place on the stove where Denver burned her fingers. And of course the spite of the house itself. There was no room for any other thing or body until Paul D arrived and broke up the place, making room, shifting it, moving it over to someplace else, then standing in the place he had made.

So, kneeling in the keeping room the morning after Paul D came, she was distracted by the two orange squares that signaled how barren 124 really was.

He was responsible for that. Emotions sped to the surface in his company. Things became what they were: drabness looked drab; heat was hot. Windows suddenly had view. And wouldn't you know he'd be a singing man.

*Little rice, little bean,*
*No meat in between.*
*Hard work ain't easy,*
*Dry bread ain't greasy.*

He was up now and singing as he mended things he had broken the day before. Some old pieces of song he'd learned on the prison farm or in the War afterward. Nothing like what they sang at Sweet Home, where yearning fashioned every note.

The songs he knew from Georgia were flat-headed nails for pounding and pounding and pounding.

*Lay my head on the railroad line,*
*Train come along, pacify my mind.*
*If I had my weight in lime,*
*I'd whip my captain till he went stone blind.*
*Five-cent nickel,*
*Ten-cent dime,*
*Busting rocks is busting time.*

But they didn't fit, these songs. They were too loud, had too much power for the little house chores he was engaged in—resetting table legs; glazing.

He couldn't go back to "Storm upon the Waters" that they sang under the trees of Sweet Home, so he contented himself with mmmmmmmmm, throwing in a line if one occurred to him, and what occurred over and over was "Bare feet and chamomile sap,/ Took off my shoes; took off my hat."

It was tempting to change the words (Gimme back my shoes; gimme back my hat), because he didn't believe he could live with a woman—any woman—for over two out of three months. That was about as long as he could abide one place. After Delaware and before that Alfred, Georgia, where he slept underground and crawled into sunlight for the sole purpose of breaking rock, walking off when he got ready was the only way he could convince himself that he would no longer have to sleep, pee, eat or swing a sledge hammer in chains.

But this was not a normal woman in a normal house. As soon

as he had stepped through the red light he knew that, compared to 124, the rest of the world was bald. After Alfred he had shut down a generous portion of his head, operating on the part that helped him walk, eat, sleep, sing. If he could do those things—with a little work and a little sex thrown in—he asked for no more, for more required him to dwell on Halle's face and Sixo laughing. To recall trembling in a box built into the ground. Grateful for the daylight spent doing mule work in a quarry because he did not tremble when he had a hammer in his hands. The box had done what Sweet Home had not, what working like an ass and living like a dog had not: drove him crazy so he would not lose his mind.

By the time he got to Ohio, then to Cincinnati, then to Halle Suggs' mother's house, he thought he had seen and felt it all. Even now as he put back the window frame he had smashed, he could not account for the pleasure in his surprise at seeing Halle's wife alive, barefoot with uncovered hair—walking around the corner of the house with her shoes and stockings in her hands. The closed portion of his head opened like a greased lock.

"I was thinking of looking for work around here. What you think?"

"Ain't much. River mostly. And hogs."

"Well, I never worked on water, but I can pick up anything heavy as me, hogs included."

"Whitepeople better here than Kentucky but you may have to scramble some."

"It ain't whether I scramble; it's where. You saying it's all right to scramble here?"

"Better than all right."

"Your girl, Denver. Seems to me she's of a different mind."

"Why you say that?"

"She's got a waiting way about her. Something she's expecting and it ain't me."

"I don't know what it could be."

"Well, whatever it is, she believes I'm interrupting it."

"Don't worry about her. She's a charmed child. From the beginning."

"Is that right?"

"Uh huh. Nothing bad can happen to her. Look at it. Everybody I knew dead or gone or dead and gone. Not her. Not my Denver. Even when I was carrying her, when it got clear that I wasn't going to make it—which meant she wasn't going to make it either—she pulled a whitegirl out of the hill. The last thing you'd expect to help. And when the schoolteacher found us and came busting in here with the law and a shotgun—"

"Schoolteacher found you?"

"Took a while, but he did. Finally."

"And he didn't take you back?"

"Oh, no. I wasn't going back there. I don't care who found who. Any life but not that one. I went to jail instead. Denver was just a baby so she went right along with me. Rats bit everything in there but her."

Paul D turned away. He wanted to know more about it, but jail talk put him back in Alfred, Georgia.

"I need some nails. Anybody around here I can borrow from or should I go to town?"

"May as well go to town. You'll need other things."

One night and they were talking like a couple. They had skipped love and promise and went directly to "You saying it's all right to scramble here?"

To Sethe, the future was a matter of keeping the past at bay. The "better life" she believed she and Denver were living was simply not that other one.

The fact that Paul D had come out of "that other one" into her bed was better too; and the notion of a future with him, or for that matter without him, was beginning to stroke her mind. As for Denver, the job Sethe had of keeping her from the past that was still waiting for her was all that mattered.

PLEASANTLY TROUBLED, Sethe avoided the keeping room and Denver's sidelong looks. As she expected, since life was like that—it didn't do any good. Denver ran a mighty interference and on the third day flat-out asked Paul D how long he was going to hang around.

The phrase hurt him so much he missed the table. The coffee cup hit the floor and rolled down the sloping boards toward the front door.

"Hang around?" Paul D didn't even look at the mess he had made.

"Denver! What's got into you?" Sethe looked at her daughter, feeling more embarrassed than angry.

Paul D scratched the hair on his chin. "Maybe I should make tracks."

"No!" Sethe was surprised by how loud she said it.

"He know what he needs," said Denver.

"Well, you don't," Sethe told her, "and you must not know what you need either. I don't want to hear another word out of you."

"I just asked if—"

"Hush! *You* make tracks. Go somewhere and sit down."

Denver picked up her plate and left the table but not before adding a chicken back and more bread to the heap she was carrying away. Paul D leaned over to wipe the spilled coffee with his blue handkerchief.

"I'll get that." Sethe jumped up and went to the stove. Behind it various cloths hung, each in some stage of drying. In silence she wiped the floor and retrieved the cup. Then she poured him another cupful, and set it carefully before him. Paul D touched its rim but didn't say anything—as though even "thank you" was an obligation he could not meet and the coffee itself a gift he could not take.

Sethe resumed her chair and the silence continued. Finally she realized that if it was going to be broken she would have to do it.

"I didn't train her like that."

Paul D stroked the rim of the cup.

"And I'm as surprised by her manners as you are hurt by em."

Paul D looked at Sethe. "Is there history to her question?"

"History? What you mean?"

"I mean, did she have to ask that, or want to ask it, of anybody else before me?"

Sethe made two fists and placed them on her hips. "You as bad as she is."

"Come on, Sethe."

"Oh, I am coming on. I am!"

"You know what I mean."

"I do and I don't like it."

"Jesus," he whispered.

"Who?" Sethe was getting loud again.

"Jesus! I said Jesus! All I did was sit down for supper! and I get cussed out twice. Once for being here and once for asking why I was cussed in the first place!"

"She didn't cuss."

"No? Felt like it."

"Look here. I apologize for her. I'm real—"

"You can't do that. You can't apologize for nobody. She got to do that."

"Then I'll see that she does." Sethe sighed.

"What I want to know is, is she asking a question that's on your mind too?"

"Oh no. No, Paul D. Oh no."

"Then she's of one mind and you another? If you can call whatever's in her head a mind, that is."

"Excuse me, but I can't hear a word against her. I'll chastise her. You leave her alone."

Risky, thought Paul D, very risky. For a used-to-be-slave woman to love anything that much was dangerous, especially if it was her children she had settled on to love. The best thing, he knew, was to love just a little bit; everything, just a little bit, so when they broke its back, or shoved it in a croaker sack, well, maybe you'd have a little love left over for the next one. "Why?" he asked her. "Why you think you have to take up for her? Apologize for her? She's grown."

"I don't care what she is. Grown don't mean nothing to a mother. A child is a child. They get bigger, older, but grown? What's that supposed to mean? In my heart it don't mean a thing."

"It means she has to take it if she acts up. You can't protect her every minute. What's going to happen when you die?"

"Nothing! I'll protect her while I'm live and I'll protect her when I ain't."

"Oh well, I'm through," he said. "I quit."

"That's the way it is, Paul D. I can't explain it to you no better than that, but that's the way it is. If I have to choose—well, it's not even a choice."

"That's the point. The whole point. I'm not asking you to choose. Nobody would. I thought—well, I thought you could—there was some space for me."

"She's asking me."

"You can't go by that. You got to say it to her. Tell her it's not about choosing somebody over her—it's making space for somebody along with her. You got to say it. And if you say it and mean it, then you also got to know you can't gag me. There's no way I'm going to hurt her or not take care of what she need if I can, but I can't be told to keep my mouth shut if she's acting ugly. You want me here, don't put no gag on me."

"Maybe I should leave things the way they are," she said.

"How are they?"

"We get along."

"What about inside?"

"I don't go inside."

"Sethe, if I'm here with you, with Denver, you can go anywhere you want. Jump, if you want to, 'cause I'll catch you, girl. I'll catch you 'fore you fall. Go as far inside as you need to, I'll hold your ankles. Make sure you get back out. I'm not saying this because I need a place to stay. That's the last thing I need. I told you, I'm a walking man, but I been heading in this direction for seven years. Walking all around this place. Upstate, downstate, east, west; I been in territory ain't got no name, never staying nowhere long. But when I got here and sat out there on the porch, waiting for you, well, I knew it wasn't the place I was heading toward; it was you. We can make a life, girl. A life."

"I don't know. I don't know."

"Leave it to me. See how it goes. No promises, if you don't want to make any. Just see how it goes. All right?"

"All right."

"You willing to leave it to me?"

"Well—some of it."

"Some?" he smiled. "Okay. Here's some. There's a carnival in town. Thursday, tomorrow, is for coloreds and I got two dollars. Me and you and Denver gonna spend every penny of it. What you say?"

"No" is what she said. At least what she started out saying (what would her boss say if she took a day off?), but even when she said it she was thinking how much her eyes enjoyed looking in his face.

The crickets were screaming on Thursday and the sky, stripped of blue, was white hot at eleven in the morning. Sethe was badly dressed for the heat, but this being her first social outing in eighteen years, she felt obliged to wear her one good dress, heavy as it was, and a hat. Certainly a hat. She didn't want to meet Lady Jones or Ella with her head wrapped like she was going to work. The dress, a good-wool castoff, was a Christmas present to Baby Suggs from Miss Bodwin, the whitewoman who loved her. Denver and Paul D fared better in the heat since neither felt the occasion required special clothing. Denver's bonnet knocked against her shoulder blades; Paul D wore his vest open, no jacket and his shirt sleeves rolled above his elbows. They were not holding hands, but their shadows were. Sethe looked to her left and all three of them were gliding over the dust holding hands. Maybe he was right. A life. Watching their hand-holding shadows, she was embarrassed at being dressed for church. The others, ahead and behind them, would think she was putting on airs, letting them know that she was different because she lived in a house with two stories; tougher, because she could do and survive things they believed she should neither do nor survive. She was glad Denver had resisted her urgings to dress up—rebraid her hair at least. But Denver was not doing anything to make this trip a pleasure. She agreed to go—sullenly—but her attitude was "Go 'head. Try and make me happy." The happy one was Paul D. He said howdy to everybody within twenty feet. Made fun of the weather and what it was doing to him, yelled back at the crows, and was the first to smell the doomed roses. All the time, no matter what they were doing— whether Denver wiped perspiration from her forehead or stooped to retie her shoes; whether Paul D kicked a stone or reached over to meddle a child's face leaning on its mother's shoulder—all the time the three shadows that shot out of their feet to the left held hands. Nobody noticed but Sethe and she stopped looking after she decided that it was a good sign. A life. Could be.

Up and down the lumberyard fence old roses were dying. The sawyer who had planted them twelve years ago to give his workplace a friendly feel—something to take the sin out of slicing trees for a living—was amazed by their abundance; how rapidly they crawled all over the stake-and-post fence that separated the lumberyard from the open field next to it where homeless men slept, children ran and, once a year, carnival people pitched tents. The closer the roses got to death, the louder their scent, and everybody who attended the carnival associated it with the stench of the rotten roses. It made them a little dizzy and very thirsty but did nothing to extinguish the eagerness of the coloredpeople filing down the road. Some walked on the grassy shoulders, others dodged the wagons creaking down the road's dusty center. All, like Paul D, were in high spirits, which the smell of dying roses (that Paul D called to everybody's attention) could not dampen. As they pressed to get to the rope entrance they were lit like lamps. Breathless with the excitement of seeing whitepeople loose: doing magic, clowning, without heads or with two heads, twenty feet tall or two feet tall, weighing a ton, completely tattooed, eating glass, swallowing fire, spitting ribbons, twisted into knots, forming pyramids, playing with snakes and beating each other up.

All of this was advertisement, read by those who could and heard by those who could not, and the fact that none of it was true did not extinguish their appetite a bit. The barker called them and their children names ("Pickaninnies free!") but the food on his vest and the hole in his pants rendered it fairly harmless. In any case it was a small price to pay for the fun they might not ever have again. Two pennies and an insult were well spent if it meant seeing the spectacle of whitefolks making a spectacle of themselves. So, although the carnival was a lot less than mediocre (which is why it agreed to a Colored Thursday), it gave the four hundred black people in its audience thrill upon thrill upon thrill.

One-Ton Lady spit at them, but her bulk shortened her aim and they got a big kick out of the helpless meanness in her little eyes. Arabian Nights Dancer cut her performance to three minutes instead of the usual fifteen she normally did—earning the gratitude of the children, who could hardly wait for Abu Snake Charmer, who followed her.

Denver bought horehound, licorice, peppermint and lemonade at a table manned by a little whitegirl in ladies' high-topped shoes. Soothed by sugar, surrounded by a crowd of people who did not find her the main attraction, who, in fact, said, "Hey, Denver," every now and then, pleased her enough to consider the possibility that Paul D wasn't all that bad. In fact there was something about him—when the three of them stood together watching Midget dance—that made the stares of other Negroes kind, gentle, something Denver did not remember seeing in their faces. Several even nodded and smiled at her mother, no one, apparently, able to withstand sharing the pleasure Paul D was having. He slapped his knees when Giant danced with Midget; when Two-Headed Man talked to himself. He bought everything Denver asked for and much she did not. He teased Sethe into tents she was reluctant to enter. Stuck pieces of candy she didn't want between her lips. When Wild African Savage shook his bars and said wa wa, Paul D told everybody he knew him back in Roanoke.

Paul D made a few acquaintances; spoke to them about what work he might find. Sethe returned the smiles she got. Denver was swaying with delight. And on the way home, although leading them now, the shadows of three people still held hands.

A FULLY DRESSED woman walked out of the water. She barely gained the dry bank of the stream before she sat down and leaned against a mulberry tree. All day and all night she sat there, her head resting on the trunk in a position abandoned enough to crack the brim in her straw hat. Everything hurt but her lungs most of all. Sopping wet and breathing shallow she spent those hours trying to negotiate the weight of her eyelids. The day breeze blew her dress dry; the night wind wrinkled it. Nobody saw her emerge or came accidentally by. If they had, chances are they would have hesitated before approaching her. Not because she was wet, or dozing or had what sounded like asthma, but because amid all that she was smiling. It took her the whole of the next morning to lift herself from the ground and make her way through the woods past a giant temple of boxwood to the field and then the yard of the slate-gray house. Exhausted again, she sat down on the first handy place—a stump not far from the steps of 124. By then keeping her eyes open was less of an effort. She could manage it for a full two minutes or more. Her neck, its circumference no wider than a parlor-service saucer, kept bending and her chin brushed the bit of lace edging her dress.

Women who drink champagne when there is nothing to celebrate can look like that: their straw hats with broken brims are often askew; they nod in public places; their shoes are undone. But their skin is not like that of the woman breathing near the steps of 124. She had new skin, lineless and smooth, including the knuckles of her hands.

By late afternoon when the carnival was over, and the Negroes were hitching rides home if they were lucky—walking if they were not—the woman had fallen asleep again. The rays of the sun struck her full in the face, so that when Sethe, Denver and Paul D rounded the curve in the road all they saw was a black dress, two unlaced shoes below it, and Here Boy nowhere in sight.

"Look," said Denver. "What is that?"

And, for some reason she could not immediately account for, the moment she got close enough to see the face, Sethe's bladder filled to capacity. She said, "Oh, excuse me," and ran around to the back of 124. Not since she was a baby girl, being cared for by the eight-year-old girl who pointed out her mother to her, had she had an emergency that unmanageable. She never made the outhouse. Right in front of its door she had to lift her skirts, and the water she voided was endless. Like a horse, she thought, but as it went on and on she thought, No, more like flooding the boat when Denver was born. So much water Amy said, "Hold on, Lu. You going to sink us you keep that up." But there was no stopping water breaking from a breaking womb and there was no stopping now. She hoped Paul D wouldn't take it upon himself to come looking for her and be obliged to see her squatting in front of her own privy making a mudhole too deep to be witnessed without shame. Just about the time she started wondering if the carnival would accept another freak, it stopped. She tidied herself and ran around to the porch. No one was there. All three were inside—Paul D and Denver standing before the stranger, watching her drink cup after cup of water.

"She said she was thirsty," said Paul D. He took off his cap. "Mighty thirsty look like."

The woman gulped water from a speckled tin cup and held it out for more. Four times Denver filled it, and four times the woman drank as though she had crossed a desert. When she was finished a little water was on her chin, but she did not wipe it away. Instead she gazed at Sethe with sleepy eyes. Poorly fed, thought Sethe, and younger than her clothes suggested—good lace at the throat, and a rich woman's hat. Her skin was flawless except for three vertical scratches on her forehead so fine and thin they seemed at first like hair, baby hair before it bloomed and roped into the masses of black yarn under her hat.

"You from around here?" Sethe asked her.

She shook her head no and reached down to take off her shoes. She pulled her dress up to the knees and rolled down her stockings. When the hosiery was tucked into the shoes, Sethe saw that her feet were like her hands, soft and new. She must have hitched a wagon ride, thought Sethe. Probably one of those West Virginia girls looking for something to beat a life of tobacco and sorghum. Sethe bent to pick up the shoes.

"What might your name be?" asked Paul D.

"Beloved," she said, and her voice was so low and rough each one looked at the other two. They heard the voice first—later the name.

"Beloved. You use a last name, Beloved?" Paul D asked her.

"Last?" She seemed puzzled. Then "No," and she spelled it for them, slowly as though the letters were being formed as she spoke them.

Sethe dropped the shoes; Denver sat down and Paul D smiled. He recognized the careful enunciation of letters by those, like himself, who could not read but had memorized the letters of their name. He was about to ask who her people were but thought better of it. A young coloredwoman drifting was drifting from ruin. He had been in Rochester four years ago and seen five women arriving with fourteen female children. All their men—brothers, uncles, fathers, husbands, sons—had been picked off one by one by one. They had a single piece of paper directing them to a preacher on DeVore Street. The War had been over four or five years then, but nobody white or black seemed to know it. Odd clusters and strays of Negroes wandered the back roads and cowpaths from Schenectady to Jackson. Dazed but insistent, they searched each other out for word of a cousin, an aunt, a friend who once said, "Call on me. Anytime you get near Chicago, just call on me." Some of them were running from family that could not support them, some to family; some were running from dead crops, dead kin, life threats, and took-over land. Boys younger than Buglar and Howard; configurations and blends of families of women and children, while elsewhere, solitary, hunted and hunting for, were men, men, men. Forbidden public transportation, chased by debt and filthy "talking sheets," they followed secondary routes, scanned the horizon for signs and counted heavily on each other. Silent, except for social courtesies, when they met one another they neither described nor asked about the sorrow that drove them from one place to another. The whites didn't bear speaking on. Everybody knew.

So he did not press the young woman with the broken hat about where from or how come. If she wanted them to know and was strong enough to get through the telling, she would. What occupied them at the moment was what it might be that she needed. Underneath the major question, each harbored another. Paul D wondered at the newness of her shoes. Sethe was deeply touched by her sweet name; the remembrance of glittering headstone made her feel especially kindly toward her. Denver, however, was shaking. She looked at this sleepy beauty and wanted more.

Sethe hung her hat on a peg and turned graciously toward the girl. "That's a pretty name, Beloved. Take off your hat, why don't you, and I'll make us something. We just got back from the carnival over near Cincinnati. Everything in there is something to see."

Bolt upright in the chair, in the middle of Sethe's welcome, Beloved had fallen asleep again.

"Miss. Miss." Paul D shook her gently. "You want to lay down a spell?"

She opened her eyes to slits and stood up on her soft new feet which, barely capable of their job, slowly bore her to the keeping room. Once there, she collapsed on Baby Suggs' bed. Denver removed her hat and put the quilt with two squares of color over her feet. She was breathing like a steam engine.

"Sounds like croup," said Paul D, closing the door.

"Is she feverish? Denver, could you tell?"

"No. She's cold."

"Then she is. Fever goes from hot to cold."

"Could have the cholera," said Paul D.

"Reckon?"

"All that water. Sure sign."

"Poor thing. And nothing in this house to give her for it. She'll just have to ride it out. That's a hateful sickness if ever there was one."

"She's not sick!" said Denver, and the passion in her voice made them smile.

Four days she slept, waking and sitting up only for water. Denver tended her, watched her sound sleep, listened to her labored breathing and, out of love and a breakneck possessiveness that charged her, hid like a personal blemish Beloved's incontinence. She rinsed the sheets secretly, after Sethe went to the restaurant and Paul D went scrounging for barges to help unload. She boiled the underwear and soaked it in bluing, praying the fever would pass without damage. So intent was her nursing, she forgot to eat or visit the emerald closet.

"Beloved?" Denver would whisper. "Beloved?" and when the black eyes opened a slice all she could say was "I'm here. I'm still here."

Sometimes, when Beloved lay dreamy-eyed for a very long time, saying nothing, licking her lips and heaving deep sighs, Denver panicked. "What is it?" she would ask.

"Heavy," murmured Beloved. "This place is heavy."

"Would you like to sit up?"

"No," said the raspy voice.

It took three days for Beloved to notice the orange patches in the darkness of the quilt. Denver was pleased because it kept her patient awake longer. She seemed totally taken with those faded scraps of orange, even made the effort to lean on her elbow and stroke them. An effort that quickly exhausted her, so Denver rearranged the quilt so its cheeriest part was in the sick girl's sight line.

Patience, something Denver had never known, overtook her. As long as her mother did not interfere, she was a model of compassion, turning waspish, though, when Sethe tried to help.

"Did she take a spoonful of anything today?" Sethe inquired.

"She shouldn't eat with cholera."

"You sure that's it? Was just a hunch of Paul D's."

"I don't know, but she shouldn't eat anyway just yet."

"I think cholera people puke all the time."

"That's even more reason, ain't it?"

"Well she shouldn't starve to death either, Denver."

"Leave us alone, Ma'am. I'm taking care of her."

"She say anything?"

"I'd let you know if she did."

Sethe looked at her daughter and thought, Yes, she has been lonesome. Very lonesome.

"Wonder where Here Boy got off to?" Sethe thought a change of subject was needed.

"He won't be back," said Denver.

"How you know?"

"I just know." Denver took a square of sweet bread off the plate.

Back in the keeping room, Denver was about to sit down when Beloved's eyes flew wide open. Denver felt her heart race. It wasn't that she was looking at that face for the first time with no trace of sleep in it, or that the eyes were big and black. Nor was it that the whites of them were much too white—blue-white. It was that deep down in those big black eyes there was no expression at all.

"Can I get you something?"

Beloved looked at the sweet bread in Denver's hands and Denver held it out to her. She smiled then and Denver's heart stopped bouncing and sat down—relieved and easeful like a traveler who had made it home.

From that moment and through everything that followed, sugar could always be counted on to please her. It was as though sweet things were what she was born for. Honey as well as the wax it came in, sugar sandwiches, the sludgy molasses gone hard and brutal in the can, lemonade, taffy and any type of dessert Sethe brought home from the restaurant. She gnawed a cane stick to flax and kept the strings in her mouth long after the syrup had been sucked away. Denver laughed, Sethe smiled and Paul D said it made him sick to his stomach.

Sethe believed it was a recovering body's need—after an illness—for quick strength. But it was a need that went on and on into glowing health because Beloved didn't go anywhere. There didn't seem anyplace for her to go. She didn't mention one, or have much of an idea of what she was doing in that part of the country or where she had been. They believed the fever had caused her memory to fail just as it kept her slow-moving. A young woman, about nineteen or twenty, and slender, she moved like a heavier one or an older one, holding on to furniture, resting her head in the palm of her hand as though it was too heavy for a neck alone.

"You just gonna feed her? From now on?" Paul D, feeling ungenerous, and surprised by it, heard the irritability in his voice.

"Denver likes her. She's no real trouble. I thought we'd wait till her breath was better. She still sounds a little lumbar to me."

"Something funny 'bout that gal," Paul D said, mostly to himself.

"Funny how?"

"Acts sick, sounds sick, but she don't look sick. Good skin, bright eyes and strong as a bull."

"She's not strong. She can hardly walk without holding on to something."

"That's what I mean. Can't walk, but I seen her pick up the rocker with one hand."

"You didn't."

"Don't tell *me*. Ask Denver. She was right there with her."

"Denver! Come in here a minute."

Denver stopped rinsing the porch and stuck her head in the window.

"Paul D says you and him saw Beloved pick up the rocking chair single-handed. That so?"

Long, heavy lashes made Denver's eyes seem busier than they were; deceptive, even when she held a steady gaze as she did now on Paul D. "No," she said. "I didn't see no such thing."

Paul D frowned but said nothing. If there had been an open latch between them, it would have closed.

RAINWATER held on to pine needles for dear life and Beloved could not take her eyes off Sethe. Stooping to shake the damper, or snapping sticks for kindlin, Sethe was licked, tasted, eaten by Beloved's eyes. Like a familiar, she hovered, never leaving the room Sethe was in unless required and told to. She rose early in the dark to be there, waiting, in the kitchen when Sethe came down to make fast bread before she left for work. In lamplight, and over the flames of the cooking stove, their two shadows clashed and crossed on the ceiling like black swords. She was in the window at two when Sethe returned, or the doorway; then the porch, its steps, the path, the road, till finally, surrendering to the habit, Beloved began inching down Bluestone Road further and further each day to meet Sethe and walk her back to 124. It was as though every afternoon she doubted anew the older woman's return.

Sethe was flattered by Beloved's open, quiet devotion. The same adoration from her daughter (had it been forthcoming) would have annoyed her; made her chill at the thought of having raised a ridiculously dependent child. But the company of this sweet, if peculiar, guest pleased her the way a zealot pleases his teacher.

Time came when lamps had to be lit early because night arrived sooner and sooner. Sethe was leaving for work in the dark; Paul D was walking home in it. On one such evening dark and cool, Sethe cut a rutabaga into four pieces and left them stewing. She gave Denver a half peck of peas to sort and soak overnight. Then she sat herself down to rest. The heat of the stove made her drowsy and she was sliding into sleep when she felt Beloved touch her. A touch no heavier than a feather but loaded, nevertheless, with desire. Sethe stirred and looked around. First at Beloved's soft new hand on her shoulder, then into her eyes. The longing she saw there was bottomless. Some plea barely in control. Sethe patted Beloved's fingers and glanced at Denver, whose eyes were fixed on her pea-sorting task.

"Where your diamonds?" Beloved searched Sethe's face.

"Diamonds? What would I be doing with diamonds?"

"On your ears."

"Wish I did. I had some crystal once. A present from a lady I worked for."

"Tell me," said Beloved, smiling a wide happy smile. "Tell me your diamonds."

It became a way to feed her. Just as Denver discovered and relied on the delightful effect sweet things had on Beloved, Sethe learned the profound satisfaction Beloved got from storytelling. It amazed Sethe (as much as it pleased Beloved) because every mention of her past life hurt. Everything in it was painful or lost. She and Baby Suggs had agreed without saying so that it was unspeakable; to Denver's inquiries Sethe gave short replies or rambling incomplete reveries. Even with Paul D, who had shared some of it and to whom she could talk with at least a measure of calm, the hurt was always there—like a tender place in the corner of her mouth that the bit left.

But, as she began telling about the earrings, she found herself wanting to, liking it. Perhaps it was Beloved's distance from the events itself, or her thirst for hearing it—in any case it was an unexpected pleasure.

Above the patter of the pea sorting and the sharp odor of cooking rutabaga, Sethe explained the crystal that once hung from her ears.

"That lady I worked for in Kentucky gave them to me when I got married. What they called married back there and back then. I guess she saw how bad I felt when I found out there wasn't going to be no ceremony, no preacher. Nothing. I thought there should be something—something to say it was right and true. I didn't want it to be just me moving over a bit of pallet full of corn husks. Or just me bringing my night bucket into his cabin. I thought there should be some ceremony. Dancing maybe. A little sweet william in my hair." Sethe smiled. "I never saw a wedding, but I saw Mrs. Garner's wedding gown in the press, and heard her go on about what it was like. Two pounds of currants in the cake, she said, and four whole sheep. The people were still eating the next day. That's what I wanted. A meal maybe, where me and Halle and all the Sweet Home men sat down and ate something special. Invite some of the other colored-people from over by Covington or High Trees—those places Sixo used to sneak off to. But it wasn't going to be nothing. They said it was all right for us to be husband and wife and that was it. All of it.

"Well, I made up my mind to have at the least a dress that wasn't the sacking I worked in. So I took to stealing fabric, and wound up with a dress you wouldn't believe. The top was from two pillow cases in her mending basket. The front of the skirt was a dresser scarf a candle fell on and burnt a hole in, and one of her old sashes we used to test the flatiron on. Now the back was a problem for the longest time. Seem like I couldn't find a thing that wouldn't be missed right away. Because I had to take it apart afterwards and put all the pieces back where they were. Now Halle was patient, waiting for me to finish it. He knew I wouldn't go ahead without having it. Finally I took the mosquito netting from a nail out the barn. We used it to strain jelly through. I washed it and soaked it best I could and tacked it on for the back of the skirt. And there I was, in the worst-looking gown you could imagine. Only my wool shawl kept me from looking like a haint peddling. I wasn't but fourteen years old, so I reckon that's why I was so proud of myself.

"Anyhow, Mrs. Garner must have seen me in it. I thought I was stealing smart, and she knew everything I did. Even our honeymoon: going down to the cornfield with Halle. That's where we went first. A Saturday afternoon it was. He begged sick so he wouldn't have to go work in town that day. Usually he worked Saturdays and Sundays to pay off Baby Suggs' freedom. But he begged sick and I put on my dress and we walked into the corn holding hands. I can still smell the ears roasting yonder where the Pauls and Sixo was. Next day Mrs. Garner crooked her finger at me and took me upstairs to her bedroom. She opened up a wooden box and took out a pair of crystal earrings. She said, 'I want you to have these, Sethe.' I said, 'Yes, ma'am.' 'Are your ears pierced?' she said. I said, 'No, ma'am.' 'Well do it,' she said, 'so you can wear them. I want you to have them and I want you and Halle to be happy.' I thanked her but I never did put them on till I got away from there. One day after I walked into this here house Baby Suggs unknotted my underskirt and took em out. I sat right here by the stove with Denver in my arms and let her punch holes in my ears for to wear them."

"I never saw you in no earrings," said Denver. "Where are they now?"

"Gone," said Sethe. "Long gone," and she wouldn't say another word. Until the next time when all three of them ran through the wind back into the house with rainsoaked sheets and petticoats. Panting, laughing, they draped the laundry over the chairs and table. Beloved filled herself with water from the bucket and watched while Sethe rubbed Denver's hair with a piece of toweling.

"Maybe we should unbraid it?" asked Sethe.

"Uh uh. Tomorrow." Denver crouched forward at the thought of a fine-tooth comb pulling her hair.

"Today is always here," said Sethe. "Tomorrow, never."

"It hurts," Denver said.

"Comb it every day, it won't."

"Ouch."

"Your woman she never fix up your hair?" Beloved asked.

Sethe and Denver looked up at her. After four weeks they still had not got used to the gravelly voice and the song that seemed to lie in it. Just outside music it lay, with a cadence not like theirs.

"Your woman she never fix up your hair?" was clearly a question for Sethe, since that's who she was looking at.

"My woman? You mean my mother? If she did, I don't remember. I didn't see her but a few times out in the fields and once when she was working indigo. By the time I woke up in the morning, she was in line. If the moon was bright they worked by its light. Sunday she slept like a stick. She must of nursed me two or three weeks—that's the way the others did. Then she went back in rice and I sucked from another woman whose job it was. So to answer you, no. I reckon not. She never fixed my hair nor nothing. She didn't even sleep in the same cabin most nights I remember. Too far from the line-up, I guess. One thing she did do. She picked me up and carried me behind the smokehouse. Back there she opened up her dress front and lifted her breast and pointed under it. Right on her rib was a circle and a cross burnt right in the skin. She said, 'This is your ma'am. This,' and she pointed. 'I am the only one got this mark now. The rest dead. If something happens to me and you can't tell me by my face, you can know me by this mark.' Scared me so. All I could think of was how important this was and how I needed to have something important to say back, but I couldn't think of anything so I just said what I thought. 'Yes, Ma'am,' I said. 'But how will you know me? How will you know me? Mark me, too,' I said. 'Mark the mark on me too.' " Sethe chuckled.

"Did she?" asked Denver.

"She slapped my face."

"What for?"

"I didn't understand it then. Not till I had a mark of my own."

"What happened to her?"

"Hung. By the time they cut her down nobody could tell whether she had a circle and a cross or not, least of all me and I did look." Sethe gathered hair from the comb and leaning back tossed it into the fire. It exploded into stars and the smell infuriated them. "Oh, my Jesus," she said and stood up so suddenly the comb she had parked in Denver's hair fell to the floor.

"Ma'am? What's the matter with you, Ma'am?"

Sethe walked over to a chair, lifted a sheet and stretched it as wide as her arms would go. Then she folded, refolded and double-folded it. She took another. Neither was completely dry but the folding felt too fine to stop. She had to do something with her hands because she was remembering something she had forgotten she knew. Something privately shameful that had seeped into a slit in her mind right behind the slap on her face and the circled cross.

"Why they hang your ma'am?" Denver asked. This was the first time she had heard anything about her mother's mother. Baby Suggs was the only grandmother she knew.

"I never found out. It was a lot of them," she said, but what was getting clear and clearer as she folded and refolded damp laundry was the woman called Nan who took her hand and yanked her away from the pile before she could make out the mark. Nan was the one she knew best, who was around all day, who nursed babies, cooked, had one good arm and half of another. And who used different words. Words Sethe understood then but could neither recall nor repeat now. She believed that must be why she remembered so little before Sweet Home except singing and dancing and how crowded it was. What Nan told her she had forgotten, along with the language she told it in. The same language her ma'am spoke, and which would never come back. But the message—that was and had been there all along. Holding the damp white sheets against her chest, she was picking meaning out of a code she no longer understood. Nighttime. Nan holding her with her good arm, waving the stump of the other in the air. "Telling you. I am telling you, small girl Sethe," and she did that. She told Sethe that her mother and Nan were together from the sea. Both were taken up many times by the crew. "She threw them all away but you. The one from the crew she threw away on the island. The others from more whites she also threw away. Without names, she threw them. You she gave the name of the black man. She put her arms around him. The others she did not put her arms around. Never. Never. Telling you. I am telling you, small girl Sethe."

As small girl Sethe, she was unimpressed. As grown-up woman Sethe she was angry, but not certain at what. A mighty wish for Baby Suggs broke over her like surf. In the quiet following its splash, Sethe looked at the two girls sitting by the stove: her sickly, shallow-minded boarder, her irritable, lonely daughter. They seemed little and far away.

"Paul D be here in a minute," she said.

Denver sighed with relief. For a minute there, while her mother stood folding the wash lost in thought, she clamped her teeth and prayed it would stop. Denver hated the stories her mother told that did not concern herself, which is why Amy was all she ever asked about. The rest was a gleaming, powerful world made more so by Denver's absence from it. Not being in it, she hated it and wanted Beloved to hate it too, although there was no chance of that at all. Beloved took every opportunity to ask some funny question and get

Sethe going. Denver noticed how greedy she was to hear Sethe talk. Now she noticed something more. The questions Beloved asked: "Where your diamonds?" "Your woman she never fix up your hair?" And most perplexing: Tell me your earrings.

How did she know?

BELOVED WAS shining and Paul D didn't like it. Women did what strawberry plants did before they shot out their thin vines: the quality of the green changed. Then the vine threads came, then the buds. By the time the white petals died and the mint-colored berry poked out, the leaf shine was gilded tight and waxy. That's how Beloved looked—gilded and shining. Paul D took to having Sethe on waking, so that later, when he went down the white stairs where she made bread under Beloved's gaze, his head was clear.

In the evening when he came home and the three of them were all there fixing the supper table, her shine was so pronounced he wondered why Denver and Sethe didn't see it. Or maybe they did. Certainly women could tell, as men could, when one of their number was aroused. Paul D looked carefully at Beloved to see if she was aware of it but she paid him no attention at all—frequently not even answering a direct question put to her. She would look at him and not open her mouth. Five weeks she had been with them, and they didn't know any more about her than they did when they found her asleep on the stump.

They were seated at the table Paul D had broken the day he arrived at 124. Its mended legs stronger than before. The cabbage was all gone and the shiny ankle bones of smoked pork were pushed in a heap on their plates. Sethe was dishing up bread pudding, murmuring her hopes for it, apologizing in advance the way veteran cooks always do, when something in Beloved's face, some petlike adoration that took hold of her as she looked at Sethe, made Paul D speak.

"Ain't you got no brothers or sisters?"

Beloved diddled her spoon but did not look at him. "I don't have nobody."

"What was you looking for when you came here?" he asked her.

"This place. I was looking for this place I could be in."

"Somebody tell you about this house?"

"She told me. When I was at the bridge, she told me."

"Must be somebody from the old days," Sethe said. The days when 124 was a way station where messages came and then their senders. Where bits of news soaked like dried beans in spring water— until they were soft enough to digest.

"How'd you come? Who brought you?"

Now she looked steadily at him, but did not answer.

He could feel both Sethe and Denver pulling in, holding their stomach muscles, sending out sticky spiderwebs to touch one another. He decided to force it anyway.

"I asked you who brought you here?"

"I walked here," she said. "A long, long, long, long way. Nobody bring me. Nobody help me."

"You had new shoes. If you walked so long why don't your shoes show it?"

"Paul D, stop picking on her."

"I want to know," he said, holding the knife handle in his fist like a pole.

"I take the shoes! I take the dress! The shoe strings don't fix!" she shouted and gave him a look so malevolent Denver touched her arm.

"I'll teach you," said Denver, "how to tie your shoes," and got a smile from Beloved as a reward.

Paul D had the feeling a large, silver fish had slipped from his hands the minute he grabbed hold of its tail. That it was streaming back off into dark water now, gone but for the glistening marking its route. But if her shining was not for him, who then? He had never known a woman who lit up for nobody in particular, who just did it as a general announcement. Always, in his experience, the light appeared when there was focus. Like the Thirty-Mile Woman, dulled to smoke while he waited with her in the ditch, and starlight when

Sixo got there. He never knew himself to mistake it. It was there the instant he looked at Sethe's wet legs, otherwise he never would have been bold enough to enclose her in his arms that day and whisper into her back.

This girl Beloved, homeless and without people, beat all, though he couldn't say exactly why, considering the coloredpeople he had run into during the last twenty years. During, before and after the War he had seen Negroes so stunned, or hungry, or tired or bereft it was a wonder they recalled or said anything. Who, like him, had hidden in caves and fought owls for food; who, like him, stole from pigs; who, like him, slept in trees in the day and walked by night; who, like him, had buried themselves in slop and jumped in wells to avoid regulators, raiders, paterollers, veterans, hill men, posses and merrymakers. Once he met a Negro about fourteen years old who lived by himself in the woods and said he couldn't remember living anywhere else. He saw a witless coloredwoman jailed and hanged for stealing ducks she believed were her own babies.

Move. Walk. Run. Hide. Steal and move on. Only once had it been possible for him to stay in one spot—with a woman, or a family—for longer than a few months. That once was almost two years with a weaver lady in Delaware, the meanest place for Negroes he had ever seen outside Pulaski County, Kentucky, and of course the prison camp in Georgia.

From all those Negroes, Beloved was different. Her shining, her new shoes. It bothered him. Maybe it was just the fact that he didn't bother her. Or it could be timing. She had appeared and been taken in on the very day Sethe and he had patched up their quarrel, gone out in public and had a right good time—like a family. Denver had come around, so to speak; Sethe was laughing; he had a promise of steady work, 124 was cleared up from spirits. It had begun to look like a life. And damn! a water-drinking woman fell sick, got took in, healed, and hadn't moved a peg since.

He wanted her out, but Sethe had let her in and he couldn't put her out of a house that wasn't his. It was one thing to beat up a ghost, quite another to throw a helpless coloredgirl out in territory infected by the Klan. Desperately thirsty for black blood, without which it could not live, the dragon swam the Ohio at will.

Sitting at table, chewing on his after-supper broom straw, Paul D decided to place her. Consult with the Negroes in town and find her her own place.

No sooner did he have the thought than Beloved strangled on one of the raisins she had picked out of the bread pudding. She fell backward and off the chair and thrashed around holding her throat. Sethe knocked her on the back while Denver pried her hands away from her neck. Beloved, on her hands and knees, vomited up her food and struggled for breath.

When she was quiet and Denver had wiped up the mess, she said, "Go to sleep now."

"Come in my room," said Denver. "I can watch out for you up there."

No moment could have been better. Denver had worried herself sick trying to think of a way to get Beloved to share her room. It was hard sleeping above her, wondering if she was going to be sick again, fall asleep and not wake, or (God, please don't) get up and wander out of the yard just the way she wandered in. They could have their talks easier there: at night when Sethe and Paul D were asleep; or in the daytime before either came home. Sweet, crazy conversations full of half sentences, daydreams and misunderstandings more thrilling than understanding could ever be.

When the girls left, Sethe began to clear the table. She stacked the plates near a basin of water.

"What is it about her vex you so?"

Paul D frowned, but said nothing.

"We had one good fight about Denver. Do we need one about her too?" asked Sethe.

"I just don't understand what the hold is. It's clear why she holds on to you, but I just can't see why you holding on to her."

Sethe turned away from the plates toward him. "What you care who's holding on to who? Feeding her is no trouble. I pick up a little extra from the restaurant is all. And she's nice girl company for Denver. You know that and I know you know it, so what is it got your teeth on edge?"

"I can't place it. It's a feeling in me."

"Well, feel this, why don't you? Feel how it feels to have a bed to sleep in and somebody there not worrying you to death about what you got to do each day to deserve it. Feel how that feels. And if that don't get it, feel how it feels to be a coloredwoman roaming the roads with anything God made liable to jump on you. Feel that."

"I know every bit of that, Sethe. I wasn't born yesterday and I never mistreated a woman in my life."

"That makes one in the world," Sethe answered.

"Not two?"

"No. Not two."

"What Halle ever do to you? Halle stood by you. He never left you."

"What'd he leave then if not me?"

"I don't know, but it wasn't you. That's a fact."

"Then he did worse; he left his children."

"You don't know that."

"He wasn't there. He wasn't where he said he would be."

"He was there."

"Then why didn't he show himself? Why did I have to pack my babies off and stay behind to look for him?"

"He couldn't get out the loft."

"Loft? What loft?"

"The one over your head. In the barn."

Slowly, slowly, taking all the time allowed, Sethe moved toward the table.

"He saw?"

"He saw."

"He told you?"

"You told me."

"What?"

"The day I came in here. You said they stole your milk. I never knew what it was that messed him up. That was it, I guess. All I knew was that something broke him. Not a one of them years of Saturdays, Sundays and nighttime extra never touched him. But whatever he saw go on in that barn that day broke him like a twig."

"He saw?" Sethe was gripping her elbows as though to keep them from flying away.

"He saw. Must have."

"He saw them boys do that to me and let them keep on breathing air? He saw? He saw? He saw?"

"Hey! Hey! Listen up. Let me tell you something. A man ain't a goddamn ax. Chopping, hacking, busting every goddamn minute of the day. Things get to him. Things he can't chop down because they're inside."

Sethe was pacing up and down, up and down in the lamplight. "The underground agent said, By Sunday. They took my milk and he saw it and didn't come down? Sunday came and he didn't. Monday came and no Halle. I thought he was dead, that's why; then I thought they caught him, that's why. Then I thought, No, he's not dead because if he was I'd know it, and then you come here after all this time and you didn't say he was dead, because you didn't know either, so I thought, Well, he just found him another better way to live. Because if he was anywhere near here, he'd come to Baby Suggs, if not to me. But I never knew he saw."

"What does that matter now?"

"If he is alive, and saw that, he won't step foot in my door. Not Halle."

"It broke him, Sethe." Paul D looked up at her and sighed. "You may as well know it all. Last time I saw him he was sitting by the churn. He had butter all over his face."

Nothing happened, and she was grateful for that. Usually she could see the picture right away of what she heard. But she could not picture what Paul D said. Nothing came to mind. Carefully, carefully, she passed on to a reasonable question.

"What did he say?"

"Nothing."

"Not a word?"

"Not a word."

"Did you speak to him? Didn't you say anything to him? Something!"

"I couldn't, Sethe. I just . . . couldn't."

"Why!"

"I had a bit in my mouth."

Sethe opened the front door and sat down on the porch steps. The day had gone blue without its sun, but she could still make out the black silhouettes of trees in the meadow beyond. She shook her head from side to side, resigned to her rebellious brain. Why was there nothing it refused? No misery, no regret, no hateful picture too rotten to accept? Like a greedy child it snatched up everything. Just once, could it say, No thank you? I just ate and can't hold another bite? I am full God damn it of two boys with mossy teeth, one sucking on my breast the other holding me down, their book-reading teacher watching and writing it up. I am still full of that, God damn it, I can't go back and add more. Add my husband to it, watching, above me in the loft—hiding close by—the one place he thought no one would look for him, looking down on what I couldn't look at at all. And not stopping them—looking and letting it happen. But my greedy brain says, Oh thanks, I'd love more—so I add more. And no sooner than I do, there is no stopping. There is also my husband squatting by the churn smearing the butter as well as its clabber all over his face because the milk they took is on his mind. And as far as he is concerned, the world may as well know it. And if he was that broken then, then he is also and certainly dead now. And if Paul D saw him and could not save or comfort him because the iron bit was in his mouth, then there is still more that Paul D could tell me and my brain would go right ahead and take it and never say, No thank you. I don't want to know or have to remember that. I have other things to do: worry, for example, about tomorrow, about Denver, about Beloved, about age and sickness not to speak of love.

But her brain was not interested in the future. Loaded with the past and hungry for more, it left her no room to imagine, let alone plan for, the next day. Exactly like that afternoon in the wild onions—when one more step was the most she could see of the future. Other people went crazy, why couldn't she? Other people's brains stopped, turned around and went on to something new, which is what must have happened to Halle. And how sweet that would have been: the two of them back by the milk shed, squatting by the churn, smashing cold, lumpy butter into their faces with not a care in the world. Feeling it slippery, sticky—rubbing it in their hair, watching it squeeze through their fingers. What a relief to stop it right there. Close. Shut. Squeeze the butter. But her three children were chewing sugar teat under a blanket on their way to Ohio and no butter play would change that.

Paul D stepped through the door and touched her shoulder.

"I didn't plan on telling you that."

"I didn't plan on hearing it."

"I can't take it back, but I can leave it alone," Paul D said.

He wants to tell me, she thought. He wants me to ask him about what it was like for him—about how offended the tongue is, held down by iron, how the need to spit is so deep you cry for it. She already knew about it, had seen it time after time in the place before Sweet Home. Men, boys, little girls, women. The wildness that shot up into the eye the moment the lips were yanked back. Days after it was taken out, goose fat was rubbed on the corners of the mouth but nothing to soothe the tongue or take the wildness out of the eye.

Sethe looked up into Paul D's eyes to see if there was any trace left in them.

"People I saw as a child," she said, "who'd had the bit always looked wild after that. Whatever they used it on them for, it couldn't have worked, because it put a wildness where before there wasn't any. When I look at you, I don't see it. There ain't no wildness in your eye nowhere."

"There's a way to put it there and there's a way to take it out. I know em both and I haven't figured out yet which is worse." He sat down beside her. Sethe looked at him. In that unlit daylight his face, bronzed and reduced to its bones, smoothed her heart down.

"You want to tell me about it?" she asked him.

"I don't know. I never have talked about it. Not to a soul. Sang it sometimes, but I never told a soul."

"Go ahead. I can hear it."

"Maybe. Maybe you can hear it. I just ain't sure I can say it. Say it right, I mean, because it wasn't the bit—that wasn't it."

"What then?" Sethe asked.

"The roosters," he said. "Walking past the roosters looking at them look at me."

Sethe smiled. "In that pine?"

"Yeah." Paul D smiled with her. "Must have been five of them perched up there, and at least fifty hens."

"Mister, too?"

"Not right off. But I hadn't took twenty steps before I seen him. He come down off the fence post there and sat on the tub."

"He loved that tub," said Sethe, thinking, No, there is no stopping now.

"Didn't he? Like a throne. Was me took him out the shell, you know. He'd a died if it hadn't been for me. The hen had walked on off with all the hatched peeps trailing behind her. There was this one egg left. Looked like a blank, but then I saw it move so I tapped it open and here come Mister, bad feet and all. I watched that son a bitch grow up and whup everything in the yard."

"He always was hateful," Sethe said.

"Yeah, he was hateful all right. Bloody too, and evil. Crooked feet flapping. Comb as big as my hand and some kind of red. He sat right there on the tub looking at me. I swear he smiled. My head was full of what I'd seen of Halle a while back. I wasn't even thinking about the bit. Just Halle and before him Sixo, but when I saw Mister I knew it was me too. Not just them, me too. One crazy, one sold, one missing, one burnt and me licking iron with my hands crossed behind me. The last of the Sweet Home men.

"Mister, he looked so . . . free. Better than me. Stronger, tougher. Son a bitch couldn't even get out the shell by hisself but he was still king and I was . . ." Paul D stopped and squeezed his left hand with his right. He held it that way long enough for it and the world to quiet down and let him go on.

"Mister was allowed to be and stay what he was. But I wasn't allowed to be and stay what I was. Even if you cooked him you'd be cooking a rooster named Mister. But wasn't no way I'd ever be Paul D again, living or dead. Schoolteacher changed me. I was something else and that something was less than a chicken sitting in the sun on a tub."

Sethe put her hand on his knee and rubbed.

Paul D had only begun, what he was telling her was only the beginning when her fingers on his knee, soft and reassuring, stopped him. Just as well. Just as well. Saying more might push them both to a place they couldn't get back from. He would keep the rest where it belonged: in that tobacco tin buried in his chest where a red heart used to be. Its lid rusted shut. He would not pry it loose now in front of this sweet sturdy woman, for if she got a whiff of the contents it would shame him. And it would hurt her to know that there was no red heart bright as Mister's comb beating in him.

Sethe rubbed and rubbed, pressing the work cloth and the stony curves that made up his knee. She hoped it calmed him as it did her. Like kneading bread in the half-light of the restaurant kitchen. Before the cook arrived when she stood in a space no wider than a bench is long, back behind and to the left of the milk cans. Working dough. Working, working dough. Nothing better than that to start the day's serious work of beating back the past.

UPSTAIRS BELOVED was dancing. A little two-step, two-step, make-a-new-step, slide, slide and strut on down.

Denver sat on the bed smiling and providing the music.

She had never seen Beloved this happy. She had seen her pouty lips open wide with the pleasure of sugar or some piece of news Denver gave her. She had felt warm satisfaction radiating from Beloved's skin when she listened to her mother talk about the old days. But gaiety she had never seen. Not ten minutes had passed since Beloved had fallen backward to the floor, pop-eyed, thrashing and holding her throat. Now, after a few seconds lying in Denver's bed, she was up and dancing.

"Where'd you learn to dance?" Denver asked her.

"Nowhere. Look at me do this." Beloved put her fists on her hips and commenced to skip on bare feet. Denver laughed.

"Now you. Come on," said Beloved. "You may as well just come on." Her black skirt swayed from side to side.

Denver grew ice-cold as she rose from the bed. She knew she was twice Beloved's size but she floated up, cold and light as a snowflake.

Beloved took Denver's hand and placed another on Denver's shoulder. They danced then. Round and round the tiny room and it may have been dizziness, or feeling light and icy at once, that made Denver laugh so hard. A catching laugh that Beloved caught. The two of them, merry as kittens, swung to and fro, to and fro, until exhausted they sat on the floor. Beloved let her head fall back on the edge of the bed while she found her breath and Denver saw the tip of the thing she always saw in its entirety when Beloved undressed to sleep. Looking straight at it she whispered, "Why you call yourself Beloved?"

Beloved closed her eyes. "In the dark my name is Beloved."

Denver scooted a little closer. "What's it like over there, where you were before? Can you tell me?"

"Dark," said Beloved. "I'm small in that place. I'm like this here." She raised her head off the bed, lay down on her side and curled up.

Denver covered her lips with her fingers. "Were you cold?"

Beloved curled tighter and shook her head. "Hot. Nothing to breathe down there and no room to move in."

"You see anybody?"

"Heaps. A lot of people is down there. Some is dead."

"You see Jesus? Baby Suggs?"

"I don't know. I don't know the names." She sat up.

"Tell me, how did you get here?"

"I wait; then I got on the bridge. I stay there in the dark, in the daytime, in the dark, in the daytime. It was a long time."

"All this time you were on a bridge?"

"No. After. When I got out."

"What did you come back for?"

Beloved smiled. "To see her face."

"Ma'am's? Sethe?"

"Yes, Sethe."

Denver felt a little hurt, slighted that she was not the main reason for Beloved's return. "Don't you remember we played together by the stream?"

"I was on the bridge," said Beloved. "You see me on the bridge?"

"No, by the stream. The water back in the woods."

"Oh, I was in the water. I saw her diamonds down there. I could touch them."

"What stopped you?"

"She left me behind. By myself," said Beloved. She lifted her eyes to meet Denver's and frowned, perhaps. Perhaps not. The tiny scratches on her forehead may have made it seem so.

Denver swallowed. "Don't," she said. "Don't. You won't leave us, will you?"

"No. Never. This is where I am."

Suddenly Denver, who was sitting cross-legged, lurched forward and grabbed Beloved's wrist. "Don't tell her. Don't let Ma'am know who you are. Please, you hear?"

"Don't tell me what to do. Don't you never never tell me what to do."

"But I'm on your side, Beloved."

"She is the one. She is the one I need. You can go but she is the one I have to have." Her eyes stretched to the limit, black as the all-night sky.

"I didn't do anything to you. I never hurt you. I never hurt anybody," said Denver.

"Me either. Me either."

"What you gonna do?"

"Stay here. I belong here."

"I belong here too."

"Then stay, but don't never tell me what to do. Don't never do that."

"We were dancing. Just a minute ago we were dancing together. Let's."

"I don't want to." Beloved got up and lay down on the bed. Their quietness boomed about on the walls like birds in panic. Finally Denver's breath steadied against the threat of an unbearable loss.

"Tell me," Beloved said. "Tell me how Sethe made you in the boat."

"She never told me all of it," said Denver.

"Tell me."

Denver climbed up on the bed and folded her arms under her apron. She had not been in the tree room once since Beloved sat on their stump after the carnival, and had not remembered that she hadn't gone there until this very desperate moment. Nothing was out there that this sister-girl did not provide in abundance: a racing heart, dreaminess, society, danger, beauty. She swallowed twice to prepare for the telling, to construct out of the strings she had heard all her life a net to hold Beloved.

"She had good hands, she said. The whitegirl, she said, had thin little arms but good hands. She saw that right away, she said. Hair enough for five heads and good hands, she said. I guess the hands made her think she could do it: get us both across the river. But the mouth was what kept her from being scared. She said there ain't nothing to go by with whitepeople. You don't know how they'll jump. Say one thing, do another. But if you looked at the mouth sometimes you could tell by that. She said this girl talked a storm, but there wasn't no meanness around her mouth. She took Ma'am to that lean-to and rubbed her feet for her, so that was one thing. And Ma'am believed she wasn't going to turn her over. You could get money if you turned a runaway over, and she wasn't sure this girl Amy didn't need money more than anything, especially since all she talked about was getting hold of some velvet."

"What's velvet?"

"It's a cloth, kind of deep and soft."

"Go ahead."

"Anyway, she rubbed Ma'am's feet back to life, and she cried, she said, from how it hurt. But it made her think she could make it on over to where Grandma Baby Suggs was and . . ."

"Who is that?"

"I just said it. My grandmother."

"Is that Sethe's mother?"

"No. My father's mother."

"Go ahead."

"That's where the others was. My brothers and . . . the baby girl. She sent them on before to wait for her at Grandma Baby's. So she had to put up with everything to get there. And this here girl Amy helped."

Denver stopped and sighed. This was the part of the story she loved. She was coming to it now, and she loved it because it was all about herself; but she hated it too because it made her feel like a bill was owing somewhere and she, Denver, had to pay it. But who she owed or what to pay it with eluded her. Now, watching Beloved's alert and hungry face, how she took in every word, asking questions about the color of things and their size, her downright craving to know, Denver began to see what she was saying and not just to hear it: there is this nineteen-year-old slave girl—a year older than her-self—walking through the dark woods to get to her children who are far away. She is tired, scared maybe, and maybe even lost. Most of all she is by herself and inside her is another baby she has to think about too. Behind her dogs, perhaps; guns probably; and certainly mossy teeth. She is not so afraid at night because she is the color of it, but in the day every sound is a shot or a tracker's quiet step.

Denver was seeing it now and feeling it—through Beloved. Feeling how it must have felt to her mother. Seeing how it must have looked. And the more fine points she made, the more detail she provided, the more Beloved liked it. So she anticipated the questions by giving blood to the scraps her mother and grandmother had told her—and a heartbeat. The monologue became, in fact, a duet as they lay down together, Denver nursing Beloved's interest like a lover whose pleasure was to overfeed the loved. The dark quilt with two orange patches was there with them because Beloved wanted it near her when she slept. It was smelling like grass and feeling like hands— the unrested hands of busy women: dry, warm, prickly. Denver spoke, Beloved listened, and the two did the best they could to create what really happened, how it really was, something only Sethe knew because she alone had the mind for it and the time afterward to shape it: the quality of Amy's voice, her breath like burning wood. The quick-change weather up in those hills—cool at night, hot in the day, sudden fog. How recklessly she behaved with this whitegirl—a recklessness born of desperation and encouraged by Amy's fugitive eyes and her tenderhearted mouth.

"You ain't got no business walking round these hills, miss."

"Looka here who's talking. I got more business here 'n you got. They catch you they cut your head off. Ain't nobody after me but I know somebody after you." Amy pressed her fingers into the soles of the slavewoman's feet. "Whose baby that?"

Sethe did not answer.

"You don't even know. Come here, Jesus," Amy sighed and shook her head. "Hurt?"

"A touch."

"Good for you. More it hurt more better it is. Can't nothing heal without pain, you know. What you wiggling for?"

Sethe raised up on her elbows. Lying on her back so long had raised a ruckus between her shoulder blades. The fire in her feet and the fire on her back made her sweat.

"My back hurt me," she said.

"Your back? Gal, you a mess. Turn over here and let me see."

In an effort so great it made her sick to her stomach, Sethe turned onto her right side. Amy unfastened the back of her dress and said, "Come here, Jesus," when she saw. Sethe guessed it must be bad because after that call to Jesus Amy didn't speak for a while. In the silence of an Amy struck dumb for a change, Sethe felt the fingers of those good hands lightly touch her back. She could hear her breathing but still the whitegirl said nothing. Sethe could not move. She couldn't lie on her stomach or her back, and to keep on her side meant pressure on her screaming feet. Amy spoke at last in her dreamwalker's voice.

"It's a tree, Lu. A chokecherry tree. See, here's the trunk—it's red and split wide open, full of sap, and this here's the parting for the branches. You got a mighty lot of branches. Leaves, too, look like, and dern if these ain't blossoms. Tiny little cherry blossoms, just as white. Your back got a whole tree on it. In bloom. What God have in mind, I wonder. I had me some whippings, but I don't remember nothing like this. Mr. Buddy had a right evil hand too. Whip you for looking at him straight. Sure would. I looked right at him one time and he hauled off and threw the poker at me. Guess he knew what I was a-thinking."

Sethe groaned and Amy cut her reverie short—long enough to shift Sethe's feet so the weight, resting on leaf-covered stones, was above the ankles.

"That better? Lord what a way to die. You gonna die in here, you know. Ain't no way out of it. Thank your Maker I come along so's you wouldn't have to die outside in them weeds. Snake come along he bite you. Bear eat you up. Maybe you should of stayed where you was, Lu. I can see by your back why you didn't ha ha. Whoever planted that tree beat Mr. Buddy by a mile. Glad I ain't you. Well, spiderwebs is 'bout all I can do for you. What's in here ain't enough. I'll look outside. Could use moss, but sometimes bugs and things is in it. Maybe I ought to break them blossoms open. Get that pus to running, you think? Wonder what God had in mind. You must of did something. Don't run off nowhere now."

Sethe could hear her humming away in the bushes as she hunted spiderwebs. A humming she concentrated on because as soon as Amy ducked out the baby began to stretch. Good question, she was thinking. What did He have in mind? Amy had left the back of Sethe's dress open and now a tail of wind hit it, taking the pain down a step. A relief that let her feel the lesser pain of her sore tongue. Amy returned with two palmfuls of web, which she cleaned of prey and then draped on Sethe's back, saying it was like stringing a tree for Christmas.

"We got a old nigger girl come by our place. She don't know nothing. Sews stuff for Mrs. Buddy—real fine lace but can't barely stick two words together. She don't know nothing, just like you. You don't know a thing. End up dead, that's what. Not me. I'm a get to Boston and get myself some velvet. Carmine. You don't even know about that, do you? Now you never will. Bet you never even sleep with the sun in your face. I did it a couple of times. Most times I'm feeding stock before light and don't get to sleep till way after dark comes. But I was in the back of the wagon once and fell asleep. Sleeping with the sun in your face is the best old feeling. Two times I did it. Once when I was little. Didn't nobody bother me then. Next time, in back of the wagon, it happened again and doggone if the chickens didn't get loose. Mr. Buddy whipped my tail. Kentucky ain't no good place to be in. Boston's the place to be in. That's where my mother was before she was give to Mr. Buddy. Joe Nathan said Mr. Buddy is my daddy but I don't believe that, you?"

Sethe told her she didn't believe Mr. Buddy was her daddy.

"You know your daddy, do you?"

"No," said Sethe.

"Neither me. All I know is it ain't him." She stood up then, having finished her repair work, and weaving about the lean-to, her slow-moving eyes pale in the sun that lit her hair, she sang:

*"When the busy day is done*
*And my weary little one*

Rocketh gently to and fro;
When the night winds softly blow,
And the crickets in the glen
Chirp and chirp and chirp again;
Where 'pon the haunted green
Fairies dance around their queen,
Then from yonder misty skies
Cometh Lady Button Eyes."

Suddenly she stopped weaving and rocking and sat down, her skinny arms wrapped around her knees, her good good hands cupping her elbows. Her slow-moving eyes stopped and peered into the dirt at her feet. "That's my mama's song. She taught me it."

"Through the muck and mist and gloam
To our quiet cozy home,
Where to singing sweet and low
Rocks a cradle to and fro.
Where the clock's dull monotone
Telleth of the day that's done,
Where the moonbeams hover o'er
Playthings sleeping on the floor,
Where my weary wee one lies
Cometh Lady Button Eyes.

"Layeth she her hands upon
My dear weary little one,
And those white hands overspread
Like a veil the curly head,
Seem to fondle and caress
Every little silken tress.
Then she smooths the eyelids down
Over those two eyes of brown
In such soothing tender wise
Cometh Lady Button Eyes."

Amy sat quietly after her song, then repeated the last line before she stood, left the lean-to and walked off a little ways to lean against a young ash. When she came back the sun was in the valley below and they were way above it in blue Kentucky light.

"You ain't dead yet, Lu? Lu?"

"Not yet."

"Make you a bet. You make it through the night, you make it all the way." Amy rearranged the leaves for comfort and knelt down to massage the swollen feet again. "Give these one more real good rub," she said, and when Sethe sucked air through her teeth, she said, "Shut up. You got to keep your mouth shut."

Careful of her tongue, Sethe bit down on her lips and let the good hands go to work to the tune of "So bees, sing soft and bees, sing low." Afterward, Amy moved to the other side of the lean-to where, seated, she lowered her head toward her shoulder and braided her hair, saying, "Don't up and die on me in the night, you hear? I don't want to see your ugly black face hankering over me. If you do die, just go on off somewhere where I can't see you, hear?"

"I hear," said Sethe. "I'll do what I can, miss."

Sethe never expected to see another thing in this world, so when she felt toes prodding her hip it took a while to come out of a sleep she thought was death. She sat up, stiff and shivery, while Amy looked in on her juicy back.

"Looks like the devil," said Amy. "But you made it through. Come down here, Jesus, Lu made it through. That's because of me. I'm good at sick things. Can you walk, you think?"

"I have to let my water some kind of way."

"Let's see you walk on em."

It was not good, but it was possible, so Sethe limped, holding on first to Amy, then to a sapling.

"Was me did it. I'm good at sick things ain't I?"

"Yeah," said Sethe, "you good."

"We got to get off this here hill. Come on. I'll take you down to the river. That ought to suit you. Me, I'm going to the Pike. Take me straight to Boston. What's that all over your dress?"

"Milk."

"You one mess."

Sethe looked down at her stomach and touched it. The baby was dead. She had not died in the night, but the baby had. If that was the case, then there was no stopping now. She would get that milk to her baby girl if she had to swim.

"Ain't you hungry?" Amy asked her.

"I ain't nothing but in a hurry, miss."

"Whoa. Slow down. Want some shoes?"

"Say what?"

"I figured how," said Amy and so she had. She tore two pieces from Sethe's shawl, filled them with leaves and tied them over her feet, chattering all the while.

"How old are you, Lu? I been bleeding for four years but I ain't having nobody's baby. Won't catch me sweating milk cause . . ."

"I know," said Sethe. "You going to Boston."

At noon they saw it; then they were near enough to hear it. By late afternoon they could drink from it if they wanted to. Four stars were visible by the time they found, not a riverboat to stow Sethe away on, or a ferryman willing to take on a fugitive passenger— nothing like that—but a whole boat to steal. It had one oar, lots of holes and two bird nests.

"There you go, Lu. Jesus looking at you."

Sethe was looking at one mile of dark water, which would have to be split with one oar in a useless boat against a current dedicated to the Mississippi hundreds of miles away. It looked like home to her, and the baby (not dead in the least) must have thought so too. As soon as Sethe got close to the river her own water broke loose to join it. The break, followed by the redundant announcement of labor, arched her back.

"What you doing that for?" asked Amy. "Ain't you got a brain in your head? Stop that right now. I said stop it, Lu. You the dumbest thing on this here earth. Lu! Lu!"

Sethe couldn't think of anywhere to go but in. She waited for the sweet beat that followed the blast of pain. On her knees again, she crawled into the boat. It waddled under her and she had just enough time to brace her leaf-bag feet on the bench when another rip took her breath away. Panting under four summer stars, she threw her legs over the sides, because here come the head, as Amy informed her as though she did not know it—as though the rip was a breakup of walnut logs in the brace, or of lightning's jagged tear through a leather sky.

It was stuck. Face up and drowning in its mother's blood. Amy stopped begging Jesus and began to curse His daddy.

"Push!" screamed Amy.

"Pull," whispered Sethe.

And the strong hands went to work a fourth time, none too soon, for river water, seeping through any hole it chose, was spreading over Sethe's hips. She reached one arm back and grabbed the rope while Amy fairly clawed at the head. When a foot rose from the river bed and kicked the bottom of the boat and Sethe's behind, she knew it was done and permitted herself a short faint. Coming to, she heard no cries, just Amy's encouraging coos. Nothing happened for so long they both believed they had lost it. Sethe arched suddenly and the afterbirth shot out. Then the baby whimpered and Sethe looked. Twenty inches of cord hung from its belly and it trembled in the cooling evening air. Amy wrapped her skirt around it and the wet sticky women clambered ashore to see what, indeed, God had in mind.

Spores of bluefern growing in the hollows along the riverbank float toward the water in silver-blue lines hard to see unless you are in or near them, lying right at the river's edge when the sunshots are low and drained. Often they are mistook for insects—but they are seeds in which the whole generation sleeps confident of a future. And for a moment it is easy to believe each one has one—will become all of what is contained in the spore: will live out its days as planned. This moment of certainty lasts no longer than that; longer, perhaps, than the spore itself.

On a riverbank in the cool of a summer evening two women struggled under a shower of silvery blue. They never expected to see each other again in this world and at the moment couldn't care less. But there on a summer night surrounded by bluefern they did something together appropriately and well. A pateroller passing would have sniggered to see two throw-away people, two lawless outlaws—

a slave and a barefoot whitewoman with unpinned hair—wrapping a ten-minute-old baby in the rags they wore. But no pateroller came and no preacher. The water sucked and swallowed itself beneath them. There was nothing to disturb them at their work. So they did it appropriately and well.

Twilight came on and Amy said she had to go; that she wouldn't be caught dead in daylight on a busy river with a runaway. After rinsing her hands and face in the river, she stood and looked down at the baby wrapped and tied to Sethe's chest.

"She's never gonna know who I am. You gonna tell her? Who brought her into this here world?" She lifted her chin, looked off into the place where the sun used to be. "You better tell her. You hear? Say Miss Amy Denver. Of Boston."

Sethe felt herself falling into a sleep she knew would be deep. On the lip of it, just before going under, she thought, "That's pretty. Denver. Real pretty."

IT WAS TIME to lay it all down. Before Paul D came and sat on her porch steps, words whispered in the keeping room had kept her going. Helped her endure the chastising ghost; refurbished the baby faces of Howard and Buglar and kept them whole in the world because in her dreams she saw only their parts in trees; and kept her husband shadowy but *there*—somewhere. Now Halle's face between the butter press and the churn swelled larger and larger, crowding her eyes and making her head hurt. She wished for Baby Suggs' fingers molding her nape, reshaping it, saying, "Lay em down, Sethe. Sword and shield. Down. Down. Both of em down. Down by the riverside. Sword and shield. Don't study war no more. Lay all that mess down. Sword and shield." And under the pressing fingers and the quiet instructive voice, she would. Her heavy knives of defense against misery, regret, gall and hurt, she placed one by one on a bank where clear water rushed on below.

Nine years without the fingers or the voice of Baby Suggs was too much. And words whispered in the keeping room were too little. The butter-smeared face of a man God made none sweeter than demanded more: an arch built or a robe sewn. Some fixing ceremony. Sethe decided to go to the Clearing, back where Baby Suggs had danced in sunlight.

Before 124 and everybody in it had closed down, veiled over and shut away; before it had become the plaything of spirits and the home of the chafed, 124 had been a cheerful, buzzing house where

Baby Suggs, holy, loved, cautioned, fed, chastised and soothed. Where not one but two pots simmered on the stove; where the lamp burned all night long. Strangers rested there while children tried on their shoes. Messages were left there, for whoever needed them was sure to stop in one day soon. Talk was low and to the point—for Baby Suggs, holy, didn't approve of extra. "Everything depends on knowing how much," she said, and "Good is knowing when to stop."

It was in front of *that* 124 that Sethe climbed off a wagon, her newborn tied to her chest, and felt for the first time the wide arms of her mother-in-law, who had made it to Cincinnati. Who decided that, because slave life had "busted her legs, back, head, eyes, hands, kidneys, womb and tongue," she had nothing left to make a living with but her heart—which she put to work at once. Accepting no title of honor before her name, but allowing a small caress after it, she became an unchurched preacher, one who visited pulpits and opened her great heart to those who could use it. In winter and fall she carried it to AME's and Baptists, Holinesses and Sanctifieds, the Church of the Redeemer and the Redeemed. Uncalled, unrobed, un-anointed, she let her great heart beat in their presence. When warm weather came, Baby Suggs, holy, followed by every black man, woman and child who could make it through, took her great heart to the Clearing—a wide-open place cut deep in the woods nobody knew for what at the end of a path known only to deer and whoever cleared the land in the first place. In the heat of every Saturday afternoon, she sat in the clearing while the people waited among the trees.

After situating herself on a huge flat-sided rock, Baby Suggs bowed her head and prayed silently. The company watched her from the trees. They knew she was ready when she put her stick down. Then she shouted, "Let the children come!" and they ran from the trees toward her.

"Let your mothers hear you laugh," she told them, and the woods rang. The adults looked on and could not help smiling.

Then "Let the grown men come," she shouted. They stepped out one by one from among the ringing trees.

"Let your wives and your children see you dance," she told them, and groundlife shuddered under their feet.

Finally she called the women to her. "Cry," she told them. "For the living and the dead. Just cry." And without covering their eyes the women let loose.

It started that way: laughing children, dancing men, crying women and then it got mixed up. Women stopped crying and danced; men sat down and cried; children danced, women laughed, children cried until, exhausted and riven, all and each lay about the Clearing damp and gasping for breath. In the silence that followed, Baby Suggs, holy, offered up to them her great big heart.

She did not tell them to clean up their lives or to go and sin no more. She did not tell them they were the blessed of the earth, its inheriting meek or its glorybound pure.

She told them that the only grace they could have was the grace they could imagine. That if they could not see it, they would not have it.

"Here," she said, "in this here place, we flesh; flesh that weeps, laughs; flesh that dances on bare feet in grass. Love it. Love it hard. Yonder they do not love your flesh. They despise it. They don't love your eyes; they'd just as soon pick em out. No more do they love the skin on your back. Yonder they flay it. And O my people they do not love your hands. Those they only use, tie, bind, chop off and leave empty. Love your hands! Love them. Raise them up and kiss them. Touch others with them, pat them together, stroke them on your face 'cause they don't love that either. *You* got to love it, *you!* And no, they ain't in love with your mouth. Yonder, out there, they will see it broken and break it again. What you say out of it they will not heed. What you scream from it they do not hear. What you put into it to nourish your body they will snatch away and give you leavins instead. No, they don't love your mouth. *You* got to love it. This is flesh I'm talking about here. Flesh that needs to be loved. Feet that need to rest and to dance; backs that need support; shoulders that need arms, strong arms I'm telling you. And O my people, out yonder, hear me, they do not love your neck unnoosed and straight. So love your neck; put a hand on it, grace it, stroke it and hold it up. And all your inside parts that they'd just as soon slop for hogs, you got to love them. The dark, dark liver—love it, love it, and the beat and beating heart, love that too. More than eyes or feet.

More than lungs that have yet to draw free air. More than your life-holding womb and your life-giving private parts, hear me now, love your heart. For this is the prize." Saying no more, she stood up then and danced with her twisted hip the rest of what her heart had to say while the others opened their mouths and gave her the music. Long notes held until the four-part harmony was perfect enough for their deeply loved flesh.

Sethe wanted to be there now. At the least to listen to the spaces that the long-ago singing had left behind. At the most to get a clue from her husband's dead mother as to what she should do with her sword and shield now, dear Jesus, now nine years after Baby Suggs, holy, proved herself a liar, dismissed her great heart and lay in the keeping-room bed roused once in a while by a craving for color and not for another thing.

"Those white things have taken all I had or dreamed," she said, "and broke my heartstrings too. There is no bad luck in the world but whitefolks." 124 shut down and put up with the venom of its ghost. No more lamp all night long, or neighbors dropping by. No low conversations after supper. No watched barefoot children playing in the shoes of strangers. Baby Suggs, holy, believed she had lied. There was no grace—imaginary or real—and no sunlit dance in a Clearing could change that. Her faith, her love, her imagination and her great big old heart began to collapse twenty-eight days after her daughter-in-law arrived.

Yet it was to the Clearing that Sethe determined to go—to pay tribute to Halle. Before the light changed, while it was still the green blessed place she remembered: misty with plant steam and the decay of berries.

She put on a shawl and told Denver and Beloved to do likewise. All three set out late one Sunday morning, Sethe leading, the girls trotting behind, not a soul in sight.

When they reached the woods it took her no time to find the path through it because big-city revivals were held there regularly now, complete with food-laden tables, banjos and a tent. The old path was a track now, but still arched over with trees dropping buckeyes onto the grass below.

There was nothing to be done other than what she had done, but

Sethe blamed herself for Baby Suggs' collapse. However many times Baby denied it, Sethe knew the grief at 124 started when she jumped down off the wagon, her newborn tied to her chest in the underwear of a whitegirl looking for Boston.

Followed by the two girls, down a bright green corridor of oak and horse chestnut, Sethe began to sweat a sweat just like the other one when she woke, mud-caked, on the banks of the Ohio.

Amy was gone. Sethe was alone and weak, but alive, and so was her baby. She walked a ways downriver and then stood gazing at the glimmering water. By and by a flatbed slid into view, but she could not see if the figures on it were whitepeople or not. She began to sweat from a fever she thanked God for since it would certainly keep her baby warm. When the flatbed was beyond her sight she stumbled on and found herself near three coloredpeople fishing— two boys and an older man. She stopped and waited to be spoken to. One of the boys pointed and the man looked over his shoulder at her—a quick look since all he needed to know about her he could see in no time.

No one said anything for a while. Then the man said, "Headin' 'cross?"

"Yes, sir," said Sethe.

"Anybody know you coming?"

"Yes, sir."

He looked at her again and nodded toward a rock that stuck out of the ground above him like a bottom lip. Sethe walked to it and sat down. The stone had eaten the sun's rays but was nowhere near as hot as she was. Too tired to move, she stayed there, the sun in her eyes making her dizzy. Sweat poured over her and bathed the baby completely. She must have slept sitting up, because when next she opened her eyes the man was standing in front of her with a smoking-hot piece of fried eel in his hands. It was an effort to reach for, more to smell, impossible to eat. She begged him for water and he gave her some of the Ohio in a jar. Sethe drank it all and begged more. The clanging was back in her head but she refused to believe that she had come all that way, endured all she had, to die on the wrong side of the river.

The man watched her streaming face and called one of the boys over.

"Take off that coat," he told him.

"Sir?"

"You heard me."

The boy slipped out of his jacket, whining, "What you gonna do? What I'm gonna wear?"

The man untied the baby from her chest and wrapped it in the boy's coat, knotting the sleeves in front.

"What I'm gonna wear?"

The old man sighed and, after a pause, said, "You want it back, then go head and take it off that baby. Put the baby naked in the grass and put your coat back on. And if you can do it, then go on 'way somewhere and don't come back."

The boy dropped his eyes, then turned to join the other. With eel in her hand, the baby at her feet, Sethe dozed, dry-mouthed and sweaty. Evening came and the man touched her shoulder.

Contrary to what she expected they poled upriver, far away from the rowboat Amy had found. Just when she thought he was taking her back to Kentucky, he turned the flatbed and crossed the Ohio like a shot. There he helped her up the steep bank, while the boy without a jacket carried the baby who wore it. The man led her to a brush-covered hutch with a beaten floor.

"Wait here. Somebody be here directly. Don't move. They'll find you."

"Thank you," she said. "I wish I knew your name so I could remember you right."

"Name's Stamp," he said. "Stamp Paid. Watch out for that there baby, you hear?"

"I hear. I hear," she said, but she didn't. Hours later a woman was right up on her before she heard a thing. A short woman, young, with a croaker sack, greeted her.

"Saw the sign a while ago," she said. "But I couldn't get here no quicker."

"What sign?" asked Sethe.

"Stamp leaves the old sty open when there's a crossing. Knots a white rag on the post if it's a child too."

She knelt and emptied the sack. "My name's Ella," she said, taking a wool blanket, cotton cloth, two baked sweet potatoes and a pair of men's shoes from the sack. "My husband, John, is out yonder a ways. Where you heading?"

Sethe told her about Baby Suggs where she had sent her three children.

Ella wrapped a cloth strip tight around the baby's navel as she listened for the holes—the things the fugitives did not say; the questions they did not ask. Listened too for the unnamed, unmentioned people left behind. She shook gravel from the men's shoes and tried to force Sethe's feet into them. They would not go. Sadly, they split them down the heel, sorry indeed to ruin so valuable an item. Sethe put on the boy's jacket, not daring to ask whether there was any word of the children.

"They made it," said Ella. "Stamp ferried some of that party. Left them on Bluestone. It ain't too far."

Sethe couldn't think of anything to do, so grateful was she, so she peeled a potato, ate it, spit it up and ate more in quiet celebration.

"They be glad to see you," said Ella. "When was this one born?"

"Yesterday," said Sethe, wiping sweat from under her chin. "I hope she makes it."

Ella looked at the tiny, dirty face poking out of the wool blanket and shook her head. "Hard to say," she said. "If anybody was to ask me I'd say, 'Don't love nothing.' " Then, as if to take the edge off her pronouncement, she smiled at Sethe. "You had that baby by yourself?"

"No. Whitegirl helped."

"Then we better make tracks."

Baby Suggs kissed her on the mouth and refused to let her see the children. They were asleep she said and Sethe was too ugly-looking to wake them in the night. She took the newborn and handed it to a young woman in a bonnet, telling her not to clean the eyes till she got the mother's urine.

"Has it cried out yet?" asked Baby.

"A little."

"Time enough. Let's get the mother well."

She led Sethe to the keeping room and, by the light of a spirit lamp, bathed her in sections, starting with her face. Then, while waiting for another pan of heated water, she sat next to her and stitched gray cotton. Sethe dozed and woke to the washing of her hands and arms. After each bathing, Baby covered her with a quilt and put another pan on in the kitchen. Tearing sheets, stitching the gray cotton, she supervised the woman in the bonnet who tended the baby and cried into her cooking. When Sethe's legs were done, Baby looked at her feet and wiped them lightly. She cleaned between Sethe's legs with two separate pans of hot water and then tied her stomach and vagina with sheets. Finally she attacked the unrecognizable feet.

"You feel this?"

"Feel what?" asked Sethe.

"Nothing. Heave up." She helped Sethe to a rocker and lowered her feet into a bucket of salt water and juniper. The rest of the night Sethe sat soaking. The crust from her nipples Baby softened with lard and then washed away. By dawn the silent baby woke and took her mother's milk.

"Pray God it ain't turned bad," said Baby. "And when you through, call me." As she turned to go, Baby Suggs caught a glimpse of something dark on the bed sheet. She frowned and looked at her daughter-in-law bending toward the baby. Roses of blood blossomed in the blanket covering Sethe's shoulders. Baby Suggs hid her mouth with her hand. When the nursing was over and the newborn was asleep— its eyes half open, its tongue dream-sucking—wordlessly the older woman greased the flowering back and pinned a double thickness of cloth to the inside of the newly stitched dress.

It was not real yet. Not yet. But when her sleepy boys and crawling-already? girl were brought in, it didn't matter whether it was real or not. Sethe lay in bed under, around, over, among but especially with them all. The little girl dribbled clear spit into her face, and Sethe's laugh of delight was so loud the crawling-already? baby blinked. Buglar and Howard played with her ugly feet, after daring each other to be the first to touch them. She kept kissing them. She kissed the backs of their necks, the tops of their heads and the centers of their palms, and it was the boys who decided enough was enough when she lifted their shirts to kiss their tight round bellies. She stopped when and because they said, "Pappie come?"

She didn't cry. She said "soon" and smiled so they would think the brightness in her eyes was love alone. It was some time before she let Baby Suggs shoo the boys away so Sethe could put on the gray cotton dress her mother-in-law had started stitching together the night before. Finally she lay back and cradled the crawling-already? girl in her arms. She enclosed her left nipple with two fingers of her right hand and the child opened her mouth. They hit home together.

Baby Suggs came in and laughed at them, telling Sethe how strong the baby girl was, how smart, already crawling. Then she stooped to gather up the ball of rags that had been Sethe's clothes.

"Nothing worth saving in here," she said.

Sethe lifted her eyes. "Wait," she called. "Look and see if there's something still knotted up in the petticoat."

Baby Suggs inched the spoiled fabric through her fingers and came upon what felt like pebbles. She held them out toward Sethe. "Going-away present?"

"Wedding present."

"Be nice if there was a groom to go with it." She gazed into her hand. "What you think happened to him?"

"I don't know," said Sethe. "He wasn't where he said to meet him at. I had to get out. Had to." Sethe watched the drowsy eyes of the sucking girl for a moment then looked at Baby Suggs' face. "He'll make it. If I made it, Halle sure can."

"Well, put these on. Maybe they'll light his way." Convinced her son was dead, she handed the stones to Sethe.

"I need holes in my ears."

"I'll do it," said Baby Suggs. "Soon's you up to it."

Sethe jingled the earrings for the pleasure of the crawling-already? girl, who reached for them over and over again.

In the Clearing, Sethe found Baby's old preaching rock and re-membered the smell of leaves simmering in the sun, thunderous feet and the shouts that ripped pods off the limbs of the chestnuts. With Baby Suggs' heart in charge, the people let go.

Sethe had had twenty-eight days—the travel of one whole moon—
of unslaved life. From the pure clear stream of spit that the little girl
dribbled into her face to her oily blood was twenty-eight days. Days
of healing, ease and real-talk. Days of company: knowing the names
of forty, fifty other Negroes, their views, habits; where they had been
and what done; of feeling their fun and sorrow along with her own,
which made it better. One taught her the alphabet; another a stitch.
All taught her how it felt to wake up at dawn and *decide* what to
do with the day. That's how she got through the waiting for Halle.
Bit by bit, at 124 and in the Clearing, along with the others, she had
claimed herself. Freeing yourself was one thing; claiming ownership
of that freed self was another.

Now she sat on Baby Suggs' rock, Denver and Beloved watching
her from the trees. There will never be a day, she thought, when
Halle will knock on the door. Not knowing it was hard; knowing it
was harder.

Just the fingers, she thought. Just let me feel your fingers again
on the back of my neck and I will lay it all down, make a way out
of this no way. Sethe bowed her head and sure enough—they were
there. Lighter now, no more than the strokes of bird feather, but
unmistakably caressing fingers. She had to relax a bit to let them do
their work, so light was the touch, childlike almost, more finger kiss
than kneading. Still she was grateful for the effort; Baby Suggs' long-
distance love was equal to any skin-close love she had known. The
desire, let alone the gesture, to meet her needs was good enough to
lift her spirits to the place where she could take the next step: ask
for some clarifying word; some advice about how to keep on with
a brain greedy for news nobody could live with in a world happy to
provide it.

She knew Paul D was adding something to her life—something
she wanted to count on but was scared to. Now he had added more:
new pictures and old rememories that broke her heart. Into the empty
space of not knowing about Halle—a space sometimes colored with
righteous resentment at what could have been his cowardice, or stupidity or bad luck—that empty place of no definite news was filled
now with a brand-new sorrow and who could tell how many more
on the way. Years ago—when 124 was alive—she had women friends,

men friends from all around to share grief with. Then there was no one, for they would not visit her while the baby ghost filled the house, and she returned their disapproval with the potent pride of the mistreated. But now there was someone to share it, and he had beat the spirit away the very day he entered her house and no sign of it since. A blessing, but in its place he brought another kind of haunting: Halle's face smeared with butter and the clabber too; his own mouth jammed full of iron, and Lord knows what else he could tell her if he wanted to.

The fingers touching the back of her neck were stronger now— the strokes bolder as though Baby Suggs were gathering strength. Putting the thumbs at the nape, while the fingers pressed the sides. Harder, harder, the fingers moved slowly around toward her windpipe, making little circles on the way. Sethe was actually more surprised than frightened to find that she was being strangled. Or so it seemed. In any case, Baby Suggs' fingers had a grip on her that would not let her breathe. Tumbling forward from her seat on the rock, she clawed at the hands that were not there. Her feet were thrashing by the time Denver got to her and then Beloved.

"Ma'am! Ma'am!" Denver shouted. "Ma'ammy!" and turned her mother over on her back.

The fingers left off and Sethe had to swallow huge draughts of air before she recognized her daughter's face next to her own and Beloved's hovering above.

"You all right?"

"Somebody choked me," said Sethe.

"Who?"

Sethe rubbed her neck and struggled to a sitting position. "Grandma Baby, I reckon. I just asked her to *rub* my neck, like she used to and she was doing fine and then just got crazy with it, I guess."

"She wouldn't do that to you, Ma'am. Grandma Baby? Uh uh."

"Help me up from here."

"Look." Beloved was pointing at Sethe's neck.

"What is it? What you see?" asked Sethe.

"Bruises," said Denver.

"On my neck?"

"Here," said Beloved. "Here and here, too." She reached out her hand and touched the splotches, gathering color darker than Sethe's dark throat, and her fingers were mighty cool.

"That don't help nothing," Denver said, but Beloved was leaning in, her two hands stroking the damp skin that felt like chamois and looked like taffeta.

Sethe moaned. The girl's fingers were so cool and knowing. Sethe's knotted, private, walk-on-water life gave in a bit, softened, and it seemed that the glimpse of happiness she caught in the shadows swinging hands on the road to the carnival was a likelihood—if she could just manage the news Paul D brought and the news he kept to himself. Just manage it. Not break, fall or cry each time a hateful picture drifted in front of her face. Not develop some permanent craziness like Baby Suggs' friend, a young woman in a bonnet whose food was full of tears. Like Aunt Phyllis, who slept with her eyes wide open. Like Jackson Till, who slept under the bed. All she wanted was to go on. As she had. Alone with her daughter in a haunted house she managed every damn thing. Why now, with Paul D instead of the ghost, was she breaking up? getting scared? needing Baby? The worst was over, wasn't it? She had already got through, hadn't she? With the ghost in 124 she could bear, do, solve anything. Now a hint of what had happened to Halle and she cut out like a rabbit looking for its mother.

Beloved's fingers were heavenly. Under them and breathing evenly again, the anguish rolled down. The peace Sethe had come there to find crept into her.

We must look a sight, she thought, and closed her eyes to see it: the three women in the middle of the Clearing, at the base of the rock where Baby Suggs, holy, had loved. One seated, yielding up her throat to the kind hands of one of the two kneeling before her.

Denver watched the faces of the other two. Beloved watched the work her thumbs were doing and must have loved what she saw because she leaned over and kissed the tenderness under Sethe's chin.

They stayed that way for a while because neither Denver nor Sethe knew how not to: how to stop and not love the look or feel of the lips that kept on kissing. Then Sethe, grabbing Beloved's hair and blinking rapidly, separated herself. She later believed that it was because the girl's breath was exactly like new milk that she said to her, stern and frowning, "You too old for that."

She looked at Denver, and seeing panic about to become something more, stood up quickly, breaking the tableau apart.

"Come on up! Up!" Sethe waved the girls to their feet. As they left the Clearing they looked pretty much the same as they had when they had come: Sethe in the lead, the girls a ways back. All silent as before, but with a difference. Sethe was bothered, not because of the kiss, but because, just before it, when she was feeling so fine letting Beloved massage away the pain, the fingers she was loving and the ones that had soothed her before they strangled her had reminded her of something that now slipped her mind. But one thing for sure, Baby Suggs had not choked her as first she thought. Denver was right, and walking in the dappled tree-light, clearer-headed now—away from the enchantment of the Clearing—Sethe remembered the touch of those fingers that she knew better than her own. They had bathed her in sections, wrapped her womb, combed her hair, oiled her nipples, stitched her clothes, cleaned her feet, greased her back and dropped just about anything they were doing to massage Sethe's nape when, especially in the early days, her spirits fell down under the weight of the things she remembered and those she did not: schoolteacher writing in ink she herself had made while his nephews played on her; the face of the woman in a felt hat as she rose to stretch in the field. If she lay among all the hands in the world, she would know Baby Suggs' just as she did the good hands of the whitegirl looking for velvet. But for eighteen years she had lived in a house full of touches from the other side. And the thumbs that pressed her nape were the same. Maybe that was where it had gone to. After Paul D beat it out of 124, maybe it collected itself in the Clearing. Reasonable, she thought.

Why she had taken Denver and Beloved with her didn't puzzle her now—at the time it seemed impulse, with a vague wish for protection. And the girls had saved her, Beloved so agitated she behaved like a two-year-old.

Like a faint smell of burning that disappears when the fire is cut off or the window opened for a breeze, the suspicion that the girl's touch was also exactly like the baby's ghost dissipated. It was only a tiny disturbance anyway—not strong enough to divert her from the ambition welling in her now: she wanted Paul D. No matter what he told and knew, she wanted him in her life. More than commemorating Halle, that is what she had come to the Clearing to figure out, and now it *was* figured. Trust and rememory, yes, the way she believed it could be when he cradled her before the cooking stove. The weight and angle of him; the true-to-life beard hair on him; arched back, educated hands. His waiting eyes and awful human power. The mind of him that knew her own. Her story was bearable because it was his as well—to tell, to refine and tell again. The things neither knew about the other—the things neither had word-shapes for—well, it would come in time: where they led him off to sucking iron; the perfect death of her crawling-already? baby.

She wanted to get back—fast. Set these idle girls to some work that would fill their wandering heads. Rushing through the green corridor, cooler now because the sun had moved, it occurred to her that the two were alike as sisters. Their obedience and absolute reliability shot through with surprise. Sethe understood Denver. Solitude had made her secretive—self-manipulated. Years of haunting had dulled her in ways you wouldn't believe and sharpened her in ways you wouldn't believe either. The consequence was a timid but hard-headed daughter Sethe would die to protect. The other, Beloved, she knew less, nothing, about—except that there was nothing she wouldn't do for Sethe and that Denver and she liked each other's company. Now she thought she knew why. They spent up or held on to their feelings in harmonious ways. What one had to give the other was pleased to take. They hung back in the trees that ringed the Clearing, then rushed into it with screams and kisses when Sethe choked—anyhow that's how she explained it to herself for she noticed neither competition between the two nor domination by one. On her mind was the supper she wanted to fix for Paul D—something difficult to do, something she would do just so—to launch her newer, stronger life with a tender man. Those litty bitty potatoes browned on all sides, heavy on the pepper; snap beans seasoned with rind;

yellow squash sprinkled with vinegar and sugar. Maybe corn cut from the cob and fried with green onions and butter. Raised bread, even.

Her mind, searching the kitchen before she got to it, was so full of her offering she did not see right away, in the space under the white stairs, the wooden tub and Paul D sitting in it. She smiled at him and he smiled back.

"Summer must be over," she said.

"Come on in here."

"Uh uh. Girls right behind me."

"I don't hear nobody."

"I have to cook, Paul D."

"Me too." He stood up and made her stay there while he held her in his arms. Her dress soaked up the water from his body. His jaw was near her ear. Her chin touched his shoulder.

"What you gonna cook?"

"I thought some snap beans."

"Oh, yeah."

"Fry up a little corn?"

"Yeah."

There was no question but that she could do it. Just like the day she arrived at 124—sure enough, she had milk enough for all.

Beloved came through the door and they ought to have heard her tread, but they didn't.

Breathing and murmuring, breathing and murmuring. Beloved heard them as soon as the door banged shut behind her. She jumped at the slam and swiveled her head toward the whispers coming from behind the white stairs. She took a step and felt like crying. She had been so close, then closer. And it was so much better than the anger that ruled when Sethe did or thought anything that excluded herself. She could bear the hours—nine or ten of them each day but one—when Sethe was gone. Bear even the nights when she was close but out of sight, behind walls and doors lying next to him. But now—even the daylight time that Beloved had counted on, disciplined herself to be content with, was being reduced, divided by Sethe's willingness to pay attention to other things. Him mostly. Him who said before gears changed to evening occupations. Denver had walked off looking for the house other children visited but not her. When she found it she was too timid to go to the front door so she peeped in the window. Lady Jones sat in a straight-backed chair; several children sat cross-legged on the floor in front of her. Lady Jones had a book. The children had slates. Lady Jones was saying something too soft for Denver to hear. The children were saying it after her. Four times Denver went to look. The fifth time Lady Jones caught her and said, "Come in the front door, Miss Denver. This is not a side show."

So she had almost a whole year of the company of her peers and along with them learned to spell and count. She was seven, and those two hours in the afternoon were precious to her. Especially so because she had done it on her own and was pleased and surprised by the pleasure and surprise it created in her mother and her brothers. For a nickel a month, Lady Jones did what whitepeople thought unnecessary if not illegal: crowded her little parlor with the colored children who had time for and interest in book learning. The nickel, tied to a handkerchief knot, tied to her belt, that she carried to Lady Jones, thrilled her. The effort to handle chalk expertly and avoid the scream it would make; the capital *w,* the little *i,* the beauty of the letters in her name, the deeply mournful sentences from the Bible Lady Jones used as a textbook. Denver practiced every morning; starred every afternoon. She was so happy she didn't even know she was being avoided by her classmates—that they made excuses and altered their pace not to walk with her. It was Nelson Lord—the boy as smart as she was—who put a stop to it; who asked her the question about her mother that put chalk, the little *i* and all the rest that those afternoons held, out of reach forever. She should have laughed when he said it, or pushed him down, but there was no meanness in his face or his voice. Just curiosity. But the thing that leapt up in her when he asked it was a thing that had been lying there all along.

She never went back. The second day she didn't go, Sethe asked her why not. Denver didn't answer. She was too scared to ask her brothers or anyone else Nelson Lord's question because certain odd and terrifying feelings about her mother were collecting around the thing that leapt up inside her. Later on, after Baby Suggs died, she did not wonder why Howard and Buglar had run away. She did not agree with Sethe that they left because of the ghost. If so, what took them so long? They had lived with it as long as she had. But if Nelson Lord was right—no wonder they were sulky, staying away from home as much as they could.

Meanwhile the monstrous and unmanageable dreams about Sethe found release in the concentration Denver began to fix on the baby ghost. Before Nelson Lord, she had been barely interested in its antics. The patience of her mother and grandmother in its presence made her indifferent to it. Then it began to irritate her, wear her out with its mischief. That was when she walked off to follow the children to Lady Jones' house-school. Now it held for her all the anger, love and fear she didn't know what to do with. Even when she did muster the courage to ask Nelson Lord's question, she could not hear Sethe's answer, nor Baby Suggs' words, nor anything at all thereafter. For two years she walked in a silence too solid for penetration but which gave her eyes a power even she found hard to believe. The black nostrils of a sparrow sitting on a branch sixty feet above her head, for instance. For two years she heard nothing at all and then she heard close thunder crawling up the stairs. Baby Suggs thought it was Here Boy padding into places he never went. Sethe thought it was the India-rubber ball the boys played with bounding down the stairs.

"Is that damn dog lost his mind?" shouted Baby Suggs.

"He's on the porch," said Sethe. "See for yourself."

"Well, what's that I'm hearing then?"

Sethe slammed the stove lid. "Buglar! Buglar! I told you all not to use that ball in here." She looked at the white stairs and saw Denver at the top.

"She was trying to get upstairs."

"What?" The cloth she used to handle the stove lid was balled in Sethe's hand.

"The baby," said Denver. "Didn't you hear her crawling?"

What to jump on first was the problem: that Denver heard anything at all or that the crawling-already? baby girl was still at it but more so.

The return of Denver's hearing, cut off by an answer she could not bear to hear, cut on by the sound of her dead sister trying to climb the stairs, signaled another shift in the fortunes of the people of 124. From then on the presence was full of spite. Instead of sighs and accidents there was pointed and deliberate abuse. Buglar and Howard grew furious at the company of the women in the house, and spent in sullen reproach any time they had away from their odd work in town carrying water and feed at the stables. Until the spite became so personal it drove each off. Baby Suggs grew tired, went to bed and stayed there until her big old heart quit. Except for an occasional request for color she said practically nothing—until the afternoon of the last day of her life when she got out of bed, skipped slowly to the door of the keeping room and announced to Sethe and Denver the lesson she had learned from her sixty years a slave and ten years free: that there was no bad luck in the world but white-people. "They don't know when to stop," she said, and returned to her bed, pulled up the quilt and left them to hold that thought forever.

Shortly afterward Sethe and Denver tried to call up and reason with the baby ghost, but got nowhere. It took a man, Paul D, to shout it off, beat it off and take its place for himself. And carnival or no carnival, Denver preferred the venomous baby to him any day. During the first days after Paul D moved in, Denver stayed in her emerald closet as long as she could, lonely as a mountain and almost as big, thinking everybody had somebody but her; thinking even a ghost's company was denied her. So when she saw the black dress with two unlaced shoes beneath it she trembled with secret thanks. Whatever her power and however she used it, Beloved was *hers*. Denver was alarmed by the harm she thought Beloved planned for Sethe, but felt helpless to thwart it, so unrestricted was her need to love another. The display she witnessed at the Clearing shamed her because the choice between Sethe and Beloved was without conflict.

Walking toward the stream, beyond her green bush house, she let herself wonder what if Beloved really decided to choke her mother. Would she let it happen? Murder, Nelson Lord had said. "Didn't your mother get locked away for murder? Wasn't you in there with her when she went?"

It was the second question that made it impossible for so long to ask Sethe about the first. The thing that leapt up had been coiled in just such a place: a darkness, a stone, and some other thing that moved by itself. She went deaf rather than hear the answer, and like the little four o'clocks that searched openly for sunlight, then closed themselves tightly when it left, Denver kept watch for the baby and withdrew from everything else. Until Paul D came. But the damage he did came undone with the miraculous resurrection of Beloved.

Just ahead, at the edge of the stream, Denver could see her silhouette, standing barefoot in the water, lifting her black skirts up above her calves, the beautiful head lowered in rapt attention.

Blinking fresh tears Denver approached her—eager for a word, a sign of forgiveness.

Denver took off her shoes and stepped into the water with her. It took a moment for her to drag her eyes from the spectacle of Beloved's head to see what she was staring at.

A turtle inched along the edge, turned and climbed to dry ground. Not far behind it was another one, headed in the same direction. Four placed plates under a hovering motionless bowl. Behind her in the grass the other one moving quickly, quickly to mount her. The impregnable strength of him—earthing his feet near her shoulders. The embracing necks—hers stretching up toward his bending down, the pat pat pat of their touching heads. No height was beyond her yearning neck, stretched like a finger toward his, risking everything outside the bowl just to touch his face. The gravity of their shields, clashing, countered and mocked the floating heads touching.

Beloved dropped the folds of her skirt. It spread around her. The hem darkened in the water.

OUT OF SIGHT of Mister's sight, away, praise His name, from the smiling boss of roosters, Paul D began to tremble. Not all at once and not so anyone could tell. When he turned his head, aiming for a last look at Brother, turned it as much as the rope that connected his neck to the axle of a buckboard allowed, and, later on, when they fastened the iron around his ankles and clamped the wrists as well, there was no outward sign of trembling at all. Nor eighteen days after that when he saw the ditches; the one thousand feet of earth—five feet deep, five feet wide, into which wooden boxes had been fitted. A door of bars that you could lift on hinges like a cage opened into three walls and a roof of scrap lumber and red dirt. Two feet of it over his head; three feet of open trench in front of him with anything that crawled or scurried welcome to share that grave calling itself quarters. And there were forty-five more. He was sent there after trying to kill Brandywine, the man schoolteacher sold him to. Brandywine was leading him, in a coffle with ten others, through Kentucky into Virginia. He didn't know exactly what prompted him to try—other than Halle, Sixo, Paul A, Paul F and Mister. But the trembling was fixed by the time he knew it was there.

Still no one else knew it, because it began inside. A flutter of a kind, in the chest, then the shoulder blades. It felt like rippling—gentle at first and then wild. As though the further south they led him the more his blood, frozen like an ice pond for twenty years, began thawing, breaking into pieces that, once melted, had no choice but to swirl and eddy. Sometimes it was in his leg. Then again it

moved to the base of his spine. By the time they unhitched him from
the wagon and he saw nothing but dogs and two shacks in a world
of sizzling grass, the roiling blood was shaking him to and fro. But
no one could tell. The wrists he held out for the bracelets that evening
were steady as were the legs he stood on when chains were attached
to the leg irons. But when they shoved him into the box and dropped
the cage door down, his hands quit taking instruction. On their own,
they traveled. Nothing could stop them or get their attention. They
would not hold his penis to urinate or a spoon to scoop lumps of
lima beans into his mouth. The miracle of their obedience came with
the hammer at dawn.

All forty-six men woke to rifle shot. All forty-six. Three whitemen
walked along the trench unlocking the doors one by one. No one
stepped through. When the last lock was opened, the three returned
and lifted the bars, one by one. And one by one the blackmen
emerged—promptly and without the poke of a rifle butt if they had
been there more than a day; promptly with the butt if, like Paul D,
they had just arrived. When all forty-six were standing in a line in
the trench, another rifle shot signaled the climb out and up to the
ground above, where one thousand feet of the best hand-forged chain
in Georgia stretched. Each man bent and waited. The first man picked
up the end and threaded it through the loop on his leg iron. He stood
up then, and, shuffling a little, brought the chain tip to the next
prisoner, who did likewise. As the chain was passed on and each
man stood in the other's place, the line of men turned around, facing
the boxes they had come out of. Not one spoke to the other. At least
not with words. The eyes had to tell what there was to tell: "Help
me this mornin; 's bad"; "I'm a make it"; "New man"; "Steady now
steady."

Chain-up completed, they knelt down. The dew, more likely than
not, was mist by then. Heavy sometimes and if the dogs were quiet
and just breathing you could hear doves. Kneeling in the mist they
waited for the whim of a guard, or two, or three. Or maybe all of
them wanted it. Wanted it from one prisoner in particular or none—
or all.

"Breakfast? Want some breakfast, nigger?"

"Yes, sir."

"Hungry, nigger?"

"Yes, sir."

"Here you go."

Occasionally a kneeling man chose gunshot in his head as the price, maybe, of taking a bit of foreskin with him to Jesus. Paul D did not know that then. He was looking at his palsied hands, smelling the guard, listening to his soft grunts so like the doves', as he stood before the man kneeling in mist on his right. Convinced he was next, Paul D retched—vomiting up nothing at all. An observing guard smashed his shoulder with the rifle and the engaged one decided to skip the new man for the time being lest his pants and shoes got soiled by nigger puke.

"Hiiii!"

It was the first sound, other than "Yes, sir" a blackman was allowed to speak each morning, and the lead chain gave it everything he had. "Hiiii!" It was never clear to Paul D how he knew when to shout that mercy. They called him Hi Man and Paul D thought at first the guards told him when to give the signal that let the prisoners rise up off their knees and dance two-step to the music of hand-forged iron. Later he doubted it. He believed to this day that the "Hiiii!" at dawn and the "Hoooo!" when evening came were the responsibility Hi Man assumed because he alone knew what was enough, what was too much, when things were over, when the time had come.

They chain-danced over the fields, through the woods to a trail that ended in the astonishing beauty of feldspar, and there Paul D's hands disobeyed the furious rippling of his blood and paid attention. With a sledge hammer in his hands and Hi Man's lead, the men got through. They sang it out and beat it up, garbling the words so they could not be understood; tricking the words so their syllables yielded up other meanings. They sang the women they knew; the children they had been; the animals they had tamed themselves or seen others tame. They sang of bosses and masters and misses; of mules and dogs and the shamelessness of life. They sang lovingly of graveyards and sisters long gone. Of pork in the woods; meal in the pan; fish on the line; cane, rain and rocking chairs.

And they beat. The women for having known them and no more,

no more; the children for having been them but never again. They killed a boss so often and so completely they had to bring him back to life to pulp him one more time. Tasting hot mealcake among pine trees, they beat it away. Singing love songs to Mr. Death, they smashed his head. More than the rest, they killed the flirt whom folks called Life for leading them on. Making them think the next sunrise would be worth it; that another stroke of time would do it at last. Only when she was dead would they be safe. The successful ones—the ones who had been there enough years to have maimed, mutilated, maybe even buried her—kept watch over the others who were still in her cock-teasing hug, caring and looking forward, remembering and looking back. They were the ones whose eyes said, "Help me, 's bad"; or "Look out," meaning *this might be the day I bay or eat my own mess or run,* and it was this last that had to be guarded against, for if one pitched and ran—all, all forty-six, would be yanked by the chain that bound them and no telling who or how many would be killed. A man could risk his own life, but not his brother's. So the eyes said, "Steady now," and "Hang by me."

Eighty-six days and done. Life was dead. Paul D beat her butt all day every day till there was not a whimper in her. Eighty-six days and his hands were still, waiting serenely each rat-rustling night for "Hiiii!" at dawn and the eager clench on the hammer's shaft. Life rolled over dead. Or so he thought.

It rained.

Snakes came down from short-leaf pine and hemlock.

It rained.

Cypress, yellow poplar, ash and palmetto drooped under five days of rain without wind. By the eighth day the doves were nowhere in sight, by the ninth even the salamanders were gone. Dogs laid their ears down and stared over their paws. The men could not work. Chain-up was slow, breakfast abandoned, the two-step became a slow drag over soupy grass and unreliable earth.

It was decided to lock everybody down in the boxes till it either stopped or lightened up so a whiteman could walk, damnit, without flooding his gun and the dogs could quit shivering. The chain was threaded through forty-six loops of the best hand-forged iron in Georgia.

It rained.

In the boxes the men heard the water rise in the trench and looked out for cottonmouths. They squatted in muddy water, slept above it, peed in it. Paul D thought he was screaming; his mouth was open and there was this loud throat-splitting sound—but it may have been somebody else. Then he thought he was crying. Something was running down his cheeks. He lifted his hands to wipe away the tears and saw dark brown slime. Above him rivulets of mud slid through the boards of the roof. When it come down, he thought, gonna crush me like a tick bug. It happened so quick he had no time to ponder. Somebody yanked the chain—once—hard enough to cross his legs and throw him into the mud. He never figured out how he knew—how anybody did—but he did know—he did—and he took both hands and yanked the length of chain at his left, so the next man would know too. The water was above his ankles, flowing over the wooden plank he slept on. And then it wasn't water anymore. The ditch was caving in and mud oozed under and through the bars.

They waited—each and every one of the forty-six. Not screaming, although some of them must have fought like the devil not to. The mud was up to his thighs and he held on to the bars. Then it came—another yank—from the left this time and less forceful than the first because of the mud it passed through.

It started like the chain-up but the difference was the power of the chain. One by one, from Hi Man back on down the line, they dove. Down through the mud under the bars, blind, groping. Some had sense enough to wrap their heads in their shirts, cover their faces with rags, put on their shoes. Others just plunged, simply ducked down and pushed out, fighting up, reaching for air. Some lost direction and their neighbors, feeling the confused pull of the chain, snatched them around. For one lost, all lost. The chain that held them would save all or none, and Hi Man was the Delivery. They talked through that chain like Sam Morse and, Great God, they all came up. Like the unshriven dead, zombies on the loose, holding the chains in their hands, they trusted the rain and the dark, yes, but mostly Hi Man and each other.

Past the sheds where the dogs lay in deep depression; past the two guard shacks, past the stable of sleeping horses, past the hens whose bills were bolted into their feathers, they waded. The moon did not help because it wasn't there. The field was a marsh, the track a trough. All Georgia seemed to be sliding, melting away. Moss wiped their faces as they fought the live-oak branches that blocked their way. Georgia took up all of Alabama and Mississippi then, so there was no state line to cross and it wouldn't have mattered anyway. If they had known about it, they would have avoided not only Alfred and the beautiful feldspar, but Savannah too and headed for the Sea Islands on the river that slid down from the Blue Ridge Mountains. But they didn't know.

Daylight came and they huddled in a copse of redbud trees. Night came and they scrambled up to higher ground, praying the rain would go on shielding them and keeping folks at home. They were hoping for a shack, solitary, some distance from its big house, where a slave might be making rope or heating potatoes at the grate. What they found was a camp of sick Cherokee for whom a rose was named.

Decimated but stubborn, they were among those who chose a fugitive life rather than Oklahoma. The illness that swept them now was reminiscent of the one that had killed half their number two hundred years earlier. In between that calamity and this, they had visited George III in London, published a newspaper, made baskets, led Oglethorpe through forests, helped Andrew Jackson fight Creek, cooked maize, drawn up a constitution, petitioned the King of Spain, been experimented on by Dartmouth, established asylums, wrote their language, resisted settlers, shot bear and translated scripture. All to no avail. The forced move to the Arkansas River, insisted upon by the same president they fought for against the Creek, destroyed another quarter of their already shattered number.

That was it, they thought, and removed themselves from those Cherokee who signed the treaty, in order to retire into the forest and await the end of the world. The disease they suffered now was a mere inconvenience compared to the devastation they remembered. Still, they protected each other as best they could. The healthy were sent some miles away; the sick stayed behind with the dead—to survive or join them.

The prisoners from Alfred, Georgia, sat down in semicircle near the encampment. No one came and still they sat. Hours passed and the rain turned soft. Finally a woman stuck her head out of her house. Night came and nothing happened. At dawn two men with barnacles covering their beautiful skin approached them. No one spoke for a moment, then Hi Man raised his hand. The Cherokee saw the chains and went away. When they returned each carried a handful of small axes. Two children followed with a pot of mush cooling and thinning in the rain.

Buffalo men, they called them, and talked slowly to the prisoners scooping mush and tapping away at their chains. Nobody from a box in Alfred, Georgia, cared about the illness the Cherokee warned them about, so they stayed, all forty-six, resting, planning their next move. Paul D had no idea of what to do and knew less than anybody, it seemed. He heard his co-convicts talk knowledgeably of rivers and states, towns and territories. Heard Cherokee men describe the beginning of the world and its end. Listened to tales of other Buffalo men they knew—three of whom were in the healthy camp a few miles away. Hi Man wanted to join them; others wanted to join him. Some wanted to leave; some to stay on. Weeks later Paul D was the only Buffalo man left—without a plan. All he could think of was tracking dogs, although Hi Man said the rain they left in gave that no chance of success. Alone, the last man with buffalo hair among the ailing Cherokee, Paul D finally woke up and, admitting his ignorance, asked how he might get North. Free North. Magical North. Welcoming, benevolent North. The Cherokee smiled and looked around. The flood rains of a month ago had turned everything to steam and blossoms.

"That way," he said, pointing. "Follow the tree flowers," he said. "Only the tree flowers. As they go, you go. You will be where you want to be when they are gone."

So he raced from dogwood to blossoming peach. When they thinned out he headed for the cherry blossoms, then magnolia, chinaberry, pecan, walnut and prickly pear. At last he reached a field of apple trees whose flowers were just becoming tiny knots of fruit. Spring sauntered north, but he had to run like hell to keep it as his traveling companion. From February to July he was on the lookout for blossoms. When he lost them, and found himself without so much as a petal to guide him, he paused, climbed a tree on a hillock and scanned the horizon for a flash of pink or white in the leaf world that surrounded him. He did not touch them or stop to smell. He merely followed in their wake, a dark ragged figure guided by the blossoming plums.

The apple field turned out to be Delaware where the weaver lady lived. She snapped him up as soon as he finished the sausage she fed him and he crawled into her bed crying. She passed him off as her nephew from Syracuse simply by calling him that nephew's name. Eighteen months and he was looking out again for blossoms only this time he did the looking on a dray.

It was some time before he could put Alfred, Georgia, Sixo, schoolteacher, Halle, his brothers, Sethe, Mister, the taste of iron, the sight of butter, the smell of hickory, notebook paper, one by one, into the tobacco tin lodged in his chest. By the time he got to 124 nothing in this world could pry it open.

SHE MOVED HIM.

Not the way he had beat off the baby's ghost—all bang and shriek with windows smashed and jelly jars rolled in a heap. But she moved him nonetheless, and Paul D didn't know how to stop it because it looked like he was moving himself. Imperceptibly, downright reasonably, he was moving out of 124.

The beginning was so simple. One day, after supper, he sat in the rocker by the stove, bone-tired, river-whipped, and fell asleep. He woke to the footsteps of Sethe coming down the white stairs to make breakfast.

"I thought you went out somewhere," she said.

Paul D moaned, surprised to find himself exactly where he was the last time he looked.

"Don't tell me I slept in this chair the whole night."

Sethe laughed. "Me? I won't say a word to you."

"Why didn't you rouse me?"

"I did. Called you two or three times. I gave it up around midnight and then I thought you went out somewhere."

He stood, expecting his back to fight it. But it didn't. Not a creak or a stiff joint anywhere. In fact he felt refreshed. Some things are like that, he thought, good-sleep places. The base of certain trees here and there; a wharf, a bench, a rowboat once, a haystack usually, not always bed, and here, now, a rocking chair, which was strange because in his experience furniture was the worst place for a good-sleep sleep.

The next evening he did it again and then again. He was accustomed to sex with Sethe just about every day, and to avoid the confusion Beloved's shining caused him he still made it his business to take her back upstairs in the morning, or lie down with her after supper. But he found a way and a reason to spend the longest part of the night in the rocker. He told himself it must be his back—something supportive it needed for a weakness left over from sleeping in a box in Georgia.

It went on that way and might have stayed that way but one evening, after supper, after Sethe, he came downstairs, sat in the rocker and didn't want to be there. He stood up and realized he didn't want to go upstairs either. Irritable and longing for rest, he opened the door to Baby Suggs' room and dropped off to sleep on the bed the old lady died in. That settled it—so it seemed. It became his room and Sethe didn't object—her bed made for two had been occupied by one for eighteen years before Paul D came to call. And maybe it was better this way, with young girls in the house and him not being her true-to-life husband. In any case, since there was no reduction in his before-breakfast or after-supper appetites, he never heard her complain.

It went on that way and might have stayed that way, except one evening, after supper, after Sethe, he came downstairs and lay on Baby Suggs' bed and didn't want to be there.

He believed he was having house-fits, the glassy anger men sometimes feel when a woman's house begins to bind them, when they want to yell and break something or at least run off. He knew all about that—felt it lots of times—in the Delaware weaver's house, for instance. But always he associated the house-fit with the woman in it. This nervousness had nothing to do with the woman, whom he loved a little bit more every day: her hands among vegetables, her mouth when she licked a thread end before guiding it through a needle or bit it in two when the seam was done, the blood in her eye when she defended her girls (and Beloved was hers now) or any coloredwoman from a slur. Also in this house-fit there was no anger, no suffocation, no yearning to be elsewhere. He just could not, would not, sleep upstairs or in the rocker or, now, in Baby Suggs' bed. So he went to the storeroom.

It went on that way and might have stayed that way except one evening, after supper, after Sethe, he lay on a pallet in the storeroom and didn't want to be there. Then it was the cold house and it was out there, separated from the main part of 124, curled on top of two croaker sacks full of sweet potatoes, staring at the sides of a lard can, that he realized the moving was involuntary. He wasn't being nervous; he was being prevented.

So he waited. Visited Sethe in the morning; slept in the cold room at night and waited.

She came, and he wanted to knock her down.

In Ohio seasons are theatrical. Each one enters like a prima donna, convinced its performance is the reason the world has people in it. When Paul D had been forced out of 124 into a shed behind it, summer had been hooted offstage and autumn with its bottles of blood and gold had everybody's attention. Even at night, when there should have been a restful intermission, there was none because the voices of a dying landscape were insistent and loud. Paul D packed newspaper under himself and over, to give his thin blanket some help. But the chilly night was not on his mind. When he heard the door open behind him he refused to turn and look.

"What you want in here? What you want?" He should have been able to hear her breathing.

"I want you to touch me on the inside part and call me my name."

Paul D never worried about his little tobacco tin anymore. It was rusted shut. So, while she hoisted her skirts and turned her head over her shoulder the way the turtles had, he just looked at the lard can, silvery in moonlight, and spoke quietly.

"When good people take you in and treat you good, you ought to try to be good back. You don't . . . Sethe loves you. Much as her own daughter. You know that."

Beloved dropped her skirts as he spoke and looked at him with empty eyes. She took a step he could not hear and stood close behind him.

"She don't love me like I love her. I don't love nobody but her."

"Then what you come in here for?"

"I want you to touch me on the inside part."

"Go on back in that house and get to bed."

"You have to touch me. On the inside part. And you have to call me my name."

As long as his eyes were locked on the silver of the lard can he was safe. If he trembled like Lot's wife and felt some womanish need to see the nature of the sin behind him; feel a sympathy, perhaps, for the cursing cursed, or want to hold it in his arms out of respect for the connection between them, he too would be lost.

"Call me my name."

"No."

"Please call it. I'll go if you call it."

"Beloved." He said it, but she did not go. She moved closer with a footfall he didn't hear and he didn't hear the whisper that the flakes of rust made either as they fell away from the seams of his tobacco tin. So when the lid gave he didn't know it. What he knew was that when he reached the inside part he was saying, "Red heart. Red heart," over and over again. Softly and then so loud it woke Denver, then Paul D himself. "Red heart. Red heart. Red heart."

TO GO BACK to the original hunger was impossible. Luckily for Denver, looking was food enough to last. But to be looked at in turn was beyond appetite; it was breaking through her own skin to a place where hunger hadn't been discovered. It didn't have to happen often, because Beloved seldom looked right at her, or when she did, Denver could tell that her own face was just the place those eyes stopped while the mind behind it walked on. But sometimes—at moments Denver could neither anticipate nor create—Beloved rested cheek on knuckles and looked at Denver with attention.

It was lovely. Not to be stared at, not seen, but being pulled into view by the interested, uncritical eyes of the other. Having her hair examined as a part of her self, not as material or a style. Having her lips, nose, chin caressed as they might be if she were a moss rose a gardener paused to admire. Denver's skin dissolved under that gaze and became soft and bright like the lisle dress that had its arm around her mother's waist. She floated near but outside her own body, feeling vague and intense at the same time. Needing nothing. Being what there was.

At such times it seemed to be Beloved who needed something—wanted something. Deep down in her wide black eyes, back behind the expressionlessness, was a palm held out for a penny which Denver would gladly give her, if only she knew how or knew enough about her, a knowledge not to be had by the answers to the questions Sethe occasionally put to her: "You disremember everything? I never knew my mother neither, but I saw her a couple of times. Did you never see yours? What kind of whites was they? You don't remember none?"

Beloved, scratching the back of her hand, would say she remembered a woman who was hers, and she remembered being snatched away from her. Other than that, the clearest memory she had, the one she repeated, was the bridge—standing on the bridge looking down. And she knew one whiteman.

Sethe found that remarkable and more evidence to support her conclusions, which she confided to Denver.

"Where'd you get the dress, them shoes?"

Beloved said she took them.

"Who from?"

Silence and a faster scratching of her hand. She didn't know; she saw them and just took them.

"Uh huh," said Sethe, and told Denver that she believed Beloved had been locked up by some whiteman for his own purposes, and never let out the door. That she must have escaped to a bridge or someplace and rinsed the rest out of her mind. Something like that had happened to Ella except it was two men—a father and son— and Ella remembered every bit of it. For more than a year, they kept her locked in a room for themselves.

"You couldn't think up," Ella had said, "what them two done to me."

Sethe thought it explained Beloved's behavior around Paul D, whom she hated so.

Denver neither believed nor commented on Sethe's speculations, and she lowered her eyes and never said a word about the cold house. She was certain that Beloved was the white dress that had knelt with her mother in the keeping room, the true-to-life presence of the baby that had kept her company most of her life. And to be looked at by her, however briefly, kept her grateful for the rest of the time when she was merely the looker. Besides, she had her own set of questions which had nothing to do with the past. The present alone interested Denver, but she was careful to appear uninquisitive about the things she was dying to ask Beloved, for if she pressed too hard, she might lose the penny that the held-out palm wanted, and lose, therefore, the place beyond appetite. It was better to feast, to have permission to be the looker, because the old hunger—the before-Beloved hunger that drove her into boxwood and cologne for just a taste of a life, to feel it bumpy and not flat—was out of the question. Looking kept it at bay.

So she did not ask Beloved how she knew about the earrings, the night walks to the cold house or the tip of the thing she saw when Beloved lay down or came undone in her sleep. The look, when it came, came when Denver had been careful, had explained things, or participated in things, or told stories to keep her occupied when Sethe was at the restaurant. No given chore was enough to put out the licking fire that seemed always to burn in her. Not when they wrung out sheets so tight the rinse water ran back up their arms. Not when they shoveled snow from the path to the outhouse. Or broke three inches of ice from the rain barrel; scoured and boiled last summer's canning jars, packed mud in the cracks of the hen house and warmed the chicks with their skirts. All the while Denver was obliged to talk about what they were doing—the how and why of it. About people Denver knew once or had seen, giving them more life than life had: the sweet-smelling whitewoman who brought her oranges and cologne and good wool skirts; Lady Jones who taught them songs to spell and count by; a beautiful boy as smart as she was with a birthmark like a nickel on his cheek. A white preacher who prayed for their souls while Sethe peeled potatoes and Grandma Baby sucked air. And she told her about Howard and Buglar: the parts of the bed that belonged to each (the top reserved for herself); that before she transferred to Baby Suggs' bed she never knew them to sleep without holding hands. She described them to Beloved slowly, to keep her attention, dwelling on their habits, the games they taught her and not the fright that drove them increasingly out of the house—anywhere—and finally far away.

This day they are outside. It's cold and the snow is hard as packed dirt. Denver has finished singing the counting song Lady Jones taught her students. Beloved is holding her arms steady while Denver unclasps frozen underwear and towels from the line. One by one she lays them in Beloved's arms until the pile, like a huge deck of cards, reaches her chin. The rest, aprons and brown stockings, Denver carries herself. Made giddy by the cold, they return to the house. The clothes will thaw slowly to a dampness perfect for the pressing iron, which will make them smell like hot rain. Dancing around the room with Sethe's apron, Beloved wants to know if there are flowers in the dark. Denver adds sticks to the stovefire and assures her there are. Twirling, her face framed by the neckband, her waist in the apron strings' embrace, she says she is thirsty.

Denver suggests warming up some cider, while her mind races to something she might do or say to interest and entertain the dancer. Denver is a strategist now and has to keep Beloved by her side from the minute Sethe leaves for work until the hour of her return when Beloved begins to hover at the window, then work her way out the door, down the steps and near the road. Plotting has changed Denver markedly. Where she was once indolent, resentful of every task, now she is spry, executing, even extending the assignments Sethe leaves for them. All to be able to say "We got to" and "Ma'am said for us to." Otherwise Beloved gets private and dreamy, or quiet and sullen, and Denver's chances of being looked at by her go down to nothing. She has no control over the evenings. When her mother is anywhere around, Beloved has eyes only for Sethe. At night, in bed, anything might happen. She might want to be told a story in the dark when Denver can't see her. Or she might get up and go into the cold house where Paul D has begun to sleep. Or she might cry, silently. She might even sleep like a brick, her breath sugary from fingerfuls of molasses or sand-cookie crumbs. Denver will turn toward her then, and if Beloved faces her, she will inhale deeply the sweet air from her mouth. If not, she will have to lean up and over her, every once in a while, to catch a sniff. For anything is better than the original hunger—the time when, after a year of the wonderful little *i*, sentences rolling out like pie dough and the company of other children, there was no sound coming through. Anything is better than the silence when she answered to hands gesturing and was indifferent to the movement of lips. When she saw every little thing and colors leaped smoldering into view. She will forgo the most violent of sunsets, stars as fat as dinner plates and all the blood of autumn and settle for the palest yellow if it comes from her Beloved.

The cider jug is heavy, but it always is, even when empty. Denver can carry it easily, yet she asks Beloved to help her. It is in the cold house next to the molasses and six pounds of cheddar hard as bone. A pallet is in the middle of the floor covered with newspaper and a blanket at the foot. It has been slept on for almost a month, even though snow has come and, with it, serious winter.

It is noon, quite light outside; inside it is not. A few cuts of sun break through the roof and walls but once there they are too weak to shift for themselves. Darkness is stronger and swallows them like minnows.

The door bangs shut. Denver can't tell where Beloved is standing.

"Where are you?" she whispers in a laughing sort of way.

"Here," says Beloved.

"Where?"

"Come find me," says Beloved.

Denver stretches out her right arm and takes a step or two. She trips and falls down onto the pallet. Newspaper crackles under her weight. She laughs again. "Oh, shoot. Beloved?"

No one answers. Denver waves her arms and squinches her eyes to separate the shadows of potato sacks, a lard can and a side of smoked pork from the one that might be human.

"Stop fooling," she says and looks up toward the light to check and make sure this is still the cold house and not something going on in her sleep. The minnows of light still swim there; they can't make it down to where she is.

"You the one thirsty. You want cider or don't you?" Denver's voice is mildly accusatory. Mildly. She doesn't want to offend and she doesn't want to betray the panic that is creeping over her like hairs. There is no sight or sound of Beloved. Denver struggles to her feet amid the crackling newspaper. Holding her palm out, she moves slowly toward the door. There is no latch or knob—just a loop of wire to catch a nail. She pushes the door open. Cold sunlight displaces the dark. The room is just as it was when they entered—except Beloved is not there. There is no point in looking further, for everything in the place can be seen at first sight. Denver looks anyway because the loss is ungovernable. She steps back into the shed, allowing the door to close quickly behind her. Darkness or not, she moves rapidly around, reaching, touching cobwebs, cheese, slanting shelves, the pallet interfering with each step. If she stumbles, she is not aware of it because she does not know where her body stops, which part of her is an arm, a foot or a knee. She feels like an ice cake torn away from the solid surface of the stream, floating on darkness, thick and crashing against the edges of things around it. Breakable, meltable and cold.

It is hard to breathe and even if there were light she wouldn't be able to see anything because she is crying. Just as she thought it might happen, it has. Easy as walking into a room. A magical appearance on a stump, the face wiped out by sunlight, and a magical disappearance in a shed, eaten alive by the dark.

"Don't," she is saying between tough swallows. "Don't. Don't go back."

This is worse than when Paul D came to 124 and she cried helplessly into the stove. This is worse. Then it was for herself. Now she is crying because she has no self. Death is a skipped meal compared to this. She can feel her thickness thinning, dissolving into nothing. She grabs the hair at her temples to get enough to uproot it and halt the melting for a while. Teeth clamped shut, Denver brakes her sobs. She doesn't move to open the door because there is no world out there. She decides to stay in the cold house and let the dark swallow her like the minnows of light above. She won't put up with another leaving, another trick. Waking up to find one brother then another not at the bottom of the bed, his foot jabbing her spine. Sitting at the table eating turnips and saving the liquor for her grandmother to drink; her mother's hand on the keeping-room door and her voice saying, "Baby Suggs is gone, Denver." And when she got around to worrying about what would be the case if Sethe died or Paul D took her away, a dream-come-true comes true just to leave her on a pile of newspaper in the dark.

No footfall announces her, but there she is, standing where before there was nobody when Denver looked. And smiling.

Denver grabs the hem of Beloved's skirt. "I thought you left me. I thought you went back."

Beloved smiles, "I don't want that place. This the place I am." She sits down on the pallet and, laughing, lies back looking at the cracklights above.

Surreptitiously, Denver pinches a piece of Beloved's skirt between her fingers and holds on. A good thing she does because suddenly Beloved sits up.

"What is it?" asks Denver.

"Look," she points to the sunlit cracks.

"What? I don't see nothing." Denver follows the pointing finger.

Beloved drops her hand. "I'm like this."

Denver watches as Beloved bends over, curls up and rocks. Her eyes go to no place; her moaning is so small Denver can hardly hear it.

"You all right? Beloved?"

Beloved focuses her eyes. "Over there. Her face."

Denver looks where Beloved's eyes go; there is nothing but darkness there.

"Whose face? Who is it?"

"Me. It's me."

She is smiling again.

THE LAST of the Sweet Home men, so named and called by one who would know, believed it. The other four believed it too, once, but they were long gone. The sold one never returned, the lost one never found. One, he knew, was dead for sure; one he hoped was, because butter and clabber was no life or reason to live it. He grew up thinking that, of all the Blacks in Kentucky, only the five of them were men. Allowed, encouraged to correct Garner, even defy him. To invent ways of doing things; to see what was needed and attack it without permission. To buy a mother, choose a horse or a wife, handle guns, even learn reading if they wanted to—but they didn't want to since nothing important to them could be put down on paper.

Was that it? Is that where the manhood lay? In the naming done by a whiteman who was supposed to know? Who gave them the privilege not of working but of deciding how to? No. In their relationship with Garner was true metal: they were believed and trusted, but most of all they were listened to.

He thought what they said had merit, and what they felt was serious. Deferring to his slaves' opinions did not deprive him of authority or power. It was schoolteacher who taught them otherwise. A truth that waved like a scarecrow in rye: they were only Sweet Home men at Sweet Home. One step off that ground and they were trespassers among the human race. Watchdogs without teeth; steer bulls without horns; gelded workhorses whose neigh and whinny could not be translated into a language responsible humans spoke.

His strength had lain in knowing that schoolteacher was wrong. Now he wondered. There was Alfred, Georgia, there was Delaware, there was Sixo and still he wondered. If schoolteacher was right it explained how he had come to be a rag doll—picked up and put back down anywhere any time by a girl young enough to be his daughter. Fucking her when he was convinced he didn't want to. Whenever she turned her behind up, the calves of his youth (was that it?) cracked his resolve. But it was more than appetite that humiliated him and made him wonder if schoolteacher was right. It was being moved, placed where she wanted him, and there was nothing he was able to do about it. For his life he could not walk up the glistening white stairs in the evening; for his life he could not stay in the kitchen, in the keeping room, in the storeroom at night. And he tried. Held his breath the way he had when he ducked into the mud; steeled his heart the way he had when the trembling began. But it was worse than that, worse than the blood eddy he had controlled with a sledge hammer. When he stood up from the supper table at 124 and turned toward the stairs, nausea was first, then repulsion. He, he. He who had eaten raw meat barely dead, who under plum trees bursting with blossoms had crunched through a dove's breast before its heart stopped beating. Because he was a man and a man could do what he would: be still for six hours in a dry well while night dropped; fight raccoon with his hands and win; watch another man, whom he loved better than his brothers, roast without a tear just so the roasters would know what a man was like. And it was he, *that* man, who had walked from Georgia to Delaware, who could not go or stay put where he wanted to in 124—shame.

Paul D could not command his feet, but he thought he could still talk and he made up his mind to break out that way. He would tell Sethe about the last three weeks: catch her alone coming from work at the beer garden she called a restaurant and tell it all.

He waited for her. The winter afternoon looked like dusk as he stood in the alley behind Sawyer's Restaurant. Rehearsing, imagining her face and letting the words flock in his head like kids before lining up to follow the leader.

"Well, ah, this is not the, a man can't, see, but aw listen here, it ain't that, it really ain't, Ole Garner, what I mean is, it ain't a weakness, the kind of weakness I can fight 'cause 'cause something is happening to me, that girl is doing it, I know you think I never liked her nohow, but she is doing it to me. Fixing me. Sethe, she's fixed me and I can't break it."

What? A grown man fixed by a girl? But what if the girl was not a girl, but something in disguise? A lowdown something that looked like a sweet young girl and fucking her or not was not the point, it was not being able to stay or go where he wished in 124, and the danger was in losing Sethe because he was not man enough to break out, so he needed her, Sethe, to help him, to know about it, and it shamed him to have to ask the woman he wanted to protect to help him do it, God damn it to hell.

Paul D blew warm breath into the hollow of his cupped hands. The wind raced down the alley so fast it sleeked the fur of four kitchen dogs waiting for scraps. He looked at the dogs. The dogs looked at him.

Finally the back door opened and Sethe stepped through holding a scrap pan in the crook of her arm. When she saw him, she said Oh, and her smile was both pleasure and surprise.

Paul D believed he smiled back but his face was so cold he wasn't sure.

"Man, you make me feel like a girl, coming by to pick me up after work. Nobody ever did that before. You better watch out, I might start looking forward to it." She tossed the largest bones into the dirt rapidly so the dogs would know there was enough and not fight each other. Then she dumped the skins of some things, heads of other things and the insides of still more things—what the restaurant could not use and she would not—in a smoking pile near the animals' feet.

"Got to rinse this out," she said, "and then I'll be right with you."

He nodded as she returned to the kitchen.

The dogs ate without sound and Paul D thought they at least got what they came for, and if she had enough for them—

The cloth on her head was brown wool and she edged it down over her hairline against the wind.

"You get off early or what?"

"I took off early."

"Anything the matter?"

"In a way of speaking," he said and wiped his lips.

"Not cut back?"

"No, no. They got plenty work. I just—"

"Hm?"

"Sethe, you won't like what I'm 'bout to say."

She stopped then and turned her face toward him and the hateful wind. Another woman would have squinted or at least teared if the wind whipped her face as it did Sethe's. Another woman might have shot him a look of apprehension, pleading, anger even, because what he said sure sounded like part one of Goodbye, I'm gone.

Sethe looked at him steadily, calmly, already ready to accept, release or excuse an in-need-or-trouble man. Agreeing, saying okay, all right, in advance, because she didn't believe any of them—over the long haul—could measure up. And whatever the reason, it was all right. No fault. Nobody's fault.

He knew what she was thinking and even though she was wrong—he was not leaving her, wouldn't ever—the thing he had in mind to tell her was going to be worse. So, when he saw the diminished expectation in her eyes, the melancholy without blame, he could not say it. He could not say to this woman who did not squint in the wind, "I am not a man."

"Well, say it, Paul D, whether I like it or not."

Since he could not say what he planned to, he said something he didn't know was on his mind. "I want you pregnant, Sethe. Would you do that for me?"

Now she was laughing and so was he.

"You came by here to ask me that? You are one crazy-headed man. You right; I don't like it. Don't you think I'm too old to start that all over again?" She slipped her fingers in his hand for all the world like the hand-holding shadows on the side of the road.

"Think about it," he said. And suddenly it was a solution: a way to hold on to her, document his manhood and break out of the girl's spell—all in one. He put the tips of Sethe's fingers on his cheek. Laughing, she pulled them away lest somebody passing the alley see them misbehaving in public, in daylight, in the wind.

Still, he'd gotten a little more time, bought it, in fact, and hoped the price wouldn't wreck him. Like paying for an afternoon in the coin of life to come.

They left off playing, let go hands and hunched forward as they left the alley and entered the street. The wind was quieter there but the dried-out cold it left behind kept pedestrians fast-moving, stiff inside their coats. No men leaned against door frames or storefront windows. The wheels of wagons delivering feed or wood screeched as though they hurt. Hitched horses in front of the saloons shivered and closed their eyes. Four women, walking two abreast, approached, their shoes loud on the wooden walkway. Paul D touched Sethe's elbow to guide her as they stepped from the slats to the dirt to let the women pass.

Half an hour later, when they reached the city's edge, Sethe and Paul D resumed catching and snatching each other's fingers, stealing quick pats on the behind. Joyfully embarrassed to be that grown-up and that young at the same time.

Resolve, he thought. That was all it took, and no motherless gal was going to break it up. No lazy, stray pup of a woman could turn him around, make him doubt himself, wonder, plead or confess. Convinced of it, that he could do it, he threw his arm around Sethe's shoulders and squeezed. She let her head touch his chest, and since the moment was valuable to both of them, they stopped and stood that way—not breathing, not even caring if a passerby passed them by. The winter light was low. Sethe closed her eyes. Paul D looked at the black trees lining the roadside, their defending arms raised against attack. Softly, suddenly, it began to snow, like a present come down from the sky. Sethe opened her eyes to it and said, "Mercy." And it seemed to Paul D that it was—a little mercy—something given to them on purpose to mark what they were feeling so they would remember it later on when they needed to.

Down came the dry flakes, fat enough and heavy enough to crash like nickels on stone. It always surprised him, how quiet it was. Not like rain, but like a secret.

"Run!" he said.

"You run," said Sethe. "I been on my feet all day."

"Where I been? Sitting down?" and he pulled her along.

"Stop! Stop!" she said. "I don't have the legs for this."

"Then give em to me," he said and before she knew it he had backed into her, hoisted her on his back and was running down the road past brown fields turning white.

Breathless at last, he stopped and she slid back down on her own two feet, weak from laughter.

"You *need* some babies, somebody to play with in the snow." Sethe secured her headcloth.

Paul D smiled and warmed his hands with his breath. "I sure would like to give it a try. Need a willing partner though."

"I'll say," she answered. "Very, very willing."

It was nearly four o'clock now and 124 was half a mile ahead. Floating toward them, barely visible in the drifting snow, was a figure, and although it was the same figure that had been meeting Sethe for four months, so complete was the attention she and Paul D were paying to themselves they both felt a jolt when they saw her close in.

Beloved did not look at Paul D; her scrutiny was for Sethe. She had no coat, no wrap, nothing on her head, but she held in her hands a long shawl. Stretching out her arms she tried to circle it around Sethe.

"Crazy girl," said Sethe. "You the one out here with nothing on." And stepping away and in front of Paul D, Sethe took the shawl and wrapped it around Beloved's head and shoulders. Saying, "You got to learn more sense than that," she enclosed her in her left arm. Snowflakes stuck now. Paul D felt icy cold in the place Sethe had been before Beloved came. Trailing a yard or so behind the women, he fought the anger that shot through his stomach all the way home. When he saw Denver silhouetted in the lamplight at the window, he could not help thinking, "And whose ally you?"

It was Sethe who did it. Unsuspecting, surely, she solved everything with one blow.

"Now I know you not sleeping out there tonight, are you, Paul D?" She smiled at him, and like a friend in need, the chimney coughed against the rush of cold shooting into it from the sky. Window sashes shuddered in a blast of winter air.

Paul D looked up from the stew meat.

"You come upstairs. Where you belong," she said, ". . . and stay there."

The threads of malice creeping toward him from Beloved's side of the table were held harmless in the warmth of Sethe's smile.

Once before (and only once) Paul D had been grateful to a woman. Crawling out of the woods, cross-eyed with hunger and loneliness, he knocked at the first back door he came to in the colored section of Wilmington. He told the woman who opened it that he'd appreciate doing her woodpile, if she could spare him something to eat. She looked him up and down.

"A little later on," she said and opened the door wider. She fed him pork sausage, the worst thing in the world for a starving man, but neither he nor his stomach objected. Later, when he saw pale cotton sheets and two pillows in her bedroom, he had to wipe his eyes quickly, quickly so she would not see the thankful tears of a man's first time. Soil, grass, mud, shucking, leaves, hay, cobs, seashells—all that he'd slept on. White cotton sheets had never crossed his mind. He fell in with a groan and the woman helped him pretend he was making love to her and not her bed linen. He vowed that night, full of pork, deep in luxury, that he would never leave her. She would have to kill him to get him out of that bed. Eighteen months later, when he had been purchased by Northpoint Bank and Railroad Company, he was still thankful for that introduction to sheets.

Now he was grateful a second time. He felt as though he had been plucked from the face of a cliff and put down on sure ground. In Sethe's bed he knew he could put up with two crazy girls—as long as Sethe made her wishes known. Stretched out to his full length, watching snowflakes stream past the window over his feet, it was easy to dismiss the doubts that took him to the alley behind the restaurant: his expectations for himself were high, too high. What he might call cowardice other people called common sense.

Tucked into the well of his arm, Sethe recalled Paul D's face in the street when he asked her to have a baby for him. Although she laughed and took his hand, it had frightened her. She thought quickly of how good the sex would be if that is what he wanted, but mostly she was frightened by the thought of having a baby once more. Needing to be good enough, alert enough, strong enough, *that* caring—again. Having to stay alive just that much longer. O Lord, she thought, deliver me. Unless carefree, motherlove was a killer. What did he want her pregnant for? To hold on to her? have a sign that he passed this way? He probably had children everywhere anyway. Eighteen years of roaming, he would have to have dropped a few. No. He resented the children she had, that's what. Child, she corrected herself. Child plus Beloved whom she thought of as her own, and that is what he resented. Sharing her with the girls. Hearing the three of them laughing at something he wasn't in on. The code they used among themselves that he could not break. Maybe even the time spent on their needs and not his. They were a family somehow and he was not the head of it.

Can you stitch this up for me, baby?

Um hm. Soon's I finish this petticoat. She just got the one she came here in and everybody needs a change.

Any pie left?

I think Denver got the last of it.

And not complaining, not even minding that he slept all over and around the house now, which she put a stop to this night out of courtesy.

Sethe sighed and placed her hand on his chest. She knew she was building a case against him in order to build a case against getting pregnant, and it shamed her a little. But she had all the children she needed. If her boys came back one day, and Denver and Beloved stayed on—well, it would be the way it was supposed to be, no? Right after she saw the shadows holding hands at the side of the road hadn't the picture altered? And the minute she saw the dress and shoes sitting in the front yard, she broke water. Didn't even have to see the face burning in the sunlight. She had been dreaming it for years.

Paul D's chest rose and fell, rose and fell under her hand.

DENVER FINISHED washing the dishes and sat down at the table. Beloved, who had not moved since Sethe and Paul D left the room, sat sucking her forefinger. Denver watched her face awhile and then said, "She likes him here."

Beloved went on probing her mouth with her finger. "Make him go away," she said.

"She might be mad at you if he leaves."

Beloved, inserting a thumb in her mouth along with the forefinger, pulled out a back tooth. There was hardly any blood, but Denver said, "Ooooh, didn't that hurt you?"

Beloved looked at the tooth and thought, This is it. Next would be her arm, her hand, a toe. Pieces of her would drop maybe one at a time, maybe all at once. Or on one of those mornings before Denver woke and after Sethe left she would fly apart. It is difficult keeping her head on her neck, her legs attached to her hips when she is by herself. Among the things she could not remember was when she first knew that she could wake up any day and find herself in pieces. She had two dreams: exploding, and being swallowed. When her tooth came out—an odd fragment, last in the row—she thought it was starting.

"Must be a wisdom," said Denver. "Don't it hurt?"

"Yes."

"Then why don't you cry?"

"What?"

"If it hurts, why don't you cry?"

And she did. Sitting there holding a small white tooth in the palm of her smooth smooth hand. Cried the way she wanted to when turtles came out of the water, one behind the other, right after the blood-red bird disappeared back into the leaves. The way she wanted to when Sethe went to him standing in the tub under the stairs. With the tip of her tongue she touched the salt water that slid to the corner of her mouth and hoped Denver's arm around her shoulders would keep them from falling apart.

The couple upstairs, united, didn't hear a sound, but below them, outside, all around 124 the snow went on and on and on. Piling itself, burying itself. Higher. Deeper.

IN THE BACK of Baby Suggs' mind may have been the thought that if Halle made it, God do what He would, it would be a cause for celebration. If only this final son could do for himself what he had done for her and for the three children John and Ella delivered to her door one summer night. When the children arrived and no Sethe, she was afraid and grateful. Grateful that the part of the family that survived was her own grandchildren—the first and only she would know: two boys and a little girl who was crawling already. But she held her heart still, afraid to form questions: What about Sethe and Halle; why the delay? Why didn't Sethe get on board too? Nobody could make it alone. Not only because trappers picked them off like buzzards or netted them like rabbits, but also because you couldn't run if you didn't know how to go. You could be lost forever, if there wasn't nobody to show you the way.

So when Sethe arrived—all mashed up and split open, but with another grandchild in her arms—the idea of a whoop moved closer to the front of her brain. But since there was still no sign of Halle and Sethe herself didn't know what had happened to him, she let the whoop lie—not wishing to hurt his chances by thanking God too soon.

It was Stamp Paid who started it. Twenty days after Sethe got to 124 he came by and looked at the baby he had tied up in his nephew's jacket, looked at the mother he had handed a piece of fried eel to and, for some private reason of his own, went off with two buckets to a place near the river's edge that only he knew about where blackberries grew, tasting so good and happy that to eat them was like being in church. Just one of the berries and you felt anointed. He walked six miles to the riverbank; did a slide-run-slide down into a ravine made almost inaccessible by brush. He reached through brambles lined with blood-drawing thorns thick as knives that cut through his shirt sleeves and trousers. All the while suffering mosquitoes, bees, hornets, wasps and the meanest lady spiders in the state. Scratched, raked and bitten, he maneuvered through and took hold of each berry with fingertips so gentle not a single one was bruised. Late in the afternoon he got back to 124 and put two full buckets down on the porch. When Baby Suggs saw his shredded clothes, bleeding hands, welted face and neck she sat down laughing out loud.

Buglar, Howard, the woman in the bonnet and Sethe came to look and then laughed along with Baby Suggs at the sight of the sly, steely old black man: agent, fisherman, boatman, tracker, savior, spy, standing in broad daylight whipped finally by two pails of blackberries. Paying them no mind he took a berry and put it in the three-week-old Denver's mouth. The women shrieked.

"She's too little for that, Stamp."

"Bowels be soup."

"Sickify her stomach."

But the baby's thrilled eyes and smacking lips made them follow suit, sampling one at a time the berries that tasted like church. Finally Baby Suggs slapped the boys' hands away from the bucket and sent Stamp around to the pump to rinse himself. She had decided to do something with the fruit worthy of the man's labor and his love. That's how it began.

She made the pastry dough and thought she ought to tell Ella and John to stop on by because three pies, maybe four, were too much to keep for one's own. Sethe thought they might as well back it up with a couple of chickens. Stamp allowed that perch and catfish were jumping into the boat—didn't even have to drop a line.

From Denver's two thrilled eyes it grew to a feast for ninety people. 124 shook with their voices far into the night. Ninety people who ate so well, and laughed so much, it made them angry. They woke up the next morning and remembered the meal-fried perch that

Stamp Paid handled with a hickory twig, holding his left palm out against the spit and pop of the boiling grease; the corn pudding made with cream; tired, overfed children asleep in the grass, tiny bones of roasted rabbit still in their hands—and got angry.

Baby Suggs' three (maybe four) pies grew to ten (maybe twelve). Sethe's two hens became five turkeys. The one block of ice brought all the way from Cincinnati—over which they poured mashed watermelon mixed with sugar and mint to make a punch—became a wagonload of ice cakes for a washtub full of strawberry shrug. 124, rocking with laughter, goodwill and food for ninety, made them angry. Too much, they thought. Where does she get it all, Baby Suggs, holy? Why is she and hers always the center of things? How come she always knows exactly what to do and when? Giving advice; passing messages; healing the sick, hiding fugitives, loving, cooking, cooking, loving, preaching, singing, dancing and loving everybody like it was her job and hers alone.

Now to take two buckets of blackberries and make ten, maybe twelve, pies; to have turkey enough for the whole town pretty near, new peas in September, fresh cream but no cow, ice *and* sugar, batter bread, bread pudding, raised bread, shortbread—it made them mad. Loaves and fishes were His powers—they did not belong to an ex-slave who had probably never carried one hundred pounds to the scale, or picked okra with a baby on her back. Who had never been lashed by a ten-year-old whiteboy as God knows they had. Who had not even escaped slavery—had, in fact, been *bought out* of it by a doting son and *driven* to the Ohio River in a wagon—free papers folded between her breasts (driven by the very man who had been her master, who also paid her resettlement fee—name of Garner), and rented a house with *two* floors *and* a well from the Bodwins— the white brother and sister who gave Stamp Paid, Ella and John clothes, goods and gear for runaways because they hated slavery worse than they hated slaves.

It made them furious. They swallowed baking soda, the morning after, to calm the stomach violence caused by the bounty, the reckless generosity on display at 124. Whispered to each other in the yards about fat rats, doom and uncalled-for pride.

The scent of their disapproval lay heavy in the air. Baby Suggs woke to it and wondered what it was as she boiled hominy for her grandchildren. Later, as she stood in the garden, chopping at the tight soil over the roots of the pepper plants, she smelled it again. She lifted her head and looked around. Behind her some yards to the left Sethe squatted in the pole beans. Her shoulders were distorted by the greased flannel under her dress to encourage the healing of her back. Near her in a bushel basket was the three-week-old baby. Baby Suggs, holy, looked up. The sky was blue and clear. Not one touch of death in the definite green of the leaves. She could hear birds and, faintly, the stream way down in the meadow. The puppy, Here Boy, was burying the last bones from yesterday's party. From somewhere at the side of the house came the voices of Buglar, Howard and the crawling girl. Nothing seemed amiss—yet the smell of disapproval was sharp. Back beyond the vegetable garden, closer to the stream but in full sun, she had planted corn. Much as they'd picked for the party, there were still ears ripening, which she could see from where she stood. Baby Suggs leaned back into the peppers and the squash vines with her hoe. Carefully, with the blade at just the right angle, she cut through a stalk of insistent rue. Its flowers she stuck through a split in her hat; the rest she tossed aside. The quiet clok clok clok of wood splitting reminded her that Stamp was doing the chore he promised to the night before. She sighed at her work and, a moment later, straightened up to sniff the disapproval once again. Resting on the handle of the hoe, she concentrated. She was accustomed to the knowledge that nobody prayed for her—but this free-floating repulsion was new. It wasn't whitefolks—that much she could tell—so it must be colored ones. And then she knew. Her friends and neighbors were angry at her because she had overstepped, given too much, offended them by excess.

Baby closed her eyes. Perhaps they were right. Suddenly, behind the disapproving odor, way way back behind it, she smelled another thing. Dark and coming. Something she couldn't get at because the other odor hid it.

She squeezed her eyes tight to see what it was but all she could make out was high-topped shoes she didn't like the look of.

Thwarted yet wondering, she chopped away with the hoe. What

could it be? This dark and coming thing. What was left to hurt her now? News of Halle's death? No. She had been prepared for that better than she had for his life. The last of her children, whom she barely glanced at when he was born because it wasn't worth the trouble to try to learn features you would never see change into adulthood anyway. Seven times she had done that: held a little foot; examined the fat fingertips with her own—fingers she never saw become the male or female hands a mother would recognize anywhere. She didn't know to this day what their permanent teeth looked like; or how they held their heads when they walked. Did Patty lose her lisp? What color did Famous' skin finally take? Was that a cleft in Johnny's chin or just a dimple that would disappear soon's his jawbone changed? Four girls, and the last time she saw them there was no hair under their arms. Does Ardelia still love the burned bottom of bread? All seven were gone or dead. What would be the point of looking too hard at that youngest one? But for some reason they let her keep him. He was with her—everywhere.

When she hurt her hip in Carolina she was a real bargain (costing less than Halle, who was ten then) for Mr. Garner, who took them both to Kentucky to a farm he called Sweet Home. Because of the hip she jerked like a three-legged dog when she walked. But at Sweet Home there wasn't a rice field or tobacco patch in sight, and nobody, but nobody, knocked her down. Not once. Lillian Garner called her Jenny for some reason but she never pushed, hit or called her mean names. Even when she slipped in cow dung and broke every egg in her apron, nobody said you-black-bitch-what's-the-matter-with-you and nobody knocked her down.

Sweet Home was tiny compared to the places she had been. Mr. Garner, Mrs. Garner, herself, Halle, and four boys, over half named Paul, made up the entire population. Mrs. Garner hummed when she worked; Mr. Garner acted like the world was a toy he was supposed to have fun with. Neither wanted her in the field—Mr. Garner's boys, including Halle, did all of that—which was a blessing since she could not have managed it anyway. What she did was stand beside the humming Lillian Garner while the two of them cooked, preserved, washed, ironed, made candles, clothes, soap and cider;

fed chickens, pigs, dogs and geese; milked cows, churned butter, rendered fat, laid fires. . . . Nothing to it. And nobody knocked her down.

Her hip hurt every single day—but she never spoke of it. Only Halle, who had watched her movements closely for the last four years, knew that to get in and out of bed she had to lift her thigh with both hands, which was why he spoke to Mr. Garner about buying her out of there so she could sit down for a change. Sweet boy. The one person who did something hard for her: gave her his work, his life and now his children, whose voices she could just make out as she stood in the garden wondering what was the dark and coming thing behind the scent of disapproval. Sweet Home was a marked improvement. No question. And no matter, for the sadness was at her center, the desolated center where the self that was no self made its home. Sad as it was that she did not know where her children were buried or what they looked like if alive, fact was she knew more about them than she knew about herself, having never had the map to discover what she was like.

Could she sing? (Was it nice to hear when she did?) Was she pretty? Was she a good friend? Could she have been a loving mother? A faithful wife? Have I got a sister and does she favor me? If my mother knew me would she like me?

In Lillian Garner's house, exempted from the field work that broke her hip and the exhaustion that drugged her mind; in Lillian Garner's house where nobody knocked her down (or up), she listened to the whitewoman humming at her work; watched her face light up when Mr. Garner came in and thought, It's better here, but I'm not. The Garners, it seemed to her, ran a special kind of slavery, treating them like paid labor, listening to what they said, teaching what they wanted known. And he didn't stud his boys. Never brought them to her cabin with directions to "lay down with her," like they did in Carolina, or rented their sex out on other farms. It surprised and pleased her, but worried her too. Would he pick women for them or what did he think was going to happen when those boys ran smack into their nature? Some danger he was courting and he surely knew it. In fact, his order for them not to leave Sweet Home, except in his company, was not so much because of the law, but the danger of men-bred slaves on the loose.

Baby Suggs talked as little as she could get away with because what was there to say that the roots of her tongue could manage? So the whitewoman, finding her new slave excellent if silent help, hummed to herself while she worked.

When Mr. Garner agreed to the arrangements with Halle, and when Halle looked like it meant more to him that she go free than anything in the world, she let herself be taken 'cross the river. Of the two hard things—standing on her feet till she dropped or leaving her last and probably only living child—she chose the hard thing that made him happy, and never put to him the question she put to herself: What for? What does a sixty-odd-year-old slavewoman who walks like a three-legged dog need freedom for? And when she stepped foot on free ground she could not believe that Halle knew what she didn't; that Halle, who had never drawn one free breath, knew that there was nothing like it in this world. It scared her.

Something's the matter. What's the matter? What's the matter? she asked herself. She didn't know what she looked like and was not curious. But suddenly she saw her hands and thought with a clarity as simple as it was dazzling, "These hands belong to me. These *my* hands." Next she felt a knocking in her chest and discovered something else new: her own heartbeat. Had it been there all along? This pounding thing? She felt like a fool and began to laugh out loud. Mr. Garner looked over his shoulder at her with wide brown eyes and smiled himself. "What's funny, Jenny?"

She couldn't stop laughing. "My heart's beating," she said.

And it was true.

Mr. Garner laughed. "Nothing to be scared of, Jenny. Just keep your same ways, you'll be all right."

She covered her mouth to keep from laughing too loud.

"These people I'm taking you to will give you what help you need. Name of Bodwin. A brother and a sister. Scots. I been knowing them for twenty years or more."

Baby Suggs thought it was a good time to ask him something she had long wanted to know.

"Mr. Garner," she said, "why you all call me Jenny?"

"'Cause that what's on your sales ticket, gal. Ain't that your name? What you call yourself?"

"Nothing," she said. "I don't call myself nothing."

Mr. Garner went red with laughter. "When I took you out of Carolina, Whitlow called you Jenny and Jenny Whitlow is what his bill said. Didn't he call you Jenny?"

"No, sir. If he did I didn't hear it."

"What did you answer to?"

"Anything, but Suggs is what my husband name."

"You got married, Jenny? I didn't know it."

"Manner of speaking."

"You know where he is, this husband?"

"No, sir."

"Is that Halle's daddy?"

"No, sir."

"Why you call him Suggs, then? His bill of sale says Whitlow too, just like yours."

"Suggs is my name, sir. From my husband. He didn't call me Jenny."

"What he call you?"

"Baby."

"Well," said Mr. Garner, going pink again, "if I was you I'd stick to Jenny Whitlow. Mrs. Baby Suggs ain't no name for a freed Negro."

Maybe not, she thought, but Baby Suggs was all she had left of the "husband" she claimed. A serious, melancholy man who taught her how to make shoes. The two of them made a pact: whichever one got a chance to run would take it; together if possible, alone if not, and no looking back. He got his chance, and since she never heard otherwise she believed he made it. Now how could he find or hear tell of her if she was calling herself some bill-of-sale name?

She couldn't get over the city. More people than Carolina and enough whitefolks to stop the breath. Two-story buildings everywhere, and walkways made of perfectly cut slats of wood. Roads wide as Garner's whole house.

"This is a city of water," said Mr. Garner. "Everything travels by water and what the rivers can't carry the canals take. A queen of a city, Jenny. Everything you ever dreamed of, they make it right here. Iron stoves, buttons, ships, shirts, hairbrushes, paint, steam engines, books. A sewer system make your eyes bug out. Oh, this is a city, all right. If you have to live in a city—this is it."

The Bodwins lived right in the center of a street full of houses and trees. Mr. Garner leaped out and tied his horse to a solid iron post.

"Here we are."

Baby picked up her bundle and with great difficulty, caused by her hip and the hours of sitting in a wagon, climbed down. Mr. Garner was up the walk and on the porch before she touched ground, but she got a peep at a Negro girl's face at the open door before she followed a path to the back of the house. She waited what seemed a long time before this same girl opened the kitchen door and offered her a seat by the window.

"Can I get you anything to eat, ma'am?" the girl asked.

"No, darling. I'd look favorable on some water though." The girl went to the sink and pumped a cupful of water. She placed it in Baby Suggs' hand. "I'm Janey, ma'am."

Baby, marveling at the sink, drank every drop of water although it tasted like a serious medicine. "Suggs," she said, blotting her lips with the back of her hand. "Baby Suggs."

"Glad to meet you, Mrs. Suggs. You going to be staying here?"

"I don't know where I'll be. Mr. Garner—that's him what brought me here—he say he arrange something for me." And then, "I'm free, you know."

Janey smiled. "Yes, ma'am."

"Your people live around here?"

"Yes, ma'am. All us live out on Bluestone."

"We scattered," said Baby Suggs, "but maybe not for long."

Great God, she thought, where do I start? Get somebody to write old Whitlow. See who took Patty and Rosa Lee. Somebody name Dunn got Ardelia and went West, she heard. No point in trying for Tyree or John. They cut thirty years ago and, if she searched too hard and they were hiding, finding them would do them more harm than good. Nancy and Famous died in a ship off the Virginia coast before it set sail for Savannah. That much she knew. The overseer at Whitlow's place brought her the news, more from a wish to have his way with her than from the kindness of his heart. The captain waited three weeks in port, to get a full cargo before setting off. Of the slaves in the hold who didn't make it, he said, two were Whitlow pickaninnies name of . . .

But she knew their names. She knew, and covered her ears with her fists to keep from hearing them come from his mouth.

Janey heated some milk and poured it in a bowl next to a plate of cornbread. After some coaxing, Baby Suggs came to the table and sat down. She crumbled the bread into the hot milk and discovered she was hungrier than she had ever been in her life and that was saying something.

"They going to miss this?"

"No," said Janey. "Eat all you want; it's ours."

"Anybody else live here?"

"Just me. Mr. Woodruff, he does the outside chores. He comes by two, three days a week."

"Just you two?"

"Yes, ma'am. I do the cooking and washing."

"Maybe your people know of somebody looking for help."

"I be sure to ask, but I know they take women at the slaughter-house."

"Doing what?"

"I don't know."

"Something men don't want to do, I reckon."

"My cousin say you get all the meat you want, plus twenty-five cents the hour. She make summer sausage."

Baby Suggs lifted her hand to the top of her head. Money? Money? They would pay her money every single day? Money?

"Where is this here slaughterhouse?" she asked.

Before Janey could answer, the Bodwins came in to the kitchen with a grinning Mr. Garner behind. Undeniably brother and sister, both dressed in gray with faces too young for their snow-white hair.

"Did you give her anything to eat, Janey?" asked the brother.

"Yes, sir."

"Keep your seat, Jenny," said the sister, and that good news got better.

When they asked what work she could do, instead of reeling off the hundreds of tasks she had performed, she asked about the slaughterhouse. She was too old for that, they said.

"She's the best cobbler you ever see," said Mr. Garner.

"Cobbler?" Sister Bodwin raised her black thick eyebrows. "Who taught you that?"

"Was a slave taught me," said Baby Suggs.

"New boots, or just repair?"

"New, old, anything."

"Well," said Brother Bodwin, "that'll be something, but you'll need more."

"What about taking in wash?" asked Sister Bodwin.

"Yes, ma'am."

"Two cents a pound."

"Yes, ma'am. But where's the in?"

"What?"

"You said 'take in wash.' Where is the 'in'? Where I'm going to be."

"Oh, just listen to this, Jenny," said Mr. Garner. "These two angels got a house for you. Place they own out a ways."

It had belonged to their grandparents before they moved in town. Recently it had been rented out to a whole parcel of Negroes, who had left the state. It was too big a house for Jenny alone, they said (two rooms upstairs, two down), but it was the best and the only thing they could do. In return for laundry, some seamstress work, a little canning and so on (oh shoes, too), they would permit her to stay there. Provided she was clean. The past parcel of colored wasn't. Baby Suggs agreed to the situation, sorry to see the money go but excited about a house with steps—never mind she couldn't climb them. Mr. Garner told the Bodwins that she was a right fine cook as well as a fine cobbler and showed his belly and the sample on his feet. Everybody laughed.

"Anything you need, let us know," said the sister. "We don't hold with slavery, even Garner's kind."

"Tell em, Jenny. You live any better on any place before mine?"

"No, sir," she said. "No place."

"How long was you at Sweet Home?"

"Ten year, I believe."

"Ever go hungry?"

"No, sir."

"Cold?"

"No, sir."

"Anybody lay a hand on you?"

"No, sir."

"Did I let Halle buy you or not?"

"Yes, sir, you did," she said, thinking, But you got my boy and I'm all broke down. You be renting him out to pay for me way after I'm gone to Glory.

Woodruff, they said, would carry her out there, they said, and all three disappeared through the kitchen door.

"I have to fix the supper now," said Janey.

"I'll help," said Baby Suggs. "You too short to reach the fire."

It was dark when Woodruff clicked the horse into a trot. He was a young man with a heavy beard and a burned place on his jaw the beard did not hide.

"You born up here?" Baby Suggs asked him.

"No, ma'am. Virginia. Been here a couple years."

"I see."

"You going to a nice house. Big too. A preacher and his family was in there. Eighteen children."

"Have mercy. Where they go?"

"Took off to Illinois. Bishop Allen gave him a congregation up there. Big."

"What churches around here? I ain't set foot in one in ten years."

"How come?"

"Wasn't none. I dislike the place I was before this last one, but I did get to church every Sunday some kind of way. I bet the Lord done forgot who I am by now."

"Go see Reverend Pike, ma'am. He'll reacquaint you."

"I won't need him for that. I can make my own acquaintance. What I need him for is to reacquaint me with my children. He can read and write, I reckon?"

"Sure."

"Good, 'cause I got a lot of digging up to do." But the news they dug up was so pitiful she quit. After two years of messages written by the preacher's hand, two years of washing, sewing, canning, cobbling, gardening, and sitting in churches, all she found out was that the Whitlow place was gone and that you couldn't write to "a man named Dunn" if all you knew was that he went West. The good news, however, was that Halle got married and had a baby coming. She fixed on that and her own brand of preaching, having made up her mind about what to do with the heart that started beating the minute she crossed the Ohio River. And it worked out, worked out just fine, until she got proud and let herself be overwhelmed by the sight of her daughter-in-law and Halle's children—one of whom was born on the way—and have a celebration of blackberries that put Christmas to shame. Now she stood in the garden smelling disapproval, feeling a dark and coming thing, and seeing high-topped shoes that she didn't like the look of at all. At all.

WHEN THE four horsemen came—schoolteacher, one nephew, one slave catcher and a sheriff—the house on Bluestone Road was so quiet they thought they were too late. Three of them dismounted, one stayed in the saddle, his rifle ready, his eyes trained away from the house to the left and to the right, because likely as not the fugitive would make a dash for it. Although sometimes, you could never tell, you'd find them folded up tight somewhere: beneath floorboards, in a pantry—once in a chimney. Even then care was taken, because the quietest ones, the ones you pulled from a press, a hayloft, or, that once, from a chimney, would go along nicely for two or three seconds. Caught red-handed, so to speak, they would seem to recognize the futility of outsmarting a whiteman and the hopelessness of outrunning a rifle. Smile even, like a child caught dead with his hand in the jelly jar, and when you reached for the rope to tie him, well, even then you couldn't tell. The very nigger with his head hanging and a little jelly-jar smile on his face could all of a sudden roar, like a bull or some such, and commence to do disbelievable things. Grab the rifle at its mouth; throw himself at the one holding it—anything. So you had to keep back a pace, leave the tying to another. Otherwise you ended up killing what you were paid to bring back alive. Unlike a snake or a bear, a dead nigger could not be skinned for profit and was not worth his own dead weight in coin.

Six or seven Negroes were walking up the road toward the house: two boys from the slave catcher's left and some women from his right. He motioned them still with his rifle and they stood where they were. The nephew came back from peeping inside the house, and after touching his lips for silence, pointed his thumb to say that what they were looking for was round back. The slave catcher dismounted then and joined the others. Schoolteacher and the nephew moved to the left of the house; himself and the sheriff to the right. A crazy old nigger was standing in the woodpile with an ax. You could tell he was crazy right off because he was grunting—making low, cat noises like. About twelve yards beyond that nigger was another one—a woman with a flower in her hat. Crazy too, probably, because she too was standing stock-still—but fanning her hands as though pushing cobwebs out of her way. Both, however, were staring at the same place—a shed. Nephew walked over to the old nigger boy and took the ax from him. Then all four started toward the shed.

Inside, two boys bled in the sawdust and dirt at the feet of a nigger woman holding a blood-soaked child to her chest with one hand and an infant by the heels in the other. She did not look at them; she simply swung the baby toward the wall planks, missed and tried to connect a second time, when out of nowhere—in the ticking time the men spent staring at what there was to stare at—the old nigger boy, still mewing, ran through the door behind them and snatched the baby from the arch of its mother's swing.

Right off it was clear, to schoolteacher especially, that there was nothing there to claim. The three (now four—because she'd had the one coming when she cut) pickaninnies they had hoped were alive and well enough to take back to Kentucky, take back and raise properly to do the work Sweet Home desperately needed, were not. Two were lying open-eyed in sawdust; a third pumped blood down the dress of the main one—the woman schoolteacher bragged about, the one he said made fine ink, damn good soup, pressed his collars the way he liked besides having at least ten breeding years left. But now she'd gone wild, due to the mishandling of the nephew who'd overbeat her and made her cut and run. Schoolteacher had chastised that nephew, telling him to think—just think—what would his own horse do if you beat it beyond the point of education. Or Chipper, or Samson. Suppose you beat the hounds past that point thataway. Never again could you trust them in the woods or anywhere else. You'd be feeding them maybe, holding out a piece of rabbit in your hand, and the animal would revert—bite your hand clean off. So he punished that nephew by not letting him come on the hunt. Made him stay there, feed stock, feed himself, feed Lillian, tend crops. See how he liked it; see what happened when you overbeat creatures God had given you the responsibility of—the trouble it was, and the loss. The whole lot was lost now. Five. He could claim the baby struggling in the arms of the mewing old man, but who'd tend her? Because the woman—something was wrong with her. She was looking at him now, and if his other nephew could see that look he would learn the lesson for sure: you just can't mishandle creatures and expect success.

The nephew, the one who had nursed her while his brother held her down, didn't know he was shaking. His uncle had warned him against that kind of confusion, but the warning didn't seem to be taking. What she go and do that for? On account of a beating? Hell, he'd been beat a million times and he was white. Once it hurt so bad and made him so mad he'd smashed the well bucket. Another time he took it out on Samson—a few tossed rocks was all. But no beating ever made him . . . I mean no way he could have . . . What she go and do that for? And that is what he asked the sheriff, who was standing there amazed like the rest of them, but not shaking. He was swallowing hard, over and over again. "What she want to go and do that for?"

The sheriff turned, then said to the other three, "You all better go on. Look like your business is over. Mine's started now."

Schoolteacher beat his hat against his thigh and spit before leaving the woodshed. Nephew and the catcher backed out with him. They didn't look at the woman in the pepper plants with the flower in her hat. And they didn't look at the seven or so faces that had edged closer in spite of the catcher's rifle warning. Enough nigger eyes for now. Little nigger-boy eyes open in sawdust; little nigger-girl eyes staring between the wet fingers that held her face so her head wouldn't fall off; little nigger-baby eyes crinkling up to cry in the arms of the old nigger whose own eyes were nothing but slivers looking down at his feet. But the worst ones were those of the nigger woman who looked like she didn't have any. Since the whites in them had disappeared and since they were as black as her skin, she looked blind.

They unhitched from schoolteacher's horse the borrowed mule that was to carry the fugitive woman back to where she belonged, and tied it to the fence. Then, with the sun straight up over their heads, they trotted off, leaving the sheriff behind among the damnedest bunch of coons they'd ever seen. All testimony to the results of a little so-called freedom imposed on people who needed every care and guidance in the world to keep them from the cannibal life they preferred.

The sheriff wanted to back out too. To stand in the sunlight outside of that place meant for housing wood, coal, kerosene—fuel for cold Ohio winters, which he thought of now, while resisting the urge to run into the August sunlight. Not because he was afraid. Not at all. He was just cold. And he didn't want to touch anything. The baby in the old man's arms was crying, and the woman's eyes with no whites were gazing straight ahead. They all might have remained that way, frozen till Thursday, except one of the boys on the floor sighed. As if he were sunk in the pleasure of a deep sweet sleep, he sighed the sigh that flung the sheriff into action.

"I'll have to take you in. No trouble now. You've done enough to last you. Come on now."

She did not move.

"You come quiet, hear, and I won't have to tie you up."

She stayed still and he had made up his mind to go near her and some kind of way bind her wet red hands when a shadow behind him in the doorway made him turn. The nigger with the flower in her hat entered.

Baby Suggs noticed who breathed and who did not and went straight to the boys lying in the dirt. The old man moved to the woman gazing and said, "Sethe. You take my armload and gimme yours."

She turned to him, and glancing at the baby he was holding, made a low sound in her throat as though she'd made a mistake, left the salt out of the bread or something.

"I'm going out here and send for a wagon," the sheriff said and got into the sunlight at last.

But neither Stamp Paid nor Baby Suggs could make her put her crawling-already? girl down. Out of the shed, back in the house, she held on. Baby Suggs had got the boys inside and was bathing their heads, rubbing their hands, lifting their lids, whispering, "Beg your pardon, I beg your pardon," the whole time. She bound their wounds and made them breathe camphor before turning her attention to Sethe. She took the crying baby from Stamp Paid and carried it on her shoulder for a full two minutes, then stood in front of its mother.

"It's time to nurse your youngest," she said.

Sethe reached up for the baby without letting the dead one go.

Baby Suggs shook her head. "One at a time," she said and traded the living for the dead, which she carried into the keeping room. When she came back, Sethe was aiming a bloody nipple into the baby's mouth. Baby Suggs slammed her fist on the table and shouted, "Clean up! Clean yourself up!"

They fought then. Like rivals over the heart of the loved, they fought. Each struggling for the nursing child. Baby Suggs lost when she slipped in a red puddle and fell. So Denver took her mother's milk right along with the blood of her sister. And that's the way they were when the sheriff returned, having commandeered a neighbor's cart, and ordered Stamp to drive it.

Outside a throng, now, of black faces stopped murmuring. Holding the living child, Sethe walked past them in their silence and hers. She climbed into the cart, her profile knife-clean against a cheery blue sky. A profile that shocked them with its clarity. Was her head a bit too high? Her back a little too straight? Probably. Otherwise the singing would have begun at once, the moment she appeared in the doorway of the house on Bluestone Road. Some cape of sound would have quickly been wrapped around her, like arms to hold and steady her on the way. As it was, they waited till the cart turned about, headed west to town. And then no words. Humming. No words at all.

Baby Suggs meant to run, skip down the porch steps after the cart, screaming, No. No. Don't let her take that last one too. She meant to. Had started to, but when she got up from the floor and reached the yard the cart was gone and a wagon was rolling up. A red-haired boy and a yellow-haired girl jumped down and ran through the crowd toward her. The boy had a half-eaten sweet pepper in one hand and a pair of shoes in the other.

"Mama says Wednesday." He held them together by their tongues. "She says you got to have these fixed by Wednesday."

Baby Suggs looked at him, and then at the woman holding a twitching lead horse to the road.

"She says Wednesday, you hear? Baby? Baby?"

She took the shoes from him—high-topped and muddy—saying, "I beg your pardon. Lord, I beg your pardon. I sure do."

Out of sight, the cart creaked on down Bluestone Road. Nobody in it spoke. The wagon rock had put the baby to sleep. The hot sun dried Sethe's dress, stiff, like rigor mortis.

THAT AIN'T her mouth.

Anybody who didn't know her, or maybe somebody who just got a glimpse of her through the peephole at the restaurant, might think it was hers, but Paul D knew better. Oh well, a little something around the forehead—a quietness—that kind of reminded you of her. But there was no way you could take that for her mouth and he said so. Told Stamp Paid, who was watching him carefully.

"I don't know, man. Don't look like it to me. I know Sethe's mouth and this ain't it." He smoothed the clipping with his fingers and peered at it, not at all disturbed. From the solemn air with which Stamp had unfolded the paper, the tenderness in the old man's fingers as he stroked its creases and flattened it out, first on his knees, then on the split top of the piling, Paul D knew that it ought to mess him up. That whatever was written on it should shake him.

Pigs were crying in the chute. All day Paul D, Stamp Paid and twenty more had pushed and prodded them from canal to shore to chute to slaughterhouse. Although, as grain farmers moved west, St. Louis and Chicago now ate up a lot of the business, Cincinnati was still pig port in the minds of Ohioans. Its main job was to receive, slaughter and ship up the river the hogs that Northerners did not want to live without. For a month or so in the winter any stray man had work, if he could breathe the stench of offal and stand up for twelve hours, skills in which Paul D was admirably trained.

A little pig shit, rinsed from every place he could touch, remained on his boots, and he was conscious of it as he stood there with a light smile of scorn curling his lips. Usually he left his boots in the shed and put his walking shoes on along with his day clothes in the corner before he went home. A route that took him smack dab through the middle of a cemetery as old as sky, rife with the agitation of dead Miami no longer content to rest in the mounds that covered them. Over their heads walked a strange people; through their earth pillows roads were cut; wells and houses nudged them out of eternal rest. Outraged more by their folly in believing land was holy than by the disturbances of their peace, they growled on the banks of Licking River, sighed in the trees on Catherine Street and rode the wind above the pig yards. Paul D heard them but he stayed on because all in all it wasn't a bad job, especially in winter when Cincinnati reassumed its status of slaughter and riverboat capital. The craving for pork was growing into a mania in every city in the country. Pig farmers were cashing in, provided they could raise enough and get them sold farther and farther away. And the Germans who flooded southern Ohio brought and developed swine cooking to its highest form. Pig boats jammed the Ohio River, and their captains' hollering at one another over the grunts of the stock was as common a water sound as that of the ducks flying over their heads. Sheep, cows and fowl too floated up and down that river, and all a Negro had to do was show up and there was work: poking, killing, cutting, skinning, case packing and saving offal.

A hundred yards from the crying pigs, the two men stood behind a shed on Western Row and it was clear why Stamp had been eyeing Paul D this last week of work; why he paused when the evening shift came on, to let Paul D's movements catch up to his own. He had made up his mind to show him this piece of paper—newspaper—with a picture drawing of a woman who favored Sethe except that was not her mouth. Nothing like it.

Paul D slid the clipping out from under Stamp's palm. The print meant nothing to him so he didn't even glance at it. He simply looked at the face, shaking his head no. No. At the mouth, you see. And no at whatever it was those black scratches said, and no to whatever it was Stamp Paid wanted him to know. Because there was no way in hell a black face could appear in a newspaper if the story was about something anybody wanted to hear. A whip of fear broke through the heart chambers as soon as you saw a Negro's face in a paper, since the face was not there because the person had a healthy baby, or outran a street mob. Nor was it there because the person had been killed, or maimed or caught or burned or jailed or whipped or evicted or stomped or raped or cheated, since that could hardly qualify as news in a newspaper. It would have to be something out of the ordinary—something whitepeople would find interesting, truly different, worth a few minutes of teeth sucking if not gasps. And it must have been hard to find news about Negroes worth the breath catch of a white citizen of Cincinnati.

So who was this woman with a mouth that was not Sethe's, but whose eyes were almost as calm as hers? Whose head was turned on her neck in the manner he loved so well it watered his eye to see it.

And he said so. "This ain't her mouth. I know her mouth and this ain't it." Before Stamp Paid could speak he said it and even while he spoke Paul D said it again. Oh, he heard all the old man was saying, but the more he heard, the stranger the lips in the drawing became.

Stamp started with the party, the one Baby Suggs gave, but stopped and backed up a bit to tell about the berries—where they were and what was in the earth that made them grow like that.

"They open to the sun, but not the birds, 'cause snakes down in there and the birds know it, so they just grow—fat and sweet—with nobody to bother em 'cept me because don't nobody go in that piece of water but me and ain't too many legs willing to glide down that bank to get them. Me neither. But I was willing that day. Somehow or 'nother I was willing. And they whipped me, I'm telling you. Tore me up. But I filled two buckets anyhow. And took em over to Baby Suggs' house. It was on from then on. Such a cooking you never see no more. We baked, fried and stewed everything God put down here. Everybody came. Everybody stuffed. Cooked so much there wasn't a stick of kindlin left for the next day. I volunteered to do it. And next morning I come over, like I promised, to do it."

"But this ain't her mouth," Paul D said. "This ain't it at all."

Stamp Paid looked at him. He was going to tell him about how restless Baby Suggs was that morning, how she had a listening way about her; how she kept looking down past the corn to the stream so much he looked too. In between ax swings, he watched where Baby was watching. Which is why they both missed it: they were looking the wrong way—toward water—and all the while it was coming down the road. Four. Riding close together, bunched-up like, and righteous. He was going to tell him that, because he thought it was important: why he and Baby Suggs both missed it. And about the party too, because that explained why nobody ran on ahead; why nobody sent a fleet-footed son to cut 'cross a field soon as they saw the four horses in town hitched for watering while the riders asked questions. Not Ella, not John, not anybody ran down or to Bluestone Road, to say some new whitefolks with the Look just rode in. The righteous Look every Negro learned to recognize along with his ma'am's tit. Like a flag hoisted, this righteousness telegraphed and announced the faggot, the whip, the fist, the lie, long before it went public. Nobody warned them, and he'd always believed it wasn't the exhaustion from a long day's gorging that dulled them, but some other thing—like, well, like meanness—that let them stand aside, or not pay attention, or tell themselves somebody else was probably bearing the news already to the house on Bluestone Road where a pretty woman had been living for almost a month. Young and deft with four children one of which she delivered herself the day before she got there and who now had the full benefit of Baby Suggs' bounty and her big old heart. Maybe they just wanted to know if Baby really was special, blessed in some way they were not. He was going to tell him that, but Paul D was laughing, saying, "Uh uh. No way. A little semblance round the forehead maybe, but this ain't her mouth."

So Stamp Paid did not tell him how she flew, snatching up her children like a hawk on the wing; how her face beaked, how her hands worked like claws, how she collected them every which way: one on her shoulder, one under her arm, one by the hand, the other shouted forward into the woodshed filled with just sunlight and shavings now because there wasn't any wood. The party had used it all, which is why he was chopping some. Nothing was in that shed, he knew, having been there early that morning. Nothing but sunlight. Sunlight, shavings, a shovel. The ax he himself took out. Nothing else was in there except the shovel—and of course the saw.

"You forgetting I knew her before," Paul D was saying. "Back

"SHE WAS crawling already when I got here. One week, less, and the baby who was sitting up and turning over when I put her on the wagon was crawling already. Devil of a time keeping her off the stairs. Nowadays babies get up and walk soon's you drop em, but twenty years ago when I was a girl, babies stayed babies longer. Howard didn't pick up his own head till he was nine months. Baby Suggs said it was the food, you know. If you ain't got nothing but milk to give em, well they don't do things so quick. Milk was all I ever had. I thought teeth meant they was ready to chew. Wasn't nobody to ask. Mrs. Garner never had no children and we was the only women there."

She was spinning. Round and round the room. Past the jelly cupboard, past the window, past the front door, another window, the sideboard, the keeping-room door, the dry sink, the stove—back to the jelly cupboard. Paul D sat at the table watching her drift into view then disappear behind his back, turning like a slow but steady wheel. Sometimes she crossed her hands behind her back. Other times she held her ears, covered her mouth or folded her arms across her breasts. Once in a while she rubbed her hips as she turned, but the wheel never stopped.

"Remember Aunt Phyllis? From out by Minnowville? Mr. Garner sent one a you all to get her for each and every one of my babies. That'd be the only time I saw her. Many's the time I wanted to get over to where she was. Just to talk. My plan was to ask Mrs. Garner to let me off at Minnowville whilst she went to meeting. Pick me up on her way back. I believe she would a done that if I was to ask her. I never did, 'cause that's the only day Halle and me had with sunlight in it for the both of us to see each other by. So there wasn't nobody. To talk to, I mean, who'd know when it was time to chew up a little something and give it to em. Is that what make the teeth come on out, or should you wait till the teeth came and then solid food? Well, I know now, because Baby Suggs fed her right, and a week later, when I got here she was crawling already. No stopping her either. She loved those steps so much we painted them so she could see her way to the top."

Sethe smiled then, at the memory of it. The smile broke in two and became a sudden suck of air, but she did not shudder or close her eyes. She wheeled.

"I wish I'd a known more, but, like I say, there wasn't nobody to talk to. Woman, I mean. So I tried to recollect what I'd seen back where I was before Sweet Home. How the women did there. Oh they knew all about it. How to make that thing you use to hang the babies in the trees—so you could see them out of harm's way while you worked the fields. Was a leaf thing too they gave em to chew on. Mint, I believe, or sassafras. Comfrey, maybe. I still don't know how they constructed that basket thing, but I didn't need it anyway, because all my work was in the barn and the house, but I forgot what the leaf was. I could have used that. I tied Buglar when we had all that pork to smoke. Fire everywhere and he was getting into everything. I liked to lost him so many times. Once he got up on the well, right on it. I flew. Snatched him just in time. So when I knew we'd be rendering and smoking and I couldn't see after him, well, I got a rope and tied it round his ankle. Just long enough to play round a little, but not long enough to reach the well or the fire. I didn't like the look of it, but I didn't know what else to do. It's hard, you know what I mean? by yourself and no woman to help you get through. Halle was good, but he was debt-working all over the place. And when he did get down to a little sleep, I didn't want to be bothering him with all that. Sixo was the biggest help. I don't 'spect you rememory this, but Howard got in the milk parlor and Red Cora I believe it was mashed his hand. Turned his thumb backwards. When I got to him, she was getting ready to bite it. I don't know to this day how I got him out. Sixo heard him screaming and come running. Know what he did? Turned the thumb right back and tied it cross his palm to his little finger. See, I never would have thought of that. Never. Taught me a lot, Sixo."

It made him dizzy. At first he thought it was her spinning. Circling him the way she was circling the subject. Round and round, never changing direction, which might have helped his head. Then he thought, No, it's the sound of her voice; it's too near. Each turn she made was at least three yards from where he sat, but listening to her was like having a child whisper into your ear so close you could feel its lips form the words you couldn't make out because they were too close. He caught only pieces of what she said—which was fine, because she hadn't gotten to the main part—the answer to the question he had not asked outright, but which lay in the clipping he showed her. And lay in the smile as well. Because he smiled too, when he showed it to her, so when she burst out laughing at the joke—the mix-up of her face put where some other coloredwoman's ought to be—well, he'd be ready to laugh right along with her. "Can you beat it?" he would ask. And "Stamp done lost his mind," she would giggle. "Plumb lost it."

But his smile never got a chance to grow. It hung there, small and alone, while she examined the clipping and then handed it back.

Perhaps it was the smile, or maybe the ever-ready love she saw in his eyes—easy and upfront, the way colts, evangelists and children look at you: with love you don't have to deserve—that made her go ahead and tell him what she had not told Baby Suggs, the only person she felt obliged to explain anything to. Otherwise she would have said what the newspaper said she said and no more. Sethe could recognize only seventy-five printed words (half of which appeared in the newspaper clipping), but she knew that the words she did not understand hadn't any more power than she had to explain. It was the smile and the upfront love that made her try.

"I don't have to tell you about Sweet Home—what it was—but maybe you don't know what it was like for me to get away from there."

Covering the lower half of her face with her palms, she paused to consider again the size of the miracle; its flavor.

"I did it. I got us all out. Without Halle too. Up till then it was the only thing I ever did on my own. Decided. And it came off right, like it was supposed to. We was here. Each and every one of my babies and me too. I birthed them and I got em out and it wasn't no accident. I did that. I had help, of course, lots of that, but still it was me doing it; me saying, *Go on,* and *Now.* Me having to look out. Me using my own head. But it was more than that. It was a kind of selfishness I never knew nothing about before. It felt good. Good and right. I was big, Paul D, and deep and wide and when I stretched out my arms all my children could get in between. I was *that* wide. Look like I loved em more after I got here. Or maybe I couldn't love em proper in Kentucky because they wasn't mine to love. But when I got here, when I jumped down off that wagon—there wasn't nobody in the world I couldn't love if I wanted to. You know what I mean?"

Paul D did not answer because she didn't expect or want him to, but he did know what she meant. Listening to the doves in Alfred, Georgia, and having neither the right nor the permission to enjoy it because in that place mist, doves, sunlight, copper dirt, moon—everything belonged to the men who had the guns. Little men, some of them, big men too, each one of whom he could snap like a twig if he wanted to. Men who knew their manhood lay in their guns and were not even embarrassed by the knowledge that without gunshot fox would laugh at them. And these "men" who made even vixen laugh could, if you let them, stop you from hearing doves or loving moonlight. So you protected yourself and loved small. Picked the tiniest stars out of the sky to own; lay down with head twisted in order to see the loved one over the rim of the trench before you slept. Stole shy glances at her between the trees at chain-up. Grass blades, salamanders, spiders, woodpeckers, beetles, a kingdom of ants. Anything bigger wouldn't do. A woman, a child, a brother—a big love like that would split you wide open in Alfred, Georgia. He knew exactly what she meant: to get to a place where you could love anything you chose—not to need permission for desire—well now, *that* was freedom.

Circling, circling, now she was gnawing something else instead of getting to the point.

"There was this piece of goods Mrs. Garner gave me. Calico.

Stripes it had with little flowers in between. 'Bout a yard—not enough for more 'n a head tie. But I been wanting to make a shift for my girl with it. Had the prettiest colors. I don't even know what you call that color: a rose but with yellow in it. For the longest time I been meaning to make it for her and do you know like a fool I left it behind? No more than a yard, and I kept putting it off because I was tired or didn't have the time. So when I got here, even before they let me get out of bed, I stitched her a little something from a piece of cloth Baby Suggs had. Well, all I'm saying is that's a selfish pleasure I never had before. I couldn't let all that go back to where it was, and I couldn't let her nor any of em live under schoolteacher. That was out."

Sethe knew that the circle she was making around the room, him, the subject, would remain one. That she could never close in, pin it down for anybody who had to ask. If they didn't get it right off—she could never explain. Because the truth was simple, not a long-drawn-out record of flowered shifts, tree cages, selfishness, ankle ropes and wells. Simple: she was squatting in the garden and when she saw them coming and recognized schoolteacher's hat, she heard wings. Little hummingbirds stuck their needle beaks right through her headcloth into her hair and beat their wings. And if she thought anything, it was No. No. Nono. Nonono. Simple. She just flew. Collected every bit of life she had made, all the parts of her that were precious and fine and beautiful, and carried, pushed, dragged them through the veil, out, away, over there where no one could hurt them. Over there. Outside this place, where they would be safe. And the hummingbird wings beat on. Sethe paused in her circle again and looked out the window. She remembered when the yard had a fence with a gate that somebody was always latching and unlatching in the time when 124 was busy as a way station. She did not see the whiteboys who pulled it down, yanked up the posts and smashed the gate leaving 124 desolate and exposed at the very hour when everybody stopped dropping by. The shoulder weeds of Bluestone Road were all that came toward the house.

When she got back from the jail house, she was glad the fence was gone. That's where they had hitched their horses—where she saw, floating above the railing as she squatted in the garden, schoolteacher's hat. By the time she faced him, looked him dead in the eye, she had something in her arms that stopped him in his tracks. He took a backward step with each jump of the baby heart until finally there were none.

"I stopped him," she said, staring at the place where the fence used to be. "I took and put my babies where they'd be safe."

The roaring in Paul D's head did not prevent him from hearing the pat she gave to the last word, and it occurred to him that what she wanted for her children was exactly what was missing in 124: safety. Which was the very first message he got the day he walked through the door. He thought he had made it safe, had gotten rid of the danger; beat the shit out of it; run it off the place and showed it and everybody else the difference between a mule and a plow. And because she had not done it before he got there her own self, he thought it was because she could not do it. That she lived with 124 in helpless, apologetic resignation because she had no choice; that minus husband, sons, mother-in-law, she and her slow-witted daughter had to live there all alone making do. The prickly, mean-eyed Sweet Home girl he knew as Halle's girl was obedient (like Halle), shy (like Halle), and work-crazy (like Halle). He was wrong. This here Sethe was new. The ghost in her house didn't bother her for the very same reason a room-and-board witch with new shoes was welcome. This here Sethe talked about love like any other woman; talked about baby clothes like any other woman, but what she meant could cleave the bone. This here Sethe talked about safety with a handsaw. This here new Sethe didn't know where the world stopped and she began. Suddenly he saw what Stamp Paid wanted him to see: more important than what Sethe had done was what she claimed. It scared him.

"Your love is too thick," he said, thinking, That bitch is looking at me; she is right over my head looking down through the floor at me.

"Too thick?" she said, thinking of the Clearing where Baby Suggs' commands knocked the pods off horse chestnuts. "Love is or it ain't. Thin love ain't love at all."

"Yeah. It didn't work, did it? Did it work?" he asked.

"It worked," she said.

"How? Your boys gone you don't know where. One girl dead, the other won't leave the yard. How did it work?"

"They ain't at Sweet Home. Schoolteacher ain't got em."

"Maybe there's worse."

"It ain't my job to know what's worse. It's my job to know what is and to keep them away from what I know is terrible. I did that."

"What you did was wrong, Sethe."

"I should have gone on back there? Taken my babies back there?"

"There could have been a way. Some other way."

"What way?"

"You got two feet, Sethe, not four," he said, and right then a forest sprang up between them; trackless and quiet.

Later he would wonder what made him say it. The calves of his youth? or the conviction that he was being observed through the ceiling? How fast he had moved from his shame to hers. From his cold-house secret straight to her too-thick love.

Meanwhile the forest was locking the distance between them, giving it shape and heft.

He did not put his hat on right away. First he fingered it, deciding how his going would be, how to make it an exit not an escape. And it was very important not to leave without looking. He stood up, turned and looked up the white stairs. She was there all right. Standing straight as a line with her back to him. He didn't rush to the door. He moved slowly and when he got there he opened it before asking Sethe to put supper aside for him because he might be a little late getting back. Only then did he put on his hat.

Sweet, she thought. He must think I can't bear to hear him say it. That after all I have told him and after telling me how many feet I have, "goodbye" would break me to pieces. Ain't that sweet.

"So long," she murmured from the far side of the trees.

# Two

124 WAS LOUD. Stamp Paid could hear it even from the road. He walked toward the house holding his head as high as possible so nobody looking could call him a sneak, although his worried mind made him feel like one. Ever since he showed that newspaper clipping to Paul D and learned that he'd moved out of 124 that very day, Stamp felt uneasy. Having wrestled with the question of whether or not to tell a man about his woman, and having convinced himself that he should, he then began to worry about Sethe. Had he stopped the one shot she had of the happiness a good man could bring her? Was she vexed by the loss, the free and unasked-for revival of gossip by the man who had helped her cross the river and who was her friend as well as Baby Suggs'?

"I'm too old," he thought, "for clear thinking. I'm too old and I seen too much." He had insisted on privacy during the revelation at the slaughter yard—now he wondered whom he was protecting. Paul D was the only one in town who didn't know. How did information that had been in the newspaper become a secret that needed to be whispered in a pig yard? A secret from whom? Sethe, that's who. He'd gone behind her back, like a sneak. But sneaking was his job—his life; though always for a clear and holy purpose. Before the War all he did was sneak: runaways into hidden places, secret information to public places. Underneath his legal vegetables were the contraband humans that he ferried across the river. Even the pigs he worked in the spring served his purposes. Whole families lived on the bones and guts he distributed to them. He wrote their letters and read to them the ones they received. He knew who had dropsy and who needed stovewood; which children had a gift and which needed correction. He knew the secrets of the Ohio River and its banks; empty houses and full; the best dancers, the worst speakers, those with beautiful voices and those who could not carry a tune. There was nothing interesting between his legs, but he remembered when there had been—when that drive drove the driven—and that was why he considered long and hard before opening his wooden box and searching for the eighteen-year-old clipping to show Paul D as proof.

Afterward—not before—he considered Sethe's feelings in the matter. And it was the lateness of this consideration that made him feel so bad. Maybe he should have left it alone; maybe Sethe would have gotten around to telling him herself; maybe he was not the high-minded Soldier of Christ he thought he was, but an ordinary, plain meddler who had interrupted something going along just fine for the sake of truth and forewarning, things he set much store by. Now 124 was back like it was before Paul D came to town—worrying Sethe and Denver with a pack of haunts he could hear from the road. Even if Sethe could deal with the return of the spirit, Stamp didn't believe her daughter could. Denver needed somebody normal in her life. By luck he had been there at her very birth almost—before she knew she was alive—and it made him partial to her. It was seeing her, alive, don't you know, and looking healthy four weeks later that pleased him so much he gathered all he could carry of the best blackberries in the county and stuck two in her mouth first, before he presented the difficult harvest to Baby Suggs. To this day he believed his berries (which sparked the feast and the wood chopping that followed) were the reason Denver was still alive. Had he not been there, chopping firewood, Sethe would have spread her baby brains on the planking. Maybe he should have thought of Denver, if not Sethe, before he gave Paul D the news that ran him off, the one normal somebody in the girl's life since Baby Suggs died. And right there was the thorn.

Deeper and more painful than his belated concern for Denver or Sethe, scorching his soul like a silver dollar in a fool's pocket, was the memory of Baby Suggs—the mountain to his sky. It was the memory of her and the honor that was her due that made him walk straight-necked into the yard of 124, although he heard its voices from the road.

He had stepped foot in this house only once after the Misery (which is what he called Sethe's rough response to the Fugitive Bill) and that was to carry Baby Suggs, holy, out of it. When he picked her up in his arms, she looked to him like a girl, and he took the pleasure she would have knowing she didn't have to grind her hip-bone anymore—that at last somebody carried *her*. Had she waited just a little she would have seen the end of the War, its short, flashy results. They could have celebrated together; gone to hear the great sermons preached on the occasion. As it was, he went alone from house to joyous house drinking what was offered. But she hadn't waited and he attended her funeral more put out with her than bereaved. Sethe and her daughter were dry-eyed on that occasion. Sethe had no instructions except "Take her to the Clearing," which he tried to do, but was prevented by some rule the whites had invented about where the dead should rest. Baby Suggs went down next to the baby with its throat cut—a neighborliness that Stamp wasn't sure had Baby Suggs' approval.

The setting-up was held in the yard because nobody besides him-self would enter 124—an injury Sethe answered with another by refusing to attend the service Reverend Pike presided over. She went instead to the gravesite, whose silence she competed with as she stood there not joining in the hymns the others sang with all their hearts. That insult spawned another by the mourners: back in the yard of 124, they ate the food they brought and did not touch Sethe's, who did not touch theirs and forbade Denver to. So Baby Suggs, holy, having devoted her freed life to harmony, was buried amid a regular dance of pride, fear, condemnation and spite. Just about everybody in town was longing for Sethe to come on difficult times. Her out-rageous claims, her self-sufficiency seemed to demand it, and Stamp Paid, who had not felt a trickle of meanness his whole adult life, wondered if some of the "pride goeth before a fall" expectations of the townsfolk had rubbed off on him anyhow—which would explain why he had not considered Sethe's feelings or Denver's needs when he showed Paul D the clipping.

He hadn't the vaguest notion of what he would do or say when and if Sethe opened the door and turned her eyes on his. He was willing to offer her help, if she wanted any from him, or receive her anger, if she harbored any against him. Beyond that, he trusted his instincts to right what he may have done wrong to Baby Suggs' kin, and to guide him in and through the stepped-up haunting 124 was subject to, as evidenced by the voices he heard from the road. Other than that, he would rely on the power of Jesus Christ to deal with things older, but not stronger, than He Himself was.

What he heard, as he moved toward the porch, he didn't understand. Out on Bluestone Road he thought he heard a conflagration of hasty voices—loud, urgent, all speaking at once so he could not make out what they were talking about or to whom. The speech wasn't nonsensical, exactly, nor was it tongues. But something was wrong with the order of the words and he couldn't describe or cipher it to save his life. All he could make out was the word *mine*. The rest of it stayed outside his mind's reach. Yet he went on through. When he got to the steps, the voices drained suddenly to less than a whisper. It gave him pause. They had become an occasional mutter—like the interior sounds a woman makes when she believes she is alone and unobserved at her work: a *sth* when she misses the needle's eye; a soft moan when she sees another chip in her one good platter; the low, friendly argument with which she greets the hens. Nothing fierce or startling. Just that eternal, private conversation that takes place between women and their tasks.

Stamp Paid raised his fist to knock on the door he had never knocked on (because it was always open to or for him) and could not do it. Dispensing with that formality was all the pay he expected from Negroes in his debt. Once Stamp Paid brought you a coat, got the message to you, saved your life, or fixed the cistern he took the liberty of walking in your door as though it were his own. Since all his visits were beneficial, his step or holler through a doorway got a bright welcome. Rather than forfeit the one privilege he claimed for himself, he lowered his hand and left the porch.

Over and over again he tried it: made up his mind to visit Sethe; broke through the loud hasty voices to the mumbling beyond it and stopped, trying to figure out what to do at the door. Six times in as many days he abandoned his normal route and tried to knock at 124. But the coldness of the gesture—its sign that he was indeed a stranger at the gate—overwhelmed him. Retracing his steps in the snow, he sighed. Spirit willing; flesh weak.

While Stamp Paid was making up his mind to visit 124 for Baby Suggs' sake, Sethe was trying to take her advice: *to lay it all down, sword and shield.* Not just to acknowledge the advice Baby Suggs gave her, but actually to take it. Four days after Paul D reminded her of how many feet she had, Sethe rummaged among the shoes of strangers to find the ice skates she was sure were there. Digging in the heap she despised herself for having been so trusting, so quick to surrender at the stove while Paul D kissed her back. She should have known that he would behave like everybody else in town once he knew. The twenty-eight days of having women friends, a mother-in-law, and all her children together; of being part of a neighborhood; of, in fact, having neighbors at all to call her own—all that was long gone and would never come back. No more dancing in the Clearing or happy feeds. No more discussions, stormy or quiet, about the true meaning of the Fugitive Bill, the Settlement Fee, God's Ways and Negro pews; antislavery, manumission, skin voting, Republicans, Dred Scott, book learning, Sojourner's high-wheeled buggy, the Colored Ladies of Delaware, Ohio, and the other weighty issues that held them in chairs, scraping the floorboards or pacing them in agony or exhilaration. No anxious wait for the *North Star* or news of a beat-off. No sighing at a new betrayal or handclapping at a small victory.

Those twenty-eight happy days were followed by eighteen years of disapproval and a solitary life. Then a few months of the sun-splashed life that the shadows holding hands on the road promised her; tentative greetings from other coloredpeople in Paul D's company; a bed life for herself. Except for Denver's friend, every bit of it had disappeared. Was that the pattern? she wondered. Every eighteen or twenty years her unlivable life would be interrupted by a short-lived glory?

Well, if that's the way it was—that's the way it was.

She had been on her knees, scrubbing the floor, Denver trailing her with the drying rags, when Beloved appeared saying, "What these do?" On her knees, scrub brush in hand, she looked at the girl and the skates she held up. Sethe couldn't skate a lick but then and there she decided to take Baby Suggs' advice: *lay it all down.* She left the bucket where it was. Told Denver to get out the shawls and started searching for the other skates she was certain were in that heap somewhere. Anybody feeling sorry for her, anybody wandering by to peep in and see how she was getting on (including Paul D) would discover that the woman junkheaped for the third time because she loved her children—that woman was sailing happily on a frozen creek.

Hurriedly, carelessly she threw the shoes about. She found one blade—a man's.

"Well," she said. "We'll take turns. Two skates on one; one skate on one; and shoe slide for the other."

Nobody saw them falling.

Holding hands, bracing each other, they swirled over the ice. Beloved wore the pair; Denver wore one, step-gliding over the treacherous ice. Sethe thought her two shoes would hold and anchor her. She was wrong. Two paces onto the creek, she lost her balance and landed on her behind. The girls, screaming with laughter, joined her on the ice. Sethe struggled to stand and discovered not only that she could do a split, but that it hurt. Her bones surfaced in unexpected places and so did laughter. Making a circle or a line, the three of them could not stay upright for one whole minute, but nobody saw them falling.

Each seemed to be helping the other two stay upright, yet every tumble doubled their delight. The live oak and soughing pine on the banks enclosed them and absorbed their laughter while they fought gravity for each other's hands. Their skirts flew like wings and their skin turned pewter in the cold and dying light.

Nobody saw them falling.

Exhausted finally they lay down on their backs to recover breath. The sky above them was another country. Winter stars, close enough to lick, had come out before sunset. For a moment, looking up, Sethe entered the perfect peace they offered. Then Denver stood up and tried for a long, independent glide. The tip of her single skate hit an ice bump, and as she fell, the flapping of her arms was so wild and hopeless that all three—Sethe, Beloved and Denver herself—laughed till they coughed. Sethe rose to her hands and knees, laughter still shaking her chest, making her eyes wet. She stayed that way for a while, on all fours. But when her laughter died, the tears did not and it was some time before Beloved or Denver knew the difference. When they did they touched her lightly on the shoulders.

Walking back through the woods, Sethe put an arm around each girl at her side. Both of them had an arm around her waist. Making their way over hard snow, they stumbled and had to hold on tight, but nobody saw them fall.

Inside the house they found out they were cold. They took off their shoes, wet stockings, and put on dry woolen ones. Denver fed the fire. Sethe warmed a pan of milk and stirred cane syrup and vanilla into it. Wrapped in quilts and blankets before the cooking stove, they drank, wiped their noses, and drank again.

"We could roast some taters," said Denver.

"Tomorrow," said Sethe. "Time to sleep."

She poured them each a bit more of the hot sweet milk. The stovefire roared.

"You finished with your eyes?" asked Beloved.

Sethe smiled. "Yes, I'm finished with my eyes. Drink up. Time for bed."

But none of them wanted to leave the warmth of the blankets, the fire and the cups for the chill of an unheated bed. They went on sipping and watching the fire.

When the click came Sethe didn't know what it was. Afterward it was clear as daylight that the click came at the very beginning—a beat, almost, before it started; before she heard three notes; before the melody was even clear. Leaning forward a little, Beloved was humming softly.

It was then, when Beloved finished humming, that Sethe recalled the click—the settling of pieces into places designed and made especially for them. No milk spilled from her cup because her hand was not shaking. She simply turned her head and looked at Beloved's profile: the chin, mouth, nose, forehead, copied and exaggerated in the huge shadow the fire threw on the wall behind her. Her hair, which Denver had braided into twenty or thirty plaits, curved toward her shoulders like arms. From where she sat Sethe could not examine it, not the hairline, nor the eyebrows, the lips, nor . . .

"All I remember," Baby Suggs had said, "is how she loved the burned bottom of bread. Her little hands I wouldn't know em if they slapped me."

. . . the birthmark, nor the color of the gums, the shape of her ears, nor . . .

"Here. Look here. This is your ma'am. If you can't tell me by my face, look here."

. . . the fingers, nor their nails, nor even . . .

But there would be time. The click had clicked; things were where they ought to be or poised and ready to glide in.

"I made that song up," said Sethe. "I made it up and sang it to my children. Nobody knows that song but me and my children."

Beloved turned to look at Sethe. "I know it," she said.

A hobnail casket of jewels found in a tree hollow should be fondled before it is opened. Its lock may have rusted or broken away from the clasp. Still you should touch the nail heads, and test its weight. No smashing with an ax head before it is decently exhumed from the grave that has hidden it all this time. No gasp at a miracle that is truly miraculous because the magic lies in the fact that you knew it was there for you all along.

Sethe wiped the white satin coat from the inside of the pan, brought pillows from the keeping room for the girls' heads. There was no tremor in her voice as she instructed them to keep the fire— if not, come on upstairs.

With that, she gathered her blanket around her elbows and ascended the lily-white stairs like a bride. Outside, snow solidified itself into graceful forms. The peace of winter stars seemed permanent.

Fingering a ribbon and smelling skin, Stamp Paid approached 124 again.

"My marrow is tired," he thought. "I been tired all my days, bone-tired, but now it's in the marrow. Must be what Baby Suggs felt when she lay down and thought about color for the rest of her life." When she told him what her aim was, he thought she was ashamed and too shamed to say so. Her authority in the pulpit, her dance in the Clearing, her powerful Call (she didn't deliver sermons or preach—insisting she was too ignorant for that—she *called* and the hearing heard)—all that had been mocked and rebuked by the bloodspill in her backyard. God puzzled her and she was too ashamed of Him to say so. Instead she told Stamp she was going to bed to think about the colors of things. He tried to dissuade her. Sethe was in jail with her nursing baby, the one he had saved. Her sons were holding hands in the yard, terrified of letting go. Strangers and familiars were stopping by to hear how it went one more time, and suddenly Baby declared peace. She just up and quit. By the time Sethe was released she had exhausted blue and was well on her way to yellow.

At first he would see her in the yard occasionally, or delivering food to the jail, or shoes in town. Then less and less. He believed then that shame put her in the bed. Now, eight years after her contentious funeral and eighteen years after the Misery, he changed his mind. Her marrow was tired and it was a testimony to the heart that fed it that it took eight years to meet finally the color she was hankering after. The onslaught of her fatigue, like his, was sudden, but lasted for years. After sixty years of losing children to the people who chewed up her life and spit it out like a fish bone; after five years of freedom given to her by her last child, who bought her future with his, exchanged it, so to speak, so she could have one whether he did or not—to lose him too; to acquire a daughter and grandchildren and see that daughter slay the children (or try to); to belong to a community of other free Negroes—to love and be loved by them, to counsel and be counseled, protect and be protected, feed and be fed—and then to have that community step back and hold itself at a distance—well, it could wear out even a Baby Suggs, holy.

"Listen here, girl," he told her, "you can't quit the Word. It's given to you to speak. You can't quit the Word, I don't care what all happen to you."

They were standing in Richmond Street, ankle deep in leaves. Lamps lit the downstairs windows of spacious houses and made the early evening look darker than it was. The odor of burning leaves was brilliant. Quite by chance, as he pocketed a penny tip for a delivery, he had glanced across the street and recognized the skipping woman as his old friend. He had not seen her in weeks. Quickly he crossed the street, scuffing red leaves as he went. When he stopped her with a greeting, she returned it with a face knocked clean of interest. She could have been a plate. A carpetbag full of shoes in her hand, she waited for him to begin, lead or share a conversation. If there had been sadness in her eyes he would have understood it; but indifference lodged where sadness should have been.

"You missed the Clearing three Saturdays running," he told her.

She turned her head away and scanned the houses along the street.

"Folks came," he said.

"Folks come; folks go," she answered.

"Here, let me carry that." He tried to take her bag from her but she wouldn't let him.

"I got a delivery someplace long in here," she said. "Name of Tucker."

"Yonder," he said. "Twin chestnuts in the yard. Sick, too."

They walked a bit, his pace slowed to accommodate her skip.

"Well?"

"Well, what?"

"Saturday coming. You going to Call or what?"

"If I call them and they come, what on earth I'm going to say?"

"Say the Word!" He checked his shout too late. Two whitemen burning leaves turned their heads in his direction. Bending low he whispered into her ear, "The Word. The Word."

"That's one other thing took away from me," she said, and that was when he exhorted her, pleaded with her not to quit, no matter what. The Word had been given to her and she had to speak it. Had to.

They had reached the twin chestnuts and the white house that stood behind them.

"See what I mean?" he said. "Big trees like that, both of em together ain't got the leaves of a young birch."

"I see what you mean," she said, but she peered instead at the white house.

"You got to do it," he said. "You got to. Can't nobody Call like you. You have to be there."

"What I have to do is get in my bed and lay down. I want to fix on something harmless in this world."

"What world you talking about? Ain't nothing harmless down here."

"Yes it is. Blue. That don't hurt nobody. Yellow neither."

"You getting in the bed to think about yellow?"

"I likes yellow."

"Then what? When you get through with blue and yellow, then what?"

"Can't say. It's something can't be planned."

"You blaming God," he said. "That's what you doing."

"No, Stamp. I ain't."

"You saying the whitefolks won? That what you saying?"

"I'm saying they came in my yard."

"You saying nothing counts."

"I'm saying they came in my yard."

"Sethe's the one did it."

"And if she hadn't?"

"You saying God give up? Nothing left for us but pour out our own blood?"

"I'm saying they came in my yard."

"You punishing Him, ain't you."

"Not like He punish me."

"You can't do that, Baby. It ain't right."

"Was a time I knew what that was."

"You still know."

"What I know is what I see: a nigger woman hauling shoes."

"Aw, Baby." He licked his lips searching with his tongue for the words that would turn her around, lighten her load. "We have to be steady. 'These things too will pass.' What you looking for? A miracle?"

"No," she said. "I'm looking for what I was put here to look for: the back door," and skipped right to it. They didn't let her in. They took the shoes from her as she stood on the steps and she rested her hip on the railing while the whitewoman went looking for the dime.

Stamp Paid rearranged his way. Too angry to walk her home

and listen to more, he watched her for a moment and turned to go before the alert white face at the window next door had come to any conclusion.

Trying to get to 124 for the second time now, he regretted that conversation: the high tone he took; his refusal to see the effect of marrow weariness in a woman he believed was a mountain. Now, too late, he understood her. The heart that pumped out love, the mouth that spoke the Word, didn't count. They came in her yard anyway and she could not approve or condemn Sethe's rough choice. One or the other might have saved her, but beaten up by the claims of both, she went to bed. The whitefolks had tired her out at last.

And him. Eighteen seventy-four and whitefolks were still on the loose. Whole towns wiped clean of Negroes; eighty-seven lynchings in one year alone in Kentucky; four colored schools burned to the ground; grown men whipped like children; children whipped like adults; black women raped by the crew; property taken, necks broken. He smelled skin, skin and hot blood. The skin was one thing, but human blood cooked in a lynch fire was a whole other thing. The stench stank. Stank up off the pages of the *North Star,* out of the mouths of witnesses, etched in crooked handwriting in letters delivered by hand. Detailed in documents and petitions full of *whereas* and presented to any legal body who'd read it, it stank. But none of that had worn out his marrow. None of that. It was the ribbon. Tying his flatbed up on the bank of the Licking River, securing it the best he could, he caught sight of something red on its bottom. Reaching for it, he thought it was a cardinal feather stuck to his boat. He tugged and what came loose in his hand was a red ribbon knotted around a curl of wet woolly hair, clinging still to its bit of scalp. He untied the ribbon and put it in his pocket, dropped the curl in the weeds. On the way home, he stopped, short of breath and dizzy. He waited until the spell passed before continuing on his way. A moment later, his breath left him again. This time he sat down by a fence. Rested, he got to his feet, but before he took a step he turned to look back down the road he was traveling and said, to its frozen mud and the river beyond, "What *are* these people? You tell me, Jesus. What *are* they?"

When he got to his house he was too tired to eat the food his sister and nephews had prepared. He sat on the porch in the cold till way past dark and went to his bed only because his sister's voice calling him was getting nervous. He kept the ribbon; the skin smell nagged him, and his weakened marrow made him dwell on Baby Suggs' wish to consider what in the world was harmless. He hoped she stuck to blue, yellow, maybe green, and never fixed on red.

Mistaking her, upbraiding her, owing her, now he needed to let her know he knew, and to get right with her and her kin. So, in spite of his exhausted marrow, he kept on through the voices and tried once more to knock at the door of 124. This time, although he couldn't cipher but one word, he believed he knew who spoke them. The people of the broken necks, of fire-cooked blood and black girls who had lost their ribbons.

What a roaring.

Sethe had gone to bed smiling, eager to lie down and unravel the proof for the conclusion she had already leapt to. Fondle the day and circumstances of Beloved's arrival and the meaning of that kiss in the Clearing. She slept instead and woke, still smiling, to a snow-bright morning, cold enough to see her breath. She lingered a moment to collect the courage to throw off the blankets and hit a chilly floor. For the first time, she was going to be late for work.

Downstairs she saw the girls sleeping where she'd left them, but back to back now, each wrapped tight in blankets, breathing into their pillows. The pair and a half of skates were lying by the front door, the stockings hung on a nail behind the cooking stove to dry had not.

Sethe looked at Beloved's face and smiled.

Quietly, carefully she stepped around her to wake the fire. First a bit of paper, then a little kindlin—not too much—just a taste until it was strong enough for more. She fed its dance until it was wild and fast. When she went outside to collect more wood from the shed, she did not notice the man's frozen footprints. She crunched around to the back, to the cord piled high with snow. After scraping it clean, she filled her arms with as much dry wood as she could. She even looked straight at the shed, smiling, smiling at the things she would not have to remember now. Thinking, "She ain't even mad with me. Not a bit."

Obviously the hand-holding shadows she had seen on the road were not Paul D, Denver and herself, but "us three." The three holding on to each other skating the night before; the three sipping flavored milk. And since that was so—if her daughter could come back home from the timeless place—certainly her sons could, and would, come back from wherever they had gone to.

Sethe covered her front teeth with her tongue against the cold. Hunched forward by the burden in her arms, she walked back around the house to the porch—not once noticing the frozen tracks she stepped in.

Inside, the girls were still sleeping, although they had changed positions while she was gone, both drawn to the fire. Dumping the armload into the woodbox made them stir but not wake. Sethe started the cooking stove as quietly as she could, reluctant to wake the sisters, happy to have them asleep at her feet while she made breakfast. Too bad she would be late for work—too, too bad. Once in sixteen years? That's just too bad.

She had beaten two eggs into yesterday's hominy, formed it into patties and fried them with some ham pieces before Denver woke completely and groaned.

"Back stiff?"

"Ooh yeah."

"Sleeping on the floor's supposed to be good for you."

"Hurts like the devil," said Denver.

"Could be that fall you took."

Denver smiled. "That was fun." She turned to look down at Beloved snoring lightly. "Should I wake her?"

"No, let her rest."

"She likes to see you off in the morning."

"I'll make sure she does," said Sethe, and thought, Be nice to think first, before I talk to her, let her know I know. Think about all I ain't got to remember no more. Do like Baby said: Think on it then lay it down—for good. Paul D convinced me there was a world out there and that I could live in it. Should have known better. *Did* know better. Whatever is going on outside my door ain't for me. The world is in this room. This here's all there is and all there needs to be.

They ate like men, ravenous and intent. Saying little, content with the company of the other and the opportunity to look in her eyes.

When Sethe wrapped her head and bundled up to go to town, it was already midmorning. And when she left the house she neither saw the prints nor heard the voices that ringed 124 like a noose.

Trudging in the ruts left earlier by wheels, Sethe was excited to giddiness by the things she no longer had to remember.

I don't have to remember nothing. I don't even have to explain. She understands it all. I can forget how Baby Suggs' heart collapsed; how we agreed it was consumption without a sign of it in the world. Her eyes when she brought my food, I can forget that, and how she told me that Howard and Buglar were all right but wouldn't let go each other's hands. Played that way: stayed that way especially in their sleep. She handed me the food from a basket; things wrapped small enough to get through the bars, whispering news: Mr. Bodwin going to see the judge—in chambers, she kept on saying, in chambers, like I knew what it meant or she did. The Colored Ladies of Delaware, Ohio, had drawn up a petition to keep me from being hanged. That two white preachers had come round and wanted to talk to me, pray for me. That a newspaperman came too. She told me the news and I told her I needed something for the rats. She wanted Denver out and slapped her palms when I wouldn't let her go. "Where your earrings?" she said. "I'll hold em for you." I told her the jailer took them, to protect me from myself. He thought I could do some harm with the wire. Baby Suggs covered her mouth with her hand. "Schoolteacher left town," she said. "Filed a claim and rode on off. They going to let you out for the burial," she said, "not the funeral, just the burial," and they did. The sheriff came with me and looked away when I fed Denver in the wagon. Neither Howard nor Buglar would let me near them, not even to touch their hair. I believe a lot of folks were there, but I just saw the box. Reverend Pike spoke in a real loud voice, but I didn't catch a word—except the first two, and three months later when Denver was ready for solid food and they let me out for good, I went and got you a gravestone, but I didn't have money enough for the carving so I exchanged (bartered, you might say) what I did have and I'm sorry to this day I never thought to ask him for the whole thing: all I heard of what Reverend Pike said. Dearly Beloved, which is what you are to me and I don't have to be sorry about getting only one word, and I don't have to remember the slaughterhouse and the Saturday girls who worked its yard. I can forget that what I did changed Baby Suggs' life. No Clearing, no company. Just laundry and shoes. I can forget it all now because as soon as I got the gravestone in place you made your presence known in the house and worried us all to distraction. I didn't understand it then. I thought you were mad with me. And now I know that if you was, you ain't now because you came back here to me and I was right all along: there is no world outside my door. I only need to know one thing. How bad is the scar?

As Sethe walked to work, late for the first time in sixteen years and wrapped in a timeless present, Stamp Paid fought fatigue and the habit of a lifetime. Baby Suggs refused to go to the Clearing because she believed *they* had won; he refused to acknowledge any such victory. Baby had no back door; so he braved the cold and a wall of talk to knock on the one she did have. He clutched the red ribbon in his pocket for strength. Softly at first, then harder. At the last he banged furiously—disbelieving it could happen. That the door of a house with coloredpeople in it did not fly open in his presence. He went to the window and wanted to cry. Sure enough, there they were, not a one of them heading for the door. Worrying his scrap of ribbon to shreds, the old man turned and went down the steps. Now curiosity joined his shame and his debt. Two backs curled away from him as he looked in the window. One had a head he recognized; the other troubled him. He didn't know her and didn't know anybody it could be. Nobody, but nobody visited that house.

After a disagreeable breakfast he went to see Ella and John to find out what they knew. Perhaps there he could find out if, after all these years of clarity, he had misnamed himself and there was yet another debt he owed. Born Joshua, he renamed himself when he handed over his wife to his master's son. Handed her over in the sense that he did not kill anybody, thereby himself, because his wife demanded he stay alive. Otherwise, she reasoned, where and to whom could she return when the boy was through? With that gift, he decided that he didn't owe anybody anything. Whatever his obligations were, that act paid them off. He thought it would make him rambunctious, renegade—a drunkard even, the debtlessness, and in a way it did. But there was nothing to do with it. Work well; work poorly. Work a little; work not at all. Make sense; make none. Sleep, wake up; like somebody, dislike others. It didn't seem much of a way to live and it brought him no satisfaction. So he extended this debtlessness to other people by helping them pay out and off whatever they owed in misery. Beaten runaways? He ferried them and rendered them paid for; gave them their own bill of sale, so to speak. "You paid it; now life owes you." And the receipt, as it were, was a welcome door that he never had to knock on, like John and Ella's in front of which he stood and said, "Who in there?" only once and she was pulling on the hinge.

"Where you been keeping yourself? I told John must be cold if Stamp stay inside."

"Oh, I been out." He took off his cap and massaged his scalp.

"Out where? Not by here." Ella hung two suits of underwear on a line behind the stove.

"Was over to Baby Suggs' this morning."

"What you want in there?" asked Ella. "Somebody invite you in?"

"That's Baby's kin. I don't need no invite to look after her people."

"Sth." Ella was unmoved. She had been Baby Suggs' friend and Sethe's too till the rough time. Except for a nod at the carnival, she hadn't given Sethe the time of day.

"Somebody new in there. A woman. Thought you might know who is she."

"Ain't no new Negroes in this town I don't know about," she said. "What she look like? You sure that wasn't Denver?"

"I know Denver. This girl's narrow."

"You sure?"

"I know what I see."

"Might see anything at all at 124."

"True."

"Better ask Paul D," she said.

"Can't locate him," said Stamp, which was the truth although his efforts to find Paul D had been feeble. He wasn't ready to confront the man whose life he had altered with his graveyard information.

"He's sleeping in the church," said Ella.

"The church!" Stamp was shocked and very hurt.

"Yeah. Asked Reverend Pike if he could stay in the cellar."

"It's cold as charity in there!"

"I expect he knows that."

"What he do that for?"

"He's a touch proud, seem like."

"He don't have to do that! Any number'll take him in."

Ella turned around to look at Stamp Paid. "Can't nobody read minds long distance. All he have to do is ask somebody."

"Why? Why he have to ask? Can't nobody offer? What's going on? Since when a blackman come to town have to sleep in a cellar like a dog?"

"Unrile yourself, Stamp."

"Not me. I'm going to stay riled till somebody gets some sense and leastway act like a Christian."

"It's only a few days he been there."

"Shouldn't be no days! You know all about it and don't give him a hand? That don't sound like you, Ella. Me and you been pulling coloredfolk out the water more'n twenty years. Now you tell me you can't offer a man a bed? A working man, too! A man what can pay his own way."

"He ask, I give him anything."

"Why's that necessary all of a sudden?"

"I don't know him all that well."

"You know he's colored!"

"Stamp, don't tear me up this morning. I don't feel like it."

"It's her, ain't it?"

"Her who?"

"Sethe. He took up with her and stayed in there and you don't want nothing to—"

"Hold on. Don't jump if you can't see bottom."

"Girl, give it up. We been friends too long to act like this."

"Well, who can tell what all went on in there? Look here, I don't know who Sethe is or none of her people."

"What?!"

"All I know is she married Baby Suggs' boy and I ain't sure I know that. Where is *he,* huh? Baby never laid eyes on her till John carried her to the door with a baby I strapped on her chest."

"*I* strapped that baby! And you way off the track with that wagon. Her children know who she was even if you don't."

"So what? I ain't saying she wasn't their ma'ammy, but who's to say they was Baby Suggs' grandchildren? How she get on board and her husband didn't? And tell me this, how she have that baby in the woods by herself? Said a whitewoman come out the trees and helped her. Shoot. You believe that? A *white*woman? Well, I know what kind of white that was."

"Aw, no, Ella."

"Anything white floating around in the woods—if it ain't got a shotgun, it's something I don't want *no* part of!"

"You all was friends."

"Yeah, till she showed herself."

"Ella."

"I ain't got no friends take a handsaw to their own children."

"You in deep water, girl."

"Uh uh. I'm on dry land and I'm going to stay there. You the one wet."

"What's any of what you talking got to do with Paul D?"

"What run him off? Tell me that."

"I run him off."

"You?"

"I told him about—I showed him the newspaper, about the— what Sethe did. Read it to him. He left that very day."

"You didn't tell me that. I thought he knew."

"He didn't know nothing. Except her, from when they was at that place Baby Suggs was at."

"He knew Baby Suggs?"

"Sure he knew her. Her boy Halle too."

"And left when he found out what Sethe did?"

"Look like he might have a place to stay after all."

"What you say casts a different light. I thought—"

But Stamp Paid knew what she thought.

"You didn't come here asking about him," Ella said. "You came about some new girl."

"That's so."

"Well, Paul D must know who she is. Or *what* she is."

"Your mind is loaded with spirits. Everywhere you look you see one."

"You know as well as I do that people who die bad don't stay in the ground."

He couldn't deny it. Jesus Christ Himself didn't, so Stamp ate a piece of Ella's head cheese to show there were no bad feelings and set out to find Paul D. He found him on the steps of Holy Redeemer, holding his wrists between his knees and looking red-eyed.

Sawyer shouted at her when she entered the kitchen, but she just turned her back and reached for her apron. There was no entry now. No crack or crevice available. She had taken pains to keep them out, but knew full well that at any moment they could rock her, rip her from her moorings, send the birds twittering back into her hair. Drain her mother's milk, they had already done. Divided her back into plant life—that too. Driven her fat-bellied into the woods—they had done that. All news of them was rot. They buttered Halle's face; gave Paul D iron to eat; crisped Sixo; hanged her own mother. She didn't want any more news about whitefolks; didn't want to know what Ella knew and John and Stamp Paid, about the world done up the way whitefolks loved it. All news of them should have stopped with the birds in her hair.

Once, long ago, she was soft, trusting. She trusted Mrs. Garner and her husband too. She knotted the earrings into her underskirt to take along, not so much to wear but to hold. Earrings that made her believe she could discriminate among them. That for every schoolteacher there would be an Amy; that for every pupil there was a Garner, or Bodwin, or even a sheriff, whose touch at her elbow was gentle and who looked away when she nursed. But she had come to believe every one of Baby Suggs' last words and buried all recollection of them and luck. Paul D dug it up, gave her back her body, kissed her divided back, stirred her rememory and brought her more news: of clabber, of iron, of roosters' smiling, but when he heard *her* news, he counted her feet and didn't even say goodbye.

"Don't talk to me, Mr. Sawyer. Don't say nothing to me this morning."

"What? What? What? You talking back to me?"

"I'm telling you don't say nothing to me."

"You better get them pies made."

Sethe touched the fruit and picked up the paring knife.

When pie juice hit the bottom of the oven and hissed, Sethe was well into the potato salad. Sawyer came in and said, "Not too sweet. You make it too sweet they don't eat it."

"Make it the way I always did."

"Yeah. Too sweet."

None of the sausages came back. The cook had a way with them and Sawyer's Restaurant never had leftover sausage. If Sethe wanted any, she put them aside soon as they were ready. But there was some passable stew. Problem was, all her pies were sold too. Only rice pudding left and half a pan of gingerbread that didn't come out right. Had she been paying attention instead of daydreaming all morning, she wouldn't be picking around looking for her dinner like a crab. She couldn't read clock time very well, but she knew when the hands were closed in prayer at the top of the face she was through for the day. She got a metal-top jar, filled it with stew and wrapped the gingerbread in butcher paper. These she dropped in her outer skirt pockets and began washing up. None of it was anything like what the cook and the two waiters walked off with. Mr. Sawyer included midday dinner in the terms of the job—along with $3.40 a week— and she made him understand from the beginning she would take her dinner home. But matches, sometimes a bit of kerosene, a little salt, butter too—these things she took also, once in a while, and felt ashamed because she could afford to buy them; she just didn't want the embarrassment of waiting out back of Phelps store with the others till every white in Ohio was served before the keeper turned to the cluster of Negro faces looking through a hole in his back door. She was ashamed, too, because it was stealing and Sixo's argument on the subject amused her but didn't change the way she felt; just as it didn't change schoolteacher's mind.

"Did you steal that shoat? You stole that shoat." Schoolteacher was quiet but firm, like he was just going through the motions—not expecting an answer that mattered. Sixo sat there, not even getting up to plead or deny. He just sat there, the streak-of-lean in his hand, the gristle clustered in the tin plate like gemstones—rough, unpolished, but loot nevertheless.

"You stole that shoat, didn't you?"

"No. Sir." said Sixo, but he had the decency to keep his eyes on the meat.

"You telling me you didn't steal it, and I'm looking right at you?"

"No, sir. I didn't steal it."

Schoolteacher smiled. "Did you kill it?"

"Yes, sir. I killed it."

"Did you butcher it?"

"Yes, sir."

"Did you cook it?"

"Yes, sir."

"Well, then. Did you eat it?"

"Yes, sir. I sure did."

"And you telling me that's not stealing?"

"No, sir. It ain't."

"What is it then?"

"Improving your property, sir."

"What?"

"Sixo plant rye to give the high piece a better chance. Sixo take and feed the soil, give you more crop. Sixo take and feed Sixo give you more work."

Clever, but schoolteacher beat him anyway to show him that definitions belonged to the definers—not the defined. After Mr. Garner died with a hole in his ear that Mrs. Garner said was an exploded ear drum brought on by stroke and Sixo said was gunpowder, everything they touched was looked on as stealing. Not just a rifle of corn, or two yard eggs the hen herself didn't even remember, everything. Schoolteacher took away the guns from the Sweet Home men and, deprived of game to round out their diet of bread, beans, hominy, vegetables and a little extra at slaughter time, they began to pilfer in earnest, and it became not only their right but their obligation.

Sethe understood it then, but now with a paying job and an employer who was kind enough to hire an ex-convict, she despised herself for the pride that made pilfering better than standing in line at the window of the general store with all the other Negroes. She didn't want to jostle them or be jostled by them. Feel their judgment or their pity, especially now. She touched her forehead with the back of her wrist and blotted the perspiration. The workday had come to a close and already she was feeling the excitement. Not since that other escape had she felt so alive. Slopping the alley dogs, watching their frenzy, she pressed her lips. Today would be a day she would accept a lift, if anybody on a wagon offered it. No one would, and for sixteen years her pride had not let her ask. But today. Oh, today. Now she wanted speed, to skip over the long walk home and *be* there.

When Sawyer warned her about being late again, she barely heard him. He used to be a sweet man. Patient, tender in his dealings with his help. But each year, following the death of his son in the War, he grew more and more crotchety. As though Sethe's dark face was to blame.

"Un huh," she said, wondering how she could hurry time along and get to the no-time waiting for her.

She needn't have worried. Wrapped tight, hunched forward, as she started home her mind was busy with the things she could forget.

Thank God I don't have to rememory or say a thing because you know it. All. You know I never would a left you. Never. It was all I could think of to do. When the train came I had to be ready. Schoolteacher was teaching us things we couldn't learn. I didn't care nothing about the measuring string. We all laughed about that—except Sixo. He didn't laugh at nothing. But I didn't care. School-teacher'd wrap that string all over my head, 'cross my nose, around my behind. Number my teeth. I thought he was a fool. And the questions he asked was the biggest foolishness of all.

Then me and your brothers come up from the second patch. The first one was close to the house where the quick things grew: beans, onions, sweet peas. The other one was further down for long-lasting things, potatoes, pumpkin, okra, pork salad. Not much was up yet down there. It was early still. Some young salad maybe, but that was all. We pulled weeds and hoed a little to give everything a good start. After that we hit out for the house. The ground raised up from the second patch. Not a hill exactly but kind of. Enough for Buglar and Howard to run up and roll down, run up and roll down. That's the way I used to see them in my dreams, laughing, their short fat legs running up the hill. Now all I see is their backs walking down the railroad tracks. Away from me. Always away from me. But that day they was happy, running up and rolling down. It was early still— the growing season had took hold but not much was up. I remember the peas still had flowers. The grass was long though, full of white buds and those tall red blossoms people call Diane and something there with the leastest little bit of blue—light, like a cornflower but pale, pale. Real pale. I maybe should have hurried because I left you back at the house in a basket in the yard. Away from where the chickens scratched but you never know. Anyway I took my time getting back but your brothers didn't have patience with me staring at flowers and sky every two or three steps. They ran on ahead and I let em. Something sweet lives in the air that time of year, and if the breeze is right, it's hard to stay indoors. When I got back I could hear Howard and Buglar laughing down by the quarters. I put my hoe down and cut across the side yard to get to you. The shade moved so by the time I got back the sun was shining right on you. Right in your face, but you wasn't woke at all. Still asleep. I wanted to pick you up in my arms and I wanted to look at you sleeping too. Didn't know which; you had the sweetest face. Yonder, not far, was a grape arbor Mr. Garner made. Always full of big plans, he wanted to make his own wine to get drunk off. Never did get more than a kettle of jelly from it. I don't think the soil was right for grapes. Your daddy believed it was the rain, not the soil. Sixo said it was bugs. The grapes so little and tight. Sour as vinegar too. But there was a little table in there. So I picked up your basket and carried you over to the grape arbor. Cool in there and shady. I set you down on the little table and figured if I got a piece of muslin the bugs and things wouldn't get to you. And if Mrs. Garner didn't need me right there in the kitchen, I could get a chair and you and me could set out there while I did the vegetables. I headed for the back door to get the clean muslin we kept in the kitchen press. The grass felt good on my feet. I got near the door and I heard voices. Schoolteacher made his pupils sit and learn books for a spell every afternoon. If it was nice enough weather, they'd sit on the side porch. All three of em. He'd talk and they'd write. Or he would read and they would write down what he said. I never told nobody this. Not your pap, not nobody. I almost told Mrs. Garner, but she was so weak then and getting weaker. This is the first time I'm telling it and I'm telling it to you because it might help explain something to you although I know you don't need me to do it. To tell it or even think over it. You don't have to listen either, if you don't want to. But I couldn't help listening to what I heard that day. He was talking to his pupils and I heard him say, "Which one are you doing?" And one of the boys said, "Sethe." That's when I stopped because I heard my name, and then I took a few steps to where I could see what they was doing. Schoolteacher was standing over one of them with one hand behind his back. He licked a forefinger a couple of times and turned a few pages. Slow. I was about to turn around and keep on my way to where the muslin was, when I heard him say, "No, no. That's not the way. I told you to put her human characteristics on the left; her animal ones on the right. And don't forget to line them up." I commenced to walk backward, didn't even look behind me to find out where I was headed. I just kept lifting my feet and pushing back. When I bumped up against a tree my scalp was prickly. One of the dogs was licking out a pan in the yard. I got to the grape arbor fast enough, but I didn't have the muslin. Flies settled all over your face, rubbing their hands. My head itched like the devil. Like somebody was sticking fine needles in my scalp. I never told Halle or nobody. But that very day I asked Mrs. Garner a part of it. She was low then. Not as low as she ended up, but failing. A kind of bag grew under her jaw. It didn't seem to hurt her, but it made her weak. First she'd be up and spry in the morning and by the second milking she couldn't stand up. Next she took to sleeping late. The day I went up there she was in bed the whole day, and I thought to carry her some bean soup and ask her then. When I opened the bedroom door she looked at me from

"Features?"

"Umm. Like, a feature of summer is heat. A characteristic is a feature. A thing that's natural to a thing."

"Can you have more than one?"

"You can have quite a few. You know. Say a baby sucks its thumb. That's one, but it has others too. Keep Billy away from Red Cora. Mr. Garner never let her calve every other year. Sethe, you hear me? Come away from that window and listen."

"Yes, ma'am."

"Ask my brother-in-law to come up after supper."

"Yes, ma'am."

"If you'd wash your hair you could get rid of that lice."

"Ain't no lice in my head, ma'am."

"Whatever it is, a good scrubbing is what it needs, not scratching. Don't tell me we're out of soap."

"No, ma'am."

"All right now. I'm through. Talking makes me tired."

"Yes, ma'am."

"And thank you, Sethe."

"Yes, ma'am."

You was too little to remember the quarters. Your brothers slept under the window. Me, you and your daddy slept by the wall. The night after I heard why schoolteacher measured me, I had trouble sleeping. When Halle came in I asked him what he thought about schoolteacher. He said there wasn't nothing to think about. Said, He's white, ain't he? I said, But I mean is he like Mr. Garner?

"What you want to know, Sethe?"

"Him and her," I said, "they ain't like the whites I seen before. The ones in the big place I was before I came here."

"How these different?" he asked me.

"Well," I said, "they talk soft for one thing."

"It don't matter, Sethe. What they say is the same. Loud or soft."

"Mr. Garner let you buy out your mother," I said.

"Yep. He did."

"Well?"

"If he hadn't of, she would of dropped in his cooking stove."

"Still, he did it. Let you work it off."

"Uh huh."

"Wake up, Halle."

"I said, Uh huh."

"He could of said no. He didn't tell you no."

"No, he didn't tell me no. She worked here for ten years. If she worked another ten you think she would've made it out? I pay him for her last years and in return he got you, me and three more coming up. I got one more year of debt work; one more. Schoolteacher in there told me to quit it. Said the reason for doing it don't hold. I should do the extra but here at Sweet Home."

"Is he going to pay you for the extra?"

"Nope."

"Then how you going to pay it off? How much is it?"

"$123.70."

"Don't he want it back?"

"He want something."

"What?"

"I don't know. Something. But he don't want me off Sweet Home no more. Say it don't pay to have my labor somewhere else while the boys is small."

"What about the money you owe?"

"He must have another way of getting it."

"What way?"

"I don't know, Sethe."

"Then the only question is how? How he going get it?"

"No. That's one question. There's one more."

"What's that?"

He leaned up and turned over, touching my cheek with his knuckles. "The question now is, Who's going buy you out? Or me? Or her?" He pointed over to where you was laying.

"What?"

"If all my labor is Sweet Home, including the extra, what I got left to sell?"

He turned over then and went back to sleep and I thought I wouldn't but I did too for a while. Something he said, maybe, or something he didn't say woke me. I sat up like somebody hit me, and you woke up too and commenced to cry. I rocked you some, but there wasn't much room, so I stepped outside the door to walk you. Up and down I went. Up and down. Everything dark but lamplight in the top window of the house. She must've been up still. I couldn't get out of my head the thing that woke me up: "While the boys is small." That's what he said and it snapped me awake. They tagged after me the whole day weeding, milking, getting firewood. For now. For now.

That's when we should have begun to plan. But we didn't. I don't know what we thought—but getting away was a money thing to us. Buy out. Running was nowhere on our minds. All of us? Some? Where to? How to go? It was Sixo who brought it up, finally, after Paul F. Mrs. Garner sold him, trying to keep things up. Already she lived two years off his price. But it ran out, I guess, so she wrote schoolteacher to come take over. Four Sweet Home men and she still believed she needed her brother-in-law and two boys 'cause people said she shouldn't be alone out there with nothing but Negroes. So he came with a big hat and spectacles and a coach box full of paper. Talking soft and watching hard. He beat Paul A. Not hard and not long, but it was the first time anyone had, because Mr. Garner disallowed it. Next time I saw him he had company in the prettiest trees you ever saw. Sixo started watching the sky. He was the only one who crept at night and Halle said that's how he learned about the train.

"That way." Halle was pointing over the stable. "Where he took my ma'am. Sixo say freedom is that way. A whole train is going and if we can get there, don't need to be no buy-out."

"Train? What's that?" I asked him.

They stopped talking in front of me then. Even Halle. But they whispered among themselves and Sixo watched the sky. Not the high part, the low part where it touched the trees. You could tell his mind was gone from Sweet Home.

The plan was a good one, but when it came time, I was big with Denver. So we changed it a little. A little. Just enough to butter Halle's face, so Paul D tells me, and make Sixo laugh at last.

But I got you out, baby. And the boys too. When the signal for the train come, you all was the only ones ready. I couldn't find Halle or nobody. I didn't know Sixo was burned up and Paul D dressed in a collar you wouldn't believe. Not till later. So I sent you all to the wagon with the woman who waited in the corn. Ha ha. No notebook for my babies and no measuring string neither. What I had to get through later I got through because of you. Passed right by those boys hanging in the trees. One had Paul A's shirt on but not his feet or his head. I walked right on by because only me had your milk, and God do what He would, I was going to get it to you. You remember that, don't you; that I did? That when I got here I had milk enough for all?

One more curve in the road, and Sethe could see her chimney; it wasn't lonely-looking anymore. The ribbon of smoke was from a fire that warmed a body returned to her—just like it never went away, never needed a headstone. And the heart that beat inside it had not for a single moment stopped in her hands.

She opened the door, walked in and locked it tight behind her.

The day Stamp Paid saw the two backs through the window and then hurried down the steps, he believed the undecipherable language clamoring around the house was the mumbling of the black and angry dead. Very few had died in bed, like Baby Suggs, and none that he knew of, including Baby, had lived a livable life. Even the educated colored: the long-school people, the doctors, the teachers, the paper-writers and businessmen had a hard row to hoe. In addition to having to use their heads to get ahead, they had the weight of the whole race sitting there. You needed two heads for that. Whitepeople believed that whatever the manners, under every dark skin was a jungle. Swift unnavigable waters, swinging screaming baboons, sleeping snakes, red gums ready for their sweet white blood. In a way, he thought, they were right. The more coloredpeople spent their strength trying to convince them how gentle they were, how clever and loving, how human, the more they used themselves up to persuade whites of something Negroes believed could not be questioned, the deeper and more tangled the jungle grew inside. But it wasn't the jungle blacks brought with them to this place from the other (livable) place. It was the jungle whitefolks planted in them. And it grew. It spread. In, through and after life, it spread, until it invaded the whites who had made it. Touched them every one. Changed and altered them. Made them bloody, silly, worse than even they wanted to be, so scared were they of the jungle they had made. The screaming baboon lived under their own white skin; the red gums were their own.

Meantime, the secret spread of this new kind of whitefolks' jungle was hidden, silent, except once in a while when you could hear its mumbling in places like 124.

Stamp Paid abandoned his efforts to see about Sethe, after the pain of knocking and not gaining entrance, and when he did, 124 was left to its own devices. When Sethe locked the door, the women inside were free at last to be what they liked, see whatever they saw and say whatever was on their minds.

Almost. Mixed in with the voices surrounding the house, recognizable but undecipherable to Stamp Paid, were the thoughts of the women of 124, unspeakable thoughts, unspoken.

BELOVED, she my daughter. She mine. See. She come back to me of her own free will and I don't have to explain a thing. I didn't have time to explain before because it had to be done quick. Quick. She had to be safe and I put her where she would be. But my love was tough and she back now. I knew she would be. Paul D ran her off so she had no choice but to come back to me in the flesh. I bet you Baby Suggs, on the other side, helped. I won't never let her go. I'll explain to her, even though I don't have to. Why I did it. How if I hadn't killed her she would have died and that is something I could not bear to happen to her. When I explain it she'll understand, because she understands everything already. I'll tend her as no mother ever tended a child, a daughter. Nobody will ever get my milk no more except my own children. I never had to give it to nobody else— and the one time I did it was took from me—they held me down and took it. Milk that belonged to my baby. Nan had to nurse whitebabies and me too because Ma'am was in the rice. The little whitebabies got it first and I got what was left. Or none. There was no nursing milk to call my own. I know what it is to be without the milk that belongs to you; to have to fight and holler for it, and to have so little left. I'll tell Beloved about that; she'll understand. She my daughter. The one I managed to have milk for and to get it to her even after they stole it; after they handled me like I was the cow, no, the goat, back behind the stable because it was too nasty to stay in with the horses. But I wasn't too nasty to cook their food or take care of Mrs. Garner. I tended her like I would have tended my own mother if she needed me. If they had let her out the rice field, because I was the one she didn't throw away. I couldn't have done more for that woman than I would my own ma'am if she was to take sick and need me and I'd have stayed with her till she got well or died. And I would have stayed after that except Nan snatched me back. Before I could check for the sign. It was her all right, but for a long time I didn't believe it. I looked everywhere for that hat. Stuttered after that. Didn't stop it till I saw Halle. Oh, but that's all over now. I'm here. I lasted. And my girl come home. Now I can look at things again because she's here to see them too. After the shed, I stopped. Now, in the morning, when I light the fire I mean to look out the window to see what the sun is doing to the day. Does it hit the pump handle first or the spigot? See if the grass is gray-green or brown or what. Now I know why Baby Suggs pondered color her last years. She never had time to see, let alone enjoy it before. Took her a long time to finish with blue, then yellow, then green. She was well into pink when she died. I don't believe she wanted to get to red and I understand why because me and Beloved outdid ourselves with it. Matter of fact, that and her pinkish headstone was the last color I recall. Now I'll be on the lookout. Think what spring will be for us! I'll plant carrots just so she can see them, and turnips. Have you ever seen one, baby? A prettier thing God never made. White and purple with a tender tail and a hard head. Feels good when you hold it in your hand and smells like the creek when it floods, bitter but happy. We'll smell them together, Beloved. Beloved. Because you mine and I have to show you these things, and teach you what a mother should. Funny how you lose sight of some things and memory others. I never will forget that whitegirl's hands. Amy. But I forget the color of all that hair on her head. Eyes must have been gray, though. Seem like I do rememory that. Mrs. Garner's was light brown—while she was well. Got dark when she took sick. A strong woman, used to be. And when she talked off her head, she'd say it. "I used to be strong as a mule, Jenny." Called me "Jenny" when she was babbling, and I can bear witness to that. Tall and strong. The two of us on a cord of wood was as good as two men. Hurt her like the devil not to be able to raise her head off the pillow. Still can't figure why she thought she needed schoolteacher, though. I wonder if she lasted, like I did.

Last time I saw her she couldn't do nothing but cry, and I couldn't do a thing for her but wipe her face when I told her what they done to me. Somebody had to know it. Hear it. Somebody. Maybe she lasted. Schoolteacher wouldn't treat her the way he treated me. First beating I took was the last. Nobody going to keep me from my children. Hadn't been for me taking care of her maybe I would have known what happened. Maybe Halle was trying to get to me. I stood by her bed waiting for her to finish with the slop jar. When I got her back in the bed she said she was cold. Hot as blazes and she wanted quilts. Said to shut the window. I told her no. She needed the cover; I needed the breeze. Long as those yellow curtains flapped, I was all right. Should have heeded her. Maybe what sounded like shots really was. Maybe I would have seen somebody or something. Maybe. Anyhow I took my babies to the corn, Halle or no. Jesus. When I heard that woman's rattle. She said, Any more? I told her I didn't know. She said, I been here all night. Can't wait. I tried to make her. She said, Can't do it. Come on. Hoo! Not a man around. Boys scared. You asleep on my back. Denver sleep in my stomach. Felt like I was split in two. I told her to take you all; I had to go back. In case. She just looked at me. Said, Woman? Bit a piece of my tongue off when they opened my back. It was hanging by a shred. I didn't mean to. Clamped down on it, it come right off. I thought, Good God, I'm going to eat myself up. They dug a hole for my stomach so as not to hurt the baby. Denver don't like for me to talk about it. She hates anything about Sweet Home except how she was born. But you was there and even if you too young to memory it, I can tell it to you. The grape arbor. You memory that? I ran so fast. Flies beat me to you. I would have known right away who you was when the sun blotted out your face the way it did when I took you to the grape arbor. I would have known at once when my water broke. The minute I saw you sitting on the stump, it broke. And when I did see your face it had more than a hint of what you would look like after all these years. I would have known who you were right away because the cup after cup of water you drank proved and connected to the fact that you dribbled clear spit on my face the day I got to 124. I would have known right off, but Paul D distracted me. Otherwise I would have seen my fingernail prints right there on your forehead for all the world to see. From when I held your head up, out in the shed. And later on, when you asked me about the earrings I used to dangle for you to play with, I would have recognized you right off, except for Paul D. Seems to me he wanted you out from the beginning, but I wouldn't let him. What you think? And look how he ran when he found out about me and you in the shed. Too rough for him to listen to. Too thick, he said. My love was too thick. What he know about it? Who in the world is he willing to die for? Would he give his privates to a stranger in return for a carving? Some other way, he said. There must have been some other way. Let schoolteacher haul us away, I guess, to measure your behind before he tore it up? I have felt what it felt like and nobody walking or stretched out is going to make you feel it too. Not you, not none of mine, and when I tell you you mine, I also mean I'm yours. I wouldn't draw breath without my children. I told Baby Suggs that and she got down on her knees to beg God's pardon for me. Still, it's so. My plan was to take us all to the other side where my own ma'am is. They stopped me from getting us there, but they didn't stop you from getting here. Ha ha. You came right on back like a good girl, like a daughter which is what I wanted to be and would have been if my ma'am had been able to get out of the rice long enough before they hanged her and let me be one. You know what? She'd had the bit so many times she smiled. When she wasn't smiling she smiled, and I never saw her own smile. I wonder what they was doing when they was caught. Running, you think? No. Not that. Because she was my ma'am and nobody's ma'am would run off and leave her daughter, would she? Would she, now? Leave her in the yard with a one-armed woman? Even if she hadn't been able to suckle the daughter for more than a week or two and had to turn her over to another woman's tit that never had enough for all. They said it was the bit that made her smile when she didn't want to. Like the Saturday girls working the slaughterhouse yard. When I came out of jail I saw them plain. They came when the shift changed on Saturday when the men got paid and worked behind the fences, back of the outhouse. Some worked standing up, leaning on the toolhouse door. They gave some of their nickels and dimes to the foreman as they left but by then their smiles was over. Some of them drank liquor to keep from feeling

BELOVED is my sister. I swallowed her blood right along with my mother's milk. The first thing I heard after not hearing anything was the sound of her crawling up the stairs. She was my secret company until Paul D came. He threw her out. Ever since I was little she was my company and she helped me wait for my daddy. Me and her waited for him. I love my mother but I know she killed one of her own daughters, and tender as she is with me, I'm scared of her because of it. She missed killing my brothers and they knew it. They told me die-witch! stories to show me the way to do it, if ever I needed to. Maybe it was getting that close to dying made them want to fight the War. That's what they told me they were going to do. I guess they rather be around killing men than killing women, and there sure is something in her that makes it all right to kill her own. All the time, I'm afraid the thing that happened that made it all right for my mother to kill my sister could happen again. I don't know what it is, I don't know who it is, but maybe there is something else terrible enough to make her do it again. I need to know what that thing might be, but I don't want to. Whatever it is, it comes from outside this house, outside the yard, and it can come right on in the yard if it wants to. So I never leave this house and I watch over the yard, so it can't happen again and my mother won't have to kill me too. Not since Miss Lady Jones' house have I left 124 by myself. Never. The only other times—two times in all—I was with my mother. Once to see Grandma Baby put down next to Beloved, she's my sister. The other time Paul D went too and when we came back I thought the house would still be empty from when he threw my sister's ghost out. But no. When I came back to 124, there she was. Beloved. Waiting for me. Tired from her long journey back. Ready to be taken care of; ready for me to protect her. This time I have to keep my mother away from her. That's hard, but I have to. It's all on me. I've seen my mother in a dark place, with scratching noises. A smell coming from her dress. I have been with her where something little watched us from the corners. And touched. Sometimes they touched. I didn't remember it for a long time until Nelson Lord made me. I asked her if it was true but couldn't hear what she said and there was no point in going back to Lady Jones if you couldn't hear what anybody said. So quiet. Made me have to read faces and learn how to figure out what people were thinking, so I didn't need to hear what they said. That's how come me and Beloved could play together. Not talking. On the porch. By the creek. In the secret house. It's all on me, now, but she can count on me. I thought she was trying to kill her that day in the Clearing. Kill her back. But then she kissed her neck and I have to warn her about that. Don't love her too much. Don't. Maybe it's still in her the thing that makes it all right to kill her children. I have to tell her. I have to protect her.

She cut my head off every night. Buglar and Howard told me she would and she did. Her pretty eyes looking at me like I was a stranger. Not mean or anything, but like I was somebody she found and felt sorry for. Like she didn't want to do it but she had to and it wasn't going to hurt. That it was just a thing grown-up people do—like pull a splinter out your hand; touch the corner of a towel in your eye if you get a cinder in it. She looks over at Buglar and Howard—see if they all right. Then she comes over to my side. I know she'll be good at it, careful. That when she cuts it off it'll be done right; it won't hurt. After she does it I lie there for a minute with just my head. Then she carries it downstairs to braid my hair. I try not to cry but it hurts so much to comb it. When she finishes the combing and starts the braiding, I get sleepy. I want to go to sleep but I know if I do I won't wake up. So I have to stay awake while she finishes my hair, then I can sleep. The scary part is waiting for her to come in and do it. Not when she does it, but when I wait for her to. Only place she can't get to me in the night is Grandma Baby's room. The room we sleep in upstairs used to be where the help slept when whitepeople lived here. They had a kitchen outside, too. But Grandma Baby turned it into a woodshed and toolroom when she moved in. And she boarded up the back door that led to it because she said she didn't want to make that journey no more. She built around it to make a storeroom, so if you want to get in 124 you have to come by her. Said she didn't care what folks said about her fixing a two-story house up like a cabin where you cook inside. She said they told her visitors with nice dresses don't want to sit in the same room with the cook stove and the peelings and the grease and the smoke. She wouldn't pay them no mind, she said. I was safe at night in there with her. All I could hear was me breathing but sometimes in the day I couldn't tell whether it was me breathing or somebody next to me. I used to watch Here Boy's stomach go in and out, in and out, to see if it matched mine, holding my breath to get off his rhythm, releasing it to get on. Just to see whose it was—that sound like when you blow soft in a bottle only regular, regular. Am I making that sound? Is Howard? Who is? That was when everybody was quiet and I couldn't hear anything they said. I didn't care either because the quiet let me dream my daddy better. I always knew he was coming. Something was holding him up. He had a problem with the horse. The river flooded; the boat sank and he had to make a new one. Sometimes it was a lynch mob or a windstorm. He was coming and it was a secret. I spent all of my outside self loving Ma'am so she wouldn't kill me, loving her even when she braided my head at night. I never let her know my daddy was coming for me. Grandma Baby thought he was coming, too. For a while she thought so, then she stopped. I never did. Even when Buglar and Howard ran away. Then Paul D came in here. I heard his voice downstairs, and Ma'am laughing, so I thought it was him, my daddy. Nobody comes to this house anymore. But when I got downstairs it was Paul D and he didn't come for me; he wanted my mother. At first. Then he wanted my sister, too, but she got him out of here and I'm so glad he's gone. Now it's just us and I can protect her till my daddy gets here to help me watch out for Ma'am and anything come in the yard.

My daddy do anything for runny fried eggs. Dip his bread in it. Grandma used to tell me his things. She said anytime she could make him a plate of soft fried eggs was Christmas, made him so happy. She said she was always a little scared of my daddy. He was too good, she said. From the beginning, she said, he was too good for the world. Scared her. She thought, He'll never make it through nothing. Whitepeople must have thought so too, because they never got split up. So she got the chance to know him, look after him, and he scared her the way he loved things. Animals and tools and crops and the alphabet. He could count on paper. The boss taught him. Offered to teach the other boys but only my daddy wanted it. She said the other boys said no. One of them with a number for a name said it would change his mind—make him forget things he shouldn't and memorize things he shouldn't and he didn't want his mind messed up. But my daddy said, If you can't count they can cheat you. If you can't read they can beat you. They thought that was funny. Grandma said she didn't know, but it was because my daddy could count on paper and figure that he bought her away from there. And she said she always wished she could read the Bible like real preachers. So it was good for me to learn how, and I did until it got quiet and all I could hear was my own breathing and one other who knocked over the milk jug while it was sitting on the table. Nobody near it. Ma'am whipped Buglar but he didn't touch it. Then it messed up all the ironed clothes and put its hands in the cake. Look like I was the only one who knew right away who it was. Just like when she came back I knew who she was too. Not right away, but soon as she spelled her name—not her given name, but the one Ma'am paid the stonecutter for—I knew. And when she wondered about Ma'am's earrings—something I didn't know about—well, that just made the cheese more binding: my sister come to help me wait for my daddy.

My daddy was an angel man. He could look at you and tell where you hurt and he could fix it too. He made a hanging thing for Grandma Baby, so she could pull herself up from the floor when she woke up in the morning, and he made a step so when she stood up she was level. Grandma said she was always afraid a whiteman would knock her down in front of her children. She behaved and did everything right in front of her children because she didn't want them to see her knocked down. She said it made children crazy to see that. At Sweet Home nobody did or said they would, so my daddy never saw it there and never went crazy and even now I bet he's trying to get here. If Paul D could do it my daddy could too. Angel man. We should all be together. Me, him and Beloved. Ma'am could stay or go off with Paul D if she wanted to. Unless Daddy wanted her himself, but I don't think he would now, since she let Paul D in her bed. Grandma Baby said people look down on her because she had eight children with different men. Coloredpeople and whitepeople both look down on her for that. Slaves not supposed to have pleasurable feelings on their own; their bodies not supposed to be like that, but they have to have as many children as they can to please whoever owned them. Still, they were not supposed to have pleasure deep down. She said for me not to listen to all that. That I should always listen to my body and love it.

The secret house. When she died I went there. Ma'am wouldn't let me go outside in the yard and eat with the others. We stayed inside. That hurt. I know Grandma Baby would have liked the party and the people who came to it, because she got low not seeing anybody or going anywhere—just grieving and thinking about colors and how she made a mistake. That what she thought about what the heart and the body could do was wrong. The whitepeople came anyway. In her yard. She had done everything right and they came in her yard anyway. And she didn't know what to think. All she had left was her heart and they busted it so even the War couldn't rouse her.

She told me all my daddy's things. How hard he worked to buy her. After the cake was ruined and the ironed clothes all messed up, and after I heard my sister crawling up the stairs to get back to her bed, she told me my things too. That I was charmed. My birth was and I got saved all the time. And that I shouldn't be afraid of the ghost. It wouldn't harm me because I tasted its blood when Ma'am nursed me. She said the ghost was after Ma'am and her too for not doing anything to stop it. But it would never hurt me. I just had to watch out for it because it was a greedy ghost and needed a lot of love, which was only natural, considering. And I do. Love her. I do. She played with me and always came to be with me whenever I needed her. She's mine, Beloved. She's mine.

I AM BELOVED and she is mine. I see her take flowers away from leaves    she puts them in a round basket    the leaves are not for her    she fills the basket    she opens the grass    I would help her but the clouds are in the way    how can I say things that are pictures    I am not separate from her    there is no place where I stop    her face is my own and I want to be there in the place where her face is and to be looking at it too    a hot thing

All of it is now    it is always now    there will never be a time when I am not crouching and watching others who are crouching too    I am always crouching    the man on my face is dead    his face is not mine    his mouth smells sweet but his eyes are locked    some who eat nasty themselves    I do not eat    the men without skin bring us their morning water to drink    we have none    at night I cannot see the dead man on my face    daylight comes through the cracks and I can see his locked eyes    I am not big    small rats do not wait for us to sleep    someone is thrashing but there is no room to do it in    if we had more to drink we could make tears    we cannot make sweat or morning water so the men without skin bring us theirs    one time they bring us sweet rocks to suck    we are all trying to leave our bodies behind    the man on my face has done it    it is hard to make yourself die forever    you sleep short and then return    in the beginning we could vomit    now we do not    now we cannot    his teeth are pretty white points    someone is trembling    I can feel it over here    he is fighting hard to leave his body which is a small bird trembling    there is no room to tremble so he is not able to die    my own dead man is pulled away from my face    I miss his pretty white points

   We are not crouching now    we are standing but my legs are like my dead man's eyes    I cannot fall because there is no room to    the men without skin are making loud noises    I am not dead    the bread is sea-colored    I am too hungry to eat it    the sun closes my eyes    those able to die are in a pile    I cannot find my man    the one whose teeth I have loved    a hot thing    the little hill of dead people    a hot thing    the men without skin push them through with poles    the woman is there with the face I want    the face that is mine    they fall into the sea which is the color of the bread    she has nothing in her ears    if I had the teeth of the man who died on my face I would bite the circle around her neck    bite it away    I know she does not like it    now there is room to crouch and to watch the crouching others    it is the crouch-ing that is now always now    inside    the woman with my face is in the sea    a hot thing

   In the beginning I could see her    I could not help her because the clouds were in the way    in the beginning I could see her    the shining in her ears    she does not like the circle around her neck    I know this    I look hard at her so she will know that the clouds are in the way    I am sure she saw me    I am looking at her see me    she empties out her eyes    I am there in the place where her face is and telling her the noisy clouds were in my way    she wants her ear-rings    she wants her round basket    I want her face    a hot thing
   in the beginning the women are away from the men and the men are away from the women    storms rock us and mix the men into the women and the women into the men    that is when I begin to be on the back of the man    for a long time I see only his neck and his wide shoulders above me    I am small    I love him because he has a song    when he turned around to die I see the teeth he sang through    his singing was soft    his singing is of the place where a woman takes flowers away from their leaves and puts them in a round basket    before the clouds    she is crouching near us    but

I do not see her until he locks his eyes and dies on my face     we are that way     there is no breath coming from his mouth and the place where breath should be is sweet-smelling     the others do not know he is dead     I know     his song is gone     now I love his pretty little teeth instead

I cannot lose her again     my dead man was in the way like the noisy clouds     when he dies on my face I can see hers     she is going to smile at me     she is going to     her sharp earrings are gone     the men without skin are making loud noises     they push my own man through     they do not push the woman with my face through     she goes in     they do not push her     she goes in     the little hill is gone     she was going to smile at me     she was going to     a hot thing

They are not crouching now     we are     they are floating on the water     they break up the little hill and push it through     I cannot find my pretty teeth     I see the dark face that is going to smile at me     it is my dark face that is going to smile at me     the iron circle is around our neck     she does not have sharp earrings in her ears or a round basket     she goes in the water     with my face

I am standing in the rain falling     the others are taken     I am not taken     I am falling like the rain is     I watch him eat     inside I am crouching to keep from falling with the rain     I am going to be in pieces     he hurts where I sleep     he puts his finger there     I drop the food and break into pieces     she took my face away     there is no one to want me     to say me my name     I wait on the bridge because she is under it     there is night and there is day     again     again     night day     night day     I am waiting     no iron circle is around my neck     no boats go on this water     no men without skin     my dead man is not floating here     his teeth are down there where the blue is and the grass     so is the face I want     the face that is going to smile at me     it is going to     in the day diamonds are in the water where she is and turtles     in the night I hear chewing and swallowing and laughter     it belongs to me     she is the laugh     I am the laugher     I see her face which is mine     it is

the face that was going to smile at me in the place where we crouched    now she is going to    her face comes through the water    a hot thing    her face is mine    she is not smiling    she is chewing and swallowing    I have to have my face    I go in    the grass opens    she opens it    I am in the water and she is com-ing    there is no round basket    no iron circle around her neck    she goes up where the diamonds are    I follow her    we are in the diamonds which are her earrings now    my face is coming    I have to have it    I am looking for the join    I am loving my face so much    my dark face is close to me    I want to join    she whispers to me    she whispers    I reach for her    chewing and swallowing she touches me    she knows I want to join    she chews and swal-lows me    I am gone    now I am her face    my own face has left me    I see me swim away    a hot thing    I see the bottoms of my feet    I am alone    I want to be the two of us    I want the join
    I come out of blue water    after the bottoms of my feet swim away from me I come up    I need to find a place to be    the air is heavy    I am not dead    I am not    there is a house    there is what she whispered to me    I am where she told me    I am not dead    I sit    the sun closes my eyes    when I open them I see the face I lost    Sethe's is the face that left me    Sethe sees me see her and I see the smile    her smiling face is the place for me    it is the face I lost    she is my face smiling at me    doing it at last    a hot thing    now we can join    a hot thing

I AM BELOVED and she is mine. Sethe is the one that picked flowers, yellow flowers in the place before the crouching. Took them away from their green leaves. They are on the quilt now where we sleep. She was about to smile at me when the men without skin came and took us up into the sunlight with the dead and shoved them into the sea. Sethe went into the sea. She went there. They did not push her. She went there. She was getting ready to smile at me and when she saw the dead people pushed into the sea she went also and left me there with no face or hers. Sethe is the face I found and lost in the water under the bridge. When I went in, I saw her face coming to me and it was my face too. I wanted to join. I tried to join, but she went up into the pieces of light at the top of the water. I lost her again, but I found the house she whispered to me and there she was, smiling at last. It's good, but I cannot lose her again. All I want to know is why did she go in the water in the place where we crouched? Why did she do that when she was just about to smile at me? I wanted to join her in the sea but I could not move; I wanted to help her when she was picking the flowers, but the clouds of gunsmoke blinded me and I lost her. Three times I lost her: once with the flowers because of the noisy clouds of smoke; once when she went into the sea instead of smiling at me; once under the bridge when I went in to join her and she came toward me but did not smile. She whispered to me, chewed me, and swam away. Now I have found her in this house. She smiles at me and it is my own face smiling. I will not lose her again. She is mine.

·  ·  ·

Tell me the truth. Didn't you come from the other side?
Yes. I was on the other side.
You came back because of me?
Yes.
You rememory me?
Yes. I remember you.
You never forgot me?
Your face is mine.
Do you forgive me? Will you stay? You safe here now.
Where are the men without skin?
Out there. Way off.
Can they get in here?
No. They tried that once, but I stopped them. They won't ever
   come back.
One of them was in the house I was in. He hurt me.
They can't hurt us no more.
Where are your earrings?
They took them from me.
The men without skin took them?
Yes.
I was going to help you but the clouds got in the way.
There're no clouds here.
If they put an iron circle around your neck I will bite it away.
Beloved.
I will make you a round basket.
You're back. You're back.
Will we smile at me?
Can't you see I'm smiling?
I love your face.

We played by the creek.
I was there in the water.
In the quiet time, we played.
The clouds were noisy and in the way.
When I needed you, you came to be with me.
I needed her face to smile.
I could only hear breathing.

The breathing is gone; only the teeth are left.
She said you wouldn't hurt me.
She hurt me.
I will protect you.
I want her face.
Don't love her too much.
I am loving her too much.
Watch out for her; she can give you dreams.
She chews and swallows.
Don't fall asleep when she braids your hair.
She is the laugh; I am the laughter.
I watch the house; I watch the yard.
She left me.
Daddy is coming for us.
A hot thing.

Beloved
You are my sister
You are my daughter
You are my face; you are me
I have found you again; you have come back to me
You are my Beloved
You are mine
You are mine
You are mine

I have your milk
I have your smile
I will take care of you

You are my face; I am you. Why did you leave me who am you?
I will never leave you again
Don't ever leave me again
You will never leave me again
You went in the water
I drank your blood
I brought your milk

You forgot to smile
I loved you
You hurt me
You came back to me
You left me

I waited for you
You are mine
You are mine
You are mine

IT WAS a tiny church no bigger than a rich man's parlor. The pews had no backs, and since the congregation was also the choir, it didn't need a stall. Certain members had been assigned the construction of a platform to raise the preacher a few inches above his congregation, but it was a less than urgent task, since the major elevation, a white oak cross, had already taken place. Before it was the Church of the Holy Redeemer, it was a dry-goods shop that had no use for side windows, just front ones for display. These were papered over while members considered whether to paint or curtain them—how to have privacy without losing the little light that might want to shine on them. In the summer the doors were left open for ventilation. In winter an iron stove in the aisle did what it could. At the front of the church was a sturdy porch where customers used to sit, and children laughed at the boy who got his head stuck between the railings. On a sunny and windless day in January it was actually warmer out there than inside, if the iron stove was cold. The damp cellar was fairly warm, but there was no light lighting the pallet or the washbasin or the nail from which a man's clothes could be hung. And a oil lamp in a cellar was sad, so Paul D sat on the porch steps and got additional warmth from a bottle of liquor jammed in his coat pocket. Warmth and red eyes. He held his wrist between his knees, not to keep his hands still but because he had nothing else to hold on to. His tobacco tin, blown open, spilled contents that floated freely and made him their play and prey.

He couldn't figure out why it took so long. He may as well have jumped in the fire with Sixo and they both could have had a good laugh. Surrender was bound to come anyway, why not meet it with a laugh, shouting Seven-O! Why not? Why the delay? He had already seen his brother wave goodbye from the back of a dray, fried chicken in his pocket, tears in his eyes. Mother. Father. Didn't remember the one. Never saw the other. He was the youngest of three half-brothers (same mother—different fathers) sold to Garner and kept there, forbidden to leave the farm, for twenty years. Once, in Maryland, he met four families of slaves who had all been together for a hundred years: great-grands, grands, mothers, fathers, aunts, uncles, cousins, children. Half white, part white, all black, mixed with Indian. He watched them with awe and envy, and each time he discovered large families of black people he made them identify over and over who each was, what relation, who, in fact, belonged to who.

"That there's my auntie. This here's her boy. Yonder is my pap's cousin. My ma'am was married twice—this my half-sister and these her two children. Now, my wife . . ."

Nothing like that had ever been his and growing up at Sweet Home he didn't miss it. He had his brothers, two friends, Baby Suggs in the kitchen, a boss who showed them how to shoot and listened to what they had to say. A mistress who made their soap and never raised her voice. For twenty years they had all lived in that cradle, until Baby left, Sethe came, and Halle took her. He made a family with her, and Sixo was hell-bent to make one with the Thirty-Mile Woman. When Paul D waved goodbye to his oldest brother, the boss was dead, the mistress nervous and the cradle already split. Sixo said the doctor made Mrs. Garner sick. Said he was giving her to drink what stallions got when they broke a leg and no gunpowder could be spared, and had it not been for schoolteacher's new rules, he would have told her so. They laughed at him. Sixo had a knowing tale about everything. Including Mr. Garner's stroke, which he said was a shot in his ear put there by a jealous neighbor.

"Where's the blood?" they asked him.

There was no blood. Mr. Garner came home bent over his mare's neck, sweating and blue-white. Not a drop of blood. Sixo grunted, the only one of them not sorry to see him go. Later, however, he was mighty sorry; they all were.

"Why she call on him?" Paul D asked. "Why she need the school-teacher?"

"She need somebody can figure," said Halle.

"You can do figures."

"Not like that."

"No, man," said Sixo. "She need another white on the place."

"What for?"

"What you think? What you think?"

Well, that's the way it was. Nobody counted on Garner dying. Nobody thought he could. How 'bout that? Everything rested on Garner being alive. Without his life each of theirs fell to pieces. Now ain't that slavery or what is it? At the peak of his strength, taller than tall men, and stronger than most, they clipped him, Paul D. First his shotgun, then his thoughts, for schoolteacher didn't take advice from Negroes. The information they offered he called backtalk and developed a variety of corrections (which he recorded in his notebook) to reeducate them. He complained they ate too much, rested too much, talked too much, which was certainly true compared to him, because schoolteacher ate little, spoke less and rested not at all. Once he saw them playing—a pitching game—and his look of deeply felt hurt was enough to make Paul D blink. He was as hard on his pupils as he was on them—except for the corrections.

For years Paul D believed schoolteacher broke into children what Garner had raised into men. And it was that that made them run off. Now, plagued by the contents of his tobacco tin, he wondered how much difference there really was between before schoolteacher and after. Garner called and announced them men—but only on Sweet Home, and by his leave. Was he naming what he saw or creating what he did not? That was the wonder of Sixo, and even Halle; it was always clear to Paul D that those two were men whether Garner said so or not. It troubled him that, concerning his own manhood, he could not satisfy himself on that point. Oh, he did manly things, but was that Garner's gift or his own will? What would he have been anyway—before Sweet Home—without Garner? In Sixo's country, or his mother's? Or, God help him, on the boat? Did a whiteman saying it make it so? Suppose Garner woke up one morning and changed his mind? Took the word away. Would they have run then? And if he didn't, would the Pauls have stayed there all their lives? Why did the brothers need the one whole night to decide? To discuss whether they would join Sixo and Halle. Because they had been isolated in a wonderful lie, dismissing Halle's and Baby Suggs' life before Sweet Home as bad luck. Ignorant of or amused by Sixo's dark stories. Protected and convinced they were special. Never suspecting the problem of Alfred, Georgia; being so in love with the look of the world, putting up with anything and everything, just to stay alive in a place where a moon he had no right to was nevertheless there. Loving small and in secret. His little love was a tree, of course, but not like Brother—old, wide and beckoning.

In Alfred, Georgia, there was an aspen too young to call sapling. Just a shoot no taller than his waist. The kind of thing a man would cut to whip his horse. Song-murder and the aspen. He stayed alive to sing songs that murdered life, and watched an aspen that confirmed it, and never for a minute did he believe he could escape. Until it rained. Afterward, after the Cherokee pointed and sent him running toward blossoms, he wanted simply to move, go, pick up one day and be somewhere else the next. Resigned to life without aunts, cousins, children. Even a woman, until Sethe.

And then she moved him. Just when doubt, regret and every single unasked question was packed away, long after he believed he had willed himself into being, at the very time and place he wanted to take root—she moved him. From room to room. Like a rag doll.

Sitting on the porch of a dry-goods church, a little bit drunk and nothing much to do, he could have these thoughts. Slow, what-if thoughts that cut deep but struck nothing solid a man could hold on to. So he held his wrists. Passing by that woman's life, getting in it and letting it get in him had set him up for this fall. Wanting to live out his life with a whole woman was new, and losing the feeling of it made him want to cry and think deep thoughts that struck nothing solid. When he was drifting, thinking only about the next meal and night's sleep, when everything was packed tight in his chest, he had no sense of failure, of things not working out. Anything that worked at all worked out. Now he wondered what-all went wrong, and starting with the Plan, everything had. It was a good plan, too. Worked out in detail with every possibility of error eliminated.

Sixo, hitching up the horses, is speaking English again and tells Halle what his Thirty-Mile Woman told him. That seven Negroes on her place were joining two others going North. That the two others had done it before and knew the way. That one of the two, a woman, would wait for them in the corn when it was high—one night and half of the next day she would wait, and if they came she would take them to the caravan, where the others would be hidden. That she would rattle, and that would be the sign. Sixo was going, his woman was going, and Halle was taking his whole family. The two Pauls say they need time to think about it. Time to wonder where they will end up; how they will live. What work; who will take them in; should they try to get to Paul F, whose owner, they remember, lived in something called the "trace"? It takes them one evening's conversation to decide.

Now all they have to do is wait through the spring, till the corn is as high as it ever got and the moon as fat.

And plan. Is it better to leave in the dark to get a better start, or go at daybreak to be able to see the way better? Sixo spits at the suggestion. Night gives them more time and the protection of color. He does not ask them if they are afraid. He manages some dry runs to the corn at night, burying blankets and two knives near the creek. Will Sethe be able to swim the creek? they ask him. It will be dry, he says, when the corn is tall. There is no food to put by, but Sethe says she will get a jug of cane syrup or molasses, and some bread when it is near the time to go. She only wants to be sure the blankets are where they should be, for they will need them to tie her baby on her back and to cover them during the journey. There are no clothes other than what they wear. And of course no shoes. The knives will help them eat, but they bury rope and a pot as well. A good plan.

They watch and memorize the comings and goings of school-teacher and his pupils: what is wanted when and where; how long it takes. Mrs. Garner, restless at night, is sunk in sleep all morning. Some days the pupils and their teacher do lessons until breakfast. One day a week they skip breakfast completely and travel ten miles to church, expecting a large dinner upon their return. Schoolteacher writes in his notebook after supper; the pupils clean, mend or sharpen tools. Sethe's work is the most uncertain because she is on call for

Mrs. Garner anytime, including nighttime when the pain or the weakness or the downright loneliness is too much for her. So: Sixo and the Pauls will go after supper and wait in the creek for the Thirty-Mile Woman. Halle will bring Sethe and the three children before dawn—before the sun, before the chickens and the milking cow need attention, so by the time smoke should be coming from the cooking stove, they will be in or near the creek with the others. That way, if Mrs. Garner needs Sethe in the night and calls her, Sethe will be there to answer. They only have to wait through the spring.

But. Sethe was pregnant in the spring and by August is so heavy with child she may not be able to keep up with the men, who can carry the children but not her.

But. Neighbors discouraged by Garner when he was alive now feel free to visit Sweet Home and might appear in the right place at the wrong time.

But. Sethe's children cannot play in the kitchen anymore, so she is dashing back and forth between house and quarters—fidgety and frustrated trying to watch over them. They are too young for men's work and the baby girl is nine months old. Without Mrs. Garner's help her work increases as do schoolteacher's demands.

But. After the conversation about the shoat, Sixo is tied up with the stock at night, and locks are put on bins, pens, sheds, coops, the tackroom and the barn door. There is no place to dart into or congregate. Sixo keeps a nail in his mouth now, to help him undo the rope when he has to.

But. Halle is told to work his extra on Sweet Home and has no call to be anywhere other than where schoolteacher tells him. Only Sixo, who has been stealing away to see his woman, and Halle, who has been hired away for years, know what lies outside Sweet Home and how to get there.

It is a good plan. It can be done right under the watchful pupils and their teacher.

But. They had to alter it—just a little. First they change the leaving. They memorize the directions Halle gives them. Sixo, needing time to untie himself, break open the door and not disturb the horses, will leave later, joining them at the creek with the Thirty-Mile Woman. All four will go straight to the corn. Halle, who also needs more time now, because of Sethe, decides to bring her and the children at night; not wait till first light. They will go straight to the corn and not assemble at the creek. The corn stretches to their shoulders—it will never be higher. The moon is swelling. They can hardly harvest, or chop, or clear, or pick, or haul for listening for a rattle that is not bird or snake. Then one midmorning, they hear it. Or Halle does and begins to sing it to the others: "Hush, hush. Somebody's calling my name. Hush, hush. Somebody's calling my name. O my Lord, O my Lord, what shall I do?"

On his dinner break he leaves the field. He has to. He has to tell Sethe that he has heard the sign. For two successive nights she has been with Mrs. Garner and he can't chance it that she will not know that this night she cannot be. The Pauls see him go. From underneath Brother's shade where they are chewing corn cake, they see him, swinging along. The bread tastes good. They lick sweat from their lips to give it a saltier flavor. Schoolteacher and his pupils are already at the house eating dinner. Halle swings along. He is not singing now.

Nobody knows what happened. Except for the churn, that was the last anybody ever saw of Halle. What Paul D knew was that Halle disappeared, never told Sethe anything, and was next seen squatting in butter. Maybe when he got to the gate and asked to see Sethe, schoolteacher heard a tint of anxiety in his voice—the tint that would make him pick up his ever-ready shotgun. Maybe Halle made the mistake of saying "my wife" in some way that would put a light in schoolteacher's eye. Sethe says now that she heard shots, but did not look out the window of Mrs. Garner's bedroom. But Halle was not killed or wounded that day because Paul D saw him later, after she had run off with no one's help; after Sixo laughed and his brother disappeared. Saw him greased and flat-eyed as a fish. Maybe schoolteacher shot after him, shot at his feet, to remind him of the trespass. Maybe Halle got in the barn, hid there and got locked in with the rest of schoolteacher's stock. Maybe anything. He disappeared and everybody was on his own.

Paul A goes back to moving timber after dinner. They are to meet at quarters for supper. He never shows up. Paul D leaves for the creek on time, believing, hoping, Paul A has gone on ahead; certain schoolteacher has learned something. Paul D gets to the creek and it is as dry as Sixo promised. He waits there with the Thirty-Mile Woman for Sixo and Paul A. Only Sixo shows up, his wrists bleeding, his tongue licking his lips like a flame.

"You see Paul A?"

"No."

"Halle?"

"No."

"No sign of them?"

"No sign. Nobody in quarters but the children."

"Sethe?"

"Her children sleep. She must be there still."

"I can't leave without Paul A."

"I can't help you."

"Should I go back and look for them?"

"I can't help you."

"What you think?"

"I think they go straight to the corn."

Sixo turns, then, to the woman and they clutch each other and whisper. She is lit now with some glowing, some shining that comes from inside her. Before when she knelt on creek pebbles with Paul D, she was nothing, a shape in the dark breathing lightly.

Sixo is about to crawl out to look for the knives he buried. He hears something. He hears nothing. Forget the knives. Now. The three of them climb up the bank and schoolteacher, his pupils and four other whitemen move toward them. With lamps. Sixo pushes the Thirty-Mile Woman and she runs further on in the creekbed. Paul D and Sixo run the other way toward the woods. Both are surrounded and tied.

The air gets sweet then. Perfumed by the things honeybees love. Tied like a mule, Paul D feels how dewy and inviting the grass is. He is thinking about that and where Paul A might be when Sixo turns and grabs the mouth of the nearest pointing rifle. He begins to sing. Two others shove Paul D and tie him to a tree. Schoolteacher is saying, "Alive. Alive. I want him alive." Sixo swings and cracks the ribs of one, but with bound hands cannot get the weapon in position to use it in any other way. All the whitemen have to do is wait. For his song, perhaps, to end? Five guns are trained on him while they listen. Paul D cannot see them when they step away from lamplight. Finally one of them hits Sixo in the head with his rifle, and when he comes to, a hickory fire is in front of him and he is tied at the waist to a tree. Schoolteacher has changed his mind: "This one will never be suitable." The song must have convinced him.

The fire keeps failing and the whitemen are put out with themselves at not being prepared for this emergency. They came to capture, not kill. What they can manage is only enough for cooking hominy. Dry faggots are scarce and the grass is slick with dew.

By the light of the hominy fire Sixo straightens. He is through with his song. He laughs. A rippling sound like Sethe's sons make when they tumble in hay or splash in rainwater. His feet are cooking; the cloth of his trousers smokes. He laughs. Something is funny. Paul D guesses what it is when Sixo interrupts his laughter to call out, "Seven-O! Seven-O!"

Smoky, stubborn fire. They shoot him to shut him up. Have to.

Shackled, walking through the perfumed things honeybees love, Paul D hears the men talking and for the first time learns his worth. He has always known, or believed he did, his value—as a hand, a laborer who could make profit on a farm—but now he discovers his worth, which is to say he learns his price. The dollar value of his weight, his strength, his heart, his brain, his penis, and his future.

As soon as the whitemen get to where they have tied their horses and mount them, they are calmer, talking among themselves about the difficulty they face. The problems. Voices remind schoolteacher about the spoiling these particular slaves have had at Garner's hands. There's laws against what he done: letting niggers hire out their own time to buy themselves. He even let em have guns! And you think he mated them niggers to get him some more? Hell no! He planned for them to marry! if that don't beat all! Schoolteacher sighs, and says doesn't he know it? He had come to put the place aright. Now it faced greater ruin than what Garner left for it, because of the loss of two niggers, at the least, and maybe three because he is not sure they will find the one called Halle. The sister-in-law is too weak to help out and doggone if now there ain't a full-scale stampede on his hands. He would have to trade this here one for $900 if he could get it, and set out to secure the breeding one, her foal and the other one, if he found him. With the money from "this here one" he could get two young ones, twelve or fifteen years old. And maybe with the breeding one, her three pickaninnies and whatever the foal might be, he and his nephews would have seven niggers and Sweet Home would be worth the trouble it was causing him.

"Look to you like Lillian gonna make it?"

"Touch and go. Touch and go."

"You was married to her sister-in-law, wasn't you?"

"I was."

"She frail too?"

"A bit. Fever took her."

"Well, you don't need to stay no widower in these parts."

"My cogitation right now is Sweet Home."

"Can't say as I blame you. That's some spread."

They put a three-spoke collar on him so he can't lie down and they chain his ankles together. The number he heard with his ear is now in his head. Two. Two? Two niggers lost? Paul D thinks his heart is jumping. They are going to look for Halle, not Paul A. They must have found Paul A and if a whiteman finds you it means you are surely lost.

Schoolteacher looks at him for a long time before he closes the door of the cabin. Carefully, he looks. Paul D does not look back. It is sprinkling now. A teasing August rain that raises expectations it cannot fill. He thinks he should have sung along. Loud, something loud and rolling to go with Sixo's tune, but the words put him off— he didn't understand the words. Although it shouldn't have mattered because he understood the sound: hatred so loose it was juba.

The warm sprinkle comes and goes, comes and goes. He thinks he hears sobbing that seems to come from Mrs. Garner's window, but it could be anything, anyone, even a she-cat making her yearning known. Tired of holding his head up, he lets his chin rest on the collar and speculates on how he can hobble over to the grate, boil a little water and throw in a handful of meal. That's what he is doing when Sethe comes in, rain-wet and big-bellied, saying she is going to cut. She has just come back from taking her children to the corn. The whites were not around. She couldn't find Halle. Who was caught? Did Sixo get away? Paul A?

He tells her what he knows: Sixo is dead; the Thirty-Mile Woman ran, and he doesn't know what happened to Paul A or Halle. "Where could he be?" she asks.

Paul D shrugs because he can't shake his head.

"You saw Sixo die? You sure?"

"I'm sure."

"Was he woke when it happened? Did he see it coming?"

"He was woke. Woke and laughing."

"Sixo laughed?"

"You should have heard him, Sethe."

Sethe's dress steams before the little fire over which he is boiling water. It is hard to move about with shackled ankles and the neck jewelry embarrasses him. In his shame he avoids her eyes, but when he doesn't he sees only black in them—no whites. She says she is going, and he thinks she will never make it to the gate, but he doesn't dissuade her. He knows he will never see her again, and right then and there his heart stopped.

The pupils must have taken her to the barn for sport right afterward, and when she told Mrs. Garner, they took down the cowhide. Who in hell or on this earth would have thought that she would cut anyway? They must have believed, what with her belly and her back, that she wasn't going anywhere. He wasn't surprised to learn that they had tracked her down in Cincinnati, because, when he thought about it now, her price was greater than his; property that reproduced itself without cost.

Remembering his own price, down to the cent, that schoolteacher was able to get for him, he wondered what Sethe's would have been. What had Baby Suggs' been? How much did Halle owe, still, besides his labor? What did Mrs. Garner get for Paul F? More than nine hundred dollars? How much more? Ten dollars? Twenty? Schoolteacher would know. He knew the worth of everything. It accounted for the real sorrow in his voice when he pronounced Sixo unsuitable. Who could be fooled into buying a singing nigger with a gun? Shouting Seven-O! Seven-O! because his Thirty-Mile Woman got away with his blossoming seed. What a laugh. So rippling and full of glee it put out the fire. And it was Sixo's laughter that was on his mind, not the bit in his mouth, when they hitched him to the buckboard. Then he saw Halle, then the rooster, smiling as if to say, You ain't seen nothing yet. How could a rooster know about Alfred, Georgia?

"HOWDY."

Stamp Paid was still fingering the ribbon and it made a little motion in his pants pocket.

Paul D looked up, noticed the side pocket agitation and snorted. "I can't read. You got any more newspaper for me, just a waste of time."

Stamp withdrew the ribbon and sat down on the steps.

"No. This here's something else." He stroked the red cloth between forefinger and thumb. "Something else."

Paul D didn't say anything so the two men sat in silence for a few moments.

"This is hard for me," said Stamp. "But I got to do it. Two things I got to say to you. I'm a take the easy one first."

Paul D chuckled. "If it's hard for you, might kill me dead."

"No, no. Nothing like that. I come looking for you to ask your pardon. Apologize."

"For what?" Paul D reached in his coat pocket for his bottle.

"You pick any house, any house where colored live. In all of Cincinnati. Pick any one and you welcome to stay there. I'm apologizing because they didn't offer or tell you. But you welcome anywhere you want to be. My house is your house too. John and Ella, Miss Lady, Able Woodruff, Willie Pike—anybody. You choose. You ain't got to sleep in no cellar, and I apologize for each and every night you did. I don't know how that preacher let you do it. I knowed him since he was a boy."

"Whoa, Stamp. He offered."

"Did? Well?"

"Well. I wanted, I didn't want to, I just wanted to be off by myself a spell. He offered. Every time I see him he offers again."

"That's a load off. I thought everybody gone crazy."

Paul D shook his head. "Just me."

"You planning to do anything about it?"

"Oh, yeah. I got big plans." He swallowed twice from the bottle.

Any planning in a bottle is short, thought Stamp, but he knew from personal experience the pointlessness of telling a drinking man not to. He cleared his sinuses and began to think how to get to the second thing he had come to say. Very few people were out today. The canal was frozen so that traffic too had stopped. They heard the clop of a horse approaching. Its rider sat a high Eastern saddle but everything else about him was Ohio Valley. As he rode by he looked at them and suddenly reined his horse, and came up to the path leading to the church. He leaned forward.

"Hey," he said.

Stamp put his ribbon in his pocket. "Yes, sir?"

"I'm looking for a gal name of Judy. Works over by the slaughterhouse."

"Don't believe I know her. No, sir."

"Said she lived on Plank Road."

"Plank Road. Yes, sir. That's up a ways. Mile, maybe."

"You don't know her? Judy. Works in the slaughterhouse."

"No, sir, but I know Plank Road. 'Bout a mile up thataway."

Paul D lifted his bottle and swallowed. The rider looked at him and then back at Stamp Paid. Loosening the right rein, he turned his horse toward the road, then changed his mind and came back.

"Look here," he said to Paul D. "There's a cross up there, so I guess this here's a church or used to be. Seems to me like you ought to show it some respect, you follow me?"

"Yes, sir," said Stamp. "You right about that. That's just what I come over to talk to him about. Just that."

The rider clicked his tongue and trotted off. Stamp made small circles in the palm of his left hand with two fingers of his right. "You got to choose," he said. "Choose anyone. They let you be if you want em to. My house. Ella. Willie Pike. None of us got much, but all of us got room for one more. Pay a little something when you can, don't when you can't. Think about it. You grown. I can't make you do what you won't, but think about it."

Paul D said nothing.

"If I did you harm, I'm here to rectify it."

"No need for that. No need at all."

A woman with four children walked by on the other side of the road. She waved, smiling. "Hoo-oo. I can't stop. See you at meeting."

"I be there," Stamp returned her greeting. "There's another one," he said to Paul D. "Scripture Woodruff, Able's sister. Works at the brush and tallow factory. You'll see. Stay around here long enough, you'll see ain't a sweeter bunch of colored anywhere than what's right here. Pride, well, that bothers em a bit. They can get messy when they think somebody's too proud, but when it comes right down to it, they good people and anyone will take you in."

"What about Judy? She take me in?"

"Depends. What you got in mind?"

"You know Judy?"

"Judith. I know everybody."

"Out on Plank Road?"

"Everybody."

"Well? She take me in?"

Stamp leaned down and untied his shoe. Twelve black button-hooks, six on each side at the bottom, led to four pairs of eyes at the top. He loosened the laces all the way down, adjusted the tongue carefully and wound them back again. When he got to the eyes he rolled the lace tips with his fingers before inserting them.

"Let me tell you how I got my name." The knot was tight and so was the bow. "They called me Joshua," he said. "I renamed myself," he said, "and I'm going to tell you why I did it," and he told him about Vashti. "I never touched her all that time. Not once. Almost a year. We was planting when it started and picking when it stopped. Seemed longer. I should have killed him. She said no, but I should have. I didn't have the patience I got now, but I figured maybe somebody else didn't have much patience either—his own wife. Took it in my head to see if she was taking it any better than

I was. Vashti and me was in the fields together in the day and every now and then she be gone all night. I never touched her and damn me if I spoke three words to her a day. I took any chance I had to get near the great house to see her, the young master's wife. Nothing but a boy. Seventeen, twenty maybe. I caught sight of her finally, standing in the backyard by the fence with a glass of water. She was drinking out of it and just gazing out over the yard. I went over. Stood back a ways and took off my hat. I said, 'Scuse me, miss. Scuse me?' She turned to look. I'm smiling. 'Scuse me. You seen Vashti? My wife Vashti?' A little bitty thing, she was. Black hair. Face no bigger than my hand. She said, 'What? Vashti?' I say, 'Yes'm, Vashti. My wife. She say she owe you all some eggs. You know if she brung em? You know her if you see her. Wear a black ribbon on her neck.' She got rosy then and I knowed she knowed. He give Vashti that to wear. A cameo on a black ribbon. She used to put it on every time she went to him. I put my hat back on. 'You see her tell her I need her. Thank you. Thank you, ma'am.' I backed off before she could say something. I didn't dare look back till I got behind some trees. She was standing just as I left her, looking in her water glass. I thought it would give me more satisfaction than it did. I also thought she might stop it, but it went right on. Till one morning Vashti came in and sat by the window. A Sunday. We worked our own patches on Sunday. She sat by the window looking out of it. 'I'm back,' she said. 'I'm back, Josh.' I looked at the back of her neck. She had a real small neck. I decided to break it. You know, like a twig—just snap it. I been low but that was as low as I ever got."

"Did you? Snap it?"

"Uh uh. I changed my name."

"How you get out of there? How you get up here?"

"Boat. On up the Mississippi to Memphis. Walked from Memphis to Cumberland."

"Vashti too?"

"No. She died."

"Aw, man. Tie your other shoe!"

"What?"

"Tie your goddamn shoe! It's sitting right in front of you! Tie it!"

"That make you feel better?"

"No." Paul D tossed the bottle on the ground and stared at the golden chariot on its label. No horses. Just a golden coach draped in blue cloth.

"I said I had two things to say to you. I only told you one. I have to tell you the other."

"I don't want to know it. I don't want to know nothing. Just if Judy will take me in or won't she."

"I was there, Paul D."

"You was where?"

"There in the yard. When she did it."

"Judy?"

"Sethe."

"Jesus."

"It ain't what you think."

"You don't know what I think."

"She ain't crazy. She love those children. She was trying to out-hurt the hurter."

"Leave off."

"And spread it."

"Stamp, let me off. I knew her when she was a girl. She scares me and I knew her when she was a girl."

"You ain't scared of Sethe. I don't believe you."

"Sethe scares me. I scare me. And that girl in her house scares me the most."

"Who is that girl? Where she come from?"

"I don't know. Just shot up one day sitting on a stump."

"Huh. Look like you and me the only ones outside 124 lay eyes on her."

"She don't go nowhere. Where'd you see her?"

"Sleeping on the kitchen floor. I peeped in."

"First minute I saw her I didn't want to be nowhere around her. Something funny about her. Talks funny. Acts funny." Paul D dug his fingers underneath his cap and rubbed the scalp over his temple. "She reminds me of something. Something, look like, I'm supposed to remember."

"She never say where she was from? Where's her people?"

"She don't know, or says she don't. All I ever heard her say was something about stealing her clothes and living on a bridge."

"What kind of bridge?"

"Who you asking?"

"No bridges around here I don't know about. But don't nobody live on em. Under em neither. How long she been over there with Sethe?"

"Last August. Day of the carnival."

"That's a bad sign. Was she at the carnival?"

"No. When we got back, there she was—'sleep on a stump. Silk dress. Brand-new shoes. Black as oil."

"You don't say? Huh. Was a girl locked up in the house with a whiteman over by Deer Creek. Found him dead last summer and the girl gone. Maybe that's her. Folks say he had her in there since she was a pup."

"Well, now she's a bitch."

"Is she what run you off? Not what I told you 'bout Sethe?"

A shudder ran through Paul D. A bone-cold spasm that made him clutch his knees. He didn't know if it was bad whiskey, nights in the cellar, pig fever, iron bits, smiling roosters, fired feet, laughing dead men, hissing grass, rain, apple blossoms, neck jewelry, Judy in the slaughterhouse, Halle in the butter, ghost-white stairs, choke-cherry trees, cameo pins, aspens, Paul A's face, sausage or the loss of a red, red heart.

"Tell me something, Stamp." Paul D's eyes were rheumy. "Tell me this one thing. How much is a nigger supposed to take? Tell me. How much?"

"All he can," said Stamp Paid. "All he can."

"Why? Why? Why? Why? Why?"

# Three

predictable happened: Sawyer told her not to come back. And instead of looking for another job, Sethe played all the harder with Beloved, who never got enough of anything: lullabies, new stitches, the bottom of the cake bowl, the top of the milk. If the hen had only two eggs, she got both. It was as though her mother had lost her mind, like Grandma Baby calling for pink and not doing the things she used to. But different because, unlike Baby Suggs, she cut Denver out completely. Even the song that she used to sing to Denver she sang for Beloved alone: "High Johnny, wide Johnny, don't you leave my side, Johnny."

At first they played together. A whole month and Denver loved it. From the night they ice-skated under a star-loaded sky and drank sweet milk by the stove, to the string puzzles Sethe did for them in afternoon light, and shadow pictures in the gloaming. In the very teeth of winter and Sethe, her eyes fever bright, was plotting a garden of vegetables and flowers—talking, talking about what colors it would have. She played with Beloved's hair, braiding, puffing, tying, oiling it until it made Denver nervous to watch her. They changed beds and exchanged clothes. Walked arm in arm and smiled all the time. When the weather broke, they were on their knees in the backyard designing a garden in dirt too hard to chop. The thirty-eight dollars of life savings went to feed themselves with fancy food and decorate themselves with ribbon and dress goods, which Sethe cut and sewed like they were going somewhere in a hurry. Bright clothes—with blue stripes and sassy prints. She walked the four miles to John Shillito's to buy yellow ribbon, shiny buttons and bits of black lace. By the end of March the three of them looked like carnival women with nothing to do. When it became clear that they were only interested in each other, Denver began to drift from the play, but she watched it, alert for any sign that Beloved was in danger. Finally convinced there was none, and seeing her mother that happy, that smiling— how could it go wrong?—she let down her guard and it did. Her problem at first was trying to find out who was to blame. Her eye was on her mother, for a signal that the thing that was in her was out, and she would kill again. But it was Beloved who made demands. Anything she wanted she got, and when Sethe ran out of things to give her, Beloved invented desire. She wanted Sethe's company for hours to watch the layer of brown leaves waving at them from the bottom of the creek, in the same place where, as a little girl, Denver played in the silence with her. Now the players were altered. As soon as the thaw was complete Beloved gazed at her gazing face, rippling, folding, spreading, disappearing into the leaves below. She flattened herself on the ground, dirtying her bold stripes, and touched the rocking faces with her own. She filled basket after basket with the first things warmer weather let loose in the ground—dandelions, violets, forsythia—presenting them to Sethe, who arranged them, stuck them, wound them all over the house. Dressed in Sethe's dresses, she stroked her skin with the palm of her hand. She imitated Sethe, talked the way she did, laughed her laugh and used her body the same way down to the walk, the way Sethe moved her hands, sighed through her nose, held her head. Sometimes coming upon them making men and women cookies or tacking scraps of cloth on Baby Suggs' old quilt, it was difficult for Denver to tell who was who.

Then the mood changed and the arguments began. Slowly at first. A complaint from Beloved, an apology from Sethe. A reduction of pleasure at some special effort the older woman made. Wasn't it too cold to stay outside? Beloved gave a look that said, So what? Was it past bedtime, the light no good for sewing? Beloved didn't move; said, "Do it," and Sethe complied. She took the best of everything—first. The best chair, the biggest piece, the prettiest plate, the brightest ribbon for her hair, and the more she took, the more Sethe began to talk, explain, describe how much she had suffered, been through, for her children, waving away flies in grape arbors, crawling on her knees to a lean-to. None of which made the impression it was supposed to. Beloved accused her of leaving her behind. Of not being nice to her, not smiling at her. She said they were the same, had the same face, how could she have left her? And Sethe cried, saying she never did, or meant to—that she had to get them out, away, that she had the milk all the time and had the money too for the stone but not enough. That her plan was always that they would all be together on the other side, forever. Beloved wasn't interested. She said when she cried there was no one. That dead men lay on top of her. That she had nothing to eat. Ghosts without skin stuck their fingers in her and said beloved in the dark and bitch in the light. Sethe pleaded for forgiveness, counting, listing again and again her reasons: that Beloved was more important, meant more to her than her own life. That she would trade places any day. Give up her life, every minute and hour of it, to take back just one of Beloved's tears. Did she know it hurt her when mosquitoes bit her baby? That to leave her on the ground to run into the big house drove her crazy? That before leaving Sweet Home Beloved slept every night on her chest or curled on her back? Beloved denied it. Sethe never came to her, never said a word to her, never smiled and worst of all never waved goodbye or even looked her way before running away from her.

When once or twice Sethe tried to assert herself—be the unquestioned mother whose word was law and who knew what was best— Beloved slammed things, wiped the table clean of plates, threw salt on the floor, broke a windowpane.

She was not like them. She was wild game, and nobody said, Get on out of here, girl, and come back when you get some sense. Nobody said, You raise your hand to me and I will knock you into the middle of next week. Ax the trunk, the limb will die. Honor thy mother and father that thy days may be long upon the land which the Lord thy God giveth thee. I will wrap you round that doorknob, don't nobody work for you and God don't love ugly ways.

No, no. They mended the plates, swept the salt, and little by little it dawned on Denver that if Sethe didn't wake up one morning and pick up a knife, Beloved might. Frightened as she was by the thing in Sethe that could come out, it shamed her to see her mother serving a girl not much older than herself. When she saw her carrying out Beloved's night bucket, Denver raced to relieve her of it. But the pain was unbearable when they ran low on food, and Denver watched her mother go without—pick-eating around the edges of the table and stove: the hominy that stuck on the bottom; the crusts and rinds and peelings of things. Once she saw her run her longest finger deep in an empty jam jar before rinsing and putting it away.

They grew tired, and even Beloved, who was getting bigger, seemed nevertheless as exhausted as they were. In any case she substituted a snarl or a tooth-suck for waving a poker around and 124 was quiet. Listless and sleepy with hunger Denver saw the flesh between her mother's forefinger and thumb fade. Saw Sethe's eyes bright but dead, alert but vacant, paying attention to everything about Beloved—her lineless palms, her forehead, the smile under her jaw, crooked and much too long—everything except her basket-fat stomach. She also saw the sleeves of her own carnival shirtwaist cover her fingers; hems that once showed her ankles now swept the floor. She saw themselves beribboned, decked-out, limp and starving but locked in a love that wore everybody out. Then Sethe spit up something she had not eaten and it rocked Denver like gunshot. The job she started out with, protecting Beloved from Sethe, changed to protecting her mother from Beloved. Now it was obvious that her mother could die and leave them both and what would Beloved do then? Whatever was happening, it only worked with three—not two—and since neither Beloved nor Sethe seemed to care what the next day might bring (Sethe happy when Beloved was; Beloved lapping devotion like cream), Denver knew it was on her. She would have to leave the yard; step off the edge of the world, leave the two behind and go ask somebody for help.

Who would it be? Who could she stand in front of who wouldn't shame her on learning that her mother sat around like a rag doll, broke down, finally, from trying to take care of and make up for. Denver knew *about* several people, from hearing her mother and grandmother talk. But she knew, personally, only two: an old man with white hair called Stamp and Lady Jones. Well, Paul D, of course. And that boy who told her about Sethe. But they wouldn't do at all. Her heart kicked and an itchy burning in her throat made her swallow all her saliva away. She didn't even know which way to go. When Sethe used to work at the restaurant and when she still had money to shop, she turned right. Back when Denver went to Lady Jones' school, it was left.

The weather was warm; the day beautiful. It was April and everything alive was tentative. Denver wrapped her hair and her shoulders. In the brightest of the carnival dresses and wearing a stranger's shoes, she stood on the porch of 124 ready to be swallowed up in the world beyond the edge of the porch. Out there where small things scratched and sometimes touched. Where words could be spoken that would close your ears shut. Where, if you were alone, feeling could overtake you and stick to you like a shadow. Out there where there were places in which things so bad had happened that when you went near them it would happen again. Like Sweet Home where time didn't pass and where, like her mother said, the bad was waiting for her as well. How would she know these places? What was more—much more—out there were whitepeople and how could you tell about them? Sethe said the mouth and sometimes the hands. Grandma Baby said there was no defense—they could prowl at will, change from one mind to another, and even when they thought they were behaving, it was a far cry from what real humans did.

"They got me out of jail," Sethe once told Baby Suggs.

"They also put you in it," she answered.

"They drove you 'cross the river."

"On my son's back."

"They gave you this house."

"Nobody *gave* me nothing."

"I got a job from them."

"He got a cook from them, girl."

"Oh, some of them do all right by us."

"And every time it's a surprise, ain't it?"

"You didn't used to talk this way."

"Don't box with me. There's more of us they drowned than there is all of them ever lived from the start of time. Lay down your sword. This ain't a battle; it's a rout."

Remembering those conversations and her grandmother's last and final words, Denver stood on the porch in the sun and couldn't leave it. Her throat itched; her heart kicked—and then Baby Suggs laughed, clear as anything. "You mean I never told you nothing about Carolina? About your daddy? You don't remember nothing about how come I walk the way I do and about your mother's feet, not to speak of her back? I never told you all that? Is that why you can't walk down the steps? My Jesus my."

But you said there was no defense.

"There ain't."

Then what do I do?

"Know it, and go on out the yard. Go on."

.   .   .

It came back. A dozen years had passed and the way came back. Four houses on the right, sitting close together in a line like wrens. The first house had two steps and a rocking chair on the porch; the second had three steps, a broom propped on the porch beam, two broken chairs and a clump of forsythia at the side. No window at the front. A little boy sat on the ground chewing a stick. The third house had yellow shutters on its two front windows and pot after pot of green leaves with white hearts or red. Denver could hear chickens and the knock of a badly hinged gate. At the fourth house the buds of a sycamore tree had rained down on the roof and made the yard look as though grass grew there. A woman, standing at the open door, lifted her hand halfway in greeting, then froze it near her shoulder as she leaned forward to see whom she waved to. Denver lowered her head. Next was a tiny fenced plot with a cow in it. She remembered the plot but not the cow. Under her headcloth her scalp was wet with tension. Beyond her, voices, male voices, floated, coming closer with each step she took. Denver kept her eyes on the road in case they were whitemen; in case she was walking where they wanted to; in case they said something and she would have to answer them. Suppose they flung out at her, grabbed her, tied her. They were getting closer. Maybe she should cross the road—now. Was the woman who half waved at her still there in the open door? Would she come to her rescue, or, angry at Denver for not waving back, would she withhold her help? Maybe she should turn around, get closer to the waving woman's house. Before she could make up her mind, it was too late—they were right in front of her. Two men, Negro. Denver breathed. Both men touched their caps and murmured, "Morning. Morning." Denver believed her eyes spoke gratitude but she never got her mouth open in time to reply. They moved left of her and passed on.

Braced and heartened by that easy encounter, she picked up speed and began to look deliberately at the neighborhood surrounding her. She was shocked to see how small the big things were: the boulder by the edge of the road she once couldn't see over was a sitting-on rock. Paths leading to houses weren't miles long. Dogs didn't even reach her knees. Letters cut into beeches and oaks by giants were eye level now.

She would have known it anywhere. The post and scrap-lumber fence was gray now, not white, but she would have known it anywhere. The stone porch sitting in a skirt of ivy, pale yellow curtains at the windows; the laid brick path to the front door and wood planks leading around to the back, passing under the windows where she had stood on tiptoe to see above the sill. Denver was about to do it again, when she realized how silly it would be to be found once more staring into the parlor of Mrs. Lady Jones. The pleasure she felt at having found the house dissolved, suddenly, in doubt. Suppose she didn't live there anymore? Or remember her former student after all this time? What would she say? Denver shivered inside, wiped the perspiration from her forehead and knocked.

Lady Jones went to the door expecting raisins. A child, probably, from the softness of the knock, sent by its mother with the raisins she needed if her contribution to the supper was to be worth the trouble. There would be any number of plain cakes, potato pies. She had reluctantly volunteered her own special creation, but said she didn't have raisins, so raisins is what the president said would be provided—early enough so there would be no excuses. Mrs. Jones, dreading the fatigue of beating batter, had been hoping she had forgotten. Her bake oven had been cold all week—getting it to the right temperature would be awful. Since her husband died and her eyes grew dim, she had let up-to-snuff housekeeping fall away. She was of two minds about baking something for the church. On the one hand, she wanted to remind everybody of what she was able to do in the cooking line; on the other, she didn't want to have to. When she heard the tapping at the door, she sighed and went to it hoping the raisins had at least been cleaned.

She was older, of course, and dressed like a chippy, but the girl was immediately recognizable to Lady Jones. Everybody's child was in that face: the nickel-round eyes, bold yet mistrustful; the large powerful teeth between dark sculptured lips that did not cover them. Some vulnerability lay across the bridge of the nose, above the cheeks. And then the skin. Flawless, economical—just enough of it to cover the bone and not a bit more. She must be eighteen or nineteen by now, thought Lady Jones, looking at the face young enough to be twelve. Heavy eyebrows, thick baby lashes and the unmistakable love call that shimmered around children until they learned better.

"Why, Denver," she said. "Look at you."

Lady Jones had to take her by the hand and pull her in, because the smile seemed all the girl could manage. Other people said this child was simple, but Lady Jones never believed it. Having taught her, watched her eat up a page, a rule, a figure, she knew better. When suddenly she had stopped coming, Lady Jones thought it was the nickel. She approached the ignorant grandmother one day on the road, a woods preacher who mended shoes, to tell her it was all right if the money was owed. The woman said that wasn't it; the child was deaf, and deaf Lady Jones thought she still was until she offered her a seat and Denver heard that.

"It's nice of you to come see me. What brings you?"

Denver didn't answer.

"Well, nobody needs a reason to visit. Let me make us some tea."

Lady Jones was mixed. Gray eyes and yellow woolly hair, every strand of which she hated—though whether it was the color or the texture even she didn't know. She had married the blackest man she could find, had five rainbow-colored children and sent them all to Wilberforce, after teaching them all she knew right along with the others who sat in her parlor. Her light skin got her picked for a coloredgirls' normal school in Pennsylvania and she paid it back by teaching the unpicked. The children who played in dirt until they were old enough for chores, these she taught. The colored population of Cincinnati had two graveyards and six churches, but since no school or hospital was obliged to serve them, they learned and died at home. She believed in her heart that, except for her husband, the whole world (including her children) despised her and her hair. She had been listening to "all that yellow gone to waste" and "white nigger" since she was a girl in a houseful of silt-black children, so she disliked everybody a little bit because she believed they hated her hair as much as she did. With that education pat and firmly set, she dispensed with rancor, was indiscriminately polite, saving her real affection for the unpicked children of Cincinnati, one of whom sat before her in a dress so loud it embarrassed the needlepoint chair seat.

"Sugar?"

"Yes. Thank you." Denver drank it all down.

"More?"

"No, ma'am."

"Here. Go ahead."

"Yes, ma'am."

"How's your family, honey?"

Denver stopped in the middle of a swallow. There was no way to tell her how her family was, so she said what was at the top of her mind.

"I want work, Miss Lady."

"Work?"

"Yes, ma'am. Anything."

Lady Jones smiled. "What can you do?"

"I can't do anything, but I would learn it for you if you have a little extra."

"Extra?"

"Food. My ma'am, she doesn't feel good."

"Oh, baby," said Mrs. Jones. "Oh, baby."

Denver looked up at her. She did not know it then, but it was the word "baby," said softly and with such kindness, that inaugurated her life in the world as a woman. The trail she followed to get to that sweet thorny place was made up of paper scraps containing the handwritten names of others. Lady Jones gave her some rice, four eggs and some tea. Denver said she couldn't be away from home long because of her mother's condition. Could she do chores in the morning? Lady Jones told her that no one, not herself, not anyone she knew, could pay anybody anything for work they did themselves. "But if you all need to eat until your mother is well, all you have to do is say so." She mentioned her church's committee invented so nobody had to go hungry. That agitated her guest who said, "No, no," as though asking for help from strangers was worse than hunger. Lady Jones said goodbye to her and asked her to come back anytime. "Anytime at all."

Two days later Denver stood on the porch and noticed something lying on the tree stump at the edge of the yard. She went to look and found a sack of white beans. Another time a plate of cold rabbit meat. One morning a basket of eggs sat there. As she lifted it, a slip of paper fluttered down. She picked it up and looked at it. "M. Lucille Williams" was written in big crooked letters. On the back was a blob of flour-water paste. So Denver paid a second visit to the world outside the porch, although all she said when she returned the basket was "Thank you."

"Welcome," said M. Lucille Williams.

Every now and then, all through the spring, names appeared near or in gifts of food. Obviously for the return of the pan or plate or basket; but also to let the girl know, if she cared to, who the donor was, because some of the parcels were wrapped in paper, and though there was nothing to return, the name was nevertheless there. Many had X's with designs about them, and Lady Jones tried to identify the plate or pan or the covering towel. When she could only guess, Denver followed her directions and went to say thank you anyway— whether she had the right benefactor or not. When she was wrong, when the person said, "No, darling. That's not my bowl. Mine's got a blue ring on it," a small conversation took place. All of them knew her grandmother and some had even danced with her in the Clearing. Others remembered the days when 124 was a way station, the place they assembled to catch news, taste oxtail soup, leave their children, cut out a skirt. One remembered the tonic mixed there that cured a relative. One showed her the border of a pillowslip, the stamens of its pale blue flowers French-knotted in Baby Suggs' kitchen by the light of an oil lamp while arguing the Settlement Fee. They remembered the party with twelve turkeys and tubs of strawberry smash. One said she wrapped Denver when she was a single day old and cut shoes to fit her mother's blasted feet. Maybe they were sorry for her. Or for Sethe. Maybe they were sorry for the years of their own disdain. Maybe they were simply nice people who could hold meanness toward each other for just so long and when trouble rode bareback among them, quickly, easily they did what they could to trip him up. In any case, the personal pride, the arrogant claim staked out at 124 seemed to them to have run its course. They whispered, naturally, wondered, shook their heads. Some even laughed outright at Denver's clothes of a hussy, but it didn't stop them caring whether she ate and it didn't stop the pleasure they took in her soft "Thank you."

At least once a week, she visited Lady Jones, who perked up enough to do a raisin loaf especially for her, since Denver was set on sweet things. She gave her a book of Bible verse and listened while she mumbled words or fairly shouted them. By June Denver had read and memorized all fifty-two pages—one for each week of the year.

As Denver's outside life improved, her home life deteriorated. If the whitepeople of Cincinnati had allowed Negroes into their lunatic asylum they could have found candidates in 124. Strengthened by the gifts of food, the source of which neither Sethe nor Beloved questioned, the women had arrived at a doomsday truce designed by the devil. Beloved sat around, ate, went from bed to bed. Sometimes she screamed, "Rain! Rain!" and clawed her throat until rubies of blood opened there, made brighter by her midnight skin. Then Sethe shouted, "No!" and knocked over chairs to get to her and wipe the jewels away. Other times Beloved curled up on the floor, her wrists between her knees, and stayed there for hours. Or she would go to the creek, stick her feet in the water and whoosh it up her legs. Afterward she would go to Sethe, run her fingers over the woman's teeth while tears slid from her wide black eyes. Then it seemed to Denver the thing was done: Beloved bending over Sethe looked the mother, Sethe the teething child, for other than those times when Beloved needed her, Sethe confined herself to a corner chair. The bigger Beloved got, the smaller Sethe became; the brighter Beloved's eyes, the more those eyes that used never to look away became slits of sleeplessness. Sethe no longer combed her hair or splashed her face with water. She sat in the chair licking her lips like a chastised child while Beloved ate up her life, took it, swelled up with it, grew taller on it. And the older woman yielded it up without a murmur.

Denver served them both. Washing, cooking, forcing, cajoling her mother to eat a little now and then, providing sweet things for Beloved as often as she could to calm her down. It was hard to know what she would do from minute to minute. When the heat got hot, she might walk around the house naked or wrapped in a sheet, her belly protruding like a winning watermelon.

Denver thought she understood the connection between her mother and Beloved: Sethe was trying to make up for the handsaw; Beloved was making her pay for it. But there would never be an end to that, and seeing her mother diminished shamed and infuriated her. Yet she knew Sethe's greatest fear was the same one Denver had in the beginning—that Beloved might leave. That before Sethe could make her understand what it meant—what it took to drag the teeth of that saw under the little chin; to feel the baby blood pump like oil in her hands; to hold her face so her head would stay on; to squeeze her so she could absorb, still, the death spasms that shot through that adored body, plump and sweet with life—Beloved might leave. Leave before Sethe could make her realize that worse than that—far worse— was what Baby Suggs died of, what Ella knew, what Stamp saw and what made Paul D tremble. That anybody white could take your whole self for anything that came to mind. Not just work, kill, or maim you, but dirty you. Dirty you so bad you couldn't like yourself anymore. Dirty you so bad you forgot who you were and couldn't think it up. And though she and others lived through and got over it, she could never let it happen to her own. The best thing she was, was her children. Whites might dirty *her* all right, but not her best thing, her beautiful, magical best thing—the part of her that was clean. No undreamable dreams about whether the headless, feetless torso hanging in the tree with a sign on it was her husband or Paul A; whether the bubbling-hot girls in the colored-school fire set by patriots included her daughter; whether a gang of whites invaded her daughter's private parts, soiled her daughter's thighs and threw her daughter out of the wagon. *She* might have to work the slaughterhouse yard, but not her daughter.

And no one, nobody on this earth, would list her daughter's characteristics on the animal side of the paper. No. Oh no. Maybe Baby Suggs could worry about it, live with the likelihood of it; Sethe had refused—and refused still.

This and much more Denver heard her say from her corner chair, trying to persuade Beloved, the one and only person she felt she had to convince, that what she had done was right because it came from true love.

Beloved, her fat new feet propped on the seat of a chair in front of the one she sat in, her unlined hands resting on her stomach, looked at her. Uncomprehending everything except that Sethe was the woman who took her face away, leaving her crouching in a dark, dark place, forgetting to smile.

Her father's daughter after all, Denver decided to do the necessary. Decided to stop relying on kindness to leave something on the stump. She would hire herself out somewhere, and although she was afraid to leave Sethe and Beloved alone all day not knowing what calamity either one of them would create, she came to realize that her presence in that house had no influence on what either woman did. She kept them alive and they ignored her. Growled when they chose; sulked, explained, demanded, strutted, cowered, cried and provoked each other to the edge of violence, then over. She had begun to notice that even when Beloved was quiet, dreamy, minding her own business, Sethe got her going again. Whispering, muttering some justification, some bit of clarifying information to Beloved to explain what it had been like, and why, and how come. It was as though Sethe didn't really want forgiveness given; she wanted it refused. And Beloved helped her out.

Somebody had to be saved, but unless Denver got work, there would be no one to save, no one to come home to, and no Denver either. It was a new thought, having a self to look out for and preserve. And it might not have occurred to her if she hadn't met Nelson Lord leaving his grandmother's house as Denver entered it to pay a thank you for half a pie. All he did was smile and say, "Take care of yourself, Denver," but she heard it as though it were what language was made for. The last time he spoke to her his words blocked up her ears. Now they opened her mind. Weeding the garden, pulling vegetables, cooking, washing, she plotted what to do and how. The Bodwins were most likely to help since they had done it twice. Once for Baby Suggs and once for her mother. Why not the third generation as well?

She got lost so many times in the streets of Cincinnati it was noon before she arrived, though she started out at sunrise. The house sat back from the sidewalk with large windows looking out on a noisy, busy street. The Negro woman who answered the front door said, "Yes?"

"May I come in?"

"What you want?"

"I want to see Mr. and Mrs. Bodwin."

"Miss Bodwin. They brother and sister."

"Oh."

"What you want em for?"

"I'm looking for work. I was thinking they might know of some."

"You Baby Suggs' kin, ain't you?"

"Yes, ma'am."

"Come on in. You letting in flies." She led Denver toward the kitchen, saying, "First thing you have to know is what door to knock on." But Denver only half heard her because she was stepping on something soft and blue. All around her was thick, soft and blue. Glass cases crammed full of glistening things. Books on tables and shelves. Pearl-white lamps with shiny metal bottoms. And a smell like the cologne she poured in the emerald house, only better.

"Sit down," the woman said. "You know my name?"

"No, ma'am."

"Janey. Janey Wagon."

"How do you do?"

"Fairly. I heard your mother took sick, that so?"

"Yes, ma'am."

"Who's looking after her?"

"I am. But I have to find work."

Janey laughed. "You know what? I've been here since I was fourteen, and I remember like yesterday when Baby Suggs, holy, came here and sat right there where you are. Whiteman brought her. That's how she got that house you all live in. Other things, too."

"Yes, ma'am."

"What's the trouble with Sethe?" Janey leaned against an indoor sink and folded her arms.

It was a little thing to pay, but it seemed big to Denver. Nobody was going to help her unless she told it—told all of it. It was clear Janey wouldn't and wouldn't let her see the Bodwins otherwise. So Denver told this stranger what she hadn't told Lady Jones, in return for which Janey admitted the Bodwins needed help, although they didn't know it. She was alone there, and now that her employers were getting older, she couldn't take care of them like she used to.

More and more she was required to sleep the night there. Maybe she could talk them into letting Denver do the night shift, come right after supper, say, maybe get the breakfast. That way Denver could care for Sethe in the day and earn a little something at night, how's that?

Denver had explained the girl in her house who plagued her mother as a cousin come to visit, who got sick too and bothered them both. Janey seemed more interested in Sethe's condition, and from what Denver told her it seemed the woman had lost her mind. That wasn't the Sethe she remembered. This Sethe had lost her wits, finally, as Janey knew she would—trying to do it all alone with her nose in the air. Denver squirmed under the criticism of her mother, shifting in the chair and keeping her eyes on the inside sink. Janey Wagon went on about pride until she got to Baby Suggs, for whom she had nothing but sweet words. "I never went to those woodland services she had, but she was always nice to me. Always. Never be another like her."

"I miss her too," said Denver.

"Bet you do. Everybody miss her. That was a good woman."

Denver didn't say anything else and Janey looked at her face for a while. "Neither one of your brothers ever come back to see how you all was?"

"No, ma'am."

"Ever hear from them?"

"No, ma'am. Nothing."

"Guess they had a rough time in that house. Tell me, this here woman in your house. The cousin. She got any lines in her hands?"

"No," said Denver.

"Well," said Janey. "I guess there's a God after all."

The interview ended with Janey telling her to come back in a few days. She needed time to convince her employers what they needed: night help because Janey's own family needed her. "I don't want to quit these people, but they can't have all my days and nights too."

What did Denver have to do at night?

"Be here. In case."

In case what?

Janey shrugged. "In case the house burn down." She smiled then.

"Or bad weather slop the roads so bad I can't get here early enough for them. Case late guests need serving or cleaning up after. Anything. Don't ask me what whitefolks need at night."

"They used to be good whitefolks."

"Oh, yeah. They good. Can't say they ain't good. I wouldn't trade them for another pair, tell you that."

With those assurances, Denver left, but not before she had seen, sitting on a shelf by the back door, a blackboy's mouth full of money. His head was thrown back farther than a head could go, his hands were shoved in his pockets. Bulging like moons, two eyes were all the face he had above the gaping red mouth. His hair was a cluster of raised, widely spaced dots made of nail heads. And he was on his knees. His mouth, wide as a cup, held the coins needed to pay for a delivery or some other small service, but could just as well have held buttons, pins or crab-apple jelly. Painted across the pedestal he knelt on were the words "At Yo Service."

The news that Janey got hold of she spread among the other coloredwomen. Sethe's dead daughter, the one whose throat she cut, had come back to fix her. Sethe was worn down, speckled, dying, spinning, changing shapes and generally bedeviled. That this daughter beat her, tied her to the bed and pulled out all her hair. It took them days to get the story properly blown up and themselves agitated and then to calm down and assess the situation. They fell into three groups: those that believed the worst; those that believed none of it; and those, like Ella, who thought it through.

"Ella. What's all this I'm hearing about Sethe?"

"Tell me it's in there with her. That's all I know."

"The daughter? The killed one?"

"That's what they tell me."

"How they know that's her?"

"It's sitting there. Sleeps, eats and raises hell. Whipping Sethe every day."

"I'll be. A baby?"

"No. Grown. The age it would have been had it lived."

"You talking about flesh?"

"I'm talking about flesh."

"Whipping her?"

"Like she was batter."

"Guess she had it coming."

"Nobody got that coming."

"But, Ella—"

"But nothing. What's fair ain't necessarily right."

"You can't just up and kill your children."

"No, and the children can't just up and kill the mama."

It was Ella more than anyone who convinced the others that rescue was in order. She was a practical woman who believed there was a root either to chew or avoid for every ailment. Cogitation, as she called it, clouded things and prevented action. Nobody loved her and she wouldn't have liked it if they had, for she considered love a serious disability. Her puberty was spent in a house where she was shared by father and son, whom she called "the lowest yet." It was "the lowest yet" who gave her a disgust for sex and against whom she measured all atrocities. A killing, a kidnap, a rape—whatever, she listened and nodded. Nothing compared to "the lowest yet." She understood Sethe's rage in the shed twenty years ago, but not her reaction to it, which Ella thought was prideful, misdirected, and Sethe herself too complicated. When she got out of jail and made no gesture toward anybody, and lived as though she were alone, Ella junked her and wouldn't give her the time of day.

The daughter, however, appeared to have some sense after all. At least she had stepped out the door, asked for the help she needed and wanted work. When Ella heard 124 was occupied by something-or-other beating up on Sethe, it infuriated her and gave her another opportunity to measure what could very well be the devil himself against "the lowest yet." There was also something very personal in her fury. Whatever Sethe had done, Ella didn't like the idea of past errors taking possession of the present. Sethe's crime was staggering and her pride outstripped even that; but she could not countenance the possibility of sin moving on in the house, unleashed and sassy. Daily life took as much as she had. The future was sunset; the past something to leave behind. And if it didn't stay behind, well, you might have to stomp it out. Slave life; freed life—every day was a test and a trial. Nothing could be counted on in a world where even when you were a solution you were a problem. "Sufficient unto the day is the evil thereof," and nobody needed more; nobody needed a grown-up evil sitting at the table with a grudge. As long as the ghost showed out from its ghostly place—shaking stuff, crying, smashing and such—Ella respected it. But if it took flesh and came in her world, well, the shoe was on the other foot. She didn't mind a little communication between the two worlds, but this was an invasion.

"Shall we pray?" asked the women.

"Uh huh," said Ella. "First. Then we got to get down to business."

The day Denver was to spend her first night at the Bodwins', Mr. Bodwin had some business on the edge of the city and told Janey he would pick the new girl up before supper. Denver sat on the porch steps with a bundle in her lap, her carnival dress sun-faded to a quieter rainbow. She was looking to the right, in the direction Mr. Bodwin would be coming from. She did not see the women approaching, accumulating slowly in groups of twos and threes from the left. Denver was looking to the right. She was a little anxious about whether she would prove satisfactory to the Bodwins, and uneasy too because she woke up crying from a dream about a running pair of shoes. The sadness of the dream she hadn't been able to shake, and the heat oppressed her as she went about the chores. Far too early she wrapped a nightdress and hairbrush into a bundle. Nervous, she fidgeted the knot and looked to the right.

Some brought what they could and what they believed would work. Stuffed in apron pockets, strung around their necks, lying in the space between their breasts. Others brought Christian faith—as shield and sword. Most brought a little of both. They had no idea what they would do once they got there. They just started out, walked down Bluestone Road and came together at the agreed-upon time. The heat kept a few women who promised to go at home. Others who believed the story didn't want any part of the confrontation and wouldn't have come no matter what the weather. And there were those like Lady Jones who didn't believe the story and hated the ignorance of those who did. So thirty women made up that company and walked slowly, slowly toward 124.

It was three in the afternoon on a Friday so wet and hot Cincinnati's stench had traveled to the country: from the canal, from hanging meat and things rotting in jars; from small animals dead in the

fields, town sewers and factories. The stench, the heat, the moisture—
trust the devil to make his presence known. Otherwise it looked
almost like a regular workday. They could have been going to do
the laundry at the orphanage or the insane asylum; corn shucking
at the mill; or to clean fish, rinse offal, cradle whitebabies, sweep
stores, scrape hog skin, press lard, case-pack sausage or hide in tavern
kitchens so whitepeople didn't have to see them handle their food.

But not today.

When they caught up with each other, all thirty, and arrived at
124, the first thing they saw was not Denver sitting on the steps, but
themselves. Younger, stronger, even as little girls lying in the grass
asleep. Catfish was popping grease in the pan and they saw themselves
scoop German potato salad onto the plate. Cobbler oozing purple
syrup colored their teeth. They sat on the porch, ran down to the
creek, teased the men, hoisted children on their hips or, if they were
the children, straddled the ankles of old men who held their little
hands while giving them a horsey ride. Baby Suggs laughed and
skipped among them, urging more. Mothers, dead now, moved their
shoulders to mouth harps. The fence they had leaned on and climbed
over was gone. The stump of the butternut had split like a fan. But
there they were, young and happy, playing in Baby Suggs' yard, not
feeling the envy that surfaced the next day.

Denver heard mumbling and looked to the left. She stood when
she saw them. They grouped, murmuring and whispering, but did
not step foot in the yard. Denver waved. A few waved back but came
no closer. Denver sat back down wondering what was going on. A
woman dropped to her knees. Half of the others did likewise. Denver
saw lowered heads, but could not hear the lead prayer—only the
earnest syllables of agreement that backed it: Yes, yes, yes, oh yes.
Hear me. Hear me. Do it, Maker, do it. Yes. Among those not on
their knees, who stood holding 124 in a fixed glare, was Ella, trying
to see through the walls, behind the door, to what was really in there.
Was it true the dead daughter come back? Or a pretend? Was it
whipping Sethe? Ella had been beaten every way but down. She
remembered the bottom teeth she had lost to the brake and the scars
from the bell were thick as rope around her waist. She had delivered,
but would not nurse, a hairy white thing, fathered by "the lowest

yet." It lived five days never making a sound. The idea of that pup coming back to whip her too set her jaw working, and then Ella hollered.

Instantly the kneelers and the standers joined her. They stopped praying and took a step back to the beginning. In the beginning there were no words. In the beginning was the sound, and they all knew what that sound sounded like.

Edward Bodwin drove a cart down Bluestone Road. It displeased him a bit because he preferred his figure astride Princess. Curved over his own hands, holding the reins made him look the age he was. But he had promised his sister a detour to pick up a new girl. He didn't have to think about the way—he was headed for the house he was born in. Perhaps it was his destination that turned his thoughts to time—the way it dripped or ran. He had not seen the house for thirty years. Not the butternut in front, the stream at the rear nor the block house in between. Not even the meadow across the road. Very few of the interior details did he remember because he was three years old when his family moved into town. But he did remember that the cooking was done behind the house, the well was forbidden to play near, and that women died there: his mother, grandmother, an aunt and an older sister before he was born. The men (his father and grandfather) moved with himself and his baby sister to Court Street sixty-seven years ago. The land, of course, eighty acres of it on both sides of Bluestone, was the central thing, but he felt something sweeter and deeper about the house which is why he rented it for a little something if he could get it, but it didn't trouble him to get no rent at all since the tenants at least kept it from the disrepair total abandonment would permit.

There was a time when he buried things there. Precious things he wanted to protect. As a child every item he owned was available and accountable to his family. Privacy was an adult indulgence, but when he got to be one, he seemed not to need it.

The horse trotted along and Edward Bodwin cooled his beautiful mustache with his breath. It was generally agreed upon by the women in the Society that, except for his hands, it was the most attractive feature he had. Dark, velvety, its beauty was enhanced by his strong clean-shaven chin. But his hair was white, like his sister's—and had been since he was a young man. It made him the most visible and memorable person at every gathering, and cartoonists had fastened onto the theatricality of his white hair and big black mustache whenever they depicted local political antagonism. Twenty years ago when the Society was at its height in opposing slavery, it was as though his coloring was itself the heart of the matter. The "bleached nigger" was what his enemies called him, and on a trip to Arkansas, some Mississippi rivermen, enraged by the Negro boatmen they competed with, had caught him and shoe-blackened his face and his hair. Those heady days were gone now; what remained was the sludge of ill will; dashed hopes and difficulties beyond repair. A tranquil Republic? Well, not in his lifetime.

Even the weather was getting to be too much for him. He was either too hot or freezing, and this day was a blister. He pressed his hat down to keep the sun from his neck, where heatstroke was a real possibility. Such thoughts of mortality were not new to him (he was over seventy now), but they still had the power to annoy. As he drew closer to the old homestead, the place that continued to surface in his dreams, he was even more aware of the way time moved. Measured by the wars he had lived through but not fought in (against the Miami, the Spaniards, the Secessionists), it was slow. But measured by the burial of his private things it was the blink of an eye. Where, exactly, was the box of tin soldiers? The watch chain with no watch? And who was he hiding them from? His father, probably, a deeply religious man who knew what God knew and told everybody what it was. Edward Bodwin thought him an odd man, in so many ways, yet he had one clear directive: human life is holy, all of it. And that his son still believed, although he had less and less reason to. Nothing since was as stimulating as the old days of letters, petitions, meetings, debates, recruitment, quarrels, rescue and downright sedition. Yet it had worked, more or less, and when it had not, he and his sister made themselves available to circumvent obstacles. As they had when a runaway slavewoman lived in his homestead with her mother-in-law and got herself into a world of trouble. The Society managed to turn infanticide and the cry of savagery around, and build a further case for abolishing slavery. Good years, they were, full of spit and conviction. Now he just wanted to know where his soldiers were and his watchless chain. That would be enough for this day of unbearable heat: bring back the new girl and recall exactly where his treasure lay. Then home, supper, and God willing, the sun would drop once more to give him the blessing of a good night's sleep.

The road curved like an elbow, and as he approached it he heard the singers before he saw them.

When the women assembled outside 124, Sethe was breaking a lump of ice into chunks. She dropped the ice pick into her apron pocket to scoop the pieces into a basin of water. When the music entered the window she was wringing a cool cloth to put on Beloved's forehead. Beloved, sweating profusely, was sprawled on the bed in the keeping room, a salt rock in her hand. Both women heard it at the same time and both lifted their heads. As the voices grew louder, Beloved sat up, licked the salt and went into the bigger room. Sethe and she exchanged glances and started toward the window. They saw Denver sitting on the steps and beyond her, where the yard met the road, they saw the rapt faces of thirty neighborhood women. Some had their eyes closed; others looked at the hot, cloudless sky. Sethe opened the door and reached for Beloved's hand. Together they stood in the doorway. For Sethe it was as though the Clearing had come to her with all its heat and simmering leaves, where the voices of women searched for the right combination, the key, the code, the sound that broke the back of words. Building voice upon voice until they found it, and when they did it was a wave of sound wide enough to sound deep water and knock the pods off chestnut trees. It broke over Sethe and she trembled like the baptized in its wash.

The singing women recognized Sethe at once and surprised themselves by their absence of fear when they saw what stood next to her. The devil-child was clever, they thought. And beautiful. It had taken the shape of a pregnant woman, naked and smiling in the heat of the afternoon sun. Thunderblack and glistening, she stood on long straight legs, her belly big and tight. Vines of hair twisted all over her head. Jesus. Her smile was dazzling.

Sethe feels her eyes burn and it may have been to keep them clear that she looks up. The sky is blue and clear. Not one touch of death in the definite green of the leaves. It is when she lowers her eyes to look again at the loving faces before her that she sees him. Guiding the mare, slowing down, his black hat wide-brimmed enough to hide his face but not his purpose. He is coming into her yard and he is coming for her best thing. She hears wings. Little hummingbirds stick needle beaks right through her headcloth into her hair and beat their wings. And if she thinks anything, it is no. No no. Nonono. She flies. The ice pick is not in her hand; it is her hand.

Standing alone on the porch, Beloved is smiling. But now her hand is empty. Sethe is running away from her, running, and she feels the emptiness in the hand Sethe has been holding. Now she is running into the faces of the people out there, joining them and leaving Beloved behind. Alone. Again. Then Denver, running too. Away from her to the pile of people out there. They make a hill. A hill of black people, falling. And above them all, rising from his place with a whip in his hand, the man without skin, looking. He is looking at her.

*Bare feet and chamomile sap.*
*Took off my shoes; took off my hat.*
*Bare feet and chamomile sap*
*Gimme back my shoes; gimme back my hat.*

*Lay my head on a potato sack,*
*Devil sneak up behind my back.*
*Steam engine got a lonesome whine;*
*Love that woman till you go stone blind.*

*Stone blind; stone blind.*
*Sweet Home gal make you lose your mind.*

HIS COMING is the reverse route of his going. First the cold house, the storeroom, then the kitchen before he tackles the beds. Here Boy, feeble and shedding his coat in patches, is asleep by the pump, so Paul D knows Beloved is truly gone. Disappeared, some say, exploded right before their eyes. Ella is not so sure. "Maybe," she says, "maybe not. Could be hiding in the trees waiting for another chance." But when Paul D sees the ancient dog, eighteen years if a day, he is certain 124 is clear of her. But he opens the door to the cold house halfway expecting to hear her. "Touch me. Touch me. On the inside part and call me my name."

There is the pallet spread with old newspapers gnawed at the edges by mice. The lard can. The potato sacks too, but empty now, they lie on the dirt floor in heaps. In daylight he can't imagine it in darkness with moonlight seeping through the cracks. Nor the desire that drowned him there and forced him to struggle up, up into that girl like she was the clear air at the top of the sea. Coupling with her wasn't even fun. It was more like a brainless urge to stay alive. Each time she came, pulled up her skirts, a life hunger overwhelmed him and he had no more control over it than over his lungs. And afterward, beached and gobbling air, in the midst of repulsion and personal shame, he was thankful too for having been escorted to some ocean-deep place he once belonged to.

Sifting daylight dissolves the memory, turns it into dust motes floating in light. Paul D shuts the door. He looks toward the house and, surprisingly, it does not look back at him. Unloaded, 124 is just another weathered house needing repair. Quiet, just as Stamp Paid said.

"Used to be voices all round that place. Quiet, now," Stamp said. "I been past it a few times and I can't hear a thing. Chastened, I reckon, 'cause Mr. Bodwin say he selling it soon's he can."

"That the name of the one she tried to stab? That one?"

"Yep. His sister say it's full of trouble. Told Janey she was going to get rid of it."

"And him?" asked Paul D.

"Janey say he against it but won't stop it."

"Who they think want a house out there? Anybody got the money don't want to live out there."

"Beats me," Stamp answered. "It'll be a spell, I guess, before it get took off his hands."

"He don't plan on taking her to the law?"

"Don't seem like it. Janey say all he wants to know is who was the naked blackwoman standing on the porch. He was looking at her so hard he didn't notice what Sethe was up to. All he saw was some coloredwomen fighting. He thought Sethe was after one of them, Janey say."

"Janey tell him any different?"

"No. She say she so glad her boss ain't dead. If Ella hadn't clipped her, she say she would have. Scared her to death have that woman kill her boss. She *and* Denver be looking for a job."

"Who Janey tell him the naked woman was?"

"Told him she didn't see none."

"You believe they saw it?"

"Well, they saw something. I trust Ella anyway, and she say she looked it in the eye. It was standing right next to Sethe. But from the way they describe it, don't seem like it was the girl I saw in there. The girl I saw was narrow. This one was big. She say they was holding hands and Sethe looked like a little girl beside it."

"Little girl with a ice pick. How close she get to him?"

"Right up on him, they say. Before Denver and them grabbed her and Ella put her fist in her jaw."

"He got to know Sethe was after him. He got to."

"Maybe. I don't know. If he did think it, I reckon he decided not to. That be just like him, too. He's somebody never turned us down. Steady as a rock. I tell you something, if she had got to him, it'd be the worst thing in the world for us. You know, don't you, he's the main one kept Sethe from the gallows in the first place."

"Yeah. Damn. That woman is crazy. Crazy."

"Yeah, well, ain't we all?"

They laughed then. A rusty chuckle at first and then more, louder and louder until Stamp took out his pocket handkerchief and wiped his eyes while Paul D pressed the heel of his hand in his own. As the scene neither one had witnessed took shape before them, its seriousness and its embarrassment made them shake with laughter.

"Every time a whiteman come to the door she got to kill somebody?"

"For all she know, the man could be coming for the rent."

"Good thing they don't deliver mail out that way."

"Wouldn't nobody get no letter."

"Except the postman."

"Be a mighty hard message."

"And his last."

When their laughter was spent, they took deep breaths and shook their heads.

"And he still going to let Denver spend the night in his house? Ha!"

"Aw no. Hey. Lay off Denver, Paul D. That's my heart. I'm proud of that girl. She was the first one wrestle her mother down. Before anybody knew what the devil was going on."

"She saved his life then, you could say."

"You could. You could," said Stamp, thinking suddenly of the leap, the wide swing and snatch of his arm as he rescued the little curly-headed baby from within inches of a split skull. "I'm proud of her. She turning out fine. Fine."

It was true. Paul D saw her the next morning when he was on his way to work and she was leaving hers. Thinner, steady in the eyes, she looked more like Halle than ever.

She was the first to smile. "Good morning, Mr. D."

"Well, it is now." Her smile, no longer the sneer he remembered, had welcome in it and strong traces of Sethe's mouth. Paul D touched his cap. "How you getting along?"

"Don't pay to complain."

"You on your way home?"

She said no. She had heard about an afternoon job at the shirt factory. She hoped that with her night work at the Bodwins' and another one, she could put away something and help her mother too. When he asked her if they treated her all right over there, she said more than all right. Miss Bodwin taught her stuff. He asked her what stuff and she laughed and said book stuff. "She says I might go to Oberlin. She's experimenting on me." And he didn't say, "Watch out. Watch out. Nothing in the world more dangerous than a white schoolteacher." Instead he nodded and asked the question he wanted to.

"Your mother all right?"

"No," said Denver. "No. No, not a bit all right."

"You think I should stop by? Would she welcome it?"

"I don't know," said Denver. "I think I've lost my mother, Paul D."

They were both silent for a moment and then he said, "Uh, that girl. You know. Beloved?"

"Yes?"

"You think she sure 'nough your sister?"

Denver looked at her shoes. "At times. At times I think she was— more." She fiddled with her shirtwaist, rubbing a spot of something.

Suddenly she leveled her eyes at his. "But who would know that better than you, Paul D? I mean, you sure 'nough knew her."

He licked his lips. "Well, if you want my opinion—"

"I don't," she said. "I have my own."

"You grown," he said.

"Yes, sir."

"Well. Well, good luck with the job."

"Thank you. And, Paul D, you don't have to stay 'way, but be careful how you talk to my ma'am, hear?"

"Don't worry," he said and left her then, or rather she left him because a young man was running toward her, saying, "Hey, Miss Denver. Wait up."

She turned to him, her face looking like someone had turned up the gas jet.

He left her unwillingly because he wanted to talk more, make sense out of the stories he had been hearing: whiteman came to take Denver to work and Sethe cut him. Baby ghost came back evil and sent Sethe out to get the man who kept her from hanging. One point of agreement is: first they saw it and then they didn't. When they got Sethe down on the ground and the ice pick out of her hands and looked back to the house, it was gone. Later, a little boy put it out how he had been looking for bait back of 124, down by the stream, and saw, cutting through the woods, a naked woman with fish for hair.

As a matter of fact, Paul D doesn't care how It went or even why. He cares about how he left and why. When he looks at himself through Garner's eyes, he sees one thing. Through Sixo's, another. One makes him feel righteous. One makes him feel ashamed. Like the time he worked both sides of the War. Running away from the Northpoint Bank and Railway to join the 44th Colored Regiment in Tennessee, he thought he had made it, only to discover he had arrived at another colored regiment forming under a commander in New Jersey. He stayed there four weeks. The regiment fell apart before it got started on the question of whether the soldiers should have weapons or not. Not, it was decided, and the white commander had to figure out what to command them to do instead of kill other whitemen. Some of the ten thousand stayed there to clean, haul and build things; others drifted away to another regiment; most were abandoned, left to their own devices with bitterness for pay. He was trying to make up his mind what to do when an agent from Northpoint Bank caught up with him and took him back to Delaware, where he slave-worked a year. Then Northpoint took $300 in exchange for his services in Alabama, where he worked for the Rebellers, first sorting the dead and then smelting iron. When he and his group combed the battlefields, their job was to pull the Confederate wounded away from the Confederate dead. Care, they told them. Take good care. Coloredmen and white, their faces wrapped to their eyes, picked their way through the meadows with lamps, listening in the dark for groans of life in the indifferent silence of the dead. Mostly young men, some children, and it shamed him a little to feel pity for what he imagined were the sons of the guards in Alfred, Georgia.

In five tries he had not had one permanent success. Every one of his escapes (from Sweet Home, from Brandywine, from Alfred, Georgia, from Wilmington, from Northpoint) had been frustrated. Alone, undisguised, with visible skin, memorable hair and no whiteman to protect him, he never stayed uncaught. The longest had been when he ran with the convicts, stayed with the Cherokee, followed their advice and lived in hiding with the weaver woman in Wilmington, Delaware: three years. And in all those escapes he could not help being astonished by the beauty of this land that was not his. He hid in its breast, fingered its earth for food, clung to its banks to lap water and tried not to love it. On nights when the sky was personal, weak with the weight of its own stars, he made himself not love it. Its graveyards and low-lying rivers. Or just a house—solitary under a chinaberry tree; maybe a mule tethered and the light hitting its hide just so. Anything could stir him and he tried hard not to love it.

After a few months on the battlefields of Alabama, he was impressed to a foundry in Selma along with three hundred captured, lent or taken coloredmen. That's where the War's end found him, and leaving Alabama when he had been declared free should have been a snap. He should have been able to walk from the foundry in Selma straight to Philadelphia, taking the main roads, a train if he wanted to, or passage on a boat. But it wasn't like that. When he and two colored soldiers (who had been captured from the 44th he had looked for) walked from Selma to Mobile, they saw twelve dead blacks in the first eighteen miles. Two were women, four were little boys. He thought this, for sure, would be the walk of his life. The Yankees in control left the Rebels out of control. They got to the outskirts of Mobile, where blacks were putting down tracks for the Union that, earlier, they had torn up for the Rebels. One of the men with him, a private called Keane, had been with the Massachusetts 54th. He told Paul D they had been paid less than white soldiers. It was a sore point with him that, as a group, they had refused the offer Massachusetts made to make up the difference in pay. Paul D was so impressed by the idea of being paid money to fight he looked at the private with wonder and envy.

Keane and his friend, a Sergeant Rossiter, confiscated a skiff and the three of them floated in Mobile Bay. There the private hailed a Union gunboat, which took all three aboard. Keane and Rossiter disembarked at Memphis to look for their commanders. The captain of the gunboat let Paul D stay aboard all the way to Wheeling, West Virginia. He made his own way to New Jersey.

By the time he got to Mobile, he had seen more dead people than living ones, but when he got to Trenton the crowds of alive people, neither hunting nor hunted, gave him a measure of free life so tasty he never forgot it. Moving down a busy street full of whitepeople who needed no explanation for his presence, the glances he got had to do with his disgusting clothes and unforgivable hair. Still, nobody raised an alarm. Then came the miracle. Standing in a street in front of a row of brick houses, he heard a whiteman call him ("Say there! Yo!") to help unload two trunks from a coach cab. Afterward the whiteman gave him a coin. Paul D walked around with it for hours—not sure what it could buy (a suit? a meal? a horse?) and if anybody would sell him anything. Finally he saw a greengrocer selling vegetables from a wagon. Paul D pointed to a bunch of turnips. The grocer handed them to him, took his one coin and gave him several more. Stunned, he backed away. Looking around, he saw that nobody seemed interested in the "mistake" or him, so he walked along, happily chewing turnips. Only a few women looked vaguely repelled as they passed. His first earned purchase made him glow, never mind the turnips were withered dry. That was when he decided that to eat, walk and sleep anywhere was life as good as it got. And he did it for seven years till he found himself in southern Ohio, where an old woman and a girl he used to know had gone.

Now his coming is the reverse of his going. First he stands in the back, near the cold house, amazed by the riot of late-summer flowers where vegetables should be growing. Sweet william, morning glory, chrysanthemums. The odd placement of cans jammed with the rotting stems of things, the blossoms shriveled like sores. Dead ivy twines around bean poles and door handles. Faded newspaper pictures are nailed to the outhouse and on trees. A rope too short for anything but skip-jumping lies discarded near the washtub; and jars and jars of dead lightning bugs. Like a child's house; the house of a very tall child.

He walks to the front door and opens it. It is stone quiet. In the place where once a shaft of sad red light had bathed him, locking him where he stood, is nothing. A bleak and minus nothing. More like absence, but an absence he had to get through with the same determination he had when he trusted Sethe and stepped through the pulsing light. He glances quickly at the lightning-white stairs. The entire railing is wound with ribbons, bows, bouquets. Paul D steps inside. The outdoor breeze he brings with him stirs the ribbons. Carefully, not quite in a hurry but losing no time, he climbs the luminous stairs. He enters Sethe's room. She isn't there and the bed looks so small he wonders how the two of them had lain there. It has no sheets, and because the roof windows do not open the room is stifling. Brightly colored clothes lie on the floor. Hanging from a wall peg is the dress Beloved wore when he first saw her. A pair of ice skates nestles in a basket in the corner. He turns his eyes back to the bed and keeps looking at it. It seems to him a place he is not. With an effort that makes him sweat he forces a picture of himself lying there, and when he sees it, it lifts his spirit. He goes to the other bedroom. Denver's is as neat as the other is messy. But still no Sethe. Maybe she has gone back to work, gotten better in the days since he talked to Denver. He goes back down the stairs, leaving the image of himself firmly in place on the narrow bed. At the kitchen table he sits down. Something is missing from 124. Something larger than the people who lived there. Something more than Beloved or the red light. He can't put his finger on it, but it seems, for a moment, that just beyond his knowing is the glare of an outside thing that embraces while it accuses.

To the right of him, where the door to the keeping room is ajar, he hears humming. Someone is humming a tune. Something soft and sweet, like a lullaby. Then a few words. Sounds like "high Johnny, wide Johnny. Sweet William bend down low." Of course, he thinks. That's where she is—and she is. Lying under a quilt of merry colors. Her hair, like the dark delicate roots of good plants, spreads and curves on the pillow. Her eyes, fixed on the window, are so expressionless he is not sure she will know who he is. There is too much light here in this room. Things look sold.

"Jackweed raise up high," she sings. "Lambswool over my shoulder, buttercup and clover fly." She is fingering a long clump of her hair.

Paul D clears his throat to interrupt her. "Sethe?"

She turns her head. "Paul D."

"Aw, Sethe."

"I made the ink, Paul D. He couldn't have done it if I hadn't made the ink."

"What ink? Who?"

"You shaved."

"Yeah. Look bad?"

"No. You looking good."

"Devil's confusion. What's this I hear about you not getting out of bed?"

She smiles, lets it fade and turns her eyes back to the window.

"I need to talk to you," he tells her.

She doesn't answer.

"I saw Denver. She tell you?"

"She comes in the daytime. Denver. She's still with me, my Denver."

"You got to get up from here, girl." He is nervous. This reminds him of something.

"I'm tired, Paul D. So tired. I have to rest a while."

Now he knows what he is reminded of and he shouts at her, "Don't you die on me! This is Baby Suggs' bed! Is that what you planning?" He is so angry he could kill her. He checks himself, remembering Denver's warning, and whispers, "What you planning, Sethe?"

"Oh, I don't have no plans. No plans at all."

"Look," he says, "Denver be here in the day. I be here in the night. I'm a take care of you, you hear? Starting now. First off, you don't smell right. Stay there. Don't move. Let me heat up some water." He stops. "Is it all right, Sethe, if I heat up some water?"

"And count my feet?" she asks him.

He steps closer. "Rub your feet."

Sethe closes her eyes and presses her lips together. She is thinking: No. This little place by a window is what I want. And rest. There's nothing to rub now and no reason to. Nothing left to bathe, assuming he even knows how. Will he do it in sections? First her face, then her hands, her thighs, her feet, her back? Ending with her exhausted breasts? And if he bathes her in sections, will the parts hold? She opens her eyes, knowing the danger of looking at him. She looks at him. The peachstone skin, the crease between his ready, waiting eyes and sees it—the thing in him, the blessedness, that has made him the kind of man who can walk in a house and make the women cry. Because with him, in his presence, they could. Cry and tell him things they only told each other: that time didn't stay put; that she called, but Howard and Buglar walked on down the railroad track and couldn't hear her; that Amy was scared to stay with her because her feet were ugly and her back looked so bad; that her ma'am had hurt her feelings and she couldn't find her hat anywhere and "Paul D?"

"What, baby?"

"She left me."

"Aw, girl. Don't cry."

"She was my best thing."

Paul D sits down in the rocking chair and examines the quilt patched in carnival colors. His hands are limp between his knees. There are too many things to feel about this woman. His head hurts. Suddenly he remembers Sixo trying to describe what he felt about the Thirty-Mile Woman. "She is a friend of my mind. She gather me, man. The pieces I am, she gather them and give them back to me in all the right order. It's good, you know, when you got a woman who is a friend of your mind."

He is staring at the quilt but he is thinking about her wrought-iron back; the delicious mouth still puffy at the corner from Ella's fist. The mean black eyes. The wet dress steaming before the fire. Her tenderness about his neck jewelry—its three wands, like attentive baby rattlers, curving two feet into the air. How she never mentioned or looked at it, so he did not have to feel the shame of being collared like a beast. Only this woman Sethe could have left him his manhood like that. He wants to put his story next to hers.

"Sethe," he says, "me and you, we got more yesterday than anybody. We need some kind of tomorrow."

He leans over and takes her hand. With the other he touches her face. "You your best thing, Sethe. You are." His holding fingers are holding hers.

"Me? Me?"

THERE IS a loneliness that can be rocked. Arms crossed, knees drawn up; holding, holding on, this motion, unlike a ship's, smooths and contains the rocker. It's an inside kind—wrapped tight like skin. Then there is a loneliness that roams. No rocking can hold it down. It is alive, on its own. A dry and spreading thing that makes the sound of one's own feet going seem to come from a far-off place.

Everybody knew what she was called, but nobody anywhere knew her name. Disremembered and unaccounted for, she cannot be lost because no one is looking for her, and even if they were, how can they call her if they don't know her name? Although she has claim, she is not claimed. In the place where long grass opens, the girl who waited to be loved and cry shame erupts into her separate parts, to make it easy for the chewing laughter to swallow her all away.

It was not a story to pass on.

They forgot her like a bad dream. After they made up their tales, shaped and decorated them, those that saw her that day on the porch quickly and deliberately forgot her. It took longer for those who had spoken to her, lived with her, fallen in love with her, to forget, until they realized they couldn't remember or repeat a single thing she said, and began to believe that, other than what they themselves were thinking, she hadn't said anything at all. So, in the end, they forgot her too. Remembering seemed unwise. They never knew where or why she crouched, or whose was the underwater face she needed like that. Where the memory of the smile under her chin might have been and was not, a latch latched and lichen attached its apple-green bloom to the metal. What made her think her fingernails could open locks the rain rained on?

It was not a story to pass on.

So they forgot her. Like an unpleasant dream during a troubling sleep. Occasionally, however, the rustle of a skirt hushes when they wake, and the knuckles brushing a cheek in sleep seem to belong to the sleeper. Sometimes the photograph of a close friend or relative— looked at too long—shifts, and something more familiar than the dear face itself moves there. They can touch it if they like, but don't, because they know things will never be the same if they do.

This is not a story to pass on.

Down by the stream in back of 124 her footprints come and go, come and go. They are so familiar. Should a child, an adult place his feet in them, they will fit. Take them out and they disappear again as though nobody ever walked there.

By and by all trace is gone, and what is forgotten is not only the footprints but the water too and what it is down there. The rest is weather. Not the breath of the disremembered and unaccounted for, but wind in the eaves, or spring ice thawing too quickly. Just weather. Certainly no clamor for a kiss.

Beloved.

# JAZZ

for R W

and

George

.

I am the name of the sound
  and the sound of the name.
I am the sign of the letter
  and the designation of the division.

"Thunder, Perfect Mind,"
*The Nag Hammadi*

**S**th, I know that woman. She used to live with a flock of birds on Lenox Avenue. Know her husband, too. He fell for an eighteen-year-old girl with one of those deepdown, spooky loves that made him so sad and happy he shot her just to keep the feeling going. When the woman, her name is Violet, went to the funeral to see the girl and to cut her dead face they threw her to the floor and out of the church. She ran, then, through all that snow, and when she got back to her apartment she took the birds from their cages and set them out the windows to freeze or fly, including the parrot that said, "I love you."

The snow she ran through was so windswept she left no footprints in it, so for a time nobody knew exactly where on Lenox Avenue she lived. But, like me, they knew who she was, who she had to be, because they knew that her husband, Joe Trace, was the one who shot the girl. There was never anyone to prosecute him because nobody actually saw him do it, and the dead girl's aunt didn't want to throw money to helpless lawyers or laughing cops when she knew the expense wouldn't improve anything. Besides, she found out that the man who killed her niece cried all day and for him and for Violet that is as bad as jail.

Regardless of the grief Violet caused, her name was brought up at the January meeting of the Salem Women's Club as someone needing assistance, but it was voted down because only prayer—not money—could help her now, because she had a more or less able husband (who needed to stop feeling sorry for himself), and because a man and his family on 134th Street had lost everything in a fire. The Club mobilized itself to come to the burnt-out family's aid and left Violet to figure out on her own what the matter was and how to fix it.

She is awfully skinny, Violet; fifty, but still good looking when she broke up the funeral. You'd think that being thrown out the church would be the end of it—the shame and all—but it wasn't. Violet is mean enough and good looking enough to think that even without hips or youth she could punish Joe by getting herself a boyfriend and letting him visit in her own house. She thought it would dry his tears up and give her some satisfaction as well. It could have worked, I suppose, but the children of suicides are hard to please and quick to believe no one loves them because they are not really here.

Anyway, Joe didn't pay Violet or her friend any notice.

Whether she sent the boyfriend away or whether he quit her, I can't say. He may have come to feel that Violet's gifts were poor measured against his sympathy for the brokenhearted man in the next room. But I do know that mess didn't last two weeks. Violet's next plan—to fall back in love with her husband—whipped her before it got on a good footing. Washing his handkerchiefs and putting food on the table before him was the most she could manage. A poisoned silence floated through the rooms like a big fishnet that Violet alone slashed through with loud recriminations. Joe's daytime listlessness and both their worrying nights must have wore her down. So she decided to love—well, find out about—the eighteen-year-old whose creamy little face she tried to cut open even though nothing would have come out but straw.

Violet didn't know anything about the girl at first except her name, her age, and that she was very well thought of in the legally licensed beauty parlor. So she commenced to gather the rest of the information. Maybe she thought she could solve the mystery of love that way. Good luck and let me know.

She questioned everybody, starting with Malvonne, an upstairs neighbor—the one who told her about Joe's dirt in the first place and whose apartment he and the girl used as a love nest. From Malvonne she learned the girl's address and whose child she was. From the legally licensed beauticians she found out what kind of lip rouge the girl wore; the marcelling iron they used on her (though I suspect that girl didn't need to straighten her hair); the band the girl liked best (Slim Bates' Ebony Keys which is pretty good except for his vocalist who must be his woman since why else would he let her insult his band). And when she was shown how, Violet did the dance steps the dead girl used to do. All that. When she had the steps down pat—her knees just so—everybody, including the ex-boyfriend, got disgusted with her and I can see why. It was like watching an old street pigeon pecking the crust of a sardine sandwich the cats left behind. But Violet was nothing but persistent and no wisecrack or ugly look stopped her. She haunted PS-89 to talk to teachers who knew the girl. JHS-139 too because the girl went there before trudging way over to Wadleigh, since there were no high schools in her district a colored girl could attend. And for a long time she pestered the girl's aunt, a dignified lady who did fine work off and on in the garment district, until the aunt broke down and began to look forward to Violet's visits for a chat about youth and misbehavior. The aunt showed all the dead girl's things to Violet and it became clear to her (as it was to me) that this niece had been hardheaded as well as sly.

One particular thing the aunt showed her, and eventually let Violet keep for a few weeks, was a picture of the girl's face. Not smiling, but alive at least and very bold. Violet had the nerve to put it on the fireplace mantel in her own parlor and both she and Joe looked at it in bewilderment.

It promised to be a mighty bleak household, what with the birds gone and the two of them wiping their cheeks all day, but when spring came to the City Violet saw, coming into the building with an Okeh record under her arm and carrying some stewmeat wrapped in butcher paper, another girl with four marcelled waves on each side of her head. Violet invited her in to examine the record and that's how that scandalizing threesome on Lenox Avenue began. What turned out different was who shot whom.

·   ·   ·

I'm crazy about this City.

Daylight slants like a razor cutting the buildings in half. In the top half I see looking faces and it's not easy to tell which are people, which the work of stonemasons. Below is shadow where any blasé thing takes place: clarinets and lovemaking, fists and the voices of sorrowful women. A city like this one makes me dream tall and feel in on things. Hep. It's the bright steel rocking above the shade below that does it. When I look over strips of green grass lining the river, at church steeples and into the cream-and-copper halls of apartment buildings, I'm strong. Alone, yes, but top-notch and indestructible—like the City in 1926 when all the wars are over and there will never be another one. The people down there in the shadow are happy about that. At last, at last, everything's ahead. The smart ones say so and people listening to them and reading what they write down agree: Here comes the new. Look out. There goes the sad stuff. The bad stuff. The things-nobody-could-help stuff. The way everybody was then and there. Forget that. History is over, you all, and everything's ahead at last. In halls and offices people are sitting around thinking future thoughts about projects and bridges and fast-clicking trains underneath. The A&P hires a colored clerk. Big-legged women with pink kitty tongues roll money into green tubes for later on; then they laugh and put their arms around each other. Regular people corner thieves in alleys for quick retribution and, if he is stupid and has robbed wrong, thieves corner him too. Hoodlums hand out goodies, do their best to stay interesting, and since they are being watched for excitement, they pay attention to their clothes and the carving out of insults. Nobody wants to be an emergency at Harlem Hospital but if the Negro surgeon is visiting, pride cuts down the pain. And although the hair of the first class of colored nurses was declared unseemly for the official Bellevue nurse's cap, there are thirty-five of them now—all dedicated and superb in their profession.

Nobody says it's pretty here; nobody says it's easy either. What it is is decisive, and if you pay attention to the street plans, all laid out, the City can't hurt you.

I haven't got any muscles, so I can't really be expected to defend myself. But I do know how to take precaution. Mostly it's making sure no one knows all there is to know about me. Second, I watch everything and everyone and try to figure out their plans, their reasonings, long before they do. You have to understand what it's like, taking on a big city: I'm exposed to all sorts of ignorance and criminality. Still, this is the only life for me. I like the way the City makes people think they can do what they want and get away with it. I see them all over the place: wealthy whites, and plain ones too, pile into mansions decorated and redecorated by black women richer than they are, and both are pleased with the spectacle of the other. I've seen the eyes of black Jews, brimful of pity for everyone not themselves, graze the food stalls and the ankles of loose women, while a breeze stirs the white plumes on the helmets of the UNIA men. A colored man floats down out of the sky blowing a saxophone, and below him, in the space between two buildings, a girl talks earnestly to a man in a straw hat. He touches her lip to remove a bit of something there. Suddenly she is quiet. He tilts her chin up. They stand there. Her grip on her purse slackens and her neck makes a nice curve. The man puts his hand on the stone wall above her head. By the way his jaw moves and the turn of his head I know he has a golden tongue. The sun sneaks into the alley behind them. It makes a pretty picture on its way down.

Do what you please in the City, it is there to back and frame you no matter what you do. And what goes on on its blocks and lots and side streets is anything the strong can think of and the weak will admire. All you have to do is heed the design—the way it's laid out for you, considerate, mindful of where you want to go and what you might need tomorrow.

I lived a long time, maybe too much, in my own mind. People say I should come out more. Mix. I agree that I close off in places, but if you have been left standing, as I have, while your partner overstays at another appointment, or promises to give you exclusive attention after supper, but is falling asleep just as you have begun to speak—well, it can make you inhospitable if you aren't careful, the last thing I want to be.

Hospitality is gold in this City; you have to be clever to figure out how to be welcoming and defensive at the same time. When to love something and when to quit. If you don't know how, you can end up out of control or controlled by some outside thing like that hard case last winter. Word was that underneath the good times and the easy money something evil ran the streets and nothing was safe—not even the dead. Proof of this being Violet's outright attack on the very subject of a funeral ceremony. Barely three days into 1926. A host of thoughtful people looked at the signs (the weather, the number, their own dreams) and believed it was the commencement of all sorts of destruction. That the scandal was a message sent to warn the good and rip up the faithless. I don't know who was more ambitious—the doomsayers or Violet—but it's hard to match the superstitious for great expectations.

Armistice was seven years old the winter Violet disrupted the funeral, and veterans on Seventh Avenue were still wearing their army-issue greatcoats, because nothing they can pay for is as sturdy or hides so well what they had boasted of in 1919. Eight years later, the day before Violet's misbehavior, when the snow comes it sits where it falls on Lexington and Park Avenue too, and waits for horse-drawn wagons to tamp it down when they deliver coal for the furnaces cooling down in the cellars. Up in those big five-story apartment buildings and the narrow wooden houses in between people knock on each other's doors to see if anything is needed or can be had. A piece of soap? A little kerosene? Some fat, chicken or pork, to brace the soup one more time? Whose husband is getting ready to go see if he can find a shop open? Is there time to add turpentine to the list drawn up and handed to him by the wives?

Breathing hurts in weather that cold, but whatever the problems of being winterbound in the City they put up with them because it is worth anything to be on Lenox Avenue safe from fays and the things they think up; where the sidewalks, snow-covered or not, are wider than the main roads of the towns where they were born and perfectly ordinary people can stand at the stop, get on the streetcar, give the man the nickel, and ride anywhere you please, although you don't please to go many places because everything you want is right where you are: the church, the store, the party, the women, the men, the postbox (but no high schools), the furniture store, street newspaper vendors, the bootleg houses (but no banks), the beauty parlors, the barbershops, the juke joints, the ice wagons, the rag collectors, the pool halls, the open food markets, the number runner, and every club, organization, group, order, union, society, brotherhood, sisterhood or association imaginable. The service trails, of course, are worn, and there are paths slick from the forays of members of one group into the territory of another where it is believed something curious or thrilling lies. Some gleaming, cracking, scary stuff. Where you can pop the cork and put the cold glass mouth right up to your own. Where you can find danger or be it; where you can fight till you drop and smile at the knife when it misses and when it doesn't. It makes you wonderful just to see it. And just as wonderful to know that back in one's own building there are lists drawn up by the wives for the husband hunting an open market, and that sheets impossible to hang out in snowfall drape kitchens like the curtains of Abyssinian Sunday-school plays.

The young are not so young here, and there is no such thing as midlife. Sixty years, forty, even, is as much as anybody feels like being bothered with. If they reach that, or get very old, they sit around looking at goings-on as though it were a five-cent triple feature on Saturday. Otherwise they find themselves butting in the business of people whose names they can't even remember and whose business is none of theirs. Just to hear themselves talk and the joy of watching the distressed faces of those listening. I've known a few exceptions. Some old people who didn't slap the children for being slappable; who saved that strength in case it was needed for something important. A last courtship full of smiles and little presents. Or the dedicated care of an old friend who might not make it through without them. Sometimes they concentrated on making sure the person they had shared their long lives with had cheerful company and the necessary things for the night.

But up there on Lenox, in Violet and Joe Trace's apartment, the rooms are like the empty birdcages wrapped in cloth. And a dead girl's face has become a necessary thing for their nights. They each take turns to throw off the bedcovers, rise up from the sagging mattress and tiptoe over cold linoleum into the parlor to gaze at what seems like the only living presence in the house: the photograph of a bold, unsmiling girl staring from the mantelpiece. If the tiptoer is Joe Trace, driven by loneliness from his wife's side, then the face stares at him without hope or regret and it is the absence of accusation that wakes him from his sleep hungry for her company. No finger points. Her lips don't turn down in judgment. Her face is calm, generous and sweet. But if the tiptoer is Violet the photograph is not that at all. The girl's face looks greedy, haughty and very lazy. The cream-at-the-top-of-the-milkpail face of someone who will never work for anything; someone who picks up things lying on other people's dressers and is not embarrassed when found out. It is the face of a sneak who glides over to your sink to rinse the fork you have laid by her plate. An inward face—whatever it sees is its own self. You are there, it says, because I am looking at you.

Two or three times during the night, as they take turns to go look at that picture, one of them will say her name. Dorcas? Dorcas. The dark rooms grow darker: the parlor needs a struck match to see the face. Beyond are the dining room, two bedrooms, the kitchen—all situated in the middle of the building so the apartment's windows have no access to the moon or the light of a street lamp. The bathroom has the best light since it juts out past the kitchen and catches the afternoon rays. Violet and Joe have arranged their furnishings in a way that might not remind anybody of the rooms in *Modern Homemaker* but it suits the habits of the body, the way a person walks from one room to another without bumping into anything, and what he wants to do when he sits down. You know how some people put a chair or a table in a corner where it looks nice but nobody in the world is ever going to go over to it, let alone sit down there? Violet didn't do that in her place. Everything is put where a person would like to have it, or would use or need it. So the dining room doesn't have a dining table with funeral-parlor chairs. It has big deep-down chairs and a card table by the window covered with jade, dracena and doctor plants until they want to have card games or play tonk between themselves. The kitchen is roomy enough to accommodate four people eating or give a customer plenty legroom while Violet does her hair. The front room, or parlor, is not wasted either, waiting for a wedding reception to be worthy of. It has birdcages and mirrors for the birds to look at themselves in, but now, of course, there are no birds, Violet having let them out on the day she went to Dorcas' funeral with a knife. Now there are just empty cages, the lonely mirrors glancing back at them. As for the rest, it's a sofa, some carved wooden chairs with small tables by them so you can put your coffee cup or a dish of ice cream down in front of you, or if you want to read the paper, you can do it easy without messing up the folds. The mantel over the fireplace used to have shells and pretty-colored stones, but all of that is gone now and only the picture of Dorcas Manfred sits there in a silver frame waking them up all night long.

Such restless nights make them sleep late, and Violet has to hurry to get a meal prepared before getting ready for her round of heads. Having a knack for it, but no supervised training, and therefore no license to do it, Violet can only charge twenty-five or fifty cents anyway, but since that business at Dorcas' funeral, many of her regular customers have found reasons to do their own hair or have a daughter heat up the irons. Violet and Joe Trace didn't use to need that hairdressing pocket change, but now that Joe is skipping workdays Violet carries her tools and her trade more and more into the overheated apartments of women who wake in the afternoon, pour gin in their tea and don't care what she has done. These women always need their hair done, and sometimes pity darkens their shiny eyes and they tip her a whole dollar.

"You need to eat you something," one says to her. "Don't you want to be bigger than your curling iron?"

"Shut your mouth," says Violet.

"I mean it," says the woman. She is still sleepy, and rests her cheek in her left hand while holding her ear with the right. "Men wear you down to a sharp piece of gristle if you let them."

"Women," answers Violet. "Women wear me down. No man ever wore me down to nothing. It's these little hungry girls acting like women. Not content with boys their own age, no, they want somebody old enough to be their father. Switching round with lipstick, see-through stockings, dresses up to their you-know-what . . ."

"That's my ear, girl! You going to press it too?"

"Sorry. I'm sorry. Really, really sorry." And Violet stops to blow her nose and blot tears with the back of her hand.

"Aw, the devil," the woman sighs and takes advantage of the pause to light a cigarette. "Now I reckon you going to tell me some old hateful story about how a young girl messed over you and how *he*'s not to blame because *he* was just walking down the street minding *his* own business, when this little twat jumped on his back and dragged him off to her bed. Save your breath. You'll need it on your deathbed."

"I need my breath now." Violet tests the hot comb. It scorches a long brown finger on the newspaper.

"Did he move out? Is he with her?"

"No. We still together. She's dead."

"Dead? Then what's the matter with you?"

"He thinks about her all the time. Nothing on his mind but her. Won't work. Can't sleep. Grieves all day, all night . . ."

"Oh," says the woman. She knocks the fire from her cigarette, pinches the tip and lays the butt carefully into the ashtray. Leaning back in the chair, she presses the rim of her ear with two fingers. "You in trouble," she says, yawning. "Deep, deep trouble. Can't rival the dead for love. Lose every time."

Violet agrees that it must be so; not only is she losing Joe to a dead girl, but she wonders if she isn't falling in love with her too. When she isn't trying to humiliate Joe, she is admiring the dead girl's hair; when she isn't cursing Joe with brand-new cuss words, she is having whispered conversations with the corpse in her head; when she isn't worrying about his loss of appetite, his insomnia, she wonders what color were Dorcas' eyes. Her aunt had said brown; the beauticians said black but Violet had never seen a light-skinned person with coal-black eyes. One thing, for sure, she needed her ends cut. In the photograph and from what Violet could remember from the coffin, the girl needed her ends cut. Hair that long gets fraggely easy. Just a quarter-inch trim would do wonders, Dorcas. Dorcas.

Violet leaves the sleepy woman's house. The slush at the curb is freezing again, and although she has seven icy blocks ahead, she is grateful that the customer who is coming to her kitchen for an appointment is not due until three o'clock, and there is time for a bit of housekeeping before then. Some business that needs doing because it is impossible to have nothing to do, no sequence of errands, list of tasks. She might wave her hands in the air, or tremble if she can't put her hand to something with another chore just around the bend from the one she is doing. She lights the oven to warm up the kitchen.

And while she sprinkles the collar of a white shirt her mind is at the bottom of the bed where the leg, broken clean away from the frame, is too split to nail back. When the customer comes and Violet is sudsing the thin gray hair, murmuring "Ha mercy" at appropriate breaks in the old lady's stream of confidences, Violet is resituating the cord that holds the stove door to its hinge and rehearsing the month's plea for three more days to the rent collector. She thinks she longs for rest, a carefree afternoon to decide suddenly to go to the pictures, or just to sit with the birdcages and listen to the children play in snow.

This notion of rest, it's attractive to her, but I don't think she would like it. They are all like that, these women. Waiting for the ease, the space that need not be filled with anything other than the drift of their own thoughts. But they wouldn't like it. They are busy and thinking of ways to be busier because such a space of nothing pressing to do would knock them down. No fields of cowslips will rush into that opening, nor mornings free of flies and heat when the light is shy. No. Not at all. They fill their mind and hands with soap and repair and dicey confrontations because what is waiting for them, in a suddenly idle moment, is the seep of rage. Molten. Thick and slow-moving. Mindful and particular about what in its path it chooses to bury. Or else, into a beat of time, and sideways under their breasts, slips a sorrow they don't know where from. A neighbor returns the spool of thread she borrowed, and not just the thread, but the extra-long needle too, and both of them stand in the door frame a moment while the borrower repeats for the lender a funny conversation she had with the woman on the floor below; it *is* funny and they laugh—one loudly while holding her forehead, the other hard enough to hurt her stomach. The lender closes the door, and later, still smiling, touches the lapel of her sweater to her eye to wipe traces of the laughter away then drops to the arm of the sofa the tears coming so fast she needs two hands to catch them.

So Violet sprinkles the collars and cuffs. Then sudses with all her heart those three or four ounces of gray hair, soft and interesting as a baby's.

Not the kind of baby hair her grandmother had soaped and played with and remembered for forty years. The hair of the little boy who got his name from it. Maybe that is why Violet is a hairdresser—all those years of listening to her rescuing grandmother, True Belle, tell Baltimore stories. The years with Miss Vera Louise in the fine stone house on Edison Street, where the linen was embroidered with blue thread and there was nothing to do but raise and adore the blond boy who ran away from them depriving everybody of his carefully loved hair.

Folks were furious when Violet broke up the funeral, but I can't believe they were surprised. Way, way before that, before Joe ever laid eyes on the girl, Violet sat down in the middle of the street. She didn't stumble nor was she pushed: she just sat down. After a few minutes two men and a woman came to her, but she couldn't make out why or what they said. Someone tried to give her water to drink, but she knocked it away. A policeman knelt in front of her and she rolled over on her side, covering her eyes. He would have taken her in but for the assembling crowd murmuring, "Aw, she's tired. Let her rest." They carried her to the nearest steps. Slowly she came around, dusted off her clothes, and got to her appointment an hour late, which pleased the slow-moving whores, who never hurried anything but love.

It never happened again as far as I know—the street sitting—but quiet as it's kept she did try to steal that baby although there is no way to prove it. What is known is this: the

Dumfrey women—mother and daughter—weren't home when Violet arrived. Either they got the date mixed up or had decided to go to a legally licensed parlor—just for the shampoo, probably, because there is no way to get that deepdown hair washing at a bathroom sink. The beauticians have it beat when it comes to that: you get to lie back instead of lean forward; you don't have to press a towel in your eyes to keep the soapy water out because at a proper beauty parlor it drains down the back of your head into the sink. So, sometimes, even if the legal beautician is not as adept as Violet, a regular customer will sneak to a shop just for the pleasure of a comfy shampoo.

Doing two heads in one place was lucky and Violet looked forward to the eleven-o'clock appointment. When nobody answered the bell, she waited, thinking maybe they'd been held up at the market. She tried the bell again, after some time, and then leaned over the concrete banister to ask a woman leaving the building next door if she knew where the Dumfrey women were. The woman shook her head but came over to help Violet look at the windows and wonder.

"They keep the shades up when they home," she said. "Down when they gone. Should be just the reverse."

"Maybe they want to see out when they home," said Violet.

"See what?" asked the woman. She was instantly angry.

"Daylight," said Violet. "Have some daylight get in there."

"They need to move on back to Memphis then if daylight is what they want."

"Memphis? I thought they were born here."

"That's what they'd have you believe. But they ain't. Not even Memphis. Cottown. Someplace nobody ever heard of."

"I'll be," said Violet. She was very surprised because the Dumfrey women were graceful, citified ladies whose father owned a store on 136th Street, and themselves had nice paper-handling jobs: one took tickets at the Lafayette; the other worked in the counting house.

"They don't like it known," the woman went on.

"Why?" asked Violet.

"Hincty, that's why. Comes from handling money all day. You notice that? How people who handle money for a living get stuck-up? Like it was theirs instead of yours?" She sucked her teeth at the shaded windows. "Daylight my foot."

"Well, I do their hair every other Tuesday and today is Tuesday, right?"

"All day."

"Wonder where they are, then?"

The woman slipped a hand under her skirt to reknot the top of her stocking. "Off somewhere trying to sound like they ain't from Cottown."

"Where you from?" Violet was impressed with the woman's ability to secure her hose with one hand.

"Cottown. Knew both of them from way back. Come up here, the whole family act like they never set eyes on me before. Comes from handling money instead of a broom which I better get to before I lose this no-count job. O Jesus." She sighed heavily. "Leave a note, why don't you? Don't count on me to let them know you was here. We don't speak if we don't have to." She buttoned her coat, then moved her hand in a suit-yourself wave when Violet said she'd wait a bit longer.

Violet sat down on the wide steps nestling her bag of irons and oil and shampoo in the space behind her calves.

When the baby was in her arms, she inched its blanket up around the cheeks against the threat of wind too cool for its honey-sweet, butter-colored face. Its big-eyed noncommittal stare made her smile. Comfort settled itself in her stomach and a kind of skipping, running light traveled her veins.

Joe will love this, she thought. Love it. And quickly her mind raced ahead to their bedroom and what was in there she could use for a crib until she got a real one. There was gentle soap in the sample case already so she could bathe him in the kitchen right away. Him? Was it a him? Violet lifted her head to the sky and laughed with the excitement in store when she got home to look. It was the laugh—loose and loud—that confirmed the theft for some and discredited it for others. Would a sneak-thief woman stealing a baby call attention to herself like that at a corner not a hundred yards away from the wicker carriage she took it from? Would a kindhearted innocent woman take a stroll with an infant she was asked to watch while its older sister ran back in the house, and laugh like that?

The sister was screaming in front of her house, drawing neighbors and passersby to her as she scanned the sidewalk— up and down—shouting "Philly! Philly's gone! She took Philly!" She kept her hands on the baby buggy's push bar, unwilling to run whichever way her gaze landed, as though, if she left the carriage, empty except for the record she dropped in it—the one she had dashed back into the house for and that was now on the pillow where her baby brother used to be— maybe it too would disappear.

"She who?" somebody asked. "Who took him?"

"A woman! I was gone one minute. Not even one! I asked her . . . I said . . . and she said okay . . . !"

"You left a whole live baby with a stranger to go get a record?" The disgust in the man's voice brought tears to the girl's eyes. "I hope your mama tears you up and down."

Opinions, decisions popped through the crowd like struck matches.

"Ain't got the sense of a gnat."

"Who misraised you?"

"Call the cops."

"What for?"

"They can at least look."

"Will you just look at what she left that baby for."

"What is it?"

" 'The Trombone Blues.' "

"Have mercy."

"She'll know more about blues than any trombone when her mama gets home."

The little knot of people, more and more furious at the stupid, irresponsible sister, at the cops, at the record lying where a baby should be, had just about forgotten the kidnapper when a man at the curb said, "That her?" He pointed to Violet at the corner and it was when everybody turned toward where his finger led that Violet, tickled by the pleasure of discovery she was soon to have, threw back her head and laughed out loud.

The proof of her innocence lay in the bag of hairdressing utensils, which remained on the steps where Violet had been waiting.

"Would I leave my bag, with the stuff I make my living with if I was stealing your baby? You think I'm crazy?" Violet's eyes, squinted and smoking with fury, stared right at the sister. "In fact, I would have taken everything. Buggy too, if that's what I was doing."

It sounded true and likely to most of the crowd, especially those who faulted the sister. The woman had left her bag and was merely walking the baby while the older sister—too silly to be minding a child anyway—ran back in her house for a record to play for a friend. And who knew what else was going on in the head of a girl too dumb to watch a baby sleep?

It sounded unlikely and mighty suspicious to a minority.

Why would she walk that far, if she was just playing, rocking the baby? Why not pace in front of the house like normal? And what kind of laugh was that? What kind? If she could laugh like that, she could forget not only her bag but the whole world.

The sister, chastised, took baby, buggy, and "Trombone Blues" back up the steps.

Violet, triumphant and angry, snatched her bag, saying, "Last time I do anybody a favor on this block. Watch your own damn babies!" And she thought of it that way ever after, remembering the incident as an outrage to her character. The makeshift crib, the gentle soap left her mind. The memory of the light, however, that had skipped through her veins came back now and then, and once in a while, on an overcast day, when certain corners in the room resisted lamplight; when the red beans in the pot seemed to be taking forever to soften, she imagined a brightness that could be carried in her arms. Distributed, if need be, into places dark as the bottom of a well.

Joe never learned of Violet's public crazinesses. Stuck, Gistan and other male friends passed word of the incidents to each other, but couldn't bring themselves to say much more to him than "How *is* Violet? Doing okay, is she?" Her private cracks, however, were known to him.

I call them cracks because that is what they were. Not openings or breaks, but dark fissures in the globe light of the day. She wakes up in the morning and sees with perfect clarity a string of small, well-lit scenes. In each one something specific is being done: food things, work things; customers and acquaintances are encountered, places entered. But she does not see herself doing these things. She sees them being done. The globe light holds and bathes each scene, and it can be assumed that at the curve where the light stops is a solid foundation. In truth, there is no foundation at all, but alleyways, crevices one steps across all the time. But the globe light is imperfect too. Closely examined it shows seams, ill-glued cracks and weak places beyond which is anything. Anything at all. Sometimes when Violet isn't paying attention she stumbles onto these cracks, like the time when, instead of putting her left heel forward, she stepped back and folded her legs in order to sit in the street.

She didn't use to be that way. She had been a snappy, determined girl and a hardworking young woman, with the snatch-gossip tongue of a beautician. She liked, and had, to get her way. She had chosen Joe and refused to go back home once she'd seen him taking shape in early light. She had butted their way out of the Tenderloin district into a spacious uptown apartment promised to another family by sitting out the landlord, haunting his doorway. She collected customers by going up to them and describing her services ("I can do your hair better and cheaper, and do it when and where you want"). She argued butchers and wagon vendors into prime and extra ("Put that little end piece in. You weighing the stalks; I'm buying the leaf"). Long before Joe stood in the drugstore watching a girl buy candy, Violet had stumbled into a crack or two. Felt the anything-at-all begin in her mouth. Words connected only to themselves pierced an otherwise normal comment.

"I don't believe an eight has been out this month," she says, thinking about the daily number combinations. "Not one. Bound to come up soon, so I'm hanging an eight on everything."

"That's no way to play," says Joe. "Get you a combo and stay with it."

"No. Eight is due, I know it. Was all over the place in August—all summer, in fact. Now it's ready to come out of hiding."

"Suit yourself." Joe is examining a shipment of Cleopatra products.

"Got a mind to double it with an aught and two or three others just in case who is that pretty girl standing next to you?" She looks up at Joe expecting an answer.

"What?" He frowns. "What you say?"

"Oh." Violet blinks rapidly. "Nothing. I mean . . . nothing."

"Pretty girl?"

"Nothing, Joe. Nothing."

She means nothing can be done about it, but it was something. Something slight, but troublesome. Like the time Miss Haywood asked her what time could she do her granddaughter's hair and Violet said, "Two o'clock if the hearse is out of the way."

Extricating herself from these collapses is not too hard, because nobody presses her. Did they do the same? Maybe. Maybe everybody has a renegade tongue yearning to be on its own. Violet shuts up. Speaks less and less until "uh" or "have mercy" carry almost all of her part of a conversation. Less excusable than a wayward mouth is an independent hand that can find in a parrot's cage a knife lost for weeks. Violet is still as well as silent. Over time her silences annoy her husband, then puzzle him and finally depress him. He is married to a woman who speaks mainly to her birds. One of whom answers back: "I love you."

**O**r used to. When Violet threw out the birds, it left her not only without the canaries' company and the parrot's confession but also minus the routine of covering their cages, a habit that had become one of those necessary things for the night. The things that help you sleep all the way through it. Back-breaking labor might do it; or liquor. Surely a body—friendly if not familiar—lying next to you. Someone whose touch is a reassurance, not an affront or a nuisance. Whose heavy breathing neither enrages nor disgusts, but amuses you like that of a cherished pet. And rituals help too: door locking,

tidying up, cleaning teeth, arranging hair, but they are prelimi-
naries to the truly necessary things. Most people want to crash
into sleep. Get knocked into it with a fist of fatigue to avoid
a night of noisy silence, empty birdcages that don't need
wrapping in cloth, of bold unsmiling girls staring from the
mantelpiece.

For Violet, who never knew the girl, only her picture and
the personality she invented for her based on careful investiga-
tions, the girl's memory is a sickness in the house—everywhere
and nowhere. There is nothing for Violet to beat or hit and
when she has to, just has to strike it somehow, there is nothing
left but straw or a sepia print.

But for Joe it is different. That girl had been his necessary
thing for three months of nights. He remembers his memories
of her; how thinking about her as he lay in bed next to Violet
was the way he entered sleep. He minds her death, is so sorry
about it, but minded more the possibility of his memory failing
to conjure up the dearness. And he knows it will continue to
fade because it was already beginning to the afternoon he
hunted Dorcas down. After she said she wanted Coney Island
and rent parties and more of Mexico. Even then he was clinging to the quality of her sugar-flawed skin, the high wild bush
the bed pillows made of her hair, her bitten nails, the heartbreaking way she stood, toes pointed in. Even then, listening
to her talk, to the terrible things she said, he felt he was losing
the timbre of her voice and what happened to her eyelids when
they made love.

Now he lies in bed remembering every detail of that October
afternoon when he first met her, from start to finish, and over
and over. Not just because it is tasty, but because he is trying
to sear her into his mind, brand her there against future wear.

So that neither she nor the alive love of her will fade or scab over the way it had with Violet. For when Joe tries to remember the way it was when he and Violet were young, when they got married, decided to leave Vesper County and move up North to the City almost nothing comes to mind. He recalls dates, of course, events, purchases, activity, even scenes. But he has a tough time trying to catch what it felt like.

He had struggled a long time with that loss, believed he had resigned himself to it, had come to terms with the fact that old age would be not remembering what things felt like. That you could say, "I was scared to death," but you could not retrieve the fear. That you could replay in the brain the scene of ecstasy, of murder, of tenderness, but it was drained of everything but the language to say it in. He thought he had come to terms with that but he had been wrong. When he called on Sheila to deliver her Cleopatra order, he entered a roomful of laughing, teasing women—and there she was, standing at the door, holding it open for him—the same girl that had distracted him in the drugstore; the girl buying candy and ruining her skin had moved him so his eyes burned. Then, suddenly, there in Alice Manfred's doorway, she stood, toes pointing in, hair braided, not even smiling but welcoming him in for sure. For sure. Otherwise he would not have had the audacity, the nerve, to whisper to her at the door as he left.

It was a randy aggressiveness he had enjoyed because he had not used or needed it before. The ping of desire that surfaced along with his whisper through the closing door he began to curry. First he pocketed it, taking pleasure in knowing it was there. Then he unboxed it to bring out and admire at his leisure. He did not yearn or pine for the girl, rather he thought about her, and decided. Just as he had decided on his name, the walnut tree he and Victory slept in, a piece of bottomland, and when to head for the City, he decided on Dorcas. Regarding his marriage to Violet—he had not chosen that but was grateful, in fact, that he didn't have to; that Violet did it for him, helping him escape all the redwings in the county and the ripe silence that accompanied them.

They met in Vesper County, Virginia, under a walnut tree. She had been working in the fields like everybody else, and stayed past picking time to live with a family twenty miles away from her own. They knew people in common; and suspected they had at least one relative in common. They were drawn together because they had been put together, and all they decided for themselves was when and where to meet at night.

Violet and Joe left Tyrell, a railway stop through Vesper County, in 1906, and boarded the colored section of the Southern Sky. When the train trembled approaching the water surrounding the City, they thought it was like them: nervous at having gotten there at last, but terrified of what was on the other side. Eager, a little scared, they did not even nap during the fourteen hours of a ride smoother than a rocking cradle. The quick darkness in the carriage cars when they shot through a tunnel made them wonder if maybe there was a wall ahead to crash into or a cliff hanging over nothing. The train shivered with them at the thought but went on and sure enough there was ground up ahead and the trembling became the dancing under their feet. Joe stood up, his fingers clutching the baggage rack above his head. He felt the dancing better that way, and told Violet to do the same.

They were hanging there, a young country couple, laughing and tapping back at the tracks, when the attendant came through, pleasant but unsmiling now that he didn't have to smile in this car full of colored people.

"Breakfast in the dining car. Breakfast in the dining car. Good morning. Full breakfast in the dining car." He held a carriage blanket over his arm and from underneath it drew a pint bottle of milk, which he placed in the hands of a young woman with a baby asleep across her knees. "Full breakfast."

He never got his way, this attendant. He wanted the whole coach to file into the dining car, now that they could. Immediately, now that they were out of Delaware and a long way from Maryland there would be no green-as-poison curtain separating the colored people eating from the rest of the diners. The cooks would not feel obliged to pile extra helpings on the plates headed for the curtain; three lemon slices in the iced tea, two pieces of coconut cake arranged to look like one—to take the sting out of the curtain; homey it up with a little extra on the plate. Now, skirting the City, there were no green curtains; the whole car could be full of colored people and everybody on a first-come first-serve basis. If only they would. If only they would tuck those little boxes and baskets underneath the seat; close those paper bags, for once, put the bacon-stuffed biscuits back into the cloth they were wrapped in, and troop single file through the five cars ahead on into the dining car, where the table linen was at least as white as the sheets they dried on juniper bushes; where the napkins were folded with a crease as stiff as the ones they ironed for Sunday dinner; where the gravy was as smooth as their own, and the biscuits did not take second place to the bacon-stuffed ones they wrapped in cloth. Once in a while it happened. Some well-shod woman with two young girls, a preacherly kind of man with a watch chain and a rolled-brim hat might stand up, adjust their clothes and weave through the coaches toward the tables, foamy white with heavy silvery knives and forks. Presided over and waited upon by a black man who did not have to lace his dignity with a smile.

Joe and Violet wouldn't think of it—paying money for a meal they had not missed and that required them to sit still at, or worse, separated by, a table. Not now. Not entering the lip of the City dancing all the way. Her hip bones rubbed his thigh as they stood in the aisle unable to stop smiling. They weren't even there yet and already the City was speaking to them. They were dancing. And like a million others, chests pounding, tracks controlling their feet, they stared out the windows for first sight of the City that danced with them, proving already how much it loved them. Like a million more they could hardly wait to get there and love it back.

Some were slow about it and traveled from Georgia to Illinois, to the City, back to Georgia, out to San Diego and finally, shaking their heads, surrendered themselves to the City. Others knew right away that it was for them, this City and no other. They came on a whim because there it was and why not? They came after much planning, many letters written to and from, to make sure and know how and how much and where. They came for a visit and forgot to go back to tall cotton or short. Discharged with or without honor, fired with or without severance, dispossessed with or without notice, they hung around for a while and then could not imagine themselves anywhere else. Others came because a relative or hometown buddy said, Man, you best see this place before you die; or, We got room now, so pack your suitcase and don't bring no high-top shoes.

However they came, when or why, the minute the leather of their soles hit the pavement—there was no turning around. Even if the room they rented was smaller than the heifer's stall and darker than a morning privy, they stayed to look at their number, hear themselves in an audience, feel themselves moving down the street among hundreds of others who moved the stoplight but looks up and down the street before stepping off the curb; how men accommodate themselves to tall buildings and wee porches, what a woman looks like moving in a crowd, or how shocking her profile is against the backdrop of the East River. The restfulness in kitchen chores when she knows the lamp oil or the staple is just around the corner and not seven miles away; the amazement of throwing open the window and being hypnotized for hours by people on the street below.

Little of that makes for love, but it does pump desire. The woman who churned a man's blood as she leaned all alone on a fence by a country road might not expect even to catch his eye in the City. But if she is clipping quickly down the big-city street in heels, swinging her purse, or sitting on a stoop with a cool beer in her hand, dangling her shoe from the toes of her foot, the man, reacting to her posture, to soft skin on stone, the weight of the building stressing the delicate, dangling shoe, is captured. And he'd think it was the woman he wanted, and not some combination of curved stone, and a swinging, high-heeled shoe moving in and out of sunlight. He would know right away the deception, the trick of shapes and light and movement, but it wouldn't matter at all because the deception was part of it too. Anyway, he could feel his lungs going in and out. There is no air in the City but there is breath, and every morning it races through him like laughing gas brightening his eyes, his talk, and his expectations. In no time at all he forgets little pebbly creeks and apple trees so old they lay their branches along the ground and you have to reach down or stoop to pick the fruit. He forgets a sun that used to slide up like the yolk of a good country egg, thick and red-orange at the bottom of the sky, and he doesn't miss it, doesn't look up to see what happened to it or to stars made irrelevant by the light of thrilling, wasteful street lamps.

That kind of fascination, permanent and out of control, seizes children, young girls, men of every description, mothers, brides, and barfly women, and if they have their way and get to the City, they feel more like themselves, more like the people they always believed they were. Nothing can pry them away from that; the City is what they want it to be: thriftless, warm, scary and full of amiable strangers. No wonder they forget pebbly creeks and when they do not forget the sky completely think of it as a tiny piece of information about the time of day or night.

But I have seen the City do an unbelievable sky. Redcaps and dining-car attendants who wouldn't think of moving out of the City sometimes go on at great length about country skies they have seen from the windows of trains. But there is nothing to beat what the City can make of a nightsky. It can empty itself of surface, and more like the ocean than the ocean itself, go deep, starless. Close up on the tops of buildings, near, nearer than the cap you are wearing, such a citysky presses and retreats, presses and retreats, making me think of the free but illegal love of sweethearts before they are discovered. Looking at it, this nightsky booming over a glittering city, it's possible for me to avoid dreaming of what I know is in the ocean, and the bays and tributaries it feeds: the two-seat aeroplanes, nose down in the muck, pilot and passenger staring at schools of passing bluefish; money, soaked and salty in canvas bags, or waving their edges gently from metal bands made to hold them forever. They are down there, along with yellow flowers that eat water beetles and eggs floating away from thrashing fins; along with the children who made a mistake in the parents they chose; along with slabs of Carrara pried from unfashionable buildings. There are bottles too, made of glass beautiful enough to rival stars I cannot see above me because the citysky has hidden them. Otherwise, if it wanted to, it could show me stars cut from the lamé gowns of chorus girls, or mirrored in the eyes of sweethearts furtive and happy under the pressure of a deep, touchable sky.

But that's not all a citysky can do. It can go purple and keep an orange heart so the clothes of the people on the streets glow like dance-hall costumes. I have seen women stir shirts into boiled starch or put the tiniest stitches into their hose while a girl straightens the hair of her sister at the stove, and all the while heaven, unnoticed and as beautiful as an Iroquois, drifts past their windows. As well as the windows where sweethearts, free and illegal, tell each other things.

Twenty years after Joe and Violet train-danced on into the City, they were still a couple but barely speaking to each other, let alone laughing together or acting like the ground was a dance-hall floor. Convinced that he alone remembers those days, and wants them back, aware of what it looked like but not at all of what it felt like, he coupled himself elsewhere. He rented a room from a neighbor who knows the exact cost of her discretion. Six hours a week he has purchased. Time for the citysky to move from a thin ice blue to purple with a heart of gold. And time enough, when the sun sinks, to tell his new love things he never told his wife.

Important things like how the hibiscus smells on the bank of a stream at dusk; how he can barely see his knees poking through the holes in his trousers in that light, so what makes him think he can see her hand even if she did decide to shove it through the bushes and confirm, for once and for all, that she was indeed his mother? And even though the confirmation would shame him, it would make him the happiest boy in Virginia. If she decided, that is, to show him it, to listen for once to what he was saying to her and then do it, say some kind of yes, even if it was no, so he would know. And how he was willing to take that chance of being humiliated and grateful at the same time, because the confirmation would mean both. Her hand, her fingers poking through the blossoms, touching his; maybe letting him touch hers. He wouldn't have grabbed it, snatched it and dragged her out from behind the bushes. Maybe that's what she was afraid of, but he wouldn't have done that, and he told her so. Just a sign, he said, just show me your hand, he said, and I'll know don't you know I have to know? She wouldn't have to say anything, although nobody had ever heard her say anything; it wouldn't have to be words; he didn't need words or even want them because he knew how they could lie, could heat your blood and disappear. She wouldn't even have to say the word "mother." Nothing like that. All she had to do was give him a sign, her hand thrust through the leaves, the white flowers, would be enough to say that she knew him to be the one, the son she had fourteen years ago, and ran away from, but not too far. Just far enough away to annoy everybody because she was not completely gone, and close enough to scare everybody because she creeps about and hides and touches and laughs a low sweet babygirl laugh in the cane.

Maybe she did it. Maybe those were her fingers moving like that in the bush, not twigs, but in light so small he could not see his knees poking through the holes in his trousers, maybe he missed the sign that would have been some combination of shame and pleasure, at least, and not the inside nothing he traveled with from then on, except for the fall of 1925 when he had somebody to tell it to. Somebody called Dorcas with hooves tracing her cheekbones and who knew better than people his own age what that inside nothing was like. And who filled it for him, just as he filled it for her, because she had it too.

Maybe her nothing was worse since she knew her mother, and had even been slapped in the face by her for some sass she could not remember. But she did remember, and told him so, about the slap across her face, the pop and sting of it and how it burned. How it burned, she told him. And of all the slaps she got, that one was the one she remembered best because it was the last. She leaned out the window of her best girlfriend's house because the shouts were not part of what she was dreaming. They were outside her head, across the street. Like the running. Everybody running. For water? Buckets? The fire engine, polished and poised in another part of town? There was no getting in that house where her clothespin dolls lay in a row. In a cigar box. But she tried anyway to get them. Barefoot, in the dress she had slept in, she ran to get them, and yelled to her mother that the box of dolls, the box of dolls was up there on the dresser can we get them? Mama?

She cries again and Joe holds her close. The Iroquois sky passes the windows, and if they do see it, it crayon-colors their love. That would be when, after a decent silence, he would lift his sample case of Cleopatra from the chair and tease her before opening it, holding up the lid so she could not see right away what he has hidden under the jars and perfume-sweet boxes; the present he has brought for her. That is the little bow that ties up their day at the same time the citysky is changing its orange heart to black in order to hide its stars for the longest time before passing them out one by one by one, like gifts.

By that time she has pushed back his cuticles, cleaned his nails and painted them with clear polish. She has cried a little talking about East St. Louis, and cheers herself up with his fingernails. She likes to know that the hands lifting and turning her under the blanket have been done by her. Lotioned by her with cream from a jar of something from his sample case. She rears up and, taking his face in her hands, kisses the lids of each of his two-color eyes. One for me, she says, and one for you. One for me and one for you. Gimme this, I give you that. Gimme this. Gimme this.

They try not to shout, but can't help it. Sometimes he covers her mouth with the palm of his hand so no one passing in the hall will hear her, and if he can, if he thinks of it in time, he bites the pillow to stop his own yell. If he can. Sometimes he thinks he has stopped it, because the corner of the pillow is in his mouth all right, and then he hears himself breathing in and out, in and out, at the tail end of a shout that could only have come from his weary throat.

She laughs at that, laughs and laughs before she straddles his back to pound it with her fists. Then when she is exhausted and he half asleep, she leans down, her lips behind his ear, and makes plans. Mexico, she whispers. I want you to take me to Mexico. Too loud, he murmurs. No, no, she says, it's just right. How you know? he demands. I heard people say, people say the tables are round and have white cloths over them and wee baby lampshades. It don't open till way past your bedtime, he says smiling. This my bedtime, she says, Mexico people sleep in the day, take me. They're in there till church time Sunday morning and no whitepeople can get in, and the boys who play sometimes get up and dance with you. Uh oh, he says. What uh oh, she asks. I just want to dance with you and then go sit at a round table with a lamp on it. People can see us, he says, those little lamps you talking about big enough to show who's there.

You always say that, she giggles, like last time and nobody even looked at us they were having such a good time and Mexico is better even because nobody can see under the tablecloth, can they? Can they? If you don't want to dance, we can just sit there at the table, looking siditty by the lamplight and listen to the music and watch the people. Nobody can see under the tablecloth. Joe, Joe, take me, say you'll take me. How you going to get out the house? he asks. I'll figure it, she croons, just like always, just say yes. Well, he says, well, no point in picking the apple if you don't want to see how it taste. How does it taste, Joe? she asks. And he opens his eyes.

The door is locked and Malvonne will not be back from her 40th Street offices until way after midnight, a thought that excites them: that if it were possible they could almost spend the night together. If Alice Manfred or Violet took a trip, say, then the two of them could postpone the gift he gives her on into the darkest part of night until, smelling of Oxydol and paste wax, Malvonne came back from her offices. As it is, having made their plans for Mexico, Dorcas tips out the door and down the steps before Violet has finished her evening heads and come home around seven to find that Joe has already changed the birds' water and covered their cages. On those nights Joe does not mind lying awake next to his silent wife because his thoughts are with this young good God young girl who both blesses his life and makes him wish he had never been born.


Malvonne lived alone with newspapers and other people's stories printed in small books. When she was not making her office building sparkle, she was melding the print stories with her keen observation of the people around her. Very little escaped this woman who rode the trolley against traffic at 6:00 p.m.; who examined the trash baskets of powerful white-men, looked at photographs of women and children on their desks. Heard their hallway conversation, and the bathroom laughter penetrating the broom closet like fumes from her bottle of ammonia. She examined their bottles and resituated the flasks tucked under cushions and behind books whose words were printed in two columns. She knew who had a passion for justice as well as ladies' undergarments, who loved his wife and who shared one. The one who fought with his son and would not speak to his father. For they did not cover the mouthpiece when they talked on the telephone to ask her to leave as she inched her way down the halls, into their offices, nor did they drop their voices to confidential whispers when they worked late doing what they called the "real" business.

But Malvonne was not interested in them; she simply noticed. Her interest lay in the neighborhood people.

Before Sweetness changed his name from William Younger to Little Caesar, he robbed a mailbox on 130th Street. Looking for postal notes, cash or what, Malvonne couldn't imagine. She had raised him from the time he was seven and a better-behaved nephew no one could have wished for. In the daytime, anyway. But some of the things he got into during Malvonne's office shift from 6:00 to 2:30 a.m. she would never know; others she learned after he left for Chicago, or was it San Diego, or some other city ending with O.

One of the things she learned explained where her grocery bag had gone—the twenty-pound salt sack she carried, nicely laundered and folded in her purse, to market. When she found it, behind the radiator in Sweetness' room, it was full of uncan-

celed letters. As she examined them her first impulse was to try
to reseal and refold their contents and get them quickly into
a mailbox. She ended, however, by reading each one including
those Sweetness had not bothered to tear open. Except for the
pleasure of recognizing the signatures, the reading turned out
to be flatly uninteresting.

Dear Helen Moore: questions about Helen's health; answers
about the writer's own. weather. deceptions. promises. love
and then the signer, as though Helen received so much mail,
had so many relatives and friends she couldn't remember
them all, identified her or him self in large, slanting script
your devoted sister, Mrs. something something; or your loving
father in New York, L. Henderson Woodward.

A few of them required action on Malvonne's part. A voca-
tional school student had sent a matchbook application to a
correspondence law school along with the required, but now
missing, dollar bill. Malvonne didn't have a dollar to spare for
Lila Spencer's entrance fee, but she did worry that if the girl
did not get to be a lawyer she would end up with an apron job.
So she added a note in her own hand, saying, "I do not have
the one dollar right this minute, but as soon as I hear that
you received this application and agreed that I should come, I
will have it by then if you tell me you don't have it and really
need it."

The sad moment came when she read the letter to Panama
from Winsome Clark complaining to her husband who
worked in the Canal Zone about the paltriness and insuffi-
ciency of the money he had sent her—money of so little help
she was giving up her job, picking up the children and returning to Barbados. Malvonne could feel the wall of life pressed
up against the woman's palms; feel her hands bashed tender

from pounding it; her hips constrained by the clutch of small children. "I don't know what to do," she wrote. "Nothing I do make a difference. Auntie make a racket about everything. I am besides myself. The children is miserable as me. the money you senting can not keeping all us afloat. Us drowning here and may as well drown at home where your mother is and mine and big trees."

Oh, thought Malvonne, she dreams of big trees in Barbados? Bigger than those in the park? Must be jungle for sure.

Winsome said she was "sorry your good friend dead in the big fire and pray for he and you how come so much colored people dying where whites doing great stuff. I guess you thinking that aint no grown person question. Send anything else you get to Wyndham Road where I and babies be two pay envelopes from now. Sonny say he have shoe shining money for his own passage so dont worry none except to stay among the quick. your dearest wife Mrs. Winsome Clark."

Malvonne didn't know Winsome or anybody on the 300 block of Edgecombe Avenue, although one building there was full of rich West Indians who kept pretty much to themselves and from whose windows came the odor of seasonings she didn't recognize. The point now was to get Winsome's notice of departure, already two pay envelopes ago, to Panama before any more cash went to Edgecombe where the aunt might get hold of it, and who knows, if she was as hateful as Winsome told it (watering down the children's milk on the sly and whipping the five-year-old for mishandling the hot, heavy pressing iron) she might keep the money for herself. Malvonne resealed the letter carefully and thought she would add another penny stamp in case that would help get it to Panama faster.

There was only one letter to sweat over and to wonder about

the woman who could write down such words, let alone do what she had done and promised more of. The writer lived in the same building as her lover. Malvonne did not know what made her waste a three-cent stamp other than the pleasure of knowing the government was delivering her heat. Perspiring and breathing lightly, Malvonne forced herself to read the letter several times. The problem was whether to send on to Mr. M. Sage (that was what he was called on the envelope; on the sheet of tablet paper he was called "daddy") his letter from "your always Hot Steam." A month had passed since it was written and Steam might be wondering if she had gone too far. Or had Daddy Sage and Steam done more of those lowdown sticky things in the meantime? Finally she decided to mail it with a note of her own attached—urging caution and directing daddy's attention to a clipping from *Opportunity Magazine*.

It was while she was preparing this anonymous advice that Joe Trace knocked on her door.

"How you doing, Malvonne?"

"Not complaining. How about you?"

"Can I step in? Got a proposition for you." He smiled his easy, country smile.

"I don't have a nickel, Joe."

"No." He held up his hand and walked past her into the living room. "I'm not selling. See? I don't even have my case with me."

"Oh, well, then." Malvonne followed him to the sofa. "Have a seat."

"But if I was," he said, "what would you like? If you had a nickel, I mean."

"That purple soap was kind of nice."

"You got it!"

"Went in a flash, though," said Malvonne.

"Fancy soap is fancy. Not meant to last."

"Guess not."

"I got two left. I'll bring them up right away."

"What brings this on? You ain't selling you giving away free for what reason?" Malvonne looked at the clock on the mantel, figuring out how much time she had to talk to Joe and get her letters mailed before leaving for work.

"A favor you might say."

"Or I might not say?"

"You will. It's a favor to me, but a little pocket change for you."

Malvonne laughed. "Out with it, Joe. This something Violet ain't in on?"

"Well. She. This is. Vi is. I'm not going to disturb her with this, you know?"

"No. Tell me."

"Well. I'd like to rent your place."

"What?"

"Just a afternoon or two, every now and then. While you at work. But I'll pay for the whole month."

"What you up to, Joe? You know I work at night." Maybe it was a trick name and a trick address, and Joe was "Daddy" picking up mail somewhere else and telling Steam his name was Sage.

"I know your shift's at night, but you leave at four."

"If it's nice enough to walk I do. Most time I catch the five-thirty."

"It wouldn't be every day, Malvonne."

"It wouldn't be no day. I don't think I like what you proposing."

"Two dollars each and every month."

"You think I need your money or your flimsy soap?"

"No, no, Malvonne. Look. Let me explain. Ain't many women like you understand the problems men have with their wives."

"What kind of problem?"

"Well. Violet. You know how funny she been since her Change."

"Violet funny way before that. Funny in 1920 as I recall."

"Yeah, well. But now—"

"Joe, you want to rent Sweetness' room to bring another woman in here while I'm gone just cause Violet don't want no part of you. What kind a person you think I am? Okay there's no love lost between Violet and me, but I take her part, not yours, you old dog."

"Listen here, Malvonne—"

"Who is she?"

"Nobody. I mean, I don't know yet. I just thought—"

"Ha. If you lucked up on some fool you'd have a place? That's what you thought?"

"Sort of. I may not ever use it. But I'd like it in case. I'd pay the money whether I used it or not."

"Fifty cents in certain houses get you the woman, the floor, the walls *and* the bed. Two dollars get you a woman on a store-bought scooter if you want it."

"Aw, no, Malvonne. No. You got me all wrong. I don't want nobody off the street. Good Lord."

"No? Who do you think but a streetwalker go traipsing off with you?"

"Malvonne, I'm just hoping for a lady friend. Somebody to talk to."

"Up over Violet's head? Why you ask me, a woman, for a

hot bed. Seem like you'd want to ask some nasty man like yourself for that."

"I thought about it, but I don't know no man live alone and it ain't nasty. Come on, girl. You driving me to the street. What I'm asking is better, ain't it? Every now and then I visit with a respectable lady."

"Respectable?"

"That's right, respectable. Maybe she's lonely though, or got children, or—"

"Or a husband with a hammer."

"Nobody like that."

"And if Violet finds out, what am I supposed to say?"

"She won't."

"Spose I tell her."

"You won't. Why would you do that? I'm still taking care of her. Nobody getting hurt. And you get two quarters as well as somebody looking out for your place while you gone in case Sweetness come back or somebody come in here looking for him and don't care what he tear up cause you a woman."

"Violet would kill me."

"You don't have nothing to do with it. You never know when I come and you won't see anything. Everything be like it was when you left, except if there's some little thing you want fixed you want me to do. You won't see nothing but some change on the table there that I leave for a reason you don't know nothing about, see?"

"Uh huh."

"Try me, Malvonne. One week. No, two. If you change your mind anytime, anytime, just leave my money on the table and I'll know you mean me to stop and sure as you live your door key will be laying in its place."

"Uh huh."

"It's your house. You tell me what you want done, what you want fixed, and you tell me what you don't like. But believe me, girl, you won't know when or if I come or go. Except, maybe, your faucet don't drip no more."

"Uh huh."

"Only thing you know is every Saturday, starting now, you got two more quarters to put in your sugar bowl."

"Mighty high price for a little conversation."

"You be surprised what you can save if you like me and don't drink, smoke, gamble or tithe."

"Maybe you should."

"I don't want nothing ornery, and I don't want to be hanging out in clubs and such. I just want some nice female company."

"You seem mighty sure you going to find it."

Joe smiled. "If I don't, still no harm. No harm at all."

"No messages."

"What?"

"No notes to pass. No letters. I'm not delivering any messages."

"Course not. I don't want a pen pal. We talk here or we don't talk at all."

"Suppose something comes up and you want or she wants to call it off?"

"Don't worry about that."

"Suppose she gets sick and can't come and needs to let you know."

"I wait, then I leave."

"Suppose one of the kids gets sick and can't nobody find the mama cause she holed up somewhere with you?"

"Who say she got kids?"

"Don't you take up with no woman if her kids is little, Joe."

"All right."

"It's asking too much of me."

"You don't have to think about none of it. You ain't in it. You ever see me mess with anybody? I been in this building longer than you have. You ever hear a word against me from any woman? I sell beauty products all over town, you ever hear tell of me chasing a woman? No. You never heard that, because it never happened. Now I'm trying to lighten my life a little with a good lady, like a decent man would, that's all. Tell me what's wrong with that?"

"Violet's wrong with it."

"Violet takes better care of her parrot than she does me. Rest of the time, she's cooking pork I can't eat, or pressing hair I can't stand the smell of. Maybe that's the way it goes with people been married long as we have. But the quiet. I can't take the quiet. She don't hardly talk anymore, and I ain't allowed near her. Any other man be running around, stepping out every night, you know that. I ain't like that. I ain't."

Of course he wasn't, but he did it anyway. Sneaked around, plotted, and stepped out every night the girl demanded. They went to Mexico, Sook's and clubs whose names changed every week—and he was not alone. He became a Thursday man and Thursday men are satisfied. I can tell from their look some outlaw love is about to be, or already has been, satisfied. Weekends and other days of the week are possibilities but Thursday is a day to be counted on. I used to think it was because domestic workers had Thursday off and could lie abed mornings as was out of the question on weekends, when either they slept in the houses they worked in or rose so early to arrive they had no time for breakfast or any kind of play. But I noticed it was also true of men whose women were not servants and day workers, but barmaids and restaurant cooks with Sunday-Monday free; schoolteachers, café singers, office typists and market-stall women all looked forward to Saturday off. The City thinks about and arranges itself for the weekend: the day before payday, the day after payday, the pre-Sabbath activity, the closed shop and the quiet school hall; barred bank vaults and offices locked in darkness.

So why is it on Thursday that the men look satisfied? Perhaps it's the artificial rhythm of the week—perhaps there is something so phony about the seven-day cycle the body pays no attention to it, preferring triplets, duets, quartets, anything but a cycle of seven that has to be broken into human parts and the break comes on Thursday. Irresistible. The outrageous expectations and inflexible demands of the weekend are null on Thursday. People look forward to weekends for connections, revisions and separations even though many of these activities are accompanied by bruises and even a spot of blood, for excitement runs high on Friday or Saturday.

But for satisfaction pure and deep, for balance in pleasure and comfort, Thursday can't be beat—as is clear from the capable expression on the faces of the men and their conquering stride in the street. They seem to achieve some sort of completion on that day that makes them steady enough on their feet to appear graceful even if they are not. They command the center of the sidewalk; whistle softly in unlit doors.

It doesn't last of course, and twenty-four hours later they are frightened again and restoring themselves with any helplessness within reach. So the weekends, destined to disappoint, are strident, sullen, sprinkled with bruises and dots of blood. The regrettable things, the coarse and sour remarks, the words that become active boils in the heart—none of that takes place on Thursday. I suppose the man for whom it is named would hate it, but the fact is, his day is a day for love in the City and the company of satisfied men. They make the women smile. The tunes whistled through perfect teeth are remembered, picked up later and repeated at the kitchen stove. In front of the mirror near the door one of them will turn her head to the side, and sway, enchanted with her waistline and the shape of her hips.

Up there, in that part of the City—which is the part they came for—the right tune whistled in a doorway or lifting up from the circles and grooves of a record can change the weather. From freezing to hot to cool.

**L**ike that day in July, almost nine years back, when the beautiful men were cold. In typical summer weather, sticky and bright, Alice Manfred stood for three hours on Fifth Avenue marveling at the cold black faces and listening to drums saying what the graceful women and the marching men could not. What was possible to say was already in print on a banner that repeated a couple of promises from the Declaration of Independence and waved over the head of its bearer. But what was meant came from the drums. It was July in 1917 and the beautiful faces were cold and quiet; moving slowly into the space the drums were building for them.

During the march it seemed to Alice as though the day passed, the night too, and still she stood there, the hand of the little girl in her own, staring into each cold face that passed. The drums and the freezing faces hurt her, but hurt was better than fear and Alice had been frightened for a long time—first she was frightened of Illinois, then of Springfield, Massachusetts, then Eleventh Avenue, Third Avenue, Park Avenue. Recently she had begun to feel safe nowhere south of 110th Street, and Fifth Avenue was for her the most fearful of all. That was where whitemen leaned out of motor cars with folded dollar bills peeping from their palms. It was where salesmen touched her and only her as though she were part of the goods they had condescended to sell her; it was the tissue required if the management was generous enough to let you try on a blouse (but no hat) in a store. It was where she, a woman of fifty and independent means, had no surname. Where women who spoke English said, "Don't sit there, honey, you never know what they have." And women who knew no English at all and would never own a pair of silk stockings moved away from her if she sat next to them on the trolley.

Now, down Fifth Avenue from curb to curb, came a tide of cold black faces, speechless and unblinking because what they meant to say but did not trust themselves to say the drums said for them, and what they had seen with their own eyes and through the eyes of others the drums described to a T. The hurt hurt her, but the fear was gone at last. Fifth Avenue was put into focus now and so was her protection of the newly orphaned girl in her charge.

From then on she hid the girl's hair in braids tucked under, lest whitemen see it raining round her shoulders and push dollar-wrapped fingers toward her. She instructed her about deafness and blindness—how valuable and necessary they were in the company of whitewomen who spoke English and those who did not, as well as in the presence of their children. Taught her how to crawl along the walls of buildings, disappear into doorways, cut across corners in choked traffic—how to do anything, move anywhere to avoid a whiteboy over the age of eleven. Much of this she could effect with her dress, but as the girl grew older, more elaborate specifications had to be put in place. High-heeled shoes with the graceful straps across the arch, the vampy hats closed on the head with saucy brims framing the face, makeup of any kind—all of that was outlawed in Alice Manfred's house. Especially the coats slung low in the back and not buttoned, but clutched, like a bathrobe or a towel around the body, forcing the women who wore them to look like they had just stepped out of the bathtub and were already ready for bed.

Privately, Alice admired them, the coats and the women who wore them. She sewed linings into these coats, when she felt like working, and she had to look twice over her shoulder when the Gay Northeasters and the City Belles strolled down Seventh Avenue, they were so handsome. But this envy-streaked pleasure Alice closeted, and never let the girl see how she admired those ready-for-bed-in-the-street clothes. And she told the Miller sisters, who kept small children during the day for mothers who worked out of the house, what her feelings were. They did not need persuading, having been looking forward to the Day of Judgment for a dozen years, and expecting its sweet relief any minute now. They had lists of every restaurant, diner and club that sold liquor and were not above reporting owners and customers to the police until they discovered that such news, in the Racket Squad, was not only annoying, it was redundant.

When Alice Manfred collected the little girl from the Miller sisters, on those evenings following the days her fine stitching was solicited, the three women sat down in the kitchen to hum and sigh over cups of Postum at the signs of Imminent Demise: such as not just ankles but knees in full view; lip rouge red as hellfire; burnt matchsticks rubbed on eyebrows; fingernails tipped with blood—you couldn't tell the streetwalkers from the mothers. And the men, you know, the things they thought nothing of saying out loud to any woman who passed by could not be repeated before children. They did not know for sure, but they suspected that the dances were beyond nasty because the music was getting worse and worse with each passing season the Lord waited to make Himself known. Songs that used to start in the head and fill the heart had dropped on down, down to places below the sash and the buckled belts. Lower and lower, until the music was so lowdown you had to shut your windows and just suffer the summer sweat when the men in shirtsleeves propped themselves in window frames, or clustered on rooftops, in alleyways, on stoops and in the apartments of relatives playing the lowdown stuff that signaled Imminent Demise. Or when a woman with a baby on her shoulder and a skillet in her hand sang "Turn to my pillow where my sweet-man used to be . . . how long, how long, how long." Because you could hear it everywhere. Even if you lived, as Alice Man-fred and the Miller sisters did, on Clifton Place, with a leafy sixty-foot tree every hundred feet, a quiet street with no fewer than five motor cars parked at the curb, you could still hear it, and there was no mistaking what it did to the children under their care—cocking their heads and swaying ridiculous, un-formed hips.

Alice thought the lowdown music (and in Illinois it was worse than here) had something to do with the silent black women and men marching down Fifth Avenue to advertise their anger over two hundred dead in East St. Louis, two of whom were her sister and brother-in-law, killed in the riots. So many whites killed the papers would not print the number.

Some said the rioters were disgruntled veterans who had fought in all-colored units, were refused the services of the YMCA, over there and over here, and came home to white violence more intense than when they enlisted and, unlike the battles they fought in Europe, stateside fighting was pitiless and totally without honor. Others said they were whites terrified by the wave of southern Negroes flooding the towns, searching for work and places to live. A few thought about it and said how perfect was the control of workers, none of whom (like crabs in a barrel requiring no lid, no stick, not even a monitoring observation) would get out of the barrel.

Alice, however, believed she knew the truth better than everybody. Her brother-in-law was not a veteran, and he had been living in East St. Louis since before the War. Nor did he need a whiteman's job—he owned a pool hall. As a matter of fact, he wasn't even in the riot; he had no weapons, confronted nobody on the street. He was pulled off a streetcar and stomped to death, and Alice's sister had just got the news and had gone back home to try and forget the color of his entrails, when her house was torched and she burned crispy in its flame. Her only child, a little girl named Dorcas, sleeping across the road with her very best girlfriend, did not hear the fire engine clanging and roaring down the street because when it was called it didn't come. But she must have seen the flames, must have, because the whole street was screaming. She never said. Never said anything about it. She went to two funerals in five days, and never said a word.

Alice thought, No. It wasn't the War and the disgruntled veterans; it wasn't the droves and droves of colored people flocking to paychecks and streets full of themselves. It was the music. The dirty, get-on-down music the women sang and the men played and both danced to, close and shameless or apart and wild. Alice was convinced and so were the Miller sisters as they blew into cups of Postum in the kitchen. It made you do unwise disorderly things. Just hearing it was like violating the law.

There had been none of that at the Fifth Avenue march. Just the drums and the Colored Boy Scouts passing out explanatory leaflets to whitemen in straw hats who needed to know what the freezing faces already knew. Alice had picked up a leaflet that had floated to the pavement, read the words, and shifted her weight at the curb. She read the words and looked at Dorcas. Looked at Dorcas and read the words again. What she read seemed crazy, out of focus. Some great gap lunged between the print and the child. She glanced between them struggling for the connection, something to close the distance between the silent staring child and the slippery crazy words. Then suddenly, like a rope cast for rescue, the drums spanned the distance, gathering them all up and connected them: Alice, Dorcas, her sister and her brother-in-law, the Boy Scouts and the frozen black faces, the watchers on the pavement and those in the windows above.

Alice carried that gathering rope with her always after that day on Fifth Avenue, and found it reliably secure and tight—most of the time. Except when the men sat on windowsills fingering horns, and the women wondered "how long." The rope broke then, disturbing her peace, making her aware of flesh and something so free she could smell its bloodsmell; made her aware of its life below the sash and its red lip rouge.

She knew from sermons and editorials that it wasn't real music—just colored folks' stuff: harmful, certainly; embarrassing, of course; but not real, not serious.

Yet Alice Manfred swore she heard a complicated anger in it; something hostile that disguised itself as flourish and roaring seduction. But the part she hated most was its appetite. Its longing for the bash, the slit; a kind of careless hunger for a fight or a red ruby stickpin for a tie—either would do. It faked happiness, faked welcome, but it did not make her feel generous, this juke joint, barrel hooch, tonk house, music. It made her hold her hand in the pocket of her apron to keep from smashing it through the glass pane to snatch the world in her fist and squeeze the life out of it for doing what it did and did and did to her and everybody else she knew or knew about. Better to close the windows and the shutters, sweat in the summer heat of a silent Clifton Place apartment than to risk a broken window or a yelping that might not know where or how to stop.

I have seen her, passing a café or an uncurtained window when some phrase or other—"Hit me but don't quit me"—drifted out, and watched her reach with one hand for the safe gathering rope thrown to her eight years ago on Fifth Avenue, and ball the other one into a fist in her coat pocket. I don't know how she did it—balance herself with two different hand gestures. But she was not alone in trying, and she was not alone in losing. It was impossible to keep the Fifth Avenue drums separate from the belt-buckle tunes vibrating from pianos and spinning on every Victrola. Impossible. Some nights are silent; not a motor car turning within earshot; no drunks or restless babies crying for their mothers and Alice opens any window she wants to and hears nothing at all.

Wondering at this totally silent night, she can go back to bed but as soon as she turns the pillow to its smoother, cooler side, a melody line she doesn't remember where from sings itself, loud and unsolicited, in her head. "When I was young and in my prime I could get my barbecue any old time." They are greedy, reckless words, loose and infuriating, but hard to dismiss because underneath, holding up the looseness like a palm, are the drums that put Fifth Avenue into focus.

Her niece, of course, didn't have the problem. Alice had been reraising her, correcting her, since the summer of 1917, and although her earliest memory when she arrived from East St. Louis was the parade her aunt took her to, a kind of funeral parade for her mother and her father, Dorcas remembered it differently. While her aunt worried about how to keep the heart ignorant of the hips and the head in charge of both, Dorcas lay on a chenille bedspread, tickled and happy knowing that there was no place to be where somewhere, close by, somebody was not licking his licorice stick, tickling the ivories, beating his skins, blowing off his horn while a knowing woman sang ain't nobody going to keep me down you got the right key baby but the wrong keyhole you got to get it bring it and put it right here, or else.

Resisting her aunt's protection and restraining hands, Dorcas thought of that life-below-the-sash as all the life there was. The drums she heard at the parade were only the first part, the first word, of a command. For her the drums were not an all-embracing rope of fellowship, discipline and transcendence. She remembered them as a beginning, a start of something she looked to complete.

Back in East St. Louis, as the little porch fell, wood chips—ignited and smoking—exploded in the air. One of them must have entered her stretched dumb mouth and traveled down her throat because it smoked and glowed there still. Dorcas never let it out and never put it out. At first she thought if she spoke of it, it would leave her, or she would lose it through her mouth. And when her aunt took her on a train to the City, and crushed her hand while they watched a long parade, the bright wood chip sank further and further down until it lodged comfortably somewhere below her navel. She watched the black unblinking men, and the drums assured her that the glow would never leave her, that it would be waiting for and with her whenever she wanted to be touched by it. And whenever she wanted to let it loose to leap into fire again, whatever happened would be quick. Like the dolls.

They would have gone fast. Wood, after all, in a wooden cigar box. The red tissue-paper skirt on Rochelle immediately. Sst, like a match, and then Bernadine's blue silk and Faye's white cotton cape. The fire would eat away at their legs, blacken them first with its hot breath and their round eyes, with the tiny lashes and eyebrows she had painted in so very carefully, would have watched themselves disappear. Dorcas avoided thinking about the huge coffin just there in front, a few feet to her left, and about the medicinal odor of Aunt Alice sitting next to her, by concentrating on Rochelle and Bernadine and Faye, who would have no funeral at all. It made her bold. Even as a nine-year-old in elementary school she was bold. However tight and tucked in her braids, however clunky her high-topped shoes that covered ankles other girls exposed in low-cut oxfords, however black and thick her stockings, nothing hid the boldness swaying under her cast-iron skirt. Eyeglasses could not obscure it, nor could the pimples on her skin brought on by hard brown soap and a tilted diet.

When she was little, and Alice Manfred agreed to sew for

a month or two, Dorcas was watched over after school by the Miller sisters. Often there were four other children, sometimes one other. Their play was quiet and confined to a small area of the dining room. The two-armed sister, Frances Miller, gave them apple-butter sandwiches to eat; the one-armed one, Neola, read them Psalms. The strict discipline was occasionally lightened when Frances napped at the kitchen table. Then Neola might grow tired of the constraint the verses imposed on her own voice and select a child to light a match for her cigarette. She would take fewer than three puffs, and something in the gesture stirred something inside her, and she told her charges cautionary tales. Her stories, however, of the goodness of good behavior collapsed before the thrill of the sin they deplored.

The truth is that the message in her instructions failed because a week after he put the engagement ring on Neola's finger, the soon-to-be-groom at her wedding left the state. The pain of his refusal was visual, for over her heart, curled like a shell, was the hand on which he had positioned the ring. As though she held the broken pieces of her heart together in the crook of a frozen arm. No other part of her was touched by this paralysis. Her right hand, the one that turned the tissue-thin pages of the Old Testament, or held an Old Gold cigarette to her lips, was straight and steady. But the stories she told them of moral decay, of the wicked who preyed on the good, were made more poignant by this clutch of arm to breast. She told them how she had personally advised a friend to respect herself and leave the man who was no good to (or for) her. Finally the friend agreed but in two days, two! she went right back to him God help us all, and Neola never spoke to her again. She told them how a very young girl, no more than fourteen, had left family and friends to traipse four hundred miles after a boy who joined the army only to be left behind and turn to a completely dissolute life in a camptown. So they could see, couldn't they, the power of sin in the company of a weak mind? The children scratched their knees and nodded, but Dorcas, at least, was enchanted by the frail, melty tendency of the flesh and the Paradise that could make a woman go right back after two days, two! or make a girl travel four hundred miles to a camptown, or fold Neola's arm, the better to hold the pieces of her heart in her hand. Paradise. All for Paradise.

By the time she was seventeen her whole life was unbearable. And when I think about it, I know just how she felt. It is terrible when there is absolutely nothing to do or worth doing except to lie down and hope when you are naked she won't laugh at you. Or that he, holding your breasts, won't wish they were some other way. Terrible but worth the risk, because there is no other thing to do, although, being seventeen, you do it. Study, work, memorize. Bite into food and the reputations of your friends. Laugh at the things that are right side up and those that are upside-down—it doesn't matter because you are not doing the thing worth doing which is lying down somewhere in a dimly lit place enclosed in arms, and supported by the core of the world.

Think how it is, if you can manage, just manage it. Nature freaks for you, then. Turns itself into shelter, byways. Pillows for two. Spreads the limbs of lilac bushes low enough to hide you. And the City, in its own way, gets down for you, cooperates, smoothing its sidewalks, correcting its curbstones, offering you melons and green apples on the corner. Racks of yellow head scarves; strings of Egyptian beads. Kansas fried chicken and something with raisins call attention to an open window where the aroma seems to lurk. And if that's not enough, doors to speakeasies stand ajar and in that cool dark place a clarinet coughs and clears its throat waiting for the woman to decide on the key. She makes up her mind and as you pass by informs your back that she is daddy's little angel child. The City is smart at this: smelling and good and looking raunchy; sending secret messages disguised as public signs: this way, open here, danger to let colored only single men on sale woman wanted private room stop dog on premises absolutely no money down fresh chicken free delivery fast. And good at opening locks, dimming stairways. Covering your moans with its own.

There was a night in her sixteenth year when Dorcas stood in her body and offered it to either of the brothers for a dance. Both boys were shorter than she, but both were equally attractive. More to the point, they outstepped everybody so completely that when they needed tough competition they were forced to dance with themselves. Sneaking out to that party with her best friend, Felice, ought to have been hard to arrange, but Alice Manfred had overnight business in Springfield, and nothing could have been easier. The only difficulty was in finding something foxy enough to wear.

The two girlfriends climb the stairs, led straight to the right place more by the stride piano pouring over the door saddle than their recollection of the apartment number. They pause to exchange looks before knocking. Even in the dim hallway the dark-skinned friend heightens the cream color of the other. Felice's oily hair enhances Dorcas' soft, dry waves. The door opens and they step in.

Before the lights are turned out, and before the sandwiches and the spiked soda water disappear, the one managing the record player chooses fast music suitable for the brightly lit room, where obstructing furniture has been shoved against walls, pushed into the hallway, and bedrooms piled high with coats. Under the ceiling light pairs move like twins born with, if not for, the other, sharing a partner's pulse like a second jugular. They believe they know before the music does what their hands, their feet are to do, but that illusion is the music's secret drive: the control it tricks them into believing is theirs; the anticipation it anticipates. In between record changes, while the girls fan blouse necks to air damp collarbones or pat with anxious hands the damage moisture has done to their hair, the boys press folded handkerchiefs to their foreheads. Laughter covers indiscreet glances of welcome and promise, and takes the edge off gestures of betrayal and abandon.

Dorcas and Felice are not strangers at the party—nobody is. People neither of them has seen before join the fun as easily as those who have grown up in the building. But both girls have expectations made higher by the trouble they'd had planning outfits for the escapade. Dorcas, at sixteen, has yet to wear silk hose and her shoes are those of someone much younger or very old. Felice has helped her loosen two braids behind her ears and her fingertip is stained with the rouge she has stroked across her lips. With her collar turned under, her dress is more adult-looking, but the hard hand of a warning grown-up shows everywhere else: in the hem, the waist-centered belt, the short, puffy sleeves. She and Felice have tried removing the belt altogether, then fixing it at her navel. Both strategies prove hateful. They know that a badly dressed body is nobody at all, and Felice had to chatter compliments all the way down Seventh Avenue to get Dorcas to forget about her clothes and focus on the party.

Music soars to the ceiling and through the windows wide

open for circulation as they enter. Immediately both girls are snatched by male hands and spun into the dancing center of the room. Dorcas recognizes her partner as Martin, who had been in her elocution class for a hot minute—which was as long as it took for the teacher to realize he would never relinquish "ax" for "ask." Dorcas dances well—not as fast as some others, but she is graceful, in spite of those shaming shoes, and she is provocative.

It is after two more dances that she notices the brothers commanding the attention of a crowd in the dining room. On the street, in vestibules as well as house parties, they are spectacular, moving like taut silk or loose metal. The stomach-jump Dorcas and Felice have agreed is the Sign of real interest and possible love surfaces and spreads as Dorcas watches the brothers. The sandwiches are gone now, the potato salad too, and everybody knows that the time for lights-out music is approaching. The unbelievable agility, the split-second timing the brothers are putting on display announces the culmination of the fast-dancing segment of the party.

Dorcas moves into the hall that parallels the living and dining room. From its shadows, through the archway, she has an unrestricted view of the brothers as they bring the performance to its rousing close. Laughing, they accept the praise that is due them: adoring looks from girls, congratulating punches and slaps from the boys. They have wonderful faces, these brothers. Their smiles, more than flawless teeth, are amused and inviting. Someone fights with the Victrola; places the arm on, scratches the record, tries again, then exchanges the record for another. During the lull, the brothers notice Dorcas. Taller than most, she gazes at them over the head of her dark friend. The brothers' eyes seem wide and welcoming to her. She moves forward out of the shadow and slips through the group. The brothers turn up the wattage of their smiles. The right record is on the turntable now; she can hear its preparatory hiss as the needle slides toward its first groove. The brothers smile brilliantly; one leans a fraction of an inch toward the other and, never losing eye contact with Dorcas, whispers something. The other looks Dorcas up and down as she moves toward them. Then, just as the music, slow and smoky, loads up the air, his smile bright as ever, he wrinkles his nose and turns away.

Dorcas has been acknowledged, appraised and dismissed in the time it takes for a needle to find its opening groove. The stomach-jump of possible love is nothing compared to the ice floes that block up her veins now. The body she inhabits is unworthy. Although it is young and all she has, it is as if it had decayed on the vine at budding time. No wonder Neola closed her arm and held the pieces of her heart in her hand.

So by the time Joe Trace whispered to her through the crack of a closing door her life had become almost unbearable. Almost. The flesh, heavily despised by the brothers, held secret the love appetite soaring inside it. I've seen swollen fish, serenely blind, floating in the sky. Without eyes, but somehow directed, these airships swim below cloud foam and nobody can be turned away from the sight of them because it's like watching a private dream. That was what her hunger was like: mesmerizing, directed, floating like a public secret just under the cloud cover. Alice Manfred had worked hard to privatize her niece, but she was no match for a City seeping music that begged and challenged each and every day. "Come," it said. "Come and do wrong." Even the grandmothers sweeping the stairs closed their eyes and held their heads back as they celebrated their sweet desolation. "Nobody does me like you do me." In the year that passed between the dancing brothers' dismissal and Alice Manfred's club meeting, the yoke Alice had knotted around Dorcas' neck frayed till it split.

Other than the clubwomen, very few knew where Joe Trace met her. Not at the candy counter of Duggie's where he first saw her and wondered if that, the peppermint she bought, was what insulted her skin, light and creamy everywhere but her cheeks. Joe met Dorcas in Alice Manfred's house right up under her nose and right before her very eyes.

He had gone there to deliver an order to Malvonne Edwards' cousin Sheila who said if Joe came to 237 Clifton Place before noon he could deliver her order, the #2 Nut Brown and the vanishing cream, right there, and she wouldn't have to wait till the following Saturday or walk all the way over to Lenox at night to pick it up, unless, of course, he wanted to come on her job. . . .

Joe had decided he would wait till next Saturday because not collecting the dollar and thirty-five cents wasn't going to strap him. But after he left Miss Ransom's house and stood for a half hour watching Bud and C.T. abusing each other at checkers, he decided to check Sheila out right fast and quit for the day. His stomach was a bit sour and his feet already hurt. He didn't want to be caught delivering or writing orders in the rain either, rain that had been threatening all during that warm October morning. And even though getting home early meant the extended company of a speechless Violet while he fussed with the sink trap or the pulley that turned the clothesline on their side of the building, the Saturday meal would be early too and satisfying: late summer greens cooked with the ham bone left over from last Sunday. Joe looked forward to the lean, scrappy end-of-week meals, but hated the Sunday one: a baked ham, a sweet heavy pie to follow it. Violet's determination to grow an ass she swore she once owned was killing him.

Once upon a time, he bragged about her cooking. Couldn't wait to get back to the house and devour it. But he was fifty now, and appetites change, we know. He still liked candy, hard candy—not divinity or caramel—sour balls being his favorite. If Violet would confine herself to soup and boiled vegetables (with a bit of bread to go along) he would be perfectly satisfied.

That's what he was thinking about when he found 237 and climbed the stairs. The argument between C.T. and Bud over the fate of S.S. *Ethiopia* had been too good, too funny: he had listened to them longer than he thought, because it was way past noon when he got there. Woman noise could be heard through the door. Joe rang anyway.

The peppermint girl with the bad skin answered the door, and while he was telling her who he was and what he'd come for, Sheila poked her head into the vestibule and shouted, "CPT! Surprise me for once, Joe Trace." He smiled and stepped in the door. Stood there smiling and did not put his sample case down until the hostess, Alice Manfred, came and told him to come on in the parlor.

They were thrilled to have him interrupt their social. It was a luncheon meeting of the Civic Daughters to plan for the Thanksgiving fund raiser for the National Negro Business League. They had settled what they could, tabled what they had to, and begun the chicken à la king lunch over which Alice had taken the greatest pains. Pleased, happy even, with their work and with each other's company, they did not know they were missing anything until Alice sent Dorcas to answer the ring, and Sheila, remembering what she had said to Joe, jumped up when she heard a male voice.

They made him feel like the singing men in spats. The

young ones who clustered on the corners wearing ties the color of handkerchiefs sticking out of their breast pockets. The young roosters who stood without waiting for the chicks who were waiting—for them. Under the women's flirty, appraising eyes, Joe felt the pleasure of his own smile as though sand-colored spats covered his shoe tops.

They laughed, tapped the tablecloth with their fingertips and began to tease, berate and adore him all at once. They told him how tall men like him made them feel, complained about his lateness and insolence, asked him what *else* he had in his case besides whatever it was that made Sheila so excited. They wondered why he never rang *their* doorbells, or climbed four flights of double-flight stairs to deliver anything to them. They sang their compliments, their abuse, and only Alice confined herself to a thin smile, a closed look, and did not join the comments with one of her own.

Of course he stayed to lunch. Of course. Although he tried not to eat anything much and spoil his appetite for the late-summer greens he was sure were simmering in the pot for him. But the women touched his hair and looked right at him, musing over his two-color eyes and ordered him: "Come on over here, man, and sit yourself down. Fix you a plate? Let me fix you a plate." He protested; they insisted. He opened his case; they offered to buy him out. "Eat, baby, eat," they said. "You not going out in that pneumonia weather without something sticking to your bones don't make no sense with all we got here, Dorcas, girl, bring this man a empty plate so I can fill it for him hear? Hush, Sheila."

They were women his age mostly, with husbands, children, grandchildren too. Hard workers for themselves and anyone who needed them. And they thought men were ridiculous and delicious and terrible, taking every opportunity to let them know that they were. In a group such as this one, they could do with impunity what they were cautious about alone with any man, stranger or friend, who rang the doorbell with a sample case in his hand, no matter how tall he was, how country his smile or however much sadness was in his eyes. Besides, they liked his voice. It had a pitch, a note they heard only when they visited stubborn old folks who would not budge from their front yards and overworked fields to come to the City. It reminded them of men who wore hats to plow and to eat supper in; who blew into saucers of coffee, and held knives in their fists when they ate. So they looked right at him and told him any way they could how ridiculous he was, and how delicious and how terrible. As if he didn't know.

Joe Trace counted on flirty laughing women to buy his wares, and he knew better than to take up with any of them. Not if he wanted to be able to lean over a pool table for a shot exposing his back to his customers' husbands. But that day in Alice Manfred's house, as he listened to and returned their banter, something in the wordplay took on weight.

I've wondered about it. What he thought then and later, and about what he said to her. He whispered something to Dorcas when she let him out the door, and nobody looked more pleased and surprised than he did.

If I remember right, that October lunch in Alice Manfred's house, something was off. Alice was vague and anybody in her company for thirty minutes knew that wasn't her style. She was the one who with a look could cut good gossip down to a titter when it got out of hand. And maybe it was her head-of-a-seamstress head that made what you thought was a cheerful dress turn loud and tatty next to hers. But she could lay a table.

Food might be a tad skimpy in the portions, and I believe she had a prejudice against butter, she used so little of it in her cakes. But the biscuits were light, and the plates, the flatware, sparkling and arranged just so. Open her napkins wide as you please and not a catface anywhere. She was polite at the lunch of course; not too haughty either, but not paying close attention to things. Distracted she was. About Dorcas, probably.

I always believed that girl was a pack of lies. I could tell by her walk her underclothes were beyond her years, even if her dress wasn't. Maybe back in October Alice was beginning to think so too. By the time January came, nobody had to speculate. Everybody knew. I wonder if she had a premonition of Joe Trace knocking on her door? Or it could have been something she read in all those newspapers stacked neatly along the baseboard in her bedroom.

Everybody needs a pile of newspapers: to peel potatoes on, serve bathroom needs, wrap garbage. But not like Alice Manfred. She must have read them over and over else why would she keep them? And if she read anything in the newspaper twice she knew too little about too much. If you have secrets you want kept or want to figure out those other people have, a newspaper can turn your mind. The best thing to find out what's going on is to watch how people maneuver themselves in the streets. What sidewalk preachers stop them in their tracks? Do they walk right through the boys kicking cans along the sidewalk or holler at them to quit? Ignore the men sitting on car fenders or stop to exchange a word? If a fight breaks out between a man and a woman do they cross in the middle of the block to watch or run to the corner in case it gets messy?

One thing for sure, the streets will confuse you, teach you or break your head. But Alice Manfred wasn't the kind to give herself reasons to be in the streets. She got through them quick as she could to get back to her house. If she had come out more often, sat on the stoop or gossiped in front of the beauty shop, she would have known more than what the paper said. She might have known what was happening under her nose. When she did find out what took place between that October day and the awful January one that ended everything, the last people on earth she wanted to see was Joe Trace or anybody connected to him. It happened, though. The woman who avoided the streets let into her living room the woman who sat down in the middle of one.

Toward the end of March, Alice Manfred put her needles aside to think again of what she called the *impunity* of the man who killed her niece just because he could. It had not been hard to do; it had not even made him think twice about what danger he was putting himself in. He just did it. One man. One defenseless girl. Death. A sample-case man. A nice, neighborly, everybody-knows-him man. The kind you let in your house because he was not dangerous, because you had seen him with children, bought his products and never heard a scrap of gossip about him doing wrong. Felt not only safe but kindly in his company because he was the sort women ran to when they thought they were being followed, or watched or needed someone to have the extra key just in case you locked yourself out. He was the man who took you to your door if you missed the trolley and had to walk night streets at night. Who warned young girls away from hooch joints and the men who lingered there. Women teased him because they trusted him. He was one of those men who might have marched down Fifth Avenue—cold and silent and dignified—into the space the drums made. He *knew* wrong wasn't right, and did it anyway.

Alice Manfred had seen and borne much, had been scared all over the country, in every street of it. Only now did she feel truly unsafe because the brutalizing men and their brutal women were not just out there, they were in her block, her house. A man had come in her living room and destroyed her niece. His wife had come right in the funeral to nasty and dishonor her. She would have called the police after both of them if everything she knew about Negro life had made it even possible to consider. To actually volunteer to talk to one, black or white, to let him in her house, watch him adjust his hips in her chair to accommodate the blue steel that made him a man.

Idle and withdrawn in her grief and shame, she whittled away the days making lace for nothing, reading her newspapers, tossing them on the floor, picking them up again. She read them differently now. Every week since Dorcas' death, during the whole of January and February, a paper laid bare the bones of some broken woman. Man kills wife. Eight accused of rape dismissed. Woman and girl victims of. Woman commits suicide. White attackers indicted. Five women caught. Woman says man beat. In jealous rage man.

Defenseless as ducks, she thought. Or were they? Read carefully the news accounts revealed that most of these women, subdued and broken, had not been defenseless. Or, like Dorcas, easy prey. All over the country, black women were armed. That, thought Alice, that, at least, they had learned. Didn't everything on God's earth have or acquire defense? Speed, some poison in the leaf, the tongue, the tail? A mask, flight, numbers in the millions producing numbers in the millions? A thorn here, a spike there.

Natural prey? Easy pickings? "I don't think so." Aloud she said it. "I don't think so."

Worn spots in the linen had been strengthened with 60-weight thread. Laundered and folded it lay in a basket her mother had used. Alice raised the ironing board and spread newspaper under it to keep the hems clean. She was waiting not only for the irons to heat but also for a brutal woman black as soot known to carry a knife. She waited with less hesitation than she had before and with none of the scary angry feelings she had in January when a woman saying she was Violet Trace had tried to see her, talk or something. Knocked on her door so early in the morning Alice thought it was the law.

"I don't have a thing to say to you. Not one thing." She had said it in a loud whisper through the chained opening in the door and slammed it shut. She didn't need the name to be afraid or to know who she was: the star of her niece's funeral. The woman who ruined the service, changed the whole point and meaning of it and was practically all anybody talked about when they talked about Dorcas' death and in the process had changed the woman's name. Violent they called her now. No wonder. Alice, sitting in the first seat in the first aisle had watched the church commotion stunned. Later, and little by little, feelings, like sea trash expelled on a beach—strange and recognizable, stark and murky—returned.

Chief among them was fear and—a new thing—anger. At Joe Trace who had been the one who did it: seduced her niece right under her nose in her very own house. The nice one. The man who sold ladies' products on the side; a familiar figure in just about every building in town. A man store owners and landlords liked because he set the children's toys in a neat row when they left them scattered on the sidewalk. Who the children liked because he never minded them. And liked among men because he never cheated in a game, egged a stupid fight on, or carried tales, and he left their women alone. Liked among the women because he made them feel like girls; liked by girls because he made them feel like women—which, she thought, was what Dorcas was looking for. Murderer.

But Alice wasn't afraid of him nor, now, his wife. For Joe she felt trembling fury at his snake-in-the-grass stealing of the girl in her charge; and shame that the grass he had snaked through was her own—the watched and guarded environment where unmarried and unmarriageable pregnancy was the end and close of livable life. After that—zip. Just a wait until the baby that came was old enough to warrant its own watched, guarded environment.

Waiting for Violet, with less hesitation than before, Alice wondered why it was so. At fifty-eight with no children of her own, and the one she had access to and responsibility for dead, she wondered about the hysteria, the violence, the damnation of pregnancy without marriageability. It had occupied her own parents' mind completely for as long as she could remember them. They spoke to her firmly but carefully about her body: sitting nasty (legs open); sitting womanish (legs crossed); breathing through her mouth; hands on hips; slumping at table; switching when you walked. The moment she got breasts they were bound and resented, a resentment that increased to outright hatred of her pregnant possibilities and never stopped until she married Louis Manfred, when suddenly it was the opposite. Even before the wedding her parents were murmuring about grandchildren they could see and hold, while at the same time and in turn resenting the tips showing and growing under the chemises of Alice's younger sisters. Resenting the blood spots, the new hips, the hair. That and the necessity for new clothes. "Oh, Lord, girl!" The frown when the hem could not be taken down further; the waistband refused another stitch. Growing up under that heated control, Alice swore she wouldn't, but she did, pass it on. She passed it on to her baby sister's only child. And wondered now would she have done so had her husband lived or stayed or if she had had children of her own. If he had been there, by her side, helping her make decisions, maybe she would not be sitting there waiting for a woman called Violent and thinking war thoughts. Although war was what it was. Which is why she had chosen surrender and made Dorcas her own prisoner of war.

Other women, however, had not surrendered. All over the country they were armed. Alice worked once with a Swedish tailor who had a scar from his earlobe to the corner of his mouth. "Negress," he said. "She cut me to the teeth, to the teeth." He smiled his wonder and shook his head. "To the teeth." The iceman in Springfield had four evenly spaced holes in the side of his neck from four evenly spaced jabs by something thin, round and sharp. Men ran through the streets of Springfield, East St. Louis and the City holding one red wet hand in the other, a flap of skin on the face. Sometimes they got to a hospital safely alive only because they left the razor where it lodged.

Black women were armed; black women were dangerous and the less money they had the deadlier the weapon they chose.

Who were the unarmed ones? Those who found protection in church and the judging, angry God whose wrath in their behalf was too terrible to bear contemplation. He was not just on His way, coming, coming to right the wrongs done to them, He was here. Already. See? See? What the world had done to them it was now doing to itself. Did the world mess over them? Yes but look where the mess originated. Were they berated and cursed? Oh yes but look how the world cursed and berated itself. Were the women fondled in kitchens and the back of stores? Uh huh. Did police put their fists in women's faces so the husbands' spirits would break along with the women's jaws? Did men (those who knew them as well as strangers sitting in motor cars) call them out of their names every single day of their lives? Uh huh. But in God's eyes and theirs, every hateful word and gesture was the Beast's desire for its own filth. The Beast did not do what was done to it, but what it wished done to itself: raped because it wanted to be raped itself. Slaughtered children because it yearned to be slaughtered children. Built jails to dwell on and hold on to its own private decay. God's wrath, so beautiful, so simple. Their enemies got what they wanted, became what they visited on others.

Who else were the unarmed ones? The ones who thought they did not need folded blades, packets of lye, shards of glass taped to their hands. Those who bought houses and hoarded money as protection and the means to purchase it. Those attached to armed men. Those who did not carry pistols because they became pistols; did not carry switchblades because they were switchblades cutting through gatherings, shooting down statutes and pointing out the blood and abused flesh. Those who swelled their little unarmed strength into the reckoning one of leagues, clubs, societies, sisterhoods designed to hold or withhold, move or stay put, make a way, solicit, comfort and ease. Bail out, dress the dead, pay the rent, find new rooms, start a school, storm an office, take up collections, rout the block and keep their eyes on all the children. Any other kind of unarmed black woman in 1926 was silent or crazy or dead.

Alice waited this time, in the month of March, for the woman with the knife. The woman people called Violent now because she had tried to kill what lay in a coffin. She had left notes under Alice's door every day beginning in January—a week after the funeral—and Alice Manfred knew the kind of Negro that couple was: the kind she trained Dorcas away from. The embarrassing kind. More than unappealing, they were dangerous. The husband shot; the wife stabbed. Nothing. Nothing her niece did or tried could equal the violence done to her. And where there was violence wasn't there also vice? Gambling. Cursing. A terrible and nasty closeness. Red dresses. Yellow shoes. And, of course, race music to urge them on.

But Alice was not frightened of her now as she had been in January and as she was in February, the first time she let her in. She'd thought the woman would end up in jail one day— they all did eventually. But easy pickings? Natural prey? "I don't think so. I don't think so."

At the wake, Malvonne gave her the details. Tried to, anyway. Alice leaned away from the woman and held her breath as though to keep the words at bay.

"I appreciate your concern," Alice told her. "Help yourself." She gestured toward tables crowded with food and the well-wishers circling it. "There's so much."

"I feel so bad," Malvonne said. "Like it was my own."

"Thank you."

"You raise other people's children and it hurts just the same as it would if it was your own. You know about Sweetness, my nephew . . . ?"

"Excuse me."

"Did everything for him. Everything a mother would."

"Please. Help yourself. There's so much. Too much."

"Those old reprobates, they live in my building, you know. . . ."

"Hello, Felice. Nice of you to come . . ."

She did not want to hear or know too much then. And she did not want to see that woman they began to call Violent either. The note she slid under Alice's door offended her, then frightened her. But after a while, having heard how torn up the man was and reading the headlines in the *Age,* the *News, The Messenger,* by February she had steeled herself and let the woman in.

"What *could* you want from me?"

"Oh, right now I just want to sit down on your chair," Violet said.

"I'm sorry. I just can't think what good can come of this."

"I'm having trouble with my head," said Violet placing her fingers on the crown of her hat.

"See a doctor, why don't you?"

Violet walked past her, drawn like a magnet to a small side table. "Is that her?"

Alice didn't have to look to know what she was staring at. "Yes."

The long pause that followed, while Violet examined the face that loomed out of the frame, made Alice nervous. Before she got up the courage to ask the woman to leave, she turned away from the photograph saying, "I'm not the one you need to be scared of."

"No? Who is?"

"I don't know. That's what hurts my head."

"You didn't come here to say you sorry. I thought maybe you did. You come in here to deliver some of your own evil."

"I don't have no evil of my own."

"I think you'd better go."

"Let me rest here a minute. I can't find a place where I can just sit down. That's her there?"

"I just told you it was."

"She give you a lot of trouble?"

"No. None. Well. Some."

"I was a good girl her age. Never gave a speck of trouble. I did everything anybody told me to. Till I got here. City make you tighten up."

Odd-acting, thought Alice, but not bloody-minded. And before she could think not to let it happen, the question was out. "Why did he do such a thing?"

"Why did she?"

"Why did you?"

"I don't know."

The second time she came, Alice was still pondering over those wild women with their packets of lye, their honed razors, the keloids here, here and there. She was pulling the curtain to cut off the light that smashed right into her visitor's eyes when she said, "Your husband. Does he hurt you?"

"Hurt me?" Violet looked puzzled.

"I mean he seemed so nice, so quiet. Did he beat on you?"

"Joe? No. He never hurt nothing."

"Except Dorcas."

"And squirrels."

"What?"

"Rabbits too. Deer. Possum. Pheasant. We ate good down home."

"Why'd you leave?"

"Landowner didn't want rabbit. He want soft money."

"They want money here, too."

"But there's a way to get it here. I did day work when I first came here. Three houses a day got me good money. Joe cleaned fish at night. Took a while before he got hotel work. I got into hairdressing, and Joe . . ."

"I don't want to hear about all that."

Violet shut up and stared at the photograph. Alice gave it to her to get her out of the house.

The next day she was back and looked so bad Alice wanted to slap her. Instead she said, "Take that dress off and I'll stitch up your cuff." Violet wore the same dress each time and Alice was irritated by the thread running loose from her sleeve, as well as the coat lining ripped in at least three places she could see.

Violet sat in her slip with her coat on, while Alice mended the sleeve with the tiniest stitches. At no time did Violet take off her hat.

"At first I thought you came here to harm me. Then I thought you wanted to offer condolences. Then I thought you wanted to thank me for not calling the law. But none of that is it, is it?"

"I had to sit down somewhere. I thought I could do it here. That you would let me and you did. I know I didn't give Joe much reason to stay out of the street. But I wanted to see what kind of girl he'd rather me be."

"Foolish. He'd rather you were eighteen, that's all."

"No. Something more."

"You don't know anything about your own husband, I can't be expected to help you."

"You didn't know they were seeing each other no more than I did and you saw her every day like I did Joe. I know where my mind was. Where was yours?"

"Don't chastise me. I won't let you do that."

• • •

Alice had finished the sheets and begun the first shirtwaist when Violet knocked on her door. Years and years and years ago she had guided the tip of the iron into the seams of a man's white shirt. Dampened just so the fabric smoothed and tightened with starch. Those shirts were scraps now. Dust cloths, monthly cloths, rags tied around pipe joints to hinder freezing; pot holders and pieces to test hot irons and wrap their handles. Even wicks for oil lamps; salt bags to scrub the teeth. Now her own shirtwaists got her elegant attentive handcare.

Two pairs of pillow slips, still warm to the touch, were stacked on the table. So were the two bed sheets. Next week, perhaps, the curtains.

By now she recognized the knock and never knew if she was eager or angry when she heard it. And she didn't care.

When Violet came to visit (and Alice never knew when that might be) something opened up.

The dark hat made her face even darker. Her eyes were round as silver dollars but could slit of a sudden too.

The thing was how Alice felt and talked in her company. Not like she did with other people. With Violent she was impolite. Sudden. Frugal. No apology or courtesy seemed required or necessary between them. But something else was— clarity, perhaps. The kind of clarity crazy people demand from the not-crazy.

Violet, her coat lining repaired too now, her cuffs secure, needed only to pay attention to her hose and hat to appear normal. Alice sighed a little sigh, amazed at herself as she opened the door to the only visitor she looked forward to.

"You look froze."

"Near bout," said Violet.

"March can put you in the sickbed."

"Be a pleasure," Violet answered. "All my troubles be over if I could get my body sick stead of my head."

"Then who would do the fancy women's hair?"

Violet laughed. "Nobody. Maybe nobody would do it and nobody would know the difference."

"The difference is more than a hairdo."

"They're just women, you know. Like us."

"No," said Alice. "No they're not. Not like me."

"I don't mean the trade. I mean the women."

"Oh, please," said Alice. "Let's get off that. I'm steeping you some tea."

"They were good to me when nobody else was. Me and Joe eat because of them."

"Don't tell me about it."

"Anytime I come close to borrowing or need extra, I can work all day any day on their heads."

"Don't tell me, I said. I don't want to hear about it and where their money comes from. You want tea or not?"

"Yeah. Okay. Why not? Why can't you hear about it?"

"Oh. The men. The nasty life. Don't they fight all the time? When you do their hair, you're not afraid they might start fighting?"

"Only when they sober." Violet smiled.

"Oh, well."

"They share men, fight them and fight over them, too."

"No woman should live like that."

"No. No woman should have to."

"Killing people." Alice sucked her teeth. "Makes me sick to my stomach." She poured the tea, then lifting cup and saucer, held it back while she looked at Violet.

"If you had found out about them before he killed her, would you have?"

"I wonder."

Alice handed her the tea. "I don't understand women like you. Women with knives." She snatched up a long-sleeved blouse and smoothed it over the ironing board.

"I wasn't born with a knife."

"No, but you picked one up."

"You never did?" Violet blew ripples into the tea.

"No, I never did. Even when my husband ran off I never did that. And you. You didn't even have a worthy enemy. Somebody worth killing. You picked up a knife to insult a dead girl."

"But that's better, ain't it? The harm was already done."

"She wasn't the enemy."

"Oh, yes she is. She's my enemy. Then, when I didn't know it, and now too."

"Why? Because she was young and pretty and took your husband away from you?"

Violet sipped her tea and did not answer. After a long silence, and after their talk had turned to trifles then on to the narrowness of life, Violet said to Alice Manfred, "Wouldn't you? You wouldn't fight for your man?"

Seeded in childhood, watered every day since, fear had sprouted through her veins all her life. Thinking war thoughts it had gathered, blossomed into another thing. Now, as she looked at this woman, Alice heard her question like the pop of a toy gun.

Somewhere in Springfield only the teeth were left. Maybe the skull, maybe not. If she dug down deep enough and tore off the top, she could be sure that the teeth would certainly be there. No lips to share with the woman she had shared them with. No fingers to lift her hips as he had lifted others. Just the teeth exposed now, nothing like the smile that had made her say, "Choose." And he did.

What she told Violet was true. She had never picked up a knife. What she neglected to say—what came flooding back to her now—was also true: every day and every night for seven months she, Alice Manfred, was starving for blood. Not his. Oh, no. For him she planned sugar in his motor, scissors to his tie, burned suits, slashed shoes, ripped socks. Vicious, childish acts of violence to inconvenience him, remind him. But no blood. Her craving settled on the red liquid coursing through the other woman's veins. An ice pick stuck in and pulled up would get it. Would a clothesline rope circling her neck and yanked with all Alice's strength make her spit it up? Her favorite, however, the dream that plumped her pillow at night, was seeing herself mount a horse, then ride it and find the woman alone on a road and gallop till she ran her down under four iron hooves; then back again, and again until there was nothing left but tormented road dirt signaling where the hussy had been.

He had chosen; so would she. And maybe after galloping through seven months of nights on a horse she neither owned nor knew how to ride, over the twitching, pulpy body of a woman who wore white shoes in winter, laughed loud as a child, and who had never seen a marriage license—maybe she would have done something wild. But after seven months she had to choose something else. The suit, the tie, the shirt he liked best. They suggested she not waste the shoes. No one would see them. But socks? Surely he has to have socks? Of course, said the mortician. Socks, of course. And what difference did it make that one of the mourners was her sworn and hated enemy laying white roses on the coffin, taking away one the color of her dress. For thirty years he was turning into teeth in Springfield, and neither she nor the mourner in the inappropriate dress could do a thing about it.

Alice slammed the pressing iron down. "You don't know what loss is," she said, and listened as closely to what she was saying as did the woman sitting by her ironing board in a hat in the morning.

**T**he hat, pushed back on her forehead, gave Violet a scatty look. The calming effect of the tea Alice Manfred had given her did not last long. Afterward she sat in the drugstore sucking malt through a straw wondering who on earth that other Violet was that walked about the City in her skin; peeped out through her eyes and saw other things. Where she saw a lonesome chair left like an orphan in a park strip facing the river that other Violet saw how the ice skim gave the railing's black poles a weapony glint. Where she, last in line at the car stop, noticed a child's cold wrist jutting out of a too-short, hand-me-down coat, *that* Violet slammed past a whitewoman into the seat of a trolley four minutes late. And if she turned away from faces looking past her through restaurant windows, *that* Violet heard the clack of the plate glass in mean March wind. She forgot which way to turn the key in the lock; *that* Violet not only knew the knife was in the parrot's cage and not in the kitchen drawer, *that* Violet remembered what she did not: scraping marble from the parrot's claws and beak weeks ago. She had been looking for that knife for a month. Couldn't for the life of her think what she'd done with it. But *that* Violet knew and went right to it. Knew too where the funeral was going on, although it could not have been but one of two places, come to think of it. Still, *that* Violet knew which of the two, and the right time to get there. Just before the closing of the casket, when the people who were going to faint fainted and the women in white dresses were fanning them. And the ushers, young men the same age as the deceased—from the dead girl's junior high school class, with freshly barbered heads and ghost-white gloves—gathered; first in a tight knot of six and then separated into two lines of three, they moved down the aisle from the back where they had assembled and surrounded the bier. They were the ones *that* Violet had to push aside, elbow her way into. And they did. Step aside, thinking maybe this was some last-minute love desperate to make itself known before it couldn't see and might forget the sleeping face it treasured. The ushers saw the knife before she did. Before she knew what was going on, the boy ushers' hard hands—knuckle-tough from marbles and steelies, from snowballs packed to bullet strength, from years of sticks sending hardballs over the hoods of motor cars, into lots with high fences and even into the open windows as well as the closed of people living four floors up, hands that had held the boys' whole body weight from the iron railings of El bridges—these hands were reaching toward the blade she had not seen for a month at least and was surprised to see now aimed at the girl's haughty, secret face.

It bounced off, making a little dent under her earlobe, like a fold in the skin that was hardly a disfigurement at all. She could have left it at that: the fold under the earlobe, but *that* Violet, unsatisfied, fought with the hard-handed usher boys and was time enough for them, almost. They had to forget right away that this was a fifty-year-old woman in a fur-collared coat and a hat pulled down so far over her right eye it was a wonder she saw the door to the church not to speak of the right place to aim her knife. They had to abandon the teachings they had had all their lives about the respect due their elders. Lessons learned from the old folks whose milky-light eyes watched everything they did, commented on it, and told each other what it was. Lessons they had learned from the younger old folks (like her) who could be their auntie, their grandmother, their mother, or their mother's best friend, who not only could tell on them, but could tell them; could stop them cold with a word, with a "Cut that mess out!" shouted from any window, doorway or street curb in a two-block radius. And they would cut it out, or take it downstairs behind the trunks, or off in a neglected park, or better still, in the shadow of the El where no lights lit what these women did not allow, don't care whose child it was. But they did it nevertheless. Forgot the lessons of a lifetime, and concentrated on the wide, shining blade, because who knew? Maybe she had more than one cutting in mind. Or maybe they could see themselves hangdog at the dinner table trying to explain to these same women or even, Jesus! the men, the fathers and uncles, and grown cousins, friends and neighbors, why they had just stood there like streetlights and let this woman in a fur-collared coat make fools of them and ruin the honorable job they had worn white gloves for. They had to wrestle her to the floor before she let go. And the sound that came from her mouth belonged to something wearing a pelt instead of a coat.

By then the usher boys were joined by frowning men, who carried *that* kicking, growling Violet out while she looked on in amazement. She had not been that strong since Virginia, since she loaded hay and handled the mule wagon like a full-grown man. But twenty years doing hair in the City had softened her arms and melted the shield that once covered her palms and fingers. Like shoes taking away the tough leather her bare feet had grown, the City took away the back and arm power she used to boast of. A power *that* Violet had not lost because she gave the usher boys, and the grown men too, a serious time.

*That* Violet should not have let the parrot go. He forgot how to fly and just trembled on the sill, but when she ran home from the funeral, having been literally thrown out by the hard-handed boys and the frowning men, "I love you" was exactly what neither she nor *that* Violet could bear to hear. She tried not to look at him as she paced the rooms, but the parrot saw her and squawked a weak "Love you" through the pane.

Joe, who had been missing since New Year's Day, did not come home that night or the next for her black-eyed peas. Gistan and Stuck came by to ask for him, to say they couldn't play cards Friday and to linger with embarrassment in the hall while Violet stared at them. So she knew the parrot was there because she kept going up and down the stairs from her apartment door to the front door to see if Joe was coming down the back and arms. Maybe *that* Violet, the one who knew where the butcher knife was and was strong enough to use it, had the hips she had lost. But if *that* Violet was strong and had hips, why was she proud of trying to kill a dead girl, and she was proud. Whenever she thought about *that* Violet, and what *that* Violet saw through her own eyes, she knew there was no shame there, no disgust. That was hers alone, so she hid behind the rack at one of Duggie's little illegal tables and played with the straw in a chocolate malt. She could have been eighteen herself, just like the girl at the magazine rack, reading *Collier's* and playing for time in the drugstore. Did Dorcas, when she was alive, like *Collier's? Liberty Magazine?* Did the blonde ladies with shingled hair capture her? Did the men in golf shoes and V-neck sweaters? How could they if she found herself stuck on a man old enough to be her father? A man who carried not a golf club but a sample case of Cleopatra products. A man whose handkerchiefs were not lightweight cotton poking from his jacket pocket, but red and large and spotted with white dots. Did he ask her to warm with her own body his spot in the bed on cold winter nights before he slid in? Or did he do it for her? He probably let her put her spoon into his pint of cream and scoop off the melty part, and when they sat in the dark of the Lincoln Theater he wouldn't mind a bit if she stuck her hand down in his box of popcorn and came up with a fistful of it the sonofabitch. And when "Wings Over Jordan" came on he probably turned the volume down so he could hear her when she sang along with the choir, instead of up so as to drown out her rendition of "Lay my body down." Turned, too, his jaw to the light of the bulb so she could press out between her thumbnails the hair root caught in a pore the dog. And another damn thing. (The malt was soup now, smooth and eyes shit no *that* Violet is me! The me that hauled hay in Virginia and handled a four-mule team in the brace. I have stood in cane fields in the middle of the night when the sound of it rustling hid the slither of the snakes and I stood still waiting for him and not stirring a speck in case he was near and I would miss him, and damn the snakes my man was coming for me and who or what was going to keep me from him? Plenty times, plenty times I have carried the welts given me by a two-tone peckerwood because I was late in the field row the next morning. Plenty times, plenty, I chopped twice the wood that was needed into short logs and kindlin so as to make sure the crackers had enough and wouldn't go hollering for me when I was bound to meet my Joe Trace don't care what, and do what you will or may he was my Joe Trace. Mine. I picked him out from all the others wasn't nobody like Joe he make anybody stand in cane in the middle of the night; make any woman dream about him in the daytime so hard she miss the rut and have to work hard to get the mules back on the track. Any woman, not just me. Maybe that is what she saw. Not the fifty-year-old man toting a sample case, but my Joe Trace, my Virginia Joe Trace who carried a light inside him, whose shoulders were razor sharp and who looked at me with two-color eyes and never saw anybody else. Could she have looked at him and seen that? Under the table at the Indigo was she drumming on a thigh soft as a baby's but feeling all the while the way it used to be skin so tight it almost split and let the iron muscle through? Did she feel that, know that? That and other things, things I should have known and didn't? Secret things kept hidden from me or things I didn't notice? Is that why he let her scoop the melty part from around the edges of his pint of ice cream, stick her hand down in his salt-and-butter popcorn.

What did she see, young girl like that, barely out of high school, with unbraided hair, lip rouge for the first time and high-heeled shoes? And also what did he? A young me with high-yellow skin instead of black? A young me with long wavy hair instead of short? Or a not me at all. A me he was loving in Virginia because that girl Dorcas wasn't around there anywhere. Was that it? Who was it? Who was he thinking of when he ran in the dark to meet me in the cane field? Somebody golden, like my own golden boy, who I never ever saw but who tore up my girlhood as surely as if we'd been the best of lovers? Help me God help me if that was it, because I knew him and loved him better than anybody except True Belle who is the one made me crazy about him in the first place. Is that what happened? Standing in the cane, he was trying to catch a girl he was yet to see, but his heart knew all about, and me, holding on to him but wishing he was the golden boy I never saw either. Which means from the very beginning I was a substitute and so was he.

I got quiet because the things I couldn't say were coming out of my mouth anyhow. I got quiet because I didn't know what my hands might get up to when the day's work was done. The business going on inside me I thought was none of my business and none of Joe's either because I just had to keep hold of him any way I could and going crazy would make me lose him.

Sitting in the thin sharp light of the drugstore playing with a long spoon in a tall glass made her think of another woman occupying herself at a table pretending to drink from a cup. Her mother. She didn't want to be like that. Oh never like that. To sit at the table, alone in the moonlight, sipping boiled coffee from a white china cup as long as it was there, and pretending to sip it when it was gone; waiting for morning when men came, talking low as though nobody was there but themselves, and picked around in our things, lifting out what they wanted—what was theirs, they said, although we cooked in it, washed sheets in it, sat on it, ate off of it. That was after they had hauled away the plow, the scythe, the mule, the sow, the churn and the butter press. Then they came inside the house and all of us children put one foot on the other and watched. When they got to the table where our mother sat nursing an empty cup, they took the table out from under her and then, while she sat there alone, and all by herself like, cup in hand, they came back and tipped the chair she sat in. She didn't jump up right away, so they shook it a bit and since she still stayed seated—looking ahead at nobody—they just tipped her out of it like the way you get the cat off the seat if you don't want to touch it or pick it up in your arms. You tip it forward and it lands on the floor. No harm done if it's a cat because it has four legs. But a person, a woman, might fall forward and just stay there a minute looking at the cup, stronger than she is, unbroken at least and lying a bit beyond her hand. Just out of reach.

There were five of them, Violet the third, and they all came in the house finally and said mama; each one came and said it until she said uh huh. They never heard her say anything else in the days that followed, when, huddled in an abandoned shack, they were thoroughly dependent upon the few neighbors left in 1888—the ones who had not moved west to Kansas City or Oklahoma; north to Chicago or Bloomington Indiana. It was through one of the last-to-leave families, bound for Philadelphia, that the message of Rose Dear's distress reached True Belle. Those who stayed brought things: a pallet, a pot, some pan bread and a bucket of milk. Advice too: "Don't let this whip you, Rose. You got us, Rose Dear. Think of the young ones, Rose. He ain't give you nothing you can't bear, Rose." But had He? Maybe this one time He had. Had misjudged and misunderstood her particular backbone. This one time. This here particular spine.

Rose's mother, True Belle, came when she heard. Left her cushiony job in Baltimore and, with ten eagle dollars stitched separately into her skirts to keep them quiet, came back to a little depot called Rome in Vesper County to take charge and over. The little girls fell in love right away and things got put back together. Slowly but steadily, for about four years, True Belle got things organized. And then Rose Dear jumped in the well and missed all the fun. Two weeks after her burial, Rose's husband arrived loaded with ingots of gold for the children, two-dollar pieces for the women and snake oil for the men. For Rose Dear he brought a silk embroidered pillow to comfort her back on a sofa nobody ever had, but would have been real nice under her head in the pine box—if only he'd been on time. The children ate the chocolate from the ingots of gold and traded the heavenly paper among themselves for reed whistles and fishing string. The women bit the piece of silver before knotting it tightly in their clothes. Except True Belle. She fingered the money and, looking back and forth from the coin to her son-in-law, shook her head and laughed.

"Damn," he said. "Aw, damn," when he heard what Rose had done.

Twenty-one days later he was gone again, and Violet was married to Joe and living in the City when she heard from a sister that he'd done it again: arrived in Rome with treasures weighing his pockets and folded under the cap on his head. His trips back were both bold and secret for he had been mixed in and up with the Readjuster Party, and when a verbal urging from landowners had not worked, a physical one did the trick and he was persuaded to transfer hisself someplace, anyplace, else. Perhaps he planned to find some way to get them all out; in the meantime he made fabulously dangerous and wonderful returns over the years, although the interims got longer and longer, and while the likelihood that he was still alive grew fainter, hope never did. Anytime anytime, on another brittle cold Monday or in the blasting heat of a Sunday night, he might be there, owl-whistling from the road, the mocking, daring dollar bills sticking from his cap, jammed into the cuffs of his trousers and the tops of his shoes. Candy stuck in clumps in his coat pocket along with a tin of Frieda's Egyptian Hair Pomade. Bottles of rye, purgative waters and eaux for every conceivable toilette made a companionable click in his worn carpet bag.

He'd be in his seventies now. Slower for sure, and maybe he'd lost the teeth that made the smile that made the sisters forgive him. But for Violet (as well as for her sisters and those who stayed in the county) he was out there somewhere gathering and putting by delights to pass out among the homefolks. For who could keep him down, this defiant birthday-every-day man who dispensed gifts and stories that kept them so rapt they forgot for the while a bone-clean cupboard and exhausted soil; or believed a child's leg would straighten itself out by and by. Forgot why he left in the first place and was forced to sneak into his own home ground. In his company forgetfulness fell like pollen. But for Violet the pollen never blotted out Rose. In the midst of the joyful resurrection of this phantom father, taking pleasure in the distribution of his bounty both genuine and fake, Violet never forgot Rose Dear or the place she had thrown herself into—a place so narrow, so dark it was pure, breathing relief to see her stretched in a wooden box.

"Thank God for life," True Belle said, "and thank life for death."

Rose. Dear Rose Dear.

What was the thing, I wonder, the one and final thing she had not been able to endure or repeat? Had the last washing split the shirtwaist so bad it could not take another mend and changed its name to rag? Perhaps word had reached her about the four-day hangings in Rocky Mount: the men on Tuesday, the women two days later. Or had it been the news of the young tenor in the choir mutilated and tied to a log, his grandmother refusing to give up his waste-filled trousers, washing them over and over although the stain had disappeared at the third rinse. They buried him in his brother's pants and the old woman pumped another bucket of clear water. Might it have been the morning after the night when craving (which used to be hope) got out of hand? When longing squeezed, then tossed her before running off promising to return and bounce her again like an India-rubber ball? Or was it that chair they tipped her out of? Did she fall on the floor and lie there deciding right then that she would do it. Someday. Delaying it for four years while True Belle came and took over but remembering the floorboards as a door, closed and locked. Seeing bleak truth in an unbreakable china cup? Biding her time until the moment returned—with all its mewing hurt or overboard rage—and she could turn away from the door, the cup to step toward the limitlessness beckoning from the well. What could it have been, I wonder?

True Belle was there, chuckling, competent, stitching by firelight, gardening and harvesting by day. Pouring mustard tea on the girls' cuts and bruises, and keeping them at their tasks with spellbinding tales of her Baltimore days and the child she had cared for there. Maybe it was that: knowing her daughters were in good hands, better hands than her own, at last, and Rose Dear was free of time that no longer flowed, but stood stock-still when they tipped her from her kitchen chair. So she dropped herself down the well and missed all the fun.

The important thing, the biggest thing Violet got out of that was to never never have children. Whatever happened, no small dark foot would rest on another while a hungry mouth said, Mama?

As she grew older, Violet could neither stay where she was nor go away. The well sucked her sleep, but the notion of leaving frightened her. It was True Belle who forced it. There were bully cotton crops in Palestine and people for twenty miles around were going to pick it. Rumor was the pay was ten cents for young women, a quarter for men. Three double seasons in a row of bad weather had ruined all expectations and then came the day when the blossoms jumped out fat and creamy. Everybody held his breath while the landowner squinted his eyes and spat. His two black laborers walked the rows, touching the tender flowers, fingering the soil and trying to puzzle out the sky. Then one day of light, fresh rain, four dry, hot and clear, and all of Palestine was downy with the cleanest cotton they'd ever seen. Softer than silk, and out so fast the weevils, having abandoned the fields years ago, had no time to get back there.

Three weeks. It all had to be done in three weeks or less. Everybody with fingers in a twenty-mile radius showed up and was hired on the spot. Nine dollars a bale, some said, if you grew your own; eleven dollars if you had a white friend to carry it up for pricing. And for pickers, ten cents a day for the women and a case quarter for the men.

True Belle sent Violet and two of her sisters in the fourth wagonload to go. They rode all night, assembled at dawn, ate what was handed out and shared the meadows and the stars with local people who saw no point in going all the way home for five hours' sleep.

Violet had no talent for it. She was seventeen years old but trailed with the twelve-year-olds—making up the last in line or meeting the others on their way back down the row. For this she was put to scragging, second-picking the bushes that had a few inferior puffs left on the twigs by swifter hands than hers. Humiliated, teased to tears, she had about decided to beg a way back to Rome when a man fell out of the tree above her head and landed at her side. She had lain down one night, sulking and abashed, a little way from her sisters, but not too far. Not too far to crawl back to them swiftly if the trees turned out to be full of spirits idling the night away. The spot she had chosen to spread her blanket was under a handsome black walnut that grew at the edge of the woods bordering the acres of cotton.

The thump could not have been a raccoon's because it said Ow. Violet rolled away too scared to speak, but raised on all fours to dash.

"Never happened before," said the man. "I've been sleeping up there every night. This the first time I fell out."

Violet could see his outline in a sitting position and that he was rubbing his arm then his head then his arm again.

"You sleep in trees?"

"If I find me a good one."

"Nobody sleeps in trees."

"I sleep in them."

"Sounds softheaded to me. Could be snakes up there."

"Snakes around here crawl the ground at night. Now who's softheaded?"

"Could've killed me."

"Might still, if my arm ain't broke."

"I hope it is. You won't be picking nothing in the morning and climbing people's trees either."

"I don't pick cotton. I work the gin house."

"What you doing out here, then, Mr. High and Mighty, sleeping in trees like a bat?"

"You don't have one nice word for a hurt man?"

"Yeah: find somebody else's tree."

"You act like you own it."

"You act like you do."

"Say we share it."

"Not me."

He stood up and shook his leg before trying his weight on it, then limped toward the tree.

"You not going back up there over my head."

"Get my tarp," he said. "Rope broke. That's what did it." He scanned the night for the far reaches of the branches. "See it? There it is. Hanging right there. Yep." He sat down then, his back resting on the trunk. "Have to wait till it's light, though," he said and Violet always believed that because their first conversation began in the dark (when neither could see much more of the other than silhouette) and ended in a green-and-white dawn, nighttime was never the same for her. Never again would she wake struggling against the pull of a narrow well. Or watch first light with the sadness left over from finding Rose Dear in the morning twisted into water much too small.

His name was Joseph, and even before the sun rose, when

it was still hidden in the woods, but freshening the world's green and dazzling acres of white cotton against the gash of a ruby horizon, Violet claimed him. Hadn't he fallen practically in her lap? Hadn't he stayed? All through the night, taking her sass, complaining, teasing, explaining, but talking, talking her through the dark. And with daylight came the bits of him: his smile and his wide watching eyes. His buttonless shirt open to a knot at the waist exposed a chest she claimed as her own smooth pillow. The shaft of his legs, the plane of his shoulders, jawline and long fingers—she claimed it all. She knew she must be staring, and tried to look away, but the contrasting color of his two eyes brought her glance back each and every time. She grew anxious when she heard workers begin to stir, anticipating the breakfast call, going off in the trees to relieve themselves, muttering morning sounds—but then he said, "I'll be back in our tree tonight. Where you be?"

"Under it," she said and rose from the clover like a woman with important things to do.

She did not worry what could happen in three weeks when she was supposed to take her two dollars and ten cents back to True Belle. As it turned out, she sent it back with her sisters and stayed in the vicinity hunting work. The straw boss had no faith in her, having watched her sweating hard to fill her sack as quickly as the children, but she was highly and suddenly vocal in her determination.

She moved in with a family of six in Tyrell and worked at anything to be with Joe whenever she could. It was there she became the powerfully strong young woman who could handle mules, bale hay and chop wood as good as any man. It was there where the palms of her hands and the soles of her feet grew shields no gloves or shoes could match. All for Joe Trace, a double-eyed nineteen-year-old who lived with an adopted family, worked gins and lumber and cane and cotton and corn, who butchered when needed, plowed, fished, sold skins and game— and who was willing. He loved the woods. Loved them. So it was shocking to his family and friends not when he agreed to marry Violet, but that, thirteen years later, he agreed to take her to Baltimore, where she said all the houses had separate rooms and water came to you—not you to it. Where colored men worked harbors for $2.50 a day, pulling cargo from ships bigger than churches, and others drove up to the very door of your house to take you where you needed to be. She was describing a Baltimore of twenty-five years ago and a neighborhood neither she nor Joe could rent in, but she didn't know that, and never knew it, because they went to the City instead. Their Baltimore dreams were displaced by more powerful ones. Joe knew people living in the City and some who'd been there and come home with tales to make Baltimore weep. The money to be earned for doing light work—standing in front of a door, carrying food on a tray, even cleaning strangers' shoes— got you in a day more money than any of them had earned in one whole harvest. Whitepeople literally threw money at you—just for being neighborly: opening a taxi door, picking up a package. And anything you had or made or found you could sell in the streets. In fact, there were streets where colored people owned all the stores; whole blocks of handsome colored men and women laughing all night and making money all day. Steel cars sped down the streets and if you saved up, they said, you could get you one and drive as long as there was road.

For fourteen years Joe listened to these stories and laughed. But he resisted them too, until, abruptly, he changed his mind. No one, not even Violet, knew what it was that permitted him to leave his fields and woods and secret lonely valleys. To give away his fishing pole, his skinning knife—every piece of his gear but one, and borrow a suitcase for their things. Violet never knew what it was that fired him up and made him want—all of a sudden, but later than most—to move to the City. She supposed that the dinner that tickled everybody must have played a part in Joe's change of mind. If Booker T. was sitting down to eat a chicken sandwich in the President's house in a city called capital, near where True Belle had had such a good time, then things must be all right, all right. He took his bride on a train ride electric enough to pop their eyes and danced on into the City.

Violet thought it would disappoint them; that it would be less lovely than Baltimore. Joe believed it would be perfect. When they arrived, carrying all of their belongings in one valise, they both knew right away that perfect was not the word. It was better than that.

Joe didn't want babies either so all those miscarriages—two in the field, only one in her bed—were more inconvenience than loss. And citylife would be so much better without them. Arriving at the train station back in 1906, the smiles they both smiled at the women with little children, strung like beads over suitcases, were touched with pity. They liked children. Loved them even. Especially Joe, who had a way with them. But neither wanted the trouble. Years later, however, when Violet was forty, she was already staring at infants, hesitating in front of toys displayed at Christmas. Quick to anger when a sharp word was flung at a child, or a woman's hold of a baby seemed awkward or careless. The worst burn she ever made was on the temple of a customer holding a child across her knees. Violet, lost in the woman's hand-patting and her knee-rocking the little boy, forgot her own hand holding the curling iron. The customer flinched and the skin discolored right away. Violet moaned her apologies and the woman was satisfied until she discovered that the whole curl was singed clean off. Skin healed, but an empty spot in her hairline . . . Violet had to forgo payment to shut her up.

By and by longing became heavier than sex: a panting, unmanageable craving. She was limp in its thrall or rigid in an effort to dismiss it. That was when she bought herself a present; hid it under the bed to take out in secret when it couldn't be helped. She began to imagine how old that last miscarried child would be now. A girl, probably. Certainly a girl. Who would she favor? What would her speaking voice sound like? After weaning time, Violet would blow her breath on the babygirl's food, cooling it down for the tender mouth. Later on they would sing together, Violet taking the alto line, the girl a honeyed soprano. "Don't you remember, a long time ago, two little babes their names I don't know, carried away one bright summer's day, lost in the woods I hear people say that the sun went down and the stars shone their light. Poor babes in the woods they laid down and died. When they were dead a robin so red put strawberry leaves over their heads." Aw. Aw. Later on Violet would dress her hair for her the way the girls wore it now: short, bangs paper sharp above the eyebrows? Ear curls? Razor-thin part on the side? Hair sliding into careful waves marcelled to a T?

Violet was drowning in it, deep-dreaming. Just when her breasts were finally flat enough not to need the binders the young women wore to sport the chest of a soft boy, just when her nipples had lost their point, mother-hunger had hit her like a hammer. Knocked her down and out. When she woke up, her husband had shot a girl young enough to be that daughter whose hair she had dressed to kill. Who lay there asleep in that coffin? Who posed there awake in the photograph? The scheming bitch who had not considered Violet's feelings one tiniest bit, who came into a life, took what she wanted and damn the consequences? Or mama's dumpling girl? Was she the woman who took the man, or the daughter who fled her womb? Washed away on a tide of soap, salt and castor oil. Terrified, perhaps, of so violent a home. Unaware that, had it failed, had she braved mammymade poisons and mammy's urgent fists, she could have had the best-dressed hair in the City. Instead, she hung around in the fat knees of strangers' children. In shop windows, and baby carriages left for a moment in the sun. Not realizing that, bitch or dumpling, the two of them, mother and daughter, could have walked Broadway together and ogled the clothes. Could be sitting together, cozy in the kitchen, while Violet did her hair.

"Another time," she said to Alice Manfred, "another time I would have loved her too. Just like you did. Just like Joe." She was holding her coat lapels closed, too embarrassed to let her hostess hang it up lest she see the lining.

"Maybe," said Alice. "Maybe. You'll never know now, though, will you?"

"I thought she was going to be pretty. Real pretty. She wasn't."

"Pretty enough, I'd say."

"You mean the hair. The skin color."

"Don't tell me what I mean."

"Then what? What he see in her?"

"Shame on you. Grown woman like you asking me that."

"I have to know."

"Then ask the one who does know. You see him every day."

"Don't get mad."

"Will if I want to."

"All right. But I don't want to ask him. I don't want to hear what he has to say about it. You know what I'm asking."

"Forgiveness is what you're asking and I can't give you that. It's not in my power."

"No, not that. That's not it, forgiveness."

"What, then? Don't get pitiful. I won't stand for you getting pitiful, hear me?"

"We born around the same time, me and you," said Violet. "We women, me and you. Tell me something real. Don't just say I'm grown and ought to know. I don't. I'm fifty and I don't know nothing. What about it? Do I stay with him? I want to, I think. I want . . . well, I didn't always . . . now I want. I want some fat in this life."

"Wake up. Fat or lean, you got just one. This is it."

"You don't know either, do you?"

"I know enough to know how to behave."

"Is that it? Is that all it is?"

"Is that all what is?"

"Oh shoot! Where the grown people? Is it us?"

"Oh, Mama." Alice Manfred blurted it out and then covered her mouth.

Violet had the same thought: Mama. Mama? Is this where you got to and couldn't do it no more? The place of shade without trees where you know you are not and never again will be loved by anybody who can choose to do it? Where everything is over but the talking?

They looked away from each other then. The silence went on and on until Alice Manfred said, "Give me that coat. I can't look at that lining another minute."

Violet stood up and took off her coat, carefully pulling her arms trapped in frayed silk. Then she sat down and watched the seamstress go to work.

"All I could think of was to step out on him like he did me."

"Fool," said Alice and broke the thread.

"Couldn't name him if my life depended on it."

"Bet he can name you."

"Let him."

"What did you think that was going to solve?"

Violet didn't answer.

"Did it get you your husband's attention?"

"No."

"Open my niece's grave?"

"No."

"Do I have to say it again?"

"Fool? No. No, but tell me, I mean, listen. Everybody I grew up with is down home. We don't have children. He's what I got. He's what I got."

"Doesn't look so," said Alice. Her stitches were invisible to the eye.

Late in March, sitting in Duggie's drugstore, Violet played with a spoon, recalling the visit she had paid to Alice that morning. She had come early. Chore time and Violet wasn't doing any.

"It's different from what I thought," she said. "Different."

Violet meant twenty years of life in a City better than perfect, but Alice did not ask her what she meant. Did not ask her whether the City, with its streets all laid out, aroused jealousy too late for anything but foolishness. Or if it was the City that produced a crooked kind of mourning for a rival young enough to be a daughter.

They had been talking about prostitutes and fighting

women—Alice nettled; Violet indifferent. Then silence while Violet drank tea and listened to the hissing iron. By this time the women had become so easy with each other talk wasn't always necessary. Alice ironed and Violet watched. From time to time one murmured something—to herself or to the other.

"I used to love that stuff," said Violet.

Alice smiled, knowing without looking up that Violet meant the starch. "Me too," she said. "Drove my husband crazy."

"Is it the crunch? Couldn't be the taste."

Alice shrugged. "Only the body knows."

The iron hissed at the damp fabric. Violet leaned her cheek on her palm. "You iron like my grandmother. Yoke last."

"That's the test of a first-class ironing."

"Some do it yoke first."

"And have to do it over. I hate a lazy ironing."

"Where you learn to sew like that?"

"They kept us children busy. Idle hands, you know."

"We picked cotton, chopped wood, plowed. I never knew what it was to fold my hands. This here is as close as I ever been to watching my hands do nothing."

Eating starch, choosing when to tackle the yoke, sewing, picking, cooking, chopping. Violet thought about it all and sighed. "I thought it would be bigger than this. I knew it wouldn't last, but I did think it'd be bigger."

Alice refolded the cloth around the handle of the pressing iron. "He'll do it again, you know. And again and again and again."

"In that case I'd better throw him out now."

"Then what?"

Violet shook her head. "Watch the floorboards, I guess."

"You want a real thing?" asked Alice. "I'll tell you a real one. You got anything left to you to love, anything at all, do it."

Violet raised her head. "And when he does it again? Don't mind what people think?"

"Mind what's left to you."

"You saying take it? Don't fight?"

Alice put down her iron, hard. "Fight what, who? Some mishandled child who saw her parents burn up? Who knew better than you or me or anybody just how small and quick this little bitty life is? Or maybe you want to stomp somebody with three kids and one pair of shoes. Somebody in a raggedy dress, the hem dragging in the mud. Somebody wanting arms just like you do and you want to go over there and hold her but her dress is muddy at the hem and the people standing around wouldn't understand how could anybody's eyes go so flat, how could they? Nobody's asking you to take it. I'm sayin make it, make it!"

It took her a moment to notice that Violet was staring. Following her gaze Alice lifted the iron and saw what Violet saw: the black and smoking ship burned clear through the yoke.

"Shit!" Alice shouted. "Oh, shit!"

Violet was the first to smile. Then Alice. In no time laughter was rocking them both. Violet was reminded of True Belle, who entered the single room of their cabin and laughed to beat the band. They were hunched like mice near a can fire, not even a stove, on the floor, hungry and irritable. True Belle looked at them and had to lean against the wall to keep her laughter from pulling her down to the floor with them. They should have hated her. Gotten up from the floor and hated her. But what they felt was better. Not beaten, not lost. Better. They laughed too, even Rose Dear shook her head and smiled, and suddenly the world was right side up. Violet learned then what she had forgotten until this moment: that laughter is serious. More complicated, more serious than tears.

Crumpled over, shoulders shaking, Violet thought about how she must have looked at the funeral, at what her mission was. The sight of herself trying to do something bluesy, something hep, fumbling the knife, too late anyway . . . She laughed till she coughed and Alice had to make them both a cup of settling tea.

Committed as Violet was to hip development, even she couldn't drink the remaining malt—watery, warm and flat-tasting. She buttoned her coat and left the drugstore and noticed, at the same moment as *that* Violet did, that it was spring. In the City.

appetite at all; giving you a taste for a single room occupied by you alone as well as a craving to share it with someone you passed in the street. Really there is no contradiction—rather it's a condition: the range of what an artful City can do. What can beat bricks warming up to the sun? The return of awnings. The removal of blankets from horses' backs. Tar softens under the heel and the darkness under bridges changes from gloom to cooling shade. After a light rain, when the leaves have come, tree limbs are like wet fingers playing in woolly green hair. Motor cars become black jet boxes gliding behind hoodlights weakened by mist. On sidewalks turned to satin figures move shoulder first, the crowns of their heads angled shields against the light buckshot that the raindrops are. The faces of children glimpsed at windows appear to be crying, but it is the glass pane dripping that makes it seem so.

In the spring of 1926, on a rainy afternoon, anybody passing through the alley next to a certain apartment house on Lenox might have looked up and seen, not a child but a grown man's face crying along with the glass pane. A strange sight you hardly ever see: men crying so openly. It's not a thing they do. Strange as it was, people finally got used to him, wiping his face and nose with an engineer's red handkerchief while he sat month after month by the window without view or on the stoop, first in the snow and later in the sun. I'd say Violet washed and ironed those handkerchiefs because, crazy as she was, raggedy as she became, she couldn't abide dirty laundry. But it tired everybody out waiting to see what else Violet would do besides try to kill a dead girl and keep her husband in tidy handkerchiefs. My own opinion was that one day she would stack up those handkerchiefs, take them to the dresser drawer, tuck them in and then go light his hair with a matchstick. She didn't but maybe that would have been better than what she did do. Meaning to or not meaning to, she got him to go through it again—at springtime when it's clearer then than as at no other time that citylife is streetlife.

Blind men thrum and hum in the soft air as they inch steadily down the walk. They don't want to stand near and compete with the old uncles positioning themselves in the middle of the block to play a six-string guitar.

Blues man. Black and bluesman. Blacktherefore blue man.

Everybody knows your name.

Where-did-she-go-and-why man. So-lonesome-I-could-die man.

Everybody knows your name.

The singer is hard to miss, sitting as he does on a fruit crate in the center of the sidewalk. His peg leg is stretched out comfy; his real one is carrying both the beat and the guitar's weight. Joe probably thinks that the song is about him. He'd like believing it. I know him so well. Have seen him feed small animals nobody else paid any attention to, but I was never deceived. I remember the way he used to fix his hat when he left the apartment building; how he moved it forward and a bit to the left. Whether stooping to remove a pile of horse flop or sauntering off to his swank hotel, his hat had to be just so. Not a tilt exactly, but a definite slant, you could say. The sweater under his suit jacket would be buttoned all the way up, but I know his thoughts are not—they are loose. He cuts his eyes over to the sweetbacks lounging on the corner. There is something they have he wants. Very little in his case of Cleopatra is something men would want to buy—except for aftershave dusting powder, most of it is for women. Women he can get to talk to, look at, flirt with and who knows what else is on his mind? And if she gives him more than the time of day with a look, the watching eyes of the sweetbacks are more satisfying than hers.

Or else he feels sorry about himself for being faithful in the first place. And if that virtue is unappreciated, and nobody jumps up to congratulate him on it, his self-pity turns to resentment which he has trouble understanding but no trouble focusing on the young sheiks, radiant and brutal, standing on street corners. Look out. Look out for a faithful man near fifty. Because he has never messed with another woman; because he selected that young girl to love, he thinks he is free. Not free to break loaves or feed the world on a fish. Nor to raise the war dead, but free to do something wild.

Take my word for it, he is bound to the track. It pulls him like a needle through the groove of a Bluebird record. Round and round about the town. That's the way the City spins you. Makes you do what it wants, go where the laid-out roads say to. All the while letting you think you're free; that you can jump into thickets because you feel like it. There are no thickets here and if mowed grass is okay to walk on the City will let you know. You can't get off the track a City lays for you. Whatever happens, whether you get rich or stay poor, ruin your health or live to old age, you always end up back where you started: hungry for the one thing everybody loses—young loving.

That was Dorcas, all right. Young but wise. She was Joe's personal sweet—like candy. It was the best thing, if you were young and had just got to the City. That and the clarinets and even they were called licorice sticks. But Joe has been in the City twenty years and isn't young anymore. I imagine him as one of those men who stop somewhere around sixteen. Inside.

So even though he wears button-up-the-front sweaters and round-toed shoes, he's a kid, a strapling, and candy could still make him smile. He likes those peppermint things last the live-long day, and thinks everybody else does too. Passes them out to Gistan's boys clowning on the curb. You could tell they'd rather chocolate or something with peanuts.

Makes me wonder about Joe. All those good things he gets from the Windemere, and he pays almost as much money for stale and sticky peppermint as he does for the room he rents to fuck in. Where his private candy box opens for him.

Rat. No wonder it ended the way it did. But it didn't have to, and if he had stopped trailing that little fast thing all over town long enough to tell Stuck or Gistan or some neighbor who might be interested, who knows how it would go?

"It's not a thing you tell to another man. I know most men can't wait to tell each other about what they got going on the side. Put all their business in the street. They do it because the woman don't matter all that much and they don't care what folks think about her. The most I did was halfway tell Malvonne and there was no way not to. But tell another man? No. Anyhow Gistan would just laugh and try to get out of hearing it. Stuck would look at his feet, swear I'd been fixed and tell me how much high john I need to remedy myself. Neither one of them I'd talk to about her. It's not a thing you tell except maybe to a tight friend, somebody you knew from before, long time ago like Victory, but even if I had the chance I don't believe I could have told him and if I couldn't tell Victory it was because I couldn't tell myself because I didn't know all about it. All I know is I saw her buying candy and the whole thing was sweet. Not just the candy—the whole thing and picture of it. Candy's something you lick, suck on, and then swallow and it's gone. No. This was something else. More like blue water and white flowers, and sugar in the air. I needed to be there, where it was all mixed up together just right, and where that was, was Dorcas.

"When I got to the apartment I had no name to put to the face I'd seen in the drugstore, and her face wasn't on my mind right then. But she opened the door, opened it right up to me. I smelled pound cake and disguised chicken. The women gathered around and I showed them what I had while they laughed and did the things women do: flicked lint off my jacket, pressed me on the shoulder to make me sit down. It's a way they have of mending you, fixing what they think needs repair.

"She didn't give me a look or say anything. But I knew where she was standing and how, every minute. She leaned her hip on the back of a chair in the parlor, while the women streamed out of the dining room to mend me and joke me. Then somebody called out her name. Dorcas. I didn't hear much else, but I stayed there and showed them all my stuff, smiling, not selling but letting them sell themselves.

"I sell trust; I make things easy. That's the best way. Never push. Like at the Windemere when I wait tables. I'm there but only if you want me. Or when I work the rooms, bringing up the whiskey hidden so it looks like coffee. Just there when you need me and right on time. You get to know the woman who wants four glasses of something, but doesn't want to ask four times; so you wait till her glass is two-thirds down and fill it up again. That way, she's drinking one glass while he is buying four. The quiet money whispers twice: once when I slide it in my pocket; once when I slide it out.

"I was prepared to wait, to have her ignore me. I didn't have a plan and couldn't have carried it out if I did. I felt dizzy with a lightheadedness I thought came from the heavy lemon flavoring, the face powder and that light woman-sweat. Salty. Not bitter like a man's is. I don't know to this day what made me speak to her on the way out the door.

"I can conjure what people say. That I treated Violet like a piece of furniture you favor although it needed something every day to keep it steady and upright. I don't know. But since Victory, I never got too close to anybody. Gistan and Stuck, we close, but not like it is with somebody knew you from when you was born and you got to manhood at the same time. I would have told Victory how it was. Gistan, Stuck, whatever I said to them would be something near, but not the way it really was. I couldn't talk to anybody but Dorcas and I told her things I hadn't told myself. With her I was fresh, new again. Before I met her I'd changed into new seven times. The first time was when I named my own self, since nobody did it for me, since nobody knew what it could or should have been.

"I was born and raised in Vesper County, Virginia, in 1873. Little place called Vienna. Rhoda and Frank Williams took me in right away and raised me along with six of their own. Her last child was three months old when Mrs. Rhoda took me in, and me and him were closer than many brothers I've seen. Victory was his name. Victory Williams. Mrs. Rhoda named me Joseph after her father, but neither she nor Mr. Frank either thought to give me a last name. She never pretended I was her natural child. When she parceled out chores or favors she'd say, 'You are just like my own.' That 'like' I guess it was made me ask her—I don't believe I was three yet—where my real parents were. She looked down at me, over her shoulder, and gave me the sweetest smile, but sad someway, and told me, O honey, they disappeared without a trace. The way I heard it I understood her to mean the 'trace' they disappeared without was me.

"The first day I got to school I had to have two names. I told the teacher Joseph Trace. Victory turned his whole self around in the seat.

" 'Why you tell her that?' he asked me.

" 'I don't know,' I said. 'Cause.'

" 'Mama be mad. Pappy too.'

"We were outside in the school yard. It was nice, packed dirt but a lot of nails and things were in it. Both of us barefoot. I was struggling to pick a bit of glass from the sole of my foot, so I didn't have to look up at him. 'No they won't,' I said. 'Your mama ain't my mama.'

" 'If she ain't, who is?'

" 'Another woman. She be back. She coming back for me. My daddy too.' That was the first time I knew I thought that, or wished it.

"Victory said, 'They know where they left you. They come back to our place. Williams place is where they know you at.' He was trying to walk double-jointed like his sister. She was good at it and bragged so much Victory practiced every chance he got. I remember his shadow darting in the dirt in front of me. 'They know you at Williams place, Williams is what you ought to call yourself.'

"I said, 'They got to pick me out. From all of you all, they got to pick me. I'm Trace, what they went off without.'

" 'Ain't that a bitch?'

"Victory laughed at me and wrapped his arm around my neck wrassling me to the ground. I don't know what happened to the speck of glass. I never did get it out. And nobody came looking for me either. I never knew my own daddy. And my mother, well, I heard a woman in the hotel dining room say the confoundest thing. She was talking to two other women while I poured the coffee. 'I am bad for my children,' she said. 'I don't mean to be, but there is something in me that makes it so. I'm a good mother but they do better away from me; as long as they're by my side nothing good can come to them. The ones that leave seem to flower; the ones that stay have such a hard time. You can imagine how bad I feel knowing that, can't you?'

"I had to sneak a look at her. It took strength to say that. Admit that.

"The second change came when I was picked out and trained to be a man. To live independent and feed myself no matter what. I didn't miss having a daddy because first off there was Mr. Frank. Steady as a rock, and showed no difference among any of us children. But the big thing was, I was picked, Victory too, by the best man in Vesper County to go hunting with. Talk about proud-making. He was the best in the county and he picked me and Victory to teach and hunt with. He was so good they say he just carried the rifle for the hell of it because he knew way before what the prey would do, how to fool snakes, bend twigs and string to catch rabbits, groundhog; make a sound waterfowl couldn't resist. Whitefolks said he was a witch doctor, but they said that so they wouldn't have to say he was smart. A hunter's hunter, that's what he was. Smart as they come. Taught me two lessons I lived by all my life. One was the secret of kindness from whitepeople—they had to pity a thing before they could like it. The other—well, I forgot it.

"It was because of him, what I learned from him, made me

more comfortable in the woods than in a town. I'd get nervous
if a fence or a rail was anywhere around. Folks thought I was
the one to be counted on never to be able to stomach a city.
Piled-up buildings? Cement paths? Me? Not me.

"Eighteen ninety-three was the third time I changed. That
was when Vienna burned to the ground. Red fire doing fast
what white sheets took too long to finish: canceling every deed;
vacating each and every field; emptying us out of our places so
fast we went running from one part of the county to another—
or nowhere. I walked and worked, worked and walked, me and
Victory, fifteen miles to Palestine. That's where I met Violet.
We got married and set up on Harlon Ricks' place near Tyrell.
He owned the worst land in the county. Violet and me worked
his crops for two years. When the soil ran out, when rocks was
the biggest harvest, we ate what I shot. Then old man Ricks
got fed up and sold the place along with our debt to a man
called Clayton Bede. The debt rose from one hundred eighty
dollars to eight hundred under him. Interest, he said, and all
the fertilizer and stuff we got from the general store—things
he paid for—the prices, he said, went up. Violet had to tend
our place and walk the plow on his too, while I went from Bear
to Crossland to Goshen working. Slash pine some of the time,
sawmill most of it. Took us five years, but we did it.

"Then I got a job laying rail for the Southern Sky. I was
twenty-eight years old and used to changing now, so in 1901,
when Booker T. had a sandwich in the President's house, I was
bold enough to do it again: decided to buy me a piece of land.
Like a fool I thought they'd let me keep it. They ran us off with
two slips of paper I never saw nor signed.

"I changed up again the fourth time in 1906 when I took
my wife to Rome, a depot near where she was born, and

boarded the Southern Sky for a northern one. They moved us five times in four different cars to abide by the Jim Crow law.

"We lived in a railroad flat in the Tenderloin. Violet went in service and I worked everything from whitefolks shoe leather to cigars in a room where they read to us while we rolled tobacco. I cleaned fish at night and toilets in the day till I got in with the table waiters. And I thought I had settled into my permanent self, the fifth one, when we left the stink of Mulberry Street and Little Africa, then the flesh-eating rats on West Fifty-third and moved uptown.

"By then all the hogs and cows had disappeared, and what used to be little shacky farms nowhere near the size of the piece I tried to buy was more and more houses. Used to be a colored man could get shot at just walking around up there. They built row houses and single ones with big yards and vegetable gardens. Then, just before the War, whole blocks was let to colored. Nice. Not like downtown. These had five, six rooms; some had ten and if you could manage fifty, sixty dollars a month, you could have one. When we moved from 140th Street to a bigger place on Lenox, it was the light-skinned renters who tried to keep us out. Me and Violet fought them, just like they was whites. We won. Bad times had hit then, and landlords white and black fought over colored people for the high rents that was okay by us because we got to live in five rooms even if some of us rented out two. The buildings were like castles in pictures and we who had cleaned up everybody's mess since the beginning knew better than anybody how to keep them nice. We had birds and plants everywhere, me and Violet. I gathered up the street droppings myself to fertilize them. And I made sure the front was as neat as the inside. I was doing hotel work by then. Better than waiting tables in a restaurant because in a hotel there're more ways to get tips. Pay was light, but the tips dropped in my palm fast as pecans in November.

"When the rents got raised and raised again, and the stores doubled the price of uptown beef and let the whitefolks' meat stay the same, I got me a little sideline selling Cleopatra products in the neighborhood. What with Violet cutting out day work and just doing hair, we did fine.

"Then long come a summer in 1917 and after those whitemen took that pipe from around my head, I was brand new for sure because they almost killed me. Along with many a more. One of those whitemen had a heart and kept the others from finishing me right then and there.

"I don't know exactly what started the riot. Could have been what the papers said, what the waiters I worked with said, or what Gistan said—that party, he said, where they sent out invitations to whites to come see a colored man burn alive. Gistan said thousands of whites turned up. Gistan said it sat on everybody's chest, and if the killing hadn't done it, something else would have. They were bringing in swarms of colored to work during the War. Crackers in the South mad cause Negroes were leaving; crackers in the North mad cause they were coming.

"I have seen some things in my time. In Virginia. Two of my stepbrothers. Hurt bad. Bad. Liked to kill Mrs. Rhoda. There was a girl, too. Visiting her folks up by Crossland. Just a girl. Anyway, up here if you bust out a hundred'll bust right along with you.

"I saw some little boys running in the street. One fell down and didn't get up right away, so I went over to him. That did it. Riot went on without me while me and Violet nursed my head. I survived it, though, and maybe that's what made me change again for the seventh time two years later in 1919 when I walked all the way, every goddamn step of the way, with the three six nine. Can't remember no time when I danced in the street but that one time when everybody did. I thought that change was the last, and it sure was the best because the War had come and gone and the colored troops of the three six nine that fought it made me so proud it split my heart in two. Gistan got me a job at another hotel where the tip was folding money more often than coin. I had it made. In 1925 we all had it made. Then Violet started sleeping with a doll in her arms. Too late. I understood in a way. In a way.

"Don't get me wrong. This wasn't Violet's fault. All of it's mine. All of it. I'll never get over what I did to that girl. Never. I changed once too often. Made myself new one time too many. You could say I've been a new Negro all my life. But all I lived through, all I seen, and not one of those changes prepared me for her. For Dorcas. You would have thought I was twenty, back in Palestine satisfying my appetite for the first time under a walnut tree.

"Surprised everybody when we left, me and Violet. They said the City makes you lonely, but since I'd been trained by the best woodsman ever, loneliness was a thing couldn't get near me. Shoot. Country boy; country man. How did I know what an eighteen-year-old girl might instigate in a grown man whose wife is sleeping with a doll? Make me know a loneliness I never could imagine in a forest empty of people for fifteen miles, or on a riverbank with nothing but live bait for company. Convince me I never knew the sweet side of anything until I tasted her honey. They say snakes go blind for a while before they shed skin for the last time.

. . .

"She had long hair and bad skin. A quart of water twice a day would have cleared it right up, her skin, but I didn't suggest it because I liked it like that. Little half moons clustered underneath her cheekbones, like faint hoofmarks. There and on her forehead. I bought the stuff she told me to, but glad none of it ever worked. Take my little hoof marks away? Leave me with no tracks at all? In this world the best thing, the only thing, is to find the trail and stick to it. I tracked my mother in Virginia and it led me right to her, and I tracked Dorcas from borough to borough. I didn't even have to work at it. Didn't even have to think. Something else takes over when the track begins to talk to you, give out its signs so strong you hardly have to look. If the track's not talking to you, you might get up out of your chair to go buy two or three cigarettes, have the nickel in your pocket and just start walking, then running, and end up somewhere in Staten Island, for crying out loud, Long Island, maybe, staring at goats. But if the trail speaks, no matter what's in the way, you can find yourself in a crowded room aiming a bullet at her heart, never mind it's the heart you can't live without.

"I wanted to stay there. Right after the gun went thuh! and nobody in there heard it but me and that is why the crowd didn't scatter like the flock of redwings they looked like but stayed pressed in, locked together by the steam of their dancing and the music, which would not let them go. I wanted to stay right there. Catch her before she fell and hurt herself.

"I wasn't looking for the trail. It was looking for me and when it started talking at first I couldn't hear it. I was rambling, just rambling all through the City. I had the gun but it was not

the gun—it was my hand I wanted to touch you with. Five days
rambling. First High Fashion on 131st Street because I
thought you had a hair appointment on Tuesday. First Tuesday
of every month it was. But you wasn't there. Some women
came in with fish dinners from Salem Baptist, and the blind
twins were playing guitar in the shop, and it's just like you
said—only one of them's blind; the other one is just going
along with the program. Probably not even brothers, let alone
twins. Something their mama cooked up for a little extra
change. They were playing something sooty, though; not the
gospel like they usually do, and the women selling fish dinners
frowned and talked about their mother bad, but they never said
a word to the twins and I knew they were having a good time
listening because one of the loudest ones could hardly suck her
teeth for patting her foot. They didn't pay me no mind. Took
me a while to get them to tell me you wasn't on the book for
that day. Minnie said you had a touch-up Saturday and how
she didn't approve of touch-ups not just because they were fifty
cents instead of a dollar and a quarter for the whole do, but
because it hurt the hair, heat on dirt she said, hurt the hair
worse than anything she knew of. Except, of course, no heat
at all. What did you have the touch-up for? That's what I first
thought about. Last Saturday? You told me you were going
with the choir out to Brooklyn to sing at Shiloh, and you had
to leave at nine in the morning and wouldn't be back till night
and that's why. And that you'd missed the last trip, and your
aunt found out about it so you had to go on this one, and that's
why. So I didn't wait for Violet to leave and unlock Malvonne's
apartment. No need. But how could you have a touch-up the
Saturday before and still make it to the station by nine o'clock
in the morning when Minnie never opens up before noon on

Saturday because she's open till midnight getting everybody readied up for Sunday? And you didn't need to keep the Tuesday regular appointment, did you? I dismissed the evil in my thoughts because I wasn't sure that the sooty music the blind twins were playing wasn't the cause. It can do that to you, a certain kind of guitar playing. Not like the clarinets, but close. If that song had been coming through a clarinet, I'd have known right away. But the guitars—they confused me, made me doubt myself, and I lost the trail. Went home and didn't pick it up again until the next day when Malvonne looked at me and covered her mouth with her hand. Couldn't cover her eyes, though; the laugh came flying out of there.

"I know you didn't mean those things you said to me. After I found you and got you to come back to our room one more time. What you said I know you didn't mean. It hurt, though, and the next day I stood freezing on the stoop worrying myself sick about it. Nobody there but Malvonne sprinkling ashes on patches of ice. Across the street, leaning up against the iron railing, I saw three sweetbacks. Thirty degrees, not even ten in the morning, and they shone like patent leather. Smooth. Couldn't be more than twenty, twenty-two. Young. That's the City for you. One wore spats, and one had a handkerchief in his pocket same color as his tie. Had his coat draped across his shoulders. They were just leaning there, laughing and so on, and then they started crooning, leaning in, heads together, snapping fingers. City men, you know what I mean. Closed off to themselves, wise, young roosters. Didn't have to do a thing—just wait for the chicks to pass by and find them. Belted jackets and handkerchiefs the color of their ties. You think Malvonne would have covered her mouth in front of them? Or made roosters pay her in advance for the use of her place of a Thursday? Never would have happened because roosters don't need Malvonne. Chickens find the roosters and find the place, too, and if there is tracking to be done, they do it. They look; they figure. Roosters wait because they are the ones waited for. They don't have to trail anybody, look ignorant in a beauty parlor asking for a girl in front of women who couldn't wait for me to leave so they could pat on to the sooty music and talk about what the hell did I want to know about a girl not out of high school yet and wasn't I married to old crazy Violet? Only old cocks like me have to get up from the stoop, cut Malvonne off in the middle of a sentence and try to walk not run all the way to Inwood, where we sat the first time and you crossed your legs at the knees so I could see the green shoes you carried out the house in a paper sack so your aunt wouldn't know you tapped down Lenox and up Eighth in them instead of the oxfords you left the house in. While you flicked your foot, turned your ankles for the admiration of the heels, I looked at your knees but I didn't touch. I told you again that you were the reason Adam ate the apple and its core. That when he left Eden, he left a rich man. Not only did he have Eve, but he had the taste of the first apple in the world in his mouth for the rest of his life. The very first to know what it was like. To bite it, bite it down. Hear the crunch and let the red peeling break his heart.

"You looked at me then like you knew me, and I thought it really was Eden, and I couldn't take your eyes in because I was loving the hoof marks on your cheeks.

"I went back up there, to the very spot. Old snow made the sky soft and blackened tree bark. Dog tracks and rabbit too, neat as the pattern on a Sunday tie scattered over the snow. One of those dogs must have weighed eighty pounds. The rest were small size; one limped. My footprints messed everything up. And when I looked back at where I'd walked, saw myself standing there in street shoes, no galoshes, wet to the ankles, I knew. I didn't feel the cold, though, because I was remembering it the way it was in our time. That warm October, remember? The rose of Sharon was still heavy with flowers. Lilac trees, pines. That tulip tree where Indians gathered looked like a king. The first time we met there I got there before you. Two whitemen were sitting on a rock. I sat on the ground right next to them until they got disgusted and moved off. You had to be working or look like you was to be anywhere near there. That's why I brought my sample case along. To look like I was delivering something important. Yeah, it was forbidden, all right, but nobody loudtalked us that time. And it gave the thing an edge, being there, a danger that was more than me and you being together. I scratched our initials on the rock those men moved away from. D. and J. Later on, after we had a place and a routine, I brought you treats, worrying each time what to bring that would make you smile and come again the next time. How many phonograph records? How many silk stockings? The little kit to mend the runs, remember? The purple metal box with flowers on top full of Schrafft's chocolates. Cologne in a blue bottle that smelt like a whore. Flowers once, but you were disappointed with that treat, so I gave you a dollar to buy whatever you wanted with it. A whole day's pay back home when I was young. Just for you. Anything just for you. To bite down hard, chew up the core and have the taste of red apple skin to carry around for the rest of my life. In Malvonne's nephew's room with the iceman's sign in the window. Your first time. And mine, in a manner of speaking. For which, and I will say it again, I would strut out the Garden, strut! as long as you held on to my hand, girl. Dorcas, girl, your first time and mine. I *chose* you. Nobody gave you to me. Nobody said that's the one for you. I picked you out. Wrong time, yep, and doing wrong by my wife. But the picking out, the choosing. Don't ever think I fell for you, or fell over you. I didn't fall in love, I rose in it. I saw you and made up my mind. My mind. And I made up my mind to follow you too. That's something I know how to do from way back. Maybe I didn't tell you that part about me. My gift in the woods that even he looked up to and he was the best there ever was. Ever. Those old people, they knew it all. I talk about being new seven times before I met you, but back then, back there, if you was or claimed to be colored, you had to be new and stay the same every day the sun rose and every night it dropped. And let me tell you, baby, in those days it was more than a state of mind."

worth, the county seat, a slave, and returned in 1888 a free woman. Her daughter and grandchildren lived in a mean little place called Rome, twelve miles north of the town she'd left. The grandchildren ranged in age from four to fourteen, and one of them, Violet, was twelve years old when True Belle arrived. That was after the men had come for the stock, the pots and the chair her daughter Rose Dear was sitting in. When she got there all that was left, aside from some borrowed pallets and the clothes on their backs, was the paper Rose's husband had signed saying they could—that the men had the right to do it and, I suppose, the duty to do it, if the rain refused to rain, or if stones of ice fell from the sky instead and cut the crop down to its stalks. Nothing on the paper about the husband joining a party that favored niggers voting. Dispossessed of house and land, the sad little family True Belle found were living secretly in an abandoned shack some neighbors had located for them and eating what food these neighbors were able to share and the girls forage. Lots of okra and dried beans, and, since it was September, berries of every kind. Twice, however, the minister's son had brought them a young squirrel to feast on. Rose told people that her husband, fed up and stunned by the uselessness of his back and hands, tired of fried green tomatoes and grits, hungry beyond belief for the meat of some meat and not just its skin, furious at the price of coffee and the shape of his oldest girl's legs, had just quit. Got up and quit. Gone off somewhere to sit and think about it or sit and not think about it. It was better to make up talk than to let out what she knew. They might come looking for her next time, and not just her pots, her pans, her house. Lucky for her, True Belle was dying and willing to die in Vesper County, after giving her whole well life to Miss Vera Louise in Baltimore.

The death True Belle was dying took eleven years, long

enough for her to rescue Rose, bury her, see the husband return four times, make six quilts, thirteen shifts and fill Violet's head with stories about her whitelady and the light of both their lives—a beautiful young man whose name, for obvious reasons, was Golden Gray. Gray because that was Vera Louise's last name (much, much later it was also the color of his eyes), and Golden because after the pink birth-skin disappeared along with the down on his head, his flesh was radiantly golden, and floppy yellow curls covered his head and the lobes of his ears. It was nowhere as blond as Vera Louise's hair once was, but its sunlight color, its determined curliness, endeared him to her. Not all at once. It took a while. But True Belle laughed out loud the minute she laid eyes on him and thereafter every day for eighteen years.

When the three of them lived in a fine sandstone house on Edison Street in Baltimore, far away from Vesper County where both Vera Louise Gray and True Belle were born, what the whitelady told her neighbors and friends was partly true: that she could not bear the narrow little ways of her home county. And that she had brought her servant and an orphaned baby she fancied to Baltimore to experience a more sophisticated way of living.

It was a renegade, almost suffragette thing to do, and the neighbors and would-be women friends surrounded Vera Louise with as polite a distance as they could manage. If they thought that would force her to alter her manner, admit she needed to look for a husband—they were wrong. The out-of-state newcomer, rich and headstrong, contented herself with luxury and even less of their company. Besides she seemed taken up completely with book reading, pamphlet writing and the adoration of the orphan.

From the beginning, he was like a lamp in that quiet, shaded house. Simply startled each morning by the look of him, they vied with each other for the light he shed on them. He was given a fussy spoiling by Vera Louise and complete indulgence by True Belle, who, laughing, laughing, fed him test cakes and picked every single seed from the melon before she let him eat it. Vera Louise dressed him like the Prince of Wales and read him vivid stories.

True Belle, of course, would have known everything right away because, first of all, nobody could hide much in Wordsworth and nothing at all could be hidden in the Big Houses of its landowners. Certainly nobody could help noticing how many times a week a Negro boy from out Vienna way was called on to ride along with Miss Vera, and what part of the woods she preferred to ride in. True Belle knew what all the slaves knew, and she knew more since she was the one whose sole job it was to tend to whatever Miss Vera Louise wanted or needed, including doing her laundry, some of which had to be soaked overnight in vinegar once a month. So if it did not need it, if the personal garments could be washed along with the rest, True Belle knew why, and Vera Louise knew she knew. There was never any need to speak of it. The only people who didn't know were the fathers. The about-to-be father— the black boy—never found out, as far as True Belle could tell, because Vera Louise never mentioned his name or came near him ever again. The old father, Colonel Wordsworth Gray, didn't know a thing. Not one thing.

It had to be his wife who finally did tell him. Finally. Although she never spoke about it to her daughter, or, after she found out, ever spoke to her daughter at all, she was the one who would have had to let the Colonel know, and when he found out he stood up then sat down and then stood up again.

His left hand patted around the air searching for something: a shot of whiskey, his pipe, a whip, a shotgun, the Democratic platform, his heart—Vera Louise never knew. He looked hurt, deeply, deeply hurt for a few seconds. Then his rage seeped into the room, clouding the crystal and softening the starched tablecloth. Realizing the terrible thing that had happened to his daughter made him sweat, for there were seven mulatto children on his land. Sweat poured from his temples and collected under his chin; soaked his armpits and the back of his shirt as his rage swamped and flooded the room. The ivy on the table had perked up and the silver was slippery to the hand by the time he mopped his brow and gathered himself together to do an appropriate thing: slap Vera Louise into the serving table.

Her mother, however, had the final cut: her eyebrows were perfectly still but the look she gave Vera Louise as the girl struggled up from the floor was so full of repulsion the daughter could taste the sour saliva gathering under her mother's tongue, filling the insides of her cheeks. Only breeding, careful breeding, did not allow her to spit. No word, then or ever, passed between them. And the lingerie case full of money that lay on Vera's pillow the following Wednesday was, in its generosity, heavy with contempt. More money than anybody in the world needed for seven months or so away from home. So much money the message was indisputable: die, or live if you like, elsewhere.

True Belle was the one she wanted and the one she took. I don't know how hard it was for a slave woman to leave a husband that work and distance kept her from seeing much of anyhow, and to leave two daughters behind with an old aunt to take care of them. Rose Dear and May were eight and ten years old then. Good help at that age for anybody who owned them and no help at all to a mother who lived in Wordsworth, miles away from her husband in a rich man's house taking care of his daughter day and night. Perhaps it wasn't so hard to ask an older sister to look out for a husband and the girls because she was bound for Baltimore with Miss Vera Louise for a while. True Belle was twenty-seven and when would she ever get to see a great big city otherwise?

More important Miss Vera Louise might help her buy them all out with paper money, because she sure had a lot of it handed to her. Then again, maybe not. Maybe she frowned as she sat in the baggage car, rocking along with the boxes and trunks, unable to see the land she was traveling through. Maybe she felt bad. Anyway, choiceless, she went, leaving husband, sister, Rose Dear and May behind, and if she worried, the blond baby helped soothe her, and kept her entertained for eighteen years, until he left home.

So in 1888, with twenty-two years of the wages Miss Vera initiated soon as the War was over (but held in trust lest her servant get ideas), True Belle convinced herself and her mistress she was dying, got the money—ten eagle dollars—and was able to answer Rose Dear's pleas by coming back to Vesper with Baltimore tales for grandchildren she had never seen. She rented a small house, bought a cookstove for it and delighted the girls with descriptions of life with the wonderful Golden Gray. How they bathed him three times a day, and how the G on his underwear was embroidered with blue thread. The shape of the tub and what they put in the water to make him smell like honeysuckle sometimes and sometimes of lavender. How clever he was and how perfect a gentleman. The hilarious grown-up comments he made when a child and the cavalierlike courage he showed when he was a young man and went to find, then kill, if he was lucky, his father.

True Belle never saw him again after he rode off and didn't know if Vera Louise had any better luck. Her memories of the boy were more than enough.

I've thought about him a lot, wondered whether he was what True Belle loved and Violet too. Or the vain and hincty pinch-nose worrying about his coat and the ivory buttons on his waistcoat? Come all that way to insult not his father but his race.

Pretty hair can't be too long, Vera Louise once told him, and because she seemed to know such things, he believed her. Almost every other thing she said was false, but that last bit of information he held to be graven truth. So the yellow curls covered his coat collar like a farmer's, although the rightness of its length in fastidious Baltimore came from the woman who lied to him about practically everything including the question of whether she was his owner, his mother or a kindly neighbor. The other thing she did not lie about (although it took her eighteen years to get around to it) was that his father was a black-skinned nigger.

I see him in a two-seat phaeton. His horse is a fine one— black. Strapped to the back of the carriage is his trunk: large and crammed with beautiful shirts, linen, and embroidered sheets and pillow slips; a cigar case and silver toilet articles. A long coat, vanilla colored with dark brown cuffs and collar, is folded neatly beside him. He is a long way from home and it begins to rain furiously, but since it is August, he is not cold.

The left wheel strikes a stone and he hears, or thinks he does, a bump that may be the dislocation of his trunk. He reins in the horse and climbs down to see if any damage has been done to his things. He discovers that the trunk is loose—the rope has slipped and it is leaning. He unties everything and secures the rope more strongly.

Satisfied with his efforts, but annoyed at the heavy rain, the spoiling it is doing to his clothes and the speed of his journey, he looks around him. In the trees to his left, he sees a naked berry-black woman. She is covered with mud and leaves are in her hair. Her eyes are large and terrible. As soon as she sees him, she starts then turns suddenly to run, but in turning before she looks away she knocks her head against the tree she has been leaning against. Her terror is so great her body flees before her eyes are ready to find the route of escape. The blow knocks her out and down.

He looks at her and, holding on to the brim of his hat, moves quickly to get back into the carriage. He wants nothing to do with what he has seen—in fact he is certain that what he is running from is not a real woman but a "vision." When he picks up the reins he cannot help noticing that his horse is also black, naked and shiny wet, and his feelings about the horse are of security and affection. It occurs to him that there is something odd about that: the pride he takes in his horse; the nausea the woman provoked. He is a touch ashamed and decides to make sure it was a vision, that there is no naked black woman lying in the weeds.

He ties his horse to a sapling and sloshes back in driving rain to the place where the woman fell. She is still sprawled there. Her mouth and legs open. A small hickey is forming on her head. Her stomach is big and tight. He leans down, holding his breath against infection or odor or something. Something that might touch or penetrate him. She looks dead or deeply unconscious. And she is young. There is nothing he can do for her and for that he is relieved. Then he notices a rippling movement in her stomach. Something inside her is moving.

He does not see himself touching her, but the picture he does imagine is himself walking away from her a second time, climbing into his carriage and leaving her a second time. He is uneasy with this picture of himself, and does not want to spend any part of the time to come remembering having done that. Also there is something about where he has come from and why, where he is going and why that encourages in him an insistent, deliberate recklessness. The scene becomes an anecdote, an action that would unnerve Vera Louise and defend him against patricide. Maybe.

He unfolds his long coat that has been tucked in the seat beside him and throws it over the woman. Then he gathers her up in his arms and carries her, stumbling, since she is heavier than he supposed, to the carriage. With great difficulty, he gets her into a sitting position in the carriage. Her head is leaning away from him and her feet are touching one of his splendid but muddy boots. He is hoping her lean will not shift, although there is nothing he can do about the dirty bare feet against his boot, for if he shifts her again, she may swerve over to his and not her side of the carriage. As he urges the horse on, he is gentle for fear the ruts and the muddy road will cause her to fall forward or brush him in some way.

He is heading toward a house a little ways out from a town named Vienna. It is the house where his father lives. And now he thinks it is an interesting, even comic idea to meet this nigger whom he has never seen (and who has never tried to see him) with an armful of black, liquid female. Provided, of course, she does not wake and the rippling in her stomach remains light. That bothers him—that she might regain consciousness and become something more than his own dark purpose.

He has not looked at her for some time. Now he does and notices a trickle of blood down her jaw onto her neck. The hickey that rose when she smashed into the tree is not the cause of her faint; she must have struck her head on a rock or something when she fell. But she is breathing still. Now he hopes she will not die—not yet, not until he gets to the house described and mapped out for him in clear, childish pictures by True Belle.

The rain seems to be following him; whenever he thinks it is about to stop, a few yards on it gets worse. He has been traveling for six hours, at least, and has been assured by the innkeeper that the journey would end before dark. Now he is not so sure. He doesn't relish night coming on with that passenger. He is calmed by the valley opening before him—the one it should take an hour to get through before he reaches the house a mile or two this side of Vienna. Quite suddenly, the rain stops. It is the longest hour, filled with recollections of luxury and pain. When he gets to the house, he pulls into the yard and finds a shed with two stalls in back. He takes his horse into one and wipes her down carefully. Then he throws a blanket over her and looks about for water and feed. He takes a long time over this. It is important to him, and he is not sure he is not being watched by someone in the house. In fact, he hopes he is; hopes the nigger is watching open-mouthed from a crack in the planks that serve as wall.

But no one comes out to speak to him, so perhaps there is no one. After the horse is seen to (and he has noticed that one shoe needs repair), he returns to the carriage for his trunk. He unlashes it and hoists it to his shoulder. It makes a further mess of his waistcoat and silk shirt as he carries it into the house. On the little porch, he makes no attempt to knock and the door is closed but not latched. He enters and looks about for a suitable place for his trunk. He sets it down on the dirt floor and examines the house. It has two rooms: a cot in each, table, chair, fireplace, cookstove in one. Modest, lived in, male, but otherwise no indication of the personality of its owner. The cookstove is cold, and the fireplace has a heap of ash, but no embers. The occupant has been gone perhaps a day, maybe two.

After he has seen to the placement of his trunk, he goes back to the carriage to get the woman. The removal of the trunk has displaced the weight, and the carriage is tipping a little on its axis. He reaches in the door and pulls her out. Her skin is almost too hot to handle. The long coat around her drags in the mud as he carries her into the house. He lays her down on a cot, and then curses himself for not having pulled its blanket back first. Now she is on top of it and the coat is all there seems to be to cover her. Its ruin may be permanent. He goes into the second room, and examining a wooden box there, finds a woman's dress. Gingerly he retrieves his coat and covers the woman with the strange-smelling dress. Now he opens his own trunk and selects a white cotton shirt and flannel waistcoat. He drapes the fresh shirt on the single chair rather than risk damaging it on a nail hammered in the wall. Carefully he examines the dry things. Then he sets about trying to make a fire. There is wood in the wood box and the fireplace, and in the darkest corner of the room a can of kerosene which he sprinkles on the wood. But no matches. For a long time he looks for matches and finally finds some in a can, wrapped in a bit of ticking. Five matches, to be exact. The kerosene has evaporated from the wood by the time he locates the matches. He is not adept at this. Other people have always lit the fires in his life. But he persists and at last has a good roaring flame. Now he can sit down, smoke a cigar and prepare himself for the return of the man who lives there. A man he assumes is named Henry LesTroy, although from the way True Belle pronounced it, it could be something else. A man of no consequence, except a tiny reputation as a tracker based on one or two escapades signaling his expertise in reading trails. A long time ago, according to True Belle, who gave him all the details—since Vera Louise shut herself in the bedroom or turned her head whenever he tried to pull information from her. Henry Lestory or LesTroy or something like that, but who cares what the nigger's name is. Except the woman who regretted ever knowing him at all and locked her door rather than say it out loud. And would have regretted the baby he gave her too, given it away, except it was golden and she had never seen that color except in the morning sky and in bottles of champagne. True Belle told him Vera Louise had smiled and said, "But he's golden. Completely golden!" So they named him that and didn't take him to the Catholic Foundling Hospital, where whitegirls deposited their mortification.

He has known all that for seven days, eight now. And he has known his father's name and the location of the house he once lived in for two. Information that came from the woman who cooked and cleaned for Vera Louise; who sent baskets of plum preserves, ham and loaves of bread every week while he was in boarding school; who gave his frayed shirts to rag-and-bone men rather than let him wear them; the woman who smiled and shook her head every time she looked at him. Even when he was a tiny boy with a head swollen with fat champagne-colored curls, and ate the pieces of cake she held out to him, her smile was more amusement than pleasure. When the two of them, the whitewoman and the cook, bathed him they sometimes passed anxious looks at the palms of his hand, the texture of his drying hair. Well, Vera Louise was anxious; True Belle just smiled, and now he knew what she was smiling about, the nigger. But so was he. He had always thought there was only one kind—True Belle's kind. Black and nothing. Like Henry LesTroy. Like the filthy woman snoring on the cot. But there was another kind—like himself.

The rain has stopped for good, apparently. He looks about for something to eat that doesn't need to be cooked—ready made. He has found nothing but a jug of liquor. He continues to sample it and sits back down before the fire.

In the silence left by the rain that has stopped, he hears hoofbeats. Beyond the door he sees a rider staring at his carriage. He approaches. Hello. Might you be related to Lestory? Henry LesTroy or whatever his name is?

The rider doesn't blink.

"No, sir. Vienna. Be back direcklin."

He doesn't understand any of it. And he is drunk now anyway. Happily. Perhaps he can sleep now. But he shouldn't. The owner of the house might return, or the liquid black woman might wake or die or give birth or . . .

When he stopped the buggy, got out to tie the horse and walk back through the rain, perhaps it was because the awful-looking thing lying in wet weeds was everything he was not as well as a proper protection against and anodyne to what he believed his father to be, and therefore (if it could just be contained, identified)—himself. Or was the figure, the vision as he thought of it, a thing that touched him before its fall?

The thing he saw in the averted glance of the servants at his
boarding school; the bootblack who tap-danced for a penny. A
vision that, at the moment when his scare was sharpest, looked
also like home comfortable enough to wallow in? That could
be it. But who could live in that leafy hair? that unfathomable
skin? But he already had lived in and with it: True Belle had
been his first and major love, which may be why two gallops
beyond that hair, that skin, their absence was unthinkable. And
if he shuddered at the possibility of her leaning on him, of her
sliding a bit to the left and actually resting while she slept on
his shoulder, it is also true that he overcame the shudder.
Swallowed, maybe, and clicked the horse.

I like to think of him that way. Sitting straight in the carriage. Rain matting the hair over his collar, forming a little pool
in the space between his boots. His gray-eyed squint as he tries
to see through sheets of water. Then without warning as the
road enters a valley the rain stops and there is a white grease
pat of a sun cooking up there in its sky. Now he can hear things
outside himself. Soaked leaves disentangling themselves one
from another. The plop of nuts and the flutter of partridge
removing their beaks from their hearts. Squirrels, having raced
to limb tips, poise there to assess danger. The horse tosses her
head to scatter a hovering cloud of gnats. So carefully is he
listening he does not see the one-mile marker with VIENNA
carved vertically in the stone. He passes it by and then sees the
roof of a cabin not five furlongs ahead. It could belong to
anyone, anyone at all. But maybe, along with the pity of its
fence enclosing a dirt yard in which a rocker without arms lies
on its side, the door fastened with a bit of rope for a lock but
gaping at its hinges, maybe it shelters his father.

Golden Gray reins in his horse. This is a thing he does well.

The other is play the piano. Dismounting, he leads the horse close enough to look. Animals are somewhere; he can smell them, but the little house looks empty, if not cast-off completely. Certainly the owner never expected a horse and carriage to arrive—the fence gate is wide enough for a stout woman but no more. He unharnesses the horse and walks it a way to the right and discovers, behind the cabin and under a tree he does not know the name of, two open stalls, one of which is full of shapes. Leading the horse he hears behind him a groan from the woman, but doesn't stop to see whether she is waking or dying or falling off the seat. Close up on the stalls he sees that the shapes are tubs, sacks, lumber, wheels, a broken plow, a butter press and a metal trunk. There is a stake too, and he ties the horse to it. Water, he thinks. Water for the horse. What he thinks is a pump in the distance is an ax handle still lodged in a stump. There was the downpour though, and a good bit of it has collected in a washtub near the chopping stump. So his horse can be watered, but where are the other animals he smells but does not see or hear? Out of the shaft, the horse drinks greedily and the carriage tips dangerously with the unequal distribution of his trunk and the woman. Golden Gray examines the trunk fastenings before going to the rope-locked door of the little house.

That is what makes me worry about him. How he thinks first of his clothes, and not the woman. How he checks the fastenings, but not her breath. It's hard to get past that, but then he scrapes the mud from his Baltimore soles before he enters a cabin with a dirt floor and I don't hate him much anymore.

Inside, light comes slowly, and, tired after forcing its way through oiled paper tacked around a window set into the back wall, rests on the dirt floor unable to reach higher than Golden

Gray's waist. The grandest thing in the room is the fireplace. Clean, set for a new fire, braced with scoured stones, from which two metal arms for holding kettles extend. As for the rest: a cot, wooden, a rust-colored wool blanket fitted neatly over a thin and bumpy mattress. Not cobs, certainly not feathers or leaves. Rags. Bits of truly unusable fabric shoved into a ticking shroud. It reminds Golden Gray of the pillow True Belle made for King to sleep on at her feet. She had been given the name of a powerful male dog, but she was a cat without personality, which is why True Belle liked her and wanted her close by. Two beds and one chair, as it turns out. The person who lived here sat alone at the table, but had two beds: one in a second room entered by a door stronger and better-made than the one to the house itself. And in that room, the second one, is a box and a woman's green frock folded on top of its contents. He looks, just as casual as you please. Lifts up the lid and sees the dress and would dig deeper, but the dress reminds him of what should have been in the front of his mind: the woman breathing through her mouth in the other room. Does he think she will wake up and run off, relieving him of his choice, if he leaves her alone? Or that she will be dead, which is the same thing.

He is avoiding her, I know. Having done the big thing, the hard thing, by going back and lifting the girl up from weeds that clung to his trousers, by not looking to see what he could see of her private parts, the shock of knowing the hair there, once it was dry, was thick enough to part with a fingernail. He tried not to look at the hair on her head either, or at her face, turned away into blades of grass. Already he had seen the deer eyes that fixed on him through the rain, fixed on him as she backed away, fixed on him as her body began to turn for flight.

Too bad she didn't have the sense of a deer and hadn't looked in the direction she was going soon enough to see the giant maple in time. In time. When he went back for her he did not know if she was still there—she could have gotten up and run away—but he believed, hoped, the deer eyes would be closed. Suddenly he was not sure of himself. They might be open. His gratitude that they were not gave him the strength he needed to lift her.

After fidgeting with his trunk he steps into the yard. The sunlight bangs his own eyes shut and he holds his hand over them, peeking through his fingers until it is safe. The sigh he makes is deep, a hungry air-take for the strength and perseverance all life, but especially his, requires. Can you see the fields beyond, crackling and drying in the wind? The blade of blackbirds rising out of nowhere, brandishing and then gone? The odor of the invisible animals accentuated in the heat mixing now with out-of-control mint and something fruity needing to be picked. No one is looking at him, but he behaves as though there is. That's the way. Carry yourself the way you would if you were always under the reviewing gaze of an impressionable but casual acquaintance.

She is still there. Hardly distinguishable from the shadow of the carriage hood under which she sleeps. Everything about her is violent, or seems so, but that is because she is exposed under that long coat, and there is nothing to prevent Golden Gray from believing that an exposed woman will explode in his arms, or worse, that he will, in hers. She should be stuffed into the ticking along with the bits of rag, stitched shut to hide her visible lumps and moving parts. But she is there and he looks into the shadow to find her face, and her deer eyes, too, if he has to. The deer eyes are closed, and thank God will not open easily, for they are sealed with blood. A lip of skin hangs from her forehead and the blood from it has covered her eyes, her nose and one cheek before it jelled. Darker than the blood though are her lips, thick enough to laugh at and to break his heart.

I know he is a hypocrite; that he is shaping a story for himself to tell somebody, to tell his father, naturally. How he was driving along, saw and saved this wild black girl: No qualms. I had no qualms. See look, here, how it ruined my coat and soiled beyond repair a shirt you will never see another one of. I have gloves made from the hide of a very young cow, but I did not use them to hoist her, carry her. I touched her with my bare hands. From the weeds to the carriage; from the carriage into this cabin that could belong to anyone. Anyone at all. I laid her on the wooden cot first thing because she was heavier than she looked, and in my haste forgot to lift the blanket first to cover her. I thought of the blood, I think, dirtying the mattress. But who could tell if it was already dirty or not? I didn't want to lift her again, so I went into the other room and got the dress I found there and draped it best I could over her. She looked more naked then than before I covered her, but there was nothing else I could do.

He is lying, the hypocrite. He could have opened his big fat trunk; removed one of the two hand-embroidered sheets, or even his dressing gown, and covered the girl. He's young. So young. He thinks his story is wonderful, and that if spoken right will impress his father with his willingness, his honor. But I know better. He wants to brag about this encounter, like a knight errant bragging about his coolness as he unscrews the spike from the monster's heart and breathes life back into the fiery nostrils. Except this monster without scales or flaming breath is more dangerous for she is a bloody-faced girl of moving parts, of luminous eyes and lips to break your heart.

Why doesn't he wipe her face, I wonder. She is more savage perhaps this way. More graphically rescued. If she should rise up and claw him it would satisfy him even more and confirm True Belle's warning about the man who saved the rattler, nursed the rattler, fed the rattler only to discover that the last piece of information he would have on earth was the irrevocable nature of the rattler. Aw, but he is young, young and he is hurting, so I forgive him his self-deception and his grand, fake gestures, and when I watch him sipping too quickly the cane liquor he has found, worrying about his coat and not tending to the girl, I don't hate him at all. He has a pistol in his trunk and a silver cigar case, but he is a boy after all, and he sits at the table in the single chair contemplating changing into fresh clothes, for the ones he is wearing, still wet at the seams and cuffs, are filthy with sweat, blood and soil. Should he retrieve the broken rocker from the front yard? Go check on the horse? He is thinking about that, his next move, when he hears slow, muffled hoof clops. Glancing at the girl to make sure the dress and the blood are intact, he opens the door and peers into the yard. Floating toward him parallel to the fence is a black boy astride a mule.

He would have said, "Morning," although it wasn't, but he thought the man lurching down the steps was white and not to be spoken to without leave. Drunk, too, he thought, because his clothes were those of a gent who sleeps in his own yard after a big party rather than in his wife's bed, and wakes when his dogs come to lick his face. He thought this whiteman, this drunken gent, was looking for Mr. Henry, waiting for him, needing the wild turkeys now, now, goddamn it—or the pelts, or whatever it was Mr. Henry promised, owed or sold.

"Hello," said the drunken gent, and if the black boy doubted for a minute whether he was white, the smileless smile that came with the greeting convinced him.

"Sir."

"You live around here?"

"No, sir."

"No? Where from then?"

"Out Vienna way."

"Is that right? Where you on your way to?"

It was better when they asked questions most times. If they said anything flat out it was something nobody wanted to hear. The boy picked at the burlap of his sack. "See bout the stock. Mr. Henry he say I'm to see bout it."

See that? The smile was gone. "Henry?" the man asked. His face was another color now. More blood in it. "You said Henry?"

"Yes, sir."

"Where is he? Is he close?"

"Don't know, sir. Gone off."

"Where does he live. What house?"

Oh, thought the boy, he doesn't know Mr. Henry but he's looking for him. "This here one."

"What?"

"This here place his."

"This? This is his? He lives here?"

The blood left his face and showed up his eyes better. "Yes, sir. When he home. Ain't home now."

Golden Gray frowned. He thought he would know it right

away, without being told and, surprised that he had, he turned around to look at it. "You sure? You sure this is where he lives? Henry Lestroy?"

"Yes, sir."

"When's he coming back?"

"Any day now."

Golden Gray ran his thumb across his bottom lip. He lifted his eyes from the boy's face and stared out across the fields still cracking in the wind. "What did you say you come by here for?"

"See bout his stock."

"What stock? There's nothing here but my horse."

"Out back." He pointed with his eyes and a gesture of his hand. "They roam now and again. Mr. Henry he say I'm to look see they get back if they break out."

Golden Gray didn't hear the pride in the boy's voice: "Mr. Henry say *I'm* . . ." because he was so terrified he laughed.

This was it, then. The place he meant to come to and any day now the blackest man in the world would be there too. "All right, then. Go on about it then."

The boy tsched his mule—for nothing, apparently, because he had to kick his sides with creamy heels before the animal obeyed.

"Say!" Golden Gray held up his hand. "When you're done, come back here. I want you to help me with something. Hear?"

"Yes, sir. I be back."


Golden Gray went into the second room to change his clothes—this time he chose something formal, elegant. It was the right time to do it. To select a very fine shirt; to unfold the dark blue trousers that fit just so. The right time and the only time for as long as anyone in Vienna knew him he wore the clothes he put on at that moment. When he took them out and laid them carefully on the cot—the yellow shirt, the trousers with buttons of bone in the fly, the butter-colored waistcoat—the arrangement, lying on the bed, looked like an empty man with one arm folded under. He sat down on the rough mattress near the trouser cuffs, and when dark spots formed on the cloth he saw that he was crying.

Only now, he thought, now that I know I have a father, do I feel his absence: the place where he should have been and was not. Before, I thought everybody was one-armed, like me. Now I feel the surgery. The crunch of bone when it is sundered, the sliced flesh and the tubes of blood cut through, shocking the bloodrun and disturbing the nerves. They dangle and writhe. Singing pain. Waking me with the sound of itself, thrumming when I sleep so deeply it strangles my dreams away. There is nothing for it but to go away from where he is not to where he used to be and might be still. Let the dangle and the writhe see what it is missing; let the pain sing to the dirt where he stepped in the place where he used to be and might be still. I am not going to be healed, or to find the arm that was removed from me. I am going to freshen the pain, point it, so we both know what it is for.

And no, I am not angry. I don't need the arm. But I do need to know what it could have been like to have had it. It's a phantom I have to behold and be held by, in whatever crevices it lies, under whatever branch. Or maybe it stalks treeless and open places, lit with an oily sun. This part of me that does not know me, has never touched me or lingered at my side. This gone-away hand that never helped me over the stile, or guided me past the dragons, pulled me up from the ditch into which

I stumbled. Stroked my hair, fed me food; took the far end of the load to make it easier for me to carry. This arm that never held itself out, extended from my body, to give me balance as I walked thin rails or logs, round and slippery with danger. When I find it, will it wave to me? Gesture, beckon to me to come along? Or will it even know who or what I am? It doesn't matter. I will locate it so the severed part can remember the snatch, the slice of its disfigurement. Perhaps then the arm will no longer be a phantom, but will take its own shape, grow its own muscle and bone, and its blood will pump from the loud singing that has found the purpose of its serenade. Amen.

Who will take my part? Soap away the shame? Suds it till it falls away muck at my feet to be stepped out of? Will he? Redeem me like a pawn ticket worth little on the marketplace, but priceless in retrieving real value? What do I care what the color of his skin is, or his contact with my mother? When I see him, or what is left of him, I will tell him all about the missing part of me and listen for his crying shame. I will exchange then; let him have mine and take his as my own and we will both be free, arm-tangled and whole.

It had rocked him when he heard who and what his father was. Made him loose, lost. He had first fingered then torn some of his mother's clothes and sat in the grass looking at the things scattered on the lawn as well as in his mind. Little lights moving like worms frolicked before his eyes, and the breath of despair had a nasty smell. It was True Belle who helped him up from the grass, soaped his tangled hair and told him what he had to do.

"Go on," she said. "I'll tell you how to find him, or what's left of him. It don't matter if you do find him or not; it's the going that counts."

So he collected what she said he should collect, packed it all and set out. During the journey he worried a lot about what he looked like, what armor he could call on. There was nothing but his trunk and the set of his jaw. But he was ready, ready to meet the black and savage man who bothered him and abused his arm.

Instead he met, ran into, a wild black girl smashing herself in the head with fright, who lay now in the other room while a black boy was rounding up stock outside. He thought she would be his lance and shield; now he would have to be his own. Look into the deer eyes with the dawning gray of his own. He needs courage for that, but he has it. He has the courage to do what Duchesses of Marlborough do all the time: relinquish being an adored bud clasping its future, and dare to open wide, to let the layers of its petals go flat, show the cluster of stamens dead center for all to see.

What was I thinking of? How could I have imagined him so poorly? Not noticed the hurt that was not linked to the color of his skin, or the blood that beat beneath it. But to some other thing that longed for authenticity, for a right to be in this place, effortlessly without needing to acquire a false face, a laughless grin, a talking posture. I have been careless and stupid and it infuriates me to discover (again) how unreliable I am. Even his horse had understood and borne Golden Gray along with just a touch or two of the whip. Steadily it had plodded, through valleys without trails, through streams without bridges or ferries for crossing. Eye gaze just above the road, undistracted by the small life that darted toward its hooves, heaving its great chest forward, pacing to hold on to its strength and gather more. It did not know where it was going and it knew nothing of the way, but it did know the nature of its work. Get there, said its hooves. If we can just get there.

Now I have to think this through, carefully, even though I may be doomed to another misunderstanding. I have to do it and not break down. Not hating him is not enough; liking, loving him is not useful. I have to alter things. I have to be a shadow who wishes him well, like the smiles of the dead left over from their lives. I want to dream a nice dream for him, and another of him. Lie down next to him, a wrinkle in the sheet, and contemplate his pain and by doing so ease it, diminish it. I want to be the language that wishes him well, speaks his name, wakes him when his eyes need to be open. I want him to stand next to a well dug quite clear from trees so twigs and leaves will not fall into the deep water, and while standing there in shapely light, his fingertips on the rim of stone, his gaze at no one thing, his mind soaked and sodden with sorrow, or dry and brittle with the hopelessness that comes from knowing too little and feeling too much (so brittle, so dry he is in danger of the reverse: feeling nothing and knowing everything). There then, with nothing available but the soaking or the brittleness, not even looking toward the well, not aware of its mossy, unpleasant odor, or the little life that hovers at its rim, but to stand there next to it and from down in it, where the light does not reach, a collection of leftover smiles stirs, some brief benevolent love rises from the darkness and there is nothing for him to see or hear, and there is no reason to stay but he does. For the safety at first, then for the company. Then for himself—with a kind of confident, enabling, serene power that flicks like a razor and then hides. But he has felt it now, and it may come again. No doubt a lot of other things will come again: doubt will come, and things may seem unclear from time to time. But once the razor blade has flicked—he will remember it, and if he remembers it he can recall it. That is to say, he has it at his disposal.

**A** thing like that could harm you. Thirteen years after Golden Gray stiffened himself to look at that girl, the harm she could do was still alive. Pregnant girls were the most susceptible, but so were the grandfathers. Any fascination could mark a newborn: melons, rabbits, wisteria, rope, and, more than a shed snakeskin, a wild woman is the worst of all. So the warnings the girls got were part of a whole group of things to look out for lest the baby come here craving or favoring the mother's distraction. Who would have thought old men needed to be cautioned too; told and warned against seeing, smelling or even hearing her?

She lived close, they said, not way off in the woods or even down in the riverbed, but somewhere in that cane field—at its edge some said or maybe moving around in it. Close. Cutting cane could get frenzied sometimes when young men got the feeling she was just yonder, hiding, and probably looking at them. One swing of the cutting blade could lop off her head if she got sassy or too close, and it would be her own fault. That would be when they cut bad—when the cane stalks flew up to slam the face, or the bill would slip and cut a coworker nearby. Just thinking about her, whether she was close or not, could mess up a whole morning's work.

The grandfathers, way past slashing but still able enough to bind stalks or feed the sugar vats, used to be thought safe. That is until the man the grandfathers called Hunters Hunter got tapped on the shoulder by fingertips that couldn't be anybody's but hers. When the man snapped up, he saw the cane stalks shuddering but he didn't hear a single crack. Because he was more used to wood life than tame, he knew when the eyes watching him were up in a tree, behind a knoll or, like this, at ground level. You can see how he was confused: the fingertips at his shoulder, the eyes at his feet. First thing came to mind was the woman he named himself some thirteen years ago because, while tending her, that was the word he thought of: Wild. He was sure he was tending a sweet but abused young girl at first, but when she bit him, he said, Oh, she's wild. Thinking, some things are like that. There's no gain fathoming more.

He remembered her laugh, though, and how peaceful she was the first few days following the bite, so the touch of her fingertips didn't frighten him, but it did make him sad. Too sad to report the sighting to his coworkers, old men like himself no longer able to cut all day. Unwarned, they weren't prepared for the way their blood felt when they caught a glimpse of her, or for how trembly their legs got hearing that babygirl laugh. The pregnant girls marked their babies or didn't, but the grandfathers—unwarned—went soft in the head, walked out of the syrup house, left their beds in the shank of the night, wet themselves, forgot the names of their grown children and where they'd put their razor strops.

When the man they called Hunters Hunter knew her—tended her—she was touchy. If he had handled it right, maybe she would have stayed in the house, nursed her baby, learned how to dress and talk to folks. Every now and then when he thought about her he was convinced she was dead. When for months there was no sign or sound of her, he sighed and relived that time when his house was full of motherlessness—and the chief unmothering was Wild's. Local people used the story of her to caution children and pregnant girls and it saddened him to learn that instead of resting she was hungry still. Though for what, exactly, he couldn't say, unless it was for hair the color of a young man's name. To see the two of them together was a regular jolt: the young man's head of yellow hair long as a dog's tail next to her skein of black wool.

He didn't report it, but the news got out anyway: Wild was not a story of a used-to-be-long-ago-crazy girl whose neck cane cutters liked to imagine under the blade, or a quick and early stop for hardheaded children. She was still out there—and real. Someone saw the man they called Hunters Hunter jump, grab his shoulder and, when he turned around to gaze at the cane field, murmur loud enough for somebody to hear, "Wild. Dog me, if it ain't Wild." The pregnant girls just sighed at the news and went on sweeping and sprinkling the dirt yards, and the young men sharpened their blades till the edges whistled. But the old men started dreaming. They remembered when she came, what she looked like, why she stayed and that queer boy she set so much store by.

Not too many people saw the boy. The first wasn't Hunters Hunter, who was off looking for enough fox to sell. The first was Patty's boy, Honor. He was looking in on Mr. Henry's place while he was gone, and on one of the days he stopped by—to do a little weeding maybe and see if the pigs and chickens were still alive—it rained all morning. Sheets of it made afternoon rainbows everywhere. Later he told his mother that the whole cabin was rainbowed and when the man came out the door, and Honor looked at his wet yellow hair and creamy skin, he thought a ghost had taken over the place. Then he realized he was looking at a whiteman and never believed otherwise, even though he saw Mr. Henry's face when the whiteman told him he was his son.

When Henry Lestory, the man so expert in the woods he'd become a hunter's hunter (and when spoken of and to, that is what they called him), got back and saw the buggy and the beautiful horse tied near his stall, he was instantly alarmed. No man he knew drove a carriage like that; no horse in the county had its mane cut and combed that way. Then he saw the mule Patty's boy rode and calmed down a bit. He stood in his own door and had a hard time making out what he was looking at. Patty's boy, Honor, was kneeling beside the cot on which a pregnant girl lay, and a golden-haired man towered above them both. There had never been a whiteman inside his house. Hunters Hunter swallowed. All the pains he had taken shot to hell.

When the blond man turned to look at him, the gray eyes

widened, then closed, then, sliding slowly up from Hunter's boots to his knees, to chest to head, the man's gaze was like a tongue. By the time the gray eyes were level with his, Hunter had to struggle to keep from feeling trapped—in his own house. Even the groan from the cot did not break the lock of the stranger's stare. Everything about him was young and soft—except the color of his eyes.

Honor looked from one to the other. "Glad you back, Mr. Henry."

"Who be these?"

"They both in here before me."

"Who *be* these?"

"Can't say, sir. The woman she bad but coming around now."

The golden-haired man had no pistol Hunter could see, and his thin boots had never walked country roads. His clothes would make a preacher sigh and Hunter knew from the ladylike hands the stranger had never made a fist hard enough to smash a melon. He walked to the table and placed his pouch on it. With one swing he tossed a brace of woodcock in the corner. But he kept his rifle in the crook of his arm. And his hat on his head. The gray eyes followed his every move.

"The woman had a bad fall from what I can tell. This here gent, he carried her in here. I cleaned the blood up best I could."

Hunter noticed the green dress covering the woman, the black-blood spots on the sleeve.

"I got the fowl in and most of the pigs. Cept Bubba. He young but getting big, Mr. Henry. Big and mean . . ."

The cane-liquor bottle, uncapped, was on the table, a tin cup next to it. Hunter checked its contents and eased the stopper in, wondering what land this queer man came from who knew so little about the rules of hospitality. Woodsmen, white or black, all country people were free to enter a lean-to, a hunter's shooting cabin. Take what they needed, leave what they could. They were waystations and anybody, everybody, might have need of shelter. But nobody, nobody, drank a man's liquor in his house unless they knew each other mighty well.

"Do we know one another?" Hunter thought the "sir" he left out was as loud as a bang. But the man didn't hear it because he had a bang of his own.

"No. Daddy. We don't."

He couldn't say it wasn't possible. That he needed a midwife or a locket portrait to convince him. But the shock was heavy just the same.

"I never knew you were in the world" was what he said eventually, but what the blond man had to say, planned to say in response, had to wait because the woman screamed then and hoisted herself on her elbows to look between her raised knees.

The city man looked faint, but Honor and Hunter had not only watched the common and counted-on birthings farm people see, but had tugged and twisted newborns from all sorts of canals. This baby was not easy. It clung to the walls of that foamy cave, and the mother was of practically no help. When the baby finally emerged, the problem was clear immediately: the woman would not hold the baby or look at it. Hunter sent the boy home.

"Tell your maw to get one of the women to come out here. Come out here and take it. Otherwise it won't live out the morrow."

"Yes sir!"

"And bring cane liquor if any's around."

"Yes sir!"

Hunter bent down then to look at the mother, who hadn't said anything since that scream. Sweat covered her face and, breathing hard, she licked beads of it off her upper lip. He leaned closer. Under the dirt, lacing her coal-black skin, were traces of bad things; like tobacco juice, brine and a craftsman's sense of play. When he turned his head to adjust the blanket over her, she raised up and sank her teeth in his cheek. He yanked away and touching his bruised face lightly, chuckled. "Wild, eh?" He turned to look at the pale boy-man who had called him "Daddy."

"Where you pick up a wild woman?"

"In the woods. Where wild women grow."

"Say who she was?"

The man shook his head. "I startled her. She hit her head on a rock slab. I couldn't just leave her there."

"Reckon not. Who sent you to me?"

"True Belle."

"Ahhhh." Hunter smiled. "Where is she? I never did hear where she went off to."

"Or with?"

"Went off with the Colonel's daughter. Colonel Words-worth Gray. Everybody knowed that. Quick they went, too."

"Guess why."

"Don't have to guess now. I never knew you was in the world."

"Did you think about her? Wonder where she was?"

"True Belle?"

"No! Vera. Vera Louise."

"Aw, man. What I look like wondering where a whitegirl went?"

"My mother!"

"Suppose I did, eh? What'd be the next step? Go up to the Colonel? Say, look here, Colonel Gray, I been wondering where your daughter got to. We ain't been riding in a while. Tell you what you do. Tell her I'm waiting for her and to come on out. She'll know the place we meet at. And tell her to wear that green dress. The one make it hard to see her in the grass." Hunter passed his hand over his jaw. "You ain't said where they at. Where you come from."

"Baltimore. My name is Golden Gray."

"Can't say it don't suit."

"Suit you if it was Golden Lestory?"

"Not in these parts." Hunter slipped his hand under the baby's blanket to see if its heart was going. "Baby boy's weak. Got to get some nursing soon."

"How touching."

"Look here. What you want? I mean, now; what you want now? Want to stay here? You welcome. Want to chastise me? Throw it out your mind. I won't take a contrary word. You come in here, drink my liquor, rummage in my stuff and think you can cross-talk me just cause you call me Daddy? If she told you I was your daddy, then she told you more than she told me. Get a hold of yourself. A son ain't what a woman say. A son is what a man do. You want to act like you mine, then do it, else get the devil out my house!"

"I didn't come down here to court you, get your approval."

"I know what you came for. To see how black I was. You thought you was white, didn't you? She probably let you think it. Hoped you'd think it. And I swear I'd think it too."

"She protected me! If she'd announced I was a nigger, I could have been a slave!"

"They got free niggers. Always did have some free niggers. You could be one of them."

"I don't want to be a free nigger; I want to be a free man."

"Don't we all. Look. Be what you want—white or black. Choose. But if you choose black, you got to act black, meaning draw your manhood up—quicklike, and don't bring me no whiteboy sass."

Golden Gray was sober now and his sober thought was to blow the man's head off. Tomorrow.

It must have been the girl who changed his mind.


Girls can do that. Steer a man away from death or drive him right to it. Pull you out of sleep and you wake up on the ground under a tree you'll never locate again because you're lost. Or if you do find it, it won't be the same. Maybe it cracked from the inside, bored through by crawling life that had to have its own way too, and just crept and bunched and gnawed and burrowed until the whole thing was pitted through with the service it rendered to others. Or maybe they cut it down before it crashed in on itself. Turned it into logs for a fire in a big hearth for children to gaze into.

Victory might remember. He was more than Joe's chosen brother, he was his best friend, and they hunted through and worked in most of Vesper County. Not even a sheriff's map would show the walnut tree Joe fell out of, but Victory would remember it. It could be there still, in somebody's backyard, but the cotton fields and the colored neighborhood around them were churned up and pressed down.

One week of rumors, two days of packing, and nine hundred Negroes, encouraged by guns and hemp, left Vienna, rode out of town on wagons or walked on their feet to who knew (or cared) where. With two days' notice? How can you plan where to go, and if you do know of a place you think will welcome you, where is the money to arrive?

They stood around at the depot, camped in fields on the edge of the road in clusters until shooed away for being the blight that had been visited upon them—for reflecting like still water the disconsolateness they certainly felt, and for reminding others about the wages sin paid out to its laborers.

The cane field where Wild hid, or watched, or laughed out loud, or stayed quiet burned for months. The sugar smell lingered in the smoke—weighting it. Would she know? he wondered. Would she understand that fire was not light or flowers moving toward her, or flying golden hair? That if you tried to touch or kiss it, it would swallow your breath away?

The little graveyards, with handmade crosses and sometimes a stone marker pleading for remembrance in careful block letters, never stood a chance.

Hunter refused to leave; he was more in the woods than in his cabin anyway, and seemed to look forward to spending his last days in the places he felt most comfortable. So he didn't haul his gear to a wagon. Or walk the road to Bear, then Crossland, then Goshen, then Palestine looking for a workplace as Joe and Victory did. Some farm that would give thirteen-year-old black boys space to sleep and food in return for clearing brush. Or a mill that had a bunkhouse. Joe and Victory walked the road along with the others for a while, then took off. They knew they had left Crossland far behind when they passed the walnut tree where they used to sleep on nights when, hunting far from home, cool air could be found high in its branches. And when they looked back down the road, they could still see smoke lifting from what was left of the fields and the cane of Vienna. They found short work at a sawmill in Bear, then an afternoon pulling stumps at Crossland, finally steady work in Goshen. Then one spring the southern third of the county erupted in fat white cotton balls, and Joe left Victory helping the smithy at Goshen for the lucrative crop picking going on outside Palestine, some fifteen miles away. But first, first he had to know if the woman he believed was his mother was still there—or had she confused fire with hair and lost her breath to it.

All in all, he made three solitary journeys to find her. In Vienna he had lived first with the fear of her, then the joke of her, finally the obsession, followed by rejection of her. Nobody told Joe she was his mother. Not outright; but Hunters Hunter looked right in his eyes one evening and said, "She got reasons. Even if she crazy. Crazy people got reasons."

They were cleaning up after eating some of what they'd caught. Joe believed later it was fowl, but it could have been something with fur. Victory would remember. Victory was wiping the roasting stick with leaves while Joe leveled the fire.

"I taught both you all never kill the tender and nothing female if you can help it. Didn't think I had to teach you about people. Now, learn this: she ain't prey. You got to know the difference."

Victory and Joe had been joking, speculating on what it would take to kill Wild if they happened on her. If the trail of her all three of them sometimes saw and followed led straight to her hide. That's when Hunter said it. About how crazy people have reasons. Then he looked right at Joe (not Victory). The low fire galvanized his stare. "You know, that woman is *somebody's* mother and *somebody* ought to take care."

Victory and Joe exchanged looks, but it was Joe's flesh that cooled and his throat that tried and failed to swallow.

From then on he wrestled with the notion of a wildwoman for a mother. Sometimes it shamed him to tears. Other times his anger messed up his aim and he shot wild or hit game in messy inefficient places. A lot of his time was spent denying it, convincing himself he misread Hunter's words and most of all his look. Nevertheless, Wild was always on his mind, and he wasn't going to leave for Palestine without trying to find her one more time.

She wasn't always in the cane. Nor the back part of the woods on a whiteman's farm. He and Hunter and Victory had seen traces of her in those woods: ruined honeycombs, the bits and leavings of stolen victuals and many times the signal Hunter relied on most—redwings, those blue-black birds with the bolt of red on their wings. Something about her they liked, said Hunter, and seeing four or more of them always meant she was close. Hunter had spoken to her there twice, he said, but Joe knew that those woods were not her favorite place. The first time he'd looked for her it was a halfhearted search after a couple of hours' spectacular fishing. Across the river, beyond the place where the trout and the bass were plentiful but before the river went underground heading for the mill, the bank turned around an incline. On top of it, some fifteen feet above the river was a sheltering rock formation, its entrance blocked by hedges of old hibiscus. Once, after pulling ten trout in the first hour of dawn, Joe had walked past that place and heard what he first believed was some combination of running water and wind in high trees. The music the world makes, familiar to fishermen and shepherds, woodsmen have also heard. It hypnotizes mammals. Bucks raise their heads and gophers freeze. Attentive woodsmen smile and close their eyes.

Joe thought that was it, and simply listened with pleasure until a word or two seemed to glide into the sound. Knowing the music the world makes has no words, he stood rock still and scanned his surroundings. A silver line lay across the opposite bank, sun cutting into the last of the night's royal blue. Above and to his left hibiscus thick, savage and old. Its blossoms were closed waiting for the day. The scrap of song came from a woman's throat, and Joe thrashed and beat his way up the incline and through the hedge, a tangle of muscadine vines, Virginia creeper and hibiscus rusty with age. He found the opening in the rock formation but could not enter it from that angle. He would have to climb above it and slide down into its mouth. The light was so small he could barely see his legs. But he saw tracks enough to know she was there.

He called out. "Anybody there?"

The song stopped, and a snap like the breaking of twigs took its place.

"Hey! You in there!"

Nothing stirred and he could not persuade himself that the fragrance that floated over him was not a mixture of honey and shit. He left then, disgusted, and not a little afraid.

The second time he looked for her was after the dispossession. Having seen the smoke and tasted the sugared air on his tongue, he delayed his journey to Palestine to detour back toward Vienna. Skirting the burned ground and fields of black stalks; looking away from the cabins that were now just hot bricks where a washtub once stood, he headed for the river and the hole in it where trout multiplied like flies. When he reached the place where the river turned he adjusted the rifle strapped to his back and dropped to his haunches.

Slowly, breathing softly through his mouth, he crawled toward the rocks shut away by greenery grown ruthless in sun and air. There was no sign of her, nothing he recognized. He managed to climb above the opening, but when he slid down and entered the rock place, he saw nothing a woman could use and the vestiges of human habitation were cold. Had she run away, escaped? Or had she been overtaken by smoke, fire, panic, helplessness? Joe waited there, till his listening made him drowsy and he slept for an hour or more. When he woke the day had moved and the hibiscus was as wide as his hand. He hauled himself down the incline and, as he turned to go four redwings shot up from the lower limbs of a white-oak tree. Huge, isolated, it grew in unlikely soil—entwined in its own roots. Immediately Joe fell to his hands and knees, whispering: "Is it you? Just say it. Say anything." Someone near him was breathing. Turning round he examined the place he had just exited. Every movement and leaf shift seemed to be her. "Give me a sign, then. You don't have to say nothing. Let me see your hand. Just stick it out someplace and I'll go; I promise. A sign." He begged, pleaded for her hand until the light grew even smaller. "You my mother?" Yes. No. Both. Either. But not this nothing.

Whispering into hibiscus stalks and listening to breathing, he suddenly saw himself pawing around in the dirt for a not just crazy but also dirty woman who happened to be his secret mother that Hunter once knew but who orphaned her baby rather than nurse him or coddle him or stay in the house with him. A woman who frightened children, made men sharpen knives, for whom brides left food out (might as well—otherwise she stole it). Leaving traces of her sloven unhousebroken self all over the county. Shaming him before everybody but Victory, who neither laughed nor slant-eyed him when Joe told him what he believed Hunter meant by those words and especially that look. "She must be tough" was Victory's reply. "Live outside like that all year round, she must be tough."

Maybe so, but right then Joe felt like a lint-headed fool, crazier than she and just as wild as he slipped into mud, tripped over black roots, scuffed through patches of dirt crawling with termites. He loved the woods because Hunter taught him how to. But now they were full of her, a simple-minded woman too silly to beg for a living. Too brain-blasted to do what the meanest sow managed: nurse what she birthed. The small children believed she was a witch, but they were wrong. This creature hadn't the intelligence to be a witch. She was powerless, invisible, wastefully daft. Everywhere and nowhere.

There are boys who have whores for mothers and don't get over it. There are boys whose mothers stagger through town roads when the juke joint slams its door. Mothers who throw their children away or trade them for folding money. He would have chosen any one of them over this indecent speechless lurking insanity. The blast he aimed at the white-oak limbs disturbed nothing, for the shells were in his pocket. The trigger clicked harmlessly. Yelling, sliding, falling, he raced back down the incline and followed the riverbank out of there.

From then on his work was maniacal. On his way to Palestine, he took every job offered or heard about. Cut trees, cane; plowed till he could hardly lift his arms; plucked chickens and cotton; hauled lumber, grain, quarry rocks and stock. Some thought he was money hungry, but others guessed that Joe didn't like to be still or thought of as lazy. Sometimes he worked so long and late he never got back to the bed he bunked in. Then he would sleep outside, sometimes lucky enough to be near the walnut tree; swinging in the tarp they kept there for when they needed it. After Palestine, when the cotton was in, baled and spoken for, Joe got married and worked even harder.

Did Hunter stay near Vienna after the fire? Move back to Wordsworth? Fix himself a little place up country—like he talked of doing—and work the world his own way? In 1926, far away from all those places, Joe thought maybe it was Wordsworth Hunter moved near to, and if he could ask him, Victory would remember exactly (assuming he was alive and prison had not rattled him) because Victory remembered everything and could keep things clear in his mind. Like how many times peahens had used a certain nest. Like where a henna carpet of pine needles was shin-bone deep. Like whether a particular tree—the one whose roots grew up its trunk—was in bud two days ago or a week and exactly where it was.

Joe is wondering about all this on an icy day in January. He is a long way from Virginia, and even longer from Eden. As he puts on his coat and cap he can practically feel Victory at his side when he sets out, armed, to find Dorcas. He isn't thinking of harming her, or, as Hunter had cautioned, killing something tender. She is female. And she is not prey. So he never thinks of that. He is hunting for her though, and while hunting a gun is as natural a companion as Victory.

He stalks through the City and it does not object or interfere. It's the first day of the year. Most people are tired from the night before. Colored people, however, are still celebrating with a day gathering, a feast that can linger into the night. The streets are slippery. The City looks as uninhabited as a small town.

"I just want to see her. Tell her I know she didn't mean what she said. She's young. Young people fly off the handle. Bust out just for the hell of it. Like me shooting an unloaded shotgun at the leaves that time. Like me saying, 'All right, Violet, I'll marry you,' just because I couldn't see whether a wildwoman put out her hand or not."

The streets he walks are slick and black. In his coat pocket is the forty-five he pawned his rifle for. He had laughed when he handled it, a fat baby gun that would be loud as a cannon. Nothing complex; you'd have to fight your own self to miss, but he isn't going to miss because he isn't going to aim. Not at that insulted skin. Never. Never hurt the young: nest eggs, roe, fledglings, fry . . .

A wind rips up from the mouth of the tunnel and blows his cap off. He runs to get it from the gutter it swept into. He doesn't see the paper ring from a White Owl cigar that sticks to the crown of his cap. Once inside the train he perspires heavily and takes off his coat. The paper sack thuds to the floor. Joe looks down at the fingers of a passenger who reaches for the bag and returns it to him. Joe nods a thank you and shoves the sack back into his coat pocket. A Negro woman shakes her head at him. At the paper sack? Its contents? No, at his dripping face. She holds out to him a fresh handkerchief to wipe it. He refuses; puts his coat back on and moves to the door to stare into the swiftness and the dark.

The train stops suddenly, throwing passengers forward. As though it just remembered that this was the stop where Joe needs to get off if he is going to find her.

Three girls pile out of the train and clack down the icy stairs. Three waiting men greet them and they all pair off. It is biting cold. The girls have red lips and their legs whisper to each other through silk stockings. The red lips and the silk flash power. A power they will exchange for the right to be overcome, penetrated. The men at their side love it because, in the end, they will reach in, extend, get back behind that power, grab it and keep it still.

The third time Joe had tried to find her (he was a married man by then) he had searched the hillside for the tree—the one whose roots grew backward as though, having gone obediently into earth and found it barren, retreating to the trunk for what was needed. Defiant and against logic its roots climbed. Toward leaves, light, wind. Below that tree was the river whites called Treason where fish raced to the line, and swimming among them could be riotous or serene. But to get there you risked treachery by the very ground you walked on. The slopes and low hills that fell gently toward the river only appeared welcoming; underneath vines, carpet grass, wild grape, hibiscus and wood sorrel, the ground was as porous as a sieve. A step could swallow your foot or your whole self.

"What would she want with a rooster? Crowing on a corner, looking at the chickens to pick over them. Nothing they have I don't have better. Plus I know how to treat a woman. I never have, never would, mistreat one. Never would make a woman live like a dog in a cave. The roosters would. She used to say that too. How the young ones couldn't think about anybody but themselves; how in the playground or at a dance all those boys thought about was themselves. When I find her, I know—I bet my life—she won't be holed up with one of them. His clothes won't be all mixed up with hers. Not her. Not Dorcas. She'll be alone. Hardheaded. Wild, even. But alone."

· · ·

Beyond the tree, behind the hibiscus, was a boulder. Behind it an opening so badly disguised it could be only the work of a human. No fox or foaling doe would be so sloppy. Had she been hiding there? Was she that small? He squatted to look closer for signs of her, recognizing none. Finally he stuck his head in. Pitch dark. No odor of dung or fur. It had, instead, a domestic smell—oil, ashes—that led him on. Crawling, squirming through a space low enough to graze his hair. Just as he decided to back out of there, the dirt under his hands became stone and light hit him so hard he flinched. He had come through a few body-lengths of darkness and was looking out the south side of the rock face. A natural burrow. Going nowhere. Angling through one curve of the slope to another. Treason River glistening below. Unable to turn around inside, he pulled himself all the way out to reenter head first. Immediately he was in open air the domestic smell intensified. Cooking oil reeked under stabbing sunlight. Then he saw the crevice. He went into it on his behind until a floor stopped his slide. It was like falling into the sun. Noon light followed him like lava into a stone room where somebody cooked in oil.

"She don't have to explain. She don't have to say a word. I know how it is. She might think it's jealousy, but I'm a mild man. It's not that I don't feel things. I've known some tough times. Got through them, too. I feel things just like everybody else.

"She'll be all alone.

"She'll turn to me.

"She will hold out her hand, walk toward me in ugly shoes, but her face is clean and I am proud of her. Her too-tight braids torture her so she unlooses them as she moves toward me. She's

**T**here she is. No dancing brothers are in this place, nor any breathless girls waiting for the white bulb to be exchanged for the blue. This is an adult party—what goes on goes on in bright light. The illegal liquor is not secret and the secrets are not forbidden. Pay a dollar or two when you enter and what you say is smarter, funnier, than it would be in your own kitchen. Your wit surfaces over and over like the rush of foam to the rim. The laughter is like pealing bells that don't need a hand to pull on the rope; it just goes on and on until you are weak with it. You can drink the safe gin if you like, or stick to beer, but you don't need either because a touch on the knee, accidental or on purpose, alerts the blood like a shot of pre-Pro bourbon or two fingers pinching your nipple. Your spirit lifts to the ceiling where it floats for a bit looking down with pleasure on the dressed-up nakedness below. You know something wicked is going on in a room with a closed door. But there is enough dazzle and mischief here, where partners cling or exchange at the urging of a heartbreaking vocal.

Dorcas is satisfied, content. Two arms clasp her and she is able to rest her cheek on her own shoulder while her wrists cross behind his neck. It's good they don't need much space to dance in because there isn't any. The room is packed. Men groan their satisfaction; women hum anticipation. The music bends, falls to its knees to embrace them all, encourage them all to live a little, why don't you? since this is the it you've been looking for.

Her partner does not whisper in Dorcas' ear. His promises are already clear in the chin he presses into her hair, the fingertips that stay. She stretches up to encircle his neck. He bends to help her do it. They agree on everything above the waist and below: muscle, tendon, bone joint and marrow cooperate. And if the dancers hesitate, have a moment of doubt, the music will solve and dissolve any question.

Dorcas is happy. Happier than she has ever been anytime. No white strands grow in her partner's mustache. He is up and coming. Hawk-eyed, tireless and a little cruel. He has never given her a present or even thought about it. Sometimes he is where he says he will be; sometimes not. Other women want him—badly—and he has been selective. What they want and the prize it is his to give is his savvy self. What could a pair of silk stockings be compared to him? No contest. Dorcas is lucky. Knows it. And is as happy as she has ever been anytime.

. . .

"He is coming for me. I know he is because I know how flat his eyes went when I told him not to. And how they raced afterward. I didn't say it nicely, although I meant to. I practiced the points; in front of the mirror I went through them one by one: the sneaking around, and his wife and all. I never said anything about our ages or Acton. Nothing about Acton. But he argued with me so I said, Leave me alone. Just leave me alone. Get away from me. You bring me another bottle of cologne I'll drink it and die you don't leave me alone.

"He said, You can't die from cologne.

"I said, You know what I mean.

"He said, You want me to leave my wife?

"I said, No! I want you to leave *me.* I don't want you inside me. I don't want you beside me. I hate this room. I don't want to be here and don't come looking for me.

"He said, Why?

"I said, Because. Because. Because.

"He said, Because what?

"I said, Because you make me sick.

"Sick? I make you sick?

"Sick of myself and sick of you.

"I didn't mean that part . . . about being sick. He didn't. Make me sick, I mean. What I wanted to let him know was that I had this chance to have Acton and I wanted it and I wanted girlfriends to talk to about it. About where we went and what he did. About things. About stuff. What good are secrets if you can't talk to anybody about them? I sort of hinted about Joe and me to Felice and she laughed before she stared at me and then frowned.

"I couldn't tell him all that because I had practiced the other points and got mixed up.

"But he's coming for me. I know it. He's been looking for me all over. Maybe tomorrow he'll find me. Maybe tonight. Way out here; all the way out here.

"When we got off the streetcar, me and Acton and Felice, I thought he was there in the doorway next to the candy store, but it wasn't him. Not yet. I think I see him everywhere. I know he's looking and now I know he's coming.

"He didn't even care what I looked like. I could be anything, do anything—and it pleased him. Something about that made me mad. I don't know.

"Acton, now, he tells me when he doesn't like the way I fix my hair. Then I do it how he likes it. I never wear glasses when he is with me and I changed my laugh for him to one he likes better. I think he does. I know he didn't like it before. And I play with my food now. Joe liked for me to eat it all up and want more. Acton gives me a quiet look when I ask for seconds. He worries about me that way. Joe never did. Joe didn't care what kind of woman I was. He should have. I cared. I wanted to have a personality and with Acton I'm getting one. I have a look now. What pencil-thin eyebrows do for my face is a dream. All my bracelets are just below my elbow. Sometimes I knot my stockings below, not above, my knees. Three straps are across my instep and at home I have shoes with leather cut out to look like lace.

"He is coming for me. Maybe tonight. Maybe here.

"If he does he will look and see how close me and Acton dance. How I rest my head on my arm holding on to him. The hem of my skirt drapes down in back and taps the calves of my legs while we rock back and forth, then side to side. The whole front of us touches. Nothing can get between us we are so close. Lots of girls here want to be doing this with him. I can see them when I open my eyes to look past his neck. I rub my thumbnail over his nape so the girls will know I know they want him. He doesn't like it and turns his head to make me stop touching his neck that way. I stop.

"Joe wouldn't care. I could rub anywhere on him. He let me draw lipstick pictures in places he had to have a mirror to see."

Anything that happens after this party breaks up is nothing. Everything is now. It's like war. Everyone is handsome, shining just thinking about other people's blood. As though the red wash flying from veins not theirs is facial makeup patented for its glow. Inspiriting. Glamorous. Afterward there will be some chatter and recapitulation of what went on; nothing though like the action itself and the beat that pumps the heart. In war or at a party everyone is wily, intriguing; goals are set and altered; alliances rearranged. Partners and rivals devastated; new pairings triumphant. The knockout possibilities knock Dorcas out because here—with grown-ups and as in war— people play for keeps.

"He is coming for me. And when he does he will see I'm not his anymore. I'm Acton's and it's Acton I want to please. He expects it. With Joe I pleased myself because he encouraged me to. With Joe I worked the stick of the world, the power in my hand."

· · ·

Oh, the room—the music—the people leaning in doorways. Silhouettes kiss behind curtains; playful fingers examine and caress. This is the place where things pop. This is the market where gesture is all: a tongue's lightning lick; a thumbnail grazing the split cheeks of a purple plum. Any thrownaway lover in wet unlaced shoes and a buttoned-up sweater under his coat is a foreigner here. This is not the place for old men; this is the place for romance.

"He's here. Oh, look. God. He's crying. Am I falling? Why am I falling? Acton is holding me up but I am falling anyway. Heads are turning to look where I am falling. It's dark and now it's light. I am lying on a bed. Somebody is wiping sweat from my forehead, but I am cold, so cold. I see mouths moving; they are all saying something to me I can't hear. Way out there at the foot of the bed I see Acton. Blood is on his coat jacket and he is dabbing at it with a white handkerchief. Now a woman takes the coat from his shoulders. He is annoyed by the blood. It's my blood, I guess, and it has stained through his jacket to his shirt. The hostess is shouting. Her party is ruined. Acton looks angry; the woman brings his jacket back and it is not clean the way it was before and the way he likes it.

"I can hear them now.

" 'Who? Who did this?'

"I'm tired. Sleepy. I ought to be wide awake because something important is happening.

" 'Who did this, girl? Who did this to you?'

"They want me to say his name. Say it in public at last.

"Acton has taken his shirt off. People are blocking the doorway; some stretch behind them to get a better look. The record playing is over. Somebody they have been waiting for is playing the piano. A woman is singing too. The music is faint but I know the words by heart.

"Felice leans close. Her hand holding mine is too tight. I try to say with my mouth to come nearer. Her eyes are bigger than the light fixture on the ceiling. She asks me was it him.

"They need me to say his name so they can go after him. Take away his sample case with Rochelle and Bernadine and Faye inside. I know his name but Mama won't tell. The world rocked from a stick beneath my hand, Felice. There in that room with the ice sign in the window.

"Felice puts her ear on my lips and I scream it to her. I think I am screaming it. I think I am.

"People are leaving.

"Now it's clear. Through the doorway I see the table. On it is a brown wooden bowl, flat, low like a tray, full to spilling with oranges. I want to sleep, but it is clear now. So clear the dark bowl the pile of oranges. Just oranges. Bright. Listen. I don't know who is that woman singing but I know the words by heart."

men; they went to Father Divine's wagon and after they'd eaten they rolled cigarettes and settled down on the curb as though it were a Duncan Phyfe. And the women tip-tapping their heels on the pavement tripped sometimes on the sidewalk cracks because they were glancing at the trees to see where that pure, soft but steady light was coming from. The rumbling of the M11 and M2 was distant, far away and the Packards too. Even those loud Fords quieted down, and no one felt like blowing his horn or leaning out the driver's side to try and embarrass somebody taking too long to cross the street. The sweetness of the day tickled them, made them holler "I give you everything I got! you come home with me!" to a woman tripping in shiny black heels over the cracks.

Young men on the rooftops changed their tune; spit and fiddled with the mouthpiece for a while and when they put it back in and blew out their cheeks it was just like the light of that day, pure and steady and kind of kind. You would have thought everything had been forgiven the way they played. The clarinets had trouble because the brass was cut so fine, not lowdown the way they love to do it, but high and fine like a young girl singing by the side of a creek, passing the time, her ankles cold in the water. The young men with brass probably never saw such a girl, or such a creek, but they made her up that day. On the rooftops. Some on 254 where there is no protective railing; another at 131, the one with the apple-green water tank, and somebody right next to it, 133, where lard cans of tomato plants are kept, and a pallet for sleeping at night. To find coolness and a way to avoid mosquitoes unable to fly that high up or unwilling to leave the tender neck meat near the street lamps. So from Lenox to St. Nicholas and across 135th Street, Lexington, from Convent to Eighth I could hear the men playing out their maple-sugar hearts, tapping it from four-hundred-year-old trees and letting it run down the trunk, wasting it because they didn't have a bucket to hold it and didn't want one either. They just wanted to let it run that day, slow if it wished, or fast, but a free run down trees bursting to give it up.

That's the way the young men on brass sounded that day. Sure of themselves, sure they were holy, standing up there on the rooftops, facing each other at first, but when it was clear that they had beat the clarinets out, they turned their backs on them, lifted those horns straight up and joined the light just as pure and steady and kind of kind.

No day to wreck a life already splintered like a cheap windowpane, but Violet, well you had to know Violet. She thought all she had to do was drink malts full of Dr. Dee's Nerve and Flesh Builder, eat pork, and she'd put on enough weight to fill out the back of her dress. She usually wore a coat on warm days like this to keep the men at curbside from shaking their heads in pity when she walked by. But on this day, this kind, pretty day, she didn't care about her missing behind because she came out the door and stood on the porch with her elbows in her hands and her stockings rolled down to her ankles. She had been listening to the music penetrate Joe's sobs, which were quieter now. Probably because she had returned Dorcas' photograph to Alice Manfred. But the space where the photo had been was real. Perhaps that's why, standing there on the porch, unmindful of her behind, she easily believed that what was coming up the steps toward her was another true-as-life Dorcas, four marcelled waves and all.

She carried an Okeh record under her arm and a half pound of stewmeat wrapped in pink butcher paper in her hand although the sun is too hot to linger in the streets with meat. If she doesn't hurry it will turn—cook itself before she can get it to the stove.

Lazy girl. Her arms are full but there is nothing much in her head.

She makes me nervous.

She makes me wonder if this fine weather will last more than a day. I am already disturbed by the ash falling from the blue distance down on these streets. A sooty film is gathering on the sills, coating the windowpanes. Now she is disturbing me, making me doubt my own self just looking at her sauntering through the sunshafts like that. Climbing the steps now, heading for Violent.


"My mother and my father too lived in Tuxedo. I almost never saw them. I lived with my grandmother who said, 'Felice, they don't live in Tuxedo; they work there and live with us.' Just words: live, work. I would see them once every three weeks for two and a half days, and all day Christmas and all day Easter. I counted. Forty-two days if you count the half days—which I don't, because most of it was packing and getting to the train—plus two holidays makes forty-four days, but really only thirty-four because the half days shouldn't count. Thirty-four days a year.

"When they'd come home, they'd kiss me and give me things, like my opal ring, but what they really wanted to do was go out dancing somewhere (my mother) or sleep (my father). They made it to church on the Sunday, but my mother is still sad about that because all of the things she should have been doing in the church—the suppers, the meetings, the fixing up of the basement for Sunday-school parties and the receptions after funerals—she had to say no to, because of her job in Tuxedo. So more than anything she wanted gossip from the women in Circle A Society about what'd been going on; and she wanted to dance a little and play bid whist.

"My father preferred to stay in a bathrobe and be waited on for a change while he read the stacks of newspapers me and my grandmother saved for him. The *Amsterdam*, the *Age*, *The Crisis*, *The Messenger*, the *Worker*. Some he took back with him to Tuxedo because he couldn't get them up there. He likes them folded properly if they are newspapers, and no food or fingerprints on the magazines, so I don't read them much. My grandmother does and is very very careful not to wrinkle or soil them. Nothing makes him madder than to open a paper that is badly folded. He groans and grunts while he reads and once in a while he laughs, but he'd never give it up even though all that reading worries his blood, my grandmother said. The good part for him is to read everything and argue about what he's read with my mother and grandmother and the friends they play cards with.

"Once I thought if I read the papers we'd saved I could argue with him. But I picked wrong. I read about the white policemen who were arrested for killing some Negroes and said I was glad they were arrested, that it was about time.

"He looked at me and shouted, 'The story hit the paper because it was news, girl, news!'

"I didn't know how to answer him and started to cry so my grandmother said, 'Sonny, go somewhere and sit down,' and my mother said, 'Walter, shut up about all that to her.'

"She explained to me what he meant: that for the everyday killings cops did of Negroes, nobody was arrested at all. She took me shopping after that for some things her bosses in Tuxedo wanted, and I didn't ask her why she had to shop for them on her off days, because then she wouldn't have taken me to Tiffany's on Thirty-seventh Street where it's quieter than when Reverend asks for a minute of silent prayer. When that happens I can hear feet scraping and some people blow their noses. But in Tiffany's nobody blows a nose and the carpet prevents shoe noises of any kind. Like Tuxedo.

"Years ago when I was little, before I started school, my parents would take me there. I had to be quiet all the time. Twice they took me and I stayed the whole three weeks. It stopped, though. My mother and father talked about quitting but they didn't. They got my grandmother to move in and watch over me.

"Thirty-four days. I'm seventeen now and that works out to less than six hundred days. Less than two years out of seventeen. Dorcas said I was lucky because at least they were there, somewhere, and if I got sick I could call on them or get on the train and go see them. Both of her parents died in a very bad way and she saw them after they died and before the funeral men fixed them up. She had a photograph of them sitting under a painted palm tree. Her mother was standing up with her hand on the father's shoulder. He was sitting down and holding a book. They looked sad to me, but Dorcas couldn't get over how good looking they both were.

"She was always talking about who was good looking and who wasn't. Who had bad breath, who had nice clothes, who could dance, who was hincty.

"My grandmother was suspicious of us being friends. She never said why but I sort of knew. I didn't have a lot of friends in school. Not the boys but the girls in my school bunched off according to their skin color. I hate that stuff—Dorcas too. So me and her were different that way. When some nastymouth hollered, 'Hey, fly, where's buttermilk?' or 'Hey, kinky, where's kind?' we stuck our tongues out and put our fingers in our noses to shut them up. But if that didn't work we'd lay into them. Some of those fights ruined my clothes and Dorcas' glasses, but it felt good fighting those girls with Dorcas. She was never afraid and we had the best times. Every school we went to, every day.

"It stopped, the good times, for a couple of months when she started seeing that old man. I knew about it from the start, but she didn't know I did. I let her think it was a secret because she wanted it to be one. At first I thought she was shamed of it, or shamed of him and was just in it for the presents. But she liked secret stuff. Planning and plotting how to deceive Mrs. Manfred. Slipping vampy underwear on at my house to go walking in. Hiding things. She always did like secrets. She wasn't ashamed of him either.

"He's old. Really old. Fifty. But he met her standards of good looking, I'll say that for him. Dorcas should have been prettier than she was. She just missed. She had all the ingredients of pretty too. Long hair, wavy, half good, half bad. Light skinned. Never used skin bleach. Nice shape. But it missed somehow. If you looked at each thing, you would admire that thing—the hair, the color, the shape. All together it didn't fit. Guys looked at her, whistled and called out fresh stuff when we walked down the street. In school all sorts of boys wanted to talk to her. But then they stopped; nothing came of it. It couldn't have been her personality because she was a good talker, liked to joke and tease. Nothing standoffish about her. I don't know what it was. Unless it was the way she pushed them. I mean it was like she wanted them to do something scary all the time. Steal things, or go back in the store and slap the face of a white salesgirl who wouldn't wait on her, or cuss out somebody who had snubbed her. Beats me. Everything was like a picture show to her, and she was the one on the railroad track, or the one trapped in the sheik's tent when it caught on fire.

"I think that's what made her like that old man so much at first. The secrecy and that he had a wife. He must have done something dangerous when she first met him or she would never have gone on sneaking around with him. Anyway, she thought she was sneaking. But two hairdressers saw her in that nightclub, Mexico, with him. I spent two hours in there listening to what they had to say about her and him and all kinds of other people who were stepping out. They had fun talking about Dorcas and him mostly because they didn't like his wife. She took away their trade, so they had nothing good to say about her, except crazy as she was she did do hair well and if she wasn't so crazy she could have got a license proper instead of taking away their trade.

"They're wrong about her. I went to look for my ring and there is nothing crazy about her at all.

"I know my mother stole that ring. She said her boss lady gave it to her, but I remember it in Tiffany's that day. A silver ring with a smooth black stone called opal. The salesgirl went to get the package my mother came to pick up. She showed the girl the note from her boss lady so they would give it to her (and even showed it at the door, so they would let her in). While the salesgirl was gone, we looked at the velvet tray of rings. Picked some up and tried to try them on, but a man in a beautiful suit came over and shook his head. Very slightly.

'I'm waiting for a package for Mrs. Nicolson,' my mother said.

"The man smiled then and said, 'Of course. It's just policy. We have to be careful.' When we left my mother said, 'Of what? What does he have to be careful about? They put the tray out so people can look at the things, don't they? So what does he have to be careful about?'

"She frowned and fussed and we waited a long time for a taxi to take us home and she dared my father to say something about it. The next morning, they packed and got ready to take the train back to Tuxedo Junction. She called me over and gave me the ring she said her boss lady had given her. Maybe they made lots of them, but I know my mother took it from the velvet tray. Out of spite, I suppose, but she gave it to me and I love it, and only lent it to Dorcas because she begged so hard and the silver of it did match the bracelets at her elbow.

"She wanted to impress Acton. A hard job since he criticized everything. He never gave her gifts the way the old man did. I know she took stuff from him because Mrs. Manfred would die before she bought slippery underwear or silk stockings for Dorcas. Things she couldn't wear at home or to church.

"After Dorcas picked up with Acton, we saw each other like before, but she was different. She was doing for Acton what the old man did for her—giving him little presents she bought from the money she wheedled out of the old man and from Mrs. Manfred. Nobody ever caught Dorcas looking for work, but she worked hard scheming money to give Acton things. Stuff he didn't like, anyway, because it was cheap, and he never wore that ugly stickpin or the silk handkerchief either because of the color. I guess the old man taught her how to be nice, and she wasted it on Acton, who took it for granted, and took her for granted and any girl who liked him.

"I don't know if she quit the old man or just two-timed him with Acton. My grandmother says she brought it on herself. Live the life; pay the price, she said.

"I have to get on home. If I sit here too long, some man will think I'm looking for a good time. Not anymore. After what happened to Dorcas, all I want is my ring back. To have and to show my mother I still have it. She asks me about it once in a while. She's sick and doesn't work in Tuxedo anymore, and my father has a job on the Pullman. He is happier than I've ever seen him. When he reads the papers and magazines he still grunts and talks back to the printed words, but he gets them first and freshly folded and his arguments aren't so loud. 'I've seen the world now,' he says.

"He means Tuxedo and the train stops in Pennsylvania and Ohio and Indiana and Illinois. 'And all the kinds of white-people there are. Two kinds,' he says. 'The ones that feel sorry for you and the ones that don't. And both amount to the same thing. Nowhere in between is respect.'

"He's as argumentative as ever, but happier because riding trains he gets to see Negroes play baseball 'in the flesh and on the lot, goddamnit.' It tickles him that whitepeople are scared to compete with Negroes fair and square.

"My grandmother is slower now, and my mother is sick, so I do most of the cooking. My mother wants me to find some good man to marry. I want a good job first. Make my own money. Like she did. Like Mrs. Trace. Like Mrs. Manfred used to before Dorcas let herself die.

"I stopped in there to see if he had my ring, because my mother kept asking me about it, and because I couldn't find it when I rummaged around in Mrs. Manfred's house after the funeral. But I had another reason too. The hairdresser said the old man was all broke up. Cried all day and all night. Left his job and wasn't good for a thing. I suppose he misses Dorcas, and thinks about how he is her murderer. But he must not have known about her. How she liked to push people, men. All except Acton, but she would have pushed him too if she had lived long enough or if he had stayed around long enough. It was just for attention or the excitement. I was there at the party and I was the one she talked to on the bed.

"I thought about it for three months and when I heard he was still at it, crying and so on, I made up my mind to tell him about her. About what she said to me. So on my way home from the market, I stopped by Felton's to get the record my mother wanted. I walked by the building on Lenox where Dorcas used to meet him, and there on the porch was the woman they call Violent because of what they said she did at Dorcas' funeral.

"I didn't go to the funeral. I saw her die like a fool and was too mad to be at her funeral. I didn't go to the viewing either. I hated her after that. Anybody would. Some friend she turned out to be.

"All I wanted was my ring, and to tell the old man he could stop carrying on so. I wasn't afraid of his wife because Mrs. Manfred let her visit and they seemed to get on okay. Knowing how strict Mrs. Manfred was, all the people she said she would never let in her house and that Dorcas should never speak to, I figured if Violent was good enough for her to let in, she was good enough for me to not be afraid of.

"I can see why Mrs. Manfred let her visit. She doesn't lie, Mrs. Trace. Nothing she says is a lie the way it is with most older people. Almost the first thing she said about Dorcas was, 'She was ugly. Outside and in.'

"Dorcas was my friend, but I knew that in a way she was right. All those ingredients of pretty and the recipe didn't work. Mrs. Trace, I thought, was just jealous. She herself is very very dark, bootblack, the girls at school would say. And I didn't expect her to be pretty, but she is. You'd never get tired looking at her face. She's what my grandmother calls pick thin, and wears her hair straightened and flat, slicked back like a man's except that style is all the rage now. Nicely trimmed above her ears and at the kitchen part too. I think her husband must have done her kitchen for her. Who else? She never stepped foot in a beauty shop or so the hairdressers said. I could picture her husband doing her neckline for her. The clippers, maybe even a razor, then the powder afterward. He was that kind, and I sort of know what Dorcas was talking about while she was bleeding all over that woman's bed at the party.

"Dorcas was a fool, but when I met the old man I sort of understood. He has a way about him. And he is handsome. For an old man, I mean. Nothing flabby on him. Nice-shaped head, carries himself like he's somebody. Like my father when he's being a proud Pullman porter seeing the world, and baseball and not cooped up in Tuxedo Junction. But his eyes are not cold like my father's. Mr. Trace looks at you. He has double eyes. Each one a different color. A sad one that lets you look inside him, and a clear one that looks inside you. I like when he looks at me. I feel, I don't know, interesting. He looks at me and I feel deep—as though the things I feel and think are important and different and . . . interesting.

"I think he likes women, and I don't know anybody like that. I don't mean he flirts with them, I mean he likes them without that, and, this would upset the hairdressers, but I really believe he likes his wife.

"When I first went there he was sitting by the window

staring down in the alleyway, not saying anything. Later on Mrs. Trace brought him a plate full of old-people food: vegetable stuff with rice and the cornbread right on top. He said, 'Thank you, baby. Take half for yourself.' Something about the way he said it. As though he appreciated it. When my father says thanks, it's just a word. Mr. Trace acted like he meant it. And when he leaves the room and walks past his wife, he touches her. Sometimes on the head. Sometimes just a pat on her shoulder.

"I've seen him smile twice now and laugh out loud once. Then nobody would know how old he is. He's like a kid when he laughs. But I had visited them three or four times before I ever saw him smile. And that was when I said animals in a zoo were happier than when they were left free because they were safe from hunters. He didn't comment; he just smiled as though what I said was new or really funny.

"That's why I went back. The first time was to see if he had my ring or knew where it was, and to tell him to stop carrying on about Dorcas because maybe she wasn't worth it. The next time, when Mrs. Trace invited me to supper, was more to watch how he was and to listen to Mrs. Trace talk the way she did. A way that would always get her into trouble.

" 'I messed up my own life,' she told me. 'Before I came North I made sense and so did the world. We didn't have nothing but we didn't miss it.'

"Who ever heard of that? Living in the City was the best thing in the world. What can you do out in the country? When I visited Tuxedo, back when I was a child, even then I was bored. How many trees can you look at? That's what I said to her. 'How many trees can you look at? And for how long and so what?'

"She said it wasn't like that, looking at a bunch of trees. She said for me to go to 143rd Street and look at the big one on the corner and see if it was a man or a woman or a child.

"I laughed but before I could agree with the hairdressers that she was crazy, she said, 'What's the world for if you can't make it up the way you want it?'

" 'The way I want it?'

" 'Yeah. The way you want it. Don't you want it to be something more than what it is?'

" 'What's the point? I can't change it.'

" 'That's the point. If you don't, it will change you and it'll be your fault cause you let it. I let it. And messed up my life.'

" 'Messed it up how?'

" 'Forgot it.'

" 'Forgot?'

" 'Forgot it was mine. My life. I just ran up and down the streets wishing I was somebody else.'

" 'Who? Who'd you want to be?'

" 'Not who so much as what. White. Light. Young again.'

" 'Now you don't?'

" 'Now I want to be the woman my mother didn't stay around long enough to see. That one. The one she would have liked and the one I used to like before. . . . My grandmother fed me stories about a little blond child. He was a boy, but I thought of him as a girl sometimes, as a brother, sometimes as a boyfriend. He lived inside my mind. Quiet as a mole. But I didn't know it till I got here. The two of us. Had to get rid of it.'

"She talked like that. But I understood what she meant. About having another you inside that isn't anything like you. Dorcas and I used to make up love scenes and describe them to each other. It was fun and a little smutty. Something about it bothered me, though. Not the loving stuff, but the picture

I had of myself when I did it. Nothing like me. I saw myself as somebody I'd seen in a picture show or a magazine. Then it would work. If I pictured myself the way I am it seemed wrong.

" 'How did you get rid of her?'

" 'Killed her. Then I killed the me that killed her.'

" 'Who's left?'

" 'Me.'

"I didn't say anything. I started thinking maybe the hairdresser was right again because of the way she looked when she said 'me.' Like it was the first she heard of the word.

"Mr. Trace came back in then, and said he was going to sit outside awhile. She said, 'No, Joe. Stay with us. She won't bite.'

"She meant me, and something else I couldn't catch. He nodded and sat down by the window saying, 'For a little while.'

"Mrs. Trace looked at him but I knew she was talking to me when she said, 'Your little ugly friend hurt him and you remind him of her.'

"I could hardly find my tongue. 'I'm not like her!'

"I didn't mean to say it so loud. They both turned to look at me. So I said it even though I didn't plan to. I told them even before I asked for the ring. 'Dorcas let herself die. The bullet went in her shoulder, this way.' I pointed. 'She wouldn't let anybody move her; said she wanted to sleep and she would be all right. Said she'd go to the hospital in the morning. "Don't let them call nobody," she said. "No ambulance; no police, no nobody." I thought she didn't want her aunt, Mrs. Manfred, to know. Where she was and all. And the woman giving the party said okay because she was afraid to call the police. They all were. People just stood around talking and waiting. Some of them wanted to carry her downstairs, put her in a car and drive to the emergency ward. Dorcas said no. She said she was all right. To please leave her alone and let her rest. But I did it. Called the ambulance, I mean; but it didn't come until morning after I had called twice. The ice, they said, but really because it was colored people calling. She bled to death all through that woman's bed sheets on into the mattress, and I can tell you that woman didn't like it one bit. That's all she talked about. Her and Dorcas' boyfriend. The blood. What a mess it made. That's all they talked about.'

"I had to stop then because I was out of breath and crying.

"I hated crying all over myself like that.

"They didn't stop me neither. Mr. Trace handed me his pocket handkerchief, and it was soaked by the time I was through.

" 'This the first time?' he asked me. 'The first time you cried about her?'

"I hadn't thought about it, but it was true.

"Mrs. Trace said, 'Oh, shit.'

"Then the two of them, they just looked at me. I thought they would never say another word until Mrs. Trace said, 'Come to supper, why don't you. Friday evening. You like catfish?'

"I said sure, but I wasn't going to. The hell with the ring. But the Thursday before, I thought about the way Mr. Trace looked at me and the way his wife said 'me.'

"The way she said it. Not like the 'me' was some tough somebody, or somebody she had put together for show. But like, like somebody she favored and could count on. A secret somebody you didn't have to feel sorry for or have to fight for. Somebody who wouldn't have to steal a ring to get back at whitepeople and then lie and say it was a present from them. I wanted the ring back not just because my mother asks me have I found it yet. It's beautiful. But although it belongs to me, it's not mine. I love it, but there's a trick in it, and I have to agree to the trick to say it's mine. Reminds me of the tricky blond kid living inside Mrs. Trace's head. A present taken from whitefolks, given to me when I was too young to say No thank you.

"It was buried with her. That's what I found out when I went back for the catfish supper. Mrs. Trace saw it on Dorcas' hand when she stabbed her in the coffin.

"I had a funny feeling in my stomach, and my throat was too dry to swallow, but I had to ask her just the same—why did she mess up the funeral that way. Mr. Trace looked at her as though he had asked the question.

" 'Lost the lady,' she said. 'Put her down someplace and forgot where.'

" 'How did you find her?'

" 'Looked.'

"We sat there for a while nobody saying anything. Then Mrs. Trace got up to answer a knock at the door. I heard voices. 'Just right here and right here. Won't take but two minutes.'

" 'I don't do no two-minute work.'

" 'Please, Violet, I wouldn't ask if it wasn't absolutely necessary, you know that.'

"They came into the dining room, Mrs. Trace and a woman pleading for a few curls 'just here and here. And maybe you can turn it down up here. Not curled, just turned, know what I mean?'

" 'You all go up front, I won't be too long.' She said that to Mr. Trace and me after we said 'Evening' to the hurry-up customer, but nobody introduced anybody.

"Mr. Trace didn't sit at the window this time. He sat next to me on the sofa.

" 'Felice. That means happy. Are you?'

" 'Sure. No.'

" 'Dorcas wasn't ugly. Inside or out.'

"I shrugged. 'She used people.'

" 'Only if they wanted her to.'

" 'Did you want her to use you?'

" 'Must have.'

" 'Well, I didn't. Thank God she can't anymore.'

"I wished I hadn't taken my sweater off. My dress stretches across the top no matter what I do. He was looking at my face, not my body, so I don't know why I was nervous alone in the room with him.

"Then he said, 'You mad cause she's dead. So am I.'

" 'You the reason she is.'

" 'I know. I know.'

" 'Even if you didn't kill her outright; even if she made herself die, it was you.'

" 'It was me. For the rest of my life, it'll be me. Tell you something. I never saw a needier creature in my life.'

" 'Dorcas? You mean you still stuck on her?'

" 'Stuck? Well, if you mean did I like what I felt about her. I guess I'm stuck to that.'

" 'What about Mrs. Trace? What about her?'

" 'We working on it. Faster now, since you stopped by and told us what you did.'

" 'Dorcas was cold,' I said. 'All the way to the last she was dry-eyed. I never saw her shed a tear about anything.'

"He said, 'I did. You know the hard part of her; I saw the soft. My luck was to tend to it.'

" 'Dorcas? Soft?'

" 'Dorcas. Soft. The girl I knew. Just cause she had scales don't mean she wasn't fry. Nobody knew her that way but me. Nobody tried to love her before me.'

" 'Why'd you shoot at her if you loved her?'

" 'Scared. Didn't know how to love anybody.'

" 'You know now?'

" 'No. Do you, Felice?'

" 'I got other things to do with my time.'

"He didn't laugh at me, so I said, 'I didn't tell you everything.'

" 'There's more?'

" 'I suppose I should. It was the last thing she said. Before she . . . went to sleep. Everybody was screaming, "Who shot you, who did it?" She said, "Leave me alone. I'll tell you tomorrow." She must have thought she was going to be around tomorrow and made me think so too. Then she called my name although I was kneeling right beside her. "Felice. Felice. Come close, closer." I put my face right there. I could smell the fruity liquor on her breath. She was sweating, and whispering to herself. Couldn't keep her eyes open. Then she opened them wide and said real loud: "There's only one apple." Sounded like "apple." "Just one. Tell Joe."

" 'See? You were the last thing on her mind. I was right there, right there. Her best friend, I thought, but not best enough for her to want to go to the emergency room and stay alive. She let herself die right out from under me with my ring and everything and I wasn't even on her mind. So. That's it. I told you.'

"That was the second time I saw him smile but it was more sad than pleased.

" 'Felice,' he said. And kept on saying it. 'Felice. Felice.' With two syllables, not one like most people do, including my father.

"The curled-hair woman came past on her way out the door, chattering, saying, Thanks so much see you Joe sorry to interrupt bye honey didn't catch your name you a blessing Violet a real blessing bye.

"I said I had to go too. Mrs. Trace plopped down in a chair with her head thrown back and her arms dangling. 'People are mean,' she said. 'Plain mean.'

"Mr. Trace said, 'No. Comic is what they are.'

"He laughed a little then, to prove his point, and she did too. I laughed too but it didn't come out right because I didn't think the woman was all that funny.

"Somebody in the house across the alley put a record on and the music floated in to us through the open window. Mr. Trace moved his head to the rhythm and his wife snapped her fingers in time. She did a little step in front of him and he smiled. By and by they were dancing. Funny, like old people do, and I laughed for real. Not because of how funny they looked. Something in it made me feel I shouldn't be there. Shouldn't be looking at them doing that.

"Mr. Trace said, 'Come on, Felice. Let's see what you can do.' He held out his hand.

"Mrs. Trace said, 'Yeah. Come on. Hurry; it's almost over.'

"I shook my head, but I wanted to.

"When they finished and I asked for my sweater, Mrs. Trace said, 'Come back anytime. I want to do your hair for you anyway. Free. Your ends need clipping.'

"Mr. Trace sat down and stretched. 'This place needs birds.'

" 'And a Victrola.'

" 'Watch your mouth, girl.'

" 'If you get one, I'll bring some records. When I come to get my hair done.'

" 'Hear that, Joe? She'll bring some records.'

" 'Then I best find me another job.' He turned tome, touching my elbow as I walked to the door. 'Felice. They named you right. Remember that.'

"I'll tell my mother the truth. I know she is proud of stealing that opal; of daring to do something like that to get back at the whiteman who thought she was stealing even when she wasn't. My mother is so honest she makes people laugh. Returning a pair of gloves to the store when they gave her two pair instead of the one pair she paid for; giving quarters she finds on the seat to conductors on the trolley. It's as though she doesn't live in a big city. When she does stuff like that, my father puts his forehead in his hand and store people and conductor people look at her like she is nutty for sure. So I know how much taking the ring meant to her. How proud she was of breaking her rules for once. But I'll tell her I know about it, and that it's what she did, not the ring, that I really love.

"I'm glad Dorcas has it. It did match her bracelet and matched the house where the party was. The walls were white with silver and turquoise draperies at the windows. The furniture fabric was turquoise too, and the throw rugs the hostess rolled up and put in the spare bedroom were white. Only her dining room was dark and not fixed up like the front part. She probably hadn't got around to doing it over in her favorite colors and let a bowl of Christmas oranges be the only decoration. Her own bedroom was white and gold, but the bedroom she put Dorcas in, a spare one off the dark dining room, was plain.

"I didn't have a fellow for the party. I went along with Dorcas and Acton. Dorcas needed an alibi and I was it. We had just renewed our friendship after she stopped seeing Mr. Trace and was running around with her 'catch.' Somebody a lot of girls older than us wanted and had too. Dorcas liked that part—that other girls were jealous; that he chose her over them; that she had won. That's what she said. 'I won him. I won!' God. You'd think she had been in a fight.

"What the hell did she win? He treated her bad, but she didn't think so. She spent her time figuring out how to keep him interested in her. Plotting what she would do to any girl who tried to move in. That's the way all the girls I know think: how to get, then hold on to, a guy and most of that is having friends who want you to have him, and enemies who don't. I guess that's the way you have to think about it. But what if I don't want to?

"It's warm tonight. Maybe there won't be a spring and we'll slide right on into summer. My mother will like that—she can't stand the cold—and my father, chasing around looking for colored baseball players 'in the flesh and on the lot,' hollering, jumping up and down when he recounts the plays to his friends, he'll be happy too. No blossoms are on the trees yet but it's warm enough. They'll be out soon. That one over there is aching for it. It's not a man tree; I think it's a child. Well, could be a woman, I suppose.

"Her catfish was pretty good. Not as good as the way my grandmother used to do it, or my mother used to before her chest wore out. Too much hot pepper in the dredging flour the way Mrs. Trace fixed it. I drank a lot of water so as not to hurt her feelings. It eased the pain."

I ought to get out of this place. Avoid the window; leave the hole I cut through the door to get in lives instead of having one of my own. It was loving the City that distracted me and gave me ideas. Made me think I could speak its loud voice and make that sound sound human. I missed the people altogether.

I thought I knew them and wasn't worried that they didn't really know about me. Now it's clear why they contradicted me at every turn: they knew me all along. Out of the corners of their eyes they watched me. And when I was feeling most invisible, being tight-lipped, silent and unobservable, they were whispering about me to each other. They knew how little I could be counted on; how poorly, how shabbily my know-it-all self covered helplessness. That when I invented stories about them—and doing it seemed to me so fine—I was completely in their hands, managed without mercy. I thought I'd hidden myself so well as I watched them through windows and doors, took every opportunity I had to follow them, to gossip about and fill in their lives, and all the while they were watching me. Sometimes they even felt sorry for me and just thinking about their pity I want to die.

So I missed it altogether. I was sure one would kill the other. I waited for it so I could describe it. I was so sure it would happen. That the past was an abused record with no choice but to repeat itself at the crack and no power on earth could lift the arm that held the needle. I was so sure, and they danced and walked all over me. Busy, they were, busy being original, complicated, changeable—human, I guess you'd say, while I was the predictable one, confused in my solitude into arrogance, thinking my space, my view was the only one that was or that mattered. I got so aroused while meddling, while finger-shaping, I overreached and missed the obvious. I was watching the streets, thrilled by the buildings pressing and pressed by stone; so glad to be looking out and in on things I dismissed what went on in heart-pockets closed to me.

I saw the three of them, Felice, Joe and Violet, and they looked to me like a mirror image of Dorcas, Joe and Violet. I believed I saw everything important they did, and based on what I saw I could imagine what I didn't: how exotic they were, how driven. Like dangerous children. That's what I wanted to believe. It never occurred to me that they were thinking other thoughts, feeling other feelings, putting their lives together in ways I never dreamed of. Like Joe. To this moment I'm not sure what his tears were really for, but I do know they were for more than Dorcas. All the while he was running through the streets in bad weather I thought he was looking for her, not Wild's chamber of gold. That home in the rock; that place sunlight got into most of the day. Nothing to be proud of, to show anybody or to want to be in. But I do. I want to be in a place already made for me, both snug and wide open. With a doorway never needing to be closed, a view slanted for light and bright autumn leaves but not rain. Where moonlight can be counted on if the sky is clear and stars no matter what. And below, just yonder, a river called Treason to rely on.

I'd love to close myself in the peace left by the woman who lived there and scared everybody. Unseen because she knows better than to be seen. After all, who would see her, a playful woman who lived in a rock? Who could, without fright? Of her looking eyes looking back? I wouldn't mind. Why should I? She has seen me and is not afraid of me. She hugs me. Understands me. Has given me her hand. I am touched by her. Released in secret.

Now I know.

. . .

Alice Manfred moved away from the tree-lined street back to Springfield. A woman with a taste for brightly colored dresses is there whose breasts are probably soft sealskin purses now, and who may need a few things. Curtains, a good coat lining to bear the winter in. The cheerful company maybe of someone who can provide the necessary things for the night.

Felice still buys Okeh records at Felton's and walks so slowly home from the butcher shop the meat turns before it hits the pan. She thinks that way she can trick me again—moving so slow people nearby seem to be running. Can't fool me: her speed may be slow, but her tempo is next year's news. Whether raised fists freeze in her company or open for a handshake, she's nobody's alibi or hammer or toy.

Joe found work at Paydirt, a speakeasy night job that lets him see the City do its unbelievable sky and run around with Violet in afternoon daylight. On his way home, just after sunrise, he will descend the steps of the Elevated, and if a milk wagon is parked at the curb, he might buy a pint from the second-day crate to cool the evening's hot cornbread supper. When he gets to the apartment building, he picks up the bits of night trash the stoop dwellers have left, drops them in the ashcan and gathers up the children's toys to place them under the stairwell. If he finds a doll he recognizes among the toys, he leaves it propped up and comfortable against the pile. He climbs the stairs and before he gets to his own door he can smell the ham Violet will not give up frying in its own fat to season the hominy swelling in the pot. He calls loudly to her as he closes the door behind him and she calls back: "Vi?" "Joe?" As though it might be another, as though a presumptuous neighbor or a young ghost with bad skin might be there instead. They eat breakfast then and, more often than not, fall asleep. Because of Joe's work—Violet's too—and other things as well, they have stopped night sleeping—exchanging that waste of time for short naps whenever the body insists, and were not surprised by how good they felt. The rest of the day goes however they want it to. After a hairdressing, for example, he meets her at the drugstore for her vanilla malt and his cherry smash.

They walk down 125th Street and across Seventh Avenue and if they get tired they sit down and rest on any stoop they want to and talk weather and youthful misbehavior to the woman leaning on the sill of the first-floor window. Or they might saunter over to the Corner and join the crowd listening to the men with the long-distance eyes. (They like these men, although Violet is worried that one or another of them will tip the wood box or the broken chair he stands on, or that somebody among the group will shout something that hurts the man's feelings. Joe, loving the long-distance eyes, is always supportive and chimes in at appropriate moments with encouraging words.)

Once in a while they take the train all the way to 42nd Street to enjoy what Joe calls the stairway of the lions. Or they idle along 72nd Street to watch men dig holes in the ground for a new building. The deep holes scare Violet, but Joe is fascinated. Both of them think it's a shame.

A lot of the time, though, they stay home figuring things out, telling each other those little personal stories they like to hear again and again, or fussing with the bird Violet bought. She got it cheap because it wasn't well. Hardly any peck to it. Drank water but wouldn't eat. The special bird mix Violet prepared didn't help either. It looked just past her face and didn't turn its head when she tweeted and purred through the bars of the little cage. But, as I said all that time ago, Violet is nothing if not persistent. She guessed the bird wasn't lonely because it was already sad when she bought it out of a flock of others. So if neither food nor company nor its own shelter was important to it, Violet decided, and Joe agreed, nothing was left to love or need but music. They took the cage to the roof one Saturday, where the wind blew and so did the musicians in shirts billowing out behind them. From then on the bird was a pleasure to itself and to them.

Since Joe had to be at work at midnight, they cherished after-supper time. If they did not play bid whist with Gistan and Stuck, and Stuck's new wife, Faye, or promise to keep an eye out for somebody's children, or let Malvonne in to gossip so she wouldn't feel bad about pretending loyalty and betraying them both, they played poker just the two of them until it was time to go to bed under the quilt they plan to tear into its original scraps right soon and get a nice wool blanket with a satin hem. Powder blue, maybe, although that would be risky with the soot flying and all, but Joe is partial to blue. He wants to slip under it and hold on to her. Take her hand and put it on his chest, his stomach. He wants to imagine, as he lies with her in the dark, the shapes their bodies make the blue stuff do. Violet doesn't care what color it is, so long as under their chins that avenue of no-question-about-it satin cools their lava forever.

Lying next to her, his head turned toward the window, he sees through the glass darkness taking the shape of a shoulder with a thin line of blood. Slowly, slowly it forms itself into a bird with a blade of red on the wing. Meanwhile Violet rests her hand on his chest as though it were the sunlit rim of a well and down there somebody is gathering gifts (lead pencils, Bull Durham, Jap Rose Soap) to distribute to them all.

There was an evening, back in 1906, before Joe and Violet went to the City, when Violet left the plow and walked into their little shotgun house, the heat of the day still stunning. She was wearing coveralls and a sleeveless faded shirt and slowly removed them along with the cloth from her head. On a table near the cookstove stood an enamel basin—speckled blue and white and chipped all round its rim. Under a square of toweling, placed there to keep insects out, the basin was full of still water. Palms up, fingers leading, Violet slid her hands into the water and rinsed her face. Several times she scooped and splashed until, perspiration and water mixed, her cheeks and forehead cooled. Then, dipping the toweling into the water, carefully she bathed. From the windowsill she took a white shift, laundered that very morning, and dropped it over her head and shoulders. Finally she sat on the bed to unwind her hair. Most of the knots fixed that morning had loosened under her headcloth and were now cupfuls of soft wool her fingers thrilled to. Sitting there, her hands deep in the forbidden pleasure of her hair, she noticed she had not removed her heavy work shoes. Putting the toe of her left foot to the heel of the right, she pushed the shoe off. The effort seemed extra and the mild surprise at how very tired she felt was interrupted by a soft, wide hat, as worn and dim as the room she sat in, descending on her. Violet did not feel her shoulder touch the mattress. Way before that she had entered a safe sleep. Deep, trustworthy, feathered in colored dreams. The heat was relentless, insinuating. Like the voices of the women in houses nearby singing "Go down, go down, way down in Egypt land . . ." Answering each other from yard to yard with a verse or its variation.

Joe had been away for two months at Crossland, and when he got home and stood in the doorway, he saw Violet's dark girl-body limp on the bed. She looked frail to him, and penetrable everyplace except at one foot, the left, where her man's work shoe remained. Smiling, he took off his straw hat and sat down at the bottom of the bed. One of her hands held her face; the other rested on her thigh. He looked at the fingernails hard as her palm skin, and noticed for the first time how shapely her hands were. The arm that curved out of the shift's white sleeve was muscled by field labor, awful thin, but smooth as a child's. He undid the laces of her shoe and eased it off. It must have helped something in her dream for she laughed then, a light happy laugh that he had never heard before, but which seemed to belong to her.

When I see them now they are not sepia, still, losing their edges to the light of a future afternoon. Caught midway between was and must be. For me they are real. Sharply in focus and clicking. I wonder, do they know they are the sound of snapping fingers under the sycamores lining the streets? When the loud trains pull into their stops and the engines pause, attentive listeners can hear it. Even when they are not there, when whole city blocks downtown and acres of lawned neighborhoods in Sag Harbor cannot see them, the clicking is there.

In the T-strap shoes of Long Island debutantes, the sparkling
fringes of daring short skirts that swish and glide to music that
intoxicates them more than the champagne. It is in the eyes
of the old men who watch these girls, and the young ones who
hold them up. It is in the graceful slouch of the men slipping
their hands into the pockets of their tuxedo trousers. Their
teeth are bright; their hair is smooth and parted in the middle.
And when they take the arms of the T-strap girls and guide
them away from the crowd and the too-bright lights, it is the
clicking that makes them sway on unlit porches while the
Victrola plays in the parlor. The click of dark and snapping
fingers drives them to Roseland, to Bunny's; boardwalks by the
sea. Into places their fathers have warned them about and their
mothers shudder to think of. Both the warning and the shudder come from the snapping fingers, the clicking. And the
shade. Pushed away into certain streets, restricted from others,
making it possible for the inhabitants to sigh and sleep in relief,
the shade stretches—just there—at the edge of the dream, or
slips into the crevices of a chuckle. It is out there in the privet
hedge that lines the avenue. Gliding through rooms as though
it is tidying this, straightening that. It bunches on the curb-
stone, wrists crossed, and hides its smile under a wide-brim hat.
Shade. Protective, available. Or sometimes not; sometimes it
seems to lurk rather than hover kindly, and its stretch is not
a yawn but an increase to be beaten back with a stick. Before
it clicks, or taps or snaps its fingers.

Some of them know it. The lucky ones. Everywhere they go
they are like a magician-made clock with hands the same size
so you can't figure out what time it is, but you can hear the
ticking, tap, snap.

I started out believing that life was made just so the world would have some way to think about itself, but that it had gone awry with humans because flesh, pinioned by misery, hangs on to it with pleasure. Hangs on to wells and a boy's golden hair; would just as soon inhale sweet fire caused by a burning girl as hold a maybe-yes maybe-no hand. I don't believe that anymore. Something is missing there. Something rogue. Something else you have to figure in before you can figure it out.

It's nice when grown people whisper to each other under the covers. Their ecstasy is more leaf-sigh than bray and the body is the vehicle, not the point. They reach, grown people, for something beyond, way beyond and way, way down underneath tissue. They are remembering while they whisper the carnival dolls they won and the Baltimore boats they never sailed on. The pears they let hang on the limb because if they plucked them, they would be gone from there and who else would see that ripeness if they took it away for themselves? How could anybody passing by see them and imagine for themselves what the flavor would be like? Breathing and murmuring under covers both of them have washed and hung out on the line, in a bed they chose together and kept together nevermind one leg was propped on a 1916 dictionary, and the mattress, curved like a preacher's palm asking for witnesses in His name's sake, enclosed them each and every night and muffled their whispering, old-time love. They are under the covers because they don't have to look at themselves anymore; there is no stud's eye, no chippie glance to undo them. They are inward toward the other, bound and joined by carnival dolls and the steamers that sailed from ports they never saw. That is what is beneath their undercover whispers.

But there is another part, not so secret. The part that touches fingers when one passes the cup and saucer to the other. The part that closes her neckline snap while waiting for the trolley; and brushes lint from his blue serge suit when they come out of the movie house into the sunlight.

I envy them their public love. I myself have only known it in secret, shared it in secret and longed, aw longed to show it—to be able to say out loud what they have no need to say at all: *That I have loved only you, surrendered my whole self reckless to you and nobody else. That I want you to love me back and show it to me. That I love the way you hold me, how close you let me be to you. I like your fingers on and on, lifting, turning. I have watched your face for a long time now, and missed your eyes when you went away from me. Talking to you and hearing you answer—that's the kick.*

But I can't say that aloud; I can't tell anyone that I have been waiting for this all my life and that being chosen to wait is the reason I can. If I were able I'd say it. Say make me, remake me. You are free to do it and I am free to let you because look, look. Look where your hands are. Now.